FOREST AT THE EDGE
~Book Eight~

The Last Day

TRISH MERCER

All characters in this book are fictitious, and any resemblance to actual
persons, living or dead, is purely coincidental, and legally I have to write
that even though deep down I think they're really out there, so characters—feel free to contact me through my website below and let's talk
about how you got into my head and what else you'd like me to write.

Cover design by Trish Mercer. And even though it may not seem like it,
there are two people in it. Check the "D" in the title very carefully, and
you'll see them, climbing up Rock Canyon in Provo, Utah.

Contact author via website: forestedgebooks.com.

Because hope is everything.

MAPS

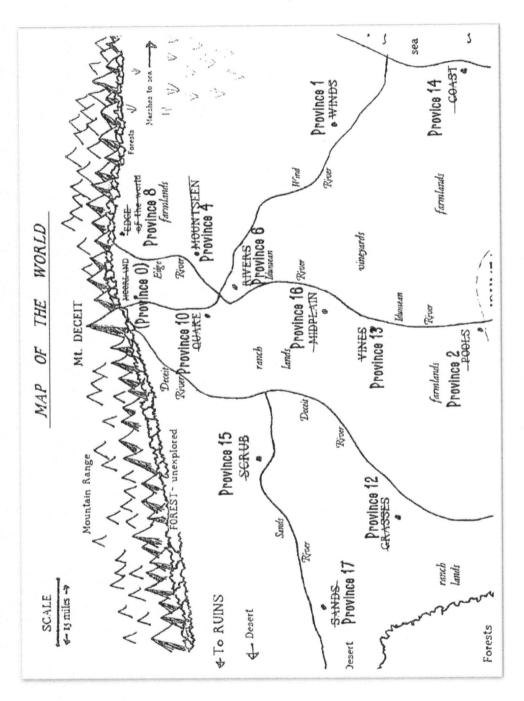

MAP OF THE WORLD

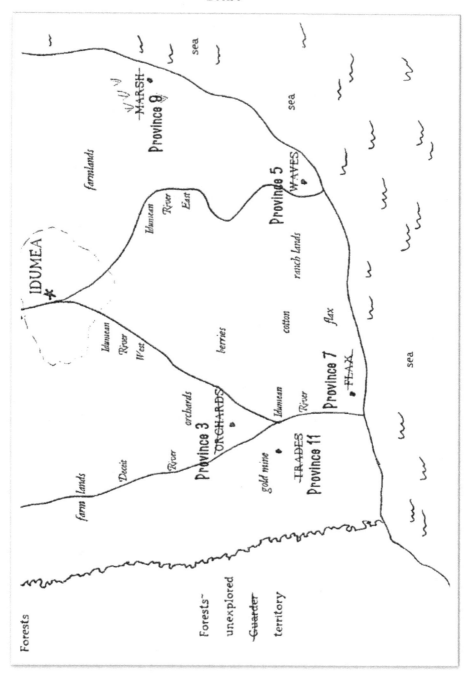

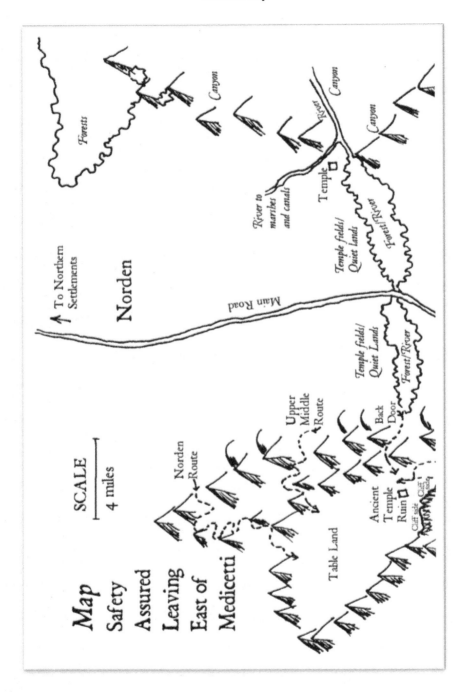

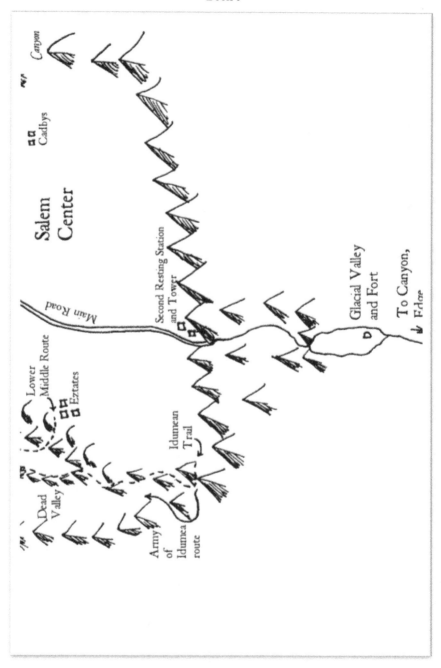

The Last Day

A pronunciation guide to some of the more unusual names . . .

Idumea	i-doo-ME-uh
Mahrree	MARR-ee
Peto	PAY-toh
Jaytsy	JAYT-see
Lorixania	Lor-ix-ZYAN-ya
Hifadhi	Hi-FAHD-hee
Cephas	SEE-fus
Qayin	KAY-in
Trovato	troe-VAH-toe
Fadh	FOD
Boskos	BOSS-kose
Barnos	BARN-ose

The Last Day

The 30th Day of Planting

It was the light that woke him up.

It was so unusual and bright and intrusive that there was no way he could have slept through it. It poured into the room through a crack in the curtains, like a sword slicing the darkness.

Young Perrin Shin sat up and looked around in the dim light of the room. Each of the cots surrounding him in Sergeant Major Poe Hili's crowded bedroom was filled with an exhausted and smoky-smelling officer. As much as he wanted to throw open the curtains and feel the sunshine for the first time in thirteen days, he didn't want to disrupt anyone's sleep. Now was not the time to have people, especially officers, angry with him.

Private Shin crept quietly to the door and opened it.

"Going somewhere?" asked an enormous soldier posted in the hallway. Another on the other side of the door raised an eyebrow at him.

"To the latrine."

"You're supposed to go down the hall there to use the officers' washroom. Can't risk any *trouble*."

What that really meant was, they didn't want to risk Private Shin running away instead of relieving himself. All Shin could think was that there were no windows in the hallway and certainly not in the washroom. The latrine, however, would have afforded a peek at the sun. But that would have to wait.

Then again, he'd spent nearly two weeks in almost complete darkness while confined to the dungeon below the tower, and the light filtering in around him was already overwhelming.

Reluctantly, he headed to the washroom but then realized it'd be the first time since he was released from the dungeon that he wouldn't be standing in his own filth. That made him smile.

A few minutes later he made his way back to where Staff Sergeant Beaved and the two guards were waiting for him.

Beaved smiled. "Ready for breakfast, Private Shin?"

"Yes, sir!"

"Come on." He led him to the main doors of the officers' quarters. "The general's waiting for you in the command tower. You'll eat with him there." He opened the doors and headed out to the compound.

The thought of facing General Thorne for the first time in nearly two weeks made Private Shin hesitate, but his yearning to be outside propelled him onward, the two massive guards on his heels. He stepped out into the sunshine that was just coming over the horizon—

And stopped, unable to continue.

It was like standing in the presence of the Creator.

The sun was so bright, warm, and inviting, as if welcoming him back. His eyes filled with tears and he felt the need to drop to his knees in worship. He wanted to rip open his uniform to expose every inch of flesh to the sunlight. Not caring who saw him or what they thought, he did the next best thing: he spread out his arms, closed his eyes, and let the tears wash down his cheeks as the light bathed him.

How was it that he never noticed before how glorious the sun was? How did he take it for granted for so many years?

Unable to ignore the urge anymore, he dropped to his knees and, disregarding the sniggers of soldiers around him, whispered the only word that came to his mind.

"Papa!"

Over and past the mountains, in the valley of Salem, Peto Shin looked up from his breakfast. He turned to the window and noticed the sun coming over the mountains that enclosed the huge valley—

And it hit him.

It hit him with such force that he dropped his fork and covered his face with his hands. No one else noticed, too involved with their meal, but his wife did.

"What is it, Peto?" Lilla whispered anxiously.

Despite the clattering of dishes, noisy conversations, and scattered laughter, the word slid into his ear as a distinct plea, a hopeful declaration of "Papa!"

Peto trembled, unable to form the words. But realizing his wife's grip on his arm was only going to grow more painful until he said something, he finally managed to whisper, "Lilla, Young Pere's been freed."

He would have knelt there for hours, but he couldn't because a moment later he heard a familiar snicker.

"I guess being in the dungeon *did* do you some good, Shin."

The private opened his eyes, took a deep breath of sun-warmed air, which was still cold enough to show his breath, and turned to see General Thorne standing a few feet away, his left hand on his hip, waiting.

Now things were going to get complicated.

During his bath last night he understood why he was being released from the dungeon: he was to lead General Lemuel Thorne and the Army of Idumea to Salem. He couldn't avoid doing so without losing his life.

Before he had dozed off, he pondered various strategies for handling the situation. With each scenario he heard Puggah whisper, *THAT WON'T WORK, BUT DON'T WORRY—WE HAVE A PLAN . . .*

But Private Shin had to do *something*.

He dropped his arms and got to his feet. Meekly he said, "Yes, sir," to Thorne, then repeated the speech he had practiced. "I had a great deal of time to think while I was in the dungeon. I'm sorry, sir, for never revealing to you that I was from Salem. I just preferred being your son than being *his* grandson. I didn't want to lose that. I lost it anyway, though." He looked down at his boots and hoped it had sounded sincere.

Thorne's left hand came off his waist to push up Shin's chin. He held Shin's jaw firmly as he evaluated his cheeks and eyes, probably looking for signs of suffering. Thorne released him to shake the side of Shin's jacket to see how loose it was.

"Hmm," Thorne said after a moment. "You look better than I expected but you're at least a size smaller than you were."

Shin wasn't about to tell the general about Qualipoe Hili, who was still asleep in his quarters after fighting the wildfire that ravaged part of the makeshift army encampment last night. For the past two weeks, Poe Hili had been smuggling Shin extra food when he delivered his rations. He even brought him a piece of jerky in the early hours of that morning.

"I think the bath I took filled me up again a bit, sir. I've been feeling spongy."

"Spongy," Thorne repeated. "Funny." Cocking his head to the command tower, he said, "Hungry?"

"Yes, sir." It hadn't been that big of a piece of jerky.

"Then let's see if you're strong enough to take the stairs. Your first climb of the day."

Shin followed General Thorne to the tower, deliberately turning his gaze away from the door that led to the records room and his old dungeon home beneath it. He was grateful to realize he could take the stairs so easily. Puggah's daily calisthenics had kept him in shape, but as he reached the top he made sure he was panting a little for show.

Thorne gestured to the large desk that was laid out with a tall stack of pancakes, syrup, salted pork, and even a pitcher of milk. It was a shocking amount of food considering everyone was on rations. Thorne must have been confident they'd soon find Salem and its storehouses bursting with food, to feel he could be so indulgent for their last breakfast in Edge.

Buddy and Pal, Thorne's clumsy and gangly teenage informants who had visited Private Shin frequently at the dungeon, sat at the other side of the desk. They were wearing big smiles, probably because the private smelled a whole better than he used to.

"Take it slowly, Shin," he heard another voice.

He looked up to see Major Twigg smiling cautiously at him.

"Men come out of there eating too quickly and they get sick," the major warned.

"Thank you, sir."

"Good to see you again," Twigg nodded.

Shin doubted that. Twigg's tense demeanor caused his pale skin to always appear stretched too tight. Upon seeing Shin, the lines around Major Twigg's mouth vanished completely and his jaw clenched. Twigg had never enjoyed being responsible for Thorne's "son."

Shin sat down and piled on the food, far too much, and did his best to not eat quickly but it was difficult.

Buddy and Pal chuckled at his enthusiasm as they filled up their plates. Apparently his new "friends" would be taking all their meals with him.

Thorne sat down on a chair near the desk and watched as Shin shoveled food into his mouth. Eventually he spoke.

"We leave in two hours and go straight north, climbing over the boulders. I anticipate making camp above the boulder line tonight, *unless* you know a way to make the journey easier for your fellow soldiers."

Shin gulped down some milk and immediately regretted it. His belly churned at its richness. Deciding it was a good time to let his stomach rest, he said to Thorne, "Sir, I don't know of any other way. There *were* routes through the boulders, but after the eruption—" He shrugged. "I must confess that once I went up through the forest after I noticed it was dead. I couldn't find any of the routes. They all collapsed. Climbing over the boulders is the only way."

Thorne tipped his head. "Can't take horses over the boulders, now, can we?"

Shin shrugged. "Perhaps that's better. Where would you stable the horses? How would you feed them? There's nothing growing on the mountains, sir." He glanced out the window to make sure of that, and his breath caught once again as the sun sparkled cheerfully.

Thorne studied him. "You may have a point. Horses would make our journey faster, though."

"But, sir, if you don't know where you're going, the speed in which you go doesn't matter, does it?"

"So where are we going, Shin?"

He turned back to his pancakes.

"Sir?" Buddy said timidly to the general. "We can watch him now, sir. You can go back to work. We'll keep him company."

From the corner of his eye, Private Shin could see the less-than-subtle wink Buddy sent to Thorne.

Thorne ignored his inept spy. "I don't understand why you insist on protecting them, Shin," he said calmly. "In the past week and a half I've found a few more people who know about Salem. It's hardly a place worth preserving. They kidnapped your mother Jaytsy and uncle Peto, and kept them in hiding all these years. They kidnapped Captain Lick's father, who was also Lieutenant Kiah's father, and forced him to Salem. For many years he tried to leave, but couldn't.

Shem Zenos himself saw to that. But finally Walickiah escaped, nearly losing his life to return to the world. So terrified he was of what he experienced in Salem that he was never fully himself again. When he finally died a few years ago, he was a broken and paranoid man. Tell me, Shin—why defend a place like that?"

Shin only stared at his plate and chewed on a pancake while memorizing Thorne's version of events: his already well-practiced story.

"And just so you realize these aren't isolated cases, Shin," Thorne continued, "it's recently come to my attention that Salem is holding others captive. Right now they're holding my wife and her two oldest daughters. The one who came to visit us at the mansion was the lucky one who escaped. And even then she preferred dying in Edge than living in Salem. Now, why is that, Shin? What did Salem do to her, her sisters, and her mother? Lieutenant Kiah is the one who brought me that devastating news about my family. He also lost his life, preferring death in Edge to life in Salem."

Shin continued to eat pedantically, feeling the penetrating gaze of Thorne, Twigg, and now Poe Hili who had climbed the stairs to listen. Buddy and Pal slowed in their eating, and Beaved, standing in the corner, folded his arms and leaned against the wall. All of them were watching for his response.

So this was the story being told to all of the soldiers, the purpose for invading Salem, provided they could find it. Thorne had years of experience in creating a compelling tale, taking convenient truths and mixing them with lies for his own recipe of rubbish.

"They abducted Eltana Yordin close to two years ago," Thorne continued in a low, steady voice, calculated to sound both concerned and furious. "As if the poor woman hadn't suffered enough with the tragic death of her husband Gari—"

Shin noticed that Thorne didn't mention that *he* was the one who arranged that tragic death.

"—They came and stole her away, too. All I can figure is that it was to force her to pay for the crimes of her husband while he was a general in the world. Gari Yordin was a violent, fierce man, Shin. Many people lost their lives because of him."

Shin ate even slower but still didn't look up, or he would have been tempted to say, *But tens of thousands have lost their lives because of you, especially everyone over age fifty.*

"They're holding my wife and daughters, Shin," Thorne continued, adding a slight tremor which almost sounded genuine. "No ransom note, no reason, nothing. Just revenge. That's all I can figure." His tone quavered for a family that he hadn't thought of in years. "I'm not going to allow that, Shin. Why Salemites feel justified in holding innocent women is beyond my imagination. Only a bitter, hateful society would do such a thing. Then again, look at what kind of men they produced."

Now his tone shifted to detached, with undercurrents of rage. "Shem Zenos was the most evil, heartless man who ever came to Edge," Thorne declared. "He destroyed the greatest man the army ever produced—your grandfather—by taking advantage of his trust and stealing away his wife."

Another shift, and Private Shin wished that he could have been taking notes. Thorne's performance was masterful, and he sounded truly distraught as he reminisced.

"I knew them, Private. I sat in this very office and watched the two of them laugh like brothers, communicate with a silly secret system of winks and facial tics only they knew, and I saw just how much trust and love—yes, *love*—Perrin Shin felt for Shem Zenos."

Thorne changed again, now agitated. "But Zenos made Perrin into a fool, Private. Tore out his heart and threw it in the mud. Zenos frequently went to their house supposedly bringing messages. But only Zenos knew how long Perrin would be away from his house so he could have Mahrree all to himself. I know, because I watched. I saw when Zenos left the fort and when he returned. He was with her more than Perrin was. Shem betrayed him in every way possible. That's the kind of men Salem produces, Private. And those are the kind of men you're trying to shield?"

Shin pushed his food around his plate, making swirls in the syrup while the rest of the soldiers and officers held their breath waiting to hear what else Thorne would say, and if Shin would react.

The general's performance was far from over. "One question has been eating at me for the past twelve days, Private," Thorne continued. "Why did *you* leave? I can't help but wonder what those people did to *my son* to force him away. They must have known who you were. What they thought of you because I was your father, I can't imagine. I've stayed awake for nights sick with worry at what they must have done to my beautiful Jaytsy. What they must have done to *you.*"

Shin struggled to keep his face still so that he wouldn't scoff at the notion that Thorne was ever sick with worry over anyone.

"How is it that they can so terrorize you that you flee to Edge with Amory—yes, I know about that, too." Thorne tried his best to sound sincere. "She was married to a monster that she ran away from. What I can't understand is, how is it that they can so abuse you as to make you risk your life to leave, yet now you can't bring yourself to expose them? They don't deserve your devotion. They deserve to be uncovered, to be cleansed by the Army of Idumea!"

Shin answered nothing, privately musing how the army could cleanse anything. It was like expecting a mud bath to make you sparkly.

"The entire army out there now knows about Salem and its evils," Thorne continued in a practiced tone that increased in volume and intensity. "Every last man out there is willing to help me liberate my wife and daughters, to find and rescue Eltana Yordin and everyone else who's a prisoner there. Every last man except you. Salem deserves my retribution for the mistreatment of my son! Salem must pay!"

Thorne was on his feet now, gesturing furiously with his left arm while his dead right arm swung erratically as if wanting to assist.

"I will see my wife and daughters freed, I promise you. I will not rest until they and Eltana Yordin and everyone else they've dragged away is breathing the sweet air of freedom again. You of all people should understand that today, Shin. I saw you out there, arms outstretched to feel the sun. How many people in Salem are suffering as you were? And for how long? Seasons? Years?"

Clearly a response was expected, but Shin was too consumed in trying to spell his last name in the syrup on his plate before the gaps closed in.

"You were down in the dungeon for only twelve days," Thorne tried again, "but Salem's been holding its victims for far longer. How can you refuse to help them, Shin, knowing how they suffer? This morning you felt how fantastic it is to be a free man. Why do you deny that to everyone else in Salem? Are you afraid? Is that it? Don't you believe I can protect you?"

Growing weary of this game, Shin sat perfectly still, unsure of what to say or do. Thorne had twisted Salem into an object deserving of destruction, and eighty thousand soldiers had no way of knowing it was yet another Thorney story. The general was brilliant. Simply brilliant.

Shin would have to be just that much more clever, somehow.

"You'll be safe, Shin," Thorne continued, his voice softening. "Those two guards at your door this morning? They weren't there to prevent you from running; they were there to *protect* you. They're at the bottom of the stairs right now, making sure no one can reach you who shouldn't. Sergeant Beaved has put together a team of soldiers designated solely for your protection. These two fine privates seated across from you are part of that team, as well as a few others. *Nine men*, Shin! I've devoted nine men to staying by your side, protecting you, and helping you with anything. You can reveal Salem to us! No harm will come to you because of it. Please, son. *Lek*," Thorne leaned in close.

Shin bristled when he heard 'son' and 'Lek' again.

"Let me give you back your rightful name. Tell me how to get to Salem and you can be Lek Thorne again. Together we can do amazing things for the world. We can rule it the way it was meant to be ruled! Trust your father. Don't you trust your father?"

Shin had heard so many things that were wrong that he wouldn't even know how to begin to address them, but Thorne's last question could be answered.

"Sir, I do trust *my* father," he whispered.

"And?" Thorne prodded.

Shin dropped his fork and rubbed his forehead in frustration, but hoped it would look like worry and fear.

"General," Hili's voice broke the thick silence. "Consider that much of what you've just said to him is not something he's heard before. Private," he said quietly, "did you know about Thorne's wife and daughters in Salem?"

Focusing on his plate, Shin shook his head.

"How about Mrs. Yordin? Or Lick's father?"

He shook his head again and held his forehead.

"Sir," Hili turned to Thorne, "give him some time to understand all of this. Let him consider and then, maybe, he'll be more willing or able."

Able, he was already. But willing? Never.

Then again, if Young Pere gave the *appearance* of willing, then earned Thorne's trust, and then sprung his trap, whatever trap that might be—

"Shin," Thorne said, almost kindly, "did you know about the nature of Salem?"

"It's not the Salem I know, sir," Shin confessed to the table.

"So why did *you* leave, son?"

He shook his head.

"Are you afraid to go back?"

Another question he could answer honestly. He nodded.

He *was* afraid to face his family again. And the thought that it might happen with Thorne by his side had never occurred to him until that moment.

Already he could hear his mother's loud sobs, see his father's look of dismay, his siblings' and cousins' accusatory stares, his grandmother shake her head in disbelief that her grandson would be in the company of her greatest enemy. And what would Guide Zenos think of him?

No. Thorne must never make it to Salem. The army? Yes, that could somehow work. But Thorne?

Never.

Shin knew what he needed to do. Getting there, however, was going to be difficult.

Thorne sighed, realizing no further progress would be made and that they were wasting time. "Finish eating. Then Beaved will take you to get acquainted with your security team. In two hours, we start climbing to Salem. I hope you're ready. You're leading the way."

It was an odd mix of feelings for Private Shin, to be freed from the dungeon and once again out in the world, cautiously walking on the icy patches to avoid the muddy sections of the dead forest, and feeling the sun trying feebly to warm the air that was still unseasonably cool. It was almost too many sensations after dark nothingness, and although he felt dazed by light and sounds, he reveled in the bombardment of his senses.

He chose his entrance to the forest deliberately: the new meadow his father had created last year. It would have been easier to pick his way through the deadened forest, like the majority of the army was. But Peto Shin had created this meadow as a diversion, sending a boulder at the top of it rolling down to trigger an avalanche of dead timbers which terrified the army. And it still did, judging by how many men purposely avoided the treefall area.

Into that scar which his father had inflicted on the forest, Shin willingly marched, his security team reluctantly following. Today, the messy and massive triangle-shape of felled trees was an arrow, pointing north to the boulder field, pointing to his home.

If it were just him heading north, the day would have been perfect. But knowing he was leading the army to that home sent his spirits to the bottom of his boots.

Something had to happen before he reached Salem. He just had to pay attention and wait for the right moment to . . . do whatever.

At the top of the triangular scar, Shin continued northward, eventually reaching the end of the trees and the beginning of the boulder field. He hadn't dared look behind to see his massive audience following, but the army was a noisy bunch, crunching branches and shouting for no good reason. Their close presence hovered menacingly behind him, and they were all watching as he stopped to survey the vast boulder field before him.

His 'security' team of nine stood behind him, waiting for him to choose a route. Thorne lurked to the side like a stalking mountain lion, accompanied by Poe Hili and Amory. Gone was her typically revealing dresses; today she wore trousers, a man's work shirt, and surprisingly sensible boots. Behind them, a dozen officers waited for Shin to choose a boulder and start heaving his dungeon-weakened body on to it.

Beyond, the eighty thousand soldiers waited for the tall private to make the first move, as if he had some bizarre and amazing skill and this would be his only performance.

He tipped his head at the immense obstacle before him, trying to delay as long as possible. "It's all the same, really, isn't it? I mean, it's just all house-sized boulders, with a few horse-sized boulders tossed in for variety. Not like there's some perfect place to start—"

"So CLIMB already!" Thorne thundered.

After jumping slightly, Shin made his way to a crevice between two boulders knowing that his heavy pack filled with rations, water flasks, a bedroll, and spare clothing would likely shift with each movement, potentially throwing him off balance and maybe off of the rock.

But this wasn't a time for stage fright. He'd planned this

performance and he hoped that the agonizingly long minutes he was currently spending—bracing and heaving and struggling—would convince the thousands behind him that climbing the boulder field would be a stupid and exhausting endeavor. Best to break their will before they even touched a rock.

Finally he was on top of the first rock, with about forty more ahead of him, and was wondering how he could make that take even longer when he heard a strange noise behind him. He glanced back to see that much of the army was cheering. He wasn't used to being applauded in the world.

He waved, half in embarrassment, half in amusement, before turning back to the boulders and being purposely slow about selecting the next one.

"Everyone, *get climbing*!" Thorne bellowed, gesturing wildly with his left arm, and the cheering stopped. The first line of thousands of men apprehensively approached the boulders, trying to find the best place to grip the smooth rock.

Well, it was only a matter of time, Shin thought to himself. They'd realize that anywhere along the seven-mile-wide barrier was as good as any, and soon it'd be swarming with men in blue.

"This isn't so hard," he heard one of the massive guards behind him say. That one was called Iron. Or Hammer. While they weren't quite as tall as Young Pere, the blond men were definitely beefy. The blacksmiths, perhaps in their late twenties, were perfectly suited for the rigors of the climb.

"Speak for yourself! Ugh," the man in his mid-thirties who they called Teach groaned behind them. He was in for a very long day, with his paunchy belly and floppy body which saw no more exercise than what was required to slap a stick on a misbehaving boy's arm. "There's got to be a smaller rock somewhere. Right over there. Look at that. Why didn't we start over there?"

Shin smirked as he heard another of his security team comfort Teach. "It's not so bad, once you look at the rocks in the right way."

"And what way would that be, Cloud Man?" Teach asked derisively.

Shin wondered why they called him that. He was just medium height, not tall enough to have his head 'hit the clouds,' and he was rather average in every way—his dark skin and short curly black hair looked like a fourth of the soldiers. While on the younger side, maybe only a couple years older than him, Shin would hardly have noticed Cloud Man if he didn't speak. But as soon as he opened his mouth, Shin understood.

"Think of the boulders as . . . brown clouds. Gray clouds. All kinds of shapes and bumps. They've fallen to the ground for us to explore. How nice!"

Shin smiled when he heard Teach grunt as he attempted to scale another rock, but his smile faded when he saw Pal crawling over, probably to ingratiate himself once again.

"Grassena survivor," Pal explained, jerking his head toward Cloud Man behind them. "Vial head."

Cloud Man was now standing on a boulder taking deep breaths and grinning to the world.

"There's a surprising amount of them still around," Pal said quietly as if complaining to his best friend. "They tried to scatter the vial heads through the ranks so that no one has an undue amount to deal with."

Shin glanced back to see if Buddy might be trying to join them for his attempt at friendliness, but instead noticed Teach lying on his stomach across a boulder, seemingly unable to find a hand or foothold. Then again, it wasn't as if he was really trying.

Another soldier, with black hair, medium brown skin, and with a determined air about him, was trying to show Teach where to put his hands. They called him Reg, Shin remembered, meaning Regular Army.

"You were one, too, weren't you?"

"What?" Shin said, realizing that Pal was still trying to get chummy with him. "Oh, yeah. Grassena boy. For a time, yes."

They inched their way up a boulder. "I never did the vials," Pal said conversationally, then hinted, "I always wondered why people did them."

"Not sure why I did them either." Shin hoped his curt tone might discourage Pal, but nope.

"Maybe . . . maybe," Pal grunted as he squeezed into the crevice that Teach with his flabby middle would never visit, "maybe to forget? Like past troubles, a disturbing childhood. I heard the vials do that."

"I'm not sure. I forgot."

"Funny," Pal said.

Shin nearly rolled his eyes, but instead looked up and did a double-take. "How . . . how'd you get up there already?"

The soldier standing on the boulder ahead of him sneered down, as if regarding a rotting corpse. "It's not really that difficult. Need a hand, Shin?"

Pal shuddered next to him. "Snarl is surprising us daily with his *abilities*," he said under his breath. Looking up at the soldier, he said, "Is rock climbing another skill?"

Snarl's lips turned into an ugly smile, and Shin understood his nickname. He was maybe thirty years old, with deep-set eyes, greasy dirt-brown hair, and a pinched face that was difficult to look at for more than a couple of seconds. "Scaling block walls up to a second level bedroom is far more difficult than this."

"What were you doing climbing up to—" Pal stopped, not wanting to know the answer.

Shin surveyed the rock before him. "I don't need your help, but I think Teach will need some soon." He glanced back to see Beaved and Reg rolling Teach off the boulder, effectively trapping him in the crevice behind. A loud moan came from the rock and Beaved shook his head in aggravation.

Snarl waved. "Hammer, go get Teach. Throw him over your shoulder or something. I'll keep an eye on Shin."

"Think of them as clouds, Teach!" came an encouraging voice. "Doesn't that 'cloud' jabbing into your back feel nice?"

Shin heard chuckling on the other side. Buddy had finally joined them, encasing him in informants.

"Look at Cloud Man jumping on these rocks. He must be part goat."

"Probably his mother," Snarl sniggered. He turned to the rock before them, scanning the area. "All clear, Shin-boy. You may climb without fear of running into anyone unpleasant."

Shin was sure he already had.

He heard protests behind. "No, I will not be carried. Get your hands off of me! I can do this myself!"

Shin finished scaling the boulder in front of him and turned around to see Teach thrown over the shoulder of Hammer.

Iron was leaning against a boulder and chuckling as Hammer tried to tackle the rock in front of him with the extra weight.

"You'll drop me, I know it!" Teach bellowed, gripping Hammer in terror while also trying to find a way to get off of his shoulder.

"Then move yourself!" Sergeant Beaved shouted at him.

"I will! I will! Just put me down. This is so undignified."

Cloud Man jumped to another boulder below Shin and started up it. "Move along, Private!" he called cheerfully. "I can't wait to see the view from the top!"

"Do you want to go ahead of me, Cloud Man?"

"Can I? Can I?"

Shin grinned at his enthusiastic dog-like expression. "Just stay out of Snarl's way."

"Oh boy, oh boy, oh boy . . ." Cloud Man whispered excitedly as he easily made his way past and joined Snarl on the next level of boulders.

Snarl didn't look pleased to have company.

"Whew," Buddy exclaimed as he pulled his body out of a tight crevice. "This is going to get tiring. I've never done anything like this before. Have you, Shin? Have *you* ever climbed rock like this before when you were younger?"

Shin smiled internally. It wasn't as if he had worried that the boredom he had experienced in the dungeon would continue once he was out, but he realized that between keeping an eye on Snarl, whose past life must have been unpleasantly interesting, and avoiding giving clues about his childhood to Thorne's clumsy young spies, and watching the less-than-toned soldiers around him trying to extract themselves from crevices designed for skinnier men, and waiting for whatever unpredictable thing Cloud Man would do next . . . well, in the moments when he wasn't fretting about leading the army to Salem, he'd be quite entertained.

The four men in gray and black mottled clothing hadn't said a word for the past hour. Flat on their bellies, they peered from the overlook at the mouth of the canyon to watch the activity well below them at the boulder field. Once the first soldiers of thousands began swarming the rock, they knew.

It was starting.

One of the men pulled out a spyglass and focused on the soldiers in the lead. He held his breath as he searched the masses in blue clothing.

The three around him also tensed, waiting for the news.

"Yes," the first man said. "It's *him*." He exhaled in relief.

But his companions were still anxious. "Woodson," one of them began, "but if it's *him*—"

To their astonishment, Woodson smiled. He rarely smiled. As the head of the scouting corps for Salem, he was responsible for everyone who was going in to the world and coming back out again. That he was smiling because tens of thousands of men in blue were invading the very forest where he was born over forty years ago befuddled his companions.

Even odder, Woodson was smiling at who was leading those soldiers in his forest—the same young man who had ruined Woodson's reputation of never losing a scout, refugee, or Salemite. The Shins' middle grandson had tricked Woodson to join his emergency scouting party to retrieve an ill rector, then that boy escaped into the world with another run-away from Salem, Amory Riling.

But right now, the deep lines on Woodson's leathery-tanned face seemed cheerful.

That made his scouting corps nervous.

"It's him," Woodson repeated confidently. "*And* he's un-armed. Take a look." He handed the glass to another man. "Every soldier out there has got some kind of weapon stashed on him. But not *him*. The men around him, however, all have army-issued long-knives and swords. That's important. That means some-thing."

The scouts around him began to smile hesitantly as well.

One of them nodded. "That means it's time for you to go and make a report. Be careful, Woodson. We'll stay here and track their progress for as long as we can."

"But not for too long," Woodson whispered back. "I can't im-agine where Thorne thinks all of them are going to camp tonight. But some might make it up to here before nightfall."

"Understood."

Woodson and another scout slid backward from their position, wiping the ashy dirt behind them so as to make the earth look undisturbed. Once they reached the narrow ravine that opened to the canyon behind them, they stood up, sprinted along the narrow river bank to their horses, and raced for the hidden glacial fort.

Peto was in the orchard looking longingly at his trees. Still nothing: no buds, no blossoms—nothing.

It wasn't too late yet. Something still *might* come, he kept telling himself. He caressed the trunk of one of his favorite peach trees and analyzed its branches.

"Papa," a quiet voice said next to him, "it's all right. Think about it this way—if there's no fruit, there's no picking up mushy rotten peaches off the ground. There's also no raccoons raiding the orchard, or bees bothering . . ." Sakal's voice trailed off, realizing that with no fruit there was also a lot more that would be suffering.

Peto smiled and put his arm around his thirteen-year-old daughter who regarded being outside as a punishment.

"You're right, Sakal!" he said sunnily, knowing his children took their cues from his mood. "Maybe the orchard just needs to rest for a year. You certainly won't mind not coming out here and fighting the hornets for apples, now, will you?"

Sakal leaned against him. "That's right," she said, borrowing his brightness. "Besides, we have plenty of dried fruit."

"Mmm, mmm! My favorite," Peto said, trying to sound sincere. "Tough, chewy fruit, shriveled for traveling and storing convenience. So much better than having juice dribbling down your chin after you've bitten into a fresh peach."

Sakal grinned at his ridiculously merry tone. "I'll miss the blackberries, though," she confessed.

"So you'll appreciate them even more next year, right?"

"Right!"

They strolled back to the house, the sun hovering in the mid-afternoon sky. A layer of brownish cloud looking like old ash was slipping in front of it, filtering out the sun's brightest rays and causing the air to chill around them again. Peto felt Sakal shiver and he wrapped his arm tighter around her.

"Where's your coat?"

"I left it inside when I saw the sun was out. I thought it'd be warmer."

"So did I." He rubbed her arm covered only by a thin cotton sleeve. Mid Planting Season was usually much warmer than this.

She snuggled closer as they walked, not only for warmth but for comfort. "Papa, do you really think next year the world will remember how to warm up again?"

"I have no way of knowing what the world will do, Sakal. I just have to *hope* it will. Hope can get us through a great many worrisome days."

"Like today?"

"Oh, today's not so bad," Peto said breezily. "Usually the trees show signs of doing something by now, but if they need to rest this year after such a long snowing season, that's all right. We have plenty to see us through, right? Right?"

Sakal smiled at her father's optimism. As long as he was cheerful, she could be, too.

The chimes from the nearby messenger tower caused them both to pause and watch the banners rise.

Red emergency banner. General's banner—now the banner for Rector Peto Shin. Guide's banner.

Sakal swallowed hard and watched her father's face. Peto stared at the tower as the last signal went up.

Solid gray banner.

Peto couldn't breathe. He'd seen that banner only once, more than twenty-five years ago, when his own father had delivered them to the towers. He knew it was only a matter of time before it was hoisted, but suddenly that time was right now, and the future was abruptly shortened.

Only his daughter clutching his arm shook him out of his astonishment.

"Papa? Gray banner?" Sakal asked nervously.

"Yes," he said slowly, unable to pull his eyes away from it. After waiting for so many years for something to happen, it was happening.

"It means that the Army of Idumea is on the move," he told her somberly. "They're on the boulders."

In the large pasture behind the Briters' house, Deck, twenty-year-old Viddrow, and twelve-year-old Atlee were counting the expecting cows as their brother-in-law Lek, further up in the corral, marked them with a dab of yellow chalk on their rumps. The task wouldn't take long since the herd was still only a few dozen animals, but they were smiling because all of the cows were expecting. The herd would be growing. Life was returning.

The four of them paused when they heard the chimes, and they watched the banners go up. Their smiles turned to worried frowns. Confused, Viddrow and Atlee looked at each other when they saw the gray banner rise. Lek dropped from the fence he was straddling and jogged over to them.

"Gray banner?" Viddrow asked his brother-in-law.

Lek looked at Deck who had turned white. "Papa Deck?"

Deck's hand covered his mouth, dragging down his face. "Yes," he whispered. "Gray."

"DECKETT!"

Jaytsy was running from the back door, ten-year-old Yenali and nine-year-old Young Shem following on her heels.

"Deckett! Do you see it?"

Only when his wife was panicked did she call him by his full name. Deck caught her as she rushed through the gate. "Jaytsy, calm down. It's only gray. It's not *black*."

"But Deck—"

"I know. I know what it means, but—"

"PETO!" Jaytsy shouted when she saw her brother striding from his orchard to the lane that led to the Zenos's house.

Peto waved. "As soon as I know, I'll tell you. Don't panic."

"Too late," Deck called back as Peto took off in a jog.

"So what does a gray banner mean?" Viddrow demanded.

Lek looked at his in-laws. "It means the army of Idumea is moving beyond Edge. They're climbing the boulder field."

Jaytsy turned to her husband. "Go. Follow Peto. Find out what's happening—"

Deck tried his best calming tone, the one he used for the most agitated cows. "The messenger with the details won't arrive for at least another ten or fifteen minutes. This doesn't mean they're invading; it only means they are on the move. Perrin made all sorts of gray banners, if I remember correctly, to designate what the army was doing and where. As long as the banners remain gray, we're fine. Viddrow can keep planning his wedding and you can keep worrying about making the dinner afterward with the new in-laws."

"That's still six weeks away, Deck," Jaytsy said. "Will our son still get to take his bride in six weeks?"

Viddrow shifted nervously, his gaze darting between his father and mother. Yenali and Young Shem whimpered quietly.

Deck turned to his fourth son. "All you really need is to hold her hands while Rector Shin says a few words. No huge gathering, no big meal—you don't even need your house finished. You can stay with us."

"Papa," Viddrow said, growing restless, "she won't know what gray means. If you don't mind, I'd like to go—"

Lek patted him on the back as Deck said, "Her parents will know what a gray banner means. Tell her we can do it here or at her parents' house. Tonight, even. It doesn't matter where, just as long as it gets done."

Viddrow took off for the barn. A moment later he was riding Clark 14, bareback, to the southern part of Salem where his fiancé lived.

In the Shins' home, Lilla stood at the large front window staring at the tower. Sakal, eleven-year-old Centia, and nine-year-old Morah were by her side.

"I never thought I would see it. I mean, I knew *someday* I'd see it. Again. Not just when Papa Pere had them laid out on the eating table explaining why he chose gray to represent Idumea, but I just didn't think it would be *now*. I mean, with everything and all, it only makes sense that I *should* see it again, but to actually *see it*, up there, flying on the tower . . ."

Mahrree smiled at her babbling daughter-in-law. She wrapped an arm around fifteen-year-old Kew who stood close to his grandmother in case she needed supporting. She was strong and steady, but she wanted Kew to feel useful anyway.

"Remember, Lilla—it only means the army is moving. It doesn't mean it's being successful. I can just imagine them trying to climb those boulders!" she chuckled. "Kind of wish I could see them flopping like lost fish on the rocks."

She watched the previously-unused banner, still with creases in it from its many years of being folded, flapping in the breeze.

Perrin had folded it. Those creases were because of him.

She knew her smile was growing, and it was terrible to be so happy at a time like this, but she couldn't help it.

Perrin was now climbing the boulders, on his way back to her.

Shem saw the banners flying all over Salem. It was impossible to miss them. He was visiting a rectory on the eastern side when he heard the chimes. He didn't worry about it until a dozen Salemites came storming into the rector's house where he was visiting.

"Guide! Gray banner! What does it mean?"

Shem was startled, but only for a moment. He knew full well it was coming, he just didn't know what day. He rushed out the door and looked at the nearest tower. "Boulders," he whispered to the crowd pressing around him.

"We'll get your horse, Guide," the rector said and gestured to his son to retrieve Shem's mount.

He raced Silver home, hoping to be there when the messenger from the glacial fort arrived. As he rode up to the barn he shared with his married sons Lek and Boskos, he could see a small crowd of family and neighbors watching for him. He left Silver in a stall, rushed out of the barn, and over to Peto at his front porch.

"No messenger yet," Peto said, "but should be soon—"

As if waiting for those words, the sound of another set of hooves came down the lane. Everyone turned to see a young man dressed in mottled gray and black, riding fast.

He rushed straight for Shem, a folded parchment in his outstretched hand. "Guide, for you!"

"As I assumed." Shem smiled calmly and gestured to his sixteen-year-old daughter. "Huldah, get him something to eat—"

"But, Guide, I'm supposed to return with a response—"

"I know," Shem said patiently. "But a response may take a few minutes to compose. Rector Shin? Follow me to my office, please."

"Uncle Shem!" Cephas called after him. "Don't we get to hear the message?"

"Eventually. Rector?"

The two men strode into the house to hear Calla say to the growing crowd, "How about we all sit down on the front steps?"

Shem could feel the tension of everyone following him in the form of Peto as they made their way to his large office at the back of the house.

Trying to keep his own worry contained, Shem sat behind his desk as Peto grabbed a nearby chair. He sat down hard and bounced his leg nervously.

Shem opened the message and read.

Peto's leg bouncing increased in tempo and severity.

Shem nodded slowly, then stopped reading.

Now Peto's chair began to creak in time.

Shem glanced at Peto and finally folded the message—

"You're killing me, here!" Peto barked.

Shem smiled. "I never kill anyone if I can avoid it. I just give people something to remember me by. Perrin's advice—"

"*SHEM!*"

Shem chuckled apologetically, then sobered. "Last night, the entire army of Idumea gathered in Edge and promptly started a fire which burned a big section of tents well into the night. I think that's the haze we see in the sky now. Then, before midday meal today, the army began to scale the boulder field."

Peto sat back, deflated. "How many?"

"Remarkable, really. By the scouts' estimates, at least eighty thousand soldiers—"

"*Eighty* THOUSAND? Where'd they get them all?"

"My guess is they conscripted most of the able-bodied men."

"But eighty *THOUSAND?*"

"Yes, Peto. Say it as often as you wish, the number will not change. And Peto, that's the correct number."

"The correct number? What do you mean?"

Shem pulled out the copy of The Writings that sat on his desk, the margins filled with his notes and thoughts. He opened to the back of the book, to Hew Gleace's vision. "You were there, Peto. Hew saw fifty thousand marching into the dead valley before the ancient temple ruin—"

"But there's EIGHTY THOUSAND now!"

"And one third 'Lost to fear'?"

Peto sagged. "Two-thirds of eighty thousand is . . . about fifty-three thousand." He closed his eyes. "Shem, is this *it?*"

"I don't know, Peto, I really don't. But it's looking like *it.*"

Peto opened his eyes because Salem's planning rector began to consider logistics. "Where are they all going to camp?"

Shem held up the message. "That's what the scouts are wondering. I suspect most of the men won't make it over the rock tonight and will sleep in the crevices."

"Not a pleasant way to pass the night," Peto scoffed.

"Feel badly for them?"

"Hardly!"

Shem smirked. "The scouts are watching their progress. We can expect updates every few hours. Once the army has cleared the boulder field, the scouts will fly the next gray banner signaling that they're in the canyon."

"Hmm," Peto said. "I'll have to pull out the general's notes to see which gray pattern designates 'Army in canyon.' Shem, should we consider . . ."

"Moving the people?" he guessed. "I think it's a little premature. The army may give up and turn back. Not until they approach the glacial valley will I give the order to start for the ancient temple site."

"That's what Father would have done." Peto stood up, assuming they were done.

"Sit down, Peto."

Worried, Peto slowly sat down again. "What have you not told me yet?"

Shem paused. "I don't think you should share this with Lilla yet, but—"

"Is it Young Pere?"

Shem nodded. "They've spotted him. He was the first one on the boulders."

Peto closed his eyes again. "No . . . no . . . no . . ."

"But Peto, I don't think it was his choice."

The optimism in Shem's tone made Peto open his eyes. "What makes you say that?"

"The scouts didn't see him carrying a weapon. Everyone wore either a sword or a long knife, but Young Pere didn't wear a belt or sheath of any kind, and he was surrounded by armed men."

Weighing that information, Peto looked out the window. "They released him early this morning."

"I know. I felt it."

"So what did they promise him to get him to cooperate?"

"Maybe he *isn't* cooperating," Shem suggested. "Maybe that's why he was locked up in the first place. He might be on *our* side."

Peto shifted his gaze to Shem and chanced a smile. "Maybe he can get them lost?"

"Maybe he can buy us time," Shem agreed.

"But," Peto's hope was short-lived, "if he wastes *too* much time or pushes Thorne too much, then Thorne will become irritated—"

"Then again, Peto, maybe not . . ."

Peto never did understand why some people enjoyed suspense. The few books of that nature that he took the time to read created in him an urgency he didn't appreciate, and he'd always thumb to the back of the book to see how it all ended before he'd invest any more time in it.

He desperately wished that today he had *The Story of Young Perrin Shin* in his hands so he could see how it would all end.

Shem broke into his brooding with, "He's still alive, Peto."

"But for how long, Shem?"

Versa knocked on the front door, and a moment later it swung open.

"Mrs. Kiah! I mean, Miss Thorne. Or is it—"

"Versa," she said to her new rector's wife, a kind woman with a perpetual smile. "Just Versa, now."

The rector's wife smiled wider. "Understood. What can we do for you?"

Versa gestured to the tower in the distance, the northernmost one built. "What does *that* mean?"

A voice from behind the rector's wife called, "Found it! I knew it was in that file somewhere, I just had to . . . ah, Mrs. Ki— I mean, Versa."

"Hello, Rector. I was just wondering about—" She cocked her head to the tower flying the gray banner.

"Aren't we all!" he exclaimed, waving a large sheet of parchment covered with writing. "Come in, come in. Three of our children ran down to the tower to get the official word, but I knew I had the information somewhere in my office."

Versa followed the rector and his wife into their gathering room. "There are quite a few people collecting at the tower," she told them. "I just didn't feel like walking all the way over there. Crowds and such, you know," her voice quieted. "In case it means . . ."

They knew her story so she didn't bother to finish her explanation. Instead, she plopped on their sofa and sighed.

The rector's wife sat next to her and patted her leg. "Don't you worry about anything or anyone, Sweety. You can't get further away from the world than here."

The rector nodded. "No one here cares who your father is, Versa. We care only for *you*. I think you might find this interesting." He handed her the parchment and sat down next to her.

"Banner codes?"

"Yes, in *his* handwriting," the rector said reverently. "General Perrin Shin. I went with my father to the meeting the general called when he visited. I was around your age. He gave one of these charts to every rector. This was in my father's possession until I took over the rectory when he died. We have all of the banners memorized, except for these." He took the parchment and turned it over. "The Gray Side, the general called it. He didn't want anyone overly concerned with these until the time was necessary, so he wrote those codes on the opposite side."

Versa stared intently at banner signals in the general's writing.

Solid gray—Army of Idumea attempting to breach the boulder field.

Versa exhaled, as did the rector and his wife.

"Just how bad *are* those boulders?" the wife asked nervously.

"Very," Versa told her. "They're enormous, like thousands of elephants turned to stone and stacked precariously upon each other."

The rector smiled at her description. "Been reading about the expeditions to the far west, I see."

Versa smiled faintly back. "Actually, I've been reading Terryp's *Stories of the World*. I needed something fanciful to distract me."

"Well, I imagine Rector Shin and the Guide will be sending further details once they have them," the rector said. "As soon as I receive word, I'll be sure to let you and your mother and sister know what's happening."

"Thank you, Rector." Versa sighed and read the rest of the codes.

Striped gray—army in the canyon.

Mottled gray—army at the glacial fort.

Spotted gray—army approaching Salem.

Black with white sword—evacuate your area immediately

Solid black—army has entered Salem

"I don't think we need to worry until we see the mottled gray banners," the rector decided. "The army may give up well before then."

"But still," his wife said, "this would be a good opportunity to tell all the families in the rectory to check their travel packs and make sure they're not in need of anything." As her husband nodded in agreement and made a note, his wife continued. "Versa, your family each has a pack, right?"

Versa nodded blankly.

Picking up on her silent cues, the rector's wife patted her leg again. "How are you doing, dear? Really?"

"All right, I suppose," she said distractedly, still staring at General Shin's writing. She felt oddly connected to it, probably because it was signaling what her father was up to. Still, there was something about General Shin's hand that almost beckoned to her.

"It seems that a few weeks after the request has been granted the reality of it all sinks in," the rector prodded gently.

Versa bobbed her head, because that was also at the back of her mind, trying to push forward for no good reason. "I don't know why it should bother me. I'm the one who requested the termination of marriage."

"But it doesn't mean you're entirely happy about it."

"My marriage didn't even last seven moons," Versa exhaled in disgust. "Although Guide Zenos said he thought it was a miracle it lasted that long." She chuckled sadly. "It's not that I really loved him. Not the kind of love I see here. It's just—"

When she didn't finish, the rector's wife suggested, "It's just that now's not the best time to be alone?"

Versa nodded.

The rector put a fatherly arm around her. "You're never alone in Salem, Versa. I have a list of families and men who have all volunteered to come to your family's aid whenever you need it. You won't have to endure anything without help."

"I know," she whispered.

"*Actually*," the rector continued in a different tone, "some of those men who signed the list are younger and *single*. You've turned quite a few heads since moving here. I see them turning when you walk into the congregational services."

Versa scoffed. "Do they *know* who I am?"

"They do," the rector chuckled. "Whenever you're ready, so are they. There are some excellent young men out there, Versa, impressed with this strong, sharp young woman."

"It's true, Versa," his wife put in. "Don't give up just yet."

"No offense, Rector," Versa said as tactfully as she knew

how, "but I see men as dogs, and right now I have no desire for *any* kind of breed."

"Rector Shin told me something like that," the rector said forgivingly. "But don't you think that might change in time?"

Versa gave him a slightly nasty look. "You've been speaking to Rector Shin, and probably Guide Zenos, and so you all say the same things to me."

The rector smiled. "I think it's because we're all inspired by the same Being."

Versa sent her look to the ceiling. "I told You, I'm *not interested* right now."

The rector and his wife laughed.

"He listens, you know," the rector told Versa. "But He listens closer to your *heart* than to your *words.*"

Versa finally cracked a smile. "Those single men are going to have to be exceptionally excellent, Rector, to turn my head."

Private Shin heaved himself over the last boulder and nearly wept for joy. He landed in a narrow channel, with the boulders on one side and the mountain curving sharply upward on the other. Salemites used to hide their horses up there, and while much of the rock had shifted, it was still wide enough for a couple of people to walk side-by-side.

"I can't believe I made it," he panted.

"Nor can I," Pal said, rolling off the boulder on to the muddy ground below.

Buddy fell next to him in an exhausted heap.

Snarl was already lying on a narrow flat stone up the mountain's side several paces, away from the mud and snow patches. "Just a good workout," he sniffed.

"Great view from here!" Cloud Man said, his hands on his waist. "You can really see the new Hill of Deceit. It's enormous! It's like the entire mountain blew to the side."

"That's because that's what happened, you vial head," Snarl grumbled.

Cloud Man blinked. "I didn't say anything vile. Did I?" He dropped down by Shin.

Shin patted Cloud Man, his favorite soldier. "No, Cloud Man.

You weren't 'vile.' He was talking about the *vials*, as in getting fogged?"

"Ah," Cloud Man said, but his dark eyes still looked lost.

"Go find us a camp site, Cloudy," Shin suggested. "We got here first, we should have first pick."

Cloud Man nodded and started surveying the mountainside. It used to be covered with trees and shrubs, but since all of them were now dead, what lay before him was a steep and uneven surface of sticks and rocks. Cloud Man's face contorted as he glanced back. "Uh, not a whole lot of options there, Shin."

"Try going to the east, Cloudy. I see some flat spaces over there, up the mountainside. Be quick about it, before some other soldier takes it."

"Yes, sir," Cloudy said, and took off in an ungainly jog.

Reg reached the top of the boulder in time to see Cloud Man bounding to the only flat area available. "How does he have any energy left? I swear we've been climbing for five hours."

"Six," Snarl said, not opening his eyes.

"So that's why I'm hungry," Teach grumbled from his sprawled position on a boulder.

Sergeant Beaved was behind him, holding a stick, and Shin wondered if Teach had been prodded along.

"You've been hungry for hours," Beaved said as he slid down from the boulder and landed in the mud. He grimaced as he looked at his filthy boots. "Well, this will be fun to sleep in, won't it?"

"I, for one, will not have a problem sleeping tonight," Buddy said, still lying in the mud. "This is not entirely uncomfortable."

"That's because you're on my legs!" Pal snapped at him.

Buddy reluctantly sat up.

Hammer and Iron appeared at the top of the boulders and quickly counted the men below them.

"Where's Cloud Man?" Sergeant Beaved asked.

Shin gestured. "Over there, securing our camp site. Everyone's here and accounted for, Sergeant."

Beaved eyed him. "That's not *your* responsibility you know, Shin. Keeping track of us?"

"Isn't it?" he asked innocently. "Shouldn't I make sure my 'protection' is accounted for and comfortable?"

Beaved nodded, seeing how the game was being played.

"When you put it that way, *of course*. I'm just wondering, why did Cloud Man feel the need to find our camp site?"

"Because *Private* Shin told him to," Snarl drawled. "Cloud Man even called Shin 'sir.'"

Shin waved that off. "Cloud Man was just responding instinctively. But look, he does have the best spot. I recommend we get up there before someone higher ranked does." He pointed down the boulder field where the blond and gray streaked hair of General Thorne was just coming into view. Somewhere he'd lost his cap, and with only one good arm, his progress had been slowed considerably. More than once Shin had looked back in smug satisfaction to see Lemuel Thorne struggling. Amory hadn't even started up the boulders, from what he could tell.

"But, sir," Shin said to Beaved, taking care to bat his eyelids innocuously, "only if *you* want to."

Beaved studied him for a moment before saying, "Hammer, drag Teach over to Cloud Man. He can annoy away anyone who tries to take our camp site."

That evening in Salem, one of many weddings was hastily planned and pushed up for the morning, just in case. A bedroom in a small new house was hurriedly completed, so the newlyweds would have a place to sleep while the rest of the house was finished in the next few days, and an extended family began to gather.

Just in case.

Shin looked out over the scene before him and felt a sense of satisfaction. As it grew darker, eighty thousand soldiers had to find ways to camp for the night.

At least half of them had to be cursing General Thorne under their breath, those who found themselves trying to find a comfortable way to sleep on the rock.

Then again, the approximately twenty thousand who made it to the top of the boulder field also might be upset with their situation. They had to camp in the crowded rock channel, or in the slushy snow, mud, and dead foliage that littered the sloping landscape.

Shin smiled to himself, because he was one of the few resting comfortably. He had cut the branches off of the few living pine trees that remained, under the close supervision of Hammer and Iron, and using Cloud Man's real army long knife. He laid the branches under his group's bedrolls, the same way the Shin, Briter, and Zenos men camped every year on their trips to mark the paths to the ancient temple site. The branches not only added a layer of cushioning, but they elevated them above the cold ground an inch or two, and smelled pleasant. Even Snarl was impressed.

Below Shin's security team and the boulder field, many fires were glowing, scattered over several miles to the east and west. Those soldiers didn't even get a chance to start climbing today, so slow was the progress of those before them. They sat in the dead forest playing Dices and setting up camps. Shin wondered if any of them had the good sense to head back to Edge and the fort, and sleep in a decent bed for the night.

Because while the forest was dead, it wasn't done with undoing the army. Word had gone out that at least fifty soldiers had already been lost before even reaching the boulder field. Some had leaned too far over a precipice, trying to see into bottomless caverns, and tumbled down into them. That stupid event sent out worried whispers that the Shins were still haunting the forests, dragging unwitting soldiers to their deaths, falling into the same crevices that the old colonel and his wife were lost to. That in turn caused other soldiers with much more bravado to start making jokes about Colonel Shin recruiting soldiers for his army of the dead, which then caused a few more dozen men to turn around and head straight back to Edge, with their commanders shouting at them to return.

Still others, curious about the now-dry geysers, had jumped up and down around the holes hoping to start them spouting again, not realizing the crust of earth around them was thin. The men broke through, falling several hundred feet to their deaths into new caverns.

In other areas of the forest, pockets of noxious gases still remained, seeping unseen from the ground, and overcame several soldiers who didn't take the hint from the dead deer in the area.

While the forest was no longer belching hot water and steam, it was still swallowing naïve men. And while Shin had always loved the forests, he was loving this one even more. It seemed to be on his side.

Officers set up rope barricades to caution soldiers about hazards, and frantic warnings were shouted back and forth that while there may not be any more steam rising, the pits were still dangerous.

That had seemed obvious to Shin, but then he remembered that the average person in the world couldn't recognize the obvious even if it were written across the trees.

Those who had reached the boulders and the slopes above breathed more easily that the forest hadn't yet cracked open and engulfed them. But that didn't mean anyone was resting well in the unfamiliar and unlevel terrain.

Slightly below Shin and to the west, on another relatively flat piece of ground, General Thorne was seated by a fire in discussion with several officers. He was drawing a crude map in the mud in front of him and gesturing toward the canyon to the east.

Shin sighed. Of course that was the next direction to take. Thorne figured that out, or maybe Amory told him. He was quite certain he hadn't accidentally revealed anything that day which could have been useful to finding Salem.

While Buddy and Pal peppered him with questions about his childhood, looking for clues, Shin answered with vague references to sandy areas, grassy plains, and old structures. Neither of Thorne's young spies suspected he was describing Terryp's land, but were sure he was feeding them something vital.

While he was cutting the pine branches, he noticed that Buddy had slipped over to Thorne's camp to talk to the general. From behind a tree, Shin did his own spying as Thorne gave Buddy a thin smile and a quick pat on the back. Apparently they felt something significant had been revealed.

As Shin watched Thorne conversing with his officers, he decided it was time to stretch his legs again. He explained to Beaved the nature of his stroll, and that he'd always be in sight, but it didn't matter. Hammer and Iron were sent to stand watch over him, albeit from a distance.

He sauntered over to the line waiting to use "the tree." It seemed spending their first night in Camp Edge without designated latrines had demonstrated to the body of the army the need to be a little more particular about such things.

He glanced around at the dozens standing with him and made sure his pack was slung over his front to hide the SHIN name patch before he said, "All I can say is, thank goodness Thorne listens more to himself than his officers." Then he braced for the response.

Several men turned to him.

"Meaning what?" asked one.

"Meaning that we get tomorrow off to rest," Shin grinned. "For scaling the boulder field, we get to sit on the mountainside and watch as the rest of the army catches up. I could use a day of naps."

That did it. The mood around him brightened considerably.

"Rest? Really?"

"It's about time Thorne did something right!"

"I'm going to sleep until midday meal."

"My feet are killing me. So are my legs, and my arms, and my side where I fell on it—"

"Yes, yes," Shin continued, "the officers told the general we should keep on to find the route, because splitting up the army isn't *that* dangerous—"

"Wait, why would it be dangerous?" asked one man.

"Scouts, I heard," said another. "They have scouts watching the forest and Edge. No doubt we've probably already been spotted. They may already be developing a strategy against us."

"Like what?"

"Like arrows?" suggested someone.

"Like *that's* going to help me sleep soundly tonight. First mud and rock, now the thought of being picked off like chickens?"

"You use arrows to kill chickens?"

"Well, don't worry, men!" Shin interrupted cheerily. "Thorne won't make us go on. He's going to do the right thing, not let his fears get the best of him and charge ahead needlessly. No, letting the army rest so we travel as one mass is the best idea."

"I certainly approve of that," said another soldier to the agreement of everyone else.

Shin did his business and sauntered back to his camp. He watched as the men dispersed from "the tree" into different directions. The way good news spread in the army, his gossip would reach even the farthest camps within an hour.

Satisfied, he sat down on his bedroll between Hammer and

Iron, below Pal, and above Buddy. The other five men filled in the gaps around them. He was sufficiently "protected," with a clear view of Thorne's camp.

And Thorne had a clear view of him. A few times he caught the general peering up at him.

And so was Poe Hili. The sergeant major was visibly exhausted, since he'd been helping pull Thorne over the rock again and again. At one point he caught Shin's eye, and sent him a quick nod and a warning glare.

Shin smiled easily back and wondered where Guide Lannard Kroop might be sleeping tonight. While Thorne had trudged up the boulders, Guide Lannard had stayed at the bottom of the boulder field, tapping soldiers on their heads to "bless" them as they embarked on their quest to liberate Salem. He shouted nonsensical phrases into the air, babbling in words "known only to the Creator."

Shin had avoided getting near him, afraid he might snigger. That morning Guide Lannard entered the dead forest wearing a purple silk robe that shimmered and billowed in the breeze. Gold edging along the border caught the sunlight and gleamed. Lannard Kroop was in his element as the soldiers gaped in admiration.

It was the first time Shin had seen him since he left for Idumea, but the role of 'Guide' had obviously grown on him during the past five moons. As he walked, or rather *floated* through the forest, he kept his eyes half-closed and his arms outstretched, as if to call to him the birds of the forest . . . or to keep his balance. He spoke in a lyrical cadence, often elongating his words in a most annoying sing-song manner.

But everyone ate it up. Soldiers flocked to him, begging for a blessing. Their women also came to Lannard, asking him to protect their men as they followed Thorne.

Even Buddy, Pal, and Reg rushed over to be touched by Lannard. But Teach rolled his eyes. He came from Edge and knew of Lannard before he was the guide.

Hammer, Iron, and Snarl merely watched as Lannard drifted past, and Beaved smiled faintly. Or maybe smirked, Shin wasn't sure. Cloud Man was too preoccupied examining a pinecone for cloud-like features to notice who chanted past him.

But Shin watched him, daring Guide Lannard to catch his eye. Not once did Lannard shift his gaze, although Shin was sure he knew the private was close enough to stick out a leg and trip him. Former

Major Kroop probably worried he'd involuntarily shudder again if he made eye contact with Private Shin.

Shin lay back on his bedroll as the forest darkened around him and looked up into the cold stars. Lannard would probably steal back to the mansion tonight to his favorite guest room, and probably with a favorite guest.

But, oh, what a waste! he thought. What a fantastic night, sleeping under the stars. Few people understood what real freedom was.

IF ONLY I HAD A PINE CONE TO THROW AT YOUR HEAD, he heard the words on the right side of his mind, THIS NIGHT WOULD BE PERFECT. BEAUTIFUL WORK AT "THE TREE," BY THE WAY. CLEVER. THEY'LL POSITIVELY HATE HIM IN THE MORNING WHEN HE GETS THEM UP.

He grinned. That's the point, he thought.

IT WON'T WORK, THOUGH. BUT IT DOESN'T HAVE TO, BECAUSE THERE'S A PLAN . . .

The knocking on Shem's door had been almost constant. That's why he'd set up Zaddick, his third son—strapping and age twenty-two—as a guard to sit on the front porch and remind people that if they had concerns or questions they had capable rectors, the words of past prophecies, and no more knowledge than Guide Zenos, so go home, pray for comfort, get your houses in order, and be ready if the banners change.

Shem was busy in his office going over every last detail, making sure he wasn't missing a thing, and reviewing again the timelines and scenarios he and Peto had outlined earlier, trying to determine when the evacuation banners should go up.

That's why he was surprised when he heard the front door open. Someone had made it past Sentry Zaddick. When his office door opened a moment later, there stood Calla with her warning smile fixed in place.

Shem stiffened, sure that behind her would be Eltana Yordin ready to yell at him.

Instead, Colonel Jon Offra marched through the door, with a quiet Teman behind him, looking apologetic.

Shem folded his arms. This would be interesting.

Since they'd stolen Offra from the world last year before Mt. Deceit erupted and destroyed most of the northern half of the world, Salem had been trying to find ways to integrate Jon into their society. He did admirably well, trying to find ways to contribute, despite the fact that he vacillated between three aspects of his personality: child-like and submissive, genial and—for lack of a better word—normal, and full-on caustic, angry army officer. Who showed up, and for how long each personality stayed, made every conversation with him a minor adventure. That's why Shem was so grateful for Teman, a widower of immense patience and kindness who spent time as a scout in the world when he was a younger man. He now devoted all his energy to keeping Jon as level as possible, which was a full-time task.

Shem braced himself before asking, "Jon, how are you this evening? What can I do for you?"

Offra was in full colonel mode as he leaned across the desk. "I'm here for you, Guide Zenos!" From his jacket he pulled a wad of folded pages and dropped them on his desk. "I've been working all afternoon—your counterattack plans."

Behind him, Teman was shrugging helplessly, undoubtedly having told Jon that Salem wasn't about to fight, that it was a place of peace.

Shem nodded to Teman and turned his attention to Jon who was spreading the pages across the desk. "Here. Here's where we begin, with a few hundred archers at the top of the ridge above the boulder field. As men come over the rocks, it'll be easy to pick them off, and the Salemites will be well hidden and inaccessible—"

"Jon," Shem tried to interrupt, but the colonel wasn't listening.

"—Should Lemuel and his idiots not have enough of that, we can position lines all across these mountain tops. Here, I've done diagrams from the points I remember on my way up, but Peto would likely have better ideas. We could eliminate the entire army, unseen, simply by positioning archers throughout the canyon—"

"But, Jon—"

"—The Army of Idumea will be the easiest target. Even twelve-year-olds could pick them off—"

"No, Jon. We will not fight."

Somehow Jon heard those quiet words, and he looked up as if he'd been slapped. "What did you say?"

"No, Jon. We will not fight."

Something in his countenance shifted, the shadowy flickering they'd come to expect when Jon changed, and it seemed his child-like, innocent expression was trying to come up, but a twitching snap of the colonel's head sent him away.

"Teman told me you refused to fight," Colonel Offra said, a sneer forming. "But I thought that was because you have no commander. You lost General Shin, but you now have Colonel Offra. And, Guide, this will work." He waved a page like a battle flag.

Shem smiled kindly. "I know it'd work, Colonel. I have complete confidence in your plans. But there's one hitch: fighting isn't the Creator's will for us. He has told us He'll fight this battle for us as long as we get to safety."

Jon gripped the page tighter, as if someone was trying to wrench it out of his hand. "But how do you know the Creator didn't intend for the battle to be fought like this? That He didn't send me to you, now? I never resigned, you know. I'm still an officer in that army! In fact, I graduated a year before Lemuel, and in a battle situation I have seniority. I'm ahead of all of them! Shem, if I could kill Lemuel, I'd be the head of that entire army and I could turn it around and send it back to Edge!"

"That's true," Shem said quietly. "That's very, very true. And here's something more: I never resigned, either. And I joined the army many years before you did—"

"That's right!" Jon gasped excitedly. "Sergeant Major, you outrank everyone in battle! So then march down there and end it all—"

"I couldn't," Shem said. "They'd kill me on sight, as they would you. Colonel, I appreciate your enthusiasm to defend us, but I know that the Creator has a plan for us, and that entails us leaving before the army ever arrives. No one should engage them, and no one should have to die."

"But the army will take over everything—the houses, the farms, the arena—"

"I know. Let them. The Creator will fix it all. Jon, do you believe me?"

Colonel Offra was beginning to sag. "For some strange reason, against all common sense and training, I do."

Shem grinned. "That's because you're a Salemite, Jon. You were baptized by us and you accepted us, and the Creator, right now, is pouring into your mind the notion that you can accept His plan. Right?"

Offra sank into a chair, and behind him, Teman exhaled quietly in relief.

"It makes no sense, though," Jon murmured. "Why . . . why just give up? Give everything up?"

"We're not giving up," Shem said. "We're letting the Creator take over. He wants to save all of us, not just the Salemites. He wants to give all of His children a chance, including those trying to invade us. Consider this: if we send an arrow into every clueless man down there—those who were *forced* into this army—we don't give them a fair chance at rejecting Thorne. Once they're in Salem, though, they'll have the opportunity to turn their backs on Lemuel. They'll have the choice to follow him or stop fighting. And a few will, Jon. I don't know how many, but we do know that one-third of them will be 'lost to fear.' Again, I'm not sure how that's going to happen, but that fear may be the very thing that saves them from doing something brutal and horrible. It just may save *them*. We have to give them that chance to redeem themselves, to make their hearts open to the Creator."

Jon sat pondering, and eventually the colonel faded, replaced by his childlike countenance. "All right, then," he finally whispered. "We have to give everyone a chance to make the right choice. What we lose in Salem doesn't matter. But losing our souls and theirs? *That* matters."

"Well said, Jon," Shem smiled.

Jon looked up and met his eyes, and another shift occurred. Now he was the friendly Offra and his eyes glittered. "But *part* of my plan has merit, Shem. There are hundreds of hiding places along those mountains."

"I know," Shem said. "That's where our scouts will be, spying on their progress."

Jon held up a finger. "And where I could be, shouting down warnings into the canyons in the same manner as I used to shout at the forts in the world. Fear?"

Shem was about to dismiss that idea until he found himself beginning to smile. "The world thinks you're dead, Jon. Probably buried under Deceit."

"Yes, yes they do." Jon was grinning now. "Imagine how terrifying it'd be for Lemuel and those who remember me to hear my voice raining down upon them from above?"

It was the soft giggling in the corner that drew the attention of both men.

Teman was trying to be noiseless but unsuccessfully. "It would be fantastic," he whispered apologetically. "I used to be a scout, you know: in the world and in those mountains. I know of some good spots where one's voice really carries."

Jon spun back in his chair, beaming. All three parts of him seemed to be there, eagerly hoping to pick up his old habit of terrifying soldiers.

Shem couldn't help but beam back. "Let the fear begin!"

When Shem headed up the stairs to bed late that night, he was still smiling that they'd found a purpose for Jon Offra. Completely drained by the day and long evening, he couldn't wait to finally fall into bed next to Calla who he'd already sent on ahead, but he stopped in the hallway when he saw Huldah timidly standing in her doorway.

He frowned at the sixteen-year-old. "What's wrong, sweety? Why are you up so late?"

"Papa . . . I don't understand. Why, why do we hate Lemuel Thorne so much?" she stammered.

Shem exhaled and leaned against the wall. "We've talked about this before, haven't we? How Captain Thorne tried to capture Aunt Mahrree and Uncle Perrin, how he chased them all down in the forest so he could send them to Idumea for trial—"

"But," she faltered, "why, why do *we* hate him. Aren't we supposed to love our enemies? Be nice to them? The Salem way?"

"Ooh, boy," Shem sighed. He wasn't going to get to bed anytime soon. He nodded for her to go back to her bedroom, and he followed. She got back into her bed, wrapping a quilt protectively around her, a shield against the world.

Shem sat down on her reading chair. "We've tried, Huldah. We've tried to love them. You remember what Uncle Peto did last year, right? Sneaking into Edge with my jacket, then Uncle Perrin's jacket, to offer them our food reserves?"

"But they didn't believe it," Huldah recalled. "They thought it was a trap of some kind."

"That's how they think in the world," Shem said. "That everyone's out to get them, that no one is ever kind unless they have another motive."

She blinked at him, confused.

Subterfuge wasn't Salem's way. It wasn't even a word in Salem.
"Can't you just talk to him or something?" she asked.

Shem snorted, but tried to cover it. "Try to talk to him . . . Huldah,
he's told the world he's killed me! He's built his entire reputation on
that lie. You really think he'd listen to me?"

"But . . . but you used to work together in the fort. Weren't you
ever friends?"

"Friends." Shem tried hard not to scoff. "Oh, Huldah. I tried. I
did, but . . ." He looked down at his hands guiltily. "That's a question
that's bothered me for decades," he confessed. "Did I try hard
enough? Probably not," he whispered.

"Why not, Papa?"

Shem sat back and stared off into a corner. "Because my big
brother hated him. I know, I know—sounds stupid when I put it that
way, but you have to understand: Perrin was an excellent judge of
character. I trusted him, implicitly. And he trusted me. When his parents were killed, and I chased him down as he rode to Idumea bent on
revenge, I was willing to help him with anything. I stopped him, if
you recall, from killing the Administrator of Loyalty."

Her voice was tiny when she asked, "I've always wondered, *how*
did you stop him?"

They normally didn't share the gruesome details of the world with
their children.

But if they asked, then—

"Perrin had thrown his sword on the large polished table of the
Administrators and told them to explain what happened to his parents.
If he didn't like the answer, he threatened that he'd retrieve his sword
and use it. Administrator Gadiman taunted him about their murder,
and Uncle Perrin was sure Gadiman had something to do with it. He
leaped onto that table to grab his sword again, and I scrambled on top
of him. While he held the sword to Gadiman's heart, I wrapped my
arm around his throat and . . . choked him."

Huldah's mouth dropped open. "You could have killed Uncle
Perrin!"

"I know," he whispered. "I very nearly did. I was only trying to
make him pass out, but he was an exceptionally strong man, and I had
to squeeze him harder than I expected. The scouting corps trains men
in those ways, you know."

Her shocked expression said that she didn't know.

"He finally did go limp," Shem continued, "and I was a bit in shock myself. At how angry Uncle Perrin was, at how close I came to taking his life. That was a very hard time, Huldah. You know that's when his nightmares began, right?"

She nodded sadly. While she had never encountered an enraged, sleep-walking Puggah, she'd seen her cousins the mornings after they had.

"They took away all of his friends after that, Huldah, the Administrators did. Took away Brillen Karna, who'd served with him even longer than I had. Took away Captain Rigoff and Grandpy Neeks and even Poe Hili. We used to be a family, Huldah. Uncle Perrin was like the papa of that fort. Karna, Rigoff and I were the uncles, Grandpy was the . . . well, the grandpy. Poe was our little brother. Then gone. All of them. Just when Uncle Perrin needed his support group the most to help him with his trauma, Chairman Mal snatched them all away. Except for me, because he thought I was one of *them*."

"That'd be incredibly hard," she whispered. "To lose everybody."

Shem nodded. "Harder than you'll ever know. Uncle Perrin held that fort together. The men loved him, the village loved him. He was so charismatic, when he allowed himself to be." Shem smiled in remembrance. "He was so solid and strong. Not just physically, but emotionally, mentally, even spiritually. So many men looked up to him. He fathered most of them—"

When Huldah's eyes grew large, he quickly amended.

"I mean, *he looked after them*. Took them under his wing, like he did with Jon Offra. He came to the fort after the mess in Idumea, as a replacement for Captain Rigoff. All of the soldiers would do anything for Perrin. That's why, later, Grandpy Neeks and Sheff Gizzada led the sergeants' army to the administrative headquarters to kill Qayin Thorne and the administrators. That's why Poe Hili led the younger soldiers out of the garrison in Idumea all the way down to Colonel Karna and Colonel Fadh, all in the name of Perrin Shin, who they thought was dead. It's why Jon Offra was here tonight, wanting to help us—because he loved Perrin Shin."

Huldah was quiet, thinking. Then she said, "So why doesn't Lemuel Thorne love Uncle Perrin?"

Shem had to ponder that one a while. "I think he did, Huldah. I think that, under everything, he did. Uncle Perrin was rather useless as a commander for nearly a year after his parents died. He didn't notice anything around him, too lost in his own nightmares and paranoia. He didn't notice that Lemuel Thorne, as a mere captain only twenty-two years old, was taking over everything. I think Lemuel was desperate to impress him, to be seen as a helper, a savior of the fort. But Perrin couldn't respond. Neither could I. I was too wrapped up in Perrin's trauma to do anything about Lemuel, who was like . . . was like a tumor, I guess, growing bigger and uglier and taking over everything. Even before we all got to Edge, Uncle Perrin had told me that Lemuel was . . . what was the phrase he used again? Something like, 'mushroom pudding.'"

Huldah wrinkled her nose in disgust.

"My reaction as well. We were supposed to like it, even though it was all wrong. We're pretty sure Thorne was sent as Chairman Mal's spy. We found out later he was sending messages back to Idumea about Aunt Mahrree. He was trying to bring her down for some reason, not Uncle Perrin.

"It's interesting," Shem reflected. "Perrin took care of so many soldiers, took them aside, trained them individually, challenged them to races, dropped extra slices of pie next to them as he passed in the mess hall, but never with Lemuel. It's like he *couldn't*. It must have been that suspicion that Lemuel was there to dig up dirt on him, but instead Lemuel wanted to take down Mahrree instead. It was as if, as if he was trying to *help* Perrin somehow. Even then, even when Perrin was refusing to take Lemuel under his wing, Lemuel still tried to get there. He still wanted the father of the fort to . . . I don't know, father him maybe?"

Shem was growing uncomfortable with this line of thinking, and was too aware of the steady gaze of his daughter in the candlelight.

"Papa?" she asked timidly. "Do you hate him? Lemuel Thorne?"

"Oh, Huldah—you're asking a lot of difficult questions tonight." He looked into his innocent daughter's face and suddenly remembered Jaytsy.

She was the same age, just sixteen, when Lemuel dragged her to a hay barn intent on—

Shem leaped to his feet and paced back and forth. The rage that had so immediately overtook him also startled him. He glanced at his daughter, now shrinking in worry at her father's abrupt behavior.

He couldn't shake the image, the vision of Lemuel trying to take his sweet little girl like he tried to attack Jaytsy—

He rubbed his forehead vigorously, trying to rub away the image, rid himself of the aggression that still he felt at the oddest of times: the sergeant major overpowering Salem's guide. The soldier who wanted to find a blade and charge over the mountain to kill one more time . . .

He'd taken many men's lives, but only once had he held a knife to a man's throat and *delighted* in it. It was when he was sitting on Lemuel's chest, after Jaytsy had fled the barn, with the point of Shem's long knife pricking Lemuel's throat. Oh, how he had wanted to thrust it in! To see the blood trickle, to hear Lemuel gasp and perhaps struggle, to watch him die—

Shem gripped his head and tried to keep his pacing from turning into stomping. No, no, no . . . that's not what he was! He took lives only when the Creator told him it was necessary, and only once in his life did he have that raw thirst for blood. Only once, so many years ago, and here it was, back again, and he could see so clearly in his mind how he could take a butcher knife, steal his way up the canyons—he knew all of the hiding places, some that no scouts knew—and slip among the soldiers and stab Lemuel and end everything, end it that very night . . .

"Papa?"

The tiny squeak somehow made it to his ears, and he stopped pacing.

"Should I go get Mama? You look a little . . . worried." She was pale and trembling, unsure of why her gentle, quiet father was suddenly agitated and now clenching his fists as if wishing there was a hilt in them.

Dear Creator! he cried in his mind. Look at her! I've terrified my baby girl! Take this away, *please take this away*—

Instantly the rage was gone, the desire for blood vanished.

He dropped to his knees in front of her bed. "I'm sorry, Huldah, so sorry." He took her hands. "I, uh . . . this is the closest I've been to the world in a while. Sometimes it feels like it's trying to grab me and drag me back."

"It did, didn't it?" she whispered.

He nodded, a few remorseful tears leaking down his face. "I'm sorry. I was a soldier for a long time, you know. Sometimes . . . sometimes I feel I need to be one again. I don't want to, I didn't always like being a soldier, but you develop an instinct, you see, and—"

She didn't see. She didn't need to. She stared at his face, hopeful but apprehensive.

Shem smiled, though he hardly felt like smiling. "You asked me a very important question a minute ago, one that really startled me. Do I hate Lemuel Thorne? To be honest, I don't know, Huldah. I don't want to hate him. I try not to. But he hurt a lot of people who I love, and it's hard to love someone who's done that. Even after all these years."

"But what if . . . what if, he was your brother? Or, like your nephew?" she suggested. "Didn't you say that the fort was like a family? If you were the uncle, wouldn't he have been the nephew?"

"Huldah, I swear you're trying to kill me tonight with the sharpness of your questions."

"Sorry, Papa."

"But you're right. And I still don't know the answer to that."

She squirmed. "Then . . . what about Young Pere? He's your nephew, and he hurt a lot of people you love. Do you . . . do you hate Young Pere?"

Shem sagged. "That?! All of this is about Young Pere?!" He laughed in relief and sank to the floor. "Oh, Huldah—no, I do not hate Young Pere! I love him, immensely. He's been stupid, but I've never stopped loving him. I wanted to go retrieve him once myself, but I was told I shouldn't. Is that what you've been worried about?"

Huldah shrugged. "Yeah, kind of. Well, yes. A little worried. I miss him. Yes, he was stupid, but he's a funny stupid. He was always entertaining."

Shem grinned. "To say the least. I promise you, Huldah, wherever Young Pere is when we finally spot him, I'll rush to his side and rescue him, if he needs it. But knowing him, he'll likely be in the middle of some immense chaotic accident, so it might take me a minute or two. But we'll get him back, and we'll love him even more, if that's possible."

Huldah relaxed and smiled. "Good. Thank you, Papa." She paused, lost in thought, and said, "If you can still love Young Pere, why is it so much harder to love Lemuel Thorne? He was stupid too, right? And he wasn't raised as well as Young Pere, either. Why is it so much harder to love him? It's been a long time, too."

The discussion had turned difficult again. "It goes back to my big brother, I guess," he said. "Perrin hated him—and Huldah, know that he rarely hated anyone. I never knew an officer with so much love as Uncle Perrin. But when he did hate someone, it was for very good reasons. Therefore, I did too."

He leaned against her bed and whispered, "But maybe I shouldn't have."

Unconsciously, he started clenching his fist again.

Huldah slipped out of bed, gave him a quick hug, and ran down the hall to get her mama, the only person who knew how to hold Shem back when the world threatened to drag him away.

The 31st Day of Planting

In the morning, familiar shouting awakened Shin and thousands of other weary soldiers.

"For what?" Thorne was roaring. "Progressing only a few hundred paces up a mountain? That's not enough to earn a day of rest!"

Shin opened his eyes and rolled over to watch the drama play out below him.

A nervous staff sergeant was delivering the news to Thorne that the army was under the impression they could sleep in—

"Well WAKE THEM UP!" Thorne yelled. "No one rests today! We're going to Salem! NOW!"

Shin rolled on to his back and smirked at the gray sky that was beginning to lighten. He listened to the groans and protests that rose all around him as sergeants roused themselves and bellowed for their men to get up. The frustrated refrain was being picked up and carried far to the east and west.

Within fifteen minutes Shin predicted, since bad news always traveled faster than good, the entire army above the boulder line for miles in either direction would be furious at General Thorne for "caving in to his officers."

He was no leader at all.

That morning, Mahrree reassured her daughter. "I think a rushed wedding is the best idea. Everyone should do it this way," she decided as she sliced loaf after loaf of bread in the Briters' kitchen for the impromptu meal afterward. "You don't have to fret for six more weeks about preparing enough food."

"And no one needs to fuss about stocking their new house fully, since it will happen later," seventeen-year-old Sewzi added as she cut up a cake.

"Or arrange flowers," her sixteen-year-old sister Tabbit said, putting the cake on plates. "Not that there *are* any flowers."

"Or worry if we forgot to invite someone, because we can now just say there wasn't time," fourteen-year-old Banu reminded them as she put the sliced bread in baskets.

"When you really look at it," Mahrree said, "it all boils down to a young man, a young woman, and their rector. Nothing else *really* matters."

Jaytsy, trying to arrange some dried fruits artfully on a large plate, shrugged. "You may have a point. I *had* been worrying about the food. Lilla said she'd bring something over."

Banu looked out the window. "She's coming over now, Mama."

Jaytsy peered out, too. "When in the world did she find time to roast a wild turkey?"

Mahrree grinned. "Oh, good. She *did* get it done. It's been baking all night but she wasn't sure it would be ready on time."

Jaytsy chuckled. "Good old Lilla. Oh, there's the bride and her family. Four wagons just drove up to the barn. Mother, please tell me Calla's got a turkey roasting, too."

"She does. There'll be plenty for sandwiches."

Jaytsy wiped non-existent sweat off her brow. "The sooner we get this over with, the better. Well, that's a terrible attitude about my son's wedding, I must say!"

"We can't do anything until Uncle Shem comes back, Mama," Tabbit reminded her.

"Don't worry. He won't miss this," Jaytsy said. "He personally wants to make sure Zaddick sees Viddrow marry. Shem said Zaddick may not remember what his duty is unless he witnesses it."

Sewzi rolled her eyes. "He's only twenty-two. I don't know why everyone's pressuring him."

"You're absolutely right, Sewzi," Mahrree told her. "Perrin and I were twenty-eight, and Shem was *thirty-six*, after all! I don't know why he's in such a rush . . ." Her voice trailed off, because years ago there was time. But today?

There was a rush.

"That's what I used to think, Muggah," Tabbit said softly.

"I'm only sixteen, but since yesterday I've been wondering if I'll ever have a wedding—rushed or unrushed—of my own."

Sewzi, a year older, sat down hard on a chair and covered her face with her hands. "What if they succeed?" she whispered. "I keep thinking they'll give up, but the banner is still flying. What if the army comes to Salem?"

"Then they'll come," Mahrree said with conviction. "And we'll go to the ancient site and wait it out."

"But . . . I wanted to become a mama," Sewzi sobbed.

Jaytsy put her arms around her.

Her heart breaking, but determined to cheer up her granddaughter, Mahrree said, "Well, who says you won't?"

Sewzi looked up, her delicate features blotchy. "How can I when it's the *Last Day*? The Last is the End, right?" Her light brown eyes glowed in desperation. "I mean, maybe I should be running outside looking for someone—anyone—to marry today, too! There are a couple of boys down the road, and maybe they're thinking the same thing—"

"Zaddick!" Tabbit cried. "Sewzi, marry Zaddick!"

Mahrree and Jaytsy's mouths fell open at the turn of the conversation.

"I *do* know him well," Sewzi mused. "He's attractive enough, but really obnoxious. Then again, Uncle Shem was supposedly like that and *he's* mellowed over the years . . ."

Jaytsy and Mahrree couldn't make a sound of protest because they were too stunned to even breathe.

"It's perfect," Tabbit encouraged. "Considering there's not much time left—"

"I don't know," Banu said. "I kind of pictured Zaddick with someone more obnoxious like him. Like Versa Thorne. She's not married anymore. They could be really interesting together."

Tabbit scoffed. "Versa Thorne *Zenos?* That would bring General Thorne here! No, I think Sewzi should marry Zaddick today. It's the most convenient—"

"What are you saying?!" Deck's voice boomed throughout the kitchen, startling them all.

It knocked Mahrree and Jaytsy out of their stunned stupor, and they looked at Deck with relief that someone was there to shout some sense into the girls.

"Sewzi! You're not about to run off and get married just because

. . . just because you think *this is the end*," Deck declared.

Behind him stood Lilla, holding the platter with the turkey on it. Her face blanched at the conversation.

"Sewzi, Sewzi," she said, pushing past Deck to put the platter on the table. "Don't worry, sweety! The last isn't the *end*. True, we don't know what happens after the Last Day, but the Creator always rewards us with what we want and deserve. You want to be married and be a mama, and somehow *you will*. We don't know the details, but I know the Creator loves you and won't deny you that privilege."

"Absolutely!" Mahrree said, finally finding her voice.

"She's right, Sewzi," Jaytsy said, smoothing her daughter's hair.

"She better be right," Deck growled. "Because any boy who wants to marry my girls has to go through me first, and I have a very lengthy waiting period. Just ask Lek. He had to wait almost nineteen years before he earned my approval to marry Salema."

Mahrree snorted. She didn't know if Deck was serious or not, but the moment shouldn't have been as tense as it was. They were preparing for a wedding, after all.

Jaytsy covered her mouth as she giggled.

Lilla's face went red suppressing her laugh as she watched Deck's stern glare start to soften.

Sewzi finally giggled, as did her sisters. "Nineteen years, Papa? That means I'll be thirty-six by the time I finally marry."

"Good," Deck said. "As long as it's not today."

An hour later, the orchard at the Shins was swarming with people. When Shem finally arrived on horseback, the crowd cheered.

"Sorry, Viddrow and Autumn!" he called as he dismounted and kissed Viddrow's eager bride on the cheek. "For some reason people in Salem are a bit panicky today and kept stopping me. I guess they didn't realize I was on my way to a wedding."

Deck patted Shem on the back. "Can't have a wedding without you, Shem. And if some panicked children of mine would have had their way," he lowered his voice, "another one of your sons would have been marrying another one of my daughters."

Shem didn't look nearly as shocked as Deck expected. "There's a *lot* of that going on today," he whispered. "I just sent out my assistants with urgent messages for the rectors to not perform any marriages unless the couple was already engaged. And as much as I want to see Zaddick married, pairing him with poor Sewzi or Tabbit isn't the way. Those girls deserve better. Actually, all girls deserve better. Zaddick's just going to have to be my guard for the rest of his life."

Deck chuckled. "Guess there was no room for the message of *no unplanned last minute weddings* on the towers?"

Shem didn't look at the message he had flying all over Salem: Emergency. Guide Zenos. Meeting. Mid-afternoon. Arena. "What I have to remind Salemites about this afternoon may be much harder to take than the stoppage of any spontaneous marriages." Shem forced a smile. "But let's not worry about any of that right now. I'm in the mood for cake!"

Deck glanced over at his son and future daughter-in-law, both of them beaming. "Rector Shin? I believe everyone's here."

Peto smiled and took his position between two peach trees as everyone else jostled for position to watch.

But Mahrree stayed at the back, leaning against the large boulder carved with her husband's name. She could see well enough, and it didn't feel right being at a wedding without her husband. His body lay beneath her feet, but his spirit was inching closer, she could feel it. He was probably sitting on a boulder, much like this one, laughing at the out-of-shape soldiers trying to make their way to Salem.

"Come home to me, Perrin," she whispered. "Meiki announced a few minutes ago that she and her husband Clyde are expecting their first baby in six moons. Come back to hold that newborn. Let another baby know Great Uncle Puggah. Please, please bring back Young Pere. The two of you are missing this.

"There they go, walking up to Peto. He just asked them if they were both there of their own desire. Viddrow answered with a shaky but happy 'Yes,' and Autumn answered with, 'I've been waiting for this for over eight moons. It took the army of Idumea to scare him enough to stand in front of you, so, yes! Definitely, yes!'

"You'd like her, Perrin. She's full of fire. Viddrow wanted to wait until the herd finished calving, although there's only a dozen expecting cows, but with the gray banners . . . Peto's saying the words . . . they're answering . . . now they're kissing." Tears filled her eyes. "And another grandchild is married. Without you by my side."

She ran her hand along the boulder feeling the words etched into the stone. Her fingers slipped into the letters for 'husband.'

"Or Perrin, if you can't come to me, let me come to you."

Shin smiled smugly at the grumbling of the soldiers around him. There wasn't enough room for twenty thousand men to make their way to the canyon, and in a crowd they felt anonymous enough to voice their frustrations.

Shin suspected Thorne would soon be calling for him and his escorts to lead the way, but he wasn't about to make anything easier by showing himself.

That would be his strategy: infuriatingly reluctant obedience.

He slouched to avoid being the tallest of the soldiers crammed for miles in the narrow passageway. Now if only Hammer and Iron would make themselves a little less conspicuous . . .

"I mean, why change his mind? This is stupid!"

"I feel like cattle being forced into a corral. What are we waiting for, anyway?"

"This should have been planned better. Why not just send a few hundred men to find the route, *then* get the rest of us?"

"Slag, look—here comes another batch of soldiers over the boulders. Hey! Just stay there. Where do you think you're going to stand? On top of me?"

"If we could have just stayed resting on the mountain side like we were promised . . ."

Shin didn't even have to plant any seeds of traitorous talk. It was springing up all around him like weeds.

In the Shins' crowded orchard, the midday wedding meal was being served when the tower chimes sounded. Peto and Shem caught each other's eyes between the apricot trees, then looked up at the tower.

The men stationed there had hit the chimes softer than usual, trying not to disrupt the wedding celebration happening below, but the banners were changing.

Gray banner, gray striped banner.

Peto and Shem met each other among the pear trees.

"Some of the army are over the rock and heading to the canyon, but the rest are still in the boulder field," Peto explained.

Shem shrugged that off. "Still time for cake, Peto. It's Grandmother Peto's recipe. Mahrree and Calla spent all yesterday evening working on it, and I'm not about to miss cake just because Lemuel wants to take a hike. Besides, there are enough things that will slow him down."

Mahrree noticed the two men talking and turned to look at the towers. Over the noise and laughter, she didn't hear the chimes, but now she saw the banners.

"Keep him safe, Perrin. I'm waiting for you."

"General, this canyon isn't exactly the widest. I don't think we can get more than three or four men abreast through here. At eighty thousand men, that means it will take—"

"Yes, thank you, Twigg!" Thorne snapped. From Edge, the canyon appeared to be very broad, but once they reached the mouth of it, the bottom half of the floor was occupied by a cold and swift river. Thorne stood at the opening of the canyon, with now thirty thousand anxious men behind him and more climbing the boulders every minute.

"I always wondered where the river came from," Hili commented as he watched it rushing past. "They must take their horses along this narrow bank, here."

"That can't be right," Thorne muttered. He looked up to the canyon walls, searching for another route. The sides rose up sharply, still covered in ash that had hardened into the same cement-like substance that rendered all of the farms in the world unusable. Wide patches of dirty snow and ice turned all of the terrain into an unfriendly gray mess. "There must be another route that's wider and faster. Look for trails that have been cleared."

"Sir?" one of the lieutenants called. He was crouched several paces ahead of the general. "Sir, look at this! Hoof prints."

Thorne walked over to peer at the impressions in the melting snow. "How recent?"

"Yesterday? And they go straight along this bank." He jogged for several paces and crouched again. "Yes! Here they are again in the mud, heading up the canyon!"

Thorne smiled in triumph. "This is it," he said confidently. "This is where they'd sit and spy on us. If I had a spyglass I could probably see right into the command tower where Wanes is perched with his feet up on my desk and Slither is gorging himself on mead. We've found it, men!" Thorne exclaimed.

Twigg and Hili exchanged cautiously relieved glances while only a handful of soldiers behind them cheered, probably not as enthusiastically as Thorne expected.

"So we don't need Shin after all?" Hili asked.

The lieutenant, still squatting at the bank, scratched his head. He looked in front of and behind him, to the left and then, absurdly, into the river.

Thorne noticed. "What is it?"

"Uh, sir? The tracks they. . . they just *stop*."

"Stop?"

"I can't see where they continue. It's as if the horses just *vanished* from this point on."

Thorne turned to the body of soldiers. "Have they found Beaved and his men yet?" he asked, newly irritated.

Down the crowded mountain there was a slight commotion moving to the mouth of the canyon. Several tall and large men were among them.

The soldiers before the commotion weren't too interested in making room for ten men to squeeze their way through, but with Snarl at the lead, leering at soldiers left and right and jabbing a few with a small knife, they eventually moved aside.

Thorne watched intently as Private Shin came to the front of the line. Beaved had suggested earlier that perhaps the private would be so excited about going home that his eyes would inadvertently give away the direction to Salem.

The private kept his gaze low, trying to squeeze through the press of men. When he saw the river flowing near Thorne, he tipped his head thoughtfully.

"Oh. I always wondered where the river came from."

Sergeant Hili seemed to smirk.

"Is this the way you choose to go, sir?" Shin asked simply, looking at the canyon walls. He gestured to a rocky outcropping high up. "Could be an interesting view from there."

Thorne glanced up at the outcropping and scoffed. "And how would someone get up there, Shin?"

Shin shrugged. "I'm betting Snarl could do it. Just a good workout. Right, Snarl?"

Buddy and Pal were watching Shin's eyes closely, as did Snarl, just as Beaved had taught them. But nothing in the way Shin surveyed the mountainside revealed anything. His pupils and eyes didn't change whatsoever, nor did his gaze linger on anything.

An exasperated sigh made everyone turn around.

Amory stood there, having followed Beaved's group. Her hair was unkempt, her remaining face paint was smudged comically, and her clothing made it apparent that she had slipped and fallen into the mud on more than one occasion. Wearily, she gazed up the canyon and leaned against a convenient soldier.

"Where's Guide Lannard?" Thorne asked her. "I thought you were going to stay with him, make sure he doesn't get lost."

"He's still back there, calling for blessings for those climbing the boulders. He's very inspiring," she said without any irony. She changed her position against the reluctant soldier. "This is it, Lemuel. River seems to be running high, though."

The soldier she leaned against shifted subtly. Amory's pack, seemingly heavier and larger than anyone else's, slipped backward as it unbalanced her. She firmed her stance and purposely looked past Shin.

"We need to head straight up this canyon. The glacial valley and fort are at the top of it."

"How far?" Thorne asked.

Amory bit her lip. "I've never been very good with distances but . . . maybe ten miles?"

Several soldiers behind her groaned.

Shin's group watched him carefully. Something twitched near his eye, but other than that he revealed nothing.

Thorne turned to him. "How far is it, Shin?"

The private shrugged. "Your guess is as good as mine, sir."

Thorne stepped close to him. "No, it's not, Shin! You've been here before! Now tell me, *how far is it*?"

Shin didn't move or speak but looked past Thorne to the canyon.

"Answer me!"

Shin remained motionless.

"Lemuel, let's just start walking," Amory said. "It doesn't matter how far it is. Just know that this is the way. Every man should fill his water flasks here. I can't remember if there's water up at the glacial valley or not, and the route we followed leaves the river and goes up the mountain side . . . somewhere."

Shin's eyes wandered up the canyon and looked over to the right, analyzing the slope.

Buddy, Pal, and Snarl noticed.

So did Thorne. "So we start walking," he said with a curt nod. "But first, we need to cross the river."

Amory's mouth dropped open. "Lemuel, why?"

"Because *that's* where the trail is. On the other side."

"No, no," Amory protested. "I'm fairly confident it was on *this* side of the canyon. It went back a ways, then switched back and forth up the mountain."

Thorne evaluated the terrain Amory waved vaguely at. It was nothing but hardened ash, snow, and ice.

"I don't see a trail."

"You're not *supposed* to see it from here! You have to . . . you have to go up, some part," she said, walking a few paces and searching the ground for a hint of where to go. "Look for tracks!"

Thorne rolled his eyes. "You told me yourself you were unsure of the distance or direction. It was raining most of the time you were traveling, and I've yet to meet a woman who was good with directions."

Amory blew out in disgust. "Who are you going to believe, Lemuel—me or him? He's not exactly eager to help you, if you haven't noticed!" She jerked her thumb irately at Shin who was still studying the opposite canyon wall.

Shin shifted his gaze to Amory, then he looked around innocently to see if she was indicating someone else.

Hili smirked and looked down at his boots.

Thorne took several quick steps to come within inches of Amory's face. "I trust his lies more than I trust your judgment, *my love.* You don't know which way is east even when the sun is rising." He turned to Twigg and Hili. "Start with fifty soldiers on that side of the river searching for a trail. Send another fifty up this side of the river to find any 'hidden' trails. In fifteen minutes we start walking in *some* direction, before the rest of the army creates a log jam behind us. Shin! How do we cross the river?"

Shin shrugged. "Bridge?"

"There's no bridge, *Shin!*"

"Stepping stones?"

"The river seems to be running high, *Shin*. I see no stepping stones!"

"Wade across?"

"It's cold, *Shin!*"

"Well, I'm out of ideas. Then again, that's why I'm only a private."

A few soldiers behind him sniggered.

Thorne stepped up to him again, aware that he had an attentive audience. "Cross that river, Shin, and find me the route or you will die without ever seeing Salem again."

Amory clenched her fists. "Lemuel! We're going to *need* him. Trust me—this is the easy part! The confusing part comes when we leave the glacial valley."

Thorne leered. "We may *possibly* need him." Abruptly he reached over, grabbed the one Beaved's team called Cloud Man, and yanked him to his side.

Cloud Man's eyes grew large, but then he blinked and smiled as if he was expecting to get a medal for bravery.

"But I don't need *this one*." Thorne shook Cloud Man's arm.

The rest of Cloud Man jiggled, too, just for fun.

"So Shin, if you don't cross that river, your little grassena friend's journey ends here." Thorne nodded to one of his personal guards, and the man drew his sword.

Cloud Man continued to grin at the attention he was receiving, oblivious to the sword pointed at his chest. "Ends here?" he said. "But I don't mind going up the canyon, sir. I'm guessing the view of the clouds from the top must be good!"

For the first time, Private Shin's expression shifted, from vacant to livid. He clenched a fist and nodded to Cloud Man.

"You'll see the clouds from the top, I promise, Cloudy." With a glare intended to stab Thorne, Shin started for the river bank, suddenly interested in it.

Thorne turned to Twigg. "Fifty men over there, now!" he bellowed and nodded to the left. "Fifty more men follow over here. Shin, start thinking or start swimming."

Private Shin began to fume. He had to confess to himself that one part of him had found the past couple of days turning into an intriguing game, something one might see acted out on the stage: just how far could he push Thorne with his feigned naivete, and how much would Thorne push back—

But now Thorne had thrown in a new player's token by using an innocent vial head as a hostage.

The game was over.

Shin paced along the riverbank, clenching his fists furiously while trying to think of how to get across. He hadn't expected Thorne would force him to find a route. He was just hoping to confuse the general, not take a frigid bath. He looked around at the trees and an idea came to him.

"Cloud Man. Let me borrow your knife again."

Cloud Man stepped past the guard's blade pointed at his chest and eagerly handed over his knife.

Thorne stepped forward too and caught Cloud Man's wrist. "Exactly what do you plan to do, Shin?"

"Make a bridge, sir," he answered coldly. "Don't worry. If I try to do anything stupid with the knife, I'm sure you'll see to it that Cloud Man sees the clouds up close and in an instant. And eighty thousand men will have a piece of me."

Thorne reluctantly let him take the knife.

He turned to the trees, analyzing the dead timbers before making his selection. Then he crouched and stabbed the long knife into the ground at the base of a dead tree, sardonically imagining Lemuel Thorne as the roots. He severed the roots all around, just as his father had weakened the trees above the fort at Edge. It really was quite easy, and he could see why Peto Shin had been able to knock down hundreds of trees a few moons ago by dislodging a boulder upon them.

Shin didn't have a boulder, but he had two blacksmiths. He stood up, grimly satisfied with his work. "Hammer, Iron—need a little push here."

The two blacksmiths walked over to the tree and shoved. It turned out he didn't need such hulking men. The dead tree crashed down and spanned the river with such little effort even Amory could have done it simply by leaning against it.

Several men cheered, but Shin was already working on the tree next to it, stabbing angrily. He was partly pleased that the strategy had worked, but more annoyed that Lemuel Thorne was still ordering him around and succeeding. The smiths readily toppled the second dead tree.

Shin stood up. "There's your bridge, sir," he said dully. "I recommend only one man go across at a time and put a foot on each log. Those trees can't be too strong since they were so easily compromised. Perhaps only lighter men should go across?"

Hammer and Iron took large steps backward.

Thorne lifted his chin. "Go first, Shin. Demonstrate just how strong the bridge is."

Beaved stepped up to the general. "Sir, is that wise? Just letting him run off like that?"

Thorne smiled thinly. "If the logs aren't strong enough to bear his weight, Shin takes another bath. If they are, you'll be second across and can chase him down if he runs. Besides, there aren't a lot of places for him to go now, are there?"

Beaved's mouth twitched and he nodded at Shin.

The private began to hand the knife back to Cloud Man, but hesitated.

Just right there, only an arm-thrust away, was Thorne's chest. How quickly could Shin stab him—

—And how quickly his guards would take Shin out if he missed Thorne's miniscule heart.

Cloud Man put an end to Shin's fantasizing by taking his knife out of his hand. Sheathing his weapon, Cloud Man said, "Think light, floaty thoughts, Private."

Another opportunity missed, Shin thought to himself as he stared longingly at Cloud Man's knife. But then the idea of stabbing Thorne seemed to wipe itself away, as if it never really wanted to be in his mind, as if his mind knew he was all talk and no action, especially when it came to openly defying Thorne.

Why didn't he do it? Act as brave as he pretended to be and stand up to Lemuel—

Thorne tipped his head toward Shin's makeshift bridge, and his guard raised his sword up to Cloud Man's chest again.

Cloud Man, oblivious to the threat to his life, grinned and gestured grandly for Shin to venture across the river.

That was why. It wasn't just Shin's life at stake.

"For you," Shin said to Cloud Man. "*Only* you."

Shin stepped first on one log, then the other. They rolled and shifted slightly, but were close enough together that their remaining limbs intertwined to stabilize them. He had done this dozens of times, in far more dangerous situations, but for some reason he felt nervous as he hesitantly crept over the rushing river.

The daring streak that accompanied him his entire life had vanished sometime in the past year, replaced by a strong sense of self-preservation. It was an odd sensation. Was this how everyone felt all the time? Was this why he didn't try to stab Thorne?

The logs bowed slightly as he reached the middle, twelve paces from either side. When he reached the far side, he exhaled and turned around, trying not to dwell on the fact that he'd have to go back again the same way.

Beaved rubbed his cheeks. "Half wish you had failed, Shin. I'm not looking forward to this." He took a tentative step onto the logs.

"Focus on one leg, then the next," Shin suggested, almost feeling badly that the staff sergeant had to follow him—he seemed to be a decent man. Beaved was growing strangely rigid. Maybe he was experiencing that self-preservation twinge as well. "And keep moving."

Beaved took his first steps and froze.

"What's wrong?" Shin called to him.

"Just how cold is the water?"

"Freezing."

"Couldn't I instead wade across?"

"You're not afraid of the water?"

"Nooo . . ."

"Then why are you afraid of crossing?"

"I'm not really sure, Shin."

"Then . . . crouch and crawl across."

"Crawl?"

"It'll be faster than standing there!"

"Crawl. Right." Beaved got down on his hands and knees, straddling the two logs. "How is this better? Now I'm closer to the water!"

"It's a shorter distance to fall," Shin pointed out. "Is that what you're afraid of? Falling?"

"Would you get moving already?!" Thorne bellowed at his sergeant.

Beaved shook slightly and started in a panicked crawl across the logs, dodging the branches sticking up. In a few moments he was on the other side.

Shin greeted him with a grin. "Good job! I promise going back will be a lot easier."

"Going *back*?" Beaved said, trembling.

Soon enough, thought Shin, or maybe in a long while, they'd discover there was no route to Salem on this side of the river.

"I'm next!" Cloud Man announced eagerly. "It'll be like floating over the world." He stepped out confidently on the logs and made his way easily over to Shin and Beaved. Even Thorne seemed surprised at his speed.

Reg, Buddy, and Pal came over next, but Teach refused.

"Someone has to stay to keep Hammer and Iron company over here. Here, take that skinny thing over there. He looks like he could use a dunking."

High above the canyon floor, four men in gray mottled clothing laid on a rock outcropping and watched the procession try to cross the river far below them. They chuckled quietly as one man, then another, fell into the rushing water and were fished out by soldiers downstream.

They also kept careful watch on the second group of men starting to make their way up the canyon wall where they were perched. At their rate it'd take them an hour to reach their position. The trail was still there, but so well camouflaged by the hardened ash that unless the sun was shining on it just right, it was nearly impossible to discern. Still someone, sometime, surely would discover it.

One of the men took out the spyglass and focused on the tall soldier who first went across the river. He smiled in satisfaction.

"What do you think they're doing?" one of the scouts whispered, mystified. "Why cross the river?"

"Why not?" asked the scout with a spyglass.

"Because it would waste time, for one thing."

"Ah, you're thinking like a Salemite. So is *he*." The man with the spyglass chuckled. "The world isn't going to trust anyone, even those they should. Amory has been gesturing wildly in the correct direction, but Thorne is instead listening to someone else."

"Who?"

"Send another message to Guide Zenos: Young Perrin Shin sighted and doing all he can to aggravate General Thorne. They just might discover the eastern sea before they find the way to Salem."

Shem didn't notice how quickly the arena was filling because of the long line of people trying to catch a few moments with him. But the arena was packed long before mid-afternoon.

For those living too far to send someone for the update, one hundred fifty scribes sat in the first three rows, ready to write down all of the guide's words. When he finished, they'd compare notes, make corrections, then get those copies to young men on fast horses. They would deliver the messages to every tower and rector, and in the dissenter villages bring the message to the elected or self-appointed leaders. Even the northernmost communities and the three dissenter villages would have the guide's warnings and advice by dinner.

Everyone in the arena knew why they were there: the gray banners flying ominously over Salem. The army of Idumea was coming, albeit slowly.

When Guide Zenos took to the stand, having gently pushed away those clamoring for his attention, the tens of thousands of gathered people hushed in anticipation.

"My beloved Salemites, you've seen the banners and the scouts have confirmed it: the army of Idumea is attempting to find Salem."

The crowd broke out in nervous whispers.

"*Why* they're coming," Shem continued, and the whispers died immediately, "I'm not entirely sure. But I know that their reserves are dangerously low and they're becoming desperate for food and farmable land. Once they lay eyes on Salem, they'll decide they've found their salvation. They'll covet our homes, our animals, and our lands. They will not, however, care one bit about your lives. As long as you live, they'll see you as a threat. But if you're dead, then all that you have stewardship over becomes theirs for the taking.

"I cannot stress enough how important it is that *should* the army be successful in this attempt to reach Salem, you and your families leave immediately for the ancient temple site. No delays! This is what we have been preparing for, for years. Now those years of preparation will pay off. When you see the black banner with a white sword on the tower near your homes, that's your signal to gather your family and your emergency packs which you've faithfully repacked every year.

"And, if you haven't repacked them, today would be a good day to do so. I've already contacted all of the rectors to make sure the storehouses remain open throughout the evening."

The crowd's nervous murmuring swelled to a constant hum.

Guide Zenos paused to let the hum quiet again, and to let the scribes catch up in their frantic writing.

A voice near the front called, "Guide, what if we fight them off? Defend our lands? Why should we just let them take it all?"

Guide Zenos held his breath as many more calls of, "Let us defend ourselves!" rose up in the arena.

Several of his twelve assistants, seated on chairs to the side of the podium, looked around, startled at the sudden aggressiveness of the Salemites.

But Shem wasn't surprised. He had long suspected this would happen. Salem had never before faced a direct threat, nor did they know how to deal with the idea of someone simply *taking* something. That never happened in Salem, so the natural impulse was to fight back.

But the Creator expected more from Salem.

Guide Zenos leaned forward and said, loudly, "NO."

The arena fell into silent befuddlement.

He let his answer settle in before continuing.

"I know your desire is to not allow anyone to take your homes, but this is not the Creator's will. Nor, you will remember, are these *your* homes, or *your* farms, or *your* livestock. All of it belongs to the Creator, as it always has. It is His will that you voluntarily leave Salem and retreat to safety. We've known this would be our fate for the past one hundred-sixty-five years, ever since Guide Pax saw this time coming. This shouldn't be a surprise. We also know that Guide Gleace saw that no weapons of any kind should be taken—"

He couldn't complete his sentence for the outcry that arose.

"No weapons?!" was the only phrase he could distinguish before the din grew too loud. Many were demanding to be armed, while many others were just as adamantly reminding them that was against the prophecy.

Another voice near the front shouted, "But what if this *isn't* the Last Day? What if it's just a preliminary attack? What if we have to rebuild once they leave or we destroy them?"

Shem sighed. He'd hesitated making any declaration that the Last Day was near, or 'around the corner,' as Mahrree had begged him to know just that morning. He didn't feel that was his announcement to make.

But as he watched tens of thousands of Salemites, who he'd always known to be a peaceful and obedient people suddenly become agitated and even irate, he knew it was because of the spirit that preceded the army of Idumea.

The Refuser's influence was already there, stirring up those whose faith wasn't quite as strong.

Shem said a silent prayer, asking if—

The answer came too forcefully to deny, and he had to grip the podium to remain upright. Staring down at his notes, he could no longer find his place because the words he needed to say were repeating in his head and would continue until he spoke them.

He swallowed hard and said, "The Last Day is coming. It will be upon us shortly. *Very* shortly."

He didn't shout or raise his voice. Yet the feeling of his words carried over the entire arena and stopped every tongue. The sudden silence was profound.

Just to be sure they heard him correctly, Guide Zenos said in the same clear voice, "The Last Day is coming. It will be upon us shortly. Very shortly. Defending ourselves is contrary to the Creator's will. If we follow the admonitions of our past guides, we will be preserved to see the hand of the Creator fight this battle for us.

"*But,*" he continued in a sharper tone, "if we insist on fighting, we will fall before the army. What's the point of losing your lives trying to keep a house or preserve a farm? The ancient temple site is and will remain a secure site. Should any danger approach it, I have full confidence the Creator will send a way to secure it again. He has promised us, through the words of many guides, that He'll fight our battle. The Deliverer will come before the Creator's Destroyer. I think we've all heard that before, haven't we?"

Before him on the benches, thousands of men, women, and children squirmed worriedly, restlessly.

"My dear Salemites, I've been in battle. It's not romantic nor heroic. It's terrifying. Tragic. Painful. If the Creator says He will do my fighting for me, then I happily accept His offer. Each of you would be wise to do so as well."

A man rose to his feet. "And what if we don't? What if we choose to fight instead?"

"Then you fight alone," Shem warned him. "Now, I'll do nothing to prevent you. Salem is still a free land. You may choose what you'll do, but I promise now that those who stay to fight the army *will die.* You simply cannot win. Idumeans are more powerful and more desperate, and they care nothing for anyone's lives but their own. The Creator will not help you, because if you choose to fight, you choose against His will and you forfeit His protection."

There was considerably more squirming in his audience.

"But *I also promise,*" he changed his tone yet again, "that if you follow the words of the guides, if you go with your families to the ancient site, you will be in the Creator's care. I'm not advising you to surrender to Lemuel Thorne; I'm advising you to surrender your will to the Creator. Let Him finish this for us."

He thought it would be enough, that the choice was obvious.

But apparently several hundred Salemites, mostly men, didn't agree.

One stood up and yelled, "All those who wish to fight, meet me out by the west greens and we'll discuss strategy!"

Shem hung his head in frustration as a few hundred men took to their feet and marched out. Shem was true to his word and said nothing, nor did he call out for any of them to be detained. Instead he shook his head and studied the podium in front of him.

Strategy? What did these people, who hadn't faced a real threat in over five generations, know about strategy?

Shem eyed the man in the lead, waving encouragingly for others to follow him. He had frequently attended Eltana Yordin's Armchair Generals meetings. Since Perrin died, she had taken over the meeting where Salemites who served for a time as scouts in the army of Idumea gathered to rehash their 'good old days' with selective memories and too much confidence. Their abilities would never match their bravado.

Shem knew about strategy, but he'd never volunteer information contrary to the Creator's will.

He closed his eyes, offered another quick prayer, then looked up at the congregation. The last of the men had filed out and now everyone turned to see what the guide would say next. Their apprehension radiated up to him, surrounding him, trying to douse him in cold, nervous sweat. Even the most faithful and confident Salemites looked desperate to be reassured just one more time. Fleeing was the correct option, right?

Shem calmly asked, "Anyone else wish to join them?"

The congregation was silent.

"Then spread the word to your families, your neighbors, and everyone you see. Prepare for the coming of the Army of Idumea and for the saving by the Creator. Be in the right place at the right time. I, for one, will be standing by the ancient temple site on the Last Day, whenever that may be. I pray every Salemite will be standing with me. We may have very little time, so I'll keep you no longer. Go home, get ready, and watch the banner towers. May the Creator be with us all."

He turned and strode off the platform, hoping his sudden movement and abrupt ending—he didn't even lead them in a hymn or a final prayer—would startle the crowd into action. He heard thousands of people standing up, talking, and hopefully filing out of the arena without delay.

Perhaps for the very last time.

That thought nearly stopped him in his tracks. He'd been speaking from that stage for decades, but was that really the last time he'd address all of Salem? It was all over, just like that?

He couldn't linger on that gloomy thought because at the bottom of the stairs stood Calla, wringing her hands in worry.

"That went well, didn't it?" she said miserably.

Shem tried to smile. "Of course it did, my love. I expected some resistance." Already a mass of semi-panicked people were rushing to speak to him, and while he had nothing more to say, he'd try to comfort them.

Someone was pushing through the crowd, shoving people left and right probably because elbows were involved. Curious and worried as to who was so determined to reach him, Shem was startled when suddenly Mahrree burst through the press and rushed up to him.

"I knew it!" she cried cheerfully and threw wide her arms to hug him. Unsure of why, he indulged her.

She jumped a little and planted a kiss on his startled cheek.

"I *knew* it! Thank you, Shem!" Mahrree turned and disappeared into the crowd, squealing in delight.

"Now *that* response," he said to his wife, "I did *not* expect."

"But you should have," Calla said. "You just confirmed that her husband's coming home."

When Shin set up his camp that night, it was in full view of his log bridge. The army had progressed exactly four hundred paces.

After extensive explorations that lasted many hours longer than the initial fifteen minutes Thorne had called for, no path was found on either side of the mountains.

Then again, Salemites didn't make paths like the world thought they would. No signs with pointing arrows, no carefully carved steps, not even logs bordering the edges.

Thorne finally declared that in the morning they'd make their own path. Most of the men were now cutting into the sides of the canyon wall with hatchets or long knives, trying to fashion a reasonably comfortable place to sleep. Very few were succeeding.

Shin heard the grumbling and complaints up and down and all around. He laid back in smug satisfaction. True, Thorne had forced Shin and a few others across the river, but Thorne was no closer to Salem—a full day wasted—and his army was growing irritated with his lack of progress. Shin counted today as a solid win, and guiltily he knew he was seeing this as a game once more.

But this was no game, and sooner rather than later the army would get closer to Salem, and then what? What could Shin do to preserve Salem, or to stop Thorne, or shift the army's loyalty?

AS IF YOU HAVE THE POWER TO DO ANY OF THAT. BUT YOU DON'T HAVE TO, YOUNG PERE. I KEEP TELLING YOU, WE ALREADY HAVE A PLAN.

Wearily, Shin looked up again at the clear cold sky. There was one thing he did know: it was another perfect night for sleeping under the stars.

"Guide, I'm sorry to come to you so late, but—"

"But nothing. You know I want updates whenever they come," Shem assured the messenger as he led him into his dark gathering room.

Calla lit a candle and brought it in.

The messenger looked at her and hesitated.

"You can speak in front of her," Shem assured him. "She'd hear it from me as soon as you left anyway."

The messenger shrugged. "Woodson recommends changing the banners to striped gray. The majority of the army is in the canyon mouth now, or trying to be, and Thorne seems determined to go onward despite not finding any trails."

Shem exhaled, and Calla gripped his arm. "How far up the canyon did they make it today?" she asked.

"Not far at all," the messenger told her. "It seems they have a soldier at the lead who's not very helpful. He had Thorne send a portion of his army across the river to find a route on the other side of the canyon."

"The other side?!" Shem exclaimed. "Any fool could see that's a much more hazardous way."

Calla smiled. "Maybe that 'fool' knew that and was trying to delay Thorne?"

Shem smiled as well. "Was it Young Pere?"

The messenger nodded. "It was. He even felled the trees to make a bridge the same way Rector Shin had felled the trees last year to destroy the forest above the fort."

Shem's jaw dropped. "He *knows*, doesn't he? He knows it was Peto!"

Calla tightened her grip. "Should we tell Lilla?"

"Not yet. I don't want Lilla to hope he'll return only to have her spirits dashed. If Young Pere pushes Thorne too far . . ."

Calla groaned in reluctant agreement.

"Today's still the 31st Day, right?" Shem said.

"It will be the 32nd in less than an hour," Calla said.

Shem thought for a moment. "Return to the Second Resting Station tonight," he said to the messenger. "At first light, change the banners to gray striped and . . ." He took a deep breath before continuing, "fly the black flag with the white sword for Region 1."

Calla gasped.

The messenger nodded soberly.

"The army would reach them first," Shem said, "so they should be the first to leave. I want the south emptied by tomorrow afternoon. I'll send a notice in the morning that the north areas and dissenter colonies should begin preparations too, since they have the furthest to go. We'll fly the sword banners there by midday meal."

"Oh, Shem," Calla whispered.

He put his arm around her. "This is what we've prepared for, Calla. It'll be fine. Thorne may still give up, turn around, and head back to Edge."

"It just . . . it just seems so *sudden.*"

"The gray banner has been flying for two days, Calla."

"I know, I know . . . it's just that after all this preparation and time it just doesn't seem real that it's *actually happening*!"

Shem pulled her close. "It's happening. Mahrree was right. It's right around the corner."

The 32nd Day of Planting

The next morning Shin woke up, stretched, and looked at the sky. Another beautiful morning, still on the Edge side of the mountains. But probably not for long.

From his vantage point he could see Thorne gesturing aggressively as he pointed up the canyon and shouted orders to Twigg and Hili. Several other officers behind them shifted anxiously. No one seemed keen to follow his orders. For men who had never before stepped into the mountains, the canyon appeared steeper, rougher, and less passable every moment.

Shin had a sinking feeling that unless those timid and whipped men banded together and told Thorne they wouldn't do it, they *would* reach the glacial valley, a mere three miles away, before nightfall. So he sent the thoughts, *Rebel! Rebel!* down to the nervous men, but none of them said or did anything.

Stupid sheep. He sighed in frustration. They could come together and throw that ridiculous wolf into the river and turn back. Wasn't there a noble Colonel Ferrim among them? Or a deceitful Glasson? Or an ambitious Lick?

No, there's not. Thorne destroys his rivals. Haven't you noticed?

"Am I really the *only* one left wanting to rid the world of Lemuel Thorne?" he whispered.

No, you're not. But it's not up to you to do it. Look, there's already a plan—

"So get them up now!" Thorne roared.

The officers saluted, turned, and grudgingly picked their ways through the scores of prone soldiers, shouting, "Up! Up!" as they went. A few headed over to the boulder field to arouse the soldiers who attempted to sleep on the rocks.

"Shin!"

He flinched and looked up.

Sergeant Beaved hovered over him and cocked his head toward the general. "Thorne wants you in five minutes. Eat your ration and get over there. You're blazing the trail."

"Sergeant," Shin whispered, "you have to realize this is ridiculous. Thorne's going to get a lot of these soldiers killed today when they lose their footing in this canyon. And conditions around us are deteriorating rapidly. No one can dig a proper latrine, and this place is disgusting. There are too many people, and some are already getting sick. This is a disaster in the making. And for what? Justice for a wife and daughters he doesn't even care about? This isn't about saving the world, Beaved. This is about Thorne's quest for revenge, and all of us have to pay the price."

Beaved squatted next to him. "So what if it is? What am I supposed to do about it, huh? March up to the general and say, 'Sir, can I be excused? I don't like heights.' There's nothing that can be done."

"Is that how all of the officers feel?" Shin whispered conspiratorially. "That they're powerless?"

"They are."

"There's only one of Thorne and tens of thousands of us! Why does he have such a hold on all of you?"

Beaved narrowed his eyes. "You should be asking that question of yourself, Shin. Why didn't you just throw yourself into that river yesterday and refuse to obey Thorne? Or let Cloud Man die? He wouldn't have minded, I'm sure. Believe it or not, you're just as big a coward as the rest of us."

As much as Shin wanted to debate that, he swallowed down his protestation. Because, one part of him had to admit, he *was* a coward. Stupid Lemuel Thorne had him afraid, too, and confessing that left him tasting bile.

"Now eat," Sergeant Beaved ordered, "do your business at the tree, and report to the general."

The sergeant stood up to wake the rest of the security team, but the private brooded. He wasn't *entirely* a coward, because if he were, he would have crumbled before Thorne and told him everything about Salem and how to get there, right? Didn't Puggah once say his grandson was braver than any man he'd known?

So what did truly brave men do? They waited for the right moment to spring their traps, and the right moment had to be coming up soon—

YOUNG PERE, WHAT YOU'RE WANTING IS MORE THAN YOU'RE ABLE TO ACCOMPLISH. I'M PLEASED THAT YOU'VE REJECTED THORNE, WHO YOU ONCE ADMIRED. BUT YOUNG PERE, YOU CAN'T DESTROY HIM. HE'LL GET YOU FIRST, AND THAT'S NOT THE CREATOR'S WILL FOR YOU. HE HAS ANOTHER PLAN BESIDES YOUR IMMINENT DEATH.

"But if everyone would just rally behind me—" he whispered.

THEY WON'T. AS MUCH AS THEY HATE THORNE, THEY LOVE THEIR PITIFUL LIVES MORE. WHAT YOU WANT THEM TO DO IS SHOW COURAGE IN THE FACE OF OPPOSITION. WHEN, IN ANY OF YOUR EXPERIENCES IN THE WORLD, HAVE YOU SEEN A GROUP OF PEOPLE WILLINGLY DO THAT?

He sighed. He'd never seen that.

PRESERVE YOURSELF, YOUNG PERE. LET THE CREATOR WORK HIS PLAN. AND LET MUGGAH AND YOUR MOTHER AND FATHER AND EVERYONE ELSE SEE YOU AGAIN. ALIVE.

"But, Puggah, what if there comes a moment that—"

NO, LISTEN TO ME: LEMUEL THORNE IS THE REFUSER'S MOST IMPORTANT TOOL. YOU REALLY THINK THE REFUSER WILL LET SOMEONE LIKE YOU UPSET HIS PLANS FOR DESTROYING SALEM? HE KNOWS YOU AS WELL AS I DO, YOUNG PERE. HE KNEW YOU BEFORE YOU WERE BORN AND HE KNOWS YOUR ABILITIES AS WELL AS YOUR PRIDE.

Shin rubbed his forehead as he always did when he couldn't out argue his grandfather.

YOU MAY THINK YOU'RE TARGETING THORNE, BUT IN REALITY THE REFUSER IS BAITING YOU. THERE'S A HUGE BATTLE BREWING ALREADY, AND IT'S OVER YOU, BOY! DON'T LET THE REFUSER TEMPT YOU INTO TAKING ON THORNE. IF YOU DIE NOW, SO DO MANY OTHER POSSIBILITIES.

He deliberated for a moment, sighed, pulled out his pack, and slowly started eating his rations.

He wasn't cowardly, he reminded himself. He was merely . . . waiting until he knew better what to do.

"Mother, I wanted to tell you before you saw it yourself," Peto said as he stood at his mother's door. She was in her gathering room, folding a blanket.

Mahrree paled and let the blanket drop on to her small sofa. "See what, Peto?"

"Thorne's army is in the canyon as of last night. Shem called for the gray striped banner to fly this morning. He's also calling for the evacuation of Region 1 and the northernmost areas."

She released a heavy sigh. "How long until Region 3 starts walking?" That was their area, the swath running through the middle of Salem.

"Not until the army passes the glacial fort and starts down the canyon to Salem. By then everyone from Regions 1 and 2 will be well on the trails to the site."

"And who will be monitoring the army's progress?" Mahrree wondered. "The glacial fort and scouts will be overrun by then."

"We have spies with horses located along the tops of the mountains. They can keep us updated as to Thorne's progress." Not long ago Woodson and his scouts had created alternative routes to Salem, paths which only the scouts, Peto, and Shem knew about.

Worried about the men she's help train in lying lessons over the years, Mahrree asked, "Woodson and the others know when to get out?"

"When Thorne reaches Salem, the scouts head for the ancient site. They've got routes across the tops of the mountains and should always be a couple hours ahead of the army. They'll get in safely," he added, seeing the concern in her eyes. "And Woodson's not fifteen anymore, Mother. He's no longer that boy we met in the forest when we were coming to Salem."

Mahrree rolled her eyes at him. "You know full well that *all* of you are still little boys to me! So when will you leave?"

"I want you heading to the site as soon as possible," Peto told her. "Both Shem and I agree that getting you out of Salem is a priority. If Lemuel—"

"That's not what I asked," Mahrree politely cut him off. "When will *you* leave?"

"That's not important, what's important is that you—"

Mahrree put her finger on her son's lips. "When will *you* leave?"

He squared his shoulders. "When would General Shin leave, Mother?"

"That's what I was afraid of."

Peto attempted a smile. Mahrree didn't even know he had a 'The Dinner' smile. He looked so much like his father.

"I'll make sure that all who want to leave will make it to the forests safely. And then I'll make it safely, too."

"What about Shem?"

"Don't worry. He doesn't intend to face Lemuel or even let him know that he's still alive."

Mahrree wasn't convinced.

Peto put his arms around her and hugged her small frame. "Remember, Guide Gleace said we would live to see the day. We'll be up there with you before you know it! In fact, you'll be so busy trying to climb all over that ruin again you won't even notice when the army marches in to the valley below."

Mahrree chuckled sadly. "I haven't been there since our 44th anniversary. Nearly two years, now. Nor have I seen the engravings Relf and the others have carved there of our history."

"See?" Peto said with strained cheeriness. "Lots for you to do up there. Relf and his family will take you up there tomorrow. He can get a start on finishing our story so those who come after us centuries later can puzzle over the shapes of our words and wonder what we were trying to tell them. You'll enjoy watching him."

Mahrree stepped away from her son. "Yes, of course I will. But Peto, don't make me go just yet. I want to stay, just a little longer."

Peto narrowed his eyes. "Mother, why?"

"I don't know, I really don't," she fibbed. "I just don't feel I should leave tomorrow. Eventually, yes, but tomorrow's too soon."

"You might as well just agree to going now," Peto said, folding his arms, "because if Shem hears you want to stay he'll be over here to have it out with you."

"Good! He hasn't been by to visit me for days. As if he has more important matters," she sniffed haughtily.

Peto smiled gently. "Please, Mother, promise me one thing?"

"What is it?"

"That you'll consider leaving tomorrow afternoon? Just to ease my mind, make me feel better?"

"I promise I'll consider it, Peto."

"But you won't do it, will you?"

"You asked only if I would *consider* it."

Peto groaned. "Let me restate that—"

"You can't," she smirked. "You asked me to promise you 'one

thing.' You can't ask for anything more."

Peto closed his eyes in frustration. "You must be *the* most aggravating woman, from the world or from Salem!"

Mahrree kissed his cheek. "How long have you been my son? And you *finally* figured that out?"

He chuckled. "After nearly forty-four years of knowing you I'm still hoping you'll become reasonable. Look, I'm only trying to keep you safe. The general wouldn't be pleased if I neglected to take care of my mother during all of this."

"You're not neglecting me. Worry instead about those at the arena who think they can fight Thorne. They're sending out messengers now, looking to build an army, right?"

He nodded drearily.

She gripped his face. "Trust me to make the right decisions, Peto. I'm old enough now, you know. Seventy-four must be 'of age,' isn't it?"

"Yes, you're of age. But—"

"Then, son, don't you have something better to do this morning? Go. Be Rector Shin. Do what your father would do: his duty."

The scouting corps was surprised to see the two men on horseback riding on the top of the ridge, well out of sight of the canyons. The paths were secret, known only to a few. They were even more surprised to see who dismounted.

"Colonel Jon Offra, at your service. And this is Teman, a former scout." Offra was wearing the gray and black mottled clothing of a scout, as was his small companion. "I'm here to strike fear, by permission of Guide Zenos. Now, where's the best position to holler down to the Glacial Fort?"

Shin scanned the terrain ahead of him, deliberating.

The first line of the army was still struggling to scale the hard, ashy slope but soon they'd catch up.

Even though he tried to explain to Thorne the importance of spacing out the soldiers as they climbed, he refused to listen. Only minutes ago, an avalanche of more than thirty soldiers slid down the mountainside, being stopped only by large boulders. It was all because the soldier in the lead had lost his footing. Shin didn't know yet what the tally of injured were from that mistake, but it wasn't the first.

The first wave of soldiers hadn't hiked more than one hundred feet above the river when two unsteady and overweight men had tumbled down into it. One had a broken leg, the other was still unconscious. It was then that Shin realized he might be able to incapacitate a good portion of the unfortunate army before they ever reached the glacial fort.

He climbed diagonally to a wide ledge above. While he had seen traces of the faint trail and had crossed it several times, no one below him recognized it for what it was. Taking the switchbacks would be safer and less strenuous, but Shin's goal was to exhaust and unnerve the soldiers. So far, none of them questioned his judgment about climbing straight up to the summit. They assumed that's how a mountain should be climbed.

"I see where you're going," Teach grunted below him, nodding to the ridge far above. "Interesting choice."

"I think it's the only choice." Cloud Man looked around. "How much further till we get to the top?"

"We won't go all the way to the top, or the summit," Shin clarified. "Just to that ridge below it. I'm guessing it will take about another hour. Then we can walk that until we get to . . . wherever it is we're going."

Teach groaned as he pulled himself up and cleared his throat.

Shin prepared himself for the comment.

"You know, *some* think that Thorne's goal is noble, trying to liberate all those who have been held hostage by Salem."

Shin continued to trudge up the steep slope in silence, grabbing brush and scrubby tree limbs to steady himself.

"*Some* think that you should be a little more helpful, considering the good intentions of the general."

He wondered what Teach's intent was. They'd had several pointless conversations in the last hour. Apparently General Thorne wasn't impressed with the quality of information Buddy and Pal were extracting, so he was trying a new tactic.

"I'm as helpful as I know to be, Teach."

"But one could be *more* helpful, Shin. Considering that Thorne has repeatedly threatened one of your security detail if you fail."

Below him, Cloud Man bounced his head, oblivious that Thorne had threatened to bounce the vial head down the mountain if the private wouldn't be more cooperative.

"Interesting," Shin said as he searched for better footing. "Thorne's so 'noble' as to *force* us to seek out Salem, and he's so 'noble' that he's also *threatening* one of his own soldier's lives to do so. Perhaps I'm not that familiar with the definition of nobility. Enlighten me, Teach."

He heard Teach moan below him again, maybe because of the question or because he was smacked by another tree branch. Hopefully both.

"Nobility. Doing that which the circumstances demand."

"That's it?"

"Language usage wasn't my specialty in the university."

"What *was* your specialty?"

"I specialized in it all."

Shin stifled a snort. "But not language usage?"

"Why bother? Everyone knows how to talk, don't they?"

Shin reached for another scrubby brush. "So who decides 'what circumstances demand'? When someone is acting in everyone's best interests and not just out of his own selfishness?"

"Are you suggesting General Thorne is selfish?" Teach asked.

"Yes."

The scoff behind him made Shin glance down.

Teach was aghast. "You actually admit that?"

"I said only what you're thinking, Teach. What *everyone* on this hill is thinking. It'd been wiser, safer, and more productive to go to Terryp's land. If we did, after three days of walking and climbing we'd be a lot further than a mere two miles from the fort!"

Teach's mouth twitched as if he agreed, but agreeing with the private wasn't his duty for the day.

"So," Teach said slowly, "how does that make you feel? Thorne's pursuing *this* endeavor rather than the one *you* recommended weeks ago?"

Shin rolled his eyes. The question was so leading, so obvious, that any honest answer he gave could be construed to be traitorous. "How do you think I feel about it, Teach?"

"I don't know. That's why I'm asking."

"You already know my answer, Teach."

"Just tell me your answer, Shin!"

"Why? Is this a test? Of my devotion to the general?"

"Ha!" Teach barked, or would have if he wasn't struggling to catch his breath. It came out more as a defiant gasp. "Everyone doubts that right now, Shin. The real question is, why? Why are you so critical of your father?"

"Isn't that what sons do?" he blinked innocently. "Criticize and rebel against their fathers?"

Teach considered that. "True, true. That's probably what many sons do. But *they* know their fathers won't kill them or their companions for it. Honestly, I don't understand you. For as evil as Salem is, you insist on shielding it. What do you fear?"

"Are you afraid they'll harm your father?" Cloud Man called up. Shin wasn't aware that he was listening in.

"Is that why you don't want the general going to Salem? Your father will get hurt?" Cloud Man asked in his typically chipper tone.

Shin smiled. The words were all correct but the meaning was all wrong. "Yeah, something like that. Very perceptive."

Cloud Man beamed at the compliment.

Teach nodded. "Then why not tell the general that? Why not tell him you're just trying to preserve him?"

"It's . . . a little more confusing than that, Teach. I get confused myself nearly every minute."

"Stupid vial heads," Teach murmured.

The first of the Salemites left early that afternoon with packs on their backs. Small children and the elderly rode on horses while everyone else walked alongside. As they passed their friends and neighbors, also readying for the journey, they nodded apprehensively and exchanged strained smiles.

Some families looked back at their colorfully painted houses, farms, gardens, and fields, but others didn't. What was the point? It wasn't as if there were any more details to memorize.

By the thousands they made their way to the southernmost route, called the Idumean trail because Guide Gleace had seen in vision that was the route the Army of Idumea would take to the dead western valley, and the reason those living near it needed to be gone well before the army arrived.

Rector Shin and his assistant Cephas Briter sat on their horses at the trailhead, waiting for the families.

As Cephas spot-checked packs to make sure they were complete—unsurprisingly, all of them were—Rector Shin asked everyone the same thing: "You understand how to read the markings, right? The number of slashes and their direction indicates how many tens of paces you need to walk, and in what direction, until you come to the next markings—"

An old woman smiled and waved as she strolled by. "Thank you, but rest assured that we all know what to do, General."

That title always made Peto squirm. "Ma'am, I'm not the general—"

But she wagged a finger at him, and an old man next to her said, "We knew your father, Rector Shin, and you are every bit as much a general as he was."

"But I never served—"

"And what have you been doing for the past twenty-odd years?" the old woman exclaimed. "Serving us. You're *our* General Shin."

"And frankly, son," the old man added, "Salem could use a general on our side right now. Don't you agree?"

Several people hearing the exchange chuckled in agreement.

Peto could do nothing else but wink his appreciation.

Once the group had passed, Cephas leaned over to his uncle. "If you're a general, does that mean I'm a lieutenant?"

Peto chuckled miserably. "My father gave me that designation when I was his assistant. The title never stuck, but you might as well be Lieutenant Briter."

Cephas sat a little taller.

Their checking of packs was unnecessary. Everyone was prepared and had been for over twenty-five years. Still, the Salemites appreciated the rector's show of concern and his attempt to look cheerful.

But nothing could disguise the melancholy in his eyes as Salem began to evacuate.

Versa examined herself in the small mirror in her bedroom. The wide breeches felt odd, as they did when she first put them on to come to Salem five moons ago, but they were more practical for walking and climbing.

The roomy tunic, however, felt wonderful. She smiled in approval that she chose the brown mottled cloth that matched her thick, long coat. She'd look like a rock if she crouched. However, crouching had become difficult lately, and as she practiced, she kept toppling over. Grumbling, she said, "I would choose now to gain weight. When I need to be my fastest, I'm instead my dumpiest."

She took the spare pair of breeches and tunic, dyed more gray than brown, folded them around her several changes of undergarments, then shoved them into her bag.

It'd been too many times that she'd packed for a move, too many times she said goodbye to a house she thought might be hers for more than a few moons. At least she was practiced at packing. Her bag was well-balanced and well-stocked.

Although the emergency shelters were full, each person was to bring enough rations for at least a week, relying on the shelters only in cases of emergency. There'd be enough true emergencies along the paths, the rector reminded their congregation, that no family should create unnecessary problems by not being prepared.

Their congregation had gathered one last time that morning, as soon as they saw the black banners with white swords flying. They received last minute instructions and, after a prayer, the rector made sure everyone was taken care of. Even—and *especially*—the Thornes.

Versa looked around the tidy and airy bedroom which had been hers, solely and completely and no one else's *ever,* for the past three moons and said a silent goodbye.

She headed to the gathering room where she knew her mother was waiting, but a deep and quiet voice startled her. She stopped and peered around the corner.

Her mother was talking to a well-built man, maybe in his mid-fifties, with light brown skin, graying hair, and gentle eyes. He was holding her mother's face.

Versa clenched her fists until she realized that Druses didn't seem to mind. In fact, she was turning a shade of pink.

"Don't you dare think you're intruding, Druses," the man was saying. "We've already discussed it and there's no talking me out of it."

"But, Creer, you need to take care of your own children—"

Creer chuckled softly. "My six boys have been married and on their own for a while now." He stepped closer to her.

Versa gripped the door frame. She'd seen her mother and that man speaking on many occasions and often he had walked her home from events at the rectory, but never had she seen him standing only inches away from her.

"My boys know how lonely I've been, Druses. My oldest son said to me this morning, 'We're taking Mrs. Thorne, aren't we? We've made room for her daughters to ride in the wagon.' He said he's never seen me smiling so much since his mother died. And it's true, Druses. You've made me smile again, and I'm not leaving without you and your girls."

Versa's mouth dropped open as her mother sighed. It wasn't a sad sigh but more of a girlish, *giddy* sigh.

She was sure her mother had never made such a noise before.

Druses stepped closer to Creer, which Versa hadn't thought possible. "Only if you're sure this is the best thing—"

She didn't get to finish her sentence.

Versa's eyes bulged as Creer tenderly kissed Druses on the lips. Druses seemed to be caught off guard and she stiffened, but suddenly her arms went around Creer and she kissed him back.

Versa stared.

Her mother *kissing?*

Creer stepped back and beamed at Druses. "I think this is the absolutely best thing."

Druses giggled.

Versa didn't know if she should intervene or call a doctor.

Creer took Druses' hands and looked deep into her eyes. "One hour, Druses. I'll be here in one hour with my sons and their families. We'll have a pack horse for your things, and you'll be riding my horse all the way there."

"Oh Creer, I couldn't—"

"Yes, you can. I'll be leading him. He's big because he's a Clark, but he's steady—"

"No, I mean I can't take your horse from—"

"I can handle the walk. I've done it half a dozen times. My boys and I stocked those emergency caves ourselves. It's really a pleasant journey. But I worry about you. I don't want you tiring too quickly."

"You . . . you *worry* about me?"

Creer stepped up to her again. "Of course I do. You're a remarkable woman, Druses, and I want to take care of you. And I," he hesitated and blushed, "well, I was also hoping that maybe, when all of this is over, whatever *that* might mean, that you'll consider—"

Druses put her finger on his lips. "Let's get through the next few days, first. But I *can* tell you right now that I'm considering all kinds of things I never dared consider before."

Creer caught her in another kiss, this time longer. Before he released her he whispered, "One hour."

"One hour," Druses repeated as he pulled away.

Creer grinned boyishly at her then bounded out the front door.

Druses released a big sigh, wrapped her arms around herself, and spun like a school girl—

Until she saw her daughter standing in the doorway, hands on her hips.

"Ah. Oh. Did you—"

"I did! Mother, what are you *thinking*?"

"I'm thinking I'm a forty-three-year-old woman who deserves to finally find some happiness."

Versa scoffed. "Don't you think this *might* not be the best time? Your *husband* is coming—"

"*Ex*-husband," Druses reminded her. "Guide Zenos released us from our marriages on the same day, although he said Lemuel stopped acting as my husband years ago. Or have you forgotten?"

Versa growled quietly. "No, it's just that you were always the one to say, 'Don't trust men. They want only one thing—'"

"Well, Creer already has six sons," Druses giggled. "Now all he wants is me."

"Mother!"

"What?"

Versa gestured wildly, baffled that her mother couldn't see the obvious. "You're . . . you're too *old* for this kind of nonsense."

"Too old? I could live another thirty years, Versa. Maybe even more. If I can have a wonderful man by my side—"

"And how can you be sure he's a wonderful man, Mother?"

"Because I *feel* it, here," Druses said, patting her chest.

"Oh, I know what you're feeling," Versa sniggered. "You're far too flushed to feel anything else but—"

"Versula Thorne! Don't you tell me what I should or should not be feeling! If I've found a good man, then why can't you be happy for me? What ulterior motive could he possibly have?"

Versa opened her mouth, then shut it. She couldn't think of any other reason except that maybe he *was* attracted to her.

To Versa's surprise, Druses began to chuckle. "Shocking, isn't it?

That he might actually enjoy my company? We've been going to many events together. I haven't exactly been telling you about that. You seem content just sitting in here reading every book you and Delia can find. But Creer is a gentle man. His wife died almost four years ago, and last night he told me that while he could never replace her, his heart has room to grow new spaces. His wife will always occupy one part, but he said last night he was growing a new section, just for me. I think that's the lumberjack in him, comparing everything to 'new growth'," she added dreamily.

"I . . . I had no idea, Mother." Versa was genuinely flabbergasted. "I didn't realize that—"

"That I might want to fall in love again? See what a husband's *supposed* to be like? He's already shown more concern for me than Lemuel ever did in the five years we were together."

Versa smiled. "You're right, I guess. But I must confess, seeing him *kiss* you—"

Druses flushed red with the memory. "Ah, Versa—he's so, *he's so* . . . This will be the longest hour of my life."

Versa chuckled as her mother fanned herself. "Would you like me to find a patch of snow to cool you down, young lady?"

Druses laughed. "No, I think I can control myself. I see you have your pack. Delia's ready, too, but went down the road to check on that new mother—"

"Mother," Versa interrupted carefully, "I'm not going to go with you and your new *boyfriend*."

Druses paled. "What?"

Versa put on a smiling face. "Don't worry, I'm going to the ancient site. It's just that, well, I haven't been exactly forthcoming with you, either."

"What do you mean?"

"I'm not always staying here reading books when you sneak out to be with Creer. I've . . . I've met someone, too."

Druses clapped her hands in delight. "Really?"

Versa nodded in embarrassment. "Really."

"Who?"

"Uh, I'm not sure that you know him. He's in his early twenties and was visiting his grandparents in the next congregation over. We've only walked together a few times, and I don't even know if it will turn into anything, but . . ."

"But?" Druses was nearly bursting.

"Well, I ran into him yesterday when I was getting supplies from the storehouse and he said he'd like me to walk with him and his family to the ancient site. There's probably about forty of them, so I'd be safe—"

Druses clapped her hands again. "Why, Versa! That's . . . that's wonderful! Oh, I want to meet him—"

"Mother, there's really no time. His grandmother isn't well and his family won't be leaving until tomorrow morning. They're waiting for a special team of horses to arrive from Salem. She's frail and needs to ride in a net litter. Right now he's helping his cousin retrieve that team from the south."

"Of course, of course," Druses said, disappointed. "But I'll meet him up there, right?"

"Maybe." Versa eyed her mother. "As eager as you are, I don't really know if I want you scaring him."

"Don't worry, I'll be the very model of restraint. I'll wait for you at the temple site?"

Versa rolled her eyes. "Mother, don't you think *everyone* will be meeting their families at the temple site?"

"Well, I don't know of anywhere else to meet," she confessed. "That's all I know that's up there!"

Versa tipped her head in agreement. "Then I'll see you there. Only, don't sit and wait for me. With my friend's grandmother doing so poorly, it could be even two days before we get there."

"But you'll *be* there?" Druses asked.

"What's that supposed to mean? Of course I'll be there!" Versa exhaled in disgust. "Where else would I go?"

An hour later, Versa was in front of her house waving goodbye to her mother and sister. Delia sat in a wagon between two younger girls, Creer's granddaughters, who were pelting her with questions about life in the world which Delia happily answered.

But Versa's attention was on Creer's sons, her potential step-brothers. She doubted that any of them knew their father had kissed her mother, repeatedly. He'd come into the house alone to retrieve Druses, greeted her with a kiss, received another kiss for his efforts, so he gave another one back as a thank you, and the pattern may have continued indefinitely had Versa not loudly cleared her throat, causing both Creer and Druses to jump apart like startled teenagers.

Now, as Creer lead Druses to his large gray horse and lifted her to the saddle—Versa hadn't realized how strong he was—Creer's sons smiled and his daughters-in-law grinned in approval.

Versa finally smiled as well. Her mother was in excellent hands.

To her surprise, Creer came back to where she was standing in the doorway, the look in his eyes grave.

"I don't like leaving you here, Versa. But Druses says you'll be traveling with another family?"

"Yes, I'll be heading over to their house soon and they'll leave in the morning."

Creer gave her a calculated look, as if he didn't fully believe her. "You be careful and take care of yourself. Understand? Don't make your mother worry about you, because she does, immensely. Now's not a good time for you to be alone, even for only an hour. Forgive me for saying this, but you aren't exactly in the best physical condition."

Versa was taken aback. "I'm fine, sir. I can take care of myself. I have for years."

"But that's not Salem's way, Versa. Let me leave one of my sons and his family here. They can keep you company and then go with you—"

"No, sir," she cut him off, almost embarrassed by his concern. Creer hardly knew her but he was acting as if he'd been in her family for years. Salem was odd that way. "That's not necessary. I'll be going over to my friend's grandparents' house right after you leave. You just . . . take care of my mother and sister, please."

Creer smiled. "I intend to, Versa. And you as well. If anything comes up, any problems, you send the word and I'll come for you."

Despite her efforts, Versa's chin quivered as she looked into his concerned face. "Thank you. My mother thinks highly of you."

"And I, her. Now don't make your mother and me worry," he said as if he already had some connection to her. To make matters worse, he gave her a quick kiss on her forehead, a fatherly gesture which so surprised her that she went rigid.

Unaware of her astonishment, Creer walked back to his horse, took the reins, and nodded to the rest of his family, most on foot, several in the wagon until the trailhead, and a couple on horseback. He started west, with his family following and waving genially to Versa still standing on the doorstep.

Druses gave Versa one final wave, then turned and asked Creer something. Whatever he answered made Druses laugh.

Versa walked back into the house and blinked back her tears

which she never let fall. She still felt that kiss on her forehead and probably would for the rest of the day. Her mother would be well taken care of, and so would Delia.

But Priscill was . . . Well, no one knew. Not even Guide Zenos could give them anything about her. That meant there was only one Thorne still to attend to.

Good thing she inherited his lying tongue.

Versa went back to her room, slipped on her very full pack, picked up her mother's brown shawl which Druses insisted she take with her to be returned at the ancient site, and wrapped it around her head to cover her blond braid.

She nodded at her reflection in the mirror, left her room, and went out the back door.

Then started walking south.

"Now this view is even better!" Cloud Man exclaimed as he was the third man to reach the ridge.

Snarl was the fourth, and a moment later the rest of Shin's security team stood along with him and Teach, who had strained himself to the point of collapse to stay with the private. Teach now lay on the snow as if he'd passed out. Or perhaps he was hoping he'd appear to be unconscious to avoid going any further.

"Yeah, great view." Sergeant Beaved leaned over to catch his breath and, Shin suspected, to avoid seeing just how high they were. "It's got to be after midday meal, isn't it?"

Shin looked up at the sky. "I'm thinking here would be a good place to camp for the night. It's a large area, and most of those on the mountainside should be able to reach here by dinner—"

"What's this I'm hearing?" a voice boomed over at him. "Camp *here*? Why?" General Thorne climbed the last few feet to the ridge. He was winded, his face was red, but his blue eyes simmered. "We have the entire afternoon. Let the stragglers camp here. We go on."

Twigg, Hili, Amory, and many more soldiers, all looking as exhausted as the general, lumbered to the ridge next, stopping to look around and catch their breath.

Shin gestured to them. "Sir, I'm not sure how much further it is, and your men are obviously tired—"

"Amory!" Thorne called. "How much further to that mountain

valley? The place with the fort and the horses?"

Amory wiped away sweaty hairs that clung to her face. Now that all the face paint had dripped off, she appeared wrinkled and haggard as she squinted into the distance, and Shin held his breath. She was going to notice—

"Why, Lemuel, we're nearly there! You see how those two peaks meet? That's at the *end* of the valley!"

Thorne looked in the direction Amory pointed. "That's maybe less than two miles from here?"

Shin held his face perfectly still, because Thorne actually had that distance correct.

"So the beginning of the valley is *less* than two miles away?" Thorne's voice grew tighter. "Along this ridge?"

Amory nodded eagerly.

Thorne aimed a sneer at Shin. "Very good, *son.* You did something right today. Make all the men exhausted, then reward them with an easy walk to the mountain valley. We should have *everyone* there by nightfall. It sounds like a much better place for a camp. I understand there are hanging nets to sleep in? I may consider letting you have one tonight."

Shin stiffened in frustration and fury. "I prefer sleeping under the stars. In fact, I may want to sleep out in the open every day for the rest of my life."

"For however long that life is, Shin," the general said testily, "you may do so." Thorne turned to everyone else. "Thirty minutes' rest, eat your rations, then we continue on." He smiled thinly at Shin. "In two miles we'll see about giving you back your first name. But the last name will wait until we reach Salem."

Bristling, Shin wisely said nothing. Instead he took off his pack, sat down on a rock which was relatively dry, and pulled out his rations.

As he nibbled on the hard bread he fretted. Anyone could find their way to the glacial fort now. At least he'd given Salem more time to evacuate. Someone should've noticed their approach by now.

He glanced over at Thorne who was making Hili get out his rations, and felt his stomach twist. More than anything in the world he hated this man who told lie after lie. He hated how he had spoken about the weakness of Colonel Shin—

A pang of guilt struck him. He'd had similar thoughts about Perrin Shin: weak, useless, too scared to return to the world and take his name back from General Thorne.

Finally Shin understood. Of what worth was the opinion of the world?

Wishing Thorne could feel the daggers he was shooting out of his eyes, he glanced again at the general but noticed instead Hili, standing nearby and holding Thorne's pack as well as his own.

Pale and worn, Hili was the oldest man out here. Why wasn't someone else acting as Thorne's pack mule?

Shin sagged. That's what *he* would've turned into had he stayed. Perrin Shin might have turned out as vile and selfish as Lemuel Thorne, but instead he fled the world.

THANK THE CREATOR YOU FINALLY UNDERSTAND WHY I DIDN'T WANT TO GO BACK TO THE WORLD. BUT YOUNG PERE, YOU DON'T HAVE TO FIX ANYTHING. THERE'S A PLAN—

No, Puggah. Let me do something good for Salem. I can't go back like this. I have to go back to Mama and Papa having done something good . . .

Eltana Yordin had been expecting the knock at her door.

Ever since the meeting at the arena yesterday, she'd been hearing rumors about men gathering, and she knew it was only a matter of time before they sought her out. A few had gone to Colonel Jon Offra for ideas, but he slammed the door in their faces and refused to discuss defense with any of them, the cowardly man. He'd vanished shortly after that, probably already running scared up to the ancient temple site.

She opened the door and smiled at the group of twenty men who stood there.

"Mrs. Eltana Yordin," said a man she knew from her Armchair Generals meetings.

"What can I do for you fine gentlemen?"

"We need some suggestions."

"Yes, you do, Mr. Custer. Come in and sit down. There might be room for all of you." She held the door opened wider and assessed them as they filed in. They ranged in ages from late teens to late sixties, and each man was lean, strong, and in far better shape than anyone in the world. That would be their first advantage.

When each of the men had found a place to sit or stand in the small gathering room, Eltana shut the door behind her. She loved rooms filled with muscle and power, with men eager do to something with their strength. This was no Armchair Generals meeting. This was a war council.

She sat down in a soft chair in the middle of the room purposely left for her. *And* they were true gentlemen.

The man who had led them out of the arena yesterday began. "Mrs. Yordin, we're not about to retreat and give all we have to our enemy. We want to stay and fight."

"Commendable, Mr. Custer," Eltana said to the burly man in his thirties. He'd never served in the army of Idumea but had always longed to be a scout. He'd told Eltana privately last year that his requests as a younger man had been denied. The trainers and guide at the time had said he was too aggressive and impulsive. Eltana had thought that summed up Salem's faults perfectly: they embraced the wrong character traits.

"And what do you want from me?" she said, although she knew quite well what they wanted. But you should always make a man work for it.

"Strategy, ma'am."

"Strategy? Now, why seek me out?" she asked, almost coyly.

"Because you know the ways of the army best!" said an eager young man. "You used to be there! You were married to a real general! You knew General Thorne!"

Mr. Custer held up his hand to calm the younger man. "Yes, that's why we're here. If anyone would know the ways of the current army, it's you."

"And no one *else* would help you?" Eltana said. "No one *else* with the reputation for recruiting and training the greatest soldiers in the history of the army?"

The men glanced at each other nervously.

She waved off their looks. Of course Shem Zenos wouldn't share his expertise. "I'm happy to help. I agree that retreating without even attempting to defend your property is cowardly and stupid. Why, each of you is in better shape than anyone in the world! How many men do you have with you?"

Mr. Custer answered, "By last count this morning, about five thousand men are willing to fight. But we haven't heard back yet from the far north or the dissenter villages. We should be getting word in a few hours, and I suspect we'll have at least double, if not triple that number."

Eltana nodded slowly, thinking. "Fifteen thousand men, at best? And how many are in the Army of Idumea right now?"

The men looked at each other again. "The scouts, at last count, say about eighty thousand men. But already a few hundred have been lost to the canyon and we're hoping many more will fall before they make it to Salem."

Eltana squinted. "I estimate they'll lose maybe another ten to fifteen thousand before they ever reach Salem. And once they're here they'll be so weary they won't put up much of a challenge."

Many of the men sighed in relief and exchanged smiles.

"But," Custer said, "as some have suggested, that's still sixty-five thousand men. And there's a large group of women supposedly coming, too."

"They're not a concern," Eltana assured him.

"Still, that's more than four soldiers to each one of us," Custer pointed out. "We'll have a real battle on our hands."

"Four flabby, exhausted men with no will of their own against each one of you: rested, strong, and wanting to save your homes!" Eltana exclaimed. "Never underestimate the desire for survival."

Several of the men nodded in appreciation.

"Exactly!"

"That's what I've been saying."

"See? We can do this."

Custer held up his hands for silence and turned to Mrs. Yordin. "I was hoping you would say something like that." He started to smile. "What I said to you were the words of discouragement Guide Zenos offered me before I left him this morning. Four to one? We can handle that! He said it'd be far worse."

Mrs. Yordin smiled, pleased to see she had more influence than Guide Zenos. "Tell me what you have, then we can start considering tactics. Weapons?"

"Pitchforks mostly, ma'am."

She made a face. "Pitchforks?"

"But we know how to use them," put in another man in his fifties. "For years we've been trained with them, in case a rogue group of soldiers happened to make their way over the mountains. General Shin wanted us to be able to defend our families. He always said the reach of a pitchfork is greater than that of a sword, with four points at the end of it, so it's more deadly than a sword, too." He made a thrusting motion.

"Sounds like the Perrin Shin I used to know," she murmured in appreciation. Louder, she said, "That's true. A sharp thrust into the chest can puncture both lungs, incapacitating your man until you can come back later to finish him off, if it's still necessary."

A couple of the men looked aghast by the idea, but Eltana continued. "What else? Knives?"

Several men nodded. "But for butchering animals," one man explained.

"A pig is a pig, sir," Eltana said. "In the field or in a uniform. Butcher them both the same way. Slash the throat, stab the heart, or gut it."

The young eager man swallowed hard at the image, and his light brown face began to go white.

"What else?" she asked.

The men looked at each other and shrugged.

"What about hatchets? Axes?" she suggested.

Custer shook his head. "General Shin didn't want us using those. He said if we threw them and missed, we just handed another weapon to our enemies."

"But if you have nothing else, a hatchet will come in handy," she told them, "especially in close combat. Don't throw them, *hold* them. You can sever a limb as easily as a tree branch, and a well-placed hatchet can stop a man's heart or cut the arteries in his neck. You don't need great force to make a man bleed to death."

A few of the men shifted, obviously not used to thinking about the many ways to take a man's life.

Eltana smirked at their uneasiness. They'd get over their squeamishness soon enough. No one in the world was squeamish anymore.

"You have bows and arrows for hunting, too, correct?" she asked. "Again, puncture a man's lung and he can't do much else but fall to the ground gasping for breath. Hit him in a vital organ and he'll collapse from the pain. Even an arrow to the leg means he can't run anymore. Oh, I can tell you a great many more ways to disable a man. But first, let's talk about your strategy. What are you planning?"

"Well, that's where we have some disagreements," Custer said, seemingly relieved to be leaving the topic of hurting other people. "Some want to defend their homes while others think we should combine together and face the army as one."

Eltana nodded. "That's your best option."

"But what if a soldier breaks away and rushes to one of our properties while we're fighting?" asked one man.

"Then chase him down and kill him when the battle is over," Eltana said glibly. "You have to defeat the *entire* army, not just *some* of the men. If you can get the army to surrender, you can deal later with the remaining soldiers as you see fit. The conquered *must* obey the conquerors. It's always been that way. Ah, but you don't know that, do you? What a waste . . ."

"So you'll help us?" asked Custer.

She scoffed. "Obviously! But we need to begin as soon as possible. Training should begin early tomorrow morning, with every man you have here to learn what I can teach you."

"We can meet in the fields behind my farm," one man suggested. "That's a rather central location."

The other men nodded in agreement.

"Good," Eltana said. "And gather as many weapons as possible. You also need to establish captains over fifties, hundreds, and thousands. Now, this is what needs to happen in the next few hours . . ."

"Done with your little nap?"

Shin's eyes flew open to see Thorne hovering over him.

"I've never seen a man sleep sitting up before, but I guess the dungeon taught you that important skill. So many benefits I never imagined."

Shin tried to shake the sleepy fog out of his head. The area was filling up with weary soldiers not appreciating the view or the slush they stood in.

"It's time to move on," Thorne said. "The rest of the army is catching up. Hili said I should let you sleep for twenty minutes so you'd be rested. Well, are you?"

He blinked, still confused. "Am I what?"

"Rested!"

"Yes, of course." Shin fumbled to his feet and picked up his pack. How did that happen? He closed his eyes only for a moment to concentrate on . . . what?

Strategy. What he was going to do later, and then suddenly he was asleep. Somehow he was sure it was Puggah's fault.

He faced north. The glacial valley would still be covered with snow. If anyone had been there, or recently left, their tracks would be obvious. If he was the first to the tracks, maybe he could cover them up. Not that it would do any good, but it would make him feel better.

He started walking, wondering who his companion would be for the next couple of miles. Likely not Teach, because Iron was trying to rouse him as he faked unconsciousness rather unconvincingly.

Shin would have appreciated Hili by his side, if only to find out how the sergeant major was. Maybe he could heft Thorne's pack for a while and perhaps accidentally drop it down a ravine. Hili didn't look well at all, and he hadn't said a word to Shin lately. But he was comforted that Hili was concerned about him, letting him take the nap which was surprisingly refreshing.

"So, just a couple miles this way, is it?" Reg was apparently his designated partner for this leg.

"Supposedly."

"You're really good at that, you know that?" Reg whispered as he walked alongside. "Not giving away anything? Keeping your emotions to yourself? Great skills for an officer to have."

Shin only shrugged.

"Did you learn to do that when you were Lieutenant Thorne?"

"No."

"Learned it before?"

"Perhaps."

"Trying to keep information away from those you called your family? You know, I don't think I even know who raised you. Those in Salem? Needed to hide your true feelings and such?"

Shin sighed. "What do you want, Reg?"

"I don't want anything, Shin. Just making small talk."

"No, you're not. None of you are here to make 'small talk,'" he accused quietly, although the general was at least forty paces behind. "All of you are acting under Thorne's direction to wheedle as much information out of me as possible."

Reg chuckled. "You *are* very smart, aren't you? Beaved warned us you were. He also said you're paranoid, but that comes from being in the dungeon. We're not supposed to take it personally, and I don't. What was it like, anyway? The dungeon?"

"Smelly."

Reg chortled again, more enthusiastically than necessary. "So Buddy and Pal told us. I can't imagine what a miserable existence that must have been. You seem to be in pretty good shape, though.

You don't look very starved."

"I felt starved."

"Maybe someone was helping you?"

Shin held his face perfectly still as he continued to walk. The kind of trouble Hili could get into, he didn't want to imagine. But maybe that's why Hili was carrying Thorne's pack; his punishment for feeding extra to the prisoner.

"Not that I wouldn't blame someone for taking pity on you," Reg rambled on. "I mean, most men die down there. I heard a few men talking that even though they didn't like you too much, they didn't think you deserved the dungeon. They wanted to find a way to help you. Digging you out was impossible, but maybe sneaking you food? There were several shifts of guards. Maybe one or two of them dropped extra rations through the floorboards? That's happened before. Against all regulations, but then again, dungeons aren't in any of the command school books, are they? I've been reading them. I hope to go to Command School when all of this is over—"

"Don't think so far, Reg," Shin cut him off.

Reg looked over at him eagerly now that he had an interesting response. "Why not plan for the future?"

"Because you have none, Reg. None of us do. This is a stupid endeavor and we will all die."

Reg was silent for a moment. "The paranoia, isn't it? You think we'll all die?"

Shin sighed. "Thorne's leading us to our deaths, Reg. I'm walking only to keep Cloud Man alive a while longer. I'm hoping a cloud will descend low enough that he can walk through it. That's the only thing I'm living for now. We're all going to die, and there's nothing anyone can do about it. It's hopeless."

Reg pondered his dire prediction. "Definitely the paranoia, because General Thorne is the greatest leader we've ever had! He wouldn't lead us into something if he didn't feel confident we would be victorious. There's no cause more worthy than liberating the captives. There's no purpose greater than saving the people of Idumea."

Shin rolled his eyes at the well-rehearsed story.

"What a marvelous heritage you have, Shin," Reg gushed on. "I must confess, I'm envious. To have General Lemuel Thorne, the greatest general the world has ever produced, as your *father*. Sure, he sent you to the dungeon, but my father always locked me up when I was misbehaving. Good fathers reprimand their sons forcefully. The greater the love, the greater the force. Only a man who loves you deeply would send you to a deep hole in the ground!"

Shin complimented himself that he didn't burst out laughing. He hadn't laughed in a long time, but this was tempting.

"I have faith in him, Shin," Reg said adoringly. "He's doing the right things for us, for the whole world. He can be trusted, Shin."

"Keep telling yourself that, Reg. It just might come true." Shin picked up his pace. There was a section coming up where they would have to travel single file, or the person on the outside would slip and fall down the canyon side. He half hoped the general's little toady would do just that.

One mile later, Reg was still keeping up but he'd stopped talking. When one gets no response, keeping up a monologue gets tiresome.

Shin stared straight ahead as they approached the glacial valley, trying to discern the tall trees that towered above the fort. There was a ladder, nearly impossible to see even when standing right below it, that ran the length of the tallest pine tree to afford the man perched on top a clear view for miles around. Shin wondered if anyone was there, if anyone had spotted him and sent a messenger into Salem.

But what he worried most of all about was, would he be recognized as the first man in the column?

Mahrree was on the front porch helping Jaytsy sort out the emergency traveling packs for the great grandchildren. Once they were sure each pack was filled properly—and they should be, since they did this every year—Jaytsy and her children would deliver them to the married children, just in case the black banner with the white sword was hoisted up their tower sooner than they expected.

Mahrree heard the horse approach but she didn't bother to look up. She knew who it was and she wasn't interested in what he had to say.

"Mahrree Peto Shin, I gave you a direct order," Shem said as he dismounted.

Jaytsy waved in greeting and elbowed her mother, but Mahrree refused to look up from her work.

"You were to get your pack as soon as that went up!" He jerked a thumb angrily to the banner that signaled the army had been spotted by the glacial fort. "Relf and his family are nearly ready, but you, apparently, aren't going with them?"

Mahrree looked up and smiled sweeter than she felt. "No."

Shem marched up to the porch. "Why not?"

She nodded to the tower. "Don't see any black flags yet, Shem."

"I can change that, you know," he said, nearly seething. "I'll run up your name with the sword banner right now. Is that the kind of attention you want?"

Mahrree's smile fell. "I'm not that childish, Shem. I'm not looking for attention."

"Then why are you doing this?" Shem began to roar. "Mahrree, I've got enough to worry about—"

"Yes, you do!" she bellowed louder than him. "Why you insist on pestering me when you have greater things to do is beyond my comprehension!"

"Look, Mahrree, Perrin would—"

"You don't know what Perrin would or would not do, Shem Zenos!" Mahrree shouted.

Jaytsy took a startled step backward.

"Perrin knew—*knows*—I'm capable of making my own choices. My mind is as sharp as ever. I can hear and see and move just fine, just a little slower, and I do NOT need to be coddled or babied or told what to do! Don't worry; I have no intention to sit on my front porch watching the Army of Idumea ravage all that I've loved for the past twenty-seven years. I'll go when *I* deem the time to be right, and right now I have grandchildren and great-grandchildren to take care of. And unless you have something else to say to me, Shem Zenos, because right now I also know you're not acting as the guide but as my little brother, you best get back to your duties!"

Mahrree returned to checking the packs.

Jaytsy, astonished, looked at Shem.

He fumed as he stared at Mahrree who refused to acknowledge him. For a moment he made as if he would walk back to his horse, but instead he continued up the steps to the porch.

Mahrree still ignored him, even as Shem took her by the shoulders and forcibly turned her. Without a word, he wrapped his arms around her and kissed the top of her head.

Mahrree stood stiffly for a moment, then, knowing it was useless, relented and put her arms around Shem.

Jaytsy gave Shem a grateful look.

"I'm not babying you, Mahrree," Shem whispered. "I need your aggravation now more than ever. And I need to know you're on top of that flat mountain watching our families and making sure everyone up there keeps their heads and wits about them. You can do that for me, for all of Salem. *I'm* being selfish, Mahrree. I've tried very hard never to be, but right now I am. Go for me, please. For those at the ancient temple. Let me know that the better half of Perrin Shin is still hard at work securing Salem."

Tears trickled down from Mahrree's eyes, making the front of Shem's tan jacket damp. "Let me wait for him here, Shem. He's coming. He's closing in on the glacial fort, less than a mile away from it."

Shem leaned back to look at her. "How do you know that?"

"I *feel* him, Shem! He's *coming back* to me! He's remembering his promise!"

Shem glanced at Jaytsy.

She shrugged.

Looking into Mahrree's face, her eyes bright with hope, Shem asked gently, "What promise?"

"He made a promise to stay with Young Pere, but he also promised me years ago we would go to the site together. He would stay in Salem until he was sure everyone who wanted to get out was on their way. He wouldn't leave until he saw the army at the canyon entrance. Then he'd get on Clark, whichever number it was, come get me from our dream house, and together we'd ride to the site."

Jaytsy blinked back her tears. "Oh, Mother, Mother, do you understand what's happening? I mean, you know that *can't*—"

Mahrree's hopeful face vanished and she looked sharply at her daughter. "Yes, *of course* I know that can't happen now! I'm not demented. I see it in both of your faces: Mahrree Shin's gone grainy! I'm not. Just . . ." Her eyes softened again as she explained, "He *is* coming back for me. I may be riding up there with Peto or Cephas or any number of grandsons who will be cajoled by their parents to come find me, but Perrin will be riding with me when I go. He'll find me here, and I *must* be here, Shem. Please, let us face the Last Day as we always planned. What will it matter, anyway? It's the *Last Day*!"

Shem smiled softly. "That's why Perrin never wanted a Gray-Clark. I get it now. He always wanted the best descendant of Clark he could find, and it had to be black."

"It was always on a big black horse that the captains rescued the maidens in distress from the Guarders," Mahrree explained, almost bashfully. "According to those ridiculous stories we had when we were growing up. I used to tease him about it until we rode from Edge through the forest. Suddenly I wanted nothing more than to be rescued by him, and on Clark. He promised that he'd always rescue me on a big black horse named Clark."

Jaytsy sniffed. "Oh Mother, he was *romantic*!? I never realized Father was romantic!"

Mahrree snorted. "Don't you ever tell him I told you this!"

Shem and Jaytsy regarded her with sad smiles.

Feeling too much of their sympathy, Mahrree pushed away from Shem's embrace. "Shem, Jayts, I just wanted you to understand. And I want you to let me decide when I go. All right? No more coercing or ordering or guilting me, because I know that's next. Let me wait for my husband?"

Jaytsy and Shem exchanged the same dubious look.

"All right, Mahrree," Shem said reluctantly. "I'll make sure Calla doesn't come by with her speech, although she's been working on it all morning. It's a doozy, too. There's no one quite like Calla for making a point."

Mahrree patted his cheek. "Tell her I appreciate it and I love all of you for trying." She glanced at her daughter. "Thank you for understanding."

"I do," Shem said, "but I don't like it. Not one bit. Jayts? Keep an eye on her, will you? Next thing you know she'll be arming herself with a pitchfork and going over to Eltana's for lessons."

"No, I won't!" Mahrree insisted. "Is that where you've been? At Eltana's?"

Shem sighed, almost in despair. "She's going to train the Salemites tomorrow morning, whoever wants to learn whatever strategy she knows. Shouldn't take too long. I told her she's deceiving them into thinking they'll be ready. They'll only be ready for their deaths. She told me it was better than the alternative."

"What's the alternative?" Jaytsy asked.

Shem shrugged. "She couldn't articulate it. She's not thinking straight—none of them are. They're so filled with fear and, in Eltana's case, a desire for vengeance that they can't understand any other course of action. They've lost faith . . ." His voice drifted off.

Mahrree gripped his arm. "They haven't lost faith in *you*, Shem. They've lost it in *everything*. Their faith has never been tried before, and now when they're facing a real threat, it's found to be wanting. Didn't Guide Gleace see this? That not everyone would go to the site?"

"If I could just find the right words—" he tried again.

"They'd still not listen, Shem," Jaytsy insisted. "You said all the right words at the arena yesterday. I could feel the power in them, the spirit of the Creator moving through you. But people can choose to ignore that power and spirit, Shem. We saw it all the time in the world. And the more they ignore it, the harder it is to hear it. You could yell in their faces or whisper into their ears, they will still choose to not believe you."

"So what do I do?" he whispered.

"You've done all you can do. Help those who want to be helped," Mahrree said. "You can't force the others to follow you. Force is the Refuser's tool, not yours."

He smiled. "That's just what Calla said. I know you're right, all of you are. It's just reassuring to hear it from a few other people I love and respect."

"I have faith in you, Guide Zenos!" Jaytsy declared. "I always have, ever since I was little."

Shem's smile widened. "Thanks, Jayts. I may come over a few more times to hear those words again."

"Come over as often as you wish."

He turned back to Mahrree. "I have to ask one more time—please go with Relf? They're leaving within the hour. Perrin will find you wherever you are. I really don't think he ever envisioned this scenario, Mahrree. I'm sure he expected to be right here with you, trying to force you on a horse you didn't like riding."

Mahrree patted his cheek again. "You're getting more worry lines every day, Shem. While those streaks of gray hair are quite handsome, those wrinkles around your eyes really must stop."

"Mahrree—"

"I'm a big girl, Shem. Your duty to me is fulfilled. Now go on to the next concern on your very long list, and don't forget to go home to Calla every now and then. She's getting as many worry lines as you are."

Shem nodded at her, at Jaytsy, and jogged down the stairs to his horse.

He tried to ignore the terrible feeling in his gut that Mahrree Shin wouldn't be at the ancient temple site that day.

It was right in front of Shin, the long, narrow glacial valley. He'd been following the trail for the past quarter mile. There simply wasn't any way to make it more difficult or confuse the army into going in another direction. Not with Amory around.

She was behind him about a hundred paces, squealing so loudly that everyone, if anyone was still at the fort, would know they were approaching.

"That's it?" Reg asked as the trail widened and opened on to the hidden valley. "I never would have guessed anything like this existed near the top of the mountain!"

Cloud Man nodded in appreciation. "It'd be concealed by heavy clouds. Where's the fort?"

Reg looked around. "Hey, there's no fort!"

Sergeant Beaved, a few paces behind them, jogged to catch up. "What do you mean, there's no fort?"

"The fort's there," Shin sighed. It'd only be a matter of time before tens of thousands of men crowding the valley, three-quarters of a mile long and just over half a mile wide, would have discovered the hidden structure in the dense stand of trees.

"Just keep going." He glanced surreptitiously to where the scouts generally hid, watching for anyone entering the glacial meadows. The spots in the trees were bare, but maybe new locations had been made since he'd left for the world.

Buddy and Pal joined Shin and his accompaniment as they entered the valley. Still covered in slushy, melting snow two feet deep, they could walk side by side, although ploddingly.

"This is incredible!" Pal breathed. "Look how the mountains rise up on either side. Like someone took a big scoop of the mountain away."

"It was a glacier," Shin said dully. "There used to be big chunks of ice that never melted. They slid slowly down the mountains, digging out sections as they went. That's what carved this."

The men looked around to verify his explanation.

"Chunks of ice?" a voice came from behind them. Teach panted to catch up. "Glaciers? Don't exist. Never heard of them."

"Not surprised," Shin intoned. "But they do exist."

"How do you know?"

"Salemites know a great deal more than anyone in the world," he said flatly. "They've seen a great deal more, too. We explore. Many of our scientists have seen glaciers, further north. This area used to be much colder a long time ago."

"Nonsense!" Teach exclaimed. "The world doesn't change like that. It remains unchanged and steady."

"Just like Mt. Deceit?" Shin suggested.

Teach opened his mouth then closed it again.

Another soldier jogged up to them. "General Thorne wants you to head to the fort if it's still here."

"It's here. It's straight ahead."

He headed for the large cluster of trees in the middle of the empty valley. In Weeding Season the valley was filled with wildflowers, and a gentle stream flowed from the bluish-green lake in the northeast. A small herd of elk also made its home in the meadows. He'd been there twice as a boy, accompanying his father to deliver recommendations to the fort from General Shin.

Puggah never wanted to go there. The last time he did, one of his former lieutenants died.

Shin hadn't asked about the details, but he'd heard quiet stories that Lieutenant Radan had been stabbed in the heart by his grandfather as he tried to run away from the glacial fort. Radan had been there with Colonel Offra, who was at the time a lieutenant himself and volunteered to go back to the world to hide the Shins' secret that they were alive. After losing both of his lieutenants, Perrin Shin never again wanted to approach the world.

Shin tried to pull his grandfather out of the air. Are the scouts gone? he thought.

Yes, Young Pere. They left a couple of hours ago. All of Salem knows the army is coming. They're already evacuating.

Good. Do they also know that I'm in the lead?

Only a few do. They also know you're unarmed and that your little security detail is.

Mama? Papa?

Shem and Peto are keeping quiet about everything until they see what happens to you.

And what will happen to me?

It's up to you, Young Pere. You can survive this if you listen to me, or you can die trying your way.

He was nearer the cluster of trees now, camouflaging the glacial fort. He headed straight for it as the soldiers looked around for something more obvious. It wasn't until he walked up to the door covered in dead branches that the hundreds of men behind him gasped and said a variety of, "There it is!" "Incredible!" "I would have walked right past it!"

He turned the handle and pulled open the door, but didn't get too far as he heard behind him, "Make way! Make way for the general!"

Shin stepped aside and let Thorne's guard, with their swords out and ready, stride past him. Thorne followed after a moment and stepped in to the reception room next, with several other soldiers following.

Shin held the door and hummed tunelessly.

"Come out now!" Thorne shouted to the empty fort. "Give yourselves up! You have no chance!"

Shin began to smirk. He heard Thorne and his guard tromping around inside until finally Thorne barged out, livid.

"It's abandoned! Nothing! Everything's gone! AMORY!"

She was rushing her best through the snow to reach the fort and stumbled through the door which Shin still held open.

Glowering, Thorne gestured with his sword for Shin to follow them.

Everything *was* gone. There was nothing to loot, nothing to use. Shin glanced up to see where the ladder was that normally rose to the top of the tallest tree, but the roof had only a man-sized hole in it, which would appear odd to those who didn't know why it was there. At his feet was a pile of chopped wood, the ladder masquerading as kindling.

Amory charged down the narrow, twisting building to the supply room. Her cry of dismay intrigued Shin enough to follow.

The shelves typically stocked with food, clothing, boots, blankets, medical supplies, and even toys for scared children were bare.

Amory rushed to the next room, an eating room/surgery area that also was emptied. Even the long table that stood in the room was dashed to pieces.

Thorne was standing with his left hand on his hip in the room just beyond, where hanging net slings could sleep up to thirty people. The hooks in the ceiling and walls were still visible, but there were no nets and all of the cots were missing.

Thorne glared at Amory and she shrugged back helplessly. Shin grinned to himself that Salem had looted itself, leaving nothing for the invading army.

"They must have seen us coming!" Amory whimpered, then

remembered. "The horses!" She ran through the large washing room, out the back door, along the narrow path between the trees and on to the stables that were also well camouflaged.

Thorne, Shin, and several other soldiers followed.

She threw open the door to see that not one of the fourteen stalls held a horse.

"We'll have to keep walking," she whined, leaning against a railing. "There should have been *something* still here!"

"Maybe no one's been back since Deceit erupted," Shin suggested innocently, although he knew from Puggah otherwise, and the bales of hay in the loft smelled somewhat fresh.

"Sir!" came a cry from the other end of the stables. "Tracks! Leading north!"

"Follow them," Thorne ordered. "See how far they go so we can be sure of our direction tomorrow morning." He turned back to Shin. "Obviously they were just here. By tomorrow morning all of Salem will know we are coming, won't they?"

"They already know, Lemuel!" Amory insisted. "I keep telling you about the scouts and message towers. *They already know!*"

"So we need to get there quickly, don't we?" Thorne said, still analyzing Shin's every muscle twitch. "Because they'll be ready for us, won't they? And *how* will they be ready, Shin? Every man and boy armed with swords and knives? Every woman holding a bow and a quiver full of arrows? Just waiting to slaughter us?"

He could no longer hold his tongue. "No, sir. They're not like you. They love peace and have no weapons. The only butchers there slaughter cows and pigs and poultry. You'll be the first beast that goes to Salem."

Knowing what was coming, Shin leaned just out of reach of Thorne's furious slap and the general connected only with air.

But he couldn't lean away from Thorne's guard. Before he could snigger at Thorne's miss, two large men shoved him against the wall while Thorne marched up and put his sneering face just inches away from his.

"You have no idea who the beasts are, Shin. I'll show you tomorrow. You have tonight to tell me what I need to know or tomorrow the first animal I slaughter in front of Salem will be you!" Then, seeing his opportunity, Thorne threw all of his fury as a fist into Shin's gut.

As Shin gasped and tipped forward, the guards released him to follow Thorne out of the stables, with Amory close behind.

"Nice sucker punch," he wheezed on his hands and knees. "Why'd I say that to him? Why'd I say that—"

"Shin?" Cloud Man came into the stables. He leaned out again. "Found him, Sergeant. He's just in here playing horsey." Cloud Man fell on all fours, too. "Hey, Shin, this is a great place to sleep. Can I claim it as our camp?"

Despite everything, Shin couldn't help but smile at the most agreeable soldier in the army. Pulling himself unsteadily to his feet, he said, "Sure, Cloudy. Check with Beaved first and tell him it's the best way to keep me contained, then start pushing together the last of the fresh straw. We can all sleep comfortably."

"But you won't see the stars," Cloud Man reminded him.

"Too many clouds tonight anyway, Cloudy. Did you invite them? It was a good idea. It'll help this night not be so cold."

Cloud Man beamed. "I did invite them! I did something right?"

"You always do everything right, Cloudy. Don't let anyone tell you differently."

Jon and Teman crawled across the summit until the glacial valley was fully in view. Silently they edged their way down to some scraggly bushes, ignoring how wet and cold their clothing became because of the slushy snow they pushed through. They positioned themselves behind the bushes and, once they felt confident about their chosen hiding place, Teman began to point.

"See that stone outcropping right there? Aim this bull's horn—" he handed over a long, curved horn, "—for those rocks. The valley's a natural bowl shape, along with those rocks, help amplify and redirect your sound waves."

Jon blinked several times and turned to Teman. "What in the world are you talking about?"

A third body caught their attention, rapidly crawling over to them. "Guide Zenos told me what you're trying to accomplish up here," Woodson said as he reached them, "And I thought I might be able to give some assistance. I figured you wouldn't know, Jon, about echo triangulation."

Jon perked up. "Ah, strangulation? Yes, I know a bit about that. Shem said I wasn't to harm anyone, but if you gentlemen agree that strangulation is the way to go——"

He was drowned out by the other two's urgent, "No, no, no!"

"*Trian*gulation," Teman repeated. "Like a triangle? That's what I was trying to tell you. Those rocks over there—point your voice at them and your words will bounce off and on to those rocks, there." He pointed to another outcropping on the other side of the valley. "They'll bounce again, and eventually come back to us, like a big triangle."

"Acoustic location?" Woodson tried, but Jon shrugged at the unfamiliar words.

"But if I understand correctly, whatever I shout over there will come back to us?"

"Yes," Teman said. "An echo. Wait—you never encountered echoes in the world, did you?"

Woodson shook his head. "Only in a very large stone building or down in the mines at Trades. Otherwise? This should be an interesting lesson for the Army of Idumea."

"And a terrifying one, too," Teman agreed. "Do you know what you want to say?" he asked Offra.

"Oh, yes," Offra smiled darkly. "I know full well what to say to unnerve soldiers. I've had decades of practice."

Lemuel strode out of the fort, enraged and edgy. Here was further evidence of Salem and its deceits, and now they hadn't even left him horses. Soldiers poured in by the thousands, looking around in wonder, and Lemuel knew he had to——

"*This is where Radan died*," said a voice. It bounced disconcertingly around the valley, not loud, but distinct.

Lemuel scowled. "Who said that?" he said to Hili, who was also frowning and looking around.

"I don't know——"

"*You remember Radan, don't you, Lemuel?*" said the voice again, almost ghostly, seemingly from the trees.

"Radan?" Hili whispered.

Lemuel searched his memory, and there, on a forgotten shelf, was the lieutenant. "In Edge," he whispered back to Hili. "He was assigned there the same time I was, but——"

"*Radan died here . . . so will all the others . . . others . . . others.*"

That last word repeated perfectly, and sounded as if it came from different directions each time.

The thousands of soldiers tromping into the valley paused in the snow and look around, bewildered.

"*Others will die . . . die . . . die . . .*"

"Whoever that is," Thorne snarled, "shut them up!"

Hili glanced around nervously, trying to discern the origination of the voice. "I'd love to shut them up. Suggestions on pinpointing where it's coming from?"

"*Lieutenant Radan died here . . . here . . . here . . .*"

Thorne turned to Hili. "Get Shin out here. Force him to explain this trickery!"

". . . *killed by Shin . . . Shin . . . Shin.*"

Hili released an anxious breath. "Slagging Creet! What does that mean?" he gasped, because at those words even Lemuel Thorne paled.

"GET SHIN OUT HERE!"

Up on the mountainside, Jon Offra, Teman, and Woodson snickered into their jacket sleeves, making sure the bullhorn Jon held was tipped away so as to not send out their stifled giggles. Thousands of soldiers were frozen in their tracks, twisting this way and that to find where the ghostly words were coming from. Thorne was now yelling that it was all just a trick and to keep coming into the valley to prevent the army from backing up behind them.

His soldiers moved very, *very* nervously.

"Better than strangulation!" Jon exclaimed quietly to his two companions who were snorting into their hands, then spoke again into the bull horn, once he'd gained control of himself again.

"*Killed by Shin . . . Radan died here . . . So will others . . . others . . . others.*"

His gut still cramping because of Thorne's fist, Shin stumbled out of the stable following Hili. It was only because the sergeant major was so insistent that Shin followed him, Iron and Hammer behind him.

Soldiers were coming into the valley, but walking slowly and peering around nervously. Well, of course, Shin thought. This is terrain unlike any they've seen before, so they're a little—

"Radan didn't die in the forests . . . forests . . . forests . . . Lemuel, he died here . . . here . . . here . . . Shin stabbed him . . . stabbed him . . . stabbed him . . ."

Shin stopped in his tracks, astonished, but Hili gripped his arm and pulled him along. "What is this, Young Pere? What's the voice?"

"I don't know," he said honestly and Thorne strode up to him, his expression a wonderful mixture of rage and terror.

"What is this trick?" he demanded.

"I don't know," repeated Shin, although he *did* know, at least part of it. Playing with the echoes was a reason people looked forward to going to the glacial fort. The pristine blue lake was one reason, of course, as was the fort and the wildflowers and elk, but no matter the time of year, the echoes were there. And this afternoon, with low cloud cover, it wasn't taking much to keep voices rebounding. Soon everyone would notice they could make an echo, too, but first that quiet, unnerving voice was getting to them.

Shin fought down his grin. As if a large percentage of the soldiers weren't already jittery enough—

"You never knew the truth . . . truth . . . truth . . . . Lemuel . . . muel . . . muel. This is where Radan died . . . died . . . died."

"I know that voice," Thorne said suddenly, spinning around and searching the few trees around him. "OFFRA?!" he bellowed, and the name came back to him, questioning, *"OFFRA? . . . OFFRA? . . . OFFRA?"*

Shin couldn't help but smile and whisper to himself, "Uncle Jon?" That had been their unofficial name for the colonel the family always talked about, and always worried about.

YES, THEY FOUND HIM LAST YEAR AND BROUGHT HIM TO SALEM. AND IT LOOKS LIKE HE'S DISCOVERED A WAY TO MAKE HIMSELF USEFUL.

Thorne, seemingly disturbed that even his voice echoed back to him, quickly regained himself. "So you didn't die under Deceit after all, huh, Colonel?" Some of his words came back on top of his first ones, garbling his message. But worse than that, soldiers arriving in the valley and hearing the echo were now trying it themselves, shouting and barking and cawing and belching to see if the sounds came back to them.

They did, and the valley suddenly became a very noisy place.

Thorne, frustrated with not hearing a response from Offra, but being greeting instead by rooster crows, swore under his breath. To his guard he said, "Send out ten men, preferably older ones who'd recognize Jon Offra, and tell them to find him and kill him!"

Up on the summit, Jon turned to Woodson and Teman. "So he worked out it's me."

"I thought it might take him a while longer," Teman said, disappointed.

"Oh, no," Jon chuckled mirthlessly. "Lemuel's smart. Very smart. Delusional—that's for sure. Probably more than even I am," Jon said, sounding exceptionally lucid. "But I knew he'd figure it out. That doesn't mean we're finished, though," he assured Teman. "They'll get tired of shouting, and eventually try to go to sleep. That's when the whispering will get to them."

That afternoon Relf looked into his grandmother's eyes. "Last chance, Muggah."

Peto and Lilla stood a little ways off, hoping their oldest son could make her see reason. The rest of the family had already said quick good-byes earlier. To keep the smaller children from worrying too much, it was decided that the actual farewells would involve only the grandparents and would be as brief as possible.

Besides, the separation would be only temporary, and they could handle anything temporarily, right?

Mahrree hugged Relf. "I know, Relf. Thank you. Take care of this sweet family of yours, all right? Until I get there?" She released him to hug Mattilin.

"Muggah, you *need* to go with us," Mattilin pleaded. "You're the matriarchal cow!"

Mahrree paused. "Now, Matti, I've been called many things over the years, but . . . *what?*"

Relf chuckled. "Elk, Muggah. She's talking elk again."

Mattilin blushed apologetically. "For my animal studies class, we followed elk and tracked one large herd for three seasons—"

"Do you ever find living with a stone cutter completely dull, Mattilin?" Mahrree interrupted.

Her grandson's wife wasn't about to be distracted. "The herd was massive and moved as one body, or so it seemed. But there was one matriarchal cow, and no elk entered a meadow or went down a canyon until she gave her approval. Even the bulls waited for her."

Mahrree squeezed her arm. "I know all about that cow. Your professor came to me some years ago, worried how I might react if the news got back to me about that cow's *nickname*."

"Nickname?" Relf frowned.

Mattilin blushed again. "For the papers and reports we presented, she was labeled M1—Matriarch 1. But in the field everyone always called her . . . Mahrree."

Relf snorted a laugh. "I never knew that!"

Mattilin shrugged. "I didn't know Muggah knew, either."

Leaning in closer, Mahrree said, "I know *all kinds* of things."

Hesitantly, Relf asked, "Was there a Perrin?"

Mattilin nodded sadly. "Biggest bull anyone ever saw. Half of the herd came from them. After he died, M1 continued on alone without another bull."

Relf sighed and Mahrree said nothing but looked down at the ground and pushed around a pebble in the slush with her boots.

"See why you have to come, Muggah?" Mattilin tried again. "You're the matriarch of the family! You should be there first, leading everyone else up there, securing the site. Be there to watch as the rest of your herd arrives."

"That's very sweet, Matti," Mahrree looked up to kiss her cheek. "But I can't go. My herd's not all here yet. Now," she said more brightly, "you be careful. I keep thinking about Grunick running over to see the view from the cliff."

"Then come with us," Mattilin insisted. "Sit on Grunick so I can nurse Sarai."

Mahrree chuckled. "That's why you're taking Kew. If a fifteen-year-old boy can't keep up with him, how could I do any better?"

Kew smiled at his grandmother, resembling Perrin—and Young Pere—so much more each day that Mahrree sometimes found it painful to look at him. "I could always use your help, Muggah."

"I'll do the next best thing," she said as she crouched to speak to her three-and-a-half-year-old grandson. She ruffled his blond hair, very much like his father's. "Now you be a good boy, Grunick. You stay far away from the cliff and climb all over that ruin instead—"

"Muggah!" Relf exclaimed.

Mahrree winked at him. "Just don't let your papa see you do it, all right?"

Grunick grinned. "All right, Muggah. You're coming soon?"

"Of course! Now, give me a squeeze. Ooh, you nearly squeezed my breath out of me. Remember, I love you, I want you to be careful, and help your mama with your baby sister."

"If I *have* too," he sighed. "I love you too, Muggah."

Mahrree gave him a kiss, then stood up and took her nine-moons-old great-granddaughter out of Mattilin's arms. "You be a good girl, too, all right, Sarai? Sleep for your parents, don't crawl through the muddy snow, and stay in your tent, understand?"

The baby grabbed Mahrree's face and her great-grandmother gave her a big kiss and one last hug.

Relf helped Mattilin up on the horse, then took his daughter out of Mahrree's arms and handed her up to Mattilin.

"Please, Muggah?" Mattilin said.

"Don't worry, you'll have plenty of help up there. The first groups from Region 1 should be there by the time you reach it," she said as Relf mounted his horse.

Peto stepped over and picked up Grunick to hand him to his father. Lilla was already over at Mattilin's side, patting the baby.

"I promise I'll be there soon," Mahrree said. "Lori and Jori and their families will be leaving tomorrow, so make sure you have a big enough area up there to camp with them."

Lilla gave Kew an enormous embrace. Before he took the reins of the pack mule carrying Relf's stonecutting tools, he came back to Muggah for one more hug. "I can take care of you, Muggah."

"I know you can. You're a wonderful young man, Kew," Mahrree said, kissing his neck. "Thank you!"

Kew blinked away some tears and gripped the reins.

"We love you," Lilla reminded them. "Be safe, you're not in a hurry—"

"They know it all, Lilla," Peto assured her, but he looked anxious as well.

"It'll be fun, Grandma Lilla!" Grunick beamed. "And when we come back, we can look at all the rocks I collected."

The adults tried to keep smiles on their faces, but there would be no coming back, as far as anyone knew.

Mahrree cleared the lump in her throat and patted Grunick's leg. "That's right, sweety. You get a nice big collection up there waiting for us to inspect. We'll be there before you know it."

Lilla choked back a sob and put on another big fake smile for

Grunick's benefit.

"Now," Peto said, "be sure to leave the animals far enough away so they won't wander to the site. There's that spring up there that would be good—"

"Papa," Relf cut him off. "I remember. I've been doing these routes my whole life."

Peto cleared his throat. "Carve those words good and deep, Relf. I want them to last a thousand years. I love you. Go." He slapped his son's horse and stood between his wife and mother, putting an arm around each of them as they watched the first of their family head first north, then turn west to the middle route that started beyond Deck's grazing pastures and past the low hills.

Mahrree sighed. "One goodbye down, how many more to go?"

Lilla sniffled. "Too many. Not enough. Oh, I'm so confused. I wish they weren't alone."

Peto hugged her shoulders. "Cephas told me at least two hundred people from our region have decided to get a head start for the site. Relf and his family will meet up with someone soon."

"It's really happening, isn't it?" Mahrree whispered. "I can't believe it, yet it feels like I've lived this day before. As if this year is lifted out of time, but I don't know where it's set us."

Lilla thought about that. "I really didn't understand that, Mahrree. But if you're trying to say it feels odd, then I agree."

"That's exactly what I meant, Lilla. Well," she said abruptly, "I should get back to Jaytsy's. I think all the packs are ready, but I wanted to make one last count. I'll bring over the packs for the two Cadby families so they'll be ready."

Without waiting for any comments, Mahrree turned and headed to the Briters' home, wiping away random tears. She wanted to stay in Salem until the very end but she also knew that was selfish. Someone would have to give her a ride up to the site since she was never very stable alone on horseback.

She was sure she could walk it, but if she waited to see the army come out of the canyon, she'd be too late at her slow pace. She'd hate to miss the Last Day because she was stuck on the trail having lost track as to how many slash marks she was supposed to count.

How would she explain that one, she thought to herself with a quiet chuckle.

Wasn't the Last Day amazing? everyone would say to each other. *Did you expect it to happen that way? What did you think of it,*

Mahrree?

And she would turn red and confess, *I missed it. I wanted to see the army march in, then I got lost on the path so I put my feet up to rest, then I heard trumpets sounding from the sky and I realized I was too late . . .*

Yes, that's what would likely happen, she decided as she reached Jaytsy's porch. The head of Salem University's history department would miss the greatest event of their history.

She found the packs lined up neatly on the front porch. Some grandchild finished the checking for her, probably Tabbit. She was a natural organizer and would be the one to label each pack by name.

Mahrree picked up the first few for the two Cadby families. They were heavier than she expected, so with four adults and seven children, she'd need to make three trips. But that was all right. Walking always gave her time to think, even if it was just between the houses.

And she usually thought of the future, but strangely today there was none. It was a most disconcerting feeling. She could *always* imagine what the future held, and sometimes could even vaguely discern what might be coming her way.

But now she felt . . . nothing. Only until breakfast tomorrow, then—

That her thoughts dropped off so abruptly left her troubled, to put it mildly. So often that day she had prayed, "Why can't I sense any further?" But the only answer that came was, *You know enough.*

More than once she wondered about Perrin. He knew that he was going to die a few days beforehand. He confided in Mahrree that even before he got stabbed by that ridiculous stick, he knew his time had grown short and that he was needed for another duty.

Had he felt something like this? This emptiness about the future?

He seemed so sure, so full of determination to accept his fate. He likely even knew just *when* he would die, too. That's why they had rested under the trees on the bench that last beautiful, hot afternoon. How long he'd been planning his death, he never told her.

Now she wished she had asked him for more details, but at the time she was too shocked that he was actually leaving her.

Mahrree placed the packs on the porch of the Shins' house, oblivious to her son watching her from the window, and turned back to wander over to the Briters. She tried to pull out of her mind any feeling of 'moving on,' or 'not waking up' or whatever else it might be that those who are to die feel to tell them their time is ending. Why didn't those who were dying write down exactly what they were experiencing?

Mahrree shook her head at the absurd notion that dying people should spend their last days analyzing their reactions to dying. She searched her mind for any clue that the Creator might have dropped about her end, but there was nothing.

Bordering on disappointed, she walked up the steps of the Briters, not noticing Jaytsy and Deck observing her through their window as she picked up the lighter children's packs and started down the stairs again.

No, she wasn't about to die soon. That was both comforting and disconcerting. So why couldn't she think past a day at a time?

She reached the Shin house again and dropped the packs on the porch, now being observed through a window by Peto, Lilla, and three concerned granddaughters. She went down the stairs and looked to the south, to the canyon that would deliver her husband and her grandson.

How would Perrin make his presence known to her? Give her a tremendous hug like he did when he left? Would she suddenly feel him lying next to her in bed again? Would she see his face in Peto or Deck or Shem?

She reached the Briters' porch and picked up the last of the Cadby bags, to the audience of six Briters behind the window fascinated that she didn't notice any of them. Back down the stairs she went, imagining every kind of possibility to feeling Perrin again.

He would say her name. She would hear his sonorous voice in her mind and it would fill her body. She would smell him, too, earthy sweet. How he could invoke his scent in her mind, she didn't know, but it was a trick she'd insist he reveal.

Then she would feel him: strong, large, and completely enveloping her—

She stopped in her tracks, lost in the imagination of his presence again. It'd been so long since she'd felt him that when it happened again she surely would lose her ability to breathe and think. She'd be reduced to a puddle, sobbing that he'd returned.

So many different variations of Perrin filled her mind. With his snowy white hair and deep dark eyes, when he kissed her before that last marking trip; the way he appeared at The Dinner in Idumea in his full dress uniform with his black hair sprinkled with the beginnings of gray; the way he looked at her the first time as he stepped on to the platform as a young twenty-eight-year-old captain with short black hair, and how he stopped in surprise to see a young woman instead of an old spinster school teacher.

What form he was in now, she didn't know. She hoped that somehow it would be a combination of all of them. Each age was his greatest, she thought, and she ached to feel him next to—

"Mother?"

She opened her eyes, her vision blurry with tears, but she could make out Jaytsy standing in front of her, with Lilla to the side, and Peto and Deck, then several grandchildren behind them, all of them wearing expressions of extreme worry.

Confused, she wondered why they were all there. Something must have happened—

"Mother," Jaytsy repeated gently, "you've been standing here for about ten minutes. We thought maybe you . . . fell asleep, or something. Are you all right?"

Nothing had happened except for nosy families.

"Fell asleep. While I was *standing here*," she said tonelessly. "Yes, that would be a good trick. I—"

Why *did* they fret so much? It wasn't as if she was a little girl lost in the woods. She was a mature woman who had solved more problems and conquered more fears than any of them. So why should they all be staring at her now?

"Enough!" she declared. "There's nothing wrong with me. I just wanted a little time to think. But all of you hover so much that I can't spend even ten minutes alone with my thoughts between your houses?"

Jaytsy and Lilla looked at each other, embarrassed.

Peto smiled sheepishly and looked down at his feet, but Deck nodded. "You're right, Mahrree," he said. "I think all of us are just a little overly anxious right now, especially about someone with such a powerful history coming out of that canyon soon."

"Mother, are you doing all right?" Peto asked. "Considering that Lemuel Thorne is coming?"

"Well, I'm not happy about his invasion," Mahrree said. "But we know what to do. We're prepared so we don't need to fear. Now, you're scaring your poor children into thinking their grandmother is losing her wits, but I'm not. All of you stop fretting about me and let's make sure all of our neighbors are as prepared as we are. Didn't Rector Shin ask us to do that at the congregational meeting?"

Peto smiled. "Are all of our packs prepared?"

Mahrree held up the ones in her hands. "When the Cadbys come in the morning, we'll have them outfitted, thanks to Tabbit."

Tabbit beamed at her grandmother.

"Then Peto, let's you and I visit that ill couple down the road. The last thing I want to do is sit in my bedroom and stew."

Cephas Briter and his horse, the second Clark of the day, trotted along the back alleys of Norden. While his task was to verify with the northern rectors and assistants that everyone was heading west, he also had been asked to get a report on the Shins' and Zenoses' Grandma Trovato. She had difficulty walking and was frequently short of breath, but her sons-in-law had sturdy net carriers to transport her to the ancient temple site. Cephas was returning to the Eztates with the news that all Trovatos were on their way.

As for Grandma Trovato's demands as to when her oldest and youngest daughters would be joining her, Cephas answered honestly that he hadn't spoken to either Aunt Calla or Aunt Lilla that morning and didn't know their plans. That answer satisfied her only a little, and Cephas made a quick exit before she could pry him for more details or hug him again.

He kept to the alleys since the main roads in Norden were packed with Salemites, all heading west. He nodded in approval that no one was pushing or panicking, but moving at a steady pace.

From the corner of his eye he noticed a young woman with a blond braid making her way south instead of west, pushing through the crowd. Her pack seemed larger than normal, and something about her struck him as familiar.

He stood up in the stirrups to try to see her better, but lost her in the crowd. There was, however, a woman with a brown shawl over her head, crouched and looking at something on the side of the road he couldn't see. Then the crowd became too thick as his horse continued to walk, and she was lost to his sight.

He sat back down, feeling a little on edge. Something was wrong, but he couldn't put his finger on it. Maybe the woman had dropped something and had gone back to retrieve it. That's why she was going the wrong direction. He scanned the dense crowd again but couldn't spot her. Knowing his report was expected back at the Eztates, he kicked his horse into a gallop and headed to Salem.

Versa counted to ten, slowly stood up, and watched as Cephas Briter rode away. She exhaled and tightened the brown scarf around her head, making sure her blond ponytail was tucked away.

That was too close.

His father had been right, Relf thought in relief. Many others were already streaming to the ancient site. Salemites weren't ones for procrastination. People nodded and waved as Relf Shin and his family entered the line of horses beginning the ascent up the Lower Middle Route.

"Good to know we'll be traveling with a Shin!" one man called.

"If anyone gets lost, you'll know the way, right?" a woman chimed in.

Relf smiled. "There's safety in numbers, and the army isn't even on our side of the mountain yet. We have plenty of time."

That's what his father would say, what his grandfather would have said, to placate the nervous Salemites. The crowd, about sixty of them, smiled at him as if the twenty-three-year-old carried as much knowledge, strength, and authority as his ancestors.

Relf felt guilty about that. Yes, he was muscular, but that was because he was a stonecutter, not a soldier. He could maneuver rocks, not armies.

Yes, he had *the voice*, but no real authority behind it except to startle already unstable officers. Yes, the blood of powerful, worldly generals ran in his veins, but he had never tapped into it, nor did he want to. His tanned skin and blond hair were very un-Shin-like. More Thorne-like, his grandmother had once commented, to his discomfiture.

Still, Salemites looked to him as the closest thing to General Shin, waiting to fall in behind his family. Relf wrapped his arm tighter around his three-year-old son and nudged his horse to enter between the two marked trees. He looked over his shoulder to make sure his wife, daughter, and younger brother were still with him.

If only Kew, with his unmistakable Perrin-like qualities, were older he'd be far better in the lead. But Relf knew that while his younger brother looked like the general, he had the temperament of a spooked lamb.

So reluctantly Relf nudged his GrayClark, and a few ragged cheers rose up behind him as he entered the forest.

It was about an hour later, as the trail skirted past a large meadow, that Mattilin gasped. "Relf! Get off the trail and let the others pass. Look who's here!"

Relf twisted in his saddle to see his wife motioning wildly to the edges of the meadow, about seventy-five paces away. Relf led his horse off the trail, and Kew followed with the pack horse.

"I can't believe it!" Mattilin exclaimed. "It must mean something. The elk herd!"

"Elk herd?" Kew asked.

As bewildered Salemites continued on behind them, occasionally glancing over, Mattilin nodded eagerly. "The one I was telling Muggah about. It's her—M1, right there!"

"Are you sure?" Kew asked. He squinted at the cow elk at the edge of the trees. "They all look the same."

Relf smiled. "Mattilin has a thing for elk, Kew. She'll know."

"There, on her left ear," Mattilin pointed. "You can just make it out. There's a large nick taken out of it, as if she was nipped by a predator and all they got was part of her ear. That's M1!"

Kew unconsciously rubbed his own ear. "And somehow that reminded all of you of Muggah?"

Mattilin chuckled. "No, it was much more than that. Look, she's doing it, checking out the meadow. In the shadows of the trees you can see the rest of the herd waiting."

Relf bit his lip. "She looks rather gaunt, don't you think?"

Mattilin's enthusiasm faded. "Yes, she does. The herd's always a bit thinner after Snowing Season, but this past year? It must have been brutal for them. I'm surprised any of them survived. Oh, if only I could convince her to come to the temple site! We could keep her and the herd safe."

His eyes wide, Kew looked over at his brother wondering if Mattilin was serious, and how one might go about enticing an elk herd to follow.

Relf shook his head at Kew. No elk would be escorting them that day.

"I wonder what she's waiting for," Mattilin peered around. "Look over there, Sarai." She pointed for her baby. "See the elk? Grunick, can you see them?"

Grunick's attention was at the other side of the meadow. "I see doggies!" he announced happily.

Relf, Kew, and Mattilin twisted to look where Grunick was gesturing.

"No!" Mattilin whimpered when she saw them. "No, no, no. Relf, we have to—"

"Shh!" Relf hushed his wife, his anxiety growing. "Why, Grunick, those aren't *exactly* doggies . . ."

Kew winced. "No, they look like wolv—"

"Don't say it!" Mattilin cut him off. "Oh, dear Creator," she looked up in despair. "Not M1. Not today, *please.*"

The matriarchal cow stood her ground, her ears—what she had of them—twitching, and her stare fixed on the "doggies" on the other side of the meadow.

The horses picked up their scent and began to back up nervously. Relf and Mattilin pulled hard on the reins, while Kew grabbed the pack mule's harness and turned it around.

Slowly the "doggies" crept out, a pack of wolves, six strong. But "strong" wasn't accurate. They were so haggard and emaciated that they could have passed for starving coyotes. Relf suspected that if they didn't make a meal of an elk today, they wouldn't have another meal, ever. It wasn't a scene his children needed to witness.

"We need to go," he told his wife and brother. "Lots of ground to still cover."

"What?" Mattilin exclaimed. "Relf, we have to save her! We can't let her—"

"We can't let her *what?*" Relf snapped, not realizing he was sounding very general-like. His wife cowered in her saddle, never hearing that tone in his voice before, at least not directed at her. "What, exactly, do you think we can do today?"

Mattilin swallowed. "Distract the wolves?"

"How?!"

"I don't know," she whimpered. "Just . . . ride by quickly? Let M1 and the herd escape?"

"Too risky."

"Wolves don't attack humans," Mattilin reminded him. "There's no danger to us—"

"Look at the eyes of those wolves, Mattilin!" Relf thundered. "They'll use their last bit of strength to take down anything they can get. Kew doesn't have a ride, and our horses are getting spooked. Should one of the children fall off—"

Mattilin clutched her baby.

Relf took a deep breath and said quietly, "The Last Day is coming. Maybe this is the Last Day for M1. If not, it will be in a few days. What does it matter at this point?"

Tears streaked down his wife's face, and Kew stared at his boots and sniffled. Grunick looked up at his father with concern as he began to realize this all might be more than just a family camping trip.

Relf exhaled. "Don't be so sure M1 can't take care of herself," he said gently. "She likely doesn't even need our help. Didn't you tell me once she stomped on a coyote that got too close to a calf?"

Mattilin nodded glumly. "She stomped it to death, in fact. But Relf, she was younger and stronger then—"

"If she's lasted this long," Relf cut her off, "she's wise enough to last a few more days." He wasn't sure if he was still talking about the elk. "She still has her herd and they can protect her. She can easily outwit a few wolves."

"But she's grown old," Kew whispered. "And the wolves are desperate." He wasn't even looking at the elk.

"We shouldn't have left her," Mattilin sniffled. "Sometimes matriarchal cows sacrifice—"

"And sometimes they outwit!" Relf snapped. "There's nothing we can do," he declared, "but get ourselves to the site. Mattilin, Kew, NOW!"

His wife and brother looked at him, astonished. They nodded and turned back to the trail following General Relf Shin.

It was dinner time, but the army rations were the same for every meal. Shin stood at the edge of the trees of the fort, his security team set up for the night in the stable along with thirty other men, since Thorne agreed with Beaved that keeping Private Shin indoors and surrounded by soldiers was the best way to "provide security."

Broodingly he watched as the army continued to pour into the valley. Reports were that their numbers were down to seventy-five thousand. So far around a thousand couldn't make the climb, and a few hundred had fallen and been injured. Shin had been hoping for higher casualties than five thousand, but the number would be growing because diarrhea was traveling among the soldiers. Those who were ill but made it this far were being isolated in a corner of the valley, but there simply wasn't enough space to keep the sickness from spreading. The route up the mountain was deteriorating rapidly, according to reports. For once, Shin was glad he was at the beginning of the invasion instead stuck in the disgusting middle. The healthy soldiers who had reached the valley were making their camps in the deep slush.

Tragically, stupidly, there were thousands more Idumeans following the army. Women and even children were probably trying to sleep on top of the ridge or somewhere down in the canyon. Shin tried not to think too much about them, remembering it wasn't his fault they were spending yet another miserable night outdoors, exposed to the cold and illness. It was Thorne's fault.

Time was running out. That the army made it this far was remarkable. Surely they'd make it the rest of the way. It was all downhill from here, albeit a potentially confusing downhill.

The canyon that led to Salem branched off in a dozen different side canyons. Some were dead ends, some led to other parts of Salem but took many more miles to do so, and from the main trail they all looked identical.

Shin would feign confusion as to which canyons were the correct ones. He might be able to stall the army another full day, keeping them from completing the next four miles in the couple of hours it would normally take.

But there was another option, far more risky but potentially with better results. Thorne was planning to address the soldiers that night once they finished filing in, using the valley's acoustics.

For the past hour, men had been playing with the echoes by shouting out words and phrases of songs—Nelt's raunchy compositions, naturally—then waiting for the well-enunciated vulgarities to come back, fainter but still just as clear. The soldiers laughed as if they had come up with the greatest jokes.

They disgusted Shin. They were so childish. Soon they'd be invading an innocent village, killing any who failed to leave and stealing everything in sight, yet they were acting as if they were on an extended camping trip with nothing better to do than look for a jug of mead.

From his position, Shin had a clear view of the glacial lake, and not for the first time that day he grimaced. He'd seen that lake before when he was younger, but didn't understand why so many had held it in awe. His father had tried to explain that there was a certain reverence about the water, but all Shin ever saw was an immensely deep pool of clear water, colored such a pure blue with touches of green that it looked unnatural.

Peto had told their congregation that how refugees regarded the glacial lake—actually, more of a massive and deep pond—was a subtle test of their readiness for life in Salem. Some refugees were rushed to Salem, like his family, while others needed time to rest at the glacial fort, primarily expecting mothers or those who had just delivered babies. The scouts would take those families to the edges of the water where, if one leaned just so, one could see so deep into the glassy water that it disappeared in shades of purple.

Salemites treasured the glacial lake and rarely touched the water, cautious not to contaminate it. A couple of times a simple raft was launched out over it for scientists to try to estimate the depth of the pool—they'd guessed well over four hundred feet deep. But no one ever drank from it, and would only gingerly dip a finger in to feel just how frigidly cold it was.

As a boy, Shin had always thought that a waste. What was the point of that water just sitting there, then?

His father explained that refugees frequently had the sensation that they were now sitting in a holy place, and staring deeply into the clear water gave them a sense of purifying, of washing away the world they left behind, much like the baptism most of them participated in later. They passed the lake to go to Salem, and it was as if the lake prevented the world from following.

Those most ready for life in Salem sat there for a long time, releasing their fears and worries in a meditative reverie, while those not yet as prepared were tempted to skip rocks across the surface before declaring it was a nice pond, and was there something else to do?

Today when Shin first glanced at the lake, his heart had skipped, and not like a rock. Suddenly he understood the cleansing of the water that no one touched, and appreciated that it had remained undefiled for hundreds, if not thousands, of years. Not even the ash seemed to have affected it. He needed that reminder that there was purity in the world, and that things could become so clean again.

How desperately Shin wanted to feel like that lake today! He recalled how he felt during his bath after coming out of the dungeon, and his longing to be baptized and purified again. The lake could have done it, he thought. He wanted to make his way over to it and dip in a finger to feel it cleansing him—

But the lake was ringed by soldiers.

And they were urinating into it.

It was a grotesque experiment, to see if enough men could turn the clear blue into a murky green. Shin wouldn't get to touch the water nor did he want to now. And, ludicrously, there were men crouching by the edge and scooping up handfuls to drink despite the fact that someone just feet away was coloring the water.

Then again, Shin thought in grim resignation, that meant there'd be another dozen or so men in no condition to march to Salem in the morning.

As he watched, he realized he had to acknowledge something: there was no way to force the world and Salem together. His plans would have failed. He had claimed that uniting everyone was a noble goal, but it really was just an excuse for adventure. If he had succeeded in bringing the two civilizations together, they would have remained miles apart in thought and in deed. No Salemite would ever have thought to relieve himself so vulgarly into the lake. And few from the world would ever have regarded it as anything more than a large, blue privy.

I'M GLAD YOU UNDERSTAND, YOUNG PERE. PROXIMITY HAS VERY LITTLE TO DO WITH UNITY.

"They have to be stopped, Puggah," he whispered. "They can't go to Salem. Look at them! They'll destroy everything."

I CERTAINLY HOPE YOU DON'T THINK THAT YOU CAN STOP THEM—

"I have to do *something*, Puggah. I just can't let this happen." He walked away from the voice shouting at him to shove away the temptation, and meandered to the southern side of the glacial fort to brood alone. Well, as alone as he could with Hammer and Iron following about five paces behind, their swords in hand.

During the next hour the valley grew darker and small campfires popped up all over. The soldiers were in surprisingly good spirits, having already forgotten the haunting voice that had echoed about some long-ago and forgotten lieutenant who had died there. They'd drowned out that warning with their own ugly echoes. This would also be the first time in two nights that the soldiers would sleep horizontally, not propped up against a prickly tree, unrelenting stone, or another soldier. That lifted everyone's mood.

Many of the men had scraped the snow off the ground and piled it around their sleeping areas in narrow walls. Their thick bedrolls had the potential to keep them sufficiently warm for the night that was proving quite tolerable.

Shin thought that was too bad as he made his way back to the stables, Iron and Hammer close behind. A hard freeze could have knocked out another segment of the army, but the women and children on the exposed ridge certainly didn't deserve that kind of a night. Neither did the Salemite families he hoped were at the ancient site many miles away. That was probably why the weather was so pleasant—to give the fleeing Salemites better conditions.

But it also gave the army better conditions.

He stood moodily at the front doors of the stables. A bonfire at the front of the fort illuminated masses of soldiers. Movement caught his attention—Thorne was leaving the fort. Shin straightened up. This was it. He stepped out of the stables.

Iron and Hammer followed Shin again as he weaved his way through soldiers to reach the back entrance of the fort. He tiptoed between bedrolls laid out along the floors, and since all of the guards and officers had followed Thorne outside, he didn't face any resistance. Iron and Hammer tracked behind him, silent but watchful.

At the front observation room, Shin looked around for the object he had spied before, crumpled and ignored in a corner: a folding ladder. Shin noticed his two guards had caught up, and he smiled guilelessly.

"I just want a better view. I'm trying to remember distances, so I'm going to use that ladder to climb to the top of the roof and get a better look. I should be *secure* there, right?"

Iron and Hammer looked at each other and shrugged as Shin undid the folded ladder, slipped the metal braces over the bends, and propped it up against the hole in the ceiling. As he put his first foot on the rung, he was struck with the memory of the ladder in the dungeon that he climbed to get through the ceiling to freedom. He would be climbing through another ceiling to freedom again, but not necessarily his.

He reached the roof, climbed out, and searched the darkness above him for the bottom of the next ladder that went up the massive, ancient pine tree. Camouflaged in the branches that hung over the roof, he saw it. He jumped and caught the lowest rung, pulled himself up, and began to climb higher into the tree until he found a sturdy perch. He slipped off the ladder and sat on a thick branch. By twisting a bit here and there, he found a way to peer through the branches for a view of Thorne below.

One of the general's guards blew his horn to get the army's attention. The three short blasts echoed in the glacial valley, the first blast coming back before the last one was sounded, making the signal sound like a continuous loop. Men in the valley laughed at the result, but they quieted as Thorne shouted, "SILENCE!"

But Shin grinned as Thorne's voice echoed back, demanding that the general be silent. In the firelight he could see a faint look of disgust in Thorne's face.

"I want to tell all of you that you have made excellent progress," Thorne announced loudly, allowing enough time for his words to rebound. "It is my understanding that the rest of the walk will be downhill!"

The valley erupted into cheers and scattered applause.

Thorne smiled at their enthusiasm and waited until the echoes faded. "To thank you for your diligence, I am offering rewards once we reach Salem. As you have been told, Salem is holding many of our people hostage. I am finding Salem not only to feed the world from their stores which they refuse to share, but to liberate the captives! Therefore I am offering *one hundred gold pieces* to whoever brings me Druses Thorne, Versula Thorne, or Delia Thorne alive!"

The gasps reverberated around the valley. One hundred gold pieces was three years' pay for most of those men.

Shin groaned. How could he compete with that?

"I am also offering the same reward for anyone locating and rescuing Eltana Yordin. And, it has been rumored there are two others very important to me who are still alive in Salem. For news that leads to their discovery, I will offer twenty gold pieces. And I will grant *two hundred gold pieces* to anyone who brings me Jaytsy Shin or Peto Shin!"

Shin buried his face in his hands. It was hopeless. The soldiers were already going mad, yelling, "Let's get there NOW!"

Puggah was right: Lemuel was smart. He knew how to appeal to their greed and knew what would get them up and ready to find Salem in the morning.

He rubbed his forehead. Knowing Thorne's propensity for lying, he doubted anyone would see any gold—

That was it—his opportunity to expose the general.

The crowd's exuberant shouts were just beginning to die down when a new voice rang out over the valley. "And where is this gold, General? Show it to them, so they can be sure this isn't another one of your lies!"

Thorne whipped around looking for the source of the voice. Someone near him pointed up to the tree. "Where are you?!" Thorne demanded.

"Show them, General, that you'll make good on your promise," Shin called down. "But I doubt you can. Why would you travel all this way carrying—or making Hili carry—eight hundred pieces of gold? It's just another one of your tricks, like telling them that your wife and daughters are being held hostage. They're not. They ran away from you to the only place that would care for and shelter them!"

Thorne was huffing in fury. He said something to the officers around him and they began to run into the fort and to the trees. But it would take them a while to reach Shin. He stood up precariously on the thick branch and gripped the one above him for stability. So filled with rage and energy he simply couldn't sit while he exposed the general.

"Salem is a place of peace, General. A place of refuge. Thousands of people have left the world over the years, escaping from liars like you who torment and threaten their lives! Why do so many people run away from you, Thorne? Find one person out there who truly respects you. No one does! They all fear and hate you! They want something better than you, Thorne!"

He ignored the scrambling of officers below him trying to find a way up the tree. A few had made it to the roof of the fort but were too short to reach the ladder in the branches.

"Soldiers, he's deceiving you! If you think you're going to rob the people of their gold for payment, think again. Salem has NO GOLD! No silver or jewels, either. If you're on your way to find riches, you're all wasting your time. Salem is a place of peace—"

"SHIN!" Thorne roared up to the trees. "GET DOWN HERE!"

"NO!" He yelled back, frantic to get the soldiers to understand. "They deserve to know the truth. You're marching to the Last Day! All of you! If you enter Salem, you begin your own destruction! It's been prophesied and seen. If you try to harm Salem, you will die!"

The words didn't have quite the affect he was hoping they would.

Scattered sniggers echoed throughout the valley.

Someone shouted, "I'll find the gold! It's there. He's just trying to hoard it for himself."

A chorus of, "He wants it for himself!" rose up.

Shin closed his eyes in frustration. They couldn't conceive of any other kind of life than what they lived. They had no imagination. The world had seen to that, years ago. Destroy their imagination, you destroy their ability to imagine something *better*. But he couldn't quit.

"There are no riches! There are, however, homes, herds, flocks, and land that the Salemites will share—"

Another round of laughter and sniggers interrupted his speech. Apparently 'sharing' was something they quit believing in when they were toddlers.

"I'll take the land!" a soldier shouted. "They can have my rock-hard farm in Trades!"

Shin couldn't hear anything else because the soldiers exclaimed what they, too, would be willing to take from Salem, their jeers and calls echoing throughout the valley.

He thought something whizzed by his head, but in his discouragement he didn't pay it any attention. Even after living there for nearly two years, he hadn't fully appreciated the world's insatiable greed. But maybe they just didn't understand . . .

"Stealing will cost you YOUR LIVES! You WILL DIE!"

"Better to die rich and young than to live poor and long, men!" a voice shouted.

Thorne.

Every man in the valley seemed to agree as they cheered. The shouting continued and developed a rhythm to it. A moment later the word became clear: "Gold! Gold! Gold! Gold!"

Thorne looked up into the trees with a triumphant sneer.

Shin sagged in defeat, almost forgetting to keep his grip on the branch above him. No one believed him. No one *wanted* to believe him.

And why should they? It wouldn't get them what they wanted. They wanted gold, land, and, Shin heard among the shouts, girls. His gut chilled as he imagined his little sisters and cousins falling prey to the rough crowd below him. Again he thought he heard a strange whizzing noise, like a lost hornet, but dismissed it.

There was a commotion near the tree. More men were there trying to boost each other to reach the ladder rung. Shin looked up to see how much higher he could climb, but he was nearly out of tree and ladder.

Suddenly something stabbed his neck, as if indeed a hornet had revived from the long cold and decided just then to sting him. His hand went up, feeling for what caused the pain. Something small and hard had punctured his flesh, but it was too big for a hornet. He yanked it out and peered at it in the dark. He couldn't be completely sure, but it seemed to be a small arrow, the kind of weapon Nelt had called a bolt, fired from a small crossbow—

His stomach churned. If the tip was poisoned, he would die in half an hour. Already his head began to sway and he felt his eyelids trying to close. His grip on the branch above was weakening.

This was the end, already. And if the bolt didn't kill him, the fall from the tree would.

His hand slipped from the branch as everything darkened. At least he had tried to do some good in his last minutes . . .

Relf looked around the ancient temple site as the sun went down.

Salemites had arrived. It was beginning. All of it. He'd prepared his entire life for such a time, and now that it was here, he felt off.

He couldn't pinpoint what was wrong. The passage of people up the routes was going smoothly. Those arriving from the northern routes also reported no problems or setbacks. Everyone seemed to feel the need to report to Relf Shin, even though one of Shem's assistants was there to record concerns and keep a tally of who arrived and from where.

Relf folded his arms and looked over at the tent he'd erected. Most people would sleep under the cold stars, but those with small children were bringing tents, hoping to corral their crawling babies into something safe. He heard quiet giggles coming from theirs as Mattilin tried to help Grunick change his clothes in the dark for bed. Sarai was already asleep, exhausted from the ride up the mountain.

Kew sat by a small fire outside of the tent poking the flames with a stick and listening to others sitting with him discussing their travel. He glanced up at his oldest brother and Relf smiled reassuringly to him. They were on the mountain now. They were safe.

Next to his tent, Relf and Kew had staked out a large section for the rest of the Shins, Briters, and Zenoses. They chose a spot forward of the ancient temple site; most Salemites preferred to set up camp behind it, in the shelter of the mountain peaks. But Relf knew Muggah wanted a clear view of the valley below where the army of Idumea would eventually arrive, trampling down the grasses struggling to emerge from the snows. The Shin sons had strung a rope around the campsite, and as the other teenagers arrived, they would be in charge of patrolling the line, making sure babies and toddlers didn't cross it and venture to the cliff.

There was nothing left for Relf to do. He'd checked the bubbling spring as soon as he arrived, and was satisfied that it was flowing adequately enough to service all of the coming Salemites. The waterfall it created off of the cliffs would likely be just a trickle by tomorrow night. The vast tableland was free of predators and debris, latrines had been dug years ago and were waiting on the perimeter, and there was nothing left to do now until the first light came and he could begin carving their story on the rocks by the temple site.

So what was wrong?

He had no idea what happened to M1. As others arrived at the site, he surreptitiously asked if they had seen the elk herd or the wolf pack. No one reported seeing or hearing anything.

He couldn't get her out of his mind, standing at the edge of the woods, calmly observing those who would destroy her.

The sunset that night was a strange dull brown, similar in hue to elk fur, darkening.

Jaytsy opened her front door and smiled quizzically. "Uncle Jon? I heard you were up whispering sweet nothings in the mountains!"

Jon Offra nodded officiously to her and behind him Teman waved. They followed Jaytsy into the gathering room, and Jon pointed at Tabbit who was on a sofa, reading.

"You're the one!" Jon boomed cheerfully.

Tabbit shrank in surprise. Her mother shrugged and tipped her head. She'd be fine, just do whatever Offra asked.

"You're the one Guide Zenos said is a swift scribe, correct?"

Closing her book, Tabbit nodded and stood up. "Yes, Uncle Jon?" None of the children were still quite sure how to respond to him and his changing moods. While they were always polite, they were also always on guard. Right now he was clearly in colonel mode, and the children didn't know much about army officers.

"I need something scribed for me, quickly and largely, so that I can read it by dim candlelight."

"Of course," Tabbit said, rushing over to a bookshelf where she kept her variety of parchments and quills. "How large?" she asked, analyzing the nibs for the broadest one.

Jon was already striding over to a copy of The Writings on a side table, thumbing through it. "I need this, right here. The Great Guide Hierum's final prophecy."

"Uncle Jon," Jaytsy said, taking the book from his hands. "You can just take the entire book with you. We have several copies. Don't you have one?"

"I do," he said, handing it to Tabbit who was already situating herself at the writing desk. "But I can't fold this up and carry it in my pocket, especially if I need to run away from the army."

Tabbit stared up at him in worry, and Jaytsy pursed her lips.

Jon jabbed a finger at the passage. "Start with this line, right here, 'When that last day comes,' and end it here," he pointed to another spot. "Make the words about this big," he indicated with two fingers. "My eyesight isn't the best by candlelight."

Biting her lower lip in concentration, Tabbit began to write, her neat, clear script nearly as perfect as the typesetters, but larger.

"Jon," Jaytsy began, "exactly what are you about to do?"

"Educate the Army of Idumea!" he declared cheerfully.

Jaytsy turned to Teman.

The small man smiled. "It's true. We don't have much time—we need to get back up to above the glacial fort tonight. We just finished chatting with Guide Zenos about what Jon should be shouting down at the soldiers while they try to sleep, and Shem suggested the last prophecy. They deserve to know what's going to happen."

Already Jaytsy was beginning to chortle. "Have they recognized your voice yet, Jon?"

"Of course!" he said. "Took Lemuel a few minutes, but once I reminded him that he'd sent both me and Radan to find you all, and that the top of the mountain was where Radan actually died, well, he figured a few things out."

Then Jon's shoulders sagged. "But, naturally, he'll dismiss everything I remind him of. This, however," and he pointed to the words Tabbit was pouring out of her quill, "some of them might remember. Some of them might have seen an old copy of The Writings, and they'll remember what's coming. I may not be able to scare off the army, but the words of the guides and the Creator certainly might make them think twice about things."

Tabbit soon was finished, blowing gently on the page to dry the ink.

She handed the parchment to Jon. "Will that suffice, sir?"

He was grinning at the page, but abruptly looked up at Tabbit. "Sir? I'm not 'sir.' At least not to you. 'Uncle Jon' will suffice."

Tabbit grinned. "Well, you're acting very colonel-ish right now. 'Sir' just seemed appropriate."

Jon smiled back. "I have to admit, at times like this I wish I still had my colonel's jacket. Just to give me that extra *you know*. But I wasn't wearing it when the scouts jumped me in the world. I left it behind."

Tabbit and Jaytsy exchanged the same look.

"Uncle Jon," Jaytsy said, "I just may have a solution for you, but first I need to check with someone. Do you have five minutes?"

"Not really, we need to get back—"

Jaytsy was already pulling him to the door, and he and Teman jogged with her along the dark lane to the Shins. A moment later they burst through the door and waved a hello at the handful of family in the gathering room. Jaytsy called, "Mother? Where are you?"

She came from the kitchen, wiping her hands on a cloth. "Jayts? Jon! You're back from the mountains—why?"

Jaytsy was already charging down to Mahrree's wing, with her mother, Jon, and Teman following.

"I'm sorry, Mother," Jaytsy explained, "I really should ask you privately first, but they need to head back to the glacial fort. Jon's going to call down Guide Hierum's last prophecy to the soldiers during the night, in case they have trouble sleeping, you see."

Mahrree burst out laughing as they all stopped in her small gathering room.

Jaytsy grinned back. "Jon was saying that he wished he still had his colonel's jacket to wear, and I thought that maybe . . . ?"

Mahrree stopped laughing when she realized what Jaytsy was asking her to give up. She glanced at Jon.

He looked a little perplexed himself, but hopeful.

Perrin would have done it. That's what she thought immediately: Perrin would do it.

Without a word she went into her bedroom and pulled out his old colonel's jacket which had been taken in last year for Peto to wear on his outing to the world. In the privacy of her bedroom she held it close to her chest one last time, breathed in the fibers of the cloth, and remembered in an instant every wonderful and terrible moment Perrin experienced while he wore that jacket.

Then she brought it out to Jon Offra.

His jaw slackened when he realized what it was.

"You saw him wearing this," Mahrree told him. "The night we left Edge. It was inside out. But it belongs on a colonel, and Colonel Offra, it needs to be used properly. Would you take it out for one last adventure?"

Gingerly Jon took the jacket out of her hands, as if being handed a most precious and valuable treasure. His hand ran along the patches and paused where the SHIN label used to be.

"We removed it when Peto used it last year. You can remain anonymous should any soldiers see you. But you can also blend in with them," she realized, "as long as they don't notice the brass buttons."

Jon couldn't speak, his fingers gliding over the buttons and stitching more reverently than Mahrree expected. Any qualms she felt about lending him the uniform were gone. If it were possible, Jon loved the jacket more than she did.

She took it out of his hands and held it up for him to try on.

He looked as if he didn't dare, then suddenly couldn't wait to put it on. Since it had been taken in for Peto, the sleeves were a bit short as was the torso, but the shoulders and chest fit perfectly.

"Oh," Jon finally breathed out, "it's beautiful! Thank you," he whispered in his childlike way. "Thank you, Mahrree!"

Teman grinned. "Colonels Offra and Shin ride again! Shall we, *sir*?"

Something joyous flared in Jon's eyes. "Indeed!" he roared. "We've got an army to lecture!" In an instant, he and Teman were racing out of the house into the night.

Mahrree couldn't help herself—she laughed along with Jaytsy.

"Oh, how I wish I could go with them!" she said wistfully. "But I imagine we'll hear the reports."

Jaytsy put an arm around her. "Sorry to spring that on you, Mother. But I'm glad you gave him the jacket."

"I am, too," Mahrree said. "Perrin's a general now, anyway. He didn't need that anymore. *We* didn't need that anymore."

She almost believed that.

Later that night Mahrree heard the knock on her door and sighed. It was late, very late. One of those days that would never end.

After she gave Perrin's jacket to Jon, she had spent the rest of the evening down the road helping a young mother organize her packs for her children since her husband was trying to recover from a stomach ailment. It was wonderful to work away the night helping someone else.

She was now ready for bed but had been looking at the bookshelf for something to read. She had been staring at the shelves for several minutes now, trying to find something to shut down her mind to let her rest.

But considering that the Last Day was coming, she couldn't figure out what she should read, aside from The Writings which she read every night.

She had just been ready to climb into bed and start another thorough reading of the prophecies when the soft knocking at the door came. She put on her bedclothes covering and went to her door.

"Ah, I wondered when you might be by," she said to the young man standing there. "Heard about my little 'time-out' this afternoon?"

Dr. Boskos Zenos smiled apologetically. "I don't know what you're talking about, Aunt Mahrree."

She rolled her eyes.

"I'm sorry about the lateness of my coming," Boskos continued, making a valiant effort, "but Papa wants everyone over seventy checked for their ability to handle the coming journey."

Mahrree tipped her head. "Uh-*HUH*. You may not know this, Boskos, but over the years your father would send me his scout hopefuls after their course in Deception. I was their final examination. After a conversation and debate with me, I would tell Shem who passed, who needed more work, and who was such a hopeless liar that their only option was to quit the scouting corps and become a doctor."

Dr. Zenos blushed.

"Well, come in," she sighed loudly. "Do your duty so you can report back to your father that you verified Mahrree Shin isn't going grainy."

Boskos chuckled as he walked in to her gathering room. "No one thinks you're going grainy, Aunt Mahrree. We're just concerned about you."

"Enough with the concern!" she exclaimed, plopping onto her cushioned chair and holding out her arm. "Pulse first, right?"

Boskos smiled and took her wrist.

"It's beating, isn't it?"

Boskos nodded slightly and continued to count.

"You can hear me breathing, right?"

He glared playfully at her.

"Look at my eyes. No dilation of the pupils and I can even tell you the dates of your son and daughter's birthdays, too. My mind is fine, Boskos."

He released her arm and nodded in satisfaction. "Anything feel sluggish?"

"Compared to what? I'm seventy-four! *Everything* feels sluggish, Bos."

He smiled patiently. "I mean, on your left side. Any trouble talking today? Moving your legs?"

"I never have trouble talking, Bos. No palsy, no drooping, no slurred speech—"

"Obviously."

"No nothing! Go home and tell your father I need no more of his babying!"

Boskos held up his hands in surrender. "All right, Most Dangerous Woman in the World! And I thought Uncle Perrin was an ornery patient."

Mahrree softened. "Sorry, Bos. I would think people would be far more concerned about your sister Meiki who's expecting a baby than they are about me."

"We're worried about her, too, Aunt Mahrree," Boskos said, a bit defensive. "Mama wants her and Clyde to leave tomorrow with Lori and Jori and their families. They can help her deal with her bouts of sickness."

"Good," Mahrree said. "I'll be glad to see them going on their way. Make this a good experience for the children, if possible. What they don't know—"

Boskos sighed. "Briter knows. He's been in a panic for a while. He even pulled out The Writings all on his own and read about the prophecies of the Last Day. Lek and Salema couldn't calm him down.

He kept asking if he was going to die."

Mahrree slumped. "Oh, Briter—the poor thing!"

"Seven-year-olds can understand a surprising amount, but not enough to *fully* understand. Now he's got Fennic all worked up, too. They're demanding to know what's going to happen, and the fact that their parents and grandparents don't know everything either, well, that's not helping much. Papa gave them a blessing of peace, that they could find faith and hope. Fennic started to calm down, but Briter? He's at that age when he's beginning to understand just how terrible the world can be. And every time he looks outside and sees the gray banners flying, he panics all over again."

"What can we do?"

Boskos smiled dismally. "I just left their house a little while ago. That's why I'm so late. We finally decided to sedate Briter, just to get him to sleep."

Mahrree's mouth dropped open. "He's inherited Perrin's sleeping problems, hasn't he?"

"I'm not sure, but he inherited the solution."

"Oh, no," she sighed. Then she remembered how opposed Shem had been about her sedating Perrin back in Edge when he couldn't sleep. "Have you told your father what you had to do?"

Boskos scoffed softly. "It was *his* idea. Said it worked for Briter's great-grandfather, it might work for Briter. Apparently he hasn't slept for the past two nights, and Salema and Lek were getting desperate to find a way to help him."

"The irony of it all! Is he sleeping now?"

"I watched him for half an hour to make sure I had the dosage right. It's rare that we use the sedation on children, and I purposely used half the recommended amount just to encourage him to sleep, not be helplessly unconscious."

Mahrree could see the worry in his eyes, so much like Shem's when he was younger. "How many more children and adults are panicking like this?"

"Too many," Boskos admitted. "Dr. Toon has been advising the doctors and midwives in ways to help people relax. I don't know if it's a lack of faith that's causing the fear or what. We don't have time to analyze the responses, unfortunately, just react to them. I hope we're reacting correctly," he finished quietly.

"How did you feel when you saw Briter drop off to sleep?"

Boskos shrugged. "Relieved he was finally calm. Guilty that we had to resort to that. Uncle Perrin was so adamant about never being sedated—"

Mahrree reached over and took his hand. "Don't make any judgments about if the decision was correct or not until you see Briter in the morning. If he's rested and better able to cope with the stress, then you'll know it was the correct decision. If nothing else, at least his parents will sleep tonight and they'll be able to help him better."

Boskos squeezed her hand and smiled. "Thanks, Aunt Mahrree. I hadn't considered that." He paused then said, "Are you sure you're all right? You can tell me, you know. Worries? Nagging pains?"

She sighed dramatically. "Ah, for me to list for you my nagging pains would take all night. Top of the list, Shem and Calla Zenos. Next, Jaytsy Briter, then Peto Shin—"

Boskos chuckled. "Understood. But really, call for me? If you feel anything's not right? Please?"

"There's no one I'd rather have checking my bunions than you."

"Then I'll wish you a good night."

"I wish you one too, Bos. You look like you need it."

If you're dead, you don't feel pain.

That was the obvious conclusion Shin came to as he felt his neck throb and his wrists ache. He kept his eyes shut while he tried to clear the fuzz in his mind to understand what had happened.

He'd been standing in the tree, the officers just starting to climb the ladder after realizing one man could lift another to grab the lowest rung, then he felt the stinging in his neck and everything went dark.

He had been poisoned but not killed. But who had the capabilities to do this? And why weren't they targeting General Thorne?

"His breathing's changing," he heard a voice near him. "Staff Sergeant, he's coming out of it."

Shin decided to open his eyes and meet his doom. The area was dark except for a nearby lantern. He was in the stable lying on his bedroll. The stable was packed with sleeping men except for some of his security team who sat around him keeping guard.

The first face he focused on was Cloud Man, and he was beaming. "Did you know you bounced when you hit the ground?"

"I tend to do that," he whispered. "What happened?"

"You slipped from the tree," Cloud Man said and gestured to

Shin's neck. "Looks like a branch stabbed you on your way down."

"Sure it was a branch?"

Cloud Man shrugged. "That's what it looks like. You're scratched up, too. Good thing you tumbled through so many branches on your way down or you would have hit the ground a lot harder. But the branches weren't too nice to your face." He held up a damp cloth he'd been using to wipe Shin's wounds. It was streaked with blood, but not excessively. "Clouds would have been kinder to fall through," he added knowingly. "You've been asleep for a few hours but should be feeling all better soon!"

Shin doubted that. In his mind he ran through the list of questions Boskos asked him whenever he woke up from an accident. Eyes? He could see relatively clearly. The fuzziness would fade. Ribs? He took a deep breath but nothing stabbed him. Shoulders? Still intact. No other appendages felt broken, miraculously. Bruising, most likely, but he was used to that. In fact, the only pain he felt, beside the annoyance of scratches on his flesh, was in his wrists and his neck. He went to reach for his neck and heard chains instead. He glanced down at his arms.

Shackled. What a surprise.

Sergeant Beaved, on the other side of him, nodded to his wrists. "Thorne now sees the depth of betrayal you're capable of," he said gravely. "Even going so far as to discredit him in front of the entire army. Until he's finished with you, you're to remain in chains. Your ankles are also bound. You will be able to walk but you can't run."

Shin sighed. "When will he be done with me?"

"Unsure," Beaved said with a tone that sounded like he was preparing for a funeral. "Amory insists they need you to get through the canyons. Then it seems Thorne wants to present you to your mother as a prelude to peace with Salem."

"Jaytsy's not my mother, Beaved," he groaned. "Think about it: none of this makes any sense. Thorne is delusional and none of you question him! Supposedly I was born in the forests, but raised in Salem? How? If I was rescued by the Briters, how did I get over the mountain to come back? Thorne *did* pursue Jaytsy Shin, but she was married for over a year before her first child was born. Highly unlikely that Thorne was the father. It's not that difficult of a puzzle, if anyone would just look at the pieces for five seconds. *None* of it goes together! I'm only nineteen, and that's the truth. Jaytsy Briter's first baby was a girl."

Beaved exhaled, not even questioning how Shin knew that detail about Jaytsy's oldest child. "None of that's going to help you, Shin."

"So I'm supposed to go along with all of this?"

"If you want to live, yes!"

"Is that what all of you do?" Shin exclaimed. "Just go along with whatever unbelievable and unlikely story preserves you for another day?"

"Yes," Beaved said shortly. "Why not?"

"Living in *lies*? That doesn't bother you?"

Beaved leaned in. "What bothers me is the idea of *dying*, Shin."

"Doesn't bother me," he said, almost believably.

"Look, Shin, just . . ." Beaved groaned quietly. "I don't know what the truth is myself, but I do know this: you have a chance to survive this. A small chance, getting smaller each time you open that big mouth of yours. But if I were you I'd cling to that chance, do whatever it takes to preserve your life. You can fix the lies later, if necessary, but you can't if you're dead. Now, Thorne plans to present you to Jaytsy Shin and, if all goes well, he just *may* set you free. *Give* you to her."

"Of course he will," Shin said dully. "And what if Jaytsy Shin can't be found? Or Thorne thinks she's dead?"

"Then you most likely will be, too," Beaved admitted. "Why did you do that?" he whispered earnestly. "Climb that stupid tree and—What were you *thinking*, Shin? That the army would suddenly, I don't know, *rally* around you? That you could possibly offer them something more tempting than General Thorne could? This fort is evidence of Salem! You just told all of them there's land available and Thorne's the one who brought them this far. Why would they suddenly shift loyalties to you? You're nobody, Shin, with no power, no authority, and nothing to give them. But you sat up there spouting off against Thorne thinking . . . what? I still can't figure you out! And you're supposed to be *smart*. You must be the stupidest 'smart' man I've ever commanded."

Shin looked up at the rafters and started counting them.

Beaved sighed and slumped in the straw next to him. "Look," he said, leaning close, "I'm not here as Thorne's informant or anything, I really just want to know—did you believe those things you were shouting up there? About the Last Day and all?"

Shin glanced at him. "I do and it's true. I told Reg earlier today and I'll tell any man who will listen. We will all die. The Creator will fight for Salem."

"But Guide Lannard got here a little while ago and said that—"

"Lannard Kroop is a fraud!" Shin hissed. "He's controlled by Thorne, not inspired by the Creator. He hasn't the foggiest idea what he's doing and neither does anyone else. Guides aren't mystical and impossible to understand. The Creator wants His people to know all He can reveal to them. He wouldn't be speaking nonsense. There is a real guide, though, Beaved," he said, lowering his voice. "And he's in Salem, leading the people and getting them ready. They know we're coming. They've known for years and they're ready."

Beaved licked his lips. "What's the guide's name?"

Shin sighed, realizing that whatever Beaved may have claimed or wanted to believe, he was still an informant. "I can't tell you. I don't want him harmed. I've done enough damage to Salem and I refuse to do more."

Beaved sat back. After a moment he whispered, "My grandfather believed in the Creator. When I was younger he would tell me about the Last Day. The land tremor, the eruption, the famine, the evil of the world marching to destroy the Creator's chosen. I can't get his words out of my mind, no matter how hard I try. We're the evil of the world, aren't we Shin? It's all true, isn't it?"

Shin studied him, trying to discern if it was another trap or if the sergeant could set aside his duty for one sincere moment. "You've seen the signs, Beaved. What do you think?"

"We're on the wrong side, Shin," Beaved whispered nervously. "How do we get on the right side?"

It *was* a trap. While he was unconscious, Beaved and Thorne must have devised this strategy to get him to explain how to get to Salem more quickly. He looked back up at the rafters.

"If I knew that, Sergeant, I wouldn't be lying in chains in the middle of a stable surrounded by armed men. Good night."

But his mind was fixated on what Beaved had said about the Last Day. Odd that the sergeant would remember so many details—

A strange sound came to his ears, almost ethereal and . . . it was words.

"Oh, no, not again," Teach moaned nearby. "Can't they shut him up?"

Pal was sitting up, hugging his knees, and Buddy looked up to the rafters as if it was the source of the words.

Shin struggled to a sitting position and peered out the dark open window, recognizing the words.

"*. . . no one knows but our Creator, and its arrival will surprise those who fight against the Creator's people . . . people . . .*"

He began to smile. "I know this," he whispered.

"Do you know how to shut him up?" Teach demanded. "They tried sending men to find him but no one can scale those slopes in the dark!"

"*On that day do not be one of those surprised to find yourself on the wrong side . . . side . . . side.*"

"Who is it?" Shin asked, realizing that someone with extensive knowledge of the echoes was making the best of them.

"*On that day do not find yourself with a blade in hand ready to charge your brother or sister . . . sister . . . sister . . .*"

"It's the clouds—" Cloud Man began enthusiastically.

"It's not the slagging clouds!" Beaved snapped at him. "It's Jon Offra again. He's up there calling down some old prophecy—"

"*On that day be one of the many standing with the guide, having seen the signs and recognizing what is coming . . . coming . . .*"

Shin glanced around at the men and realized none of them were sleeping but were listening to the quiet voice.

Outside, a few soldiers were shouting for silence, then being told to be quiet themselves and let everyone sleep.

He almost sniggered. Their earlier excitement about invading Salem had to be waning. If nothing else, there'd be a lot of tired, grouchy men in the morning.

"*Before the Last Day will be a land tremor more powerful than any ever experienced . . . It will awaken the largest mountain and change all that we know in the world . . . Those changes will bring famine, death, and desperation to the world . . . And that desperation will cause the world's army to seek to destroy the faithful of the Creator . . . Creator . . . Creator.*"

Next to Shin, Cloud Man laid down and was happily murmuring the echoes. "Creator . . . Creator . . . Creator!"

Shin hoped he'd make it through everything just so he could finally meet Uncle Jon. The man was a genius. "How long has this been going on?" he asked the quiet barn.

Someone outside his window began to sob softly.

"A couple hours," Beaved muttered. "This is his fifth time through it, and always the same. He lets things get all quiet and calm, then he starts up again."

Shin mouthed the next lines along with Offra, the words coming again so clearly to his mind as if he'd never forgotten them.

"Be among those faithful to the Creator!"

"Shut up already!" Teach hollered, and the fatigued men around him started throwing straw at him, more annoyed at his outburst than at Offra's calm threats.

"Be among those standing firm for what you know, having not so quickly forgotten His words to us!

"Be among those who see the marvelous deliverance from the enemy the Creator will send us!"

"I'd like to see that deliverance," Shin whispered to himself.

"For He will send deliverance before He sends destruction to those who fight Him!"

Someone whispered, "What kind of destruction? Shin, do you know?" It sounded like Reg.

"I don't know," Shin admitted. "No one does."

"Then what about deliverance?"

"Again, I don't know. But I have a feeling we'll find out."

Someone whimpered into the straw and Shin grinned into the night.

The 33rd Day of Planting

Mahrree put on another cheerful face late in the morning of the 33rd as she hugged the seven Cadby grandchildren. Their Cadby grandparents were already on the trail, suspecting that they would be so slow that their sons and their families would catch up to them before they reached the ancient temple. Mahrree kissed and hugged the three babies Maggee, Marey, and Peto Cadby, the four pre-school-aged great-grandchildren, her twin granddaughters Lori and Jori and their husbands, then the other twins, seventeen-year-olds Kanthi and Nool Shin, who were going to help their sisters.

Traveling with them were Shem and Calla's oldest daughter Meiki and her husband, Clyde. Already Meiki was pale, holding up to her nose the bundle of herbs Salema had packed for her, trying to stave off her nausea.

Calla winced at her daughter. "Are you sure now's the best time for you to leave?"

Meiki swayed slightly. "The way I'm feeling, Mama, there's never going to be a good time."

"But we're going very slow," Lori assured her cousin. "There'll be plenty of time for you to lean over the horse and vomit."

Meiki frowned. "Thanks for that."

Jori chuckled in sympathy. "She just means that we understand how you're feeling. We'll keep a close eye on her, Aunt Calla. We have plenty of water for her, and as soon as we get to the site, she can lay down and not move again until the Last Day."

Everyone's fragile smiles dissolved. That used to be a family joke—saying someone wasn't going to do something again until the Last Day. A moment too late, Jori realized the literalness of what she'd just said. "Oh . . . oh, I didn't mean—"

But Shem pulled her into a forgiving hug. "Thank you, Jori and

Lori, for taking care of my daughter. I can already tell Nool's going to stay as far away from her as he can."

Nool, holding on to a pack horse, was scowling at the thought of his cousin vomiting all the way up the trail. His sister Kanthi didn't look too pleased about the idea, either.

Meiki looked at her mother. "Come with me now, Mama?"

Calla whimpered. "Oh, Meiki, I—"

Shem vigorously nodded his head. "I'm *trying* to get her to go. Right now, even. Let's get you up there, Calla!"

Calla wrung her hands. "Oh, but I can't, yet. Shemmy, I need to be with you—but my Meiki! She's so pale—Isn't there a net sling available?"

Mahrree put a bracing arm around Calla whose eyes now darted between her family. All of the net slings were being used by those more frail than Meiki.

"Calla, there's never going to be a perfect solution," Mahrree told her. "No matter what you do, you're going to be torn between going and staying."

Bravely, Meiki sat taller and made her mother's decision for her. "Stay here and take care of Papa. There's nothing you can do for me on the trail but wipe my chin."

Her husband Clyde, who had been silent until then, stepped forward. He was so scrawny—the opposite of his burly father-in-law—that Mahrree had frequently thought Shem could have snapped him like a twig. But Clyde was gentle and a genius in calculus, so Mahrree had always liked the young mathematics professor. She held her breath, hoping the timid, mousy man would do something more than calculate how often his expecting wife would get sick.

"Wipe your chin, Meiki? Isn't that my job? Mama Calla," he said to his mother-in-law, "we'll be fine. We're surrounded by help, right? That's what The Writings say. I can take care of your daughter for you."

Calla sighed in resignation, and Shem glowered at his son-in-law. He was hoping to have more reasons to send his wife to the site now, not give her excuses her stay. Still, he put on a grateful smile.

"That's absolutely true, Clyde." Shem clapped him heavily on the shoulder. "Oh, sorry. Here, let me help you up."

Mahrree caught the glances of Con and Sam Cadby. Both of them were built like bears; Con a black bear, Sam a grizzly.

They responded to Mahrree's look with one of their own. *Yes,*

Muggah—we'll watch out for little Clyde.

There was no more time to waste. Calla took Shem's hand and smiled apologetically at Meiki.

She smiled back, a little sadly, but was buoyed up by her husband's enthusiasm. Soon the next wave of descendants were on their way to the ancient site.

"Traveling with three babies," Mahrree sighed as the wagon and horses set off.

Peto put an arm around Lilla, who had been uncharacteristically quiet. "As soon as you want to leave, you can. I'd feel better knowing you're up there with everyone. You can go with the large group leaving this afternoon."

But Lilla firmed her chin. "Not until I know, Peto," she whispered.

Mahrree, Shem, and Calla regarded each other sadly. Lilla was waiting for news of Young Pere. She still hoped he might come wandering back to the house at any moment.

"He's traveling with them, Lilla," Shem assured her. "That much we know."

Lilla turned to the south. The banners at the towers had taken down the mottled gray, and up went the spotted gray banners this morning. The army was in the canyon approaching Salem.

Up with that banner had also gone the black with white sword banners in nearly every region of Salem, except for Region 3, where the Shins and their families lived. Theirs was the shortest route to the site, and to keep the flow of people from converging too quickly from the various routes, Peto and Shem staggered the times as to when people should leave. But they weren't about to deny anyone who wanted to go earlier. They still had at best two days before the army would enter Salem. Then the solid black banner would be raised, and any who remained in the valley would know it was now or never. Even the tower watchmen, after hoisting the solid black, would leave immediately on horses tethered and waiting at each tower.

Lilla was insisting on staying until at least tomorrow. Today she would continue to help those in the rectory needing assistance. Although according to her detailed checklist which every rector's wife kept to make sure that not one person in Salem was unaccounted for, everyone was prepared.

Mahrree knew what her daughter-in-law was feeling. Hour by hour, the Shin, Briter, and Zenos families were separating, never again to be all together in the big houses or in the orchard laughing and eating cake as they did just three days ago at Viddrow's wedding.

Life at the Eztates was slowly ebbing away.

Mahrree sighed and put her arm around Lilla. She looked to the canyon entrance miles to the south. Nothing yet, and not expected today, but soon.

Earlier that morning Barnos Shin had met with Jaytsy, Deck, and the four oldest Briter sons to discuss moving their wives and their seven toddlers and babies.

Of greatest concern was Eraliz Briter, Holling's wife, who was expecting their second child in about eight weeks. She was already experiencing regular pains, and Salema, now fully trained as a mid-wife, suggested they all travel together. She and Lek had decided getting Briter away from Salem was probably the best solution to his recurring anxiety. And should the worst happen with Eraliz, she would be surrounded by help. Sewzi Briter would go as official babysitter.

The rest of the families would leave tomorrow; the Zenoses and their four remaining children, plus Boskos' wife and two toddlers; the rest of the Briters, Jaytsy and Deck and their five children; and the Shins—Peto and Lilla and their last four children.

Cephas Briter would stay as Rector Shin's assistant, running messages from other rectors and checking the routes. Cephas exhausted three horses yesterday and showed no signs of stopping, and probably wouldn't until Peto would finally order him to the ancient site.

Mahrree gazed at the houses, already so much quieter. Behind the orchard and gardens, the smaller houses there were abandoned, or would be soon. She could barely stand to look at them.

She cleared her throat. "Dishes to do, I'm sure. Going back in, now." She left Peto, Lilla, Shem, and Calla in the road watching their children leave.

Mahrree's heart was near to breaking. All of Salem was dying. Its life and blood were leaking away. Slow deaths were the worst.

She wandered into the kitchen and pumped water to clean up from breakfast. Her chin trembled as she saw the little cups and plates the grandchildren had used not long ago. That they would never use again.

In some distant era would there be a woman like her exploring the ruins of crumbling houses with vines growing over them, and find these sweet little mugs and dishes? Would she have any idea how many people had used them, that they were all part of a large and boisterous family that laughed and argued and debated and hugged and cried? Would she realize the smaller dishes were for children?

Mahrree's tears dropped into the basin. It seemed wrong to wipe away the little children's messes. She wanted to leave them there, to remember Annly pushing the pancakes and syrup around on the dish to make a swirly shape, or Ensio licking his plate so clean that Muggah wouldn't have to bother washing it. Already the water filling the basin was washing away the evidence that her great-grandchildren had been there. Already it was gone, too late to be preserved.

Just last year she'd been so eager for the Last Day. All she could selfishly think of was the return of Perrin. Not once had she considered the fear, confusion, and worry of her children, grandchildren, and great-grandchildren. Now she wished she could do something to ease it. Maybe she had hoped for the Last Day too hard, and it was coming because she willed it. Perhaps it was all her fault that Eraliz was suffering from pains far too early. Should that baby be born too soon, die because of the coming of the Last Day—

You didn't cause this. It was coming anyway, and you know it. You just now feel the pain everyone else has. Look past the next few days, Mahrree. Remember, it will be glorious. Eventually.

Mahrree sniffed and smiled. "Thank you, Father. I just feel guilty for my previous joy."

Why should you feel guilty about joy? You were right! It's just getting through these next few days that will be most difficult. And as horrible as they may seem, the day will come when they will be remembered only as a brief memory. The joy that follows will erase the heartache of the next few days.

Mahrree began to tremble. "And then I'll get to see you again, right, Father?"

I'm counting the seconds, Mahrree!

She grinned. "Just how *many* seconds, Father?"

Ah, too many for you to count, my darling daughter. Just wait and stay focused on the end.

"Will Briter and Eraliz and Meiki and everyone else be all right?"

They are all in the Creator's hands, Mahrree. No place could be safer.

Mahrree picked up a little dish. "They'll still need to grow up, won't they? Still need dishes?"

Trust the Creator to provide a most glorious ending, Mahrree.

She was about to ask what that meant when she heard the chimes clanging. She had told herself she wouldn't go out to the tower to see the updates, but she couldn't help herself. She set down the dish and rushed to the front windows.

Messenger coming with news for Guide Zenos.

Mahrree looked to their house and saw that Shem and Calla, who had been walking home, now started to jog to meet the messenger.

Peto, at the front porch with Lilla, trotted down the stairs over to the Zenoses. But Lilla walked in the front door and plopped down on the sofa.

Mahrree had never seen her look so discouraged. "They'll be fine, Lilla. I've just received assurance they are in the Creator's hands."

Lilla smiled grimly. "I know, Mahrree. I just hate sitting and waiting for the next thing . . . Let's not!" She suddenly stood up. "Let's go to the Zenoses and see what the next message is. Maybe Thorne fell down in the canyon and *died* or something."

Mahrree snorted at Lilla's uncharacteristic wish of violence upon someone. "Let's go!"

They set off arm in arm for the Zenoses. Halfway there they saw the messenger racing to the house, and Lilla and Mahrree picked up their pace to get there before the most important news was revealed. As they approached the house they could hear through the open window the messenger talking to Shem.

Mahrree stopped and put her finger to her lips, signaling to Lilla that here was as good a place as any.

"—take advantage of the echoes in the valley. We could hear them plainly even a mile down the canyon."

"I remember the days when spying was a real challenge," Peto remarked.

"But is he all right?" Calla asked. "Could they see in what condition he was in?"

"The scout said he seemed to bounce as he hit the ground."

Lilla gripped Mahrree's arm.

Someone bouncing as he hit the ground? It had to be . . .

Lilla released Mahrree's arm and bolted for the front door. She blew in like a tornado with a winded Mahrree behind her.

"Young Pere?!" Lilla cried. "Was it Young Pere? Did you see him?"

Peto gingerly took her shoulders. "How long have you been

listening in—"

"WHY DIDN'T YOU TELL ME?"

Even Mahrree blinked at Lilla's volume.

In his best calming voice, Peto started, "Shem didn't want to—"

"SHEM! TELL ME!"

Now Calla stepped over and took her youngest sister's shoulders. "Lilla, they *have* seen Young Pere. We didn't want to tell you because we didn't know how he's involved or what's happening."

"No," Lilla whispered, suddenly drained of enthusiasm. "No, not my boy. He's . . . he's not betraying us, is he?"

"No, Mrs. Shin," the scout said, with a hesitant smile. "Not at all! That's why I'm here. Woodson wanted me to let you know that he spied him early this morning leaving the valley and approaching the canyon. He's in the lead, but he's shackled, wrists and ankles."

Mahrree covered her mouth with her hand. "Oh, no."

"No, that's *good,*" the scout insisted. "That he's alive, that Thorne's still trying to use him. This is good news, in a way."

Lilla trembled. "I don't understand."

"Lilla," Shem said gently, "last night Thorne announced to the army there was a reward for locating Druses, Versa, and Delia."

"Oh, no," Mahrree said again.

"But it gets worse. He also wants Eltana Yordin found."

"But how did he know about Eltana?" Mahrree said. "Who revealed that she and the Thorne women are here? Oh," she said, remembering. "Anoki Kiah! He must have made it back."

"Possibly. Or Amory Riling," he reminded them. "She knew about Eltana before she left. But it gets even worse," Shem said, sending a bracing glance to Mahrree. "The reward for them is one hundred pieces of gold. However, there's a *two* hundred pieces of gold reward for . . . Peto and Jaytsy. Each."

Lilla's eyes grew large. "What?!"

Peto gave her a sappy smile. "Seems we've been kept hostage here and Lemuel's coming to free us. Isn't that nice?"

Mahrree scoffed. "He always knew you were alive! And now he's making up some ridiculous story about rescuing you?"

"What does this have to do with Young Pere?" Lilla asked.

Shem tried a different smile, this one almost genuine. "Last night he made a stand against Thorne. He climbed the tree that holds the observation ladder and started shouting to all of the army that Thorne was lying, that Salem had no gold or wealth, and that," he stopped,

his voice unsteady, "that they were ushering in the Last Day by attacking Salem."

Lilla looked at Peto, almost afraid to hope.

His eyes were shiny. "He's not completely lost. He *remembers.*"

"And he *believes,*" Shem choked out.

Mahrree clapped her hands in joy but couldn't speak. Young Pere
wasn't another of Thorne's obedient little soldiers after all; he was a
Shin—loud and obnoxious and trying to proclaim the truth to the
world.

Lilla's eyes were now glistening, her mouth hanging open as if
words were supposed to come out but none could find their way yet.

Calla took her sister's arm. "Then Lilla, he fell from the tree, and
bounced unconscious on the ground, from what the spies could tell.
The soldiers carried him into the stables—"

"No!" Lilla whimpered. "Is he . . . is he . . ."

"That's what I'm here to tell you," the messenger said with eager
exasperation. "This morning he was walking out, shackled wrists and
ankles! He's up and fine, and they're forcing him to find the way to
Salem, but he's not willingly helping them."

Finally Lilla's tears flowed, along with her words. "So he's coming home—PETO! HE'S COMING HOME!"

The front door flew open again and there stood Jaytsy, flushed
from her run from her house. "I could've heard that shout a mile
away! Is it true? Young Pere?"

Calla smiled cautiously. "Seems to be. But Young Pere's in
chains and at the head of the army."

Jaytsy's mouth twisted at the news, unsure if she should be happy
or sad about that. "So that's . . ."

"Good! Really!" the messenger gestured wildly.

"If you say so," Jaytsy smiled.

"I'm glad you're here, Jayts," Shem said soberly. "We need to get
you out, this afternoon. Go with Salema and the rest."

"Wh—Why?"

"Lemuel's coming to free us, Jayts!" Peto declared with fake
cheer. "We're being held captive, didn't you know? And the reward
for finding us is two hundred gold pieces. For each of us."

"Two HUNDRED?" Jaytsy blinked in shock. "That's a fortune."

"See my concern?" Shem said, his voice growing tighter. "I can't
risk you staying here. You and Mahrree need to get out, now."

Mahrree glared at him mischievously. "There's no reward out for *me*, Shem."

"But if someone found you alive," he rounded on her, "Lemuel would give up the mansions in Idumea to get his hands on you!"

Mahrree stood taller. "Sounds like I might be rather important, then."

"So am I," Jaytsy added with a wink.

Shem threw up his hands. "What is WRONG with you women?! Don't you get it? Each of the nearly eighty thousand—"

The messenger cleared his throat. "Guide? About seventy-two thousand, last estimate. Lost a few more last night to—"

"Still a LOT!" Shem bellowed. "Each of those soldiers will be looking for you! And will Lemuel keep you alive?"

"He'll want *me* alive," said Jaytsy coolly.

Mahrree felt a chill run down her spine. "No, Jaytsy—"

Shem grabbed Jaytsy by the shoulders. In a low voice he said, "I stopped him once from getting to you—"

"No, you didn't, Uncle Shem," Jaytsy said. "I stopped him, remember? He was already in bad shape by the time you got to him. You may have threatened his life, but I was the one who kept him from ruining mine. I handled him before. If I have to, I can handle him again."

Peto and Mahrree exchanged looks of bewilderment. There was a story neither of them knew.

"Look, Shem, I'm not planning to bring him a loaf of bread when he invades Salem, but I'm also not leaving until I'm sure that all my children are safely on the route, and that Mother, Lilla, and Peto are ready to go. Deck and I already decided that."

"Deck will change his mind when he hears Lemuel's looking for you," Shem warned.

"I, and only I, will decide when I leave my home and Salem. There's too much to do still. You need me here."

Shem's chest heaved in frustration. "Do you still have faith in me, Jaytsy Shin Briter?"

"Complete, Guide. But right now I think you're acting as my uncle. I will go when I feel the time is right. Don't you have faith in me, Uncle Shem?"

Shem sighed. "Why I ever think I can make any headway with Shin women, I'll never know."

Mahrree beamed proudly at her daughter.

Jaytsy winked back.

"Just so you both know," Shem announced, "I don't like this. Not one bit."

"Of course you don't," Mahrree said blithely and turned to the messenger. "You said they lost some soldiers last night? What do you mean by 'lost'?"

The messenger smiled. "A lot have become ill, but about three thousand, maybe more now, are refusing to go on. It seems a certain voice kept them up all night and sufficiently scared them."

"Jon Offra!" Mahrree clapped her hands. Everyone else chuckled.

"He recited Guide Hierum's prophecy about ten times before his voice gave out," the scout explained. "He and Teman are napping in a camping shed we have tucked away in a hidden canyon. He plans to get back to work shortly, though."

Shem smiled genuinely. "He should be very proud of himself. He conquered three thousand men and never raised a blade. Tell him that when he wakes up."

Shin looked down at the slushy ground as he tried to pick his way through the rocks. He never noticed before how necessary being able to hold one's arms out was for balancing. Twice he had slipped and fallen, and wasn't able to brace himself as he hit the ground because his wrists were too tightly bound.

The second time it happened, Thorne sniggered behind him. He looked back to see Thorne's sneer and Hili's nod of sympathy. He struggled to his feet, Cloud Man rushing over to help him, and continued down the slippery, muddy canyon.

Cloud Man kept a protective hand on his arm to keep him from falling after that. He seemed to be the escort of the morning and Shin thought that at least *one* thing was going his way.

But he began to grow nervous, because around the next bend would be the first split into two. He knew the pattern of which canyons to choose on the way down. His father had had each of the children recite it when he took them up there.

First choice was right, but Shin tried to think of a believable way to appear to not remember, and maybe even get Thorne to split the army, one part taking the endless canyon to the left. If he could get the army to split and get lost enough times, he might be the only one left to reach Salem.

He evaluated the slope for signs that anyone would have left to warn Salem of their approach. The army could be there before mid-day meal. But there were no tracks. If someone had been spying on them, they must have found alternative ways back to Salem, probably along the tops of the peaks.

Still worrying and plotting, he rounded the corner of the canyon well before the divide and stopped, astonished. He wanted to laugh but was too stunned to make a noise.

Cloud Man stopped just as quickly beside him, with Sergeant Beaved and the rest of the security team bumping against them as they came around the bend.

"What the slag is THAT?" Beaved shouted.

Shin was grinning. He couldn't help it, but it was brilliant. He knew he had to compose himself because Thorne and his group was coming up behind them.

"What's the hold up?" Thorne demanded as he saw the security team rooted to the ground. "Why aren't you moving? Creet! How did *that* get there?"

"Why . . . why it's a *wall*!" Hili said in amazement.

"Made out of what?" Thorne shouted, as if staring at a personal insult. "It must be at least . . . twenty-five feet high! Who builds a wall in the middle of a canyon?"

"Looks like block," mused another officer.

Shin walked up to it, struggling to conceal his smile, and ran his chained hands along the tall block wall that fully spanned the canyon about thirty feet across.

"I think it's made of ash," Shin guessed, peering at the particles.

"What?" Thorne exclaimed. "They turned the ash into *blocks*?!"

"Seems like it, sir." Shin could barely keep the admiration out of his voice. If Puggah were still alive, this would have been the kind of thing General Perrin Shin would come up with for slowing down the Army of Idumea: a gray block wall.

Cloud Man stepped up to the wall and, without a moment's hesitation, licked it.

Shin stared at him. The rest of the security team scowled.

"Yep," Cloud Man nodded. "Tastes just like ash."

"How would you know *that*?" Beaved demanded.

"Doesn't everyone?"

"That's likely how he survived the volcano," Snarl muttered. "He ate his way out of the ash."

Cloud Man shrugged sheepishly.

"I . . . I don't believe this!" Thorne said, as if his proclamation would make it disappear. But it wasn't vanishing, despite him waving almost helplessly with his left arm at the massive blockade. "We have to get around it, or over it, or tear it down, or *something!*"

"How do we do that, sir?" asked an officer.

"I don't know! Build a ladder!"

"Out of what, sir?" came the almost timid reply.

Thorne looked wildly around. All that grew in the canyon were scrubby trees which could never hope to be even stepstools.

"Tear it down!" Thorne hollered.

Already a couple of soldiers were inspecting the block and shaking their heads.

"Brittle and easy to knock down, right?" the general asked.

One of the soldiers, a man in his forties, was squinting at it worriedly. "Sir, this is solid. I'm guessing each block is probably at least a foot wide, if not more, and the mortar holding it together—well, this is excellent construction," he said in reluctant approval. "I helped build your new armory at the garrison, and sir—I wish we could have constructed it like this." He thumped his fist on wall. "Look—it's carved into the mountain side, anchored on every row. The block extends into the stone. I mean—this is quality work!"

Shin tried not to grin. This was a Salem job, which meant the wall was designed to last for a century.

Thorne's fist was clenching and unclenching repeatedly.

His builder ran his hand over the wall, nearly caressing it. "Perhaps if we had sledge hammers, which I can't imagine anyone would have thought of bringing . . . I supposed we could send word back, have someone retrieve hammers and picks, then we get to work and I think we could have a sizable hole within two or three days, or if we bring up shovels we might be able to dig under it—"

"We climb the side of the canyon up and over the wall!" Thorne decided, already abandoning the tear-it-down or dig-under-it plans.

Several of the soldiers let out low whistles.

"It's not that high," Thorne insisted.

His builder shrugged in unwilling agreement that climbing was the faster alternative.

"No, it's not that high," Hili agreed. "However, the sides are very muddy and steep. We'll have to make a chain of men to help get everyone over. This could slow us down a few hours—"

"I don't care!" Thorne raged. "Start now. Shin, start scaling the side and get around this slagging thing!"

Shin held up his shackled hands. "I'll go more quickly if I'm not chained."

"Sir," said Hili imploringly, "at least take off his leg chains."

"No!" Thorne was nearly frothing in anger. "His little cloud friend will help him. I'm not unchaining you for anything, Shin. I rather enjoy watching you struggle. Now climb!"

While the task seemed impossible, Shin was happy to attempt it. He stared at the wall and nearly snickered in delight. Beautiful, absolutely beautiful. And it would waste a *lot* of time.

He looked for handholds or anything else to grip as he evaluated the muddy bank.

"How about this?" Cloud Man squatted and webbed his hands together as a foothold. "I can push you up to that bush there."

He felt badly about putting his muddy boot on Cloud Man's hands, but realized that Cloudy might just lick them clean again.

Shin scrambled as best he could up the slippery slope, covering himself in mud before he finally reached the top. Heaving himself on top of the wall, he laid on it precariously and looked to the north—

And snorted.

"What is it, Private?" Thorne bellowed.

"Walls!"

"What?"

"More walls!" Shin called, almost gleefully. "The canyon splits about forty paces from here and there are walls closing off both sides!"

"What in the world are Salemites thinking?!" Thorne exclaimed.

Hili smiled vaguely. "They're thinking that they don't want the world invading them, sir. We best think of a faster way over these walls because we may encounter a few more."

"Block!?" a woman's voice shrieked. Amory had just come around the bend joining hundreds of soldiers stacking up and staring in bewilderment. "Since when does Salem make block?"

She pushed her way through the growing mass of stunned soldiers to where Shin was still lying on top of the wall.

"They made a *few* walls," he told her, cocking his head in the direction. "They found a good use for the ash." He thumped his fist on it and beamed.

"This is . . . this is ridiculous!" Amory exclaimed. "We're miles away from Salem. To construct this they had to *haul* the block all this way and then *build* it?"

"I can't imagine anyone working that hard," another soldier said.

Shin smiled at the barriers before him. "That's because you can't imagine anyone working hard at all," he mumbled to himself. "With the way they cooperate, they probably erected these in just a few afternoons."

His chest swelled with pride as he looked at what Salem had accomplished. They had found ways to keep themselves occupied, likely during the failed Harvest Season, and ensured that everyone in Salem would have enough time to make it out as the army approached.

How many more walls there were, he couldn't imagine but was eager to find out. *His* people did this. Salemites, surprising Thorne and the army of Idumea. Peaceful, non-assuming people reducing the world's general to tantrums, now screaming for ropes or anything else that could be used to scale the walls more quickly.

Without making a single weapon or causing a single death, Salem was sinking the will of the army. While several soldiers were just as irate as Thorne, many men were sitting down in the cold mud shaking their heads in amazement, fatigue, and disappointment.

Shin chuckled. "Puggah, do you see this?"

Oh, I see it, Young Pere. Peto, it's perfect! Exactly how I imagined it could be. Brilliant work with the block, Shem. Of course Salem would find a use for the ash. I wished you two could see this. The looks on their faces—it's got to be the funniest thing I've ever witnessed. Well done, boys!

Peto and Shem walked outside and looked to the canyon, after finally calming down Lilla who was fairly dancing back to her house.

"I suspect they must be near the first wall by now," Peto said quietly.

Shem smiled. "I wish I could see their faces right now."

Peto chuckled. "I wish I knew what Father thinks of it."

Shem looked wistfully to the south. "Mahrree was right, he *is* getting closer. I can almost feel him again, and I swear I can hear him laughing. Like distant bells. He always thought it would be so funny for soldiers to run into a gray block wall in the middle of nowhere!"

Peto smiled. "I remember when he came up with that idea when we were first coming to Salem. You and Mother thought we had the strangest sense of humor, but it was a great idea. So Shem, what does he think of the wall?"

Shem closed his eyes and pondered until he grinned. "He thinks, It's perfect, Peto. Exactly how he imagined it could be. Brilliant work with the block. He wishes we could see the looks on their faces. He thinks it the funniest thing he's ever seen. Well done, boys!"

Peto whispered to the canyon, "Thanks, Father. Keep an eye on him, please. And son, be careful. Let your mother see you again."

Shin was down the first wall and analyzing the next two in front of him where the canyon divided, both routes blocked entirely. He evaluated one, then the other, then the first one again.

Cloud Man copied his movements as if he could see what Shin was seeing. Eventually his gaze drifted upward and he smiled at a big fluffy cloud.

"So which way?" Beaved asked, joining them. The rest of the security team followed, Teach having made the most noise getting up the wall, then getting down on the other side with a rapid splat.

Shin shrugged.

"What did he say?" Thorne asked, out of breath as he made his way over to them. A chain of soldiers had hoisted and heaved him over, doing all the work, yet still Thorne huffed as if he'd labored on his own. He spat on the nearest wall. "Stupidest thing I've ever seen. What slagging Zenos came up with *this* idea?!"

Shin nearly laughed again. For once the general got it right. *The slagging Zenos* probably *did* come up with this idea.

"Which way, Shin?" Thorne demanded.

He shrugged again. "The way I look at it, you'd want to block off the route that directly leads to where you don't want people to go."

"But both routes are blocked!"

"So maybe both lead to Salem," he suggested benignly.

"Amory!" Thorne called. "Do both routes lead to Salem?"

Amory, slipping down the muddy side, nearly tripped as she hurried over to them. "I . . . I don't think so, but I'm not sure. I never really paid much attention when they were teaching about the canyons in school."

"Figures," Thorne mumbled in disgust.

Amory pushed back her disheveled hair, inadvertently adding a muddy streak, and glowered at him.

"So now what?" Thorne demanded.

"Split the army?" Shin offered. "One group head to the left, the other to the right."

"And which way do you want to go?"

"Whichever way you command, sir." He blinked innocently.

Thorne clenched his fist. "I'm growing weary of you, Shin. You want to earn your name back, you're going to have to do much better than that, *son*."

Shin clenched his own fists. It was probably a good thing they were shackled. He never, *ever* wanted to hear that last word from the general again.

He felt strength, courage greater than he'd ever experienced, coursing through him. It was as if power from Salem was drifting up the mountain to reinforce him. He felt the energy of General Shin, Peto Shin, Shem Zenos, Deckett Briter, and every other brother, cousin, and relative flowing up to him, reclaiming him, wanting him to come home.

He felt his mother, more distinctly than he had in seasons—

And he also felt his grandmother.

Mahrree Shin was still alive, still wanting him to remember who he was. She was sending out tendrils of influence, as if she were still sitting in a pumpkin patch, hoping to snag him and drag him back.

And he wanted to go.

He didn't need the name of Lek Thorne. His cousin Lek Zenos would be confused by it anyway. He had a far greater legacy waiting for him, and after nearly two years he was finally understanding the power of that heritage. He wanted to claim it, to beg its forgiveness for ever leaving it, and he wanted to honor it as bravely as Mahrree Shin would.

He was Young Perrin Shin, and he never wanted to be anyone else.

Young Pere turned to Thorne with new determination. "I don't *want* your name. I can't imagine why anyone would. I'm *not* your son, no matter what you believe. You're growing weary of me? Every man here is weary of *you*! You want to find Salem? Then *find it*—"

He was prepared for the slap. He steeled himself to absorb Thorne's furious smack across his face, and he barely moved. He continued to glare at the general, who expected the private to fall to the ground or look down in shame. But instead he stood tall.

Thorne seemed taken aback by his brashness.

"Oh yes, *General*." Young Pere squinted with disdain. "*That* makes me want to call you 'father.' There's a reason I never would, Thorne. You're *not* my father. My name is Young Perrin Shin, and Amory was right—they called me Young Pere. That's because there was an Old Pere, not that long ago. Yes, *he* was my grandfather, but you were never my father, nor can you ever hope to earn the right. Hit me all you want, Thorne, but you can never change who I am or what you are. So choose the canyon *yourself*."

From the corner of his eye, Young Pere could see Hili beaming. But Thorne stood shocked, not used to such flagrant insubordination, and evidently didn't know how to proceed.

The several dozen men now on their side of the wall glanced at each other anxiously, waiting for the general's response. He was taking an inordinate amount of time formulating one.

Young Pere stood as tall as he could and felt another presence very distinctly on his right. General Perrin Shin was staring down Lemuel Thorne, too.

Thorne wilted ever so slightly, as if he could feel the spirit of the general daring him to touch his grandson again.

Young Pere almost smiled at the strength of the presence. He could even smell Puggah, earthy sweet, and wondered if Thorne could smell him, too.

Finally Thorne whispered, in as sinister a voice as he could muster, "I have one more thing to do with you, Shin. Then I *will* kill you myself. Nothing will give me greater pleasure. Your days are numbered, make no mistake about that!"

Young Pere nodded once, not at all intimidated. Thorne was full of unmet promises; just ask anyone he'd told he'd give a medal. He still owed Young Pere a few.

"So which canyon, Thorne?" he said, his contempt obvious. "Left or right?"

"Right," Thorne said in a dead voice. "You and fifty men scout it for half an hour, then return." He turned to another group of men and shouted at them to take the left one.

Young Pere caught Hili's eye.

Hili winked at him subtly, proudly, before turning to choose fifty men to follow the general's orders.

Young Pere turned to assess which side of the canyon to climb because he had a home to get to. He felt someone right behind him.

"Private Shin, you're going to get yourself killed!" Beaved hissed. "I'm beginning to really like you, so why can't you leave well enough alone?"

Young Pere turned to the sergeant. "That's the whole problem with the world, Sergeant: everyone leaves well enough alone. No one takes a stand, no one declares what's wrong or right, no one dares to make a noise for fear they may suddenly . . . what, not be liked anymore?"

"Or worried that they might not be alive anymore, Private," Beaved whispered.

But Young Pere was undaunted. "I don't care what Thorne or anyone thinks of me. No, I take that back. I care what my family and my guide think of me. If I die, at least I will have died for saying the right things. And my name's Young Pere, not Private Shin. I recommend we head up the left side of this wall. If Hammer goes first, then Iron can shove Teach up to him and they can drop him over the other side."

Beaved gave him a half smile. "You're not the lieutenant anymore, you know. You shouldn't be giving orders."

"I don't even want to be in the army anymore, Sergeant. And I'm not giving orders, just recommendations."

Beaved nodded. "Follow Young Pere's recommendations," he called.

Cloud Man grinned at Young Pere.

Jaytsy walked back to her house with a shadow. She didn't turn around as she opened her front door, but called, "I know you're there, Mother. And I know what you want to ask me about. Come on in."

Mahrree slipped in to the house behind her daughter. The family had completed their discussion at the Zenoses' home, but one thing sat heavily on Mahrree's mind and she couldn't let it go, even though it happened almost thirty years ago.

"I realize it's none of my business now, Jayts," Mahrree hedged as she followed her daughter into her kitchen, "but what was Shem talking about, concerning you and Lemuel Thorne?" She whispered his name in case any children were around to hear.

Jaytsy turned to her mother. Her expression was stern, yet also surprisingly amused. "True, it's no longer your business—"

When she saw her mother clench her teeth, she chuckled.

"But it will kill you to not know, and I don't want you to miss the Last Day, after all." Jaytsy glanced around to make sure they were alone. Voices in the eating room suggested some children were looking for a snack, and Jaytsy cocked her head for her mother to follow her into the larder. They sat down on crates, their knees touching in the large closet, and shut the door.

"I'm trying to remember just how much you might know," Jaytsy began. "You know Lemuel was interested in me, right?"

Mahrree nodded. "Of course. After The Dance in Idumea?"

"Did you know he was courting me?"

At that, Mahrree hesitated. "Actively?"

Jaytsy bobbed her head. "Father was having those nightmares, none of us were sleeping well, and Lemuel decided to start walking me home from school each day."

Mahrree's eyes flared. "Bringing you home to an empty house?"

Jaytsy patted her mother's knee as if she was five. "Remember, this was about thirty years ago now. No need to get angry."

"Yes, yes . . . go on."

"He never came into the house. I always abandoned him on the porch. All he ever did was bore me to tears with stories about horses and army life. He never asked me questions, and I never really did anything but nod."

"So you weren't attracted to him?"

"Did you ever *smell* him, Mother?" Jaytsy's nose twitched in remembrance. "He always smelled of purple. Lilacs or lavender or something else that a real man shouldn't smell of."

"Like an old lady?" Mahrree smiled slyly.

"Exactly!" Jaytsy giggled as if she were fifteen again. "He was so perfectly handsome and perfectly shaved and perfectly *scented*. Ick!"

Mahrree laughed in relief. "So what happened?"

"Well, after several weeks of that, I told him I wasn't ready for walking and talking and such. Maybe in a couple of years, but not yet. I was trying to go into the house when he pulled me back and kissed me."

Mahrree flinched. "Where?"

"In the front garden—"

"I mean, where on you?"

"My mouth," Jaytsy grimaced. "I ran into the house and washed it off rather violently."

Mahrree nodded in approval. "Good girl. But Jayts, an unwelcomed kiss isn't exactly 'life ruining'—"

Jaytsy's lip pursing told her that wasn't the entire story.

"Oh no. What else did he do?"

"Not quite a year later," Jaytsy began, holding her mother's anxious gaze, "before the Remembrance Ceremony that marked one year since that land tremor, I had gone to bring Father his dinner. I greeted some enlisted boy on the stairs, and Thorne saw me."

When Jaytsy paused, Mahrree said, "Aaannnd?"

Jaytsy repositioned herself. "He confronted me as I was starting for home. He dragged me over to a feed barn and accused me of flirting."

"You would have been sixteen then," Mahrree said. "That's what sixteen-year-old girls do."

Jaytsy raised her eyebrows. "Not if they are the future wife of Lemuel Thorne, or so he said."

Mahrree scoffed.

"He then said it was obvious that I was ready for courting, and I guess he thought I was ready for even more. *Much* more," Jaytsy added meaningfully.

Her mother squinted. "Just how 'much' more?"

Jaytsy shifted on the wooden crate. Not able to stall any longer, she gave her mother a *Look*.

Mahrree's jaw dropped again. "He . . . he . . ."

"Wasn't successful, Mother!" Jaytsy quickly supplied when she saw her mother growing pale.

Sagging in relief, Mahrree asked, "So what did you do?"

"Everything Father taught me," Jaytsy declared proudly. "I screamed. I ripped his shirt. I kicked. And oh, *how perfectly* I kicked—I got him twice. He went down, hard and retching!"

"That's my girl!" Mahrree cheered.

"And that was when Shem burst into the barn," Jaytsy continued. "He told me later he had a feeling something was wrong. While Thorne was moaning on the ground, I got myself out of there. Shem sat on Lemuel's chest, pulled out his long knife, and threatened Lemuel's life while holding the blade against his throat—"

"I know this story!" Mahrree suddenly exclaimed. "At least this part. Yudit told me years ago that Shem was tempted to kill Lemuel at one point, but she never told me the circumstances and now I know why. This must have been it."

Jaytsy nodded. "Shem eventually let Lemuel go, then came and found me hiding behind the barn. I was more worried about Shem than anything, and he told me Lemuel shouldn't be bothering me anymore."

Mahrree released a sigh. "I had no idea. I'm so sorry, Jayts. Why didn't you tell me?"

Jaytsy laughed softly. "Remember how later that year, after the attack on Moorland, we were all invited to stay at the Cushes' mansion in Idumea for The Dinner? And how Lemuel wanted to take me—alone—with him?"

Mahrree searched the past but found it quickly. "You and Deckett became engaged about that time, right? And married the night of the Dinner? Yes . . . Ooh, I remember now! I was furious that Lemuel had the presumption that we would let our daughter travel with him *alone*."

"Exactly. At the time I thought, 'So this is what an enraged mother bear looks like.'"

"That's right," Mahrree said, fuming at the memory. "I was ready to beat him into the ground!"

"I pictured you shredding him and sprinkling him over Idumea," Jaytsy said thoughtfully.

Mahrree calmed down enough to chuckle. "Oh, I like that idea! So . . . why did you never tell me what happened in that barn?"

"Well, first, I didn't think your killing Lemuel Thorne would go over too well with his family, but mostly I saw how much progress Father had made. He was almost back to his old self by that time. His nightmares were more under control, you didn't have to sedate him as much, he was laughing again . . ." Jaytsy took a deep breath. "I so miss hearing him laugh."

Mahrree could only nod and wipe away a stray tear.

"Well," Jaytsy continued, "I was worried how both of you would react if you knew Lemuel attacked me in the barn, so I made Shem promise not to tell, and he made sure that he and Lemuel had the same schedules so he could keep a close eye on him. But Mother, I'm fairly confident he let Father know. Even though I made him promise not to say a word, I'm sure Shem wiggled his face in some sort of strange manner to get the message across."

"He would," Mahrree agreed.

"After the offensive, when we were helping bandage up the wounded from Moorland," Jaytsy went on, "Father was hovering rather closely, an eye always on the soldiers who claimed to need more help than they really did." She chuckled softly at the memory of the young men trying to catch her attention. "At one point, Father came over to me, asking if I was all right. I had just finished with Thorne a few minutes before, tightening the bandage on his chest with so much zeal that he squirmed in pain. I told Father that I was fine and also that I was proud of what he had accomplished in Moorland. Then he said something like, 'I was just hoping to be brave enough to fight *my* way out of the barn.' Then he kissed me on the forehead and went off to yell at some soldier somewhere. We never said anything more of it, but I'm sure he knew."

Mahrree sighed. "And he never told me."

"That's because we were all scared of you, Mother," Jaytsy said with mock sobriety. "We still are."

Mahrree slapped her arm good-naturedly. "But I'm a little concerned, Jayts. Why is there such a reward for you now? Might it be that Lemuel is still . . ." She bobbed her head back and forth.

Jaytsy waved that off. "I think he's just trying to flush out the Shins. It's the same amount as for Peto, after all. Besides, I can't imagine he still thinks of me. I gave him no reason to then and certainly not now."

Mahrree wrinkled her nose at that. "I remember what Druses Thorne said when she was over for dinner some moons ago. She took a long look at you and said, 'I see why Lemuel pined for you.'"

"He may have pined, but many years ago," Jaytsy said dismissively, embarrassedly. "Druses hasn't seen him for over fifteen years herself. He's given up on the thought of me, I'm sure. He's had a dozen other women—"

"—who didn't measure up to Jaytsy Shin Briter," Mahrree pointed out. "That may be what he's thinking, you know. We need to seriously consider, what if he still wants you?"

A booming voice on the other side of the door made them both jump. "He can't have her!"

The larder door swung open and Jaytsy and Mahrree, now practically sitting on top of each other in their surprise, stared at Deck.

His normally tranquil light brown eyes were dark with anger. "He's looking for you? When were you going to tell me?"

Jaytsy struggled to stand up in the crowded pantry and helped her mother find her feet. "So, did Shem—"

"Yes, Shem told me!"

Mahrree rocked back. She'd never seen her son-in-law so livid.

Neither had Jaytsy, but she wasn't one to be easily intimidated.

"Deck," she said soothingly as she pushed out of the larder, her hands on his chest. "I'm not going to do anything stupid. I'm going to leave with you and everyone else just as we agreed, and I don't want you to spend another moment worried about any of this."

"What are you two women planning?" he demanded.

"Nothing!" Mahrree declared. "We'll keep your wife far away from Lemuel Thorne. Did you . . . did you *know*," she searched for a tactful way to put it, "about his *efforts* with Jaytsy?"

Deck nodded hotly.

Mahrree threw her hands in the air. "So once again I'm the only one who doesn't know things? Why is that?"

"Because," Deck said with a hint of a smile, "you're the most dangerous woman in the world and we're all terrified of you."

"Told you," Jaytsy said.

Mahrree smacked Deck gently on the arm.

"Ow, ow!" he cried melodramatically. "See?"

But immediately he sobered again. "Please leave, Mahrree. Both you and Jaytsy. Get out of here as soon as you can."

"We will," she assured him. "When we're sure everyone's—"

Mahrree didn't get to finish her sentence. Her son-in-law suddenly embracing her, probably for the first time, crushed the rest of her words.

Jaytsy sniffled at her husband's unexpected affection.

"I cried when Perrin died," Deck choked out. "Don't make me . . . don't *you* . . ."

Mahrree patted him on the back and squeezed him. "Not planning on it, son," she said, meaning that last word wholeheartedly. "I love you, and I'll be fine. So will Jaytsy. Thank you, Deck. Now go milk something before I start sobbing."

Chuckling, he released her and turned to his wife. "I've never said this before, but I'm saying it now: leave me. As fast as possible."

"Never," she whispered back. "Never."

"I was afraid of that." He darted out of the house before the women could see his emotion.

"Well," Mahrree sighed. "I . . . never."

Deck marched straight for his cattle, aimlessly and pointlessly, to work out the idea which struck him like a pitchfork in the chest.

While he couldn't remember the first time, he knew that was the last time he'd ever hug his mother-in-law.

Because Mahrree couldn't bear to watch Lilla rechecking the bags for those who would leave that afternoon, and because the day was beginning to smother her much like her dear son-in-law had, she convinced Peto that the storehouse needed her expertise and without accepting a ride from anyone, she walked over there.

Except someone tried to stop her.

Halfway there, she saw the large black Clark come trotting down the road. She exhaled when she saw who was riding him. The only man who had ever properly tried to court her.

"Oh, Honri," she murmured as he reined the horse to a stop and dismounted.

"Mahrree, just hear me out—"

"And who have you been talking to?" she interrupted, because she was never good at hearing people out.

He slapped his hands quietly, guiltily together. There were no cheerful dimples in his cheeks today, no boyish smile on his seventy-four-year-old face. "Mahrree, we need to get you out of—"

"Oh, not *this* again. Not you too," and she turned for the storehouse.

"Hey. Hey!" he called after her. He ran over and grabbed her by the arm and spun her around.

Mahrree was alarmed. Honri had never been rough with her, but having spent a few years in the world as a scout had taught him worldly ways.

"Look, this isn't some game, Mahrree. This is serious! Lemuel is on his way, right now! Yes, the walls are slowing them up, but I'm getting reports from my grandson who's in the corps. They'll be here, soon, and if Lemuel knows you're here—"

"I don't care about Lemuel—"

"You need to leave NOW! That's what Perrin would say," Honri exclaimed, his grip on her arm growing tighter. "And I'll take you up there, *for him*!"

Wait a minute—Honri didn't own a black Clark. He always got the GrayClarks.

Someone had told him about her plan with Perrin to ride to the ancient site on a black Clark together.

Stupid, meddling Shem!

"Right now," Honri said, his voice a bit calmer, now that he noticed a few passing Salemites were eyeing them both worriedly. Still, he didn't release his hold on her. "I'm not doing this because I once wanted to propose to you. I'm doing this because Perrin was like a brother to me, and his wife needs to be rescued and taken far away so that she's safe for him."

He was right. All the words sounded correct. *Everyone* was right that she needed to get out of Salem. But the idea didn't sit well in her heart, for some strange reason. It just wasn't the right time . . . yet.

She gazed into Honri's eyes, and his blue eyes pleaded back with her. Almost she agreed. Almost she thought—

"No," she said quietly. She cleared her throat. "No. I hear you, I thank you, Perrin thanks you . . . especially for stealing someone's black Clark. But, no."

He was so startled that his grip on her arm loosened enough for her to escape. Immediately she started again for the storehouse.

"Mahrree!" he called after her again. "But why?!"

She turned around. "I honestly don't know, Honri. I don't. Please, don't ask me anymore. But if I need you, I promise I'll send for you."

He took an eager step toward her. "You mean it? You'll let me take you up?"

She sighed. "Sure. Of course. You taking me makes the most sense. My family won't be burdened by me, then. You and me. You've got the right color horse, obviously."

Honri smiled hesitantly, not quite believing her. "I've got your word, now."

"Of course you do! Now head home, and . . . I'll let you know when I'm ready to go. Tell Shem, too, so he'll quit fretting."

At that, Honri smiled broader, showing his dimples that made Mahrree slightly wobbly in the knees. He mounted his massive Clark easily and pointed at her. "Day or night," he said. "Call for me day or night."

"Day or night," she repeated.

Honri was about to kick his Clark to leave, but first gave Mahrree one long, last searching look.

She gazed back at him, adoringly, appreciatively.

She had tutored in him in her lying courses before he became a rector/scout in the world. They both knew when words were only words without meaning behind them.

Honri's shoulders sagged, but Mahrree lifted her chin and beamed at him.

Without another word he gently kicked his horse and was on his way.

Mahrree rubbed her forehead and continued to the storehouse. But it wasn't as busy as she expected, to her disappointment and relief.

However, there was a steady stream of Salemites requesting items, and the rector in charge told the volunteers to hand out everything. There was no need to hold anything back for a rainy day; it was pouring outside. Besides, this way there'd be less for the army to loot.

Mahrree retrieved saddles, tents, boots, and hatchets. Lots of hatchets. And knives. And bows and arrows. And pitchforks.

But she didn't say anything about it. Most people didn't say much, either, she noticed. Normally a place of cheerful conversations, the storehouse today was subdued and discussions were brief. Any smiles exchanged were unnatural and worried, and when someone said good-bye it seemed to be a final farewell.

Still, Mahrree tried to keep on a brave face and offer a few genuine smiles. At one point she came out of the back storage room, her arms filled with beige changing cloths to give to a new grandmother, and noticed a familiar face in the crowd of twenty Salemites waiting for their goods.

It was Assistant Choruk, and he was watching for her. Choruk was the next in line to be Guide, having been called by Guide Gleace right after Shem. Had they been in the world, Mahrree had occasionally thought, that would have meant that the older, slight man with thinning black hair, skin tinted yellow like sulfur, and dark narrow eyes would have been plotting Zenos's death to hasten his rise to the top.

Instead, he was Shem's right hand in running the affairs of Salem. While Peto was in charge of securing Salem from Idumea, Assistant Choruk oversaw the interactions within Salem and delegated them to the other assistants.

Mahrree eyed him suspiciously as he flashed his ever-ready smile which crinkled his eyes into mere slits. But Mahrree knew him well enough to notice there was no usual spark in his eyes. Something was up.

"Mrs. Shin, glad I found you here," he said, gently pushing himself to the front of the line, "Guide Zenos—"

"Oh, what does he want *now*?" she snapped.

On any other day, those waiting in line likely would have snorted a few laughs, but today Salemites looked aghast at her disrespect.

Mahrree bit her lip. "I'm sorry. It's just that every time I turn around, he's got some other excuse as to why I should already be heading to the site."

A man nodded to her. "I was just wondering myself why you haven't, Professor Shin."

"What, and miss all of this?" she said, placing the armful of changing cloths into the grandmother's large bag. "This is where the action is. If your grandbabies need more, we have plenty," she said to the woman. "I can't imagine anything worse than facing the Last Day with a baby in soiled cloths. Next?"

Choruk stepped in front of Mahrree, his smile already gone. "He said you'd be resistant but to assure you this isn't a plot to get you up to the site. We're hoping," he lowered his voice to a whisper, "that the wife of *one* general might be able to talk some sense into those following the wife of *another* general."

"Eltana?" she breathed. "What's she doing?"

Choruk glanced around to see far too many curious eyes. "Come with me, please?"

Mahrree followed him out to his wagon. He helped her in and slapped the horses before he said anything else.

"Sorry about that," he said. "A few people in there may have been there on Mrs. Yordin's bidding. How many hatchets, knives, and pitchforks have been requested today?"

"Quite a few, actually. Along with bows and arrows. Why?"

"Weapons," he said dully.

Mahrree closed her eyes. "Oh, how senseless. Tell me what's happening."

"Since early this morning, when they all gathered, Mrs. Yordin's been showing her new army different ways to incapacitate someone. She's telling them to not bother with killing but just with maiming. Since they're outnumbered they should focus on slowing down the army, letting them bleed to death."

"How gruesome. How does she know such things? I never asked Perrin the details of what they taught."

"She lived through a lot of skirmishes and battles," Choruk suggested. "She probably witnessed a lot firsthand. Her graphic descriptions have so disturbed a few men that they left and went to Guide Zenos, asking him how they could erase the images from their minds."

"But they can't!"

"That's unfortunately true," Choruk agreed. "But that's not what's so worrisome. Guide Zenos headed over there to find nearly fourteen thousand men had gathered to learn how to fight."

She was more than stunned. "So many?"

"We were a little surprised at the number as well. Supposedly two of the dissenter colonies have decided to stay put and fight it out. They're trying to make swords as quickly as they can."

"No . . . no—we're a place of peace—"

"Not anymore," Choruk said dully. "But I still haven't told you the worst part. It's not just the men that want to fight. Many have brought their wives and children. Mrs. Shin, there are over twenty thousand Salemites massed on the eastern side of Salem, many camping in the first wide canyon there, south of the river and temple, trying to learn to fight."

Mahrree covered her mouth because one-fifth of Salemites were delusional enough to think they were soldiers, and she was growing nauseated. "Do they have *any idea* what battle is like? What a man's body looks like after he's been hit by a sword? I do. Perrin was badly injured twice, and I tended to dozens of wounded after Moorland. Even though it's been many years, I'll never forget the horror of that blood."

"They obviously don't know or they wouldn't be so gallant right now," said Choruk, his tone filled with frustration. "It makes no sense. We've been teaching for years there's a solution. We've been preparing, but now so many have lost faith and hope?"

"They haven't lost faith," Mahrree decided. "They've just shifted it to themselves instead. They want to rely more on themselves than on the Creator, and trust in their own arms, not His. Oh, this is so ludicrous. Why? Why do they refuse His plan?"

"Ah, Mrs. Shin," Choruk said, "that's been the question ever since the first five hundred families came to this sphere. Why would any of them refuse His plan? Why do they believe the Refuser more than the Creator? What does he offer that's better than the Creator? Nothing. Only temporary flashes of entertainment or possessions, then nothing. I don't get it. I just don't get it."

Mahrree sighed as the wagon headed east. "Neither do I. Unless they simply can't believe what the Creator holds out to them later is better. Maybe they fear *this* is all there ever *will* be. They have no imagination to consider what may be in store later. So what does Shem think I can do over there?"

"He's hoping you can convince some of the mothers to leave with their younger children. Maybe help them realize how gory this may become, how their children won't be spared—"

"Oh, they won't!" Mahrree wailed. "Soldiers always go for the easiest kill. There'll probably be many soldiers who don't want to fight at all, but of those who do, slaughtering children and women will be no problem. I can't believe this is happening in Salem. Oh, Perrin—they might have listened to you."

Choruk put his arm around her. "But you've always been better with words, Mrs. Shin. If they won't listen to you, they won't listen to anyone. I'll be praying that the Creator can fill you with the correct words."

"Pray that I'll be listening for them, too."

The group of fifty men Sergeant Major Hili had sent over the wall of the left canyon had been hiking for nearly half an hour when they stopped, confused. The canyon split again, and they had no idea what to do. The men turned to the staff sergeant in charge.

"Now what?" someone asked.

The staff sergeant spat. "It's a maze. I always hated mazes."

"We're supposed to be turning back now to tell Thorne which direction to go," said another private in his early forties.

The staff sergeant scratched his head and glanced around at his new soldiers. Most were from the southern villages, as he was, and were likely tired of walking north, as he was. He never did find the north appealing.

"What if the other walled route is the correct one?" another man suggested. "Thorne and the rest might already be heading down the other canyon."

The staff sergeant shrugged. "Anyone feel like exploring either one of these canyons?"

A sergeant raised his hand. "I've got no problem going further. Rather uncrowded and quiet over here . . ."

A few more soldiers nodded. "I'll go with him."

"So will I."

"I've had enough of being crammed together like a herd of sheep."

"And hearing *that voice*," one man said quietly. Several others nodded in remembrance of Offra's warnings drifting down to them last night.

The staff sergeant counted. "How many? Fifteen? Good. Tell you what—Sergeant, you're in charge. You all wander that way as far as you want. If you see anything interesting, send a few men back through the canyons. Just remember which canyons you choose so you don't get lost."

"Won't General Thorne wonder what happened if we don't return with all fifty?" asked one nervous young man.

The staff sergeant waved that away. "The general cares only about one private right now. You're safe, don't worry. Enjoy the hike," he said, saluting away the fifteen others, and he turned back with his thirty-four to report to Sergeant Major Hili.

Mahrree and Assistant Choruk rolled up in the wagon to a most impressive and alarming site: vast farmlands covered with immense clusters of would-be soldiers. Directly before her were about two hundred men pretending to hack with imaginary hatchets. Beyond them were some groups trying hand-to-hand combat but were clearly worried about actually harming each other; others were honing their pitchfork techniques on accommodating bales of hay; and another large group near the end of the lane was taking aim with bows and arrows at haystacks with shapes tacked on to them at the appropriate heights for vital human organs. Many women were standing along-side the men, also taking their shots.

"I don't believe this," Mahrree said under her breath as she surveyed the thousands of Salemites pretending to be fighters. "They're all going to die. Simple as that, the foolish people."

She spied Eltana Yordin, dressed in dark gray men's trousers and a dark blue men's tunic, striding toward her.

"Oh, what a surprise," she snarled. "This must be the *great* Mahrree Shin."

Choruk helped Mahrree down from the wagon and whispered, "Good luck," as Mrs. Yordin drew closer.

"Impressive army I've massed, isn't it?" Mrs. Yordin signaled to the thousands behind her. "Perrin could have done this years ago and then such a day like this would never have happened."

Mahrree ignored Mrs. Yordin's sharpness. "Eltana, good to see you up and about, doing something for Salem," she said calmly. "Although, I must say, this is doomed to failure."

"You have no faith, do you?" Mrs. Yordin put her hands on her hips. "None at all in these brave, ambitious people!"

"That's misplaced faith," Mahrree said. "Brave ambition isn't a guarantee for success. What you call brave, I consider fool-hardy. What you label ambitious, I'd call arrogant. These people have no idea what they're up against, Eltana. How dare you let them believe that they do?"

Mrs. Yordin pointed to a group of men hacking at a bale of hay with butcher knives. "What makes you think they don't have a chance? I know the world's soldiers now. Trust me, there are no Perrin Shins or Shem Zenoses out there. There may be a few serious soldiers here and there, but the rest of them are no more fit for battle than these people."

"And then it will still be four against one, at best," Mahrree pointed out. "There's strength in numbers, Eltana. Maybe if these people had a few years of training, discipline, then *maybe* they could—"

"And why don't they?" Mrs. Yordin retorted. "Why didn't your *beloved* Perrin and his *best buddy* Shem teach these people all they know? I still can't fathom that. This could be a great fighting force, but no. 'Salem is peaceful.' Well, it's not now!"

Mahrree gestured madly. "It is everywhere else but here! We don't *have* to fight! Oh, why am I telling you this. You're as stubborn and narrow-minded as the rest of the world." She pushed past Mrs. Yordin. "It's them I want to talk to." She indicated a large group of women and younger children watching the 'soldiers' practicing, and she started a quick march for them.

Mrs. Yordin jogged to catch up to her. "And just what do you think you're doing, Mahrree?"

"Watch and see, Eltana."

"Don't you dare interfere with my soldiers!"

Mahrree stopped. "*Your* soldiers? Eltana, no one in Salem owns anything, especially soldiers! But this is what it's about for you, isn't it? Revenge for Gari? You don't care one bit for these people. You never really tried to live the Salem way. You harbored resentment and anger all this time, and now you're using these gullible people to try to, what, kill Lemuel Thorne? Is that your goal?"

"Yes!" Mrs. Yordin declared. "For me AND for all these people, and even for you, Mahrree! We kill Thorne, we change the world."

"Change it to what? Not all change is for the best, Eltana, I promise you. The kind of place where bitter old women like you get their way and peace-loving people suddenly want to know how to bleed a man to death is not a place I'd want to live in!"

Mrs. Yordin folded her arms. "You were always so self-righteous," she announced smugly. "Always had to tell everyone else what they were doing wrong and why nothing was ever right. No wonder the world forced you from it. They were sick of listening to you. Everyone in Edge was! And now you're breathing your sanctimonious ranting here."

"Yes, I am." Mahrree spun and headed to a small tower hastily constructed, probably intended to give Mrs. Yordin or whomever else was directing the training a better view.

Mrs. Yordin followed her. "Get away from there!" she shouted as Mahrree quickly climbed the dozen steps to the top. "I won't let you interrupt their training!"

"They don't have to listen," Mahrree said. "But I'm going to talk anyway." She hollered as loudly as she could, "EVERYONE! I ASK ONLY FIVE MINUTES!"

"No!" Mrs. Yordin shouted, climbing up behind Mahrree.

There was room for only one person at the top of the stairs, and Mahrree gripped the railing of the platform in front of her. No one was going to get her to move until she had her five minutes.

"She has no right to speak to you!" Mrs. Yordin called as she struggled to get past Mahrree. Later Mahrree considered how comical it must have been to see two gray-haired women trying to find their muscles. Mahrree won out of sheer stubbornness.

"I have every right to speak!" Mahrree shouted. The would-be fighters stopped to watch the commotion at the small tower. "This isn't the world, Eltana. Everyone here has a right to speak. Now, they don't have to *listen* to me—that's *their* right—but I'm taking my five minutes!" She slapped Mrs. Yordin's hand.

Mrs. Yordin pulled back and scowled.

"Now," Mahrree shouted at the thousands of Salemites who couldn't help but be attracted by the scuffle at the small tower. "I'm here to ask you, what in the world all of you think you are doing?! This is madness! Why are your children here? You really want them to witness your deaths? And die themselves?"

"That won't happen!" someone called. "We're prepared!"

And suddenly it hit her: the reason she was there. The reason why she didn't leave with Relf yesterday or the others this morning. The reason why she couldn't go with Perrin when he died.

So startled by the revelation that she nearly blurted, "I can't believe I've been so dense!" But she kept those words in her head because she didn't need Eltana agreeing with her. Mahrree had stayed alive in order to remain as a witness against the world; so that she could warn these stupid, *stupid* people about what was coming.

As she gazed across the field, she recognized a great many of the pretending soldiers. Nearly everyone in the past twenty-five years had taken her History of the World course or had read her text. No one in Salem had more credibility about the world than she did. She'd been preserved for this moment: to bring these senseless people back to their senses.

"And what are you prepared *for*?" she demanded. "You have no idea what battle is like, no idea how it feels to have a sword slice through you and only injure you, not kill you. No idea what it's like to run terrified from someone larger and stronger—"

"No one is larger and stronger than us!" someone else shouted, and hundreds loudly agreed.

"You're willing to bet your lives on that?" she yelled, and the crowd fell silent. "Because that's what you're doing. The world's scrawniest soldier will be able to slice in half that gangly boy right there with a sword." It was an exaggeration but the pain of battle wasn't.

The young teenager she pointed at squirmed.

"I don't understand why you're doing this. Someone, please, explain this. Not you, Eltana—a real Salemite."

"For our homes!" someone shouted. "Our farms, flocks, everything we need to survive!"

"That's what General Shin told us to fight for," called another man. The crowd shouted in approval.

Mahrree held up her hands. "I know General Shin told you that, but he wasn't referring to the Last Day. He was trying to keep you safe *until* this day. Don't you remember the words of the guides? This is not your battle to fight—it's the Creator's. If you ignore His plan, you fail His plan!"

"I won't do it!" said another man. "I won't leave behind everything we've worked so hard to build. And not just for me, but for my congregation, my family, my neighbors—I can't just abandon all that we have."

"Why not?" Mahrree said.

A man in the middle shouted, "Why not? Do you have any idea how hard it is to start again?"

"As a matter of fact, I do!" Mahrree told him, and nearly grinned as she realized how perfectly the Creator had prepared her for this moment. "I know *exactly* what it's like to leave a home I love, to leave books that I considered my closest friends, to say good-bye to memories, possessions, the graves of all those I loved, and to have nothing more than the clothing on my back to walk to a future that I knew nothing about."

The crowd was silent as she continued. They'd heard her story before in her class, but not told quite like this. Today, it was more than just history.

"Twenty-seven years ago I came to Salem, nervous and at times terrified as to what I would find. All I knew was that the Creator told us to go, and in faith I went. Not blindly, because every previous time I followed His plan, He was right.

"I ran through the forest in the darkest night I've ever seen, with hazards on either side, the army right behind me, and a lightning storm before me. But I came out of it safely and my faith stronger than ever. And then I came to Salem, which was a far greater life than I could've ever imagined. Now, none of that would have happened if I had said to the Creator, 'No thanks—I think I'll just handle the army on my own.' I realize you're worried, but staying here and fighting is far more terrifying than trusting in the Creator!

"Soon I'll be making that journey again," Mahrree's voice threatened to quaver but she held it strong. "I'll weep when I again leave my beloved house, when I walk for the last time through our orchard and garden, when I touch for the last time the boulder over my husband's grave. But I know that whatever sacrifice the Creator asks of me, He will reward me again a hundred times over.

"So what if you lose your homes? Your flocks and property which you *don't even own*? Isn't the risk of losing your souls worse? There's a saying in the world: It doesn't matter how you begin the race but how you end it. How tragic it'd be if you've spent your entire lives living as the Creator wanted you to, then now, at the very end of the race, you jump off the path and ignore all that you've been taught? Why fail the Plan now?"

Mahrree knew she was saying the right things. Her chest burned and she felt such energy she could have flown right off the small tower. She watched their eyes as she spoke. So many were hardened and impenetrable, but others' eyes were softening.

"How do you know this isn't His plan?" one man demanded.

Mahrree firmed her grip on the railing. Her five minutes were probably up but she didn't care. "Guide Zenos declared just the other afternoon that this is the coming of the Last Day. I was there, and so were many of you when he prophesied that anyone who fights—Salemites or the army—will die. What more do you need?"

"I don't believe him," a man near the front shouted. "This can't be it—"

"How can it NOT be it?" Mahrree shouted, throwing her hands in the air. "Have all of you missed the signs? Land tremors! Deceit awakened! Famine in the world! Now the army marching upon the Creator's chosen? THIS IS IT, PEOPLE!"

To her relief, many of the women sitting with their children over to the side began to nod.

"Professor Shin's right!" one mother said loudly. "I know it. I've known it all along. I don't want to be here," she called to Mahrree apologetically, "and neither do my children. It's just that my husband—"

"Hush, woman!" a man, apparently her husband, shouted at her, and immediately looked embarrassed by his outburst.

"NO!" she called back, boldly standing up.

Mahrree wanted to cheer but instead clenched her hands in hopeful fists by her face.

"No, you said this wasn't the Last Day," his wife shouted, and clearly uncomfortable to do so, especially in front of a crowd. "You said that once the army destroys everything we'll have to rebuild again. But I know that's not right! I've been trying to convince myself to believe you, but I can't. I'm sorry, but the Creator comes before you."

"Before your own husband?" he bellowed in surprise.

"The Creator will never lead me astray," she said. "But *you* have."

"Why, you—" he started charging for his wife who stood in the large group of women, but many more women rose up like a shield in front of her.

He stopped, unsure of how to continue against a line of irate women.

"I believe Professor Shin too!" announced one of them. "And I'm taking my children with me." More women got up, probably a hundred, pulling their children by the hands and standing rebelliously against a line of men who didn't know what do to next. Violence, especially against one's spouse, was quite unheard of in Salem.

Mahrree bit her lip, the tension was thickening by the second. "Choose to take them to the ancient temple site, men!" she encouraged. "Bring your wives and children to safety. You still have time!"

A couple of men in the crowd of thousands glanced at her, then started in jogs to their wives. Mahrree beamed as one young man broke through the line of men holding pitchforks and rushed to his wife. Without a word he grabbed her by the hand, snatched his little boy with his other, and continued on without once looking back.

Many of the wives cheered and were joined by another husband, then another, until about thirty or forty men had left their places in training to rejoin their wives.

They didn't get to leave easily, though. Once the body of would-be soldiers saw the deserters in their ranks, they grabbed the men trying to leave. The deserters thrashed and even punched their way through the lines to reach their wives who were shouting encouragement.

Mahrree stared in awe and horror at the sight. Never before had she seen anyone in Salem try to stop another person from making a choice, especially the right one. Never before had she seen grown men in Salem come to blows, but now fighting was breaking out in a dozen places.

She bit her fist and prayed fervently for the men trying to reach their families. Each husband seemed to grow stronger as he neared, plowing through lines of angry Salemites and finally reaching the women on the other side. Each man who wanted to leave made it through, took his wife and family, and walked swiftly toward Salem.

"It's only a few!" Mrs. Yordin shouted to the remaining army.

Mahrree had forgotten she was still standing behind her. "We still have thousands left!"

"Thousands left who will miss the Last Day!" Mahrree shouted louder.

Many in the throng shook their heads. "We're missing nothing! Everyone will see the Last Day. Or have YOU not read The Writings lately?"

Mahrree firmed her stance as thousands of men sniggered at her. "You're remembering it wrong. All of the FAITHFUL will see the Last Day. You, each of you here, refusing the Creator's help and insisting on doing things your own way, you are *no longer faithful*! If you continue, this path will only earn you a spot in the dark deserts of the Creator's prison. While your families and friends are in Paradise with the Creator, you'll be alone with your regret, tormented by what you *could* have been, what you *could* have done, if only you had remained faithful until the Last Day. Is a couple of sheep or a shelter of wood really worth losing your place with your family in Paradise?"

From her vantage point, Mahrree could see a few more men on the edges sneak away. She stared down the mob, trying to find more men willing to listen, willing to remember.

But the decision to step away from the crowd was intensely intimidating. To walk away meant to be completely alone. If only she could help them realize they weren't alone, because some of the men who left noticed each other and quickly banded together. If only the ones in the middle could see that, she was sure more would make the difficult decision to abandon their friends. They'd find help, almost immediately.

But first, they had to make that difficult decision on their own.

She could tell that many more recognized the truth, but the longer they stood with the multitude, the light of that truth began to dim. Soon they would be able to convince themselves that she never said anything real, because the truth was too hard to take. It was just easier to follow the crowd. Follow it to their destruction.

"Your five minutes are up, Mahrree," Mrs. Yordin said coldly behind her.

"And your time is growing short, too!" Mahrree yelled. "If you feel what I am saying is true, LEAVE! If not now, then before the army arrives. It's still not too late, but soon it will be! Wives and children, get out while you can, even if you go alone—"

"Mahrree! Get off my tower!"

She sighed. There was nothing more to say. But it was all right, she decided. She'd fulfilled the reason for her remaining behind: several hundred people were now swiftly making their way back to Salem. She'd preserved a few more families and maybe more would find their courage as well.

She pushed passed Mrs. Yordin and trotted down the steps back to the wagon where Choruk was waiting.

"Just can't stay away from the debating arena, can you, Mahrree?" Mrs. Yordin called after her. "I can't imagine why you keep doing this, seeing how often you fail."

Mahrree didn't respond but kept walking.

"Don't listen to her, Mahrree," Assistant Choruk said as he kept his glare fixed on Eltana. "By my rough count, nearly four hundred people have left because of your words." He shifted his gaze to her and smiled. "That's a fantastic success. Better than Guide Zenos, but don't tell him I'm making comparisons. He got maybe fifty to leave."

Mahrree smiled resignedly and allowed him to help her up into the wagon. "Well, I feel like I accomplished something today. There are many children who are now going to have their fathers at the end of everything, whereas ten minutes ago that might not have been the case. I only wish we could have reached more," she said wistfully. "I wish I could *still* do more to help the rest get where they need to be."

"Don't we all," Choruk sighed. "If I were a betting man, I'd bet that several more of them will desert that ridiculous army. I think you've done a lot more good than you think you have. Time will show just how much more."

Young Pere smirked. Another wall.

Next to him, Cloud Man chuckled. Reg, Buddy, and Pal smiled miserably at it.

Teach, being supported by Hammer and Iron, groaned loudly. Snarl just curled a lip, and Sergeant Beaved shook his head as he said, "These Salemites of yours are something else, Young Pere."

"Yes, they are," Young Pere grinned. "They can erect a three bedroom house in just days. They willingly work together to harvest crops, shear sheep, and weave blankets so they have plenty of time to spend the afternoon and evening dancing and eating and laughing together." He stared at the wall as if he could see it all again.

"You admire them, don't you?" Beaved whispered.

"I do," Young Pere said in a hushed tone. "I miss them. I never realized how much until just now."

"And they don't steal people away, do they?"

The entire security team was now listening.

Young Pere smiled. "Actually, they do! But only because they want to be stolen. *Rescued.* Thousands of people have fled the world over the years. It all began with Guide Pax, the one the king's guards supposedly killed. But he didn't die. He was running away from the king, 165 years ago now. And all those who were called Guarders back then? Just families. Terrorized, threatened families who hated what they saw in the world and ran away to something better. They started Salem as a place of peace. The name is even a code, and it stands for Safety Assured Leaving East of Medicetti. *Salem.*"

He ignored Teach frowning, and Iron asking quietly, "Where's Medicetti? How could this be east? East of what?"

Young Pere continued staring at the wall as if they were his family. "They arrived with nothing and then built everything. What's not to admire about that?"

Sergeant Beaved exhaled. "What's waiting for us on the other side of all these walls, Young Pere?"

"Not an army, I promise that," Young Pere said.

Snarl folded his arms. "So why do you keep saying we'll all die?"

Young Pere finally pulled his eyes away to focus on Snarl. "The Creator delivered our ancestors here. He promised the valley would remain safe until the Last Day. Then He would destroy those who tried to destroy His people."

Snarl scoffed. "Another vial head. You did them, didn't you? I can see the scars on your ears. Only vial heads get tagged. You can have relapses of visions for years. 'Ooh, the Creator is coming!'" he waved his hands in the air. "'He's coming to get us! Run, run!'"

Hammer and Iron laughed nervously, almost apologetically, while Buddy, Pal, and Reg looked between Young Pere and Snarl, who had slept soundly through Colonel Offra's all-night readings.

Cloud Man looked up and wondered where the clouds went.

The rest of the forty men sent to follow Young Pere were now gravitating nearer to listen.

"I've heard that, too," Teach said, folding his arms. "And not just from Offra, but from older folks. They used to talk a lot about the Creator. But Shin, those stories were concocted by our ancestors who used to live in the west before they settled in Idumea and branched out to the villages. They poisoned those western lands, the ones *you* wanted to go find. Scholars concluded that the so-called 'Creator' was just a regular man, the mastermind and leader of those first thousand settlers. He was a clever dictator who died three years later."

Young Pere tipped his head at Teach. "Does it give you comfort to believe that story?"

Teach's shoulders twitched. "I suppose so."

"And I get comfort from my version," Young Pere said easily. "I won't tell you what to believe. That's not Salem's way. But I will give you all the evidence I have and let you draw your own conclusions. The first Great Guide predicted that all of this," he gestured as best he could with the chains confining him, "would happen, and two later guides verified it, seeing the same things. The land tremors, the eruption, the famine, and now the march on Salem. If all of this has happened, why won't the coming of the Last Day happen too?

"I choose to believe He will fight this battle, Teach," Young Pere went on to a captive audience. "How He'll do it, or who He'll choose to do it, I don't know. I rather hope He lets me help should I live so long. *That* gives me comfort. And Snarl, laugh all you want, I don't care. Your opinions don't affect my beliefs." He turned back to the wall. "I just want to get over this and back to Salem. I always like sitting on the front row for the best shows."

Beaved, smiling faintly, waved to the soldiers behind them. "Thirty of you head back to Thorne. Tell him we've found another wall. This must be the way."

It was afternoon and Mahrree was dreading the moment. Still, she put on the well-practiced Dinner smile matching the fake smiles of the Briters, Shins, and Zenoses.

Shem was standing a little way off, quietly speaking to his oldest grandson Briter. The rest of the grandchildren and their children were arranging themselves on the ten horses and figuring out who would walk. There was no point in taking the wagon. They would have to abandon it in less than a mile anyway, as the Cadbys had done yesterday. The route that began from the hills beyond the Briters' pasture area was less than four miles to the ancient site, albeit steep in some places.

That four miles up the mountain was the concern for Eraliz and the smaller grandchildren. The families heading out now hoped to make it to the ancient site by nightfall, but should Eraliz—on a horse led by Holling—begin to suffer pains again, the party would camp for the night on a high sheltered plateau halfway to the site. The morning light would illuminate the steeper areas on the approach to the ancient site. For now, Eraliz's pains had subsided, after receiving a blessing from Uncle Peto, but no one wanted to rush unnecessarily. Salema would keep a close watch on her the entire way.

Mahrree hugged and kissed each little and big face, and went around again just to make sure no one was skipped or hadn't been told by their Muggah that she loved them. She smacked Bubba Briter on the arm when he declared she was getting as bad as his cousins' Grandma Trovato, then gave him a third hug just to prove the point.

Barnos Shin told his cousin that Muggah smelled better than his Grandma Trovato, and gave her another hug.

"It's not for long, Muggah," he assured her.

Cambo put an arm around her. "We'll save you a good spot. I know you don't want to miss any of the excitement."

"She could just come now," Holling suggested. "We're traveling slowly anyway."

Mahrree put her hands on her hips. "What, I'm that slow now?"

The family laughed and Hycy shook her head. "No, Muggah. It's just that . . ."

Mahrree kissed baby Jothan again. "You say hi to your great-great-grandpa for me. We got word that Old Jothan left yesterday, so knowing him he's sitting at the edge of the cliff watching for someone to come walking in."

Wes nodded. "He went with my older brother and his family. Great Grandma Asrar is heading up today. She's not in a hurry, but my great-grandpa's just a little excited."

Mahrree grinned. "See? I'm not the only one excited for the Last Day. Now, all of you, off with you!"

Cambo tried one last time. "Come with us, Muggah. Go sit with Mr. Hifadhi. The two of you have plenty of stories from the good old days in Edge to exaggerate in the retelling, I'm sure."

"Not yet," Mahrree whispered.

Hycy sighed. "I know I'd feel better with you by our side. I still remember that hot afternoon when I came out to weed a pumpkin patch with you." She looked meaningfully at her cousin Viddrow.

He smiled back. "I remember that afternoon. We were *thirteen*."

All of the cousins chuckled quietly. They knew what happened at thirteen, when they learned more details about their grandmother's past, first from General Shin, then 'corrected' by Professor Shin.

Mahrree looked down at the ground, slightly embarrassed by everyone towering over her.

"I believe," Viddrow continued, "that I began with something casual and nonchalant, such as, 'So, you really destroyed the world?'"

Everyone chuckled again, having tried a similarly suave-yet-stumbling way of approaching the small woman they thought was merely their Muggah.

"I remember being traumatized to hear you were 'the most dangerous woman in the world.'" Hycy recalled. "Muggah, I'd love to have such a dangerous woman sitting next to me at the site tonight."

Finally Mahrree looked up, and it was to roll her eyes. "Now, I *really* don't know where that came from: most dangerous woman in the world? Ha!"

Her grandchildren laughed at her overly dramatic expression.

"That was Hogal's title. He was your great, great, great . . ." Mahrree paused to count out. "Well, you know. Uncle Hogal Densal. A most enthusiastic and occasionally exaggerating rector. Supposedly he was quite earnest when he told your grandfather that's what he thought about me, but then again, I was expecting Peto at the time and was prone to rather unpredictable mood swings—"

Her grandchildren smiled obligingly at the story they'd heard so many times before.

Mahrree felt embarrassed again. She was just an old woman who bored her descendants with the same old stories, and they politely acted as if it was the first time they'd heard them.

She stood as tall as she could. "I may have *helped* change the world so many years ago because I couldn't keep my mouth shut and yelled at some administrator's assistant, but I assure you, I'm *not* dangerous. I've never made a man shake in his boots. Except for occasionally your grandfather."

They chuckled again. They would have done anything to get her to go with them. She couldn't understand why, though. She really didn't do that much for them. Likely they were trying to do their parents a favor. All the attention was making her uncomfortable.

"Best be going, everyone. No more waiting."

"Then Muggah," Salema narrowed her eyes, "what are *you*

waiting for?"

Mahrree sighed and glanced at the distant southern canyon, then back at her adult grandchildren. "*He's* coming," she whispered. "The scouts have seen him. He's shackled, but he'll be the first over that wall at the canyon entrance. I plan to go with him to the ancient site. With him and my husband."

Her grandchildren looked at each other with skepticism.

Hycy patted her grandmother's arm. "Muggah, Young Pere knows the way. He even bragged he could do it with his eyes closed."

Cambo nodded. "He even did it once, for most of a day."

Barnos chuckled along with his cousins. "He tripped a few times but he never took the blindfold off."

Mahrree didn't smile. "He's been walking blind for long enough." Her somber tone quieted her grandchildren. "When I get up there, it'll be with Young Pere and Perrin, I know it. Somehow, he'll escape, he'll find his way here . . . I refuse to let him come to an empty house."

Hycy sighed. "That's how Mama feels."

"And my mama," Salema added. "And as I've heard Papa Shem say on more than one occasion, I don't like it, Mahrree Shin. I don't like it one bit." She hugged her grandmother one last time. "But as the mother of three sons, I do understand."

Mahrree pulled out The Dinner Smile again. "Then mount up! Your children are happy and napped, but that won't last long."

Reluctantly, her grandchildren headed for their horses while Briter and Fennic Zenos ran over to Mahrree.

She squatted, ignoring the cracking of her knees, and hugged them both. "Be good! Have fun! I love you!"

Fennic gave Mahrree a kiss on her cheek and took off running to the pack horse he would share with Briter. As Lek put him on, Mahrree turned to Briter's sober face.

"Grandpa Shem said you're happy about the Last Day," he said.

"I am, Briter. I have been for a long time. It will be scary at times, I know, but it will also be amazing. My father has already told me I'll get to see him again. He's counting the seconds."

Briter chanced a small smile. "Really?"

"I haven't seen him since I was fifteen, so I can hardly wait."

Briter glanced back to his five-year-old brother. "Fennic thinks Puggah will be there."

"I know he will be, Briter," her voice trembled at the idea. "Somehow, sometime, we'll both know he's there. I promise it will be wonderful."

"So, Muggah, why is everyone afraid? Why are some people staying to fight?"

She sighed. "That's a good question, Briter. I don't really know. I guess we're afraid because we don't know what's coming next."

"But you're old! You're supposed to know everything."

She grinned. "I wish that were true. But there are still lots of things I don't know. But this I know: your papa and mama and grandparents will do all they can to take care of you. You may still have scary moments, but in the end it will be all wonderful. Can you be brave until the end? I believe every story has a happy ending, if you just wait long enough."

Briter pondered that for a moment, then nodded.

Mahrree kissed him. "I love you, Briter. Now go and save me a spot with a good view."

Briter kissed her cheek and ran to his father. Lek lifted him and put him behind Fennic. Salema was already seated on a horse, while Deck checked the belt securing Salema's youngest son, Plump Perrin, in front of her. Lek took the reins of the horse and waved one last time to Mahrree.

A few moments later the train of horses, grandchildren, and great-grandchildren started the trek north, then west. The three sets of grandparents and one great-grandmother waved and watched silently until their descendants climbed the hill and out of view.

"Sun's going down soon," Cloud Man noticed.

"It just gets darker in the canyons sooner than anywhere else," Young Pere explained. "But Sergeant, I think it would be a good idea to find a place to camp. We shouldn't go any further today. We can't, actually."

Beaved looked around. "This is a pretty good area. We can stop at the next wall."

"That should be coming up soon," Reg said. He, Buddy, and Pal had jogged ahead earlier to see how many more walls there were. When they saw the next one in a narrow, steep passage, fifty feet high and requiring a system of ropes to climb it, they already knew Salem would wait at least one more day. As the afternoon had advanced, the walls had become higher, making their progress even slower.

Beaved glanced behind them. Thorne and his accompaniment were only a few minutes behind. "Snarl, go tell the general we think we should stop at the next wall for the night. Let the rest of the army try to catch up while we figure out a way to fashion ropes."

Snarl rolled his eyes like a pouty teenager and slowly started back to Thorne.

"I don't like him," Cloud Man said quietly to Young Pere. "He's not a nice man."

"Because he doesn't like vial heads like us?"

Cloud Man shrugged at that. "Tell me more about the jobs people have," he said, changing the subject. "Some people have different jobs every year?"

Teach picked up his step to get closer to Young Pere. Hammer, Iron, Buddy, Pal, and Reg were already there, intrigued to hear more about life in Salem. Young Pere had spent the afternoon telling them the way Salem *really* was.

"You can have any kind of job, and someone's always willing to train you in doing it. Before I joined the army I worked with a rancher, scout, doctor, and even spent some time with men who used to serve in the Army of Idumea, all to help me decide what I wanted to do first. Some people stay with a job for years, others change all the time. And there aren't specific jobs for men or women. I knew women doctors and men basket weavers, women shepherds and men quilt makers. Whatever you want to explore and try, you can."

None of the soldiers replied for a moment, lost in the idea.

Eventually Teach cleared his throat. "How can women be smart enough to be doctors?"

"I suppose you could ask that of the president of the Salem university," Young Pere said slyly. "*She* could probably explain it to you." Seeing Teach's aghast expression, he continued. "Half of the professors are female. The head of the history department was a little old woman, about seventy-four now." Young Pere smiled at the thought. "She even wrote the textbooks, updating them every few years. What everyone in Salem knows about the world comes from her and those from the world she interviews."

Teach grunted. "Huh," was all he could come up with.

"So there's really no shops?" Reg asked. "I still can't get over that. You just walk into a storehouse and they give you whatever you want?"

Young Pere nodded. "Within reason. If you have a need, they'll fill it. Food, clothing, house—whatever."

"For free?"

"For free. Everyone works, everyone benefits."

Beaved shook his head. "I can't imagine a life without worrying about getting paid."

"Sounds kind of nice to me," Cloud Man smiled.

Buddy nodded. "To me, too."

Pal shrugged. "I just don't think it would work. How can it? Gold and silver is what makes the world do things."

"Not in Salem," Young Pere said. "Care for each other makes Salemites do things."

Iron scoffed. "I don't believe it. It's not possible."

"Believe or don't believe," Young Pere said. "Salem isn't hampered by your inability to believe in it."

"I can't believe in elephants!" Hammer said.

"Seriously, Shin? You know men who have touched elephants?" Pal said.

Young Pere grinned. It was easier and easier to smile whenever he thought about Salem. "One even climbed on top of a big male! He didn't *stay* there long, but—"

"So how far away are they?" Beaved asked, glancing behind him to see how much longer they had until the general caught up.

"One thousand, four hundred miles . . . about," Young Pere said.

Hammer scoffed. "But no one can travel that far without dying!"

"Sure they can," Young Pere said easily. "Salem has sent nine expeditions in the last twenty years. Before that, two different groups even went all the way around the world. It's twenty-four thousand miles around, with huge lands and larger seas, and animals and trees and flowers and glaciers and deserts and even more ruins no one has ever imagined before! There are hundreds of men in Salem who have gone on the expeditions, along with several dozen women. Scientists, writers, explorers, artists—they've written books, drawn pictures, made full-size paintings of the animals, and seen all kinds of things you can't even dream about."

Beaved exhaled. "That's just . . . just. . . too . . ."

"Ridiculous!" Teach exclaimed. "Can't be true! Elephants are mythical."

"What about wapiti, Teach?" Young Pere asked.

"Mythical as well."

"Teach, what if I told you I've seen wapiti? We call them elk, though."

"I'd call you a liar, Shin. You think Thorne weaves a good story? Yours are preposterous."

Young Pere grinned. "I've also *eaten* wapiti. Great jerky. I hope we'll find a herd of them in the hills near Salem. The forests here are dead, but further north we should be able to find some preposterous animals for you."

Teach grunted again and looked around for hiding elk.

"Young Pere," Buddy elbowed him, "what about lions? Are they real?"

"Yep! And zebras, too. Black and white striped horses. Very un-ridable, though. Better success with the elephants."

Buddy chuckled while Cloud Man sighed. "Let's go there, Young Pere. Right now! A little more than a thousand miles? That's not too far. We could do it in a few seasons, right?"

"Faster than that, Cloudy, with the right animals and supplies."

Beaved eyed him. "*That's* how you know so much about the western lands, isn't it? You've probably even been there!"

Young Pere winked at him. "Twice. And I've eaten byson."

"I'll go with you, Young Pere," Cloud Man decided. "To find those elephants. Can we get supplies from the storehouses?"

"Sure. Let's first get this little problem of the Last Day out of the way, then it's you and me, Cloudy. Far west until we find elephants."

Cloud Man grinned and several of the soldiers chuckled at his eagerness.

They heard a whistle and looked back at the general. He was gesturing for them to set up camp there. He could see the wall and it was obvious they were going no farther that day.

"No more talking about the future," Cloud Man said in a low voice to Young Pere. "I don't want Thorne to hear you. He might want to go with us to find the elephants, but he'd be no fun at all."

Young Pere almost laughed.

"It's getting dark, isn't it?" said one of the fifteen soldiers lost in the canyon.

They had walked for hours looking for an outlet but found none. So they continued in a slightly downhill manner hoping to find something, but only encountered more mountains, more canyons, more twists and turns.

The sergeant sighed. "I noticed that a few minutes ago. There's no hope of returning to the rest of the army," he said, looking behind him. It wasn't as if he knew the way, either. He lost track of which way to go back about two hours ago but didn't dare admit it.

Another man smiled. "I don't mind. We can camp here with far more space and *silence.*"

"Yes!" another soldier agreed. "I swear, some men never sleep, and are determined to not let anyone else sleep either." He glared at the other men around him to make sure none of them were that kind.

They all held up their hands, offering no argument.

"And I don't think Offra knows where we are, either," suggested another man.

Their sergeant smiled. "Well, then. I suppose we will enjoy a quiet night here under the stars and in . . . I really have no idea where we are," he confessed.

"Does it matter, sir?"

"No, it doesn't. I think we deserve an early night. Any objections?"

There were none.

Shem heard a strange sound coming from his bedroom as he made his way up the stairs. He quietly pushed open the door and saw his wife sitting on the bed, her shoulders shaking.

"Calla, my love? Are you crying?"

She quickly wiped her face and turned to him with a sweet smile. "No, not at all."

Shem sat down and wrapped his arms around her. "Salemites are such terrible liars."

She snuggled into his chest. "I'm sorry, Shemmy. I just feel so empty. Lek and Salema and the boys, Meiki and Clyde, then tomorrow Boskos and Noria—one part of me knows all of this is right and good, but another part of me looks at their quiet houses and . . . they're all gone. I just can't get past this horrible feeling. *All* of Salem is vanishing. All that we've built, it's just waiting for the worst—it's all ending, *everything*! I just . . . I shouldn't put this on you—"

"Oh, Calla, Calla," he said, rocking her. "You're the one I worry about the most, yet I'm hardly ever here with you. I've been neglecting you, haven't I?"

"No, no. You've always cared for everyone and everything. I'm happy to share you."

He kissed her again. "You're amazing, you know that?"

"Shem?" She sat up and wiped her nose. "When are you going?"

"When the solid black banner flies. I promise. That's what Perrin always said. When Thorne or the army is spotted, the black banners fly and the tower men leave. So will Peto and I. We'll keep Clark 14 and Silver saddled and waiting for that moment."

Calla pulled away. "Only two horses?"

"Yes, why?"

"What about me?"

"Deck said he'll personally choose the horses for you, Lilla, Jaytsy, and Mahrree. The fields before the route beyond his pasture are filling with abandoned horses and wagons. He's going tomorrow morning to retrieve the most steady mounts he can find. I really wished I could see Mahrree on a horse again," he chuckled.

"Shem."

"Yes?"

"Tell him to find a fast Clark for me, too. I can still ride, you know."

"Of course you can, but when Deck takes you—"

"No, Shemmy. That's not what we discussed."

Shem sighed. "I know what we discussed, but you're going with Deck. Zaddick and Cephas have already agreed to help him when Deck says it's time. We've decided that—"

"Wait a minute—*you've* decided? As in you and Deck?"

"And Peto," Shem confessed. "We discussed it earlier this evening. Deck and Zad will choose horses from the base of the route, bring them to the barns tomorrow morning, then . . . you're leaving. All of you. The children as well, by midday meal. Peto and I will remain to see the black banner rise. Calla, it's going to happen very soon."

"NO!" she shouted at him.

Shem nearly fell off the bed in surprise.

"You and me! We've discussed this! Lilla won't go either, not without Peto and—" She stopped.

"And Young Pere?" Shem asked.

"Mahrree won't go until she sees him coming home. She won't leave without Perrin."

Shem closed his eyes. "You women are the most stubborn,

illogical—"

"We're illogical and stubborn because we love our equally stubborn men!" Calla declared.

Shem began to chuckle. "Yes, we're stubborn, too. And I'm going to *win* this one, Calla Trovato Zenos."

"Oh, I'd like to see you try!"

"Don't make me pull rank, my love."

Calla narrowed her eyes. "The Guide can't force anyone."

"But the Sergeant Major can. I never retired or turned in my resignation, you know."

Calla began to smile. "You have no authority here."

"Oh, yes I do. I actually have more authority than Lemuel. I've been serving much longer, just *somewhere else*. But in a battle, I'd have seniority."

"So go already," Calla exclaimed. "Go take charge of the Army of Idumea and order them back to Edge!"

Shem grinned. "I've thought of that. Somehow, I don't think they'd listen to me. Jon's planning to give them another disturbing night, but I don't know if they'll listen to him either."

Calla kissed him. "But I listen to you."

"Will you listen now, my love?"

"Shem, I—"

"Don't want me to worry, right? Want me to know that you're safe and secure so that I can rescue any stragglers or Salemite fighters with a sudden change of heart? I won't have to worry about any of my children or nieces and nephews or in-laws because they're already on the trail, several hours ahead of me?"

Calla bit her lip. "You make it sound as if you think they'll make it tomorrow."

"Woodson sent a message this evening," Shem whispered. "The sword banners will go up in the morning, calling for complete evacuation, although I don't think there's anyone left except us at the Eztates and Eltana's army. Cephas reported that Salem is extremely quiet and the routes are packed all the way up the mountains. Calla, the army is only two walls away."

Calla's mouth hung open. "Why didn't you tell us they're so close?"

"We don't need everyone panicking. Whoever is still here needs to sleep well so they can leave first thing in the morning. But Peto and I told Deck."

"Where's Young Pere?"

"Still at the lead, chained, and with nine other men. They stay very close to him. He's doing most of the talking but he's too far away for the scouts to know what he's saying. Thorne and his contingency are following at a safe distance, as if they think any attacks will hit Young Pere and his group first."

Calla actually growled. "Sending Young Pere first as bait! If I ever get my hands on that Thorne—"

"You're not going to."

Calla grumbled under her breath.

Shem blinked at her rancor. "I don't know when I've ever seen you like this."

"Shem, the happiness of my little sister rests in Lemuel's hands! If he destroys Young Pere after letting him get so close to home—"

Shem took her arms. "It's all in the *Creator's* hands, Calla. Do you believe that?"

She took a deep breath. "Yes. I do."

"Then there's nothing more we can do except go with Deck when he tells you it's time. Peto and I may be elsewhere when the banners rise, but Deck has promised to stay here and get everyone moving. Remember, he has a bullwhip and I don't know of another man more accurate than him. I've given him permission to use it."

Calla leaned against her husband. "Don't let anything happen to you. Remember, I want to stand next to you on the Last Day."

He kissed her again. "Guide Gleace told me I'd be there, remember? Peto and I both. You don't need to worry about us. Just save us a good spot, all right? I don't want to miss any of it."

"All right, Shemmy. I'll go with Deck. I'll even force Lilla to go, and Mahrree. Although Deck will likely need to pull out his calf roping skills to get them to go."

That night Mahrree looked out the dark windows to an even darker Salem. Its light was leaving, heading up the routes.

Nearly every section of Salem was on the move now. By dawn the last of Salem would be walking west, if anyone was left. Many had scurried out at nightfall, wanting to sleep in the cover of the forest just in case. In a strange way, Mahrree thought, it was happening so fast. The end was coming, very soon.

She peered out the windows hoping to see if there was any other candlelight like hers out there, flickering. But there was nothing.

Then again, it was also very late, so whoever was still around was probably already trying to sleep in order to get an early start in the morning. But how anyone could sleep with the knowledge that this was their last night in their beds, *ever*, she couldn't imagine. They must be up, just like her, looking out their windows one last time, maybe even seeing her candlelight and wondering what she was doing to pass the long hours.

Reading, but even The Writings couldn't keep her focus, although she felt the need to keep them open on her lap.

She sighed and looked at the page. The first horse riders. She wasn't too keen about that. Instead she thumbed through the pages, letting them flip through her fingers. What *should* she be reading on her last night in her beloved dream house? The book fell open at a page, and she shook her head at it. Not *that* one.

She thumbed through the book again, and again it fell open at the same spot. Maybe because she read it so often in the last year and a half.

Still not wanting to address those words, she once again tried to look for something else, then suddenly found herself unable to move. The Writings, falling open yet again to the same determined page, demanded to be read. Every surface of her body tingled with it—*read this now.*

Mahrree's mouth went dry as she smoothed the paper.

Before the Last Day even the aged of my people will strike terror in the deadened hearts of the fiercest soldiers.

On the Last Day those who have no power shall discover the greatest power is all around them.

On the Last Day those who stayed true to The Plan will be delivered as the destroyer comes.

I have created this Test, I have given this Plan, and I will reward my faithful children.

The words hit her with such a force she could barely breathe. Especially the first line.

Before the Last Day even the *aged* of my people will strike terror in the deadened hearts of the fiercest soldiers.

She couldn't pull her eyes from that line, her mind repeating it again and again without her willing it to. Each word seemed different tonight, and all together they created something very specific and deliberate. And very pointed, as if straight at her.

The last time that passage hit her so strongly was the morning after Perrin proposed to her. She had read it, felt something heavy overcome her, so she slammed shut the book in complete surprise. Then she opened it again and started reading from the very beginning—**We are all family**—and giddily began to think about starting a family with Perrin.

Also interestingly, that night when Perrin proposed so many years ago was the first time that she dreamed about this beautiful house with the weathered gray wood and window boxes filled with herbs.

And now she was sitting in that very house, lingering over the memory of the first time that passage hit her, as if she'd completed an enormous loop and she'd come back to the beginning of it, and if she reached out she could span the forty-six years and tap her twenty-eight-year-old shoulder, give herself a wink, and start it all over again.

For the first time, Mahrree realized how significant that night was so many years ago. Not because she and Perrin had started on a life more abundant and adventurous than she ever could have imagined, but because she'd been given two glimpses into her future.

One glimpse was the house and the more than a dozen children—her twenty-five grandchildren and ever increasing numbers of great-grandchildren—running around in its gardens.

But the other glimpse was one she had ignored all those years ago. And that was all right, because she wasn't meant to remember it until tonight.

She looked at the calendar on the wall and considered the date. The 33rd Day of Planting Season. She searched her memory to see if it might have been significant. It was a few days after the land tremor so many years ago, and a couple weeks before Jaytsy's birthday, and her and Deck's anniversary. Perrin didn't propose until the 39th Day . . . Maybe the date didn't matter.

Before the Last Day even the aged of my people will strike terror

in the deadened hearts of the fiercest soldiers.

She couldn't stop staring at the words which in the past she'd always skimmed, assuming they were symbolic, or indicative of an overall attitude . . .

Because the following lines were always much more intriguing, especially the tantalizing idea of the Deliverer and who that might be. She had to admit that a few times she wondered if it couldn't have been her own husband.

But after Perrin passed, Mahrree finally deduced the Deliverer's identity: it was Shem. He had delivered the Shins and so many other families, so of course there was no one else who it could be, and Mahrree couldn't have been happier about that.

But had Shem figured that out? Doubtful. He'd never assume such an honor for himself. Not until the Last Day would he probably put it all together, and even then the Creator would most likely have to point His Great Finger and call down from the sky: *Yes, Shem Zenos—It Is You!*

Mahrree chuckled to herself, but annoyingly found her eyes drawn to the first line of the passage yet again.

Before the Last Day even the aged of my people will strike terror in the deadened hearts of the fiercest soldiers.

Specifically the words, **even the aged.**

Try as she might, she couldn't force her eyes beyond that line.

The words settled on her with such a gentle yet overwhelming force that she felt it in every fiber.

Yes, Mahrree Peto Shin. The Aged of My People Who Will Strike Terror—It Is You.

She slammed the book shut.

"Oh, slagging Zenoses, *not again!*" Teach moaned.

They had just made themselves as comfortable as possible in the canyon, laying out their bedrolls up against each other to make enough room for all of the soldiers trying to find a horizontal place to sleep. Young Pere's security team had circled around him, Snarl already snoring, when the voice came drifting down to them.

Jon Offra had another position on the summit above them and was calling down something new. Young Pere grinned as he recognized the prophecy of Guide Pax, and what the guide saw when he first set eyes upon the massive valley that would become Salem.

"The inhabitants of this new city will live in peace until the end comes, when the enemy will threaten to annihilate them."

The echo in the canyon was shorter, but it carried Offra's words well, bouncing between the walls.

"But before that time, the Creator will send one to prepare them. From the highest ranks of the enemy will He call one to mark the path of escape for the valiant."

"Puggah," Young Pere whispered proudly. Ever since he was little he'd been taught those lines were about his grandfather—he'd been named High General when he left the 'ranks of the enemy' to go to Salem and prepare their paths to the ancient temple site.

"The Deliverer will ensure the safety of the Creator's people, until the coming Destruction—"

Somewhere behind him, Thorne sat up. "Offra, SHUT UP!"

Young Pere was sure the quiet snickering he heard nearby came from Sergeant Beaved.

"Nope!" sang down a cheery voice, startling them all. "Because, Lemuel, you need to understand this prophecy. It's referring to the Last Day, and that 'coming destruction'? It's coming to destroy you! *The inhabitants of this new city will live—"*

"Until I destroy them!" Thorne bellowed.

"Shut up already, both of you!" someone further up the canyon bravely shouted back, and Young Pere snorted into his hands as did most everyone else around him. They may not have been standing up to Lemuel Thorne, but they certainly didn't admire or even respect him. And his losing his temper in front of everyone wasn't helping things.

"—will live in peace until the end comes, when the enemy will threaten to annihilate them. Now, Lemuel—I'm going to repeat this passage from Guide Pax only about, oh, a dozen times before I move up the canyon. You've brought a lot of boys with you, haven't you? They all get a bedtime story, all night long if my voice holds out. *But before that time the Creator will send one to prepare them. From the highest ranks of the enemy will He call one to mark the path of escape for the valiant . . ."*

Young Pere fell asleep to the soothing words of Guide Pax and dreamed about going home.

The 34th Day of Planting—a very long day

The sun wouldn't be rising for another couple of hours, but Peto Shin had to do something—*anything*—besides lying in bed staring at the darkness.

"Where are you going?" Lilla asked sleepily as he slipped out of bed.

He kissed her on the cheek. "I'll be back by breakfast. Or midday meal, I promise. I just need to . . . something," he faltered.

There were too many thoughts, too many images for him to even consider resting. This was going to be one of the most significant days the world had ever experienced, and he needed to get an early start on it.

He still didn't think of himself as General Shin, but maybe the descendant of three General Shins could *stop* a war.

If not, it just might be a very long day.

Mahrree slept fitfully that night, likely the last in her beloved house. And it was because she dreamed.

But this was no dream like before, about her weathered gray house and gardens and children. It was much bleaker.

She was on a boat of some sort—really just boards lashed together with rope—and sat gripping them desperately. It was a cloudy night, cold and bleak, and she was balancing precariously on the boards. They bounced and heaved on black waves. She strained to see anything around her, but there was no end to the water. It must have been like the seas she had seen only in paintings; water that went on forever.

But just before her, she could make out something in the distance.

A shore, littered with enormous rocks. Not the most hospitable, but certainly better than the heaving water.

Suddenly she felt a body next to her. She looked over and saw, clinging to the boards with her, Jaytsy. With terror-filled eyes she looked back at her mother.

Mahrree had an idea. "Jaytsy, it's not that far. If you get into the water, I can push you to the shore. Swim your hardest and you'll be all right."

Jaytsy slipped down into the dark wetness. Mahrree gave her a push, stronger than she'd ever been. The force of her shove sent Jaytsy all the way to the shore where she grabbed hold of the rocks and waved back to Mahrree in relief.

Mahrree couldn't rejoice for long because she noticed another person by her side. Salema.

"Do the same as your mother," Mahrree told her. "Get in the water and I'll push you to shore."

Salema, with great trepidation, splashed into the water. Mahrree gave her a mighty push, and soon Salema was at the shore, Jaytsy helping her stand up.

"What about me, Muggah?"

Mahrree smiled at the person next to her. Relf.

"I can get you all there!" she declared, and she did. She pushed Relf, Jori, Cambo . . . all of them, even little Plump Perrin, all the way to the shore where the rest of the family eagerly held out their hands to pull them to safety. The air around Mahrree began to grow colder, the waves lapped higher, and she realized a harsher storm was on its way. There was only one person left to get to shore.

"Swim with me, Mother," Peto said to her. "We'll go together."

"I can't," Mahrree told him. "I can only push."

"Then how will you get to the shore?"

"I'll find a way. Now go—they're waiting for you." She shoved him into the water and gave him a mighty push, propelling him all the way to the shore.

Just before he reached it, Mahrree felt even colder. The lashings holding her boat together were coming apart. The boards separated, and Mahrree found herself flailing to grab hold of them.

But the waves pushed them beyond her reach. She gasped and kicked and tried to keep her head above water, but all her strength was gone. She looked to the shore, assured that all of her family was safely there. Her eyes locked with her son just as he stood up out of the water, just as she ducked below the waves—

Mahrree sat up abruptly in bed, her face drenched and a chill rushing through her. She knew what the dream meant. Her family would be safe . . .

But she wouldn't reach the shore.

She awoke again to the first light of dawn trying to burn into her window. She'd never closed the curtains last night, still looking for other candles lit somewhere, anywhere. Over on the bedside table was the book. The Writings.

She recalled with extreme clarity the words she heard over and over in her head.

Yes, Mahrree Peto Shin—It Is You.

They were still repeating, impossible to ignore. A small, wicked part of her wanted to murmur, "Shut up!" But there was nothing she could do. She sat up, gulped, and wondered how she would fill the hours until she greeted the Army of Idumea.

Sometimes, my darling daughter, the world really is out to get you. Like today, for instance.

"I *really* need to clean something."

It was going to be a very long day.

Young Pere opened his eyes and saw the sunrise over the canyon's edge. For some reason he took note of the color of the sky, something he had rarely done since he left Salem.

Muggah always drilled that into their heads, almost maniacally: what color is the sky? No one dared to answer her without first looking out a window, which was what she expected.

But for almost two years he had assumed, like everyone else in the world, that the sky was blue. It may appear to be another color for the moment, but underneath it all it was always blue, right?

No. It was important to see what color the sky was at that moment, and this morning it was a surprisingly deep red, almost like blood. Or poppies in bloom. He couldn't decide which.

He sat up and noticed the rest of the army was rising early, too. Even Amory must have awakened hours ago to prepare her clothing, hair, and face using the supplies she had lugged on her back for the past few days. Obviously she wanted to make an impression when she returned to Salem. Gone were her muddied men's clothes. She was now dressed in impractical purple silk, with breeches so wide they looked like a skirt, and a flowing tunic embellished with gold and silver accents. Over that she wore a shimmering red cloak to stave off the cold.

If only Guide Lannard had caught up to them, Young Pere thought with a smirk, Salem would see the two of them sparkling from miles away. Amory's hair was piled high on her head with strategic locks cascading down her overly painted face. She probably thought she looked beautiful, but there was nothing real or genuine on her any- where. Even her chest seemed to be inordinately accentuated. Maybe that was where she stuffed her filthy clothing.

She was absurd, and for no good reason. If they were following the plans, no Salemites would ever see her since they would already be on the trail to the ancient temple site.

Young Pere eyed the large wall to his left and sighed. He knew exactly where he was and the army would definitely reach Salem to- day.

The soldiers got up and handed their bedrolls to a major and his lieutenant who was calling for them. In a few minutes they would begin to tie them together for a long rope. It was the only way to get over this wall, over fifty feet high and placed in such a steep section of the canyon there was no hope of climbing around it.

Young Pere wondered how tall the last wall would be. No matter its height, Salem would be seen and recognized from the top of it. The wall they were currently readying to scale was in a dip in the canyon, preventing a clear view into the valley beyond. But the wall at the narrow entrance would likely be the most formidable just to slow down the army that much more.

Young Pere thought of it with excitement and worry. For the past four days he wanted nothing more than to be back in Salem. He would be the first over the wall, by Thorne's orders.

But what if Salem didn't want him back?

It would be a very long day.

The sun was beginning to rise in the east. The old man sat near the edge of the cliff about sixty paces before the temple ruins and looked out at the valley below. The surprisingly warm air for the past couple of days had melted all the snow on the immense table section of the mountain where he sat.

He considered that a tender mercy from the Creator. There wasn't even mud to make camping there unpleasant. All that remained was soft, damp grass, quite comfortable for sleeping on.

Jothan Hifadhi knew all about camping. He and his wife Asrar, who was still dozing soundly in a tent behind the temple site, had spent years living in forests and caverns above Edge. Last night was perfect.

He glanced behind him to see a steady, quiet stream of people already arriving. They most likely slept on the trails and woke at the first light, and now they were emptying out of the forest on to the table land. Two routes ended much further north, in the safer and more sheltered areas of the plateau. The Norden route and the Upper Middle routes went along the tops of the mountains to reach the back, while the Lower Middle and Idumean Trail converged to the south of the site, following the mountain tops to spill out just before the ancient temple, the route which Jothan could now observe.

The last trail, the one in the middle not yet used by anyone, was called the Back Door. While it was short, it was also very steep. It originated near the river that bisected Salem, the Quiet Lands that remained untouched and as pristine as when Guide Pax first saw the land. The only structure there was the temple on the far eastern side of Salem at the mouth of one of the canyons. Since no one lived near the Back Door, it wasn't expected that anyone would really use it. And since the last few hundred paces required climbing a rock face, it also wasn't an option for the elderly or young children or those squeamish about heights.

Jothan nodded in satisfaction that the Salemites were filing in, almost reverently. The only other sound he heard that early morning was the tapping of Relf Shin's chisel and hammer. He started working as soon as there was enough light to see the stone into which he was carving their story.

Thousands of Salemites were already here, and more would pour in for the rest of day, stragglers arriving perhaps tomorrow. And then?

He could hear people calling softly to each other as they arrived, congratulating and greeting each other, mostly at the ruins.

Apparently everyone had told each other to meet there, somewhere along the elaborately carved pillars that soared fifty feet in the air, or among the large blocks of rubble covered in vines and shrubs,

.or along the wide, stone steps leading up to where the front entrance used to be.

Jothan smiled to think that by tomorrow people would be climbing on top of each other trying to find their family and friends.

Last night he watched a middle aged woman stand there for two hours, wringing her hands with worry, until a man with graying hair, probably her husband, came to lead her gently away. She would likely arrive soon again, waiting for someone to come. But maybe she already found whomever she was searching for. He prayed last night that she would.

Jothan looked back down into the valley. It was hard to imagine that soon it would be filled with the Army of Idumea. Right now it was peaceful and quiet. But the valley was deceptive. Anyone from Salem who went there could feel it—cold heaviness that weighed one down. It was even hard to walk in there, as if carrying an extra hundred pounds on one's shoulders. Anyone who spent more than a day there became excessively irritable, angry, and violent.

Long ago it was realized that the valley had been the site of many other 'Last Days.' It was the place where evil came to destroy the faithful of the world who took refuge at the large tableland behind him. And where evil fell, it never seemed to fully leave. It was as if the spirits of those who died there were too terrified to go to the dark desert prison. But here, there was no progress. Just anger and heaviness and guilt.

No Salemites ventured there if they didn't have to. And none did today, either.

That's why Jothan squinted, then squinted again in the distance at where one of the canyons emptied out into the valley. It wasn't the canyon where Guide Gleace had prophesied the Army of Idumea would come, but one to the west. He was sure he saw the early sunshine flash off of something shining in the distance. He watched for a few minutes, then finally turned around.

"Cabbish," he called to a young woman behind him, picking up firewood. "And you, um . . ." He snapped his fingers at a young man helping her, "Perrin's grandson. Look just like him."

Cabbish chuckled as the young man blushed. "His name's Kew Shin, Grandpa Jothan."

Her great-grandpa nodded his head that used to be crowned with black hair but was now faded gray, much like his skin. "Sorry about that. Q? As in the letter? Like 'R' or 'W'?"

The gangly boy shrugged. "Just a family name. Kew."

"As in Kew-ute," Cabbish whispered.

Kew, not sure he heard her correctly, glanced at her, but Jothan chuckled quietly. There had already been one Shin-Hifadhi marriage. There might be another some year if—

Jothan didn't know how to think about the future. There wasn't one, as far as he knew.

"Kew, Cabbish—come over here."

"What is it, Mr. Hifadhi?" Kew said as they approached. Still carrying the wood, they squatted next to him. Kew had been relieved of Grunick duty that morning since his siblings Lori, Jori, Nool, and Kanthi arrived last evening with his brothers-in-law, their children, his cousin Meiki and her husband Clyde, and many Trovato cousins.

"Your eyes might be sharper than mine, so look out there," Jothan gestured. "At the second canyon from the east, at the end of the valley. Do you see a glint of something shiny?"

"I'm still trying to see the end of the valley," his great-granddaughter chuckled.

"Me, too," Kew admitted as he squinted in the distance.

"Sit down properly, both of you," Jothan directed. "Relax your bodies, then relax your minds, then let your eyes drift along the edge of the valley there in the distance. It might take a moment . . ."

The teenagers sat down and stared out into the distance. The rising sun passed a peak and shone brighter into the valley.

"There!" Kew said suddenly. "I saw something. That second canyon."

"I see it!" Cabbish said. "Two glints, right?"

Jothan sighed. "That's right."

"What would cause that, Grandpa?"

Jothan watched for another moment before answering. "Metal."

"Metal?" asked Kew. "Like . . ."

"Swords," Jothan said heavily.

Kew and Cabbish looked at each other in alarm.

"But . . . but that's not the right canyon, is it?" Kew asked, slightly panicked.

"No, it's not the Idumean canyon. Nor is that the main body of the army. It's probably a group of soldiers who got lost."

"So, not too big a worry?" Cabbish asked.

Jothan shook his head. "Any soldier is a worry, my dear. They find out where we are, they get a little ambitious and try to come up here, or they return and tell Thorne too soon where we are before everyone else is ready."

Kew and Cabbish exchanged fearful looks.

"Mr. Hifadhi, what do we do?" Kew said.

"We watch them for another fifteen minutes. Unless they have a spyglass, they can't tell what's going on here. They may just go into the next canyon and get lost on their way to Salem again."

"But what if they don't?"

"Then, Kew Shin, you find a horse abandoned at one of the springs and ride as fast as you can to find your uncle Shem. This might be turning into a very long day."

"Well, it *is* a valley . . ." said one of the soldiers looking around.

"Yes, it is," said another.

The sergeant put his hands on his waist. He and his fourteen men had arisen early and set out to find their way to Salem, or their way out. He wasn't expecting this.

"If we had walked just a few hundred paces last night, we could have camped here instead of in the canyon!"

"The canyon was fine," said an older soldier. "Something about this valley, though . . ."

"Look at it. It's perfect!" said a younger man. "What a great place to start a village. Flat, and no ash hit here. Look how lush it is. Corn would grow twice as tall here, I'm sure of it."

One of the soldiers said, "What did Thorne say about 'claiming' houses and land?"

The sergeant's eyebrows rose. "He said whoever found something first got to claim it."

"We saw this first, sir."

The sergeant nodded. "Yes . . . yes we did. Split fifteen ways . . . that's quite a bit of land, men—"

"Wait a minute! I saw it first! All of it is mine!"

The sergeant looked at him. "We all got here at the same time! It's all of ours—"

"You . . . you're just going to *steal* it from me?"

"STEAL? I didn't hear you claim this!"

"I claim it now!" shouted another soldier.

"No! I do!"

The sergeant drew his sword. "ENOUGH! There's enough here for all of us! *I'm* the leader of this group according to Thorne's staff sergeant, so I declare that when the battle is over I will divide up this parcel into fifteen shares, then each of you will get to choose one share."

"No! That's not—"

"Sarge!" cried one man. He was holding a spyglass and looking off into the distance. "Sarge, I think I see movement above the cliff!"

"What?" The sergeant marched over and snatched the spyglass out of his hands. "How can that be?" He held it up and focused. A moment later he lowered it. "There are people up there," he said softly as if they could hear him so far away. "Not a lot, but enough that might be trying to stake a claim on our land."

The other fourteen soldiers shifted in agitation. "Not our land, they don't! This is OURS! We saw it first, we get to take it. Sarge, can we take them?"

The sergeant spied again at the cliff side. "I see only a few people. A couple of children, an old man . . . nothing we can't handle." He put down the glass and looked at his men. "Ten swords, two archers, three long knives . . . yes, we can take care of this."

One of the men licked his lips. "So what do we do?"

"Simple. We walk over there, climb the cliff, kill whoever's there, then send word to Thorne that we've claimed this land."

But the older man shook his head slightly. "I don't think this will end well . . ."

"Not for them, no. What, are you scared?"

The older man stiffened up. "Absolutely not," he said as he drew his sword. "Time for me to get my own land."

Versa opened her eyes, stretched and stood up. She'd always enjoyed sleeping in barns: the hay really was quite comfortable, once she laid a blanket over it to keep the scratchy ends from poking her. She'd learned that trick long ago as a child, during one of the many times she and her family were on the run, stealing into barns for the night to stay far away from soldiers.

She peeked out the barn door to the house. It seemed empty, just like the rest of the neighborhood. Last night she wasn't sure, so she didn't dare enter the house. But she didn't mind a second night in a cozy barn. In many ways, she felt most at home with all she owned on her back, and her future wherever her feet would take her. For the past two days she'd been on the run again, so to speak, and she'd eased back into her old ways.

She picked up her pack and walked confidently to the house, not wanting to use up her rations if she didn't need to.

In the kitchen she found plenty of dried fruits, jerky, and a forgotten loaf of bread, not too stale. Alone at the kitchen table she ate her breakfast and considered her route for the day. In case she ran into a straggler, her southern progress would be suspicious. She would sneak through gardens and orchards, just to be safe. The roads in Salem were bare now, with everyone moving to the west.

She snooped through the cabinets to see if there was anything else worth taking, and shoved a piece of hard cracker bread into her bag.

After hefting the pack on her back, she slipped out of the house. The barn she had chosen was well off the main roads, where Cephas Briter, Peto Shin, and Shem Zenos and his assistants frequently rode to make sure the evacuation was progressing smoothly.

Versa couldn't see or hear another living soul. Salem was disturbingly silent.

She set her focus on the southern canyon and started to walk, hoping it wasn't going to be a long day.

"Zaddick, what about this one?" Deck led a horse over to him. The pasture lands before the route entrance was filled with hundreds of horses grazing among the abandoned wagons. Already new travelers and wagons were stopping to unhitch their horses, give them a pat goodbye, and start up the trail on foot and with pack horses. A few of them nodded to the Briters, Zenoses, and Shins in the field retrieving usable animals. "We didn't check this one yet, did we? His shoes look good."

Zaddick tipped his head. "No, I'm pretty sure we didn't. He looks well rested, too."

"Hogal," Deck called over to his nephew, "come take this one."

The fourteen-year-old jogged over and nodded at the painted horse. "I like him."

"Well, I don't, Papa," scowled ten-year-old Yenali Briter, sitting on a nearby rock. "His face is only half brown."

Eleven-year-old Centia rolled her eyes. "It's only for a few hours, Yenali. Muggah or someone else can ride him."

"Not that one for Muggah," Deck told them. "He's too lively. Put that one on my side of the barn, Hogal. Your aunt Jaytsy can handle him, but I'm still looking for the right horse for Muggah."

Hogal mounted the painted horse to bring it back to the barn. He met twelve-year-old Atlee Briter going back to the pasture lands.

"I like that one," Atlee told him as he passed.

"Good, because your sister doesn't. He'll be Aunt Jaytsy's today."

Atlee nodded. "There's plenty of feed in the barn now, although I don't think the girls like shoveling it too much."

"Then they should bring the horses back to the barn."

"They'd like that even less."

As Hogal approached the barn between the Shins and Briters, he saw his aunt Jaytsy coming out. "Oh, I like that one!"

"Good, because Uncle Deck says it's yours today."

She walked over to Hogal and took the reins as he dismounted. "Been a while since I've ridden. Did he handle well?"

"Really gentle," Hogal said. "I thought he should be for Muggah, but Uncle Deck said he's looking for just the right horse for her."

"Hmm. Might take him all morning," Jaytsy mused. "We need something old and mellow, yet fast."

"I don't think they usually come in that combination," Hogal told her.

"I know," she chuckled. "But the Creator will help them find the right animal before this afternoon, don't you think?"

Hogal smiled at his aunt and started back to the fields.

Jaytsy led the horse into the barn and tethered it near the first one Atlee brought in.

Nine-year-old Morah Shin moaned. "Already another one? I just got water for the first!"

Her cousins Tabbit and Banu Briter, pitching straw, frowned. "Want to trade?" fourteen-year-old Banu offered. Sixteen-year-old Tabbit held out her pitchfork.

"No!" Morah dashed out of the barn with a bucket.

Sixteen-year-old Huldah Zenos and her eighteen-year-old sister Ester laughed at their cousin. "Maybe I'll go help her," Ester suggested. "I can carry two buckets and I have a feeling the horses will start coming faster."

Nine-year-old Young Shem Briter leaned on his pitchfork. "I still don't know why I'm stuck working with all the girls."

"Because you like being inside, remember?" Sakal Shin said.

Young Shem looked around the barn. "This really isn't inside."

"Oh, get moving, Young Shem," his mother said as she playfully slapped his rear. "Everyone is doing a different kind of work today. I hear another horse coming."

Jaytsy left the barn with a chuckle. She never imagined seeing the girls and her youngest son working in the barn. The miracles just kept happening, and maybe another was arriving. Thirteen-year-old Sakal was approaching on a small, stocky horse.

"What do you think?" she asked her aunt. "Uncle Deck thinks Muggah could handle this one."

Jaytsy nodded thoughtfully at the tan animal. "Small, steady, and hopefully not ready to drop dead halfway up the mountain . . . Yes, yes this *might* do. But tell your uncle Deck that if he finds any horses a little younger than Muggah, that would be good too."

Sakal laughed and jogged back to the field.

Jon Offra leaned against the gray scraggly tree appearing nonchalant, even though the dead branches were poking him in the back. In one hand was a chunk of wood—a new whittling project Teman had given him, to teach him how to use a knife for something other than ending someone's life.

Jon was trying to carve it into a bear, but he kept whittling too many sharp points on it.

It was odd behavior for the army of Idumea to behold—a tall, distinguished man with blond-gray hair at the side of the canyon, whittling.

He wasn't guarding the small canyon that branched off behind him. Quite the contrary.

Last year, Salem's hope had been to wall up all of the canyons as a lure or diversion. But then the snows came early, and the construction had to stop. The main walls had been erected, however, so that had to suffice.

Still, there were many routes breaking off into blind canyons, and there was no reason not to make use of them.

In front of such a one, Teman, who was hiding in a cluster of shrubs, had placed Jon, who was now commenting loudly as he worked on his whittling project. "Yessiree, *much* calmer and quieter in that little canyon behind me."

He tipped his head backward to indicate the sheltered, narrow passage where already a few dozen men had decided to end their army careers and take a well-deserved break. In the patches between the snows, soldiers had laid out their packs and were closing their eyes in the first rays of the sun that reached them.

"Yessirree, no 'Last Day Doom' can reach them there. No, the Creator won't send His Destruction to *that* canyon," he continued in a convivial and very loud voice. "Great place to spend the Last Day in peace, I'd wager."

Soldiers passing him on their way to yet another depressing gray wall hesitated, partly because of the backlog of men trying to climb the wall, partly because the brass buttons on Offra's jacket were so mesmerizing and enticing, just like his words.

"Safety assured leaving east of Medicetti," he announced. "Right there behind me—that's where the safety is. Where space is. Where rest and comfort and anything else you *really* want is. No one will care that you've left the army. No one really wants to do *this*." He gestured with his carving knife at the imposing block wall before them.

That's when the murmuring would begin, the mutters of, "I don't want to really do this, either."

"Another wall? *They're* not climbing the wall, are they? Not getting in trouble either, are they?"

Jealous glances would be sent to those who had quit the army for meadow life; eyes would dart back and forth, making sure punishment wasn't around some corner; and then, a half dozen or so men would sidle closer and closer to the tall whittling man, still announcing, "Safety behind me, Destruction in front of me. Decision seems pretty clear . . ."

Abruptly, the defectors sprinted from the crowd of a few hundred men to the quiet solitude of the side canyon, grinning in triumph and being greeted with cheers by those who had left the army only a few minutes before.

Occasionally an officer strode angrily up to Offra, ready to shout him down or worse. But Jon would calmly lift his head and glare with the power of a Shin.

Maybe it had something to do with the jacket, but no officers dared contend with Jon. They suspected he was Colonel Offra, but something about that jacket—the brass buttons, the older insignias . . . Well, that jacket wasn't supposed to be there.

None of them were supposed to be there.

More than one officer surely intended to take down Jon Offra, wanted to pull out his sword and dispatch the oldest officer in the army who was supposed to be dead already and make him that way.

But they didn't. They couldn't. It was as if there were some kind of invisible shield, some kind of protection around him that pulsed a feeling of inevitable doom to whichever man considered raising a sword to Offra.

Maybe it was the little old man who sat higher on the rock on the slope. Maybe he radiated down that threatening feel, as if he were a rain cloud hovering nearby, with lightning ready to strike.

Offra was oddly untouchable.

To the men who slipped past Offra and trotted back into the narrow canyon, the officers only sent glances of envy. Then, obediently, they continued on with the rest of the army to the next wall.

Soon the next wave of soldiers were funneled into the walled canyon, groaning at the sight of yet another blockade. And soon, they'd find themselves bemused by the tall man who was whittling what *was* a bear but now resembled a porcupine, who'd start telling them, "Yessiree, *much* calmer and quieter in that little canyon behind me . . ."

Up on the cliff side, the three figures hadn't moved for fifteen minutes. They kept their focus on the occasional flashes of light that bounced off the swords in the distance.

"Concentrate on that lead flash," Jothan said. "If they're going into the next canyon, we'll see it next past the large boulder there. If not, it will stay to the right of it."

"How often did you do this, Mr. Hifadhi? Watching bits of light in the distance?"

Jothan chuckled lightly but maintained his gaze. "For years, Kew. *Years.* When we didn't have anyone traveling the routes to safety, I'd sit high in the trees at the edge of the forest and just watch. I always knew which flash of light was Colonel Shin's. It bounced off your Great Grandfather Relf's sword like nothing else."

Kew smiled and tried to keep focused on the first sword.

"Grandpa," Cabbish whispered after a moment, "it's not turning, is it?"

Jothan was silent as they continued to watch. The glints continued in a straight path.

Kew shifted nervously, waiting for the word. "I think it's still coming toward us, Mr. Hifadhi."

Jothan sighed. "You're both right," he finally admitted. "Relf may need to stop carving and start getting these people behind the ruins and as far back as possible. Yes, yes . . . Cabbish, go tell Relf to get everyone moving and come back to me for an update every five minutes. I'll try to get an estimate on the rate of their progress. Kew, find the fastest horse you can, take it down to the Eztates, and tell Shem that the sergeant major will be needed here."

Kew was getting up, but stopped midway. "What was that? The sergeant major?"

Jothan nodded, not once taking his eyes from the distance. "Only an experienced sergeant major can handle this. Tell Shem that Jothan Hifadhi said the day has finally come for him to remember his training: Perrin's orders. He'll know what it means. GO!"

Kew jumped and ran with Cabbish to give Relf the news, then he continued on to find a horse.

Relf dropped his tools and rushed to the ruins. "Move! Move to the back! Now!" His brother Nool joined him, trying to get people up and going.

Con and Sam stood up groggily from their camp sites, Relf's shouting having woken them up. They saw their brothers-in-law waving frantically at stunned people milling around the ruins. The Cadby brothers looked to the cliff and saw the old scout sitting there, studying something in the distance.

"This doesn't look good," Sam said to Con.

His brother nodded and together they started rousing their exhausted wives and scooping up their babies.

Less than a minute later Kew was on the most rested Clark he could find, racing down the mountain.

Down the slope, merely half an hour's walk away from the top of the trail, Lek was guiding the horse carrying his sons and leading the train of Zenoses, Shins, and Briters. They had made some progress up the mountain the night before, but Eraliz was in tears of silent misery when they reached the camping meadow. Salema took one look at her and announced to the party, "We're camping here for the night." No one complained. The wriggly little ones were more than ready to run around, and Eraliz wept in relief as Holling laid her down on a soft bedroll.

The large group was up at daybreak and were on the trail when Kew was racing down it on a parallel track so as to not get in the way of the steady stream of Salemites.

Lek frowned at the approaching rider.

"Someone's going the wrong way," he called out to the family behind him. "And in a hurry."

But Hycy, a few horses behind, recognized her brother. "Kew?"

Lek spun as Kew shouted something as he rode past.

Holling Briter, at the back of the train with Eraliz and Salema, understood his shout.

"What'd he yell?" Cambo Briter called down to him.

"Soldiers!"

"No," Lek whimpered, the reins going slack in his hands.

Cambo turned to Lek. "Throw the reins to Briter and mount up with me. Wives and children," he shouted to the rest of the family, "stay on the trail but stop before you get to the ancient site. Stay hidden in the forest until all is clear. Boys, let's go see what's happening."

"Papa?" Briter called in a panic as Lek handed him the reins.

"You'll be all right," Lek assured him, trying to remain calm himself. "Mama's coming."

Salema was already riding up on the other side, holding Plump Perrin in the wrap secured to her front. She and her son slid off her horse and took the reins from Briter so Lek could climb up behind Cambo.

The seven men quickly shifted children to wives and sisters and rearranged riders and horses, but Holling paused and gazed at his ailing wife.

Eraliz smiled bravely. "I'm fine. No pains. They need you more than me. Ride!"

The men kicked their horses and galloped up the trail.

Jaytsy sighed when she saw Boskos, Noria, and their two little ones walking up the lane from their house with Shem and Calla. Another farewell.

"Come to choose a good horse for your ride to the site?" Jaytsy called to them. "I'm getting quite the collection this morning."

Boskos smiled. "Noria's family should be here soon, but I suppose we can go horse hunting in case what they bring isn't satisfactory."

"The world calls it *shopping,* Boskos. You're not out to shoot anything," Jaytsy smiled.

Shem was looking around. "Peto still out?"

"Lilla said he didn't think he'd have much success with Eltana," Jaytsy explained, "but he wasn't sleeping this morning anyway."

"Well, maybe he's having *some* success. Where's Mahrree? She wanted to say good-bye."

"She's hiding in the house, cleaning things," Jaytsy gestured. "She doesn't want to face the horses, and she also doesn't want to leave a dirty house this afternoon."

Noria and Calla nodded in understanding, but Shem waved his arms in disbelief. "I'll never understand that. Who's going to see the house?"

Calla patted him. "It has nothing to do with pride, but everything to do with gratitude. The house is being thanked for its service to us. We just want our houses to feel . . . clean. Before the soldiers do whatever they'll do to them."

Shem shrugged. "Little Callia and I will get Mahrree. Boskos, see if there's anything you want to hunt in the barn."

Jothan, now lying down at the edge of the cliff to be less conspicuous, twisted to see the progress behind him. He nodded in relief that seven more of Perrin's and Shem's male descendants had arrived and were helping move people to the back of the tableland.

"Leave the bedrolls and packs," he muttered. "They'll be able to come back for them in a while. Just *go.*"

He noticed his great-granddaughter explaining the situation to a newly-arrived family and he beckoned for her to come over to him, crawling.

As she neared, he said, "Cabbish, tell Relf or whoever is acting in charge that the soldiers have picked up their pace. I estimate they'll be up here in less than an hour. I'm counting on them struggling up the trail on the cliff side, but we shouldn't assume that we have more time than that."

Cabbish fingered her long black braid in worry. "Grandpa, maybe you should come back with me now."

"I know how to be invisible, Cabbish," he assured her. "And I've been waiting many years to see this. I'll roll behind that large rock when they reach the top of the trail. But you better be running for the back by then."

She kissed him quickly on the cheek and peered cautiously over the edge. Far below were the fifteen soldiers in a steady jog. She uttered a little yelp of fear and rushed back to the Shin and Zenos men who created a line just before the ruin. They were instructing newcomers where to go, looking behind them frequently for updates.

Cabbish's dark skin was flushed when she announced to her cousin Wes and his in-laws, "Less than an hour, now."

Relf, Lek, and Cambo—the oldest sons of each family—shared the same anxious look.

"Kew should be reaching the Eztates soon," Relf said.

Lek nodded. "Then another five minutes and Papa should be on his way up here."

"How fast can this route be done?" Cambo asked.

"Trying to remember," Bubba said. "Papa did it just for fun, once, many years ago. Remember, Cambo?"

"We were just young," Cambo said, rubbing his forehead in Perrin fashion. "But I *want* to say he made it in much less than an hour, on that really fast horse he borrowed. He was trying to prove he didn't need to go on the marking trip that year, wasn't he?"

Bubba shrugged. "I don't remember. But less than an hour?"

"The horse nearly died, though," Cambo reminded them.

"*Much less* than an hour would be good," Lek said, watching Jothan Hifadhi at the edge of the cliff.

"There are a lot more horses available for the ride down," Relf agreed.

Deck heard the noise coming down the hillside, sounding like a bear crashing through the woods, and he spun in alarm. The steady stream of Salemites to his right heading up the route also looked, but relaxed when they realized it was just a teenager rushing down on a horse.

But Deck knew something was wrong. "Kew?"

Panting, Kew reined the horse to a stop in front of his cousin. "Zaddick! Where's Uncle Shem?"

"At Boskos' house. They were going to leave soon—"

But Kew had already kicked the horse into a frothy run to the Eztates. Zaddick and Deck grabbed the nearest horses and mounted.

"Papa?" Atlee shouted. Hogal, Centia, and Yenali stared as Deck and Zaddick joined the race back to the Eztates.

"Does this mean I get to choose the horse I want now?" Yenali said.

"Mahrree? Mahrree, the house looks *fine*," Shem called. "Where are you? You have to leave something for Lilla to do when she gets back from the rectory."

"Here, Shem," he heard her voice down the hall.

He found her in Young Pere's room. "Oh, Mahrree."

"Just so he knows we were waiting," she smiled feebly and gestured, a little embarrassed, to the large sign above his bed, charcoal written on a white bed sheet.

Young Pere, we had to leave. You know the way to us. Please hurry. We're watching and praying for you. All our love, everyone.

"I ran out of space to write everyone's names," she apologized. "But I think he'll recognize my handwriting. And he'll see we left his bedroom the same . . ."

Shem sighed. "He'll know, Mahrree. Good idea."

"Muggah!" Callia said, holding out her arms.

"Ooh, come here, you sweet thing," Mahrree said, taking Boskos's daughter from Shem. "You going bye-bye? Is it time?"

Shem nodded. "Come on. Boskos is horse 'hunting'."

"He's what?"

Shem chuckled. "Just come say goodbye. I promise I won't make you get on a horse yet. Although the traveling breeches do look nice on you."

"Shem Zenos!" Mahrree exclaimed. "*Looking* at a *woman* in *breeches.*"

Shem blushed. "I, I, I mean—"

Mahrree burst out laughing. "Ah, you're still so easy sometimes. I'm sorry, but I'm really not. Thanks, Shem. I needed the laugh. The look on your face."

"You're awful, you know that?" he said, playfully slapping her arm as they walked down the hall to the large gathering room. "Making me feel like a twenty-year-old again."

She was just opening her mouth to give him a smart comeback when she noticed through the window a horse racing to the Eztates. "Who is that?"

Shem stepped in front of her and opened the door. Mahrree and Callia followed.

"It's Kew!" Shem sprinted from the front porch.

Kew had brought the horse to a stop right before Calla and Boskos. Mahrree jogged after him awkwardly, still carrying her grand-niece.

"Kew!" Shem shouted. "What's wrong?"

"Soldiers, Uncle Shem!"

Deck and Zaddick, on their borrowed horses, came to a quick stop behind him to listen.

"What?" Shem cried.

Calla stared at Kew. "How? Where?"

Kew shook his head, trying to catch his breath. "Not too many," he finally managed. "Hifadhi thinks they're lost. Came out of a wrong canyon. Maybe got diverted by one of the walls, looking for a shortcut."

Shem pressed his lips together.

"How many?" Calla asked.

"Around fifteen," Kew panted. "Counted the number of glints on their swords approaching the cliff side. Not turning to any other canyons. We may have been spotted."

Shem closed his eyes in thought. Mahrree finally reached them with Callia, and Noria took her daughter from Mahrree and held her close as Mahrree read the bleak faces of those around her.

"Oh dear," she murmured quietly. "My mind is desperate for distractions, but not like this."

"Papa?" Boskos whispered, "Do we still go, or . . ."

"Uncle Shem?" said Kew, finally breathing normally, "Mr. Hifadhi said it's time for the sergeant major to come. Only the sergeant major can fix this. The day to pull out your training? Perrin's orders? He said you'd know what that meant."

Shem opened his eyes. "He didn't *really* say that, did he, Kew?"

Kew nodded.

"Papa? What does that mean?" Boskos asked.

Jaytsy and Mahrree held their breath.

Shem, nearly petrified, only muttered, "I can't do it—"

With speed no one anticipated, Calla spun Shem to her and gripped him by both arms. "Listen to me. This is it, Shem! Sergeant Major Zenos, you never did turn in your resignation, remember? You were always supposed to remain a soldier. Hew Gleace told you that and so did Tuma Hifadhi. The day would come, remember, Shem? The day would come when your skill would preserve Salem for one more day. If you don't stop those soldiers, we may not get everyone safely to the site. They can't be allowed to return to Lemuel, Shem. If he finds out too soon, Salem perishes. Remember his dream, Shem. Accept it! Do it! Face the world!"

"You're supposed to hold me back from the world!" he nearly shouted at her.

"Not today!" she exclaimed. "Today, I'm shoving you to it!"

Jaytsy nudged her mother. "What is she talking about?" she whispered. "Whose dream?"

Mahrree shrugged. "I have no idea."

Deck, Zaddick, and Boskos shrugged as well.

"Calla," Shem exhaled, "You know how I feel about this. I never again wanted to take a sword—"

"So why did the Creator allow you to learn to use it so well?" she rounded on him with surprising gusto. "To defend this people, Sergeant Major! Even Perrin saw it in his dream!"

Now Mahrree and Jaytsy stared at each other, and Boskos and Zaddick blinked in surprise.

Shem closed his eyes again. "I know you're right, Calla," he said quietly. "I could never do this without you. Thank you, my love, for always pushing me in the right direction—"

Calla shook him. "Thank me later. Get a horse and *get up there*!"

Shem opened his eyes, kissed her quickly, and headed to the barn. "Fresh horses. All of you men, you're coming with me!"

Boskos's eyebrows went up. "We're *what*?"

"It's all right," Calla assured him, pushing him toward the barn.

Jaytsy and Mahrree followed with Zaddick, Deck, and Kew.

"You'll want to see this," Calla promised, jogging with them to the barn. "Perrin had a dream where he saw Shem fighting off soldiers at the cliff side, giving the Salemites another day to gather," she told them hurriedly. "Shem could do it because he was still legally in the army and wouldn't be breaking the Creator's decree that no Salemites fight at the ancient temple site. That had been Guide Hifadhi's and Guide Gleace's admonitions, to always remain a soldier, and Perrin, as the General of Salem, was given the understanding of why. Shem never wanted to believe any of it, but Jothan knew about the dream as well, and—well, there was more to it, but we don't have time. Grab a horse!"

Shem was already getting on top of a rare white Clark, powerful and rested. Silver was in his barn too far away, and Clark 14 was still out with Peto.

"Boskos, take this one," Jaytsy grabbed the reins of another strong horse and pointed to a third. "Kew, try that one. Zad, over here—"

Without a word, Shem rode swiftly out of the barn, the men following him through Deck's pasture lands.

Calla watched for a few seconds, then grabbed the reins of the painted horse with the half brown face.

"Mama?!" Huldah exclaimed.

Ester dropped her pitchfork.

"Calla!" Jaytsy cried. "What are you doing?"

Calla struggled to mount the saddle-free horse, but soon was astride.

"Calla, get down from there!" Mahrree ordered.

But Calla was beaming. "Call me grainy, Mahrree, but I always dreamed of watching my sergeant major in action. Ever since I was fourteen years old, I wanted to see Shem Zenos fight. I *can't* miss this, Mahrree. Explain it to Lilla if I'm not back in time?"

Mahrree couldn't help but grin. "Then go, Calla! *Go!*"

Calla kicked the horse and took off, following the men already well on their way.

Jaytsy, Noria, Huldah, Ester, and Mahrree jogged after her to watch in awe.

"I can't believe she's going," Jaytsy said, shaking her head at the diminishing figure of Calla, about a hundred paces behind the men.

Noria chuckled. "Maybe if she wasn't wearing breeches, she wouldn't have gone."

"So hard to mount a horse in a dress," Ester agreed.

"Maybe that's why we usually don't wear breeches, unless we're traveling," Mahrree smirked. "Too tempting to rush out and do something brave and foolish. Ride, Calla! Go watch your sergeant major! Then come back and tell me all about it, but not too much. Just like

Lek, I don't like the bloody parts."

The women and girls chuckled.

As the riders entered a dip in the hills and vanished from sight, Mahrree scoffed quietly and exclaimed, "So THAT'S why Perrin needed to see Jothan!"

Jaytsy frowned. "What was that?"

"Just before Perrin passed," she explained to the family around her, "he requested to see Jothan Hifadhi. They met, just the two of them, and I never knew what they talked about. But I did find a note Perrin had left, his list of what to finish. On it were the words, 'Jothan, about Shem.'" She shook her head in wonder. "I never knew that he dreamed about Shem. I wonder how long ago that was. It must have been about this day."

Huldah Zenos squirmed. "Papa didn't want to do it."

Mahrree nodded confidently. "Your papa can and will do it, whatever *it* is. He always did his duty, especially when his commander told him to." She sighed, slightly resentful that she didn't know about Perrin's dream. "But I'm dying to know what *it* is. Ah, well. There's work to do, everyone, and I've got a pantry to reorganize."

Young Pere sighed. The ropes made out of twisted bedrolls were sturdy. All ten of them. And they easily went up and over the sixty foot wall. The soldiers would be able to climb it relatively faster than they'd been scaling the sides of the canyons to go around them.

Still, the ropes had to be secured by ten men on the *other* side as counterweights for those pulling on the ropes to climb up. That was the problem. They had already thrown over the ropes before the army realized there was no counterweight on the other side.

Young Pere had seen the problem before they even started tossing, but he wasn't about to point that out. It had been much more fun to watch Thorne rage in fury about the lack of forethought. But now his latest temper tantrum was over.

"Come now, *Shin*," General Thorne simpered. "Certainly you can do *this*."

Young Pere turned and held up his shackled hands to the general. "Come now, *Thorne*. Certainly you can see *reason*."

Hili coughed a warning at Young Pere's obvious contempt. "Sir," the sergeant major said, "there's no way he can get to the top. There's most likely another wall on the other side. If he's unchained for a few moments so he can get up and over, it's not as if he can run off anywhere."

Cloud Man raised his hand eagerly. "I'll be in charge of him! I'll even carry his chains and be the next one over."

The general rolled his eyes at Cloud Man's request. He grumbled, then pointed at Beaved. "Take off the chains, give them to that *soldier* there," he said, scoffing at Cloud Man, "but you're next right after those two, Sergeant!"

Beaved walked over to Young Pere and undid the lock to release the chains from his wrists.

Young Pere fought the urge to massage his wrists in front of Thorne. He didn't want Thorne to have the satisfaction that he had been uncomfortable. A moment later his ankles were freed and Beaved handed the chains to Cloud Man. He happily draped them around his neck and bounced to the jingling.

Young Pere wished he was as clueless and jolly as Cloud Man. He stretched his arms and legs before attempting the climb.

Not that he hadn't had time to rest. The army had been blocked by the wall for most of the morning. By the time they were ready to toss the last bedroll rope, they had realized the problem of no anchorage. They tried securing a large stone to the end of the rope, hoping vainly to heave it over the wall, but it was too heavy for anyone to successfully throw sixty feet in the air. The strongest men could barely get the bedroll ropes over. For half an hour Thorne argued with and shouted at his officers, trying to find a solution.

Finally the officers agreed to try a method, suggested by a rancher, that the last rope could be lassoed around a scrubby bush growing on the side of the canyon over the wall. Tossed just the right way, the rope could circle the leafless bush and the other end come back down to the same side. Then someone could hold both ends of the blanket rope using the bush as the anchor, and climb up to the top of the wall, throw one end of the rope on the other side, and lower himself down again, thus being on the correct side of the wall to start acting as a counterweight for one rope to allow the soldiers to start climbing.

Thorne promised the rancher-turned-soldier a medal for his innovative thinking, and Young Pere smirked to think that Thorne had promised him medals, too, that never materialized.

It took Thorne and the officers another fifteen minutes to find someone in the thousands of soldiers stacked up behind them who who believed he could lasso the bush with the cumbersome bedroll rope, since the rancher with the initial idea had a hurt arm from a fall the day before.

It then took another twenty minutes of fruitlessly throwing the heavy rope before the man finally succeeded in catching the bush at the correct angle.

The sun was fully shining in the canyon by the time Young Pere's chains came off, the Army of Idumea having been delayed for over two hours that morning by ash turned into block.

Young Pere gripped both sides of the bedroll rope and started to climb, bracing his feet against the wall. The bush above him creaked under his weight, but disappointingly held as he climbed as slowly as he dared, taking the time to enjoy being able to fully stretch his limbs as well as to delay the army that much longer.

Once he reached the top he realized that there was, indeed, another wall, probably seventy feet high, down the canyon. But it was the last one, Young Pere was sure. Even from here he could make out the valley in the distance just above it, and even recognized a brown rock slowly moving in the distance. A cow.

Soon the army would be to the last wall, and maybe in another hour have enough bedroll ropes knotted together to go up and over to finally see Salem.

"Where's the next wall?" Thorne called up to him.

Young Pere sighed almost in despair. "Just ahead."

"Well, get down and get anchoring the rope, Shin! I don't have all day!"

Young Pere started to lower himself down. "Actually, we have until the end of the world," he whispered.

Eltana Yordin surveyed Salem's Region 1. Dozens upon dozens of houses and barns, abandoned two days ago—they'd be the perfect hiding place for her soldiers. Her army could watch the canyon entrance and the block wall before them, waiting for their moment to ambush.

Eltana nodded to her captains riding on either side. "Tell them to spread out, but there should be at least fifty men assigned to each property, as many as can fit into each structure. They can wait in barns, too. We need to hurry. Idumea should be arriving today."

The captains rode off to give the instructions, and Eltana, in her brown tunic, breeches, and short jacket, turned to watch their progress. With Salem-like precision and obedience, the nearly fourteen thousand people on foot behind her broke off into their groups and started jogging for the houses and barns scattered over the southern end of Salem. Armed with pitchforks, axes, bows, and arrows, the men, boys, and even several hundred women took their positions.

One figure, on horseback, surveyed the situation. He had trailed Eltana since early that morning, well before the sun rose, as she called for them to break camp and march to their chosen battle field.

He had followed, calling out for Salemites to change their minds, to leave with him and head west. No one would listen but he didn't give up. He tried from different angles and at a variety of places, hoping to change someone's—*anyone's*—mind, but for the past few hours they demonstrated their resolve to defend their land.

During the last fifteen minutes, the lone rider had stopped his pleading and watched instead as the Salemites rushed to take up their positions. He frequently glanced up to the canyon entrance and the tower, just beyond the Second Resting Station, watching for the solid black banner to suddenly rise. All that waved now was the gray one signaling the army was still in the canyon.

The rider looked over to Eltana Yordin and caught her glaring at him. It was at that canyon entrance where they became acquainted again, almost two years ago. It was then he promised her Salem was a place of miracles.

But now?

Peto Shin stared back at her with pity.

Reluctantly, he turned Clark 14 and headed back to the Eztates.

Shem thought only one thing as the white stallion galloped through the forest parallel to the Salemites hiking up the mountain.

Climb! Climb! Climb!

He didn't think about his lack of weapons, or the condition of the Salemites on the tableland, or if the soldiers were already there. He didn't even bother to look back to see if Boskos, Zaddick, Kew, and Deck were still following. He only wanted them in case something happened to him or the horse he was riding. He really didn't expect them to fight, just to support.

He spent every free thought willing the horse to go faster up the slope. It could be done, he knew. He could get there before soldiers. He just had to *get* there.

Deck, sprawled on the dirt, evaluated the lamed horse next to him.

"Obviously you were not the best choice." He watched as Shem, Boskos, Kew, and Zaddick continued to ride up the mountain, soon out of view. None of them had noticed his horse go down.

But several families, a dozen paces away on a parallel path, did.

"Mr. Briter? Is that you? What's happened?"

Deck got up, wiped the mud and leaves from his clothing, and smiled in embarrassment as the horse hobbled away from him. "Just a little accident, that's all."

"Do you need help getting to the top?" a man asked him.

"No. No, I'm really needed down at the Eztates. I guess this is the Creator's way of telling me that."

"Are you in a hurry? Need to borrow a horse?"

"It's only about two and a half miles from here. Just a pleasant jog down the mountain. Not really my style, what's going on at the top right now." He tried not to reveal anything more so as to not alarm his audience. "I'm better down at the Eztates."

A painted horse suddenly whipped past him. He could barely make out the figure riding it. He blinked, then blinked again.

"Was that . . . was that *Mrs. Zenos*?" the man asked him.

"I . . . I think so."

"Why?"

"I have no idea."

"Seriously, Cambo?" Viddrow Briter looked at the long branch his oldest brother put into his hands. "How is this going to help?"

His brothers, cousins, and in-laws were thinking the same thing.

"Intimidation," Cambo said, thrusting another branch into his brother Holling's hands. "We just need to *look* intimidating. I don't expect any of us to use these. We just need to hold them off until

Uncle Shem gets here."

Barnos Shin scowled as his cousin Cambo gave him a branch. "Doesn't even have a pointy end."

"There's no time for that!" Relf told his brother as he shoved a branch into his brother-in-law Con's hands. "Mr. Hifadhi says they're climbing the cliff side. We have maybe ten minutes—"

"I could whittle a pointy end in ten minutes," Barnos said to Wes. "My *pocket knife* is more deadly than this thing—"

"But we're not supposed to be armed with weapons," Lek reminded them.

"So what is *this?*" Bubba Briter asked, holding up his club-like branch.

"Firewood!" Cambo declared. "Just . . . not broken up yet."

Lek glared at Cambo's explanation. It sounded like a rationalization his grandmother Mahrree would make. Lek was still not comfortable with the idea his cousin Relf and brother-in-law Cambo cooked up, yet he held a piece of thick firewood.

Nool, the youngest man there at age seventeen, cringed as he looked at his stick. "And I thought it would be safer up here than down at the Eztates."

"Look," Relf said to the young men, pacing in front of them in a very general-like way, but none of them knew it. "We just need to hold them off until help arrives. We're well-rested—"

Sam scoffed. "Speak for yourself. I spent yesterday on the mountain with four children and slept with twin babies last night. This," he pried open his blood-shot eyes, "is not well-rested."

"Come on, Sam," Cambo said, patting his ample arm and holding out another long branch, "You just need to flex those muscles and they'll quiver in their boots."

Relf nodded. "I remember Puggah saying that all of us, even our little Wes, are bigger and stronger than most of the soldiers in the army."

Wes tried to stand a little taller. He unfortunately didn't take after his massive great-grandfather, Jothan Hifadhi, watching the soldiers slowly climb up the cliff side, but he had a little meat on him.

Unlike Meiki's husband Clyde, who regarded the stick in his hands as if it were a snake in disguise. "Except that General Shin never met *me.*"

Relf and Cambo stopped. The only muscle the mathematician apparently exercised was his brain.

"That's all right," Cambo said, trying to sound reassuring but needing more experience in lying. "You're still big *enough.*"

Relf nodded unconvincingly.

Lek closed his eyes.

Clyde stared dubiously at the wood in his hands, calculating its weight and potential force. Judging by the tightening on his face, the results weren't promising.

Cambo turned back to Sam, easily twice as large as Clyde. "Sam, just flex and . . . growl or something."

"Growl?"

Con elbowed his brother. "Pretend you're playing bear with Ensio."

Sam shrugged and emitted a low growl. His relatives chuckled.

Cambo winced dramatically. "Rather feeble, Sam. Come on! Be a real bear, one that's ready to attack your sheep. Put some heart into it, man!"

Sam hunched over, flexed his arms, and growled impressively. Even Lek chuckled in appreciation, and Clyde sidled over to stand behind Sam.

"*I'm* scared!" Cambo announced with an approving grin. "And that's all we need to do. Scare them!"

Relf pointed to the men in turn, his General Relf voice coming through. "Remember, there's twelve of us, and only fifteen of them. We can hold them off. If they approach, we just start beating them with the firewood. Uncle Shem can't object to that. And we're only allowing the descendants of Perrin Shin and Shem Zenos to fight— those with the ancestral blood of the Army of Idumea in them; no other Salemites."

Con raised his eyebrows dubiously at his brother-in-law, then turned to Sam. "So why are we here? I really don't know what to do with this!" He gestured feebly with his branch.

"You're *fathers* of descendants of Perrin Shin!" Relf snapped at the Cadby brothers, in full general style.

They instinctively stood at attention.

"You too, Wes," Relf added in his gravelly low voice and began pacing again. "And you will be soon, Clyde: a father to a descendant of Shem Zenos. And by marriage, you're all their sons."

Cambo, and a reluctant Lek, nodded in agreement.

"We'd be thirteen if Cephas were here," Bubba said wistfully. "Where is he, anyway? I hardly ever see him anymore. He's always off doing something for Uncle Peto."

"He was going to spend last night at our house," Sam said. "He and two of the assistants were making a final sweep of the eastern regions to make sure there aren't any stragglers. But I doubt they'll find anyone. Once Mrs. Yordin started collecting that massive group of fighters, everyone near us packed up and left in a hurry."

"And we'd have fourteen, then, if Young Pere were here," Nool smiled faintly, thinking about his older brother. "Kind of wish he was. He'd be brave enough to go down the trail and throw rocks at the soldiers or something."

His brother Barnos smiled. "I still remember when he did that to me."

"And me," his cousin Holling nodded.

Relf sighed. "He's coming. They've seen him," he said in his usual and more gentle tone. "And despite everything that's happening, there's nothing I want more than to see my big little brother again. Even in chains. Maybe it'll be even *better* if he *is* in chains."

His family laughed softly.

"But if these soldiers get in the way—" the general began to creep back into his tone, "—that might not happen. Our mothers and Muggah have enough to worry about. Let's not make them deal with another missing, or *dead*, son today."

The young men soberly nodded at Relf and tightened their grips on their firewood.

"Hifadhi's signaling," Cambo noticed. "Five minutes."

"Roll out of the way now, Jothan," Lek mumbled. "Time to get behind that rock."

Clark 14 trotted wearily toward the barn, and Peto was surprised to see his sister come out of it.

"I missed saying goodbye to Boskos, didn't I?" he asked.

Jaytsy shrugged as she took his horse. "Probably, but I'm not sure. Noria just left with her children and family, but Boskos might be coming back."

Peto squinted. "Why?"

Jaytsy told him what was happening up at the ancient site with the fifteen soldiers, and Peto groaned in frustration. "So where's Deck?"

"He followed them," Jaytsy confessed.

Peto glared at her. So far nothing that morning had gone as he hoped, and now the carefully laid plan to protect the Eztates was also unraveling. "Deck's supposed to stay *here* at *all* times!" he said irritably. "That's what Shem, Deck, and I agreed to last night!"

Jaytsy put her hands on her hips, still annoyed that the men had held a family council without the women. "Well, Shem ordered for 'all men' to follow him!" she snapped back. "And Deck is 'all men.'"

They glowered at each other.

It had been years—*decades*—since they had last argued. Some years ago Peto realized that his sister was one of his best friends, and it wouldn't do now for Rector Shin and Mrs. Briter to revisit their childish fighting. If Shem *had* ordered Deck to follow, no one outranked Guide Zenos.

He could see in Jaytsy's eyes dread mingled with despair. It'd been a difficult morning—a difficult week. Peto hated to see his sister on the verge of tears, and he knew how to fix that.

"Jayts, with your 28th wedding anniversary around the corner, it's good to hear that you still think of your husband as 'all man.' Of course, that's probably a sentiment you should share only with *him*, and in more *private* moments. I *really* didn't need to hear that—"

Immediately Jaytsy's eyes softened and she snorted.

Peto smiled. "I'm sorry, Jayts. I didn't mean to get angry at you. Just . . . not a good morning."

She nodded in understanding. "Not a good anything, Peto. I have to admit, it's all starting to get to me."

"I know, I know," he said, looking around the Eztates which was noticeably quieter. "This empty hole in my gut . . . *All* of Salem . . ."

"You look drained," Jaytsy said when he didn't finish. "When did you get to sleep last night?"

"I don't think I ever did," he confessed. "Then I got up early this morning—"

"I heard. Eltana's Army?"

Peto smirked briefly at the name and climbed down from Clark 14.

"Couldn't get any of them to see reason?" Jaytsy guessed by his bleak demeanor.

"No. They're all in position waiting just beyond the Second Resting Station. They took over every structure they could find. I imagine the army will form their ranks in the open fields between the houses and barns. Then, when all of the soldiers are there . . . ambush." He sighed. "It'll be ugly."

Jaytsy winced at the image. "I'm so sorry, Peto. I know you did your best."

"But did I, Jayts? I keep thinking, *If Father were here, what would he say?* I almost wish I still had his jacket to wear, that maybe the blue of it and the resemblance I bear to him might have had some impact. But I'm no General Shin."

Jaytsy put an arm around him. "If people don't want to listen, there's nothing that can force them. I remember when Father tried to convince Edge to give away land to the refugees from Moorland and others in need, after that first pox outbreak that killed off so many families. No one listened to him then, Peto, and he was more powerful than most men I know. Almost as powerful as you."

Peto scoffed. "I'm not powerful, Jayts. Not like he was. He would just walk into a room and people turned and stared in awe of him. I know I did."

"They do that with you too, Peto," she jostled him gently.

"No they don't," he chuckled sadly. "I'm not General Shin."

"No, you're not. But you're *Rector* Shin. You walk just like him, Peto. You sound a lot like him, too. And when you speak, you say the words of the Creator. *That's* what made Father powerful—he listened and was inspired. You are, too. Everyone can feel that spirit with you. Those people this morning, they've had practice in ignoring it. That's why they ignored you. But tens of thousands of people are walking west because they feel that spirit in you. *You* have secured Salem. Father was right—you would have made a good officer."

Peto put his arm around his sister. "Thanks, Jayts. I might believe that someday. I need to run into the house for a moment, but then I'll be back to help you with getting the rest of the horses."

Jaytsy waved that off. "Hogal and Atlee said they could take care of it."

"Then I'll be out to help as soon as possible!"

Jaytsy chuckled as Peto jogged off to his house.

He opened the door. "Mother? The house is spotless. Enough, already."

She peeked her head out the kitchen door. "Just rearranging the cabinets, Peto. Then I'll be out to . . . whatever it is to do with the horses."

Peto smiled, secretly looking forward to seeing his mother on horseback. "Lilla still out?" he asked, already knowing the answer because he didn't smell anything baking.

"Yes," Mahrree answered through the closed door. Peto heard some large crockery being shoved into a new location. "At the rectory, in case anyone else needs last minute help. She said she'll be back before midday meal. I doubt anyone is left, but the rectory affords the best view of the main road, you know, just in case . . ."

Peto finished the sentence in his mind. *Just in case Young Pere comes running down it.*

He trudged up the stairs, the unnatural silence of the house nearly sucking all hope out of him. He walked to his bedroom and paused at the door. He didn't have any time to be sentimental, which was probably good. Remembering all the memories of that house would have reduced him to a sobbing mess if he spent any time thinking about it.

But there was one thing he needed to do. Time was growing short and it had been pressing on his mind all morning as he watched the make-shift army and wished for the influence of General Shin.

He walked over to his wardrobe and felt underneath the sweaters Mama Trovato had knitted him over the years. He pulled out the thick parchment envelope and sat down on his bed, staring at it.

He had no idea what could come of it now. It was from another time and another place that had nothing to do with this point in his life. He slipped the Papa Pere Prophecy from the envelope and reread the scrawls he made when he was fourteen years old. The top of the parchment containing the names of Lek and Lorixania Shin, with the signature of General Relf Shin, had been sliced off and given to his father years ago. His mother now had it, lying on top of her dresser drawers.

But the rest of the prophecy that no one knew about, except for Lilla, was still intact.

The greatest general the world ever saw, leading the world in its final conflict to bring a lasting peace.

That's what Grandfather Relf had said all those years ago in Idumea. He was so sure it would be his son Perrin Shin. Then, not so long ago, Peto wondered if Relf, in those delirious dreams, had not seen his great-grandson instead. He was also named Perrin Shin and looked nearly identical to his grandfather. For a few brief, terrifying moments Peto had wondered if his son might not have found a way to overthrow Lemuel to claim the title of general himself.

But now that was clearly impossible. Everything on that parchment was impossible. But Peto couldn't ignore the admonition of his grandfather, which he felt again, nearly overwhelming him. He heard the words many times that morning as he watched Eltana lead out the fighters.

Take it with you, Peto. Whenever you think you might be gone for a long time, take it with you. It will become important to your children and grandchildren. Take it with you, Peto.

"Grandfather," he whispered to the parchment as he carefully folded it again on the lines Relf had originally made, "I'm putting it in my shirt pocket right now. For years I thought I understood this, and for the last year and three seasons, ever since he died, none of it has made any sense. It still doesn't. But it's in my pocket and I will carry it with me through the Last Day. And when I see you again, I may demand some explanation for all of this!" He smiled as he tucked it into his shirt pocket and buttoned up his thick jacket to keep it secure.

"Apparently that last stretch up the cliff is the toughest." Bubba Briter dropped his considerable weight on the ground and sat in the drying grass. "Because that's the longest five minutes I've ever experienced."

Viddrow chuckled anxiously at his brother. "It can be as long as it wants to be."

Lek continued to check over his shoulder, anticipating seeing his father arrive. "They're out of shape, remember?"

"Oh, I remember," Barnos Shin said, slapping his timber against his hand. "I'm counting on it."

"Con," Sam nudged his brother, "do I have time to take a nap?"

"Close your eyes. I'll wake you when I see something," Con promised.

Relf clenched the firewood in his hands, watching the edge of the cliff. "Get up, Bubba!"

Bubba swallowed hard as he noticed the first head wearing a blue cap coming over the edge. He got to his feet and Con elbowed his brother.

"That wasn't nearly long enough," Sam complained, opening his eyes. They grew wide when he saw another, then another, and another head come over the edge.

The soldiers spied them too, about thirty paces from the cliff, standing in a row. The fourth man up was the sergeant, and he sneered at the sight. "Look, men: the army of Salem is here to greet us with sticks."

The first three soldiers, who had looked at the line a little warily, started to laugh.

"This won't even be a challenge," one of the soldiers said as he stood opposite of Cambo about twenty paces away, his hand on the hilt of his sword.

"Now, now," the sergeant said. "Wait for everyone else. All of you deserve to have a little fun."

The descendants of Perrin Shin and Shem Zenos said nothing but tightened their grips on their firewood, if only for something to hold on to.

One of the younger soldiers cracked his knuckles in anticipation. "Been waiting to bloody my sword on something more than a squirrel."

"A squirrel?" said another soldier.

"I got bored waiting to climb that stupid mountain after the boulders."

"You probably killed the last surviving squirrel in the area."

"Yeah, I know."

The line of young men held their positions as the rest of the soldiers arrived at the top, winded and weary to take their place opposite of them.

Lek glanced to the side. "Papa," he whispered, "now would be a good time. Papa?"

The last of the soldiers came up to the summit and sniggered at the twelve *mostly* well-built men holding sticks.

Clyde was almost fully behind Sam now, cowering slightly.

A noise behind them, like a wild animal crashing through the brush, spun the sons around. Lek heaved a sigh of relief as suddenly a large white horse with Shem Zenos came rushing out of the forest and straight toward them.

The soldiers stared in surprise. Shem couldn't have been a more startling or impressive sight. He sat tall on the horse, bulky and powerful as he pulled it to a quick stop. Right behind him was Boskos, Zaddick, and an exhausted Kew. Now it was sixteen to fifteen.

Shem slipped off his horse and walked boldly through the line between his nephews and headed for the sergeant.

Boskos, Zaddick, and Kew dismounted and got in line by their brothers.

The sergeant instinctively drew his sword and the rest of his soldiers scrambled for their weapons. The two bowmen stepped back quickly into the shrubs.

Shem was undeterred. He held up his hands to show he was unarmed and strode up to the sergeant. "Get off my mountain, Sergeant, you and your men. You have no claim to this land."

"Oh, yes we do!" the sergeant said, his voice tinged with fear. "By order of General Thorne. Whatever we find, we can take."

"General Thorne is not the authority here. I am," Shem said calmly yet firmly. "I'm telling you now, get off my mountain or I will kill you."

The sergeant tried to laugh. "Oh really? How do you and those little boys back there plan to——"

"Get off my mountain."

"No! It's mine!" The sergeant raised his sword, but Shem was faster. He dropped to the ground, kicking the legs out from under the sergeant, who flailed and fell to the ground releasing his grip on his sword as he tried to brace his fall. Shem deftly caught the blade with outstretched fingers, got back to his feet, flipped the sword expertly in the air and caught it by the hilt.

The other soldiers gaped in amazement as they realized their sergeant was now unarmed, and Shem was unharmed, not even nicked by the blade he caught, all in half a moment.

Shem held the sword straight out and pointed it at the throat of the sergeant lying stunned on the ground. "Get off my mountain!"

The sergeant swallowed before he shouted.

"Attack!"

Calla had left her horse away from the rest of the abandoned animals, far from the Salemites who were nervously waiting for word that it was safe to proceed. She didn't want anyone to know she was there to watch her sergeant major fight. What prideful behavior! She wasn't known for being prideful, except when it came to her husband. But she couldn't help it, nor was she really trying, to be honest. She'd waited years for this moment, ever since Perrin had told them of his dream, and since she was a mere girl she'd fantasized about Shem Zenos with a sword. She almost shocked herself with her worldliness, but not enough to remain at the Eztates.

She scrambled up a steep ridge that overlooked the tableland before the cliff side, knowing no one else would be there because of the ruggedness of the terrain. She crouched and darted from one scrubby bush to another, using them as shields so as to not be seen by her family below who now came into view. As she moved along the slope for a better angle, she clutched branches and braced herself against large rocks to keep from sliding or tumbling down to the family campsite about one hundred paces below, which would have been mortifyingly embarrassing.

She paused to watch Shem confront the sergeant, gasped in delighted surprise at how he disarmed him, and was planning to make her way down for an even closer view when she heard the sergeant yell, "Attack!"

She froze in a cluster of bushes as two soldiers on either side of Shem charged at him simultaneously. He stepped back at the last moment and the two soldiers veered to each other instead. As they looked in dismay that their target had shifted, Shem sliced the neck of the soldier on the right, then plunged his sword into the chest of the other one. Both men dropped to the ground.

Aghast at their swift deaths, but too impressed by her husband to mourn the men, Calla clenched her fist and whispered, "Yes! Perfect! Shemmy, on the left. He's coming next. Yes, yes—"

Slice, and another man fell, writhing from losing his arm. Shem finished him off with a stab to his heart.

"Oh, Shemmy! Poor Lek's going to go . . . oh, never mind. He's already down. To the right now and . . ." Calla winced and held her hand to her mouth. "You're right. Decapitation *is* messy. Glad Lek didn't see that. Shemmy, look—another one. Yes! Whoa, where did he come from? Well, he's gone now. Oh, you're amazing, Sergeant Major. Too effective—" and she swallowed down the bile that was rising in her throat, "—but fantastic."

Down below her, the fifteen young men, fourteen still conscious but two looking like they would join Lek sprawled on the ground at any moment, kept to the line but stared in amazement as Shem spun, slashed, and killed another soldier, then another, and another.

Boskos shook his head in awe. "Zad, look at him! That's *our*

Papa."

"Bos, I'm going to be sick. He just cut off that soldier's *head*!"

"Do you realize the sheer force it takes to *do* that? To sever the vertebrae—"

"Bos, just *shut up* about it. Oh, he just got another one! I can't watch this . . ."

Boskos couldn't help but smile. "That's *my* Papa. Watch out! There's another—oh, never mind."

None of the other young men could speak as they watched the sixty-four-year-old man step, dodge, spin, stab, slash, and plunge like a man thirty years younger.

Sergeant Major Zenos wounded another man who fell to his knees, dropping his useless long knife, as Zenos turned to catch with his blade another approaching soldier. Boskos started for the wounded soldier until a sudden slice of Zenos's sword removed the necessity of his son rendering first aid.

Boskos stopped in midstride. "Oh . . . I'm pretty sure I can't fix *that* anymore."

Above him, unseen in the shrubs of the ridge, Calla continued quietly cheering on her husband. "Excellent, Shemmy! Boskos, get out of there! Shemmy, the bowmen, in the bushes. You'll have to get them, soon. One of them might actually stop shaking enough to nock an arrow. Shemmy, the—Ooh, that was ugly. Efficient, but gruesome. Nice slash, though. Ah, Shemmy—you're amazing. The bowmen, Shemmy. One's got an arrow nocked!"

Shem didn't even try to parry and thrust like the soldiers had been taught. His goal was to stop them, not show off for them. He went straight for vital organs and hit them almost always the first time. If not, the soldier struggled only a moment before a second stab ended his suffering.

Boskos watched the bodies pile up, counting as they went. "Five left, Papa!" he called, looking around for the bowmen. "In the bushes, Papa! Bows!"

Shem didn't say anything but slashed another soldier across the chest and charged directly for one of the bushes. As he raised his sword, the bowman let the arrow fly in a frantic attempt to accomplish something. The arrow flew aimlessly toward the empty ridge behind the stunned young men, and Shem finished off the bowman's brief career with one plunge to the heart.

"Four left!" Boskos called.

Shem spun to see the two last knife holders shaking in terror and anger. Shem beckoned them to come. They nodded, then charged at Shem.

"Shemmy!" Calla gasped from her hiding place. "The other bowman . . . He's nocked the arrow! Shemmy!" She couldn't understand why she was gasping for breath. Maybe the excitement of the ride up there, and now watching him fight—she *was* fifty-six after all. Not exactly a young woman anymore. "Shemmy, excellent jab! But the bowman . . ."

The two knife holders were now on the ground, stilled and bleeding profusely, while Shem charged at the last bowman trembling in the bushes. Before Shem reached him, he released his directionless arrow. Shem slashed him across the throat. All of the soldiers, but one, were now dead.

The sergeant remained prone on the ground and panting in terror where Shem had originally felled him.

Shem walked serenely over to him—in fact, he'd felt wholly focused and calm during the entire incident, filled with the tranquil assurance he always felt when the Creator sent him to do an unpleasant and violent task—and pointed the dripping sword at the sergeant's throat, a few drops of blood landing on his flesh.

"I leave you alive to return and report to Lemuel. But take your time. Tomorrow will be soon enough to give him this warning: Tell him this is my mountain, and if he comes here, he will die, just like all of them."

The sergeant trembled. "And who are you?"

"Tell him Sergeant Major Shem Zenos sends this message."

The sergeant began to choke. "That . . . that's not possible! Thorne killed Zenos himself! *Everyone* in the world knows that!"

Shem tipped his head. "Everyone knows a lie, Sergeant. Lemuel *missed* and he knows it. Remind him of that. Now stand up!"

The sergeant struggled to get to his feet, staring at Zenos. "You can't be him—"

"Who else in Salem could handle a sword like me? Only someone trained by Perrin Shin, that's who."

The sergeant tried to catch his breath. "But . . . but I'm not even sure . . . where Thorne is, sir."

Shem smirked at the sergeant's "sir." It meant he accepted Shem's identity. He motioned with the sword. "That large boulder you passed at the back of the valley? Go back to it, turn to the left, and walk through that canyon. At the end of it you will find Salem and the army likely scaling the last wall. Dismissed!"

The sergeant obediently saluted and ran for the trail going down the cliff side. In a moment he was gone, frantically slipping and jogging down the path he just came up.

A faint laugh came from behind the boulder just beyond the trailhead.

Shem walked over to it. "Jothan?"

Jothan stood up stiffly and grinned. "Fantastic, Sergeant Major! Absolutely marvelous! Ah, that was worth the wait, my friend. Worth the wait!"

Shem grinned back and firmed his grip on the hilt as Jothan moved around the rock to join him. "I hate to confess it, Jothan, but this feels mighty good in my hand again."

"It looks *great* in your hand!"

Shem's grin faded as he stared at the blade he never wanted to hold again. How he'd picked it up again so easily, and had used it so naturally after all these years, suddenly worried him. "But it's over, now. I can't let this stay." He turned to the bodies strewn before the cliff side, but instead noticed the line of stunned young men staring at him with expressions of pride and horror.

Lek was just starting to sit up. "Is it over?"

"Yes, Lek. It's over."

The young men relaxed and immediately began to compare notes. "Did you see that—"

"Or what about—"

"And then when he—"

Shem held up his hands. "Boys!" he called. "We can discuss this later. First, we need to clean up this mess."

Boskos was already at the bodies checking for pulses. The obviously dead ones he didn't even approach.

Shem walked over to him. "How was I?"

Boskos exhaled. "Remarkably deadly, Papa."

"Sorry about that."

"No, don't be. You were impressive. I mean, I never fully appreciated you could do all of that. I heard the stories, but *seeing* you—"

"That's enough, Bos," Shem said in a low voice. "There's no glory in this. It had to be done. And now all of this has to leave the temple site or the Creator's protection can't be here."

"Understood," Boskos said, standing up. He felt his father's large bicep. "But I have to say, in order to decapitate a man—"

Shem looked at him severely. "Did I do that?"

Boskos gestured to the evidence not far from them.

Shem flinched. "We need to get rid of this, now. Bos, all of you," he said, turning to the young men gazing squeamishly at the bodies on the ground. "Please don't say much of this to Calla. She's always had a strange idea that it would be interesting to watch me."

"Really?" Lek said, not understanding that at all.

Shem chuckled uncomfortably. "Kind of a romantic notion that somehow this is all *admirable*."

"Well, we won't say much," Zaddick assured him, "but what about them?"

Shem looked beyond to see the crowd of hundreds of people coming from behind the temple ruin. Some began to clap, and suddenly all of the Salemites there, thousands strong, were cheering and applauding their guide's success.

Shem went hot and red, and tried to hide his face in his hands, but the hilt of the sword he was still holding stopped him. He looked at the sword, then the cheering Salemites, and he knew what he had to do. He flung the sword as far as he could, sending it plummeting to the valley floor below.

The crowd stopped their cheering, unsure of why he did that.

"Fourteen men just died here," he called to them, "never knowing their Creator, never knowing the reason for their lives. That's nothing to be celebrated. It's to be mourned. I need volunteers with strong stomachs—"

Lek sat back down on the dirt.

"—to help me clean up the area. These bodies need to join that sword in the valley below. We also need volunteers to sweep away the blood. We may need this area for camping tonight. Thousands of Salemites are on the routes. Set up your camps close together, help each other, and those willing to help me, get over here now, please."

Salemites reluctantly turned back to establishing their camps. A few men jogged over to Guide Zenos, butchers and a doctor, and began to pick up the bodies to toss off the cliff.

The wives and children of the young men slowly made their way back to their husbands, carefully avoiding the bloody areas.

Meiki cried out when she saw her father. "Papa! You're bleeding!"

Shem glanced down at his shirt. "No, Meiki. It's not my blood."

Looking as if she was about to vomit, she whimpered, "That makes it worse, somehow."

Shem buttoned up his jacket. "Better?"

Meiki nodded and rushed into his arms. "That was so scary, Papa! I can't believe you did that."

"I can't believe you watched that."

"I couldn't help it."

"Just don't let your mama know. As sick as you've been feeling with this baby, then to see all of that—"

"Oh, Uncle Shem," Lori said, coming over, "Meiki lost *all* of her breakfast not long ago."

Meiki laughed shakily into her father's chest until she saw her husband. She rushed over to Clyde and embraced him for hiding so bravely behind Sam.

"Then I'll hug you!" Lori announced as she flung her arms around her uncle. "Thank you, Uncle Shem."

"And I'm next!" Salema announced.

Up on the ridge in the thick shrubs, hidden to everyone on the tableland, Calla could only mouth the words, "Shemmy, I'm so sorry. Shemmy, I'm so sorry. I love you. I love you. I'm sorry . . . ." She laid on her side, her strength fading fast, two arrows protruding from her chest deflating her lungs. She didn't even have the strength to shake the shrubs around her to get anyone's attention. Not that it would do any good.

She'd learned enough from Boskos to know there was no hope. It'd be over in just moments. It was better this way, to go alone. Her family would have been devastated to watch her suffering, and the last thing she wanted was to cause them more worry as they readied for the Last Day.

Yet she was. Eventually they'd find her, and oh, what a terrible moment that would be for them! Why didn't she think of them instead of her silly pride? Why wasn't she taking care of her two daughters down at the Eztates instead of acting like an impetuous teenager herself, wanting to watch the man she adored in battle? He would be aghast at her behavior, not understanding any of it.

Tears trickled down her face as she cringed in pain and grief.

But the idea floated in her mind: it was worth it to watch him. It was *almost* worth it. He was magnificent!

"My babies," her lips moved. "I'm so sorry to leave you now. I shouldn't have done this. I'm sorry. I love you all so much. Oh, Shemmy . . ."

Young Pere sighed with a mixture of joy, fear, and amusement at the last wall. It was truly imposing. Seventy feet high.

Everyone reacted to it the same way he did, stopping in astonishment.

"Creet!" Beaved whispered. "That's . . . that's . . ."

"Kind of big," Cloud Man suggested.

"Oh there's *no* way," Teach said. He sat down on a rock. "The next one will be a mile high!"

Snarl squinted at the wall, then the slope, then started scaling the steep terrain in a way no one else could follow.

Young Pere braced himself as Snarl scurried to the top. He would figure it out in five, four, three, two—

"Hey . . . hey!" Snarl shouted from his precarious perch. "That's *it*! This is the last wall! General, I can see something beyond. It's got to be Salem!"

Young Pere's head dropped as a loud cheer erupted from the soldiers behind him.

Thorne broke into a run to the last wall. "Are you sure?"

"I see a herd of cattle," Snarl exclaimed. "This has got to be it."

Amory jogged over and evaluated the canyon contours. "I know these rocks. I used to live not far from here. Salem is just on the other side. Lemuel, we made it!"

Thorne turned to her with a thin smile. "Yes, *my love*, we did. But had you told me about this when we *first* got together, I could have had my kingdom for much longer."

Amory heard the cutting tone in his voice. "Lemuel? I thought I explained all of that to you—"

Thorne nodded to his guards, and two of them gripped her arms. "You did, but not to my satisfaction." He drew his sword.

Amory gasped.

"You're not fit to be my queen. Only one woman is." He plunged his sword into Amory's chest.

Young Pere barely looked away in time, but he still heard her ragged gasping.

"Jaytsy will be my queen," Thorne declared calmly. "Not an old sow like you."

Young Pere heard the sword plunge again and the gurgling from Amory stopped, followed by a soft thudding of a body meeting the ground.

"He just killed her!" Reg whispered, horrified. "I can't believe it—just like that!"

"I've seen him do that before," Young Pere whispered back, his eyes squeezed shut. "Too many times."

Pal rushed over to the side of the canyon and lost his breakfast all over a dead bush. Buddy joined him a moment later.

Cloud Man shook his head sadly, gazing at the finery of Amory, now slumped in the mud. "He definitely wouldn't be fun when we go find the elephants, Young Pere."

Beaved gripped his shoulder. "You're next, Young Pere," he whispered harshly. "Be careful, be very, *very* careful in the next few minutes or you won't be meeting your mother."

"She's not my mother," Young Pere whispered, his gut heavy. "But I do want to see her. And I'll be careful, I promise."

"What are you girls whispering about over there?" Thorne demanded, putting his bloody sword back into the sheath.

"Strategy for scaling this wall, sir," said Beaved loudly.

His team nodded rapidly in agreement.

"And?" Thorne said indifferently, as if nothing more had happened except for 'his love' getting a mosquito bite.

"This climb isn't so hard," Snarl announced, still at his perch.

"It will be for people like Teach," Young Pere said, willing himself not to look at the body, covered in reddening silks and splayed on the ground. "I recommend that whoever can should follow Snarl," he said, "but be careful so as to not erode the side too much, or no one else will be able to follow. For the rest, we still have lots of bedrolls. We need to get tying them together before we have too big of a log jam behind us again."

"Do it!" Thorne ordered. "But *Shin*, I want you up and over that wall *now*. You need to be one of the first to climb it."

Young Pere turned to him, seeing out of the corner of his eye the body of Amory being dragged over to a small ledge. She would be on display, in all her bloody silks, for the rest of the army passing by. Young Pere crossed his arms as best he could with his wrists chained, and cocked his head. His hatred for Lemuel was doubling every moment.

"And *why* do I need to be one of the first, *Thorne?*"

Thorne glowered at his disrespect. "To gauge the reaction time of the Salemites, *Shin.*"

"Only if you unchain me again."

"Only your ankles. You can move well enough with your wrists shackled."

"I'll do it!" Cloud Man said eagerly. Beaved handed him the key and Cloud Man undid the lock holding the ankle shackles. He put the chain around his neck and again bounced merrily.

"Be quiet and climb!" Thorne ordered.

Cloud Man saluted sloppily and nodded to Young Pere.

Young Pere started in the same hand and footholds Snarl used. He slipped a few times, but too soon was near the top of the wall. Snarl had scooted higher, not wanting to be in Young Pere's way and also not wanting to be the first to set foot in Salem.

Young Pere's stomach leaped into his throat when he noticed the actual entrance was only a hundred paces away. Suddenly he wanted to be there, as fast as he could. Taking a deep breath to control his anticipation, he cautiously started back down the other side. His sense of self-preservation startled him. Normally he would have risked leaping from a good height and taking off in a fast sprint, but for some reason a sense of injury and danger hovered around him, the same sensation he felt when he was trying to cross the river on the logs he felled. His normally reckless nature was missing, and at a time like this he wished he had it back.

Or maybe not. Perhaps now was the time for restraint, but that seemed entirely inconsistent with his nature.

Cloud Man was right behind him, but Snarl stayed at the top, searching in the distance for any movement and quietly muttering, "Sheep, swine, horses, goats . . ."

"Wait for me," Cloud Man called as Young Pere reached the bottom.

Young Pere was a mixture of emotions as his feet hit the ground. The anxious feeling remained, his feet rooted in place, but a small, rebellious part of him rose up demanding that he run, run, run. But the choice was simple: Cloud Man would suffer from Thorne's sword if he ran away. Suddenly nothing was more important than waiting for the former vial head.

Cloud Man rushed over to him. "Hold out your hands," and Young Pere obediently did so, wondering why. With his back to Snarl, Cloud Man expertly undid the lock on his wrists and shoved the lock in his pocket.

Young Pere's jaw dropped. "Cloudy, what are you doing?" he whispered.

"In the future, I hope to have the pleasure of explaining everything to you, but now's not that time," he said hurriedly, and quite lucidly. "We're going to find elephants later, remember? But the timing needs to be just right. This isn't it, but I'm preparing you for when it is. Hold the chain together in your hand so it looks like it's still locked."

Astonished, Young Pere grinned at him.

Cloud Man winked conspiratorially. "When the time *is* right to drop it and run, I'll let you know. But for now—" He kneeled and put the chain back around Young Pere's ankles just as Beaved cleared the top of the wall.

Young Pere glanced up and saw the look of relief on Beaved's face that Cloud Man was shackling him again. He nodded back to Thorne that his prisoner was once again secured, and that no one had yet attacked them.

"You're not a grassena boy or a vial head, are you?" Young Pere whispered to Cloud Man. "Who are you and why do you want to help me?"

He looked up at Young Pere and yanked on the ankle chains to make sure they were secure. "Elephants." To Beaved on the wall, he called, "All ready to go, sir."

"Wait for us," Beaved said as he started sliding down the slope, cursing as he did so, with Snarl right behind him. "Buddy, Pal, and Reg can make it over, but Hammer, Iron, and Teach will catch up later when they have the ropes."

Cloud Man nodded and smiled up at the sky in his usual, goofy way. "Beautiful morning, isn't it?"

Young Pere grinned. "It's getting better every minute."

Versa surveyed the scene before her and wondered which way to go. She had made it within sight of the Second Resting Station, her former home, and before her the houses and barns were filled with the absurd men and women who thought they could handle the general and his army. Somehow she would have to make her way through them.

She sat down on the rocking chair on someone's front porch. The house was empty, one of the few at the end of a lane not occupied by eager and anxious fighters. The bulk of Salem's army was ahead, spread out in structures to the left and right, with large fields and orchards in between. The army would be camping among their enemy.

But they weren't here yet, so Versa put her feet up on the railing for a rest. She was terribly out of shape and her ankles were swelling. Just a year ago she could have run half the distance of Salem, but it had taken her two days and a morning to walk to the canyon entrance, a distance of less than thirty miles. She'd never before been so large and clumsy.

Still, she had made it to the southern end of Salem before the general arrived, and without being caught. Three times this morning she was nearly intercepted by Rector Shin as he tried to yell reason at the unreasonable beings armed with only farm implements. Apparently everyone thought getting a start two hours before dawn was a good idea. Fortunately his focus was solely on the crowd marching, and not the occasional stray figure walking behind or he would have spotted her.

Now Versa just needed a plan. She was never very good with those. She hoped to be in the right place at the right time and expected it would all just *come together*. But nothing could be done until the banner in the Second Resting Station tower changed. Until the black banner went up, she could keep her feet up and rest.

Because the rocking chair was wide—likely designed for two, because Salemites were hopelessly romantic like that—she set her camouflaged pack next to her. Draping her cloak over herself and the pack, she looked like a large forgotten bundle of clothing, with eyes peeking out.

Until she closed her eyes and sighed in exhaustion.

Maybe just a little nap . . .

"Jayts, how many horses do you have right now?" Peto asked as he came over to the barn. Grandfather Relf's prophecy was securely in his shirt pocket, his mother was needlessly reorganizing a linen closet, and he'd made no progress with Lilla who was still firmly entrenched at the rectory, staring down the silent road in hope. She could spend another hour or so, watching. They sat together for a time, holding hands and silently praying, until Peto knew he needed to get back to the Eztates. He nodded in approval at his daughters and nieces as they showed him the ready stalls.

"Well, since Shem and company rustled our best horses," Jaytsy gestured to the barn which was considerably emptier, "all we have left is that little one for Mother and this beige one. Clark 14 obviously needs some rest." Tabbit Briter was brushing him down as he munched on a bag of oats.

"Seems I've got a little time right now," Peto said. "So I'll head up to the route and start choosing some more horses. Are Hogal and Atlee still up there?"

"Supposed to be," Jaytsy said. "With my Yenali and your Centia."

"Oh, dear," Peto said dramatically, "they've been unsupervised for probably an hour now, so . . ."

"One of us better get over there," Jaytsy finished with a chuckle.

Peto started in a fast walk to the route entrance. He wanted to see how people were progressing anyway. Cephas had caught up to him in the center of the city earlier that morning and told him the eastern side of Salem, for as far as he and the remaining assistants could see, was abandoned. He'd be returning to the Eztates for midday meal.

Peto started to jog in hope of shaking the weariness out of his mind. He'd already been up for the past six hours of one of the longest mornings he had ever remembered. It was just going to get longer, he suspected.

Soon he was over the hill and down one of the many dips between the hills on the way to the route, out of sight of the Eztates.

"Ready?" Young Pere said to the men standing with him.

"They won't attack with you in the lead, right?" Buddy asked.

Young Pere smiled patiently. "Pretty sure they won't, Buddy. No Salemites will be attacking anyone today."

What he would see in less than one hundred paces, he wasn't sure. Certainly the tower, but in what condition was the rest of Salem? And would anyone be there? It was too much to hope that his father might be waiting, or his brother Relf, but maybe . . .

A moment later he stepped out of the narrow canyon entrance and into Salem. His security team around him gasped at the sight as he gazed on his home. The houses were all still there, albeit far more colorful than he remembered. Not only houses but even the barns were painted in blues, reds, oranges, greens and yellows. There were animals, orchards, farms, canals . . . hundreds and thousands of buildings, fields, vineyards, extending for forty miles to the north. It was exactly as he remembered it. Home!

Except one thing was missing: noise. The usual hum of the valley was replaced by eerie silence. Salem had evacuated and was deserted, as it should be. There was a wandering cow here, a bleating goat in the distance there, but otherwise the immense valley was still, as if it were a giant painting come only partially to life. Young Pere was partly disappointed but mostly grateful. The Salemites had followed General Shin's plan.

He glanced to his right at the tower. The banners were changing, as they should be. There were two: one black with a white sword, calling for evacuation of the area, and another gray banner that Young Pere vaguely remembered signified something about the army on the move. Both went down. A lump lodged in his throat. He didn't even notice the soldiers filling in behind him, each exclaiming in wonder over the size of Salem, because the new banners were rising. The short red emergency flag went first, then the solid black banner, still with creases in it from having sat folded for so many years.

Puggah folded it. He'd folded each one of them, tightly, then shoved them far back in the cabinets of each banner tower, never to see the light of day. Except for *one* day, this day. And now, more than twenty-five years later, it finally flapped, dark and brooding over the tower.

The Army of Idumea had entered Salem.

No chimes were sounded, but Young Pere knew the other tower men would be watching. Already in the distance the other banners were falling to be replaced with the somber, solid black ones. The tower men would then take their waiting horses and ride away to join the rest of the Salemites at the ancient temple ruin.

Tears streaked down Young Pere's face. He was *home* and he didn't care that he was home in chains. *He was back.* Maybe someone at the tower would reach his family and let them know he was there—

"Young Pere!" he heard a reverent whisper next to him. "This is unbelievable!"

He glanced over to see Poe Hili, his jaw appropriately slack.

"The towers! The valley! So big . . . so much . . . the *towers*!"

In the world, the towers were one quarter the size, with simple banners for a handful of messages. When Puggah came to Salem, he designed far larger towers with taller poles for more complex messages.

"I'll give you one guess, Poe, as to who had those towers built and devised the messaging system," Young Pere whispered.

Poe quickly turned to him, still astonished. "I just can't . . . I want to believe, but . . . here it all is . . . I . . . I . . . ."

Young Pere grinned at his stumbling and saw tears of hope building in Poe's eyes.

A movement by the Second Resting Station tower caught Young Pere's attention. He turned just in time to see a man posted to the tower run to the east, slipping quickly into the thick forest. He would have to do some sneaking around to get past the army and to the west, but it wouldn't be difficult, especially if he had a horse tethered in the trees, which Young Pere suspected.

"Run!" he whispered. "Run away!"

"HEY!"

Young Pere jumped when he heard Thorne's shout right behind him. "Someone's escaping from the tower. After him!"

Immediately five soldiers broke away and ran to the forest, but stopped before entering it. None of them felt brave enough yet to step into the trees.

Thorne grumbled his displeasure and Young Pere winced when he realized only one messenger had left. Another still had to be at the tower.

"Come on, Shin. We have a message to send." Thorne grabbed him by the arm and headed over to the tower, not startled enough by the grandeur of Salem to stare in wonder at it.

"Impressive," Thorne commented dully as he looked at the tower designed by Perrin Shin himself. "Idea stolen from the world?"

"I suppose so," Young Pere said.

"Black banner. What's that supposed to mean?"

"That you've arrived."

"Really?" Thorne smiled tightly. "How nice. I always looked good in black." He glanced into the distance to see the other banners starting to rise. "Will everyone be flying *my* banner?"

"Yes."

"Good. I always like to announce my arrivals."

A few more soldiers had run ahead of Thorne to the tower, and now two of them pulled a heavy-set older man from behind it.

Young Pere grimaced.

It was Assistant Ahno.

Young Pere shook his head slightly, trying vainly to assert his innocence in helping the army to Salem. But Ahno's face hardened as he recognized Young Pere. He was the same assistant Young Pere had tricked in order to sneak out of Salem. Of all the Salemites, Ahno was the most innocent and least capable of withholding anything important. One look from the general and Ahno would confess even his most innocuous daydreams.

Why *him*? And here?! He wasn't even a tower worker! Young Pere's heart sank. Maybe . . . maybe Salem wasn't as ready as it should be if it thought Ahno should be the first Salemite Thorne would meet—

"You!" Thorne barked at him.

Ahno withered.

"Send another message! I want Jaytsy Shin brought to me at the Second Resting Station! Now!"

Ahno's mouth worked without speaking, then he stuttered, "The . . . the message tower men . . . are all leaving—"

"Get their attention! I heard you have some chime system or something. Bang it! Get them back! Send my message, now!"

Ahno jumped in fear and allowed the guards to escort him back to the tower. With surprising speed, the portly old man climbed the ladder and a few seconds later started banging the chimes.

"All right, all right!" Thorne shouted. "Even the dead heard that! Send up the message."

Young Pere licked his lips nervously as high above him Assistant Ahno fumbled with the flags and banners. There was no way of knowing if the other towers would relay the message. Young Pere didn't know if he wanted them to or not.

A minute later the banners went up. Red emergency. Black banner. Jayt Brt. Blue striped General Shin banner. Second Resting Station banner.

Young Pere exhaled. Ahno was calling for help by sending up the blue striped general's banner. At least he knew how to work the codes.

Thorne squinted at the colors and shapes that went up. "Explain it, Shin."

Young Pere cleared his throat. "General Thorne requests Jaytsy Shin to come to the Second Resting Station."

"That's it?"

"That's quite a lot for *just* a handful of flags, don't you think?"

"Don't be cheeky with me, *Shin!*"

"No cheekiness intended, *Thorne.*"

Ahno banged on the chimes again, fast and furious, trying to alert the other towers.

Young Pere looked into the distance to see if any other banners were coming down. A moment later the banners in a tower to the northwest went down. The message would be on its way to the Eztates, for good or for bad.

Thorne called up to Ahno. "Now get down here and show me the Second Resting Station!"

"Ask him," Ahno gestured to Young Pere, anger clouding the old man's eyes.

"He's proving unreliable. A Salem trait, I'm sure. Get down here!"

Ahno tipped his head apologetically at Young Pere, then started down the ladder again.

"It's just over here," Ahno said as he reached the bottom and pointed to the enormous structure.

"The large barn?" Thorne frowned at it.

Ahno did a nervous jog-walk over to it.

Thorne paused for Hili and the other officers to catch up, but they were hardly paying any attention to him, still staring in surprise at

Salem.

But Thorne hadn't given anything a second look, as if he were past feeling amazement or wonder at anything.

Young Pere took advantage of Thorne's pause and he jogged to catch up to Ahno, his chains jangling.

"It was Amory Riling who told him about the tower messages and station," Young Pere said quietly. "It wasn't me, I promise."

Ahno glanced back. "Where is she?"

"Dead. Thorne killed her just before the last wall."

Ahno sighed and kept walking, the two soldiers marching on either side. "You've been spotted, shackled," he muttered. "*They* know you're coming."

"Good," Young Pere breathed, knowing *they* was his family. The scouts had seen the chains and realized he wasn't cooperating. "Thanks."

"Shut up, up there!" Thorne called to them.

"Shutting up," Young Pere mumbled.

"That's Thorne?" Ahno whispered.

Young Pere grunted.

"Never thought I'd live to see the day," Ahno murmured.

"Pray you live to see the end of it, sir."

"Amen."

Ester and Huldah Zenos, Tabbit and Banu Briter, and Morah Shin stared at the tower along with Jaytsy.

The black banner had just risen.

"That ought to bring Lilla running from the rectory," Jaytsy said.

The girls nodded soberly.

"I'll go find Aunt Lilla, in case she isn't looking out the window," Ester said, and took off in a run for the rectory.

Young Shem Briter came out of the barn, his mouth hanging open.

The front door of the Shins' house opened and Mahrree stared at the tower, then looked over at Jaytsy. "He's here," she called dully.

Sakal rushed out of the Shin's house, stopping right behind her grandmother.

"Mama," Tabbit said anxiously to Jaytsy, "something's changing."

Sure enough, the banners were lowering, then a few moments later new banners went up.

Mahrree gasped at the message. "Jaytsy!"

Jaytsy gaped at the tower calling for her to come to the Second Resting Station.

And suddenly she knew what she had to do.

Mahrree ran over to the tower and shouted to the men at the top. "Go! Leave now! Thorne can't see that he can control our message system!"

"Sorry," one of them called down. "We weren't sure what to—"

"GO!" Mahrree bellowed and the men obediently scrambled down the ladder.

"That message is from that general?" Morah whispered. "The one we don't like?"

Banu nodded at her little cousin as the tower men mounted their horses and took off for the Lower Middle route. "The black banner is to say he's here. And he wants . . ." She glanced nervously at her mother. "Mama?"

Jaytsy continued to stare at the flapping banners as Mahrree jogged back from the tower. "Jaytsy, run! Now!"

"I'll get a horse." Huldah raced to the barn.

"Yes," Jaytsy said slowly. "I need a horse . . ."

Mahrree stopped. "Oh no . . . Jaytsy! Look at me!"

Jaytsy turned calmly to her mother.

"No, no, no," Mahrree moaned. "I know that look. What are you going to do?"

"Answer the call," said Jaytsy confidently. "Mother, I can take care of this—"

"WHAT?! NO!"

Jaytsy gripped her mother's shoulders. There was something she could do for Salem. The idea had impressed itself in her mind so deeply and urgently that no other option even occurred to her.

"He wants me *alive,* Mother. Two hundred pieces of gold, re-member? Of anyone in Salem, he might just listen to *me.* I know a few things about him. Maybe . . . maybe I can help bring this to some kind of peaceful resolution."

Mahrree looked wildly around. "Where's Peto?"

"Went to get horses. I doubt he can see the tower banner, not if he's in that dip between the hills. Once he gets to the beginning of the route, he'll see it."

"Deck?"

"Went to help Shem."

"Jaytsy, you can't go alone!" Mahrree shrieked.

"I'll go with her," Tabbit offered bravely.

Her grandmother and mother rounded on her. "NO!" they shouted together.

Tabbit looked relieved.

"Look, Mother," Jaytsy said, jostling her a little. "They barely arrived. They know very little of the condition of Salem, and the entire army will still take several hours to get here. Now's the perfect time for me to go."

"And do what?" Mahrree demanded.

"Reason with him—"

"Shins are not very reasonable, Jaytsy!"

"Negotiate—"

"Again, *not* our strength!"

"Sway him with my beauty, then!"

Mahrree paused. "You *are* still very beautiful, Jaytsy."

Huldah stood there with the beige horse, trying to understand what was going on.

Jaytsy whisked the reins out of her hand. "Then it's settled," she said as she mounted.

"Oh, no it's not!" Mahrree cried as Jaytsy kicked the horse. "Come back here, young lady! *JAYTSY!*"

But she was already heading to the main road.

Mahrree was shocked for only half a second before she spun and ran back to the barn. She looked at Clark 14, sweaty and exhausted, then at the smaller horse, wobbly and frail.

Her granddaughters, grandson, and niece followed her in.

"It's the only option, Muggah," Banu said quietly, nodding to the pony.

Mahrree closed her eyes and sighed. "I could never catch her, could I?"

"Not on *that*, Aunt Mahrree," Huldah said. "I could go . . ."

"No!" Mahrree gripped her arm. "No, no, no. We need to stay together. No one else leaves!" She looked up and called, "Dear Creator, this is not good! Send the men back! Send Lilla and Calla and

Ester back! We're running out of time. And please, *please,* send Jaytsy back!"

As they reached the Second Resting Station, Ahno looked back
to the general and offered a most awkward smile. "And we're here.
Now if you don't mind, I have someone waiting for me—"

Thorne scoffed and quickened his pace to grab the man's arm.
"You're staying with me, *my little friend.* What's your name?"

"Ahno?"

"Stupid name. No wonder you're not sure of it," he said, steering
him up the stairs. Thorne stopped on the front porch and cocked his
head toward his guards who stepped up and threw open the door.
"You go in first, Ahno."

Bemused, Ahno shrugged and walked in willingly. Thorne gestured to the guards to follow him, and four men went in while six
remained surrounding the general.

A minute later a soldier stuck his head out. "All clear, sir."

Thorne gestured to Sergeant Beaved and the security team that
was still with him. "Stay out here and keep watch." Thorne tipped his
head to Young Pere to follow him in. They strode into the large gathering room, Thorne's guards still looking around cautiously as the
general evaluated the building for his potential headquarters.

Ahno came over and whispered to Young Pere, "What was that
all about, me going in first?"

"Checking for traps or assassins."

"What's an ah, ah—" Ahno didn't even want to try to say the
word.

"Someone trying to kill him," Young Pere told him.

Ahno was shocked. "Why, we'd *never*—"

"Shut up!" Thorne snapped. "You, Ahno. Is there a cellar here?"

"Y-yes," Ahno stammered. "Filled with all kinds of supplies—"

"How many entrances?"

Ahno blinked at the odd question. "Only one."

As the other officers filed in, taking in the massive gathering room
filled with sofas and soft chairs, Thorne stepped up to Ahno who
trembled under his glare. "And where are all the Salemites, Ahno?"

Ahno swallowed and shifted nervously. "They . . . they left."

Thorne stood practically on top of him. "Where?!"

Ahno shook his head, terrified.

Thorne grabbed his shirt and shoved him up against the wall.

Young Pere flinched in sympathy as Ahno's head banged against the timbers. This was it. The dumpy, old man who shouldn't have been here was about to crumble—

"WHERE?!"

Ahno couldn't speak, couldn't move.

"I know about the temple site, Ahno! Now I want to know, WHERE IS IT? WHERE'S THE TEMPLE, AHNO?!"

Young Pere held his breath as Ahno trembled.

"Northeast. Ten miles from here. Mouth of largest canyon. Beyond the forest and river." He ended in a defeated whimper.

But Young Pere's mouth dropped open in amazement. Ahno didn't reveal the *ancient* temple site, but the *current* temple.

"Large canyon?" Thorne said. "So everyone can run and hide in it like scared sheep?"

Ahno nodded as tears of betrayal slipped down his cheeks.

Thorne spun to see Young Pere's reaction to the news.

Young Pere was sufficiently stunned. Ahno hadn't *lied,* but he didn't tell Thorne what he *really* wanted to know. The old man was craftier than Young Pere had expected. It was almost as if he'd been taking lessons in lying.

Thorne took Young Pere's shock as a good sign. "It's the truth," he sneered. "Look at Shin. Amory was right—Salemites can't lie to save their lives. Or in this case, the lives of *everyone they know.* Find a room to lock this one up." He pointed to Ahno. "He's a wealth of easy information. As for Shin, he's used to dark basements. Guards, and *you,*" Thorne pointed irritably at Cloud Man who had wandered into the Resting Station and was beaming at it with happiness. "Take Shin down to the cellar." He turned back to Ahno. "Where's the door to the cellar?"

Ahno's shoulders heaved as if he were about to break into sobs. "Through the kitchen. Have to go out on the porch, down the stairs, there's an access outside. Young Pere, I'm sorry . . . I'm sorry!"

"Shut up!" Thorne bellowed at him.

Young Pere nodded, suppressing his smile at Assistant Ahno's new acting skills. "It's all right, Mr. Ahno. I *understand*—"

"Take him!" Thorne shouted, and Cloud Man steered Young Pere gently toward the kitchen.

Shem looked around the ancient temple site. After half an hour of cleaning there was no sign of any battle. He nodded in satisfaction and walked over to the camp site of the Shins, Briters and Zenoses. They were in front of the ruin, about thirty paces away, with a clear view of the dead valley below. He smiled at the location.

"We told Muggah we'd save her a good spot," Jori said. "We thought this provided the best views."

"She'll love it," Shem agreed. "Plenty of room for all of us. Lek, you have my tent, right?"

"Yes, Papa. I was going to set it up right about where you're standing."

"And the extra bedrolls—"

"And everything else you said to take for those who forget. Mama packed it all. It's all over here, just waiting for you to move so I can start setting it up," Lek hinted.

Boskos put his hand on his father's shoulder. "We're fine now, Papa. No one else is coming until the full army arrives. Go back down, get Mama, tie up Aunt Mahrree and Aunt Lilla, and get back up here when you can."

Shem looked around at the extended family setting up camp perfectly well without his direction. Several more children nodded at him to leave. "Yes, you're all doing quite well. And that's quite enough excitement for one morning."

"The morning's only half over, Papa," Zaddick reminded him.

Shem exhaled. "Unfortunately you're right. Let's get back down. I'm a little anxious to see what the towers are doing."

"Now this is not your average dungeon," Cloud Man declared as he surveyed the enormous cellar packed floor to ceiling with food.

The two guards behind him pushed past to look.

Young Pere grinned. "Smells a whole lot better, too." He breathed in the aroma of dried meats, onions, herbs, and everything else wonderful and ready for consuming.

"How much is in here?" one of the guards asked. The other guard licked his lips as they looked at the rows and rows of bags, jugs, and bottles. The cellar ran the entire length of the building, dug extra deep so that the shelves could run extra high.

"Enough for about twenty people for a year, or something like that." Young Pere picked up a jar off a nearby shelf, opened it, and dipped in a finger. "Strawberry!"

"What?" one of the guards rushed over to him. "Strawberry?"

Young Pere nodded. "Preserves. Mashed and bottled with sugar to—"

"Gimme that," the guard said, and started drinking straight out of the jar.

Young Pere took another jar. He opened it, peered inside, and held it up. "Anyone for blueberry?"

That got the other soldier over. He snatched it and took a drink.

"Usually we smear it on bread," Young Pere said, but the guards didn't care.

Cloud Man was stuffing his pockets full of jerky. He glanced up apologetically at Young Pere.

"Go ahead, Cloudy. Have fun. I'm looking for . . . hmm, must be *way* down there at the end. Yes, that must be where the *mead* is stored."

The two guards stopped their greedy drinking of the preserves and looked at him. "Mead?"

"Of course, they disguise it in something else," Young Pere continued off-handedly, "as small bottles inside large bags of grain. To keep the teenagers from finding it, you know. Otherwise they'd be breaking in here all the time trying to get at it. Tastes so much better than what they make in the world—"

The guards dropped their jars of preserves and ran to the far end of the cellar, hurriedly grabbing bags and trying to open them.

Cloud Man smirked at Young Pere. "I thought you told us that Salemites don't make mead," he whispered.

Young Pere only smiled.

"Nicely done" said Cloud Man. "Now give me that jar of strawberry."

Peto had taken a few moments to kneel in the trees in the dip between the hills so that he could pour out his heart to the Creator. He was already spent and needed extra strength from above to finish the day, or at least get to midday meal. When he reached the entrance to the route, he was startled to find Salemites picking up their pace, a few even running. He blinked in confusion at their panicked manner, then spun around to look at the nearest tower.

"They're here!" he gasped. Just how long had he spent praying in the woods?! To the Salemites and his children in the field, he shouted, "When did the banners change?"

Hogal and Atlee, holding the reins of two horses they had chosen, looked at each other. "Maybe five minutes ago, Papa," Hogal said. "Did you see the one by our house?"

Peto twisted to look at the call for Jaytsy. "NO!"

He looked around for some animal that seemed strong and fast. His son and nephew held out the reins of the horses they had.

"This one, Uncle Peto?" Yenali suggested, pointing to a horse she was holding.

He was still frantically trying to make his selection when he noticed someone coming down the route.

"Peto?" Deck asked as he finished his stroll down the mountainside. "Back from anti-recruiting at Eltana's army?"

"Where have you been?!" Peto roared at him.

Deck stopped, startled. "I got thrown from my horse a couple miles up, then one family asked me to help calm a skittish horse, then I took an elderly couple over that steep part because there was no way they could—"

But Peto was gesturing frantically to the tower, and Deck dropped off his explanation.

"They're here," Deck said in a dead tone, then, "JAYTSY!"

"Grab a horse, Deck, and let's go!"

"Mrs. Yordin," whispered one of her captains, Mr. Custer, although they were in a second story bedroom watching the army come in about half a mile away. "When do we strike?"

"Not yet. Not until the bulk of them are here."

"But we could pick them off as they come over the wall."

"And how long will that take?" she snapped at him. "Hours! They'll be doing this for hours! We can't fight that long without getting exhausted. Besides, after the first few dozen are 'picked off,' they'll decide on another strategy and stop coming over the walls. No, we wait until we see at least sixty thousand of them have arrived. That's when we strike. What's the count?"

Another man keeping tally marks quickly counted. "Two thousand two hundred so far, ma'am. Averaging at about . . . forty a minute. They could move faster with more than ten ropes. Room for at least eight more."

"They'll figure that out in about an hour. Take a seat, Mr. Custer," Mrs. Yordin said. "Take a nap on that bed if you want to. It'll be a while."

Either Jaytsy's horse was exceptionally fast or she really didn't want to do this.

For whichever reason, she seemed to reach the southern end of Salem surprisingly soon. She stopped the horse and watched as the soldiers streamed over the wall like ants on the move. Glancing nervously around, she knew Eltana's army had to be hiding somewhere, perhaps even around her. She was about to ride into the middle of everything.

Even though she was sure she was doing the right thing, suddenly none of this seemed like a good idea anymore.

Exhaling quietly, she mumbled to herself, "How does an unarmed woman disarm a one-armed general?" Summoning all of her worldly thoughts, she came to a conclusion and untied the bands holding her hair up in a bun. Around her shoulders and down her back cascaded her thick, black hair with thin highlights of silver.

Then, remembering the look in Deck's eyes whenever she let loose her hair, she hastily gathered it back into a youthful ponytail.

"I'm trying to *prevent* trouble," she grumbled to herself, "not cause more. Then again, he may remember me as a teenager, not see me as a middle-aged grandmother."

Within minutes her ponytail was in a braid, as it had been when she was decades younger. Feeling a bit silly, yet strangely confident with her appearance, she kicked the sides of her horse.

From the large gathering room of the Second Resting station, two lieutenants with spyglasses gazed out at Salem and commented on what they saw. Two more men sat near them writing down everything about the terrain and possible resources, trying to keep the awe and excitement out of their voices.

General Thorne had already taken over the large eating room, spreading out plans from his pack across the long table and sending officers to ask the lieutenants to locate obstacles or routes. They were attempting to make a map to discover the fastest route to the temple site in the northeastern part of Salem.

In the meantime, soldiers continued to pour into Salem.

Colonels, majors, and captains directed them to different fields and pastures to reorganize them into groups of hundreds, thousands, and tens of thousands. None of the soldiers were allowed to raid the houses and barns that sat invitingly. Not yet, Thorne was adamant. Any man seen venturing where he shouldn't would be hunted down and killed. In the meantime the soldiers sat in fields salivating at the tremendous amount of wealth that lay before them, all for the taking. And not a single Salemite to fight them for it.

One of the lieutenants with the spyglass stopped reciting the terrain and focused on one particular spot. He paused, looked again, then raced over to the eating room.

"General, sir! I just spotted a woman, maybe a half mile away, on horseback. She was looking in this direction then she started her horse here."

Thorne licked his lips eagerly. "How old?"

The lieutenant shrugged. "Late thirties, but possibly older?"

"Color of eyes?"

The lieutenant shrugged again. It was impossible to tell the color of someone's eyes at that distance, even with the spyglass. "Don't know."

"HILI!" Thorne shouted.

Sergeant Major Hili came into the eating room from the back porch where he was directing soldier placement for encampment. "Yes, sir?"

"Would you remember Jaytsy Shin if you saw her?"

Hili blinked in surprise. "She's not here, is she?"

"Someone's coming alone on horseback. Female."

"The last time I saw her she was just a teenager, but I might."

"Get down there," Thorne told him. "Be the first face she sees of the army. If it's her, bring her to me immediately!"

Poe Hili, skeptical but curious, trotted down the stairs and searched the abandoned farms before him until he saw the lone figure riding in a gallop straight for the station.

It couldn't be her, could it?

He started in a jog, pushing his way through assembling soldiers who made a path for him half a second too late. The growing mass of soldiers ended about one thousand paces away from the station, and it was there, before a row of houses, that he stopped and waited, watching the horse and rider come confidently closer. He didn't realize he was holding his breath until he felt light-headed.

Her age was right, although she appeared younger than mid-forties. And her hair—that thick braid, going down her back, as it always did. And her eyes . . .

Hili gasped.

It *was* Jaytsy!

He firmed his stance since his knees felt like buckling, and her horse came to a stop in front of him.

The soldiers massing behind him turned to look at the Salemite woman who had come, but Hili could barely speak.

Despite her demeanor, as sharp as a general's sword, she was as beautiful as ever, as if time hadn't done anything more than accentuate her features. Her dark eyes were exactly like Colonel Shin's, and her nose and mouth as fine as her mother's. Compared to the painted faces and elaborate hairstyles of the women of the world, she was no comparison at all. She was far more exquisite.

She stared hard at the sergeant major until something in her eyes changed.

"I don't believe it," she whispered. "*Poe*? Poe Hili?"

Poe stood taller and nodded. "Miss Jaytsy! They've released you? You're alive!"

Jaytsy looked confused. "Released me? Ah, that's right. Supposedly I've been held against my will, is it?"

"Isn't it?"

Jaytsy smiled, and Poe felt his chest burn. He never would have had a chance with her years ago, and he guessed that at some point every boy in Edge must have longed for her as he did. They were just too terrified to try anything, considering who her father was.

She shook her head in amazement. "Ah, Poe! I can't believe I'm seeing you, right there. After all these years. Look at you, a sergeant major! My father would be so proud."

"Yes, Miss Jaytsy," was all he could utter.

Jaytsy looked up at the station. "Lemuel, right?"

Poe nodded again, still finding it difficult to form a complete sentence, as if he were nineteen years old again.

Jaytsy shifted her gaze back to him. "Poe, years ago you came back to Edge, and my father trusted you with our family's lives. Remember that night after the land tremor, when you sat up all night with his sword watching for threats while we all slept?"

Finally he found words. "I remember it as if it were last night, Miss Jaytsy."

"Good. That night we put our lives in your hands. Poe, are you still that same man?"

"Ma'am?"

"The same man who fought sleep to protect us? The same man who stole horses all the way to Idumea to deliver a message to help save Edge?"

Poe stood at attention. "I am still the man who Perrin Shin would be proud of."

Jaytsy nodded once. "So if I get off this horse, will you promise that I will come back to this horse safely? Will you be my escort there and back again?"

"Miss Jaytsy, I've already pledged to take care of one Shin, and I believe I did so very well. I promise you'll return safely or I'll die trying to keep that promise."

"Take care of *one Shin*?" she whispered. After a hesitation she dismounted, tied her horse to a railing, and took Poe's arm to begin the long walk up to the station.

Every soldier turned and stared at her, and the whispers raced ahead.

"Who's that?"

"The sergeant major called her Miss Jaytsy."

"Thorne's lost love?"

"It's her!"

"Creet, there goes *that* reward."

Deck and Peto rode as fast as they could, beyond the Briters' grazing fields and to the houses at the Eztates.

"Where's Jaytsy?" Deck shouted as he wheeled his horse to a stop in front of the barn, Peto right behind him.

Mahrree, standing in front of the barn with some of her grandchildren, bit her lower lip and wrung her hands. "Umm . . . she . . ."

"She didn't?" Deck nearly screamed.

"I tried to stop her!" Mahrree cried, and her grandchildren nodded.

Peto stammered, "What . . . what does she think she can do?"

Mahrree shrugged helplessly.

"JAYTSY!" Deck yelled, and kicked his horse into a fast run again.

Peto kept up with him.

"What's the plan?" Peto called over to his brother-in-law.

"I thought you had one!" Deck called back. "Just . . . grab her and run!"

"That's what I've got, too."

Poe could hardly believe that gripping his arm was Jaytsy Shin, in the flesh. While she walked tall and determined, he could feel her hand trembling slightly as she held on to him, almost as if for dear life. He'd protect that dear life with his own.

"Someday you'll have to tell me the whole story, Jaytsy," he said quietly as soldiers parted and stared at them. "For all these years I thought you were dead. I cried when I heard the news. I didn't even cry when my own mother died, but I did when I heard the news about you. And the colonel. And your brother."

"And my mother?" she asked.

"Did she deserve my tears?"

"For all that she did for you, Poe? For all those afternoons at our house at her after school care? For taking care of you after the land tremor? She loved you, Poe. She once called you her 'lost son.' Any tears for her?"

Something jolted him about the words, "her lost son." There had been times when, as a boy, he had wished she *was* his mother.

Eventually he said, "Did she also love the sergeant major?"

"Yes. As a brother. So did my father."

"Are you sure?"

"As sure as I didn't die all those years ago. As sure as I'm walking with you right now. Shem Zenos never betrayed us, Poe."

He sighed. "I want to believe that, Miss Jaytsy."

She squeezed his arm. "Then *choose* to believe, Poe. Think of all the possibilities and hold tight to the best one. Don't just simply accept what everyone thinks might be true."

After a moment's silence, where Poe tried to ignore the stares of thousands of soldiers as they walked, he said, "It took me years to stop looking at the sky each morning to see what color it was."

"Why did you stop checking the color?"

"Because the sky is blue."

"No, it's not, Poe," Jaytsy said, her tone thick with disappointment. "Mahrree Peto taught you that when you were just six years old. She taught you to test for yourself to see what is right and what isn't. She made you look at the sky every morning and every afternoon, didn't she? Why'd you stop?"

Poe thought about that. "Because everyone said it was blue."

"Did you see the sky this morning at dawn, Poe?"

"I did, Miss Jaytsy."

"What color was it?"

"Red. Like blood."

"So it wasn't blue, was it?"

"It would *become* blue, Miss Jaytsy. Just like it has now."

"It's blue *with white*, Poe. Don't ignore the clouds. Watching the clouds can tell you when a storm is coming."

"Can it, Miss Jaytsy?"

She sighed. "The color of the sky, and what's in it, can give you all kinds of messages, but only if you choose to notice them. How you're forced to see the world taints your entire perception of life. I saw the sky at dawn, too. I thought it was more of a reddish-orange, Poe, like poppies. So why is it that when you see a blood-red sky you can still convince yourself it's blue, while the same sky makes me think of a field of flowers?"

Poe swallowed the lump in his throat. The only thing he could say was, "The world has missed people like you, Jaytsy."

"Is that why the world is here now? To demand we return? Or to plunder all we have and make sure that anyone who survives sees only blood instead of poppies?"

"This wasn't my idea, Miss Jaytsy," he whispered urgently as they neared the station. "I wanted to go find Terryp's land. Find by-son, bring them back for food. Convince everyone to settle in the west."

Jaytsy smiled. "You know who else wanted to do that, Poe?"

"The colonel?"

"Yes, and he planned to take his wife with him. Terryp's map was always in his possession, Poe. My father stole it from a storage room at the old garrison in Idumea when he was a young lieutenant. He didn't even show it to us until our last night in Edge. It was *Perrin* who made the copy sent to the Administrators. It was *Perrin* who wanted to run away with his wife. Shem never even saw the original map."

"Oh Jaytsy, if only I could believe—"

"Then choose to. And be careful what you say, we're being watched by the station. Tell me, what will I find there?"

"A most remarkable surprise, Miss Jaytsy."

Two of the guards raced down the stairs to the cellar, Beaved on their heels. They found Young Pere and Cloud Man sitting on large barrels with their boots propped up on a shelf and sampling a variety of jars opened in front of them.

"Definitely this stuff, Young Pere," Cloud Man said, turning the jar in his hands. "What's it called again?"

"Applesauce," Young Pere said, digging his fingers into some-thing he'd waited nearly two years to sample again. The red goo coated his fingers, his wrist chains clanking against it, and he sucked off the sweet and tart raspberries. Paradise!

"Yeah, applesauce," Cloud Man said with appreciation. "That's my favorite so far. So they just smash up the apples?"

"Something like that," Young Pere said, dribbling raspberry jam down his chin. "When they start getting mushy. We had an orchard, and it was my task to shake down all the overripe apples from the trees to collect for applesauce. Great fun, especially when someone I didn't like was still under the trees."

"We just throw them away," Cloud Man said. "It never occurred to me there could be another use for them. Hey, Sergeant!" Cloud Man held up a jar. "Pull up a barrel. There's some great stuff in here."

"And mead somewhere back here!" The guards called to the two new guards who had followed after the sergeant. "Having a slagging hard time finding it, but it's gotta be here." There was a sound of crashing crates.

The two new guards ran to the back of the cellar and started helping to rip apart bags of wheat and oats.

Beaved fumbled with some keys. "Thought you said Salemites don't make mead," he groused. "And as tempting as sampling the wares here is, there's no time. Shin, I'm to take off your ankle shackles."

"Why? What's going on?" Young Pere asked, keeping his feet up for Beaved's convenience.

Beaved smiled. "Visitor!"

Young Pere swallowed another mouthful of jam. "Who?"

"It's a surprise. Cloud Man, run upstairs and get a bowl with water and a cloth. We're supposed to clean him up a bit."

Young Pere leaned forward as Cloud Man went up the narrow stairs. "Let me guess—my long lost mother?"

"Maybe . . ."

Young Pere smiled. "She's not my mother, you know. I keep telling you that. Here, try this. Raspberry jam."

Beaved waved off the offer. "We'll let her decide if she's your mother or not."

"I'm only nineteen, Beaved. Please believe me—everything Thorne has ever told you is a lie." He leaned forward and said in a low voice, "When the time is right, run away, Beaved. All of you— Hammer, Iron, Reg . . . well, leave Snarl. But everyone else, escape when you can. Your time is running out. *We've invaded Salem.* The Last Day is coming. Applesauce?"

Beaved finally got the chain off his ankles and straightened up. "Shin, I really like you sometimes. You've got good intentions but you're still totally fogged." He flicked his scarred ear. "Get a hold of yourself, Young Pere! Face the reality of what's coming. Save *yourself.*"

Young Pere nodded, the ends of the unlocked chain around his wrists clenched by three fingers. "I plan to."

Thorne watched Hili's progress from the westward window at the station. He licked his lips, ran his left hand through his hair several times, and even checked the buttons on his jacket and straightened a few medals.

Major Twigg knew better than to comment, but kept his distance and watched with veiled amusement. Thorne was acting like a young lieutenant getting ready for a big dance, not a hardened general ready to face the woman who rejected him and married a mere farmer.

As Hili and the striking woman neared the stairs, Thorne turned and headed back to the study at the other end of the building.

"Bring her to me here!" he called to his officers, all of whom had also been spying on him. He stepped into the study and slammed the door.

Cloud Man smiled as he wiped Young Pere's face, as if he were washing up a toddler. "Chin up. Up, up. Too bad there's no time for a shave. You grow the most ridiculously splotchy beard. Now, behind your ears . . . And over to your forehead . . ."

Beaved rolled his eyes and turned around in embarrassment.

Young Pere struggled to keep his face from contorting. Cloud Man was the best.

"Now close your eyes. We need to get all that dust off. Why, you're not as tan as I thought you were. Most of that coloring is dirt. Tsk, tsk. What would your mother say? Oh, I guess we'll find out soon enough, won't we?"

Young Pere snorted.

"Now your hair . . . hmm. I think I have a comb somewhere. Ah, here it is! I don't think I've even used this. Let me comb through this . . . It's as if you haven't bathed in days, Young Pere."

"Because I haven't, Cloudy. None of us have."

"Tsk, tsk. Your hair would be better if it was shorter. Guess there was no time for a decent cut after they released you from the dungeon. We'll just comb it up and over your ears. Now, let me look at you. Hmm. Guess we need a woman's opinion. Do they generally consider you handsome?'

"Generally."

"You might pass for handsome. *Ruggedly* handsome, since you're not cleaned up properly—"

"Are you about finished?" Beaved interrupted hotly. "Because I'm supposed to bring him at any moment!"

Cloud Man nodded and patted Young Pere's hand which still held the unlocked chain together. "I think we're *almost* ready."

Jaytsy's heart fluttered anxiously to her throat as she and Poe walked up the steps to the Second Resting Station. Today, the refuge for refugees felt entirely wrong. There were far too many uniforms, bringing with them a spirit of violence to the building which had always been a haven.

Poe opened the door and Jaytsy steeled herself, drawing upon every confident and arrogant Shin trait she could muster, hoping none of the dozen officers who turned to stare at her would see her nervousness.

Standing tall and aloof, she said coolly, "I saw the message that I was needed here?"

A major scurried over, his face drawn and tight, his name badge reading TWIGG. He gestured to the door of the study. "He wants to see you in here, ma'am."

Jaytsy nodded and waited for him to knock.

"Come in!" Thorne's voice rang out.

Twigg opened the door and motioned for Jaytsy to go in.

Gripped with fear, and momentarily paralyzed by the fact that she had no idea what she was going to do next, she glanced at Hili.

"I'll stay right here, should you need me," Poe whispered.

Pulling strength from the expression in his eyes—he didn't want to be here, either—Jaytsy marched boldly into the study.

Thorne had his back turned, thumbing mindlessly through a random book resting on a shelf. He looked over at her casually as she shut the door, as if pretending to be nonchalant, but the stiffness of his demeanor gave him away.

Jaytsy sucked in her breath as she took him in—his blond hair longer and going gray, and his blue eyes strangely shallow and blank. Unable to look at them any longer, her gaze drifted to his dead right arm and his gloved hand. That was even harder to take in, so she looked up into his face and was surprised that her first emotion was sympathy, almost as if he were a brother who had been lost for far too long in the world. His former handsomeness was carved by age lines, deep and angry, more than someone his age should possess. The world hadn't been easy on Lemuel Thorne.

Then again, he hadn't been easy on the world, either.

His eyes changed, and she saw hunger and pleading there that she didn't expect. He couldn't keep up the façade of disinterestedness and stepped around the desk that stood between them to grab her hand.

"Jaytsy!" he said, kissing her hand tenderly.

She tried not to flinch. Everything about being sixteen years old rushed back to her. She had to remind herself she was a grandmother, not a helpless teenager, and she yanked back her hand.

"Lemuel," she said shortly.

He didn't notice her coldness as his eyes wandered all over her, evaluating her so intensely that she fidgeted in discomfort.

"Jaytsy, Jaytsy! I've fantasized about this moment for so many years. But I never dreamed I would *actually* see you again. You're still *so beautiful*," he gushed. "You haven't changed a bit. I was right to love you all these years."

"What do you want, Lemuel?" she said, trying to sound bored. "I'm a rather busy woman."

He smiled thinly. "Busy woman. Funny. You always could make me laugh."

She realized then that she had never heard him laugh. "If you want jokes, I can send in someone funnier." She turned for the door.

"No, Jaytsy," he grabbed her arm. "Please, sit down." He gingerly led her to a chair which she reluctantly took, and he sat down across from her, leaning forward as if to breathe her in.

She shrank back to avoid being so close. "Why are you here, Lemuel? What do you want from Salem?"

"Jaytsy, I want *you.* I came to rescue you, and look: I've been in Salem for less than an hour and already you're freed."

"I was never a captive, Lemuel."

"Is that what they've told you?" he simpered. "Manipulated your mind to the point you believed you actually *wanted* to be here?"

He was worse than she anticipated. "You've come up with so many lies that you actually believe them, don't you?"

"Oh, my poor, dear Jaytsy." He tried to take her hand again.

She pulled them out of his reach.

He smiled, or tried to. He didn't seem to know how to do so sincerely. "It's all right. In time you'll come to see things as you're *supposed* to see them. I'm sorry I didn't come for you sooner, but I learned only recently that you were here. But now I can fix things, Jaytsy, to be the way they always should have been."

Glaring, she asked, "And what way is that?"

Thorne's odd smile broadened. "I'm going to unite the world with Salem! We never should've been divided all those years ago. We all belong together, and today I am righting the injustices that have been wrong for far too long."

Jaytsy tipped her head analytically. "So you're delusional."

She noticed a flash of irritation in his eyes. "I'm a *visionary*, Jaytsy," he insisted, giving up on his smile. "It's a world of difference. You simply can't see what I can see, but you will in time. Everyone does."

"All right," she decided. "You're not insane, just so wholly self-absorbed that you can't imagine any other possibilities than what you want, and you'll force everyone to give you that or you throw a tantrum. In other words, you're an overgrown toddler."

As if he didn't hear a word she said—and she remembered that he never did listen to her—his left hand swiftly snatched hers again and held it tightly. "Jaytsy." She tried to pull it away, but his strength surprised her. "I don't want to do this the hard way, nor do you. I came here fully intending to make you my queen—"

"Queen?!"

"—and together you and I will rule Salem and the world as one reunited kingdom," he forged on, ignoring her rapid blinking. "With you by my side, Salem will certainly acknowledge my authority to lead. We can do this without spilling one drop of blood, Jaytsy. And it's all up to you."

She wrenched her hand away, demonstrating she had strength as well. "So if blood *is* shed, it's *my* fault?"

"Yes," he said simply.

"YOU'RE the one who's brought swords to the valley, NOT ME!" she raged. "*You're* the one trying to force these people, *these people* who I have *loved* for twenty-seven years to accept an egotistical power-hungry idiot as their leader! You haven't changed a bit, you know that, Lemuel? You've only become more ridiculous. I never loved you and you never loved me. You didn't even *know* me. You merely loved that I was Perrin Shin's daughter and you thought somehow that I could guarantee you his power. Well you could never take his power, Lemuel. He's the strongest man I know, and he didn't die in some stupid crevice in the forest. You see those towers flying the black banner? He built every single one of them! You see the creases in that banner? He made those when he first folded those banners and delivered them personally to each tower to warn his beloved Salemites that evil was here. You are that evil, Lemuel!"

At some point in her ranting she remembered that Shins weren't very good negotiators. They weren't much for reasoning either. She was proving that quite well.

Something changed in Lemuel's eyes and the previous pleading vanished. All that remained was raw hunger. "Where is he?"

"Far too busy to talk to you," she said icily.

"Where is *she?*"

"Again, my mother is occupied by more important things than worrying about you."

"You're lying," he hissed. "They're dead."

"You have no idea what's real, do you? Here's one thing that is: Salem will never surrender to you," she declared. "In fact, you will die."

Thorne scoffed at that. "Do you know how many battles I've been in? How often I've cheated death? It can't touch me, Jaytsy. I'm greater than death," he insisted. "I'm greater than Salem. You don't want to cooperate? That's fine. I *will* possess Salem. I already know where your people are hiding."

Jaytsy swallowed down her first bit of worry. "Who told you?"

Thorne waved his hand vaguely. "Oh-no, Ah-no, some tubby little man who was hiding in the tower. Very easy to get Salemites to talk, Jaytsy. They take one look at me and start divulging their darkest fears. It's to the northeast, Jaytsy," he said, watching her closely for a reaction. "In fact, one of my less skilled interrogators has coerced him to draw us a map. Once his hand stops shaking, it should be quite simple to march my eighty thousand men over there. We'll be there by dinner time. You have that long to change your mind, and *their* minds."

Jaytsy's face remained motionless while Thorne spoke, but she knew her eyes were revealing something. Whatever it was, by his sneer it was obvious he seemed to think he had made quite the impression on her.

But she was impressed instead with Assistant Ahno. He'd succeeded, and fantastically.

Sitting taller, Jaytsy said again, "Lemuel, turn back now before it's too late. Although I believe it may already be beyond your stopping any of this."

"Why would I *want* to stop any of this?" he chuckled humorlessly.

"I'm about to become the greatest general the world has ever seen!"

Jaytsy sighed. "I've heard enough and I have a kitchen to clean," she announced, standing up. "Poe can see me back to my horse."

Thorne stood up too and moved close to her, but she couldn't step back because of the chair behind her. While he was only a few inches taller than her, he hovered in a way intended to make her lose her balance. "Pleasantly surprised to see him? I thought you might enjoy seeing someone from your past. Hili's been an excellent soldier. I've taught him all he knows." He was nearly on top of her now, but she refused to budge, refused to be cowed. "There's another surprise I have for you, my dear Jaytsy. I think seeing this one just *might* change your mind about a great many things."

She frowned, dubious. "How?"

"Jaytsy, Jaytsy." His eyes tried to soften as he took her hand again in a firm grip she couldn't slip out of. "You and I once had something very special. How your mother turned you against me, I'll never know, but I know you felt for me as strongly as I felt for you."

Her frown turned into a glower. "Oh, I felt something *strongly* for you, all right—"

"Jaytsy, Jaytsy," he simpered as if he hadn't noticed she was speaking, "that night in the barn at the fort? It was just you and me and the lantern light. It was beautiful, it was right, it was perfect—"

"What are you *TALKING* about?" she shouted, kicking away the chair behind her and taking a huge step backward, but still Lemuel held her hand securely. "It was rape! Or it *would* have been had my father not taught me where to kick!"

"You're remembering it all wrong," Thorne said sappily. "That's not what happened. You and me, alone—"

Jaytsy tried to pull free from his grip, unsuccessfully. She still knew how to kick but she didn't see the need. Yet. "Even Shem saw what you were trying to do to me!"

The softness vanished from his eyes. "Zenos destroyed everything, Jaytsy," he snarled. "It was *him*, wasn't it? He got to your mother, so she got to you. Because of Zenos we lost what we could've had!"

Jaytsy stared in his empty eyes and realized it was useless. There was no reasoning with a man who had rewritten his entire history and believed every lie he'd ever concocted.

"I'm leaving now," she said. "There's nothing more—"

"Oh, yes there is!" He released her hand and instead clenched her arm, causing her to writhe in discomfort. "I have proof about what really happened in the barn, Jaytsy! I brought it with me."

"What are you talking about?" she demanded, trying to wrench out of his grip.

"Guards!" he shouted at the closed door, "Tell Beaved it's time." He turned back to Jaytsy. "When you see this, you'll know your memories have been warped. Open the door!" he called.

A guard swung open the door, and Lemuel, still gripping Jaytsy's arm, pulled her out.

The officers in the gathering room immediately turned to do something else, but it was obvious by their sudden shuffling that they'd all been listening to the arguing going on behind the door.

Jaytsy sent an imploring glance to Poe but he was already following closely as Thorne dragged her through the eating room and to the kitchen. He led her out to the back porch and pushed her up against the railing as thousands of soldiers stopped to gawk.

Poe hovered protectively behind her.

Anxious, yet hopeful, Jaytsy surveyed the thousands of blue uniforms before her, looking for one specific size and shape. But a commotion below her by the cellar door drew her attention instead.

A staff sergeant emerged, leading a tall, dark-haired soldier.

Jaytsy held her breath. He was the right height—

Another soldier followed, but all Jaytsy noticed was that the one in the middle was in chains and kept his head down.

"He's been uncooperative," Thorne muttered. "I've had to keep his wrists bound on occasion. But once he takes a look at you . . ." He cleared his throat loudly.

The soldier in chains didn't look up but was positioned by his guards to face Lemuel and Jaytsy.

Jaytsy bit her lower lip. *Oh please, oh please, oh please,* she prayed.

"SHIN!" Thorne bellowed.

Finally the soldier lifted his head and locked eyes with Jaytsy.

She almost didn't recognize him. As if he'd forgotten how to hold himself as a Shin, he slouched, almost apologetically, and was far more ragged than she'd expected. His hair was too long for a soldier, his chin too scruffy, and he'd lost some weight. His eyes were sunken and weary, but underneath it all she could see him; Young Pere was still there, trying to get back.

For once she wished she'd learned her father and Shem's

ridiculous face twitching hobby, but there was one twitch every Shin knew: half a wink, right eye.

He returned it.

Good to see you, too.

And then she tried to communicate everything else, as he seemed to try to give her nearly two years' worth of explanations.

Your parents are waiting, Young Pere, she willed her eyes to say. *Everyone wants you home, Muggah's waiting, so please try to find a way out of here, and run, run home—*

She barely noticed that Lemuel was speaking to her.

"He's ours, Jaytsy!" Lemuel said, full of emotion. "Our son!"

She clung to the railing, the only way she could prevent herself from rushing down the stairs and embracing Young Pere, but she knew she had a part to play. But what to do next?

Suddenly she felt a presence so powerful, so strong, that it nearly took her breath away. She even smelled him, earthy sweet.

Father!

BE HONEST, JAYTS. HE'S NOT YOUR SON. WE'LL DO THE REST.

Jaytsy held her chin still that wanted to tremble as his words filled her, but now she knew what had to happen.

She tilted her head and scowled at Young Pere. "Who is that?"

Thorne stared at her, stunned.

She regarded Young Pere with as much disdain as she could arouse. "You think *that* is *our* son?" She scrunched up her nose. "Lemuel, I have *seven* sons—"

Thorne licked his lips hungrily.

"—and the father of each of them is Deckett Briter. We also have five daughters. He's the only man who's ever touched me and he's the only man who ever will. That," she said, pointing in disgust at Young Pere and trying not to wink at him conspiratorially, "is definitely *not my son!*" She turned haughtily and marched back into the station, Poe stepping quickly aside to let her in.

"But, Jaytsy!" Thorne cried as he chased after her.

Poe broke into a relieved grin and followed.

"Now!" Cloud Man whispered to Young Pere.

Young Pere threw down the chains, spun, and took off in a dead run southeast toward the forest that lay four hundred paces from the station.

Not a single man noticed for a couple of seconds, too captivated by the drama that had been playing out on the back porch. It was as if none of them were *allowed* to see the private sprinting past them.

Until Beaved shouted, "HEY!"

That seemed to break the trance.

Cloud Man looked at the ground to see the chains. "Whoa. Now how did *that* happen?"

"After him!" Beaved cried.

Obediently Cloud Man took off in a run after Shin.

But Young Pere had a three-second head start, and that was all he needed. Already he was past the groups of soldiers massing in the fields and only now did they seem to notice he was escaping. Cloud Man was hard on his heels but no one else felt the need to pick up the chase.

Beaved looked around wildly. "Archers!" he screamed. "Archers, fire on him!"

A dozen men around him ran for their weapons and fumbled with their arrows.

The shouting brought Thorne back out to the porch.

"What's going on—" In the distance he saw the retreating figure of Shin nearing the forest, Cloud Man in pursuit.

"NO!" Thorne shouted. "After him! EVERYONE!"

Jaytsy appeared on the porch next to Lemuel and spied her nephew outpacing the pursuing soldier. She bit her lip and clenched her fists and didn't even fight her grin. As Thorne kept shouting orders to his sluggish soldiers, Jaytsy whispered, "Run! Run, Young Pere! Go! You're almost to the trees!" No one would catch him, she was sure.

The soldiers, now pursuing by the hundreds, would never have hope of reaching him. Volleys of arrows filled the air but fell short of the tall private and the soldier chasing him, hitting instead several soldiers running after them.

Wincing in worry, Jaytsy pounded her fists on the railing, willing Young Pere just a little faster . . . almost there . . .

He disappeared into the dense trees, the other soldier still hot in pursuit but the rest of the army broke off the chase.

Jaytsy beamed in triumph. She felt like shrieking for joy, jumping up and down, and cheering Young Pere's win in the most important race ever run in Salem or the world.

But Thorne was enraged.

"GUARDS!" he screeched, his voice cracking as he ran down the porch steps, gesturing madly with his left arm.

NOW, JAYTS. RUN. RUN!

There was only one general she took orders from.

"Yes, Father!" she whispered and darted back into the station. Grabbing Poe by the arm, she said, "Fulfill your promise—get me to my horse!"

Poe led her out the front door and down the steps. For good measure, he drew his sword and grabbed Jaytsy's hand with his free hand. While the rest of the army was still rushing to the east to see what the uproar was about, Poe and Jaytsy rushed west, and soon they reached her horse.

Jaytsy gave Poe a quick kiss on the cheek. "Thank you, Poe. You're still that same man. My mother will be so proud of you when I tell her what you did today!"

Poe's jaw dropped. "She's . . . she's still *alive*?"

Grinning, Jaytsy winked at him, got on her horse, and kicked it into a full run to the northwest.

Deck sat on the ground of the empty road and shouted, "TWICE! Twice in one day—one *morning*!—I choose a horse that goes lame! NO!" He picked himself up and kicked the cobblestones in fury. Tears of frustration filled his eyes when he realized he was still at least a mile away from the Second Resting Station and there wasn't a spare animal anywhere.

"JAYTSY!" he roared, as if she could hear him so far away. What was happening with her and Lemuel, and this very moment—

Down the road, less than twenty paces, Peto shook his head at his horse.

"To throw one shoe, I can understand. But *three*?" He looked up at the sky. "What are You trying to tell us? Why can't we get to her?" He closed his eyes and squeezed angry tears from them. "Jaytsy, Jaytsy . . . why'd you go?"

Deck, despairing, covered his face with his hands. "Peto, I have to go after her!" he wailed. "I know it's stupid to not have a plan, but I just can't let him *take her!*"

"I know. I feel the same way, but we have to think this through. We don't even have weapons, and now no horses—"

"I don't care!" and suddenly Deck was sprinting down the road.

"DECK!" Peto chased after him, and soon caught up, because Deck was flagging and stumbling.

"It's no use, is it?" Deck blubbered, letting his brother-in-law put his arms around him. "This is all wrong, this is all wrong . . . Peto, what would Perrin do? He always had plans!"

"I don't know," he confessed, feeling Deck's anguish piling on top of him. "Come on, let's think this through—Wait," he said, noticing movement down the road.

A rider on a horse.

"Deck, look! Maybe we can snag that horse?"

With renewed hope, Deck regained his footing and they watched the horse race toward them.

"JAYTSY!?" they cried together.

She nearly rode past them, not realizing who they were. Abruptly she pulled the horse to a stop and stared.

"What are you two doing here?"

"What were *you* doing *there?*" Deck waved angrily at the south. He dragged her off the horse and caught her in a big hug.

But she pulled out of it, her eyes dancing as she grabbed her brother's arm. "Watching Young Pere run away!"

Peto lost the ability to move.

Deck blinked. "Really? Young Pere? Are you sure?"

"Oh, I'm sure! He saw me too. Peto, Peto, did you hear me? He's free! He's running in the *wrong direction*," she said, bobbing her head, "but if anyone can make it back to us, he can!"

Peto's shoulders began to shake and tears slid down his face. "You saw him? He's all right?"

"Running as fast as Father ever did! No one will catch him. And Peto, *Father's* back too! I felt him! I heard him! I *smelled* him, earthy sweet! THEY'RE BOTH HOME!"

Her husband and brother sagged in relief.

"Oh," she added as an afterthought, "and Lemuel's completely delusional."

Young Pere dodged and weaved and hurdled trees and shrubs and rocks. Aunt Jaytsy wasn't entirely disappointed to see him, he concluded. Something in her eyes seemed excited to see him, *before* she pointed at him and said with so much drama that he nearly snorted that he was *not* her son. Now she could go back to the Eztates and tell them—

"Keep going! Keep going!" Cloud Man behind him shouted. "As far as you can! Beyond the arrows!"

"They're firing arrows?" Young Pere shouted back as he ran through a cold stream.

"They *were*! One hissed right by my ear. Keep running!"

"Are you on my side, Cloudy?"

"I have to be! They're going to figure out in just a minute that I'm the one who unlocked your wrist shackles. Run!"

"STUPID, SLAGGING SOLDIERS!" Thorne screamed, his voice echoing. "How in the slagging world did NONE of you notice he was running away?"

His screeching all the way back to the Second Resting Station put every soldier on edge. Thorne was given plenty of space as he strode through the staging areas of the groups of hundreds that were trying to reorganize themselves.

Several soldiers were retrieving the men injured by the flying arrows, and already it was known that three soldiers had died from the poorly aimed volleys.

Thorne continued to spit and storm and thrash recklessly with his good arm as he shouted every profanity he knew and created a few new ones on his way up the stairs and into the station.

"Where is she?" Thorne demanded as he looked around the large gathering room to see only officers.

Each of the men looked nervously at each other, shrugging and twitching.

Finally Twigg spoke. "She seems to have left, sir. During the commotion. But I'm sure we can get her back—"

"IDIOTS!" Thorne shrieked. He dove into the study and slammed the door behind him.

The officers in the gathering room all sagged and gulped. Only

Twigg had seen where Jaytsy Shin had gone. His eyes darted worriedly to the front doors.

"Hili, what are you doing?" he whispered to himself.

Alone in the study, Lemuel Thorne took several deep, calming breaths and considered the past several minutes.

She was radiant. Absolutely radiant.

And she wanted him. She just couldn't reveal it right then, but she would, once she had some time to think and realize all that he offered. It was all just too much, too overwhelming for her to be in his presence again. He had that effect on people, especially on women. When he found her again and got her alone, she'd be his forever.

From the window he had a view of the forest where Shin and that ridiculous cloudy soldier had disappeared several minutes ago.

Lemuel began to smile.

"Excellent work," he nodded toward the trees. "Well done. I knew you'd succeed after everyone else failed. You stay on his tail now. After all, you're his new best friend."

Shem and Zaddick rode their horses in an uneven trot down the mountain, parallel to the cleared path filled with now thousands of Salemites. Boskos decided to stay at the top and wait for his wife and her family.

There would be no one left when they reached the bottom, Shem concluded. A few times people tried to call out to him, but Shem didn't feel he could stop today. He needed to get Calla to the site, along with Mahrree and everyone else. The horses were frothing and tiring, but he could change mounts at the bottom of the mountain. Deck probably had another beautiful animal waiting for him. Maybe that's why he didn't make it to the top.

"Yes!" Mahrree called up to the tower. "That's what it needs to be."

Her granddaughter and niece were up there, changing the banners on the tower to read the original black bannered message.

"Much better. Now come down here before Shem returns."

Next to her, Lilla shook her head. "We're not supposed to be messing with the banners, Mahrree. No one's even allowed up there unless they're a trained messenger. *Your* husband's rule."

Ester Zenos folded her arms. "That's what I've been saying."

"Yes, I *know* that's what you've been saying," Mahrree said, her patience running out. "I've been *hearing* you for the past five minutes."

Huldah Zenos and Tabbit Briter came down from the tower and ran over to Mahrree and the others waiting between the houses.

"That was kind of fun," Tabbit said.

"But I feel guilty," Huldah admitted.

"Well, you should!" Ester declared. "Papa deserves to see the last message."

Mahrree put her hands on her hips. "That, up there now, is the last *legitimate* message sent by the towers. The other one was forced by Thorne. It deserved to come down."

Ester glared at her. "So you're not going to tell Papa about Aunt Jaytsy?"

"Yes, yes, of course I will," Mahrree said hurriedly. "Just not by the banners. Oh, Ester, you understand nothing about men. It's all in the *way* you present the information. You saw how maddened Deck and Peto were when they went flying through here. Your father doesn't need to experience that right now. He's just coming back from battle, Ester. Putting a sword into a man's hands—that changes him. He's going to be fighting that change all the way down. If he saw that Lemuel was calling for Jaytsy, he'd be ready to take up another sword."

"No he wouldn't," Huldah said. "Papa told me the other night that he didn't like being a soldier, or thinking like soldiers—"

Mahrree took a step closer. "But he *must* be a soldier. It's what he was trained for, and it's part of who he is. He can't deny it."

Ester shifted nervously. "But Papa won't kill anyone today."

"Yes, he will. He's done it before," Mahrree said steadily as Shem's daughters squirmed. "He *must* do it again today or innocent people will die. He needs time to deal with that raw emotion, and seeing those black banners is already going to be a struggle for him.

He'll lose his temper like you've never seen him lose it before, I promise. Why make it more difficult?"

Ester sighed. "I just don't like lying to him."

Mahrree flailed in frustration. "It's not lying! It's . . . *revealing the truth at the appropriate moments.*"

"Sounds like lying," Huldah whispered to her sister.

"Look," Mahrree tried again, "he's going to be angry enough about Calla if he doesn't know about that already, then when he realizes Jaytsy's gone, and that Deck and Peto followed—"

They all turned as they heard two horses on a fast approach.

Mahrree bit her lip.

Shem and Zaddick slipped off their horses and ran over to them.

"Black banners!" Shem shouted. "Get your packs! This is it!"

"Um, Shem?" Mahrree started.

"No, no, no! I'm not listening to it anymore, Mahrree, I'm serious. NOW!"

"Shem, you don't quite understand, there's a little problem—"

"The kitchen's CLEAN, Mahrree!" Shem roared. "Get your pack! Lilla! Get the horses! Where's Calla?" He looked hastily around.

Mahrree frowned. "She's not with you?"

"What?" Shem spun to Mahrree. "Why should she be with me?"

Ester and Huldah sent their best accusatorial looks at their Aunt Mahrree.

"All right," she said, wringing her hands. "Here we go. Shem, did you know that Calla always wanted to see you in action?"

Shem squinted and took her by the shoulders. "Where is she?"

Mahrree paled. "She followed you, Shem. Left half a minute after you did."

"Did you try to stop her?"

Mahrree nodded eagerly. "Uh, *Huldah* did."

His daughter nodded enthusiastically too.

Ester folded her arms. "But Aunt Mahrree told her to go."

"YOU *WHAT?*"

Mahrree flinched. "Shem, she said it was her dream since she was fourteen! I mean, how *sweet* is that? She wanted to see her sergeant major in action. Maybe it was the spirit of your ancestor Lorixania reaching her, you know, following her husband into battle?"

Shem glared.

"Come on, Shem. I'm going to tell my *best* friend, Don't pursue your one chance to live out your dream?"

Shem released her shoulders. "I don't believe it. She did it. I suspected she might, but—"

"You didn't see her?" Mahrree pressed.

Shem looked to Zaddick.

He shook his head.

"She was probably hiding," Mahrree suggested. "And seeing the look on your face right now, I can understand why."

Shem spun around. "Maybe she's coming back."

"It might be better if she stays," Ester said. "At least she's up there now."

Shem nodded. "We talked about that last night. I told her how important it was for me to see her up there, safe. You're probably right that she's staying. Her way of apologizing for following me." He sighed heavily. "We'll carry her pack up there. Deck?" he called, searching.

When no one answered, Shem directed his glare once more to Mahrree, his patience sliver-thin. "Where is Deck, *Mahrree*?"

She cleared her throat. "That's the *other* problem."

"How many do we *have*, Mahrree?"

She shrugged. "Uh, Shem, there was *another* banner message." She nodded to Ester to prove she was getting to it.

Ester watched her closely.

Mahrree blurted it out. "Shem, Lemuel sent a message calling for Jaytsy to come to the Second Resting Station."

"He *WHAT?*"

"But I made the girls take it down. It's my fault they changed the banners—"

Shem searched frantically, his panic rising. "So where is she?"

"Jaytsy left," Mahrree cringed. "For the Station."

"AND YOU TOLD HER TO GO, TOO?" Shem raged.

"NO!" Mahrree shouted back. "I tried to stop her!"

"She did, Papa," Huldah said timidly, alarmed at seeing her father so infuriated. "She even thought about getting on a horse."

"See?" Mahrree took his arm, "I really *didn't* want her to go!"

Shem rubbed his face with his hands. "How long ago?"

"An hour ago, at least. Probably longer—"

Shem darted for the barn.

Mahrree followed him. "Shem! Stop! Peto and Deck already went after her—"

He twisted to Mahrree. "*Both* of them?"

Mahrree winced and nodded.

That was all he could take. "NO!" Shem shouted and banged his fist on the door so hard it seemed to rattle the entire barn.

The girls cowered at his fury. Several rushed over to Lilla, who was astonished. Zaddick stopped in his tracks and Young Shem hid behind him.

"Deck's supposed to STAY HERE!" Shem yelled. "Only *I'M* supposed to deal with Thorne, *IF* it comes to that! None of this is following the plan! We discussed this, we planned this—"

Mahrree bravely stepped up and grabbed his arms. "You? Deal with Thorne? Shem! Think like a *general*! Pull out that sergeant major again and put him to work. Does the general of one army *ever* confront the general of the other without one of them dying? What happened to Brillen Karna? Killed by Snyd! No, Shem. Outthink him! Out-strategize him! Even if he holds Jaytsy, Peto, and Deck as hostages, you DO NOT cave in to him! He might be luring you to him already. Don't fall for it. We go west. Right now. *You* need to lead this people at the Last Day. I'm ready to get on a horse for you, right now! Shem . . ."

She paused until his angry, darting eyes finally rested on hers.

"Shem," she whispered, "you are the *Deliverer*."

He blinked several times and finally focused on her. "What did you say?"

Mahrree put her hands on his face to hold him steady. "You, Shem Zenos, are the Deliverer. I *know* it."

Ester sniffled.

But Shem stared at Mahrree. "You don't know—"

"Oh, yes I do! When I say the words my arms tingle. Shem, you need to do what the Creator wants the Deliverer to do. Don't worry about Lemuel or Deck or Peto or Jaytsy—worry about the Salemites on the mountain. The Creator will take care of our family if you take care of everyone else. I have full confidence in that. We can wait for them until midday meal, then we'll get our packs and go. You *must* come with us and go nowhere else. Especially not to the Second Resting Station."

Shem's eyes softened as he looked into Mahrree's. "If it's not Calla, it's you," he whispered. "Either one of you says exactly what Perrin would have said to me." He took her hands in his, his demeanor markedly changed. "I'm not so sure about that Deliverer thing, but you're right. We can give them another hour, then I take all of you up the mountain. I can always come back . . ."

Mahrree smiled and kissed his hands. "But we need some more horses," she gestured to the barn.

Shem saw Clark 14 resting and the small horse chosen for Mahrree. "Zaddick? Get up to the children, start choosing horses, have each one ride a horse and lead a horse back. I'll be up to help—"

The sound of horses' hooves turned all of them around to see who was coming.

"PETO!" Lilla screamed. "Mahrree, they're BACK!"

Mahrree released the biggest sigh of relief in her life and looked up to the sky. "THANK YOU!"

Shem ran out to the road, followed by everyone else.

Peto was on his own horse, a tired animal that looked as if it was already experiencing its Last Day, and Jaytsy and Deck were sharing Jaytsy's mount.

Peto slid off his miserable animal and rushed to Lilla. "He's free! He's running free! He's escaped!"

Mahrree stopped abruptly and Lilla screamed. "REALLY?"

"Peto, where's Young Pere?" Shem asked.

"Running *southeast*!" Jaytsy laughed. "But he's running unshackled and right into the forests!"

Mahrree clutched her chest.

Jaytsy dismounted and rushed over to her. "Mother, Father's back too! I could even smell him, right next to me! He told me what to say to free Young Pere!"

"Tell me!" Mahrree cried. "Tell me everything!"

"Jaytsy," Shem said urgently, "what about Lemuel?"

"Oh, yeah. A delusional maniac. Wants me as his queen. But let me tell you about Young Pere and Father—and Qualipoe Hili!"

Young Pere slid in a narrow ravine and Cloud Man dropped in next to him, panting heavily.

"No one's following," Young Pere grinned. "We did it!"

"Whew," Cloud Man sighed. "Thank Creet, because I can't run another foot. We must be at least a mile away. Maybe two?"

Young Pere analyzed Cloud Man, now that they were relatively safe. "So will you tell me who are you and why should I trust you?"

"Yes, I will," Cloud Man said, his words flowing faster when he wasn't pretending to be a vial head. "You're far too trusting. My brother was right about you."

Intrigued, Young Pere said, "Who's your brother?"

Cloud Man sat up and held out his hand. "Introductions first. My name is Lieutenant Nelt."

"Nelt?!"

"*Perrin* Nelt, if you can believe that," he smirked. "Named after your grandfather."

"Wait, what?"

"Apparently your grandfather impressed my parents at some fancy dinner at Idumea," Lieutenant Nelt told him, "taking care of my brother when he was fussing so that my parents could dance. When I was born about four years later, your grandparents had already been lost—or so everyone thought—but my father wanted to honor his memory. He named me Perrin, but always called me Pere. I guess we're a pair of Peres."

"*Nelt?*" Young Pere repeated in disbelief.

Nelt smiled sadly. "The Captain Nelt you knew was my older brother."

Young Pere sighed. "I'm so sorry. I was with him when he died at the border battle for Idumea. Arrows."

"Yes, I know," Nelt whispered. "I was at the border battle, too. I found him after they pulled you away to bring you to Thorne. I've had a morbid fear of arrows ever since. But I also know that death is one of the hazards of our work. He knew it, too."

Young Pere gestured limply. "I'm sufficiently stunned. Why are you here? Why are you helping me?"

"Because I made a promise to my brother that I would," Perrin Nelt said, sounding like he regretted it. "Right before that confrontation Thorne had with Sargon, I caught up to him. He told me all about you and he also told me to watch out for you should something happen to him. It's taken me a few seasons to catch up, but I finally found a way to fulfill my promise."

Young Pere stared at him. "I'm . . . I'm speechless."

Nelt grinned. "Finally! As much as you've been going on and on about Salem . . ."

Young Pere smiled hesitantly back. "You know, you're my favorite soldier."

"Of course I am. That's because I'm not entirely a soldier. I was training to be an assassin like my brother. Until, well, *everything*."

He looked down at his hands.

Young Pere rubbed his neck. "Wait a minute—you! *You* shot me with that small arrow! Up at the glacier fort!"

"Bolt. We call it a bolt." He opened his jacket to show the small crossbow tied inside. "The bigger crossbows we were developing can shoot a bolt right through body armor like Thorne wears. But those weapons are rather obvious. This small thing, it's not powerful enough to kill a man, but that's not its purpose. It's to deliver this mixture, right here." He pointed to a small bottle in a hidden pocket. "The bolt needs only to puncture the skin, then the liquid on the tip does the rest. One drop knocks you out. If the bolt is saturated in it, it kills you in thirty minutes."

Young Pere blinked. "Were you trying to *kill me* when you shot me out of the tree?"

"Of course not!" Nelt exclaimed. "Just shut you up. I used only one drop. You nearly killed yourself that night. I spent two full minutes trying to target you. You know how hard that is to do in the dark when you're standing up in a tree and I'm hiding in a bush? I fired three bolts before the fourth hit you. Fantastic shot, though, if I do say so myself."

Young Pere rubbed his neck again. "Yes, I'll admit it was. I heard two of them whizzing past my head. I thought they were hornets. And you're the one who said it looked like a stick poked me!"

Nelt smiled innocently, much like Cloud Man. "When you get right down to it, the bolt really is just a pointy stick."

"So if you have that thing," Young Pere gestured to the small crossbow, "why not use it on Thorne?"

Nelt sighed, long and thoughtful. "To be honest, I hadn't made up my mind until recently whose side I was on. Usually my devotions lie with the richest man, so my sense of survival told me to be on Thorne's side. But my sense of honor, whatever I may have left, is telling me to be on your side. In the end, you won. And since I got to taste apple mush, obviously that was the right choice."

Young Pere smiled. "Apple *sauce*. I'm still astounded. You played a vial head so well."

"Something my brother taught me," Nelt explained smugly. "Behave the opposite of what you really are. How should the smartest man in the world act?" He pointed modestly to himself. "Like a vial head. My brother was very obvious in so many ways that no one ever noticed his subtlety."

"So," Young Pere squinted, "he wasn't really that *experienced* with women?"

"Oh, that part was true. Well, as far as I know. So much he was going to teach me, so much I never learned." Nelt looked off into the distance, his thoughts drifting like clouds.

Young Pere patted him on the back. "Salem girls don't go for *any* of the things he said in his songs. Trust me. When all of this is over, maybe we can learn a few things about Salem women."

Nelt looked at him. "*What happens* when all of this is over, Shin?"

Young Pere opened his mouth and closed it. "I really don't know. Haven't thought that far."

Nelt gave him a friendly punch in the shoulder. "So let's not, then. Let's think about today. What do we do first?"

BE CAREFUL, YOUNG PERE.

Young Pere tipped his head. "See that mountain range over there?"

"On the *other* side of the valley filling up with the nasty soldiers that we're trying to avoid?" Nelt said in Cloud Man fashion.

"Yeah, I'm afraid so. That's where we need to get. Then up and over those mountains to safety. That's where the Salemites are."

"No it's not," Nelt said. "They're at the temple, northeast of here."

ENOUGH, YOUNG PERE! ENOUGH! I SAID BE CAREFUL!

Young Pere pondered those words that nearly screamed in his head, reminding him that he didn't have any real reason to trust this man. He may not even be Captain Nelt's brother.

He had to stop thinking like a trusting Salemite and start thinking like a spy. A thought came to him, inspired by a general.

"Salem split itself in two. Half goes one way, the other goes another way. That way at least one half of Salem will survive while Thorne attacks the other half. My family is on the west side, but we can hide out in the east with the other half of Salem until it's over."

Nelt nodded at that explanation. "So where do we go now?"

"We need to head north. Maybe try to get around the Salemites massed behind the temple, then if there's an opening we can try to head west."

Nelt nodded again. "Your land, you're in charge. Oh, that's an interesting cloud . . ."

Everyone sat around the Briters' eating table, listening and wearing a hopeful smile. The morning had started out grisly, first with Eltana's army refusing to back down, then Shem's battle which he described to them without much detail.

But the mood in the house brightened considerably as they listened to Jaytsy explain her experience with Lemuel Thorne and Young Pere's sprint to freedom. Deck never once let go of her hand, even though she frequently used it to make a point.

When Jaytsy finished, Mahrree shook her head. "Young Pere's running free, and Poe Hili is a sergeant major! I never would have imagined it."

"Especially when Perrin and I were chasing Poe down and throwing him into incarceration," Shem said.

Mahrree, Jaytsy, and Peto smiled, but only for a moment.

Shem turned his mug in his hands, pensive. "And our dear Assistant Ahno succeeded. Lemuel thinks everyone is on the *opposite* side of the valley. I knew Ahno could do it if he just concentrated, but he always got so flustered every time you pushed him in his testing, Mahrree."

She smiled sadly. Ahno had definitely been her most trying student. "He told me once he wanted to do something brave. Now he's done it."

"This will give us the time we need to get those who are still trying to get up to the ancient site," Peto said. "Lemuel's a little earlier than I anticipated. I thought he wouldn't make it in until this afternoon."

"They fashioned ropes out of what looks like bedrolls," Jaytsy explained. "They were using those to climb over the walls."

"Rather cleverer than I expected," Shem said. "I wish there was a way to get Ahno out—"

Mahrree put a hand on his. "Shem, he knew it was a one-way trip," she said quietly. "Lemuel won't keep him alive longer than he needs him. He may already be gone to his wife," she finished in a whisper. "He was looking forward to being with her again."

"No one faithful will miss the Last Day," Deck reminded them. "Ahno will be there somehow, Shem."

"I know . . ." Shem said, with a faraway look of planning in his eyes that made Mahrree uncomfortable.

Peto scoffed. "Bedroll ropes. Guess they still have an ingenious man or two among them. Lemuel needs to be kept distracted until at least tomorrow morning. I saw some families leaving from Eltana's army this morning. They just need more time. But if Thorne sends up a few scouts to the temple, and if they find no one there—"

"Yes, yes . . . a *distraction*," Shem said airily.

Mahrree squeezed his hand. "Don't think it, Shem. Whatever it is."

"Not thinking anything, Mahrree."

Shem was an excellent liar, so she glared at him.

So did Ester.

"Well," Lilla said, standing up, "we don't have much time left. We should get something ready for midday meal, and you men can go get the horses. I suppose we'll just have to hope Young Pere is still a fast runner," she said with a tight smile, her eyes swimming.

Peto sighed and rubbed his eyes. "Is it really only midday meal time? It's *got* to be closer to dinner."

Lilla kissed him on the head. "You poor thing. I don't know when you've had such a long day. What made you get up so early anyway?"

Peto closed his eyes. "I don't know. Just couldn't sleep anymore. Too many things to do and think about. I really should be out there looking for Young Pere, but somehow knowing he's on the run has made me so tired."

"Then rest a little while. The Creator is probably trying to keep you safe," Lilla said, patting his head. "Two hundred pieces of gold for you, remember? You'd have to ride through all those soldiers to reach him." Her voice cracked. "I'll try to go slow with getting your food," and she headed to the kitchen with Jaytsy.

Peto put his head down on the table. "You don't think Lemuel will stall the army while I get a little nap? I've been on a horse since well before dawn."

Deck chuckled. "Take your nap, Peto. Zaddick and I can get the horses while Shem stays on guard here."

From the kitchen they heard Jaytsy's voice. "I don't think you need to worry about that. Come look at the children!"

Everyone, including sleepy Peto, went to the kitchen window. They smiled as they saw Hogal and Centia Shin, and Yenali and Atlee Briter each riding a horse and leading three behind them. They were bringing sixteen very obedient horses.

"Ah," Peto smiled. "We still get miracles, don't we? First we get back with Jaytsy safely, then Young Pere has escaped, and now we have horses!"

Shem nodded. "I'm beginning to feel more and more confident about this day, Peto."

Sergeant Beaved had never been so uncomfortable on such a soft chair. He squirmed, watching the door to the study.

A few minutes ago, out had come the four guards who had been hunting for mead in the cellar when Shin escaped. General Thorne had shouted at them for ten full minutes, and when they sulked out of the study, they were somber and dejected. Beaved didn't know if it was because Thorne had just reduced all of them in rank and pay to privates, or because they had never found any mead. Beaved suspected the latter.

He was next.

Outside on the front porch, the rest of his security team waited just as nervously.

Hammer, Iron, and Teach had just been located, having been forced by an over-eager lieutenant colonel into one of his groups.

Buddy, Pal, and Reg had been trying to keep guard around the station, but the constant flow of soldiers had prevented them from noticing Shin escaping, even though nearly every soldier in the vicinity had stopped to watch the latest installment of the Thorne-and-his-woman drama unfold at the back porch.

Snarl had been discovered gorging himself in a pantry off the kitchen, and Cloud Man had run away with Shin. It was obvious he was the one who had unlocked Shin's wrist chains. It must have happened early this morning when Beaved gave him the key to undo the chain around his ankles.

Beaved shifted again in the chair.

Just how long did it take to put together an execution squad? There were thousands of men with swords, many of them eager to use them. But like a cat watching a mouse suffer before killing it off, Thorne must have been delaying this deliberately.

He already ran the speech he would hear in his mind. *Most incompetent soldier ever produced by the army! Not one of your security team noticed? Do you even know the definition of 'security'?*

Beaved avoided looking at any of the officers rushing past him to look out the windows, then going back to the plans in the eating room.

Not as if he would be involved in the attack on the temple. His body would be food for some stray animals by dinner time. Just get it over with already—

The door to the study opened and General Thorne nodded once to the sergeant.

Beaved got up shakily and walked into the study.

"Sit!" Thorne ordered.

Beaved did so in a hard chair set by the desk, his mouth dry.

Thorne sat at the desk across from him. "What do you have to say for yourself, Beaved?"

The sergeant fought the trembling in his voice. "I have no excuse for my gross incompetence. I could never apologize enough, and I realize that I will be punished. Please, sir, may I beg that it be swift?"

To his surprise, the side of Thorne's mouth lifted into half a smile. "That was rather well-said for a mere staff sergeant. I suppose I underestimated you. I did not, however, underestimate your incompetence. In fact, I was counting on your failure."

"Uh . . . I don't understand, sir—"

"Of course you don't. How could you? You've been serving for what, not yet five years?" Thorne leaned forward on the desk. "You really think I would trust a silver chip as valuable as Shin to a mere staff sergeant and his so-called security team?"

Beaved gulped, realizing he had no idea what was going on. But it seemed to be another game of Dices, and Beaved had never been able to master the trickery of that game.

Thorne sniffed at his astonishment. "Why in the slagging world would I assign a *vial head*, a fogged-up grassena idiot obsessed with clouds of all things to such an important team?"

"I, uh, I wondered that myself, sir," Beaved choked out.

"Yes, you are incompetent. Cloud Man is no vial head. He was training to be an assassin. He's Captain Nelt's brother."

Beaved squinted. "The Captain Nelt of, 'There once was a girl from Grasses?'"

"Yes, and many other overly-descriptive poems esteemed by the soldiers," Thorne frowned. "Captain Nelt was an assassin working for Major Yordin, but his younger brother, Lieutenant Perrin Nelt, was an assassin-in-training working for me. It's because Lieutenant Nelt was a traitor to his brother that I was able to foil the attempt on my life at the Idumean border last year. Lieutenant Nelt slipped me a note about the kind of weapons the assassins have and what their plans were, so I made sure I wore my leather body armor and shifted all of the angles when Sargon and I met."

Beaved ran all of that over in his mind, knowing that he better not ask about the vague reference to angles and body armor.

"It's that kind of loyalty," Thorne continued, "that earned Perrin Nelt a position on your team, and will also earn him his command of any village in the world once we finish here."

Beaved tried to keep up. "So . . . Cloud Man *did* allow Shin to escape, but . . . you *knew* about it?"

Thorne sighed. "I don't have all day, Beaved. I have a battle to fight soon. Yes, *of course*! None of your team got anything useful out of him. But I knew Nelt would, once Shin tired of the feeble attempts of the rest of your team. Shin was never going to divulge where the Salemites are hiding. That's what I've really wanted to know. Amory gave me everything else, but not the location of the temple. She was withholding that for when, I don't know. But this isn't her game of dices. During the past few weeks I could feel Shin's desire to go home growing, and I knew once he saw this place he'd do all that he could to get back to his family. That's what I want, Beaved. *His family.* That's exactly where he's running to, and I have the most capable spy and assassin in all the world running with him."

"So . . . I didn't mess up?" Beaved asked with the smallest amount of hope.

"Of course you did, you slagging idiot!" Thorne pounded the desk. "But I *counted* on you to mess up!"

"Yes, sir," Beaved whispered, still trying to figure out if any of this was good news.

Thorne's shoulder twitched. "Is your team outside?"

"Yes, sir."

"*All* of them?"

"Yes, except for Cloud Man. I mean, Nelt."

Thorne rolled his eyes. "He's still Cloud Man, Beaved. Can you remember that?"

Beaved was confused but answered, "Yes, sir."

"Good. Because when we apprehend Shin at the temple, after we let him witness the execution of his family, he will be shackled and once again under your guard."

It took Beaved a moment to answer. "You mean, I—"

"YES! Or do you want to be executed instead?"

Beaved shook his head vigorously. "No, sir! I welcome the

opportunity to redeem myself, sir. But, sir, execution of his family?"

Thorne was already writing down something on his stack of notes. "Yes. Once he witnesses that, he'll be far more docile and easy to control. Broken will and such."

Beaved seriously doubted that Young Pere would become docile. Quite the opposite. But it was clear that Thorne wasn't going to believe anything other than what he imagined, what was convenient. Beaved saw so many holes in the logic he wasn't sure which one to point out first, but also knew doing so would rapidly end his life.

Still, he dangerously felt the need to mention at least one item. "But, sir, his 'mother' this morning, she didn't think he was hers."

Thorne shrugged that away. "She needs some time to come to accept the idea. For so many years she was sure he was taken away from her, then to see him so suddenly? The shock of it all," he continued to write. "She'll come around."

Young Pere was right: Thorne was ridiculous.

"So, what family is he running *to*, then? That woman's, or the people who raised him?"

Thorne put down his quill with an irritated sigh. "Does it matter?"

Still trying to sort it all out, Beaved said, "But, sir, the other night he was talking of his family here. He mentioned many small children. Nieces and nephews, babies—those won't be executed, will they?"

"Why not?"

"But, sir, *babies*?"

Thorne tilted his head. "Sergeant, is this too hard for you?"

Beaved did his best to sit at attention. "No, sir; not at all."

"Then get back to your team, tell them we'll intercept Shin and Cloud Man in a few hours, and tell them to be prepared to let nothing, I mean *nothing*, distract them again! And don't you ever 'But, sir' me again! Dismissed."

"Yes, sir!" Beaved stood up and saluted.

To his team waiting anxiously on the front porch, he said, "Follow me." He looked around for a suitable place to talk and eventually decided the barn was the best bet. Several soldiers were already in there, stealing a nap in the straw, but Beaved led his team to a quiet corner.

"We're going to die, aren't we?" Reg trembled.

"I'm not dying." Snarl fondled his long knife. "Thorne will die first. All of this was poorly planned."

Buddy and Pal looked at each other with worry, and even Hammer and Iron grew pale.

Teach flopped down on the straw. "I'll go first. I'm so tired I don't care if I die now. None of this is worth it."

"Look," Beaved said in a hushed tone, "none of us is dying."

"Why not?" Reg said, almost sounding disappointed.

Beaved looked into their faces, realizing he didn't know who in the world, or in Salem, he could trust. But he had to try someone.

"Thorne's been lying to us. And I'm starting to think he's genuinely unstable. I may not be the brightest man in the world, but there are so many holes in his thinking I'm surprised his shrunken brain hasn't fallen out of one of them yet."

Teach snorted in appreciation.

"And I'm also beginning to believe the only man we should ever have trusted has run away."

Teach sighed. "Cloud Man."

"No," Beaved hissed.

Teach sat up in surprise. "No?"

"What I'm about to tell you goes no further than here. If it does, Reg, we *will* be executed. But I don't care anymore. I can't sit by and watch what's going to happen. How many of you have heard of Captain Nelt? Well, you've heard his songs, I'm sure, if you've spent more than two days in the army. It seems he had *a brother*, and they were both in the assassins league—"

"Wait," Pal broke in nervously. "Assassins league? They're not real. That's just a story to scare children to be good, right?" His voice drifted off when he saw the very somber expression on Teach's face.

"They're real," Beaved said quietly. "Ever since the time of the kings. Maybe from the time of Idumea's organization. My grandfather told me there has always been a secret group who *eliminate undesirables*. They used to be a core section of the Guarders. I know what you're going to say—a lot of Guarders were just thieves in black, but at the core were always the true Guarders, the ones who took the oaths and were trained and did the bidding of the highest bidder. King Querul and his descendants, as well as Chairman Mal— all of them had assassins, often as undercover soldiers—"

Reg was holding up a finger in question. "Like Shem Zenos?"

Beaved paused and looked at the barn which housed them, new storylines intersecting with the ones he knew and throwing everything he thought he understood into the air like chicken feathers. "Like we were *told* about Shem Zenos, but honestly . . . I don't know anymore, men. If Shem Zenos was *from here*, then . . . ." He exhaled loudly as he looked at the bewildered expressions of his team. "You're all thinking the same thing I am, aren't you?"

"I don't think so, because I'm thinking," Hammer started slowly, "that I have no idea what to think anymore."

The rest of the team nodded in perplexed agreement.

"Yeah, that's what I was thinking too," Beaved admitted. "Anyway, I do know this: assassins have been around for generations, but now they've been kind of a killer-for-hire bunch, not loyal to anyone but to whomever pays them the most. The generals have been quietly using them for years to take out annoyances."

"It's been my observation," Teach said, "that Thorne takes out his own annoyances."

"Well, he can't do everything everywhere," Beaved said irritably. "That's why he's retained Lieutenant Nelt—"

Buddy, who wasn't quite yet following along, likely because he'd gone deathly gray at the reality of assassins, raised his hand timidly. "Who's Lieutenant Nelt again?"

Beaved rolled his eyes. "Who's missing from our little group, Buddy?"

"What's the count now?" Mrs. Yordin asked as she continued to watch the soldiers stream over the wall and into Salem.

One of the men sitting next to her checked the tally. "Forty-one thousand."

Mrs. Yordin nodded. "Certainly sped up their rate by adding more ropes. Maybe they brought them from another wall further up the canyon."

Captain Custer standing next to her rubbed his hands. "How much longer? If I'm this itchy to get going, so will be the others!"

"Good. Use that 'itchiness.' Maybe another two hours. Just keep thinking itchy thoughts. Use Thorne to scratch them."

Custer paced in front of the window. "We've been waiting over five hours now!"

Mrs. Yordin sighed. "War is an art, and like any art, patience is necessary. You don't want to rush it and have a sloppy conclusion with results you didn't want. You need to watch the signs, pace the progress, make the move at precisely the right—"

"Not according to them!" Custer said, pointing out the window.

Mrs. Yordin looked below.

The fighters from several barns were slipping silently out and starting in a stealthy run. Their target was a group of weary soldiers who had just arrived and were lining up in rows between grape vines, temptingly less than one hundred paces in front of the house where Mrs. Yordin was stationed.

"NO!" she cried.

She took off running down the stairs. By the time she rushed out the front door, she already heard the familiar clang of steel. She stopped to see the soldiers with swords drawn, over one hundred of them, engaging nearly two hundred men with pitchforks and hatchets.

"Idiots!" she shouted.

There was nothing else to do now that all strategy was gone. She grabbed the rope hanging on the bell at the front porch and clanged it as the signal. Then she pulled her husband's long knife from its sheath on her waist and looked around for her first victim.

The battle for Salem had begun, a little early.

Major Twigg had been watching Salem in front of him, evaluating where the next batch of soldiers should be placed so he could give that information to Hili, when he saw the movement in the west. He grabbed the spyglass out of the lieutenant's hand and focused it. "General . . ." he started.

Thorne had just gone to the eating room and was pointing to something on the new map Ahno had completed.

"General!" Twigg said louder, staring through the spyglass. "UNDER ATTACK! General, we're UNDER ATTACK!"

Thorne ran from the eating room. "*What*?"

The other lieutenant with the second spyglass nodded. "I see them! Just a bunch of villagers outfitted with pitchforks and hatchets but . . . slagging Creet, they keep coming . . . there are *thousands* of them! They've been hiding in the buildings!"

Thorne ran to the front porch and pointed at his trumpeter. "Sound attack! To the west!"

Immediately the trumpeter sounded the patterned call.

"Horse!" Thorne bellowed. "I need a horse! Anyone find one yet?!"

A colonel shook his head. "Plenty of cows but not a single horse or mule or donkey anywhere, sir."

"Keep looking! I can't ride to battle on a cow!" He ran to the window where Twigg was still watching the progress of fighters.

"Every house, General. Every barn. They're pouring out of them like an infestation! They must have been waiting all morning. We've been setting the soldiers right in front of them! Creet! It's an ambush!"

"Steady, Major," the general said putting his left hand on Twigg's shoulder. "They can't be too successful with just farm tools. Our men are more practiced."

"Not most of them, sir. Most have been in the army for only three weeks!"

"Three weeks more than any of them, Twigg," Thorne said confidently.

He took the spyglass from the other lieutenant, balanced the end on a window pane, and watched the battle.

Soldiers were racing to get to the fight without waiting for orders. Officers ran behind them shouting out commands that no one could understand.

Thorne scanned the other side for signs of anyone in command of the Salemites. They had even less structure and discipline.

He grunted in satisfaction.

Battle *is* chaos, and whoever's side is more chaotic suffers the greatest. It was the most untidy battle he'd seen in years but already he was confident the Army of Idumea would prevail. Salem was so desperate they were even using women as archers. A few of their arrows were successful in hitting their targets, but most weren't.

"Salem is a city of peace," Thorne scoffed quietly. "Look at your people, Private Shin. Did you really think I was gullible? Why did you think I brought so many expendables?"

Shem, inspecting the newly arrived horses in the barn, stopped and listened. He shushed Deck who was pouring water for the animals, and a moment later ran out of the barn, with Deck following.

"Hear that?" Shem said. "In the distance? Horn blasts?"

"What's it mean?"

"Years ago it meant, 'Attack!'"

Deck let out a low whistle. "Eltana's Army is striking?"

Shem exhaled. "Bad timing. Lemuel's probably still got a third of his army behind the wall, well protected. They can just wait it out."

"Maybe Eltana got tired of waiting?"

Shem rubbed his face.

"You want to go see," Deck said, "don't you?"

Shem glanced at Deck. "Mahrree told me to think like a general, like a sergeant major. The commander in charge of defense should know what the offense looks like."

"Good thing your wife isn't here . . ."

Shem grinned. "Are you kidding? She'd be wanting to ride along. Good thing she's up and away from the action."

Deck smirked. "Want me to tell Peto?"

"Not until he wakes up. The poor man needs another hour of sleep, don't you think? He looks so comfortable on your sofa." Already he was backing up to the barn, eyeing the new stock.

"I'll say what Calla would," Deck sighed. "Be careful, don't get involved, don't stay out long—"

"One hour!" Shem called, jogging into the barn. "Tell the women to clean something in the meantime." He snatched the reins of an already saddled horse.

Deck waved good-bye. "None of this is going according to plan, Shem," he whispered to his retreating figure. "None of it."

It was the screaming that woke up Versa, although it took her a moment to figure that out. She forced open her eyes and her back immediately felt stiff and achy. Confused, she blinked and looked around to orient herself.

The front porch. The rocking chair. Her cloak over her and the pack. The army—

The army!

It was running right past her on either side of the house, pursuing fleeing Salemites and slashing them as they went. Versa dropped to the planking floor and crawled over to the wall, dragging her cloak with her. She pushed the rocking chair in front of her as a meager shield, and cowered under her cloak as she blinked the sleepiness out of her eyes.

It was just to be a short nap, that was all . . . She looked at the position of the sun in the sky. It was high, casting deep shadows on the front porch to hide her, so midday—

Midday?!

She must have slept for five hours! The army and the general himself came in and she slept through it.

She chastised herself for such carelessness, although she couldn't help but think she was feeling much more refreshed, except for the kink in her back. And her neck. And her legs. She could walk those out. But when?

She was going to have to rethink everything. She'd been hoping to see the general come over the wall, walk over to him and say, "I'm Versa Thorne, your daughter. And I'm here to tell you that you're making a big mistake."

Not the most persuasive or compelling beginning, but she was hoping she'd be inspired with something else right after that. That's what she'd been praying for the past few days: Dear Creator, help me find a way to stop this. Salem has done so much for us; let me do something for Salem.

But each time she listened for inspiration as to what to do or say, nothing came. Well, something *did* come, but she ignored it. It was a faint suggestion that she didn't need to do anything at all, that there was already a plan, that she should get to the ancient site right now—

But Versa wanted to do her part. If Thorne wouldn't listen to his daughter, one that he loved once, then who would he listen to?

As Versa watched the men and soldiers running past her, she began to wonder if her long nap wasn't somehow part of His plan. How could anyone possibly sleep through the coming of the army? Maybe the only way one *could* sleep through it was if the Creator put them to sleep.

She looked up at the sky. "Is this Your doing?" she asked quietly, angrily. "Please, let me do some good for Salem! What should I do now?"

The answer came clearly. *Wait.*

Versa grumbled and did her best to get comfortable.

Boskos looked up from the hand he was bandaging and stared in surprise as his wife walked over to him.

"Is that fast or what?" She grinned.

"How did you . . . how did you get up here so fast?"

Noria kissed him and sat down to watch him work.

The middle-aged man who was Boskos's patient nodded sheepishly at her. "Been a little while since I've used a hatchet," he explained. "Tried to show my grandson how to be safe with it."

"And a lesson well-learned," Boskos said, "judging by the look of horror on his little face when he came to see your stitches."

Noria chuckled. "I'm so sorry, but that's kind of funny."

"My wife thought so, too. Not a lot of sympathy from her, either," the man admitted.

Boskos nudged his wife. "So how did you get here so fast? Where are the children?"

"Toli is riding with my father, and Callia fell asleep in the carrier with my sister. I decided to try riding as fast as you and, well, here I am!"

"Not that I mind, but I don't have our camp site set up yet. I was expecting you to be another couple of hours."

"I can set up camp for us. But what I really want to know is, what happened with Papa Shem? And what did Mama Calla think of it?"

Boskos squinted. "My mother?"

"Yes, she followed you. Haven't you seen her? I saw the horse she rode grazing with the others down the slope."

"Are you sure?"

"Positive," Noria said. "It has a very distinctive face: half brown and half white. I was watching for her to return. I saw Papa Shem and Zaddick ride down, but not her. You really haven't seen her?"

Boskos' face darkened. Noticing his brother, he called, "Lek! Anyone say anything about seeing Mama up here?"

Lek came over. "Mama? She's not here."

"Yes, yes she is," Noria insisted. "She followed your father, wanting to watch him in action. I watched her ride up here. The horse she took is on the other side."

Lek surveyed the area, but there were tens of thousands of people now on the massive tableland, with more pouring in every minute. "She could be anywhere . . ."

"People want a word with her more than they want to see your father," Noria said.

But Boskos shook his head. "Mama would always check in on us first. Lek, I don't like this."

"Neither do I," he said, still scanning the crowd.

Noria rubbed her legs nervously. "Maybe . . . maybe there was an emergency somewhere that she's helping with and she couldn't get away to come see you."

"I'm going to put out the word we're looking for her," Lek decided. "Uncle Peto put people in charge of different sections. I'll find someone and tell them we're looking for her." He took off in a jog toward the ruin.

Noria tried to smile away Boskos's deepening worry. "She's fine, Bos. I'm sure of it."

The rest of the army progressed rather quickly through the canyon, once they mastered the numerous ropes going up and over the walls. The thousands of women and children far behind them were also no longer struggling, especially since it was downhill.

It was almost fun, Guide Lannard thought to himself, once he passed Jon Offra who had raised his eyebrows at him in a most disappointed way. Behind Offra were a few hundred soldiers, lounging in the grasses of a side canyon, but Lannard didn't know why.

He was too distracted by Offra's jacket to think about the soldiers. There was something about those brass buttons. Something weirdly familiar, something angry, even.

How did Offra get a jacket with brass buttons?

Worse, how did Offra even get here?! Didn't he die?

Colonel Offra had been calling something about quiet canyons when he spied Lannard, and no matter how hard Lannard tried not to look at him, Offra's eyes gripped his gaze and wouldn't let go.

It was like being stared down by a ghost.

Lannard pushed his way through some scrawnier privates to get past the old colonel as fast as he could, goose bumps rising on his skin at an alarming rate.

After that, the going was far more enjoyable.

Once Lannard put his silky purple robe into his pack to keep it from snagging, and changed his silk pants and tunic for regular army clothes, he challenged some of the younger soldiers to see who could scale the next wall the fastest.

Of course, the Guide of the Creator won every time, and Lannard was sure it was because the Creator was with him, not because the soldiers let him win.

It was shaping up to be a rather pleasant day. The air was cool and comfortable, the sun was shining yet again, and the news had come up through the soldiers that there were only two walls left.

Lannard smiled and rubbed his hands in anticipation of the wall looming before him.

"Stand back, stand back everyone!" he announced. "Watch the guide in action!" He took a running start, leaped for the wall, caught the bedroll rope part of the way up, and quickly pulled himself to the top. He stood up there, arms outstretched and bowed to the applause of the soldiers and the first group of women catching up to them. With a broad grin he turned around and slid down the rope easily, landing in front of a middle-aged man, not quite fifty.

He chuckled and patted Lannard on the back. "And here I thought guides were wrinkly old men with white hair and canes."

"Not *this* guide!" Lannard said. "Only one more wall? I'm rather disappointed about that. But I'm sure there will be new challenges ahead of us!" He started a fast walk, weaving between the soldiers who naturally made way for him, and burst into a grin when he saw the last wall. It was enormous.

He looked around at the mass of men waiting up against it, not climbing. "What's going on?"

"Battle, sir! I mean, Guide! Salemites are fighting. We thought it safer on this side."

Lannard's chin dropped. "Fighting? Salemites aren't supposed to fight. They don't have weapons."

"They have pitchforks, hatchets, and bows and arrows," a captain told him.

Major Kroop folded his arms. "And we have swords! Well, most of us do, anyway. Come on! I've been waiting to see Salem for far too long. I'm not going to worry about a few hatchets." As if a dozen angry Salemites were enough to stop the mighty Idumean army! He grabbed a bedroll rope and began to steadily climb up the wall and slid down again, landing among a crowd of cowering soldiers.

It was the noise he heard first. It was clearly more than a dozen rebellious farmers. He jogged to the narrow entrance, unimpeded because no one was willing to leave the wall, and the view on the other side froze him in place. For a full minute he could do nothing more than stare at the vastness of Salem, the sheer enormity of the number of houses, animals, and fields.

Then his gaze shifted to the scene closer at hand.

Tens of thousands of men, many in blue, others in plain clothing, fighting and screaming and dying a mere half mile down the slope.

His face tightened. There was a reason he wanted to be in charge of supplies. When he was younger, the thought of fire and death and body parts had fascinated him. He'd even once pleaded, unsuccessfully, with a young Captain Thorne to let him ride to the ruins of Moorland just to gawk at the carnage. But then when he was twenty-two he witnessed his first bloody battle and lost his appetite for fighting. To be honest, everything about it terrified him, even more than supply lists.

That same horror filled him now, and there was nothing he wanted to do more than turn around and climb back over the wall to where it was safe and crowded by soldiers.

Actually, that wasn't a bad idea—

He spun and started again for the wall but stopped. The army, apparently inspired by their guide's bravery, were scaling the wall again, but perching on top of it, awaiting his response.

If it ever got back to Thorne that Lannard had retreated, it would be Lannard's last day.

"It's great!" he called in a shaking voice. "And we're prevailing! Come on!" He bounded out of the canyon and darted behind the first large boulder he spied, well away from the fighting. So what if people thought he was a coward. He was the guide. He needed to be protected and preserved.

Feeling somewhat shielded, he peered around the rock and glanced again at Salem. But all he could focus on were towers, massive ones, all flying thin, long black banners.

Perrin Shin built those towers, Lannard knew. The old colonel was everywhere.

Lannard gripped the boulder in front of him, as if worried someone could yank it away and expose him.

Offra's jacket—the one he was wearing when Lannard saw him earlier . . . *it* had brass buttons. They hadn't had brass buttons since Shin's day—

The old colonel was everywhere.

Lannard put his head against the boulder and shrank like a terrified sixteen-year-old as yells and cries and screams from the battle drifted up to him. People were stabbing, bleeding, dying—this wasn't going to be such a good day after all.

"This was a bad idea . . . oh, this was a *bad* idea . . ."

The major and the captain continued to shout orders, but no one was listening. It really didn't matter, though. It wasn't as if the soldiers were disciplined or practiced enough to do anything organized, but what they were doing was enough.

The Salemites had no fight in them. True, there was a man here and there who aggressively forged onward with his pitchfork or hunting knife, stabbing and slashing with abandon. But for every one of those, there was another hundred cowards who hacked half-heartedly with their hatchets or, even worse, after a plunge or two with a pitchfork dropped their weapons in horror and begged for forgiveness. As if they felt *badly* for wounding their enemy.

There's no room for empathy on the battlefield, the major and the captain knew. When you get right down to it, no room for it in life, either. Not if you want to be a success.

And so, even as the two officers shouted orders, they didn't worry that no one was following them. Salemites were surrendering left and right, up and down. Many just fell on the ground, weeping and crying for mercy.

That was where the true skill of the Army of Idumea manifest itself. No empathy and no mercy. It's a war, after all. A few hundred Salemites had been rounded up already as prisoners for Thorne's interrogators, but the rest would simply take back their properties if allowed to live—especially those women, and some very young looking men and the stray children here and there—and no soldier was ready to give up what he was fighting for. Even the clumsiest soldiers achieved kills by the fifth or sixth messy stab.

The major and captain continued on, eventually ceasing their shouting and instead strolled leisurely behind the line of soldiers that was advancing northward, leveling every Salemite they found.

The major stumbled, and the two men began to pay more attention to the ground below them. The amount of bodies on it was growing, and there were very few blue uniforms among the bodies clad in rough, dirt-colored clothing.

As the two men progressed they pointed at the dead, sniggering occasionally and musing as to what some corpse hoped to accomplish with the pointed hoe lying next to him. The sunshine glinted off something to their right, and the officers picked their way through the bodies to investigate.

"Look at this one," the captain sneered. "The Salemites used old ladies."

The major crouched to investigate and gestured to her hand. "That's army issued, Captain."

"So it is. A long knife in Salem! Even bloodied. Guess she got in a stab or two. But how would an old lady in Salem get a long knife? Oh, wait a minute. Don't tell me—" Following a hunch, the major who served for a time in Sands pushed over the body to see the woman's face. "Creet."

"What is it?"

The major sighed in frustration. "Another hundred gold pieces no one will collect on. Slagging Mrs. Yordin got herself killed. Worthless woman. Maybe we'll still get half for her body?"

"Don't count on it," the captain said.

The major stood up and, without another thought, he and the captain continued to survey the dead strewn before them.

Shem rode the horse, a worthy Clark, south along the back roads on the western side of Salem. He knew the dust his horse kicked up could possibly draw attention, since the back roads weren't paved in cobblestone, but by the sounds of battle coming to the east of him, no one would be looking over soon.

He stopped his horse at one of the towers and quickly climbed up to the top where he had a clear view of the battle beyond.

Eltana's army was losing, hugely.

He groaned in grief at the hundreds of Salemite bodies motionless on the ground, with only a handful of blue uniformed bodies among them. Many more Salemites were retreating, running north through the houses and farms, being chased and cut down by soldiers. Shem closed his eyes, not able to witness the destruction of his people.

"Is there nothing to be done for them?"

Not for them, Shem. I'm sorry. They rejected the words of the guides and, just this morning, the pleadings of a rector. They made their decisions and now their fate is sealed. As much as they wanted to believe there was more time, there does come a time when time runs out.

"I suppose I should go back—"

Not yet. There's more for you to see.

"Perrin?"

Yes, he's here, but on the other side of the valley. He's the one who wants you to see a few things.

Shem's chin trembled. "Still securing Salem, is he?"

That's his calling, after all. Death doesn't change our callings. Look.

Shem's eyes were directed to the middle of the battle where a line of Salemites, tied together, were being led by soldiers.

"Prisoners!"

Yes, to be taken in for questioning. Lemuel has two questions: first, where are the Salemites hiding?

"But Ahno already told him about the temple site, the current one. Jaytsy told us Thorne believed him."

Ah, but like a good worldly general, he believes nothing until he has multiple verifications of that information.

Shem smacked his forehead. "They'll talk! They'll crumble and tell him about the *ancient* site!"

They will. And instead of marching north, the army will head west. Lemuel will find a horse and be up at the cliff tonight.

"No! We're not ready! There are still people trying to get to safety, and Young Pere will never make it in time!"

There are many others waiting in their houses to ambush any soldiers coming to take them. Some soldiers will break ranks if Lemuel heads west to yet another canyon. They'll think he's cheating them out of their reward, and they'll begin taking over houses, resulting in more bloodshed.

But there are also a few faithful families scattered throughout Salem trying to convince those remaining to leave. They still have a chance to get out, but only if Lemuel continues north with the army. Once the remaining Salemites see that their fighters were conquered by the Army of Idumea, they will finally give up and run to the routes tomorrow morning. There will be injured, too. They'll need time to get up to the ancient temple.

He nodded. "Understood. So how do we convince Lemuel to go north when all of his prisoners are crying about the west?"

In a moment. There's another question Lemuel has: where are the Shins? He's beginning to accept the fact, every time he looks at Perrin's towers, that the Shins weren't held here by force. He wants to find the Eztates and someone will reveal that to him as well.

Shem began to get antsy. "So I need to get them out now!"

In another moment, Shem. Lemuel is scared, deep down scared, that the Shins are alive and well in Salem.

He picked up on the key word. "Scared?"

Lemuel wouldn't be the only one terrified to realize Mahrree Shin is still alive. After all the stories, after all the lies, to see her still alive would shake a lot of men.

Shem's mouth went dry. "What . . . what are you suggesting?"

First, Lemuel has to believe there's still a group of Salemites hiding in the canyon behind the temple. Shem, how would you like to play Guarder spy, just one last time?

Despite all of the grim news he had just received, he couldn't help himself; he began to smile. "Tell me what to do."

No one at the ancient temple site had seen Calla Zenos.

No one. Even though every last Salemite up there searched all around them for the guide's missing wife, there was no word of her.

At the large camping site in front of the ancient temple, the Zenoses, Briters, and Shins were growing worried.

Meiki lay on her bedroll, overcome with fatigue, nausea, and dread. "Something's wrong. I know it is!"

Relf's wife Mattilin sat near her, smoothing her black hair. "Don't fret yet, Meiki. Everyone's looking for her. We'll find her. Don't worry."

Lori, sitting nearby nursing one of her twins, nodded at her cousin. "Just rest for now, Meiki."

After Meiki closed her eyes, Lori shared a look with her sister-in-law.

"It's because the matriarchal cow didn't inspect the site and lead the herd here," Mattilin whispered.

As time wore on, their anxiety increased. Boskos eventually wandered to where their father had battled earlier that morning.

Lek joined him. "What are you looking for, Bos?"

"I had a thought a few minutes ago," he said in a low tone. Too many people and children were watching him from their camp. "Lek, where were those bowmen?"

Lek exhaled. "I wasn't exactly paying attention at the time."

Boskos looked around for someone who had been conscious during the fight. He noticed Sam holding one of his twins and waved him over. "Where were those two bowmen, Sam?"

Sam paled. "Oh, no—"

Boskos shook his head. "Don't say that. *Don't say that!* Just tell me, do you remember where they were? I thought one was right here."

Sam nodded. "The other was over there, maybe twenty paces." He walked to the spot. "Look, blood splatter. We didn't remember to clean this area, I guess."

Boskos turned to face the direction the bowmen fired. "So if, uh, one of the arrows had released well . . ."

Lek was already covering his face. "They both did, Bos. I saw that much."

Boskos cleared his throat. "The trajectory would be . . ." He pointed to the slope rising above the camp site. It was steep, intersected by many ridges and covered by waist-high scrubby brush.

"Dear Creator, no!" Lek cried and took off in a run with Boskos following.

Sam dropped off Maggie by Lori and ran after the brothers.

Meiki sat up. "Where are they going?"

Lori bit her lip and watched them run up the slope. "I don't know, I don't know."

Relf and Cambo, speaking to yet another person who hadn't seen Calla Zenos, saw Lek, Boskos, and Sam running, so they immediately followed.

At the beginning of the ridges, Lek began to mumble, "Please no, please no, please no . . ."

Boskos took his arm. "Lots of brush to check. Lek, you stay here. I don't think you're up to—"

"I'm looking!" he shouted, and started out along one of the steep ridges.

"Looking for what, Bos?" Cambo asked tentatively.

"To see where those two arrows fell," was all Boskos replied.

Relf closed his eyes at the suggestion, then gestured to the rest of the brothers and cousins to come up. Many more men and a few women came, too.

"Two arrows were fired this morning. We're looking to see where they landed," was all the explanation Relf gave.

No one asked for more. In just moments, the slope was covered with people looking cautiously under every bush and shrub.

Down below, Meiki began to sob as she saw her husband join in the search. Mattilin held her tight and looked with worry at Lori, who had a tear trickling down her cheek.

The wait was grueling. The search, silent. The nearly two hundred people assisting knew what they were hoping, and not hoping, to find. They looked for five minutes, then for ten. Lek reached the other side of the ridge and peered over the edge in case anything had fallen on the other side.

Near the bottom, Salema stood with the rest of the women and children, watched him intently, praying he wouldn't be the one to discover anything. She held the hands of Briter and Fennic, each biting their lips in worry. The wives watched their husbands, and the sisters sat close together praying for the best.

It wasn't going to happen.

A woman near a stand of thick brush screamed before turning around to retch into the shrub behind her.

Immediately the searchers converged on her site, each wearing the same expression of devastation.

"MOVE! MOVE!" Boskos yelled as he hurdled bushes and slipped a few times in his frantic run to the spot.

Lek remained paralyzed in place.

The crowd moved to let Boskos through, and two men caught him before he got too close. Everyone at the ancient temple site heard him scream.

"*MAMA!*"

From behind a tree, Shem peered at the fields before him strewn with bodies and fighting men. It was chaotic, with men on both sides flailing, inefficiently and reckless, none of them trained enough to handle their weapons.

On the one hand, it was fortunate. There might be a few survivors.

On the other, the only thing worse than dying in battle was dying *slowly*.

Shem tried to ignore the fighting and instead searched the bodies for what he needed. It would be nearby; that's why he was directed to come here. Beside a barn door he saw it, two houses away.

The next part was tricky. Shem glanced around, then started moaning and limping as fast as he could to the barn door. A soldier started running for him and Shem dropped to the ground as if he suddenly lost consciousness.

The soldier jumped over him and continued on.

Shem peeked open an eye to see if anyone else was near, then rolled to his stomach and continued his already-wounded-and-dying crawl to the barn, hoping no one would think him worth engaging.

It worked. A minute later he reached the barn door and crawled past the dead officer lying before it. Shem scanned to the barn to see if anyone was there. Only a disinterested goat. He dragged the officer into the barn.

"What do we have here?" he whispered and he took off his jacket. "A colonel, is it? Thank you, Perrin. I always wanted to be a colonel. General's too high," Shem explained to the corpse as he undid the buttons and worked off the blue jacket. Shem couldn't see any visible signs of trauma. Maybe the man expired because of a heart attack from climbing too many walls. At least his uniform was clean.

"But a colonel, you see," he explained as he put the jacket on and buttoned it up; it fit perfectly, "has a great deal of power without having to be the *ultimate* authority." He bent down and started to undo the trousers. "Sorry about this, but this is what we call a field promotion." He slipped the ample pants up over his. "Maybe you should have lost a few inches around the middle here. Ah well, I can make it do."

Take the cap. Few men in the world have gray hair anymore. Nearly all died last year.

"Gray-*ing* hair. Still mostly light brown." He pulled the cap off the officer and put it on. "I would have had my hair trimmed if I had known," he said, tucking up his wavy locks under the cap. "But I'll be going so fast no one will notice my lack of grooming, right?"

Don't give anyone an opportunity to get a good look at you. Be a blur in their memory.

"Understood. Do I look all right?"

Perfect. Perrin would be pleased.

"All right, then," he said, peering out of the barn and plotting his course. "Guarder on the loose—lock up your houses!" He took off in a run to the east, straight into the middle of the fighting.

He headed for a knot of officers trying to direct the battle without getting involved themselves. When they saw him approaching, they stopped their shouting at soldiers who weren't listening anyway.

"Pass the word along—Salemites will be claiming the rest of the people are west of here, but the truth is they're still in the canyon northeast behind the temple. They're planning to attack us from behind if we start going west!"

Shem didn't wait to hear their responses. He took off to the east, to another officer pointing in earnest at a house.

"Don't fall for their lie that the rest of them are in the west! They're planning another ambush, and the fallback position is the temple in the northeast! Need to continue on there!"

The officer nodded as Shem took off again. He shouted to a staff sergeant, spread the word to two more captains, and advised another colonel that in the northeast would be the real battle, not the west as the captured Salemites would be claiming.

When Shem saw that man take off in a run to the heavily fortified Second Resting Station, he knew he still had his rumor-spreading talent.

He also knew there was no chance for him to find his assistant Ahno, so he offered up a quick prayer that Ahno wouldn't suffer, and began to jog back to the west.

He pulled the cap down low on his brow and avoided eye contact with anyone lest he be recognized by a passing Salemite.

Some were frantically flailing with their gardening tools while others were kneeling on the ground and sobbing. A few surrendered as they saw him, but he couldn't break character to help them.

There was no time left for them.

He shoved that horrible thought far back into his mind; he would weep profusely for them later. Right now, he had a job to do.

He slowed down only enough to say to anyone in authority, "Don't believe it's in the west—it's in the northeast!" He darted around houses and easily avoided panicked pitchfork wielding Salemites hoping to treat him like hay.

Eventually he stopped between two houses that were relatively quiet so he could catch his breath. Leaning against one house and panting, he noticed a double-wide rocking chair on the front porch, tempting him to sit down and take a rest next to a large pack someone had forgotten in their haste to leave.

Instead, he chuckled lightly. "All right," he panted, "I confess— I'm not twenty-four anymore. Don't think I'd win the Strongest Soldier race today. But, Perrin, not too bad for an old man like me, right?"

He scanned the area as he rested his lungs.

"Anything else? *Anyone* else? Now's the time." He paused and listened.

Nothing came to him.

"All right, then. Time to put away the guarder and pull out the Guide."

He ran as fast as he could back to where his horse was tethered. Just before he mounted, he realized he was still wearing the uniform. He slipped off the jacket, reversed it, smiled at the dull black lining that hadn't changed in forty years, and put it back on. The cap he threw into a shrub, not wanting the Eztates to think they were already under attack.

"Now, exactly what kind of a distraction does Perrin want me to set up at the temple to scare our Lemuel?"

Only one person noticed him riding away. Versa pushed away the rocking chair she was hiding behind and crawled to watch Guide Zenos disappear down the road.

Dismayed, she looked up. "What in the world was he doing?! And why did he stop here?"

She bit her lip as a new understanding came to her, why he was a mere two feet away, catching his breath.

"Were You trying to send me help? Look, I realize You've sent me several chances to escape in the form of Shins, Briters, and now Zenoses. But please, let me still do something good first?"

General Thorne stood at the windows watching the battle—or what Salemites might term a battle but he thought of as a feeble temper tantrum. Reports were coming in constantly, but within fifteen minutes the rest of the Salemites who had no idea how to fight would be easily put down.

He was smiling. Two officers had confirmed it—Eltana Yordin was dead. They both recognized her. She was even clutching an army-issued long knife.

Behind the Resting Station was a long line of Salemites, tied to each other by the wrists and fully traumatized. Obviously none of them had expected their defeat, nor did they expect to be held captive with dozens of soldiers pointing swords at them.

Many of them were weeping, others sat in shock, and the rest were pleading to be released. There wasn't a brave soul out there. Thorne was already evaluating the canyon that many of them were gesturing to. They wanted to be allowed to run there, promising that they'd give up their lands and houses if they could just be freed. They were so weak and gullible, just like everyone else in Salem.

Thorne noticed one of his colonels come running up to the station. Breathless, he hurried up the stairs and into the large gathering room.

"Sir, still planning to go west?" he asked between gasps for air.

"That's where all of the prisoners are desperate to go. Why?"

"It's a trick, a lie! Their fallback position is northeast, at the temple that old man Ahno mentioned. They're trying to get us going in the wrong direction, then they'll attack from behind."

Thorne furrowed his brows. "How do you know this?"

"Word's spreading through the officers. A colonel told me himself. Some of the Salemites were overheard."

Another officer came bursting through the door. "Sir! We have to continue to the northeast! That's where the rest of their army is hiding!"

The colonel gestured excitedly at the captain. "See?"

Thorne turned to look out the other window to the lines of weeping Salemites, begging to go west.

"They're more devious than I gave them credit for," he mumbled. "Those tears look quite genuine . . ."

Major Twigg cleared his throat. "Sir? Which way will we proceed when the battle here is finished? West or northeast?"

"They're desperate to go west, aren't they?" Thorne said, observing his prisoners through the window.

Twigg stood by Thorne. "Absolutely terrified. Never seen people so scared before."

"Quite convincing, aren't they?" Thorne said thoughtfully. "*Too* convincing, really . . ."

"Sir?"

"Pull out the first map for the northeast," Thorne ordered. "We'll hit the temple at dinner time. But keep the map for the west, because we'll go there tomorrow, just in case anyone is left alive."

Twigg waved to the men working on the maps, and a flurry of pages shuffled on the eating room table.

Hili came in. "General, I think I've spotted Kroop. He must have recently come over the last wall."

Thorne started walking to the back porch through the eating room. "You mean, *Guide Lannard?*"

"Uh, yes. Of course," Hili cleared his throat apologetically. "He's up by that boulder. Perhaps watching the soldiers come out of the canyon?" he said with a great deal of meaning. Lannard wasn't known for his bravery. "I think we're seeing the last of the soldiers coming through now, sir."

"Current count?" Thorne asked.

A lieutenant near Hili glanced at his forms. "Sixty-four thousand, approximately sir."

Thorne nodded to another lieutenant. "Go get Guide Lannard, bring him directly here. He doesn't know where we're meeting. That was to have been Amory's duty."

After the lieutenant left, Thorne whispered to Hili, "Why is Lannard hiding, Poe?"

"Scared?"

"He better get over it, quick. He's leading the soldiers to the temple."

"Is that the best idea, General?" Poe whispered.

Thorne scoffed. "What, *I'm* going to attack a *temple*? That's the only reason he's here, Poe. This is *guide's* work, not general's work. Find yourself a replacement; your priority now is to prepare Kroop for his duty. I can already see he's shaking more than our prisoners."

Mahrree walked through her small gathering room one last time while Shem scouted out the situation in the south and Peto got a well-deserved nap. She patted the books on the shelves again, sniffed Perrin's large stuffed chair catching the very last remnants of his scent that still lingered deep in the fibers, ran her hand along the low table where they both rested their feet, and made her way to the bedroom.

Ignoring their massive bed, she bit her lip to keep her lower jaw from trembling and went to the wardrobe. There she fingered the lock of Perrin's white hair Yudit had trimmed for her, carefully folded the paper back over it again, and tucked it into her pocket.

She wondered why she did that. What, was she going to return it to him? Sniggering at herself, she decided that since she didn't have his jacket to wear—which she had planned to do until Jaytsy gave it to Jon Offra—this would be a way that Perrin could accompany her to the ancient site. Still, she was holding out for a much more dramatic accompaniment. Somehow . . .

She walked over to his side of the bed, now frequently her side too, and ran her hand along his pillow that she hugged every night.

"Maybe soon, Perrin," she whispered. "It *has* to be soon."

She wiped away her tears and looked around, knowing it was time to leave. Even the room was telling her that, almost seeming to grow impatient that she still lingered. This was the last place she was saying goodbye to.

Spying The Writings by her bedside table, she walked over to it, feeling again as she had so many times that morning: *Mahrree Peto Shin, It Is You.*

She sighed, took Perrin's walking stick that the elder Boskos Zenos had given him years ago before he died, and, since she didn't have Perrin's jacket which Jon was still wearing, kissed the stick instead, set it back down, and left her bedroom forever.

Shem rode to the Eztates with mixed emotions. The same old thrill he always felt when he sneaked around and started rumors was still coursing through him, but it was greatly tempered by what he feared would be coming next. He rode past his bright yellow house giving it one last, loving look, in case it *was* his last look—Calla and he and gone through it together late last night, remembering and weeping and laughing—and continued on to the barn where Zaddick stood, momentarily startled by his father's appearance in uniform.

Mahrree came out of her house and stopped, too, when she saw him getting off his horse.

"What have you been doing, Shem!?"

He held up his hands in surrender. "Perrin's idea, I promise. Look," he said taking off the jacket, "I've been promoted to colonel. And I just bought Salem another day."

"Oh, you've got a lot of explaining to do, young man!" Mahrree said, putting her hands on her hips.

Shem nodded soberly. "Gather everyone together. It's nearly time to go."

"Now, Lannard, there's nothing to worry about," Poe Hili said as he led the quivering guide up the stairs to one of the many bedrooms. Only one was occupied with the old man they caught that morning, chained to a large wardrobe. "Right in here, Lannard. This one's nice. Take off your pack and sit down."

Lannard dropped his pack, sat on the soft bed and flopped back on it helplessly. "Poe, I can't do it! Can't you feel him? He's everywhere!"

Poe rummaged through Lannard's pack, pulling out the silk clothing. "Feel who, Lannard?"

"HIM!" Lannard wailed, sitting up. "*Perrin Shin*!"

Poe stopped. "I know. His spirit is everywhere, isn't it?"

"Poe, Offra was right! They made it out *to here*! I was just thinking about it, and really, Salem isn't that far from Edge. They probably could make it in a day in the right conditions. In *less* than a day if there were no blasted walls!"

Poe shook out Lannard's guide outfit. "I know, I know. I came to the same conclusion. But Lannard, I know for a fact that Colonel Shin is dead," he said sadly.

"A long time?"

Poe shrugged. Considering Lannard's unstable condition, he thought it wise to say nothing about Jaytsy's recent visit, or what she suggested about Lannard Kroop's former school teacher. Learning that the woman he unintentionally framed for treason was possibly alive just might send Lannard over the edge.

"Look, Lannard. It's not as if you'll be commanding the army or calling the shots. It's very simple. You are the chosen guide. The chosen guide has helped General Thorne find Salem. The rest of the Salemites are hiding at their temple, actually *behind* it, in a canyon. There may be some in the army that are a bit skittish about attacking an area considered sacred. You will go to the front of the temple, declare that it is the Creator's will that the army defeat Salem, claim the temple for Idumea, then stand back and let everyone else do their thing. You don't even have to wear a sword."

Lannard had started nodding, but changed to shaking his head. "But what if the Salemites attack me?"

"Don't worry, they're very ineffective."

"I saw them out there," Lannard said, jerking his head in the direction of the prisoners. "They're big and strong!"

"And clumsy cowards. They came out loud and furious, but as soon as we started cutting them down, they lost their will to fight. I've heard a few reports of Salemites who killed some of our soldiers, dropped their weapons, then knelt to be killed themselves. These people have no honor in battle, Lannard. You're a rather sizable man. Just growl at them and they'll go running with their tails between their legs like the dogs in Edge. You can do this, Guide Lannard. You *have* to do this." Poe paused. "Did you see Amory?"

Lannard shook his head. "Is she downstairs somewhere?"

"No. She was on display between the last two walls. Dead."

Lannard stared at him. "Thorne?"

Poe nodded.

"Why?"

"Because she didn't give him what he wanted *when* he wanted it," Poe said meaningfully.

Lannard exhaled and rubbed his face. "What will you be doing when we're at the temple, Poe?"

"Thorne wants me by your side, holding you up if necessary."

Lannard whimpered in relief. "Good."

Poe stopped rummaging in the pack. "Please don't make me do that, Lannard. For once in your life be brave, man! You've got the easiest task in the army and the flashiest outfit to go with it." He held up the light blue tunic.

Lannard smiled faintly. "It really is nice silk, isn't it? Thickest I could find. It's bug vomit, you know."

Poe rolled his eyes. "It is not. Well, not *precisely.* It's from moth caterpillar cocoons. I saw the weavers in Grasses."

"And you know how the caterpillars *make* those cocoons?" Lannard pressed.

Poe sighed. "Just get dressed and come downstairs. The huge pantry in the kitchen is stocked with the most incredible amount of food. Something down there will make you feel better."

"Any mead?"

"Haven't located any yet."

Lannard flopped back on to the bed and sighed miserably.

Thorne eyed the lieutenant colonel he had sent out earlier. He had just returned and was urgently beckoning to the general to speak to him in private in the study.

"Well?" Thorne asked as he closed the door.

The lieutenant colonel looked pale. "The prisoner was right. I saw the sign myself. On the main road, it points west down a lane. 'Shin-Briter-Zenos Eztates.'"

Thorne looked like someone had knocked the wind out of him. "Did you go down the lane?"

The officer shook his head vigorously, but covered his fear with, "We thought you'd want that privilege yourself."

Thorne was nearly trembling now. "Who else knows?"

"Only my lieutenant and me. He's sworn to keep quiet."

Thorne paced the room, his eyes darting back and forth.

The lieutenant colonel waited patiently, nervously.

"They may already be gone," Thorne mumbled. "Or maybe they're staying to see what happens . . ."

"Sir, we found a few horses," the officer said. "Brought one back for you."

Thorne stopped his pacing and looked up at him. "I need to see that sign myself. Take me there!"

Peto shook his head in amazement. "Shem, you are indeed one of the bravest, if not the craziest, men I've ever had the privilege to know."

Shem shrugged while everyone chuckled between bites of their hasty midday meal.

Except for Ester sitting next to him at the table. "Mama won't be happy, Papa."

Shem put his arm around his daughter. "I think it's *you* who's not happy that I'm wearing this uniform. Your mother would've been trying to chase me down again. I think this is why the Creator told her to stay up there instead. She would have wanted to play my prisoner or something."

Everyone laughed again, and Ester smiled. "Probably true."

Shem looked across the table at Peto. "Feeling rested?"

Peto nodded. "Yes, much better. We're just waiting on one more person." He glanced at the window where Jaytsy watched earnestly, nibbling on her sandwich and fretting about her son who was the same age as Young Pere.

"Cephas knows the way, Jayts," Peto gently reminded her. "We talked about every contingency last night. If we're not here, he knows to go up."

"But you said he'd be back by midday meal!" she said. "It's an hour later now. What if he ran into a problem?"

Deck, who was standing with Jaytsy and also watching out the window for their son, put his arm around her. "Cephas is the most level-headed young man I know. He'll get here, and if not, he'll get to the ancient site."

Peto put his hand on Lilla's. She'd been very quiet.

"Same thing for Young Pere," Peto said softly to his wife. "Except for the level-headed part."

Everyone chuckled lightly, but Jaytsy turned to Lilla sitting miserably at the table. "I promise, Lilla, Father *is* with him. I could feel him so strongly I could have reached out and hugged him. I looked into Young Pere's eyes only for a moment, but he is a very different young man. And he's trying to get back, that much I could read. Father will get him there, Lilla!"

Lilla smiled bravely. "Maybe Cephas will run into him?"

Mahrree sighed. "That's what I've been praying, Lilla."

Deck turned back to the window, something catching his attention. "Part of the prayer is answered. Cephas is back, but alone."

Lilla managed another smile. "That's all right! Thank goodness he's back! I'll get him a sandwich!" She slapped the table. "Time to go!" she said in an unnaturally high pitch.

Everyone nodded and most of the family reluctantly stood up, looking around one last time.

Jaytsy was already out the front door and hugging her son. But he gently pushed her aside to hurry into the house.

"Guide Zenos? Any way we can delay the army? There are maybe two dozen families still trying to get out! They're—" He stopped short when he saw his uncle was wearing an inside-out uniform.

"Trying to convince their loved ones to leave their houses?" Shem said.

Cephas nodded, confused as to how the guide knew that. He absent-mindedly took the massive, six-layer sandwich his aunt Lilla shoved into his hands. "Uncle Shem, what did you *do*?"

Shem smiled. "Your mother and father can tell you. I've bought some time for the last of our people. But I think you might find your mother's morning even more interesting than mine."

Perplexed, he took a bite of sandwich, his mouth barely fitting around it, and headed back outside to where Jaytsy was beckoning him to come find a fresh horse. He garbled, "You had an interesting morning, Mama?"

Mahrree and Shem heard his voice trailing off as he walked with everyone to the barn.

There were now only two people left at the table seated across from each other.

Reluctantly, Mahrree stood up.

Shem didn't. "We need to talk, Mahrree."

"Yes, we do."

"Why did you say that?"

She sighed. "What did he tell you, Shem? I know you've heard him. What does Perrin want us to do next?"

He looked down at his hands. "I haven't heard *him*, but I received his message. And I don't like it, Mahrree. Not one bit."

"How many times have you said that in the past few days, Shem?"

"Far too many." He looked up at her, something distressing happening in his eyes. "Why didn't you go to the site when I told you to? Why didn't you go with Relf?"

"I didn't feel the time was right," she said honestly.

"But it's right, now?"

Mahrree swallowed. "It's time to get on a horse. I know that much."

Shem dropped his gaze to the table, his chin wobbling. "I can't do it, Perrin," he whispered. "There's *no way*—"

Mahrree clenched her fists. She had *almost* successfully avoided this, too caught up in the frenetic events of the morning to give much thought to the words which were repeating in her head.

But now . . . she knew it was time.

"Shem, I don't know it all but I do know *something*. There's that line, from Pax's prophecy . . ." Her mouth had grown too dry for her to continue.

He looked up at her. "The aged?"

She nodded.

He closed his eyes. "It's you, Mahrree."

"I know it is."

His eyes flashed open in surprise at how calmly she said those words. "That's why you wouldn't go with Relf?"

"I didn't know it then, but . . . Well I'm not sure *what's* supposed to happen, but I know *I'm* supposed to make it happen," she confessed, her voice trembling.

"Have you read Gleace's prophecy lately?" he asked.

"Too many times."

His eyes were swimming. "Perrin fretted over that for years, Mahrree. One third of the Army of Idumea, *scared* away. Pair it with Pax's vision that the *aged* shall strike fear in the soldiers? Mahrree, there's only one aged person in the entire valley of Salem who could possibly scare the Army of Idumea."

As if she needed any more confirmation. "The reason Hogal Densal declared me to be the most dangerous woman in the world wasn't because of what I did many years ago *in* the world," she whispered. "It's because of what I'm supposed to do today, *to* the world. It's why I've been preserved. I now understand that I've been kept alive for this very day."

His shoulders began to shake. "Perrin, I can't do it!"

"What does he want you to do, Shem?" Mahrree asked, surprising herself with her composure.

"The temple," he choked.

"That's where the army's going?"

Shem nodded as tears spilled down his cheeks.

"Take me on Clark 14, Shem," she said. "He's rested now."

His head snapped up. "I don't know what will happen there!"

"Neither do I." She leaned across the table. "But I have faith that it will end well, Shem. Let me do this for Salem. For all it's done for us. You and Salem rescued us. Now I can return the favor for a few families to give them the time they need. Yesterday I helped get a few away from Eltana's army, and even then I wished I could've done more. Well, now I can—"

Peto stuck his head in the door. "Mother? Shem? Are you still in here?"

"Yes," Mahrree called back, trying to sound cheerful. "Just need a few more moments."

Peto came into the eating room to see Shem wiping away his tears. Mahrree had already dried her face.

"What's going on?" he asked severely.

Shem cleared his throat and stood up. "One last task, Peto."

Peto looked at his mother, suddenly frantic. "No . . . NO! Just leave with us, NOW!"

Mahrree took his arm. "Whatever do you think I'm going to do?"

she said in an overly sweet tone which he saw right through.

Peto's chin wobbled. "It's the prophecies, isn't it!? The aged! Scaring the soldiers! Father could never figure that out but he has now, hasn't he? Most dangerous woman in the world—it's *you!*"

Mahrree pulled him into a powerful hug. "Isn't that amazing, Peto? I might get to fulfill a prophecy. How many people get to say that about themselves? *And you know it, too.*" For some reason, that knowledge gave her strength she needed.

Peto squeezed her back. "Mother, no! I can't let you do this—"

"I'm not even sure what I'm doing, son."

"Peto," Shem said gravely, "take the others to the site. We'll join you when we can. It may not be until after dark, but I'll be there. Tell Calla I promise I'll be there with her tonight."

Peto sniffled but didn't release his mother. "What will I tell the others?"

"That Mahrree's being unreasonable, as usual. She wanted to see something before she left, and I agreed to take her because I wanted to check on a couple houses, too. We'll take Clark 14."

"That's why he's here," Peto said gruffly, finally releasing her. "He was chosen by Father for this day." He could barely choke out the words. Holding Mahrree by the shoulders, he said, "Be careful, don't make us wait too long, all right? Stay close to Shem and . . . do whatever you have to do. We'll have your bedroll waiting."

Mahrree kissed his cheek. "Bring Clark 14 to the front. Tell them I'm in the washroom one last time and that I wanted to mount from the front porch. Some silly plan Perrin and I had. That way we can go in the other direction without everyone noticing."

Peto nodded miserably and hugged her again. "I can't believe I'm letting you go."

"As if you had a choice, Peto," Mahrree whispered. "How long have you known I needed to do this?"

"Since this morning," he confessed. "That's why I was up so early and decided to chase after Eltana Yordin. I kept thinking of the prophecies and suddenly seeing you with the words. But I've been trying to ignore it all morning."

She stepped out of his hug and smiled bravely. "I only wish you could witness what I get to do! But I'm sure your father will. He can tell you about it later."

Peto's face contorted at the idea, and he pointed at Shem. "Take care of my mother, Shem."

"Apologize to my wife, Peto."

Peto sighed, looked at his mother one last time, and, knowing time was already too short, darted out the back door.

Mahrree turned to Shem. "I really *do* need to use the washroom again. Two minutes."

Peto strode to the barn, took the big black horse without a word, and led him out.

"Peto? Where are you taking Clark 14?" Lilla asked.

Deck and Jaytsy, who were helping their children mount, looked over at him.

"Mother wants him at the front," he said, not meeting any of their gazes. "Shem will take her."

"Why?" Jaytsy asked.

Peto turned around. "I don't know!" he snapped. "I'm just tired of arguing with her! Everything has to be her way. Don't you know that by now? She always complicates everything, even if lives are at stake. Now, we're running out of time. Whatever it takes to get her out of here, at this point I'll just do it! If Shem's dense enough to indulge her, then let him! We've already blown the day's plan completely anyway. I'm seeing the rest of you to safety. Now mount up and be ready to MOVE!"

Jaytsy and Lilla glanced at each other, speechless at Peto's uncharacteristic outburst. The children cowered.

But Deck nodded calmly. "We'll wait for you, Peto."

Peto broke into a run with Clark 14 to the front of the house, brushing away his tears as he did.

Shem was waiting, and Mahrree was coming out the front door.

"Thank you, son. I could always count on you to do the right things."

Peto handed the reins to Shem, sent his mother one last feeble smile, then ran back to the others.

Mahrree and Shem exchanged The Dinner smile. He helped her get into the saddle, then mounted up behind her.

"This first part will be a little rough, but I've got you," he said, wrapping a strong arm around her. He kicked the horse's sides and he took off in a gallop toward the center of Salem.

Back at the barn, Peto had mounted on the last horse available,

Shem's Silver, brought over earlier by Zaddick, and nodded to Deck that it was time to leave. But as they heard Clark 14 heading in the other direction, everyone turned in their saddles.

Peto only nodded again to Deck. "Go, Deck. They'll catch up."

"But Peto—" Jaytsy started.

"I said *GO!*"

"We need to get off the main road," Shem said in Mahrree's ear. "Thorne will have sent out scouts and we don't want to meet any."

Mahrree didn't answer but tried to keep her breathing steady as the horse jarred her.

Down the Shin-Briter-Zenos Eztates lane Clark 14 galloped, up along the main road for a few dozen paces, then on to a tracked lane between barns and sheds. Shem slowed Clark 14 to a trot and Mahrree finally caught her breath.

"Shem, maybe you should put the jacket on right-side out. Look like an officer who's captured me."

"Not a bad idea," he said, stopping Clark 14 between two sheds. He slipped off the horse in the narrow gap and reversed the jacket.

Mahrree looked around. "It's so quiet. I've never known Salem to be so still."

"It's eerie, I agree," Shem said as he put on the jacket properly. "It's felt all wrong for the past few days."

"But in a way it also feels like it's trying to force us away. Telling us to leave."

Shem buttoned up the jacket. "I agree with that, too. Each building whispers, 'Go west, Shem. Go west.'"

"And here you are going east," Mahrree said sadly.

"All right, the buildings are actually saying, 'Go west in a *little while,* Shem.'"

Mahrree smiled as he mounted up behind her again. "Can 14 just walk? I'm really not in a hurry, you know."

Shem glanced around. "I estimate we have maybe two hours before Thorne and the army arrive. They'll be highly motivated to stay on the attack now that they've had a taste of success. At a walk, 14 will get there in about an hour and a half."

"Is that all right if he just walks?"

"Of course it is. Anything for the great Mahrree Shin."

"Oh, Shem, stop it."

He chuckled and wrapped his arm protectively around her, then clucked Clark 14 onto a narrow lane. "If we walk we might hear what's happening, and we won't draw any attention to us, either."

She leaned back and put her head against his shoulder. "Sounds good to me."

General Thorne, confident that the first battle for Salem was a decisive victory for the Army of Idumea, rode with the lieutenant colonel and his assistant past the battlefield and onto the main cobblestone road. Lemuel surveyed the region as their horses galloped.

Salem was rich, spectacularly rich. Every house was large and well-kept. Every orchard and farm was tidy. There wasn't a rickety barn, ill-repaired fence, or a falling down shack anywhere.

"A great many places to explore in the next few days, General," the lieutenant colonel commented. "It seems to go north for many miles, too."

Thorne nodded. "Truly remarkable. When we take it over we'll make it even better."

"Of course, sir."

They rode for several miles looking for signs of life but saw none. It was all ripe for Lemuel's picking. Eventually the lieutenant colonel slowed his horse and pointed. "Right there, sir."

Thorne got closer and sneered at the sign. "'Eztates'? With a z?" Then he knew.

"There was a housing district in Idumea called *Zebra Eztates*—"

"Sir, shall we go with you? You have no idea what you'll find."

That was exactly Lemuel's concern.

"No. I will do this alone. If I'm not back in ten minutes, come find me. Everything is abandoned, anyway."

He kicked his horse into a trot and headed down the lane, scanning the perimeter for movement. There was none except for a stray dog and a few wandering chickens. After a minute he saw another sign, much larger, spanning the entire lane and supported on tall timbers above the road.

SHIN-BRITER-ZENOS EZTATES.
BEGUN—338. END—NEVER.

"Ends today," he jeered. His horse trotted to the end of the lane where he stopped, stunned.

There were two large houses, one painted a deep red, the other weathered gray wood with window boxes. Each had a large second story, then additions on the sides. Back between the houses was a massive blue barn, the door swinging in the breeze.

Cautiously, Lemuel looked to his left. There stood a tall tower with the black banner waving, and beyond it was another large house, painted bright yellow. Along the lane leading to it were two smaller houses, each painted a different shade of yellow.

He again faced the two large houses. Behind the gray one was a sprawling orchard, and further on were several smaller houses painted in various hues. Beyond the red house was a small herd of cattle grazing on the earliest green sprouts, immense fields stretching behind and leading up to the rolling hillside.

Lemuel could hardly take it all in.

It had been *theirs*. All of it. All this time, just over the mountain, they had been *here*.

He rode up to the gray house and leaned over in the saddle to look in the windows. Furniture to hold twenty people. And—

He reared back, startled, his breathing rapid.

No, only paintings. They were faces, just paintings of faces. The realism and accuracy of the artwork was far more splendid than anything in the world. The thought drifted by that he should find an artist to do a portrait of himself before he killed all of the Salemite prisoners.

Taking a few deep breaths, he regained his composure and peered again into the windows.

Faces. Dozens of them. For a moment he was tempted to leave the horse and walk into the house, but even though the images grinned at him, something refused to let him enter. But he could just make out . . . *them*.

As they must have looked when they first arrived.

Then another, a little older. And with small children on their laps.

Then older still, of *him* looking in the distance, with *her* looking directly at the painter, her head resting on his chest as if she were proudly displaying a possession—

The horse backed up, agitated, and Lemuel swung it around. He found himself in front of another set of windows and peered in.

A massive painting of a ruin, and even though he couldn't see them clearly, he knew *they* were there, those small blotches leaning against a pillar.

He glanced at the red house across the way, most likely just as spacious and full, and he felt strangely sweaty and clammy.

A large boulder positioned between the two properties caught his eye. Something was carved on it, and around it were additional stones, all roughly the size of kickballs, each with something painted on it. He walked his horse over to the boulder and stopped when he saw the words.

PERRIN SHIN

291-363

Lemuel stared at the death date.

Two years ago. Only two short years ago. He gaped at it for a full minute, various emotions racing through him.

Fury that the colonel survived.

Shock that he was here until two years ago.

Grief that he missed him by only two short years.

All that time—*all that time*—he was just over the mountain . . . He'd been so close, for so long . . .

Lemuel cleared his throat and shifted in the saddle. He glared at the stone now, reading the rest of the words carved deeply and more skillfully than anything he'd seen in Idumea.

BELOVED SON
HUSBAND
FATHER
GRANDFATHER
GREAT-GRANDFATHER
BROTHER

Lemuel stopped at that one. Brother? Perrin was an only child. Who would call him brother?

A churning in his gut told him who. He read the next word.

UNCLE

The only way Perrin could be an uncle was if his so-called brother became a father. Lemuel's stomach twisted again.

FRIEND
PUGGAH
SON OF THE CREATOR

He didn't expect to feel such a confusion of responses at this moment. Triumph, regret, pain—

To distract himself, he started reading the words on the rocks placed on top, around, and below the massive boulder. Some were painted carefully, others more sloppily.

Some of the names were familiar. Relf. Jaytsy. Deckett. Peto.

Others he didn't know. Cambo. Kanthi. Ester.

Other rocks had small hand prints with names written carefully underneath. Fennic. Gersh. Riekel. Raishel. Likely grandchildren or great-grandchildren.

Lemuel's gaze rose to the top. He flinched when he saw the name on the highest stone. In a careful hand was written, Mahrree.

He felt very hot. There *she* was, sitting on top of everything in prominence. No death date next to her name. Not yet.

He searched the other stones in earnest and paused at the name Lek, then saw one he was looking for, in familiar handwriting.

Young Pere.

His mouth filled with the taste of bile as he continued to read stone after stone, searching. Holling. Eraliz. Hycy. Wes. Hogal. Zaddick. Yenali—

Then he spied it, at the bottom. A smaller stone labeled Calla rested upon it, but the larger bottom stone bore only four letters, printed clearly but small.

Shem.

Lemuel gripped the reins tighter as his mouth filled. He spat all that he had on that rock, then filled his mouth again and fouled the rock bearing Mahrree's name.

"How dare you!" he shouted at it. "I'll find you, you sow! You'll pay! All of you!"

Lemuel wheeled his horse around but one more large stone, set to the side of the boulder, caught his eye. He twisted in his saddle and looked at the words carved on it.

THE CAT.
336-350.

Lemuel squinted at it. The Cat? He remembered as he looked at the date of birth—336.

The year of the Moorland offensive. The year he was sliced by the Guarder and Perrin saved him. The year he sent a scrawny kitten to Jaytsy because his mother said giving girls baby animals brings out their mothering instincts and they go looking for someone to be a father.

They *took* the cat with them.

Lemuel had searched the burned-out ruins of their house a few weeks after they were gone, on the off chance of finding that cat still lurking. It wasn't there nor at the Briters' looted farm. Lemuel assumed it had run away or died.

But they *took it with them*. Not only that, they buried it and marked its grave with a carved stone.

The sentiment struck Lemuel oddly. Suddenly he was a twenty-three-year-old officer again, remembering how he felt for the colonel who had shown him more kindness than his own father ever had. That young officer never shed a tear before in his life, but he did when Perrin was lost to the forest.

And Perrin had taken a part of Lemuel with him, and even had the memory carved in stone.

Lemuel looked back at the great boulder. "They didn't deserve you," he whispered to it. He looked down at the ground below where Perrin's corpse lay. "And you deserved none of this. You deserved so much more. Your name will be remembered, Perrin. I'll *make* them remember it. I promise you. I—"

He'd noticed one more stone, again etched precisely.

IN MEMORY OF CLARK, A DECENT HORSE

"So THAT'S what happened to his horse?!" he shrieked. "It came here too? Yordin said he never got it back and we searched for weeks, because how do you misplace such a massive animal?"

Too many facts were now clashing with his well-known stories, and too many emotions were battling in his gut. He shut it all down, shoved it all away, unable to think or process or know how to react.

Instead, he kicked his new horse—which, now that he looked at it, seemed a great deal like the black animal they could never find—and raced out of the Eztates. A few moments later he reached the lieutenant colonel and his assistant.

"Sir?" the officer asked anxiously.

"Cut down the sign! Then we start the march north," he shouted, near to frothing. "I'll return later and burn the houses myself."

Still cowering behind the rocking chair on the front porch, Versa had seen the general and the two officers ride down the main cobblestone road. She looked around to make sure no more soldiers were around checking the dead, and recognized her opportunity.

She slipped away from the house and pulled out her own sneaking-around-skills to run between houses and move undetected along tree lines and shrubs. Spending her childhood thieving to help her mother have enough to feed her family was coming in handy once again.

But her progress was awkward, her additional weight slowing her down considerably. Still, she did her best to make her way along the quiet roads to where she was sure the general was headed: the Eztates. She couldn't even see the horses anymore, so far behind she was, but depending on how long he spent there, she had a reasonably good chance of catching up. Maybe this was why she had such a long nap, to give her the energy she needed now. This was a better way to confront him, with only two other officers and away from everyone else. This might be the best, and only, chance she would get.

She jogged along as quietly as possible, occasionally going back to the main road to see how much further she had to reach the two officers waiting at the smaller Eztates sign, then ducking back behind the houses. Less than half a mile. A quarter mile—

In the unnatural silence of Salem, she heard the horse's hooves distinctly as they echoed. She quickened her run and darted out to the main road. Down it some ways, Thorne was back, shouting about tearing down the signs and calling for the army to march north. This was it. Next he'd be riding toward her.

Versa made her move to intercept him. She began her run north to him, still several hundred paces away. Just as she opened her mouth to shout to get his attention, she tripped, and everything became dark.

"What the—?"

Versa tried to turn around, but she was blocked. Somehow, for some bizarre reason known only to the deranged person who did this, she was standing in a pit that barely held enough room for her and the pack. She had bobbled into it, her weight and pack bonking her back and forth against the narrow sides until her feet landed in soft sand. She was shaken up and maybe had a new bruise or two, but otherwise was surprisingly sound and standing in—

A well?!

Someone was digging a well, right here next to the main road?! Who digs a well *here*?! She looked up to see daylight, a few inches above how high her arms could reach, and just then the shadow of the three horses sped past her.

"NO!" she cried, but her voice was captured by the well. Even if her voice had carried out of the pit, it would have been drowned out by the sounds of the horses on the stone road.

"Aaugh!" she punched the soft dirt walls around her. "NO! It's as if You don't *want* me to stop him!" she shouted to the sky. "I don't understand that! Why not let me stop him?!" She beat the dirt in fury for another minute, then, realizing she was expending valuable energy, started instead to look for a way to get out.

"This is ludicrous," she finally laughed mirthlessly. "I mean, I'm in a HOLE and NO ONE is around to HELP ME!" That's when she noticed a carved out section in the side of the pit, big enough for a hand. She looked down and noticed more carved out parts, evenly spaced, starting down by her feet.

"Salemites!" she laughed derisively. "Only Salemites would think to start digging a well beside the road, then also dig in steps to climb out of it!"

She put a foot in the first hole and pushed up. It was awkward going, and if she'd felt clumsy before, she was wholly ungainly now trying to maneuver her way up the dirt holds. Eventually she heaved herself and the pack out, and sat by the side of road, looking longingly to the south where the distant horses were turning back to the station. She picked herself up and began brushing off the dirt before deciding it helped to camouflage her better, then turned north.

"If that's where they're marching, then so am I. Why they're going north, I can't fathom," she said as she started on her way. "The temple site is to the west—"

She stopped, grinned, and started walking again.

"*Unless* they think everyone's at the *current* temple site, which is to the north! I could make it there in about one and a half hours." She looked behind her, "And they are about half an hour behind me . . . YES! This is why, right?" She looked up to the sky. "A better plan? At the temple site? If I wasn't here, then I wouldn't have heard that they're going north, and that's what You wanted me to hear, right?"

She rubbed her hands together.

"I've still got a chance."

The mood at the ancient temple site was oppressively somber. Word that the beloved wife of the guide had been felled by two arrows to her chest rushed faster than wildfire, and each family that arrived could feel the devastation in the air like a hot, humid day. The horrible news was shared as new families arrived, and the sound of weeping was heard in every section of the tableland.

At the combined family camp of Shins, Briters, and Zenoses, the dark mood was crushing. Calla Trovato Zenos's body lay on the ground, covered with a white blanket except for her gentle face. Quietly Salemites streamed by at a respectful distance, trying to comprehend the tragedy.

Her daughter Meiki lay by the body, weeping to dehydration, while Clyde could do nothing more than keep a protective hand on her shoulder. At Calla's feet, her sons Lek and Boskos held each other as they shook with great racking sobs, their wives kneeling behind them with their arms wrapped around them. Their five children were nearby, cradled by relatives while they cried.

Calla's four sisters were clustered opposite of Meiki, touching the white cloth and weeping as their husbands and children and many more of the Zenos clan sat further behind, holding each other. Grandma Trovato was in a surgery tent by the ruins, being tended to by doctors after she passed out in horror after seeing her oldest daughter.

Around the Zenoses sat the rest of the Shin and Briter families, tears streaming down their faces as they watched their cousins so deep in mourning that they couldn't yet be comforted, and waiting for the first indication of what they could do to help.

Three of Shem's assistants stood to the side, talking quietly and answering questions for those just arriving. They tried to intercept everyone who came to mourn, making sure no one bothered the Zenos children. Another assistant sat where refugees emerged from the routes, waiting for the arrival of Shem.

At one point one of the assistants suggested to Salema that he ride down and find Guide Zenos and the other three children to deliver the news. Salema put a stop to that.

"He needs to be the guide right now. There's nothing he can do for her. Telling him down there will only make his ride here even more distressing. He can't handle that right now. Just keep watch for him, for all my family. Let *us* tell them when they arrive."

There was no way the very long day could get any worse.

Shem and Mahrree had ridden in silence for a few minutes, both lost in thought. Finally Mahrree said, "Tell me about this morning, of Perrin's dream about you."

He sighed. "You don't really want to hear about that, do you?"

"Shem, what else do you think is on my mind? Distract me. You could always drive me to distraction."

He chuckled. "All right. Well, I really didn't understand what Tuma and Hew meant. You see, Tuma Hifadhi had told me years ago that I should always remain a soldier, never turn in my resignation, and that someday I would need to claim that authority. Hew Gleace clarified that later. About a year before we all left Edge, he said that when I did 'vanish,' I should just slip away like everyone else and remain a sergeant major, with the rank and seniority it affords. I thought, 'All right, whatever.' I didn't think anything about it again, not until later when Hew had his stroke, days before he passed away."

Shem's voice grew husky at the memory.

"I went to see him, late at night once he was awake again. His speech was so slurred we struggled to understand him, but he said I needed to get ready. Being the assistant who had served the next long-est, I would be the next guide, but I really didn't want to be! I came home with a very heavy heart. When I woke up late that morning, Perrin was sitting in my bedroom, waiting. Scared me to death!" he chuckled. "Calla had let him in, hoping he could say something to comfort me. He didn't. He said he had been up for hours, unable to sleep after a dream he had.

"It was before the Last Day," his voice quavered again, "and Perrin dreamed that a group of soldiers had made their way to the cliff side. No Salemites up there were to fight, we knew that. But he saw one man who was something *other* than a Salemite, running to help. Perrin didn't see his face at first, but he killed all but one of the soldiers so that no one else had to lift a weapon and violate the Creator's decree that the temple site remain as a haven for His people, free of violence. Perrin then said the man turned around, and he saw it was me. I had even ridden in on a white horse," he whispered. "As a soldier, I was still allowed to fight."

Mahrree patted his hand that held her waist. "Oh, Shem—you did it! And even chose the right horse."

She could feel him shrugging humbly behind her. "I don't think you know this, but after Perrin's dream, he and I sparred a few times a year in my barn. We had two sticks which were the right length and close to the right weight. Just to keep in form, you know," he said apologetically.

"No, I didn't know that."

"A couple of times we bruised each other," he admitted with a chuckle. "So we made up stories for our wives about how that happened. The last time we practiced was about a week before our last marking party, right before he left us. Mahrree, he was still so strong and fast. *So* fast."

She smiled at the image of the two grandfathers sword fighting with sticks. "Oh, I wish I had known! I would have loved to watch. How remarkable. This whole day, Shem, is just remarkable."

"It's the longest day I've ever experienced, that's for sure," he said wearily.

Mahrree patted his hand again. "It can be as long as it wants. Right now it's very good. Perrin never told me that dream, you know."

"I figured as much."

"Usually he told me everything."

"It wasn't meant for you. But apparently he told Jothan, too, or I never would have received the message to go up there."

"And you told Calla, right?"

"Perrin did," he said drearily. "That's why she forced me up there."

"Let's see—you've been guide for nearly nine years now, so that's how long she's been waiting for this day."

"Probably."

Mahrree chuckled. "I can hardly wait to ask her what she thought. I hope she saw what she wanted to see!"

Shem groaned behind her.

Young Pere and Nelt continued along the forests on the eastern side of Salem, within view of vineyards and flocks of sheep, but out of view of anyone who might still be around to see them.

"How much further?" Nelt asked.

"Not really sure," Young Pere said, picking his way through the underbrush. "I know the mountains on the west side, not the east. The forest will lengthen out up here soon, and that's what we're looking for. There's a narrow river that empties off of this mountain and heads west toward the valley. The trees that line that river have been left standing. Salemites like the fact that there's a forest running through Salem. Rather cuts the valley in two halves, south and north, but the main road has been cleared and there are lots of bridges built across it."

Nelt shook his head. "Down in the world the villages clear off *all* the trees."

"I know," Young Pere said in disappointment. "Anything beautiful that nature creates, the world sees fit to knock it down."

"So where's the temple?"

"On the other side of that river and forest, in untouched lands. They call them the Quiet Fields."

"Huh," Nelt said. "Can't think of anything in the world purposely left untouched and quiet."

"Me neither." Young Pere sighed as he walked around a large rock. They climbed up a rise and paused at a clearing.

"There," Young Pere gestured. "See how the forest extends out from the mountains like a long finger? It borders the bank of the river and continues nearly all the way to the western mountains."

"The army will likely go through that spot," Nelt pointed to a narrow gap in the trees. "That must be a main bridge. So how long till we get to the temple?"

"At our rate, about another hour and a half," Young Pere guessed. "Maybe more, since I don't know this terrain."

Nelt glanced back to the south of the valley and squinted. "From what I can see, it looks like they're forming ranks."

Young Pere focused on the distance as well, where soldiers like swarms of ants were massing. "I think you're right."

"How long from there to the temple site on the main road?"

"Less than two hours, quick march?"

Nelt and Young Pere looked at each other. "We need to hurry!"

Shem, Mahrree, and Clark 14 had been traveling in silence for a while. Eventually Mahrree voiced the only thought in her head. "Shem, what am I supposed to do there?"

"I still don't know."

"Thank you for taking me, by the way," she said. "There's no one else I'd want with me right now."

He cleared his throat. "Of course, Mahrree. You're my dearest and oldest friend."

She frowned. "You *had* to say 'oldest'?"

He chuckled. "In my eyes, you look exactly as you did when I first met you. You haven't aged a day over thirty."

"Oh, as if I'm going to believe any of that," she scoffed. "But it was nice to hear, anyway."

"It's true, Mahrree. You're just as feisty and determined and lovely as when I first met you at the market."

"You remember that?"

"With Jaytsy throwing new potatoes and Peto throwing a fit. And you talking to yourself. An unforgettable sight."

Mahrree chuckled. "You really surprised me that day. I'd never met another twenty-year-old willing to help with screaming children. I should have realized then what an unusual man you were. Do you remember you said something about helping me get home?"

"I do. And I meant it in more ways than one."

"You did, didn't you? I think you started off in the wrong direction, too, pulling Jaytsy in the wagon."

He smiled. "I started heading east, toward the canal system. I really didn't know which way you lived, but that was the direction I hoped someday to take you. East, then north to our home."

"I never put it all together until many years after we came here. I just thought you were a clueless soldier."

"I was that, too," he confessed. "I fumbled around so often those first years I was surprised I didn't give myself away."

"No, Shem. You always did the right things," Mahrree insisted. "You were an amazing young man. And you still are. You've never ceased to surprise me, Shem Zenos."

She could nearly feel him blushing behind her. "And you've always surprised me. No other officer's wife would be asking how to negotiate with Guarders. And who else would be brave enough to stand in front of all of Edge years later to declare the Administrators were liars? But the most surprising thing you ever did was that night when you stood up to your husband, called him that vulgar name, and told him you'd defend your right to speak, even to your death. Whew! I was ready to start applauding, except I thought Perrin might kill me."

Mahrree winced. "Oh, that was an awful night, wasn't it?"

"Turned out wonderfully though, didn't it?" he said. "Watching him slice those Administrator emblems off his jacket? It gave me chills. When I put on this jacket today I wished somehow the name would have been Shin. Instead I'm stuck with Gerblatz. What kind of name is Gerblatz?"

Mahrree laughed and twisted to look at the badge she hadn't noticed. "Oh, I *am* sorry! Must be the sound overripe fruit makes when it hits the ground."

Shem chuckled. "At least I'm a colonel."

"And an excellent one at that."

"Thank you."

They rode in silence again for a few minutes.

"Talk to me, Shem. It's so quiet, and the voices in my mind are making me nervous."

"I always suspected you weren't completely alone in there."

"Exactly! Keep talking!"

He paused again. "I . . . I don't know what to say, Mahrree."

"I don't either. Here we have all this time with no interruptions and nothing to say."

"Maybe . . . maybe we don't have to say anything. Maybe after all these years we've said all we need to say and can just enjoy each other's silence."

Mahrree pondered that for a moment. "That doesn't sound like either one of us, Shem."

He chuckled. "Oh, Mahrree. You're just *something else.*"

"What does that mean? Perrin would say that too. I want a definition for once. I think I deserve that right now, don't you?"

"I really don't know what it means, Mahrree. We haven't been able to figure out what that 'something else' is."

Mahrree grumbled as Shem chuckled.

After a moment she sighed. "You're my dearest friend too. You've been so much more than just a brother, if that's possible, more than just a friend. I don't even know how to define you. I know I say Calla is my *best* friend, but you're my *dearest*."

"Thank you, Mahrree," he whispered.

"Explain it to her, will you? When you see Calla?" She fought to keep her voice steady. "We were going to stand together and try to count the soldiers. Tell her I'm sorry."

"Mahrree, what are you talking about?" But the hesitancy in his voice gave him away.

She sighed. "You and I both know you'll be riding back alone, Shem."

He firmed his grip around her waist, as if to not let her go. "I don't know anything of the sort and neither do you."

"Shem, it's all right—"

"No, it's not! I'm not delivering you to your death, Mahrree!"

"No, you're not," she said calmly. "You're delivering me to my husband."

She felt his head rest against hers. "No, no, no . . ."

"Please, Shem. Let me see Perrin again? I've been so lonely for him."

She thought she felt him kiss the back of her head. "I'm so sorry. I didn't realize you were so lonely. If I had known—"

"I haven't been *lonely*, not with family all around me and poor Honri doing his best. I'm just lonely *for him*. Does that make sense?"

"It does. But it doesn't make me feel any better about any of this. I'm feeling sick just thinking about it."

"Ew, please don't be sick. I'm right in front of you."

Shem chuckled sadly. "Mahrree, Mahrree . . . you don't have to die. I'm not convinced that's what's going to happen."

She patted his hand. "I'm not afraid, Shem." She paused. "All right, *honestly*—because at a time like this it's best to not have any last minute mistakes on my mind that I might not have time to fix— I'll admit I'm afraid of the *pain,* but not of *dying*. I'm fairly confident I know what will happen right after that, and I have a feeling once I get to the other side, I'll wonder why I was so cautious in life that I wanted to prolong it. Paradise will be so much more wonderful than even Salem."

She heard sniffing behind her and felt Shem shake silently.

She put her arm over his that was wrapped around her and squeezed it. "Stop it, Shem. You'll get me going. I need to see clearly in the next few hours."

He snorted a laugh that turned into a sob. She was sure she felt him kiss the back of her head that time.

"Definition of 'something else,'" he said quietly. "The ability to see the world from angles no one else dared to try. Deciding not to be afraid of what everyone else is afraid of, not to do what everyone else does, and deciding to be exactly what you want to be without a care in the world as to what anyone else thinks."

"A little wordy for a definition, Shem, but I'll take it."

"Give me time and I'll make it more succinct."

"How much more time do we have, Shem?"

"The forest is about fifteen minutes away, right there."

She swallowed. "I see it. Kind of hard to miss. So half an hour altogether?"

"At best."

"Can this Clark go any slower?"

He tightened his grip on her again. "I'll see what I can do."

"They're still not behind us, Peto," Lilla said, turning around to check again. From their vantage point they could see well down the trail. No one was behind them—they seemed to be the last ones leaving Salem. Everything was still.

Silver, bringing up Peto at the rear, continued to plod up the hill. He stared straight ahead, making sure that Zaddick and Deck in the lead didn't need anything.

"Did you hear me, Peto?" Lilla exclaimed. "I don't see them!"

Peto sighed. "I know, Lilla. Just keep your eyes on the trail ahead. Gets a little tricky on the steep part."

Lilla swallowed hard and brushed away her tears.

"There's our canyon," Young Pere said to Nelt, pointing north. "Thorne's going to go to the temple in front of it. We're probably half an hour away."

"So we go to the canyon?"

Young Pere turned and slowly drew Nelt's sword from his sheath as Nelt watched in confusion. He held it up to the sunlight, admiringly. "We go to the *temple*. May I borrow this?"

Nelt swallowed. "Young Pere, what are you planning to do?"

"I'm going to end this, Nelt," he declared. "I'm tired of running from him, of being afraid of him, of being cautious of my every word and step around him. And now he has all of Salem terrified, too? How in the world has a man like him been allowed to live this long?! But no longer."

Nelt shook his head but took off his belt and sheath, and handed them to Young Pere. "Just don't tell anyone I gave this to you, all right?"

Versa plopped down on a large rock by the river and put her feet up on an obliging log.

"I never realized before how much I depended on thieving to keep me in shape." Tired and hungry, she opened her pack, pulled out some nuts, and nibbled on them. The temple sat to the right of her: precisely cut white stone with pillars and a portico. Majestic, grand, and, like everything else in Salem, very quiet.

"Exactly what am I supposed to do next?" she asked the trees sheltering her. "He'll be coming here then . . . what?"

She received no answer.

Thorne's troops continued their brisk march north through Salem. Through the houses and through the barns, finding a few horses here and there, taking food out of kitchens and cellars, and smashing windows just for fun.

For their excellent work in taking out the Salemite fighters, Thorne rewarded them with a sampling of Salem. The only requirement was to keep up their pace. Guide Lannard led the way, easy to see in his purple silk cloak and light blue pants. The horse he was given trotted serenely north toward a long line of trees, while several officers and guards jogged alongside.

Thorne followed about a hundred paces behind, also mounted, making sure the soldiers kept up the pace. They did so, with armfuls of food not seen in the world since Deceit erupted.

Each new house offered another opportunity. A few times soldiers surprised people still hiding in them, but rarely were there any drawn-out confrontations. A couple slices of a sword usually ended anything before it started. The last of the Salemites, only a dozen by Thorne's count, were fleeing before the army. Most were heading west, but they were far further north than the canyon his prisoners frequently gestured to. Lemuel smiled smugly. They were fleeing to the forests, but they wouldn't stay there long. His soldiers would flush them out, scared and hungry, in the next few days.

By the time they'd reach the temple, the Army of Idumea would have plowed through the southern half of Salem. Men forgot all about their exhaustion. Those in the back raced to be up front so as to be the first to go through another house. It was like a relay race to the forested river. Even the most frail men suddenly found the energy they needed to run seven miles from the canyon entrance to the northeast temple, looting as they went.

Lemuel beamed at the land he was conquering, all before dinner. For the moment, he forgot all about the ridiculous Eztates, because it was shaping up to be a fantastic day.

Snarl gazed longingly at yet another house, open and ready for the taking, but he heard Sergeant Beaved say once again, "No!"

They were heading north with the rest of the army, keeping up a steady jog, but staying on the main road. Snarl's gaze hardened as he shifted his glare to Beaved. "It's stupid. Everyone else is—"

"*We* are not everyone else," Beaved countered. "We agreed. These are the homes and possessions of people—of Shin's people—and we loot nothing."

Reg straightened his jacket. "Snarl, you're free to leave us. Just run off and do whatever. No one's keeping you here."

Snarl massaged his hands which wanted to lift and pocket something. "Still have a duty to do. Maybe," he grumbled.

Reg and Beaved exchanged looks of bewilderment. "Shin was our duty," Reg reminded them as their brisk walk came to stop. The pack of soldiers ahead of them had paused for some reason, which was good because Teach was struggling to catch up. Iron and Hammer had been jogging beside him, poking him unhelpfully when he flagged. Buddy and Pal had already caught up to Reg, Beaved, and

Snarl, and watched with expressions of pained amusement as Teach lumbered up to them. Panting exhaustedly, he leaned against a hitching post as the security team waited for the bottleneck ahead to clear.

"What are . . . we talking . . . about?" Teach panted. "Please let it be . . . a nap . . . in that . . . house. Or here." He slumped to the ground.

Beaved eyed Snarl steadily as he said, "We're reminding each other what we pledged in the barn: we loot nothing, we follow the army to see what happens next, and if we find Shin, we help him."

Teach asked, "And if we find . . . he's with that Cloudy assassin?"

Beaved gripped the hilt of his sword. "Then Lieutenant Nelt— and that's his real name so get used to using it—Nelt gets what he was intending to give."

His team nodded in wary agreement. Just how skilled Nelt was as an assassin still wasn't known. Each man had privately decided that letting Sergeant Beaved approach him first was the best idea. They'd jump in after they assessed Nelt's ability, and if Beaved didn't die too quickly.

"Slagging assassin," Snarl grumbled. "I'd wondered why Thorne assigned him to our team but I never asked him."

Reg chuckled mirthlessly. "As if Cloudy Nelt would have given you a straight answer had you asked—"

"I meant Thorne," Snarl snarled. "I never asked Thorne."

"Well, not like you had private discussions with him—" Reg's voice trailed off when he noticed Snarl's curled lip that was attempting a smile. "You did? You spoke with Thorne?!"

Snarl sniffed importantly. "When he approached me about being on the team, yeah."

Beaved folded his arms, his eyebrows furrowed. "Why'd Thorne recruit you anyway?"

"Because he caught me climbing the walls to his mansion. Twice." Snarl tried to smile again. "And three times, I slipped out of incarceration. He needed someone like me. Someone who knows the criminal mind. Someone who can *be creative*."

Beaved sighed. "Figures. So you think Thorne still wants to use you?"

Snarl tipped his head. "If Nelt fails, Thorne gave me permission to *finish things off* as I see fit." He fondled the handle of his long knife which stuck out above his waistband.

The rest of the team eyed him anxiously.

"Not like I knew about Nelt specifically," Snarl continued, "but

Thorne told me he had a few plans in place, and once they failed, I'd get my shot at Shin. I'd also get fifty slips of gold if I take care of things *neatly*."

"What, you're supposed to kill him?" Beaved demanded.

Pal and Buddy shrunk back behind Iron and Hammer, who looked like they smelled something unpleasant.

Snarl shrugged. "If that's what it took to take care of things—"

Beaved stepped up to him. "Thorne thinks that's his son. I sincerely doubt he wants him dead. So what, exactly, were you *supposed* to do?! What did you and Thorne decide upon?"

For once, Snarl seemed unsure, as if finding out for the first time that two and two don't make five. "Take care of things," he repeated. "Neatly."

"No, you're not," Beaved said, his nose nearly touching Snarl's. "I'm in command of this team, and my order is that we help Shin live and even escape from Thorne, if necessary. Is that clear?"

Snarl bobbed his head noncommittally. In a mutter he said, "Fifty slips of gold *is* a lot of gold—"

He was interrupted by Teach, who was fuming. "Slagging general promised me only twenty slips!"

Now everyone pivoted to stare at Teach, who was struggling to get up from his uncomfortable patch of cobblestone.

"You too?" Beaved exclaimed. "Thorne was paying you off, too? For what?"

"Information," Teach declared bitterly. There didn't seem to be any reason to hold back now. "Details about his family, this valley— whatever I could get out of him."

"And how much *did* you get out of him?" Beaved pressed.

Teach squirmed. "Not a whole lot. Not sure if it'll be worth twenty slips of gold."

"Especially since we're already here, right?" Beaved said in exasperation.

Buddy and Pal were whispering to each other, and Beaved cleared his throat at them. "All right, you two: and how much did Thorne promise you for befriending Shin?"

They frowned at each other before admitting, "Only ten slips of gold—"

"Which is still a lot of gold for two boys and only two weeks' worth of work!" Beaved insisted.

"Yes, but Shin stank!" Buddy reminded them.

"I know," Beaved said steadily. "I was there when they brought him up from the pit for your dinners. And I haven't been promised any extra slips of gold."

"Me neither," Reg said, disappointed. "Offered to be promoted two steps above to sergeant, but—"

Beaved pivoted to him. "Really? I'm only getting my choice of posting—" He stopped when the rest of the team snickered at him.

"So *you* did all of this," Teach waved vaguely, "for a bribe from Thorne as well. Then don't look at us with so much self-righteousness."

Ignoring that, Beaved turned to Hammer and Iron. "How much did Thorne promise you and what was your task?"

"Fifteen slips of gold, each," said Iron.

"For keeping Shin under control," admitted Hammer. "We're likely not going to see any of that gold."

"Don't worry," Beaved said bitterly. "None of us would have seen any gold. Thorne didn't bring any with him, and if Shin's correct, there isn't any here, either."

Noticing a soldier trotting nearby, weighed down with stolen coats and cloaks, Beaved whistled him over.

"Good pickings, huh?"

The solder guffawed. "Anything you could want!"

"How about gold?" Beaved asked.

At that, the soldier scowled. "These Salemites hide it real good. No one's found anything gold or silver. Not even jewelry!"

Beaved folded his arms, cast an *I told you so look* to his team, and said, "False walls in cellars? False bottoms in drawers? In mattresses? Barns?"

"Trust me," the soldier said, readjusting his pile of cloaks that were sliding in all directions, "we're tearing up everything. Even slashing paintings, looking for hidden compartments behind. Nothing. They likely buried it all in their fields. Got a few men digging in outhouses, looking."

Beaved shuddered. "Maybe tell your fellows that they get themselves out of the outhouses, because we've heard that Salemites don't use gold or silver at all. They simply don't have it."

"Yeah, right!" the coat man scoffed, and headed on his way, trying to jog north without tripping.

The mass of soldiers began to move again, and Beaved motioned to his team to follow.

"So why are we doing this?" Snarl grumbled. "Keeping together, letting these *lovely houses* go to waste?"

"You're still free to leave, Snarl. But *we* stick together because we're a team," Beaved declared, even though it was a lame reason. He came up with a better one. "Because each of us, in one way or another, is intrigued by what Shin claimed about Salem, and we want to know if all he said was true. And personally, I'm a little worried about all this Last Day talk."

He glanced behind to see the rest of his team huddled closely as they walked, wearing similarly worried expressions. Except for Snarl, of course.

"We need to be on the correct side of all of this," Beaved said.

"I don't think that being in the army is the correct side," Reg suggested.

"Nor do I," Beaved agreed in a low voice. "But until we can *find* the correct side, we play the observers. We don't loot, we gather whatever evidence we can, and we won't fight whatever hapless Salemites are at the temple. In fact, if any try to escape, I suggest we do all we can to help them. If there *is* a Creator, I think He'll notice we're trying to do the right thing, even if we're not sure it is the right thing."

He hesitated.

"Does that make sense?"

"In other words," Teach said, "we do the opposite of General Thorne, who didn't bother to bring our reward gold, who hasn't figured out that there's no way Shin could be his son, and who hired an assassin to chase his fake son, who he also likely won't pay. Did *that* make sense?"

Everyone slowly nodded.

"So we do the opposite of what Thorne commands," Beaved restated firmly, and the rest of the team met his eyes with new determination. Snarl almost did.

Beaved flashed a smile. "Suddenly, I'm feeling a whole lot better about this day."

"There it is," Shem choked out.

"Yep," Mahrree squeaked back.

Shem stopped Clark 14 at the edge of the woods, in front of the ornately carved temple several hundred paces away. Crafted out of white stone, it stood two levels tall and eighty paces deep. The carved columns at the front were patterned after the columns found at the ancient site. They stood five abreast the large front portico of the temple, supporting the roof above them. A wide set of stone stairs, about twenty, led from the ground up to the open portico. There were no railings in order to keep the view to the temple clear. Since it was the only place in Salem where children were not allowed—otherwise it would be impossible to keep the temple as quiet and restful as the adults needed it—there was no concern about safety. On the ground around the temple were the cast-off blocks not used in its construction, the jagged rock reminding Salemites of the boulders that separated them from the rest of the world. The thick-glassed windows were draped in heavy red cloth to allow in a little light, but to keep out most of the noise. The temple was a place of serenity, of prayer, of reminders of what the Creator wanted His people to do.

And soon it was going to be desecrated by the very world it served to be a sanctuary from.

"May it forgive us," Mahrree whispered.

"It's served its purpose well for over one hundred fifty years. It's time of use is over," Shem whispered back. "We've come here for guidance, we've made vows here with our spouses that we want to be with them in the life we have after, whatever 'life' that may be. It's over." He looked to the side, at the vast fields that always lay before it. The grass was just emerging from the melting snow, revealing a slushy mess. "I suppose there's room for around seventy thousand soldiers . . ."

Mahrree scanned the area too. "All the times I came here I never imagined these wildflower fields covered in blue uniforms. I always thought it was a lovely idea to keep so much of the valley pristine and untouched, just as Pax discovered it. But never did I imagine it was to accommodate the Army of Idumea."

"That was never its purpose. It *was* supposed to be a reminder of how the Creator designed this valley. The world is just out to destroy it."

"I supposed we should go now," Mahrree said in a shaky voice.

Shem cleared his throat. "Walk on, Clark. Take your time."

Guide Lannard looked nervously at the thick string of trees before him. "Uhh . . ."

"We take the bridge, Guide?" a major next to him suggested.

"Yes, of course! The bridge across with *no trees*."

Several soldiers looked at the forest before them. "There might not be any volcanoes or mud pots," one of them suggested.

A colonel shook his head. "Too risky. We know nothing of the terrain."

"What's the hold up now?" Thorne called impatiently to them, seeing the army had stopped again.

"Should we funnel the soldiers over this wide bridge, sir?" called the colonel, "Or risk going through the forest and fording the river, which we don't know is safe or not." It was obvious which option he preferred.

Thorne sighed irritably. "Across the bridge! Have them form lines in the wide field beyond. I don't want anyone attacking without our full forces here. We strike as one body and spare no Salemites. Spread the word. Guide Lannard, lead the way!"

Guide Lannard nodded, glanced to the forest on either side, and kicked the horse into a trot across the wide wooden bridge that spanned the narrow river. He was over to the other side in just moments, his shoulders sagging in relief. He continued on, with officers and soldiers jogging behind him, to form long lines in the vast fields before them.

Clark 14 walked slowly to the temple carrying his reluctant load, and at the steps he stopped without Shem's prodding. Shem slid off, then took Mahrree by the waist and helped her down. She started for the stairs, but Shem grabbed her and pulled her into a hug.

Mahrree wrapped her arms around him. "You're not making this any easier, Shem."

"No, I'm not."

Gerblatz's jacket caught her tears until she finally pushed him away. Movement in the distance caught her attention.

Shem spun to see what made her gasp. "They're here."

"Far away still," she said. The soldiers were lining up about a quarter of a mile away, the ants trying to organize.

He turned back to her. "I'll position myself in the forest and—"

"No, you won't! You'll leave here and go straight west. In that uniform you can ride right through them and they'll never question you."

Shem grabbed her arms. "I'm not leaving you!"

"Yes, you are!"

"No!"

"Perrin will take care of me! GO! Let me go to my husband!"

Shem trembled at those words.

Mahrree was startled to hear herself say them, but suddenly there was nothing she wanted more.

"You're still my dearest friend, Shem," she said tenderly, raising her hands to hold his face, still so boyish despite his years. "You always will be my dearest friend and I love you." She kissed him on the lips, a goodbye.

Shem caught her again in a massive bear hug. "Oh, Mahrree. I love you too. Tell Perrin . . ." The words caught in his throat until they forced their way out. "Tell Perrin I'm sorry."

"I won't," she said into his chest since he refused to release her, "because neither of us will be sorry for what you've done." She slid her hands to his chest and gently but firmly shoved him away. "Go. I'll sit behind the pillars and watch. You need to get out of here and up to the *real* site."

He showed no signs of budging. "Mahrree, I—"

"NOW!" she insisted, and he jumped a little in surprise. "Shem Zenos, *move it!*"

Before he could seize her again, Mahrree spun and started quickly up the stairs to the portico. She couldn't bear to see the anguish in Shem's face, nor allow him to discover the immense dread in hers. At the top of the stairs she turned around, intending to lecture him one last time as he stood there, rooted, but instead noticed the soldiers pouring in like water through a broken dam.

There was no more time. For anything.

Instinctively she slipped behind a column, then realized Salem's guide was still standing forlornly, staring up at her.

"Shem, go already!" she hissed at him.

Tears streaming down his face, he glanced behind him to see the army growing rapidly. He turned back and knew, too, that time had run out.

"Most dangerous woman in the world?" he said. "Try to duck, all right?"

"Only if you *go!*" She was now feeling desperate—desperate to get him out of there and to safety. This was no place for the Guide of Salem.

Reluctantly, Shem mounted Clark 14 and, without another word or look, kicked the horse into a run to the edge of the forest.

Mahrree sighed in relief. "I'm going to miss you, Shem."

Versa stood at the edge of the forest behind a tree watching the officer ride past in a hurry.

"Guide Zenos?" she whispered, astonished. She turned to see who he had delivered to the temple. Initially she assumed that the two riders were an officer and a prisoner that the general had sent to check the distance to the temple, but now she was baffled. She couldn't see what was happening with the two people once they dismounted because the black horse was in the way, but now she focused on the person at the temple.

It looked like an older woman who ducked again behind a pillar.

"What are they *doing?*" she asked the trees. She stepped back a few feet into the protection of the dense woods and crept along to get a closer view. After a few minutes she slipped again to the edge of the forest and peered at the figure from a different angle. She recognized the small woman behind the pillars.

"Mrs. Shin?" she whispered in surprise. "This makes no sense! He's just . . . he's just *left* her there? No protection, no weapons, nothing? He just *left her there!*"

Versa was tempted to rush across the slushy field less than one hundred paces to the temple and go to Mrs. Shin's aid, but she felt something holding her back. It took her a moment to identify the emotion: fear.

She had rarely felt fear but now it filled her completely, trying to keep her stuck to the ground like the prickly shrubs around her. She panted, furious with her cowardice, but even more terrified to actually do something.

Instead she sat down on a felled log and wept.

"That's it, isn't it?" Nelt whispered to Young Pere.

He nodded. "The back of the temple. Look—the army's arriving." In the distance they could see the lines forming, surprisingly fast.

"Guess they want to get this over with and back to raiding kitchens," Nelt mused.

"Wait until they find the storehouses," Young Pere said. "Thorne will never get them out of there."

Nelt smiled slightly and surveyed the canyon below them. "I don't see anyone. No one!"

Young Pere nodded. "Pretty good, huh? Just like the fort at the glacial valley was nearly impossible to see."

But Nelt shook his head. "This isn't . . . this isn't the same. We're talking about *thousands* of people, Shin. The ground doesn't even look disturbed."

He was right, and Young Pere's thoughts were thrown into a panic before an idea came to him, likely from the Head of Salem's Security. "Salem is a place of secrets and strategy. *Of course* you won't see their footprints going *behind* the temple. That's because there's a secret entrance."

Nelt, who didn't have a clear view of the front of the temple, smiled in appreciation. "Really?"

Young Pere waggled his eyebrows. "Really."

"Where is it?" he said, gazing at the canyon walls.

"Tell me—what do you see?"

Nelt continued to look around, shrugging, until his eyes finally rested on the temple. "No . . . really?"

"I told you the temple is a place of refuge, right? All it is, is an elaborate and secret entrance to the canyon. There are a number of caves throughout the mountain, huge caverns connected by narrow passages. Many open up outside of the canyon. Some even open up *in the ground.*" He held his hands out to the temple.

Nelt stepped back in astonishment. "Brilliant! Build an innocent-looking structure over the main entrance to the caves. Do the caves have other exits?"

"Wouldn't be any good if they didn't," Young Pere invented easily. "They empty out all over the canyon in crevices you can't discern from the mouth of it. Every year they were finding more passages and more exits. They were up to something like thirty-two before I left. Miles up the canyon," he waved vaguely. "We can hide tens of thousands of people *in* the mountain, and no one will ever see them. Do *you* see anything?"

"You're right, Young Pere," Nelt said, his voice tinged with genuine awe. "That's ingenious! Point out one of the exit crevices to me."

"We can't see them from this angle," Young Pere told him, the answers coming effortlessly. "We need to get closer to the valley floor. Thorne will want to search the temple himself, I'm sure. That's when I plan to greet him."

Nelt leaned against a large rock. "Shin, I don't like the sound of this. Exactly what are you trying to do?"

Young Pere observed the lines of soldiers growing rapidly. "Look, we need to move quickly. We're running out of time. I'm going to go into the temple and wait just inside the front doors. There's bound to be something I can hide behind—a sofa, shelves, something—"

"You've never been in there?"

"You have to be an adult to know the secrets," Young Pere said. "I'd left Salem just as I reached that age, so I never went in there. But I've heard descriptions. It looks like a vast and nicely decorated gathering room. I'll wait in there until Thorne comes in. Then I kill him. Simple as that."

"Then his guards kill you," Nelt said coldly.

"But what if they're glad that I killed Thorne?"

Nelt looked dubious.

"All right then . . . I run."

"To where?" Nelt gestured wildly. "This place will be teeming with soldiers, and a few just might be upset that you killed their general!"

Young Pere narrowed his eyes. "I know where to run, all right? You just keep to the trees. Obviously the army is still nervous about forests, otherwise they wouldn't all be crammed on that one bridge. They'd take the several other foot bridges that cross the river."

Nelt folded his arms. "Shin, I haven't worked this hard just to see you get killed by Thorne."

"I can do this," Young Pere insisted. "I can end it. And I'm not going back to my family until I've done some good. *This* will be good."

"*This* will be suicide, Shin!"

"Does that mean you're not coming?"

Nelt sighed. "I'm right behind you. Lead the way."

The sky was the wrong color for such an evening. It should have been the color of a bruise.

That stray thought drifted through Mahrree's preoccupied mind, and she grabbed hold of it, grateful for the diversion.

"It's blue with a few simple clouds," she frowned at the glimpses of the sky she had from her hiding spot. "It's all too cheerful. The color should be a deep and angry blue-gray, with swirling clouds suggesting a violent storm approaching, and maybe some jagged lighting in the distance. Menacing. Foreboding. Not these fluffy white clouds like clueless lambs floating in the sky. Who ordered such pleasant weather?" she demanded, chuckling tensely at herself.

Her hands trembled. So did her arms, and her knees, and even her teeth chattered for a moment in sheer terror.

"I'm the brave wife of the major," she whispered to herself, remembering her refrain from years ago when she was running in the dark during a Guarder attack. "I'm the brave wife of the major. Hmm. After all these years, I *still* don't believe it." She watched yet another line of soldiers form. "Quite a bit of attention and effort for just one little old lady, Lemuel. What a nice gesture."

The sun was lowering in the sky. This was when she usually started making dinner with Lilla.

"Good thing I'm not in the least bit hungry. All of this might have ruined my appetite. I wonder where Shem is . . ." But another thought flitted by and she grasped that one instead. "I wonder where Young Pere is. Where Perrin is . . ."

She squeezed her eyes shut. Perrin and she had taken vows together in that temple with Guide Gleace officiating, promising the Creator to be as faithful as they could, desiring to be together forever. They'd done the same for their parents and ancestors to give them that opportunity as well. Soon she might see if those promises were sure.

"Please be here, Perrin. Please. Please be waiting for me . . ."

Thorne watched his soldiers eagerly jogging to the broad fields, many still holding evidence of having raided kitchens along the way.

They looked hungrily to the north where the houses and farms began again, beckoning them to come find what else might be waiting. Thorne had promised that when that battle was over, they could continue eating and looting to their hearts' delight. But first they had a few Salemites to kill.

And now that the last of the seventy thousand or so soldiers were beyond the bridge, Thorne estimated that the great and swift battle would commence in just minutes.

"As if I'm really going to ride away and just *leave* you there," Shem whispered to himself. "Calla, Peto, and Jaytsy would all have my head for it! And Perrin would haunt my dreams all night."

He and Clark 14 had slipped into the forest between the lines of soldiers. A few men watched him but thought nothing of the officer on horseback. Almost a hundred horses had been found by now. They *were* probably startled he headed right into the trees, but they could no longer see him. He dismounted, tethered 14, and crept along the trees to have a clear view of the front of the temple.

"Thorne captures you, I'll come rescue you, Mahrree. I still have a few Guarder tricks up my sleeve, and I'm wearing a colonel's jacket and I have a sturdy Clark. Rescues in those old stories always happened with big black horses, right? I've got a few plans, don't worry, Mahrree."

"How much closer do you want to get?" Nelt whispered to Young Pere as they crept their way down the mountainside, moving from tree to tree to avoid the more barren and revealing areas of scrubby brush.

"I've got to get all the way down, Nelt. I think Thorne's getting ready. The soldiers are lining up—look! They're starting their approach. Maybe five minutes before they reach the temple?"

His mind searched for an appropriate word to utter in frustration, realizing that his time was running out, but all of those words belonged in the world.

"Forget this hiding in the shrubs, I don't care if they see us. I've got to get down there!" Young Pere rushed along the slope to be parallel with the front of the temple, needing only to charge down the hill through the forest, race across the field, and rush up the stone steps. He looked behind him to see Nelt struggling to catch up.

"Wait for me!" Nelt said, trying to get through a briar patch in a stand of trees. "Shin, I'm stuck! Help me!"

Young Pere rolled his eyes and jogged up a few paces. Nelt was caught by a thorny vine that held his leg.

"Just let it rip your clothes, Nelt! No one's going to be inspecting our uniforms right now." He bent over to grasp the vine, only to find something wrapping around his thigh—a thick cord. In an instant it was strapped to a tree and the cord was clasped by the same lock that used to hold Young Pere's wrist shackles.

Young Pere looked up in alarm.

Nelt gave him a sad smile. "Maybe your uniform won't be inspected, but mine will be as soon as I report back to Thorne."

Young Pere was so furious he couldn't even speak.

Nelt shrugged. "I weighed the prospects of survival again. Being associated with a general's assassin?" He pointed at Young Pere. "That's the surest way to die, Young Pere. I know."

He lifted his sword from Young Pere's side. He didn't even remember he was wearing it.

"I'm sorry. Nothing personal. I actually like you, so I'll be by to get you later, once the caves are flushed. I don't believe either you or Thorne needs to die today." Nelt took off in a run down the mountain to the temple.

Young Pere opened his mouth to shout at him but found he couldn't speak.

DON'T GIVE AWAY YOUR POSITION. SIT TIGHT!

"But, Puggah!" he whispered in exasperation, "I can't do anything now!" He yanked against the tree that didn't budge.

EXACTLY. NOW SIT TIGHT!

"I can't *sit* with my leg strapped to a tree! Did you do this? Is this your fault?!"

YES, YOUNG PERE—I CONVINCED A WOULD-BE ASSASSIN TO BETRAY YOU. COME ON, GIVE ME MORE CREDIT THAN THAT. WE USED HIM, HE USED US—WAY OF THE WORLD. YOU SHOULD KNOW THAT BY NOW.

"We used him?"

TO ESCAPE! I WANTED YOU TO TRUST HIM AS FAR AS HE WOULD HELP YOU. AND HE HELPED YOU GET QUITE FAR. YOU NEVER WOULD'VE MADE

IT HERE WITHOUT HIS HELP. AND NOW HE'S GOING TO REPORT TO THORNE THERE ARE CAVES ALL OVER THIS CANYON. THORNE WILL BE MORE DETERMINED THAN EVER. LOOK. THE LITTLE STINKER NAMED AFTER ME IS REACHING THORNE RIGHT NOW. AND . . . THERE GOES THE INFORMATION. I THINK I CAN SEE THORNE SALIVATING FROM HERE.

Young Pere slumped against the tree. "You *did* plan this, didn't you?! He could be searching this canyon for days." He had to concede that was an excellent strategy.

SECURITY OF SALEM IS MY SPECIALTY, YOUNG PERE, AND MY CALLING. I WAS NEVER RELEASED FROM THAT. THERE ARE STILL MANY GOOD PEOPLE TRYING TO GET OUT. THEY NEED AT LEAST ANOTHER DAY TO DO IT. UNFORTUNATELY, SEARCHING FOR CAVES IS NOT WHAT'S GOING TO HAPPEN HERE. YOU TOLD NELT THAT STORY TO GET HIM AWAY. WE DON'T NEED HIM ANYMORE. THERE ARE A FEW MORE THINGS THAT NEED TO HAPPEN FIRST.

Young Pere smacked the tree in frustration. "Then let me help!"

OH, YOU WILL, YOU WILL. BUT FIRST, ONE HUNDRED SIXTY-FIVE YEARS AGO GUIDE PAX SAW EXACTLY WHAT'S TO TAKE PLACE HERE. GUIDE GLEACE SAW IT, TOO. THERE'S NOTHING YOU CAN DO—OR SHOULD DO— TO STOP IT. IT WAS PROPHESIED AND IT WILL HAPPEN.

Young Pere leaned forward earnestly as Thorne, Guide Lannard, and the other officers stopped their horses a few paces away from the temple steps. They turned their backs to the temple to watch the rest of the army fill in behind them and spread out, saturating the formerly Quiet Fields with raucous blue.

Young Pere held his breath at the sight. "So many . . . *so many!* What's going to happen?"

SOMETHING FANTASTIC, YOUNG PERE. WATCH. AND WHATEVER YOU DO, DON'T MAKE A SOUND!

Her chest seized in terror, making it nearly impossible for Mahrree to breathe. She was hiding in the alcove of the large oak doors, the tall, white columns in front of her about ten paces. The sun, hanging low above the mountains, cast deep shadows all around her, and she cowered in the darkest one. On the other side of the columns were the stairs and then . . . the officers. It was strange to see so many men in blue uniforms after so many years away from the army. And the blue continued beyond them, filling the fields and coming in as a massive pack ever closer to the temple.

Seventy thousand against one. Not good odds.

Her hands shook, her mouth was dry, her palms were wet, her knees crackled as they trembled, and she was sure that at any moment she would collapse. Between the columns she could make out the profile of Lemuel on his horse, his right arm limp by his side and his blond hair going gray. He had arrived first with some mounted men and officers on foot. As soon as he reached the lane which ran before the temple, he turned to watch the progress of the soldiers. Mahrree had assumed he'd dismount and march up the stairs, but he seemed to be waiting for the right moment to make his grand approach. His face was hardened and no longer as handsome as she remembered when he was a young man.

Beside him sat another mounted man whose face she couldn't make out before he, too, turned his back to the temple. He was wearing an absurd light blue silk outfit that looked more appropriate as bed clothing for a king, and was covered with an outrageous purple cloak edged in gold that would have been better as curtains in a mansion. Maybe that's where he got them. Mahrree almost smiled at the thought.

She searched the other profiles and backs of heads standing near Thorne and the curtain man, trying to see if she could recognize Poe among them. There was a gray-haired man near the curtain man that at first Mahrree dismissed, then considered that Poe *would* have gray hair by now.

She still thought of him as the nine-year-old boy sitting on her front porch wearing silk shirts and asking questions about Terryp. She wondered if he remembered those days, as she frequently did. If he would just turn around, glance at the temple or mountain behind, she might be able to glimpse the Poe Hili she once knew. But he didn't move except to put a steadying hand on the curtain man's leg, as if worried he'd jump off the horse and make a run for it.

Mahrree bit her lip and wrung her hands in worry. She certainly couldn't make a run for it, trapped now by the line of officers before her, the stone edifice behind her.

Let's just get this over with, she thought. *Whatever 'this' may be.* It was by far the largest crowd she ever had to perform for, and she didn't have the slightest idea what would happen or what she would say. She was never this unprepared for anything. She kept praying for inspiration and kept getting the feeling that the right words would come at the right moment. Now she just had to wait for that moment.

Trying to calm herself, she took deep breaths, thinking that Boskos would tell her slower, slower, slower—

The sound of thousands of men just a stone's throw away echoed in the covered stone portico, reverberating deafeningly in her tiny alcove, a horrible combination of metal, marching, and voices, punctuated by shouts and calls of officers.

Suddenly a horn blasted three times in front of the steps, and Mahrree nearly jumped out of her skin as it bounced around the portico. Then she heard Lemuel's voice. She would have recognized him anywhere.

"Our Great Guide has some words for you all!" Thorne bellowed.

"Guide?" Mahrree mouthed. She peered over to see the silk curtain man getting off his horse and she rolled her eyes. The world's guide wears *silk?* For half a moment she wished Shem was there to see this—

Suddenly her chest burned. The man began to climb up the stairs and Mahrree knew *this* was her moment. She was to confront the guide, because in her mind she clearly saw herself doing it. He was up half the stairs, now at the top. He turned and held up his hands dramatically, waiting for silence.

Mahrree stepped out of her shadowy alcove, not knowing what was going to happen but feeling as if she were following some scene in a play that she'd always known but didn't remember until the moment she performed it.

She headed straight for the blue silk, and her mouth dropped open in astonishment as she recognized the guide. She stopped by his side.

He glanced down at her, startled to realize he wasn't alone, and then he went deathly pale.

Mahrree put her hands on her hips. "*Lannard Kroop*! What *in the world* have they done to you?"

Lannard froze.

Mahrree knew he recognized her. There was no possible way he would be wearing such an expression of horror and dismay if he didn't.

"Oh, Creet," he whispered. "Oh Creet, oh Creet . . ." He started to back up toward the southern end of the open portico, his hands still upraised.

Mahrree felt confidence and power that filled her head to toe as she walked toward him at the same rate. "Lemuel did this to you, didn't he? Oh Lannard, you were always such a follower."

"Lannard!" Thorne shouted, a tinge of worry in his tone to see his guide behaving so oddly when he was supposed to be delivering some motivational speech that Mahrree would bet Lemuel had written for him. "What's going on?" He glared at the little old woman scaring Lannard to the edge of the portico.

Lannard's eyes shot over to Thorne, as if pleading for deliverance from a stalking mountain lion, and he continued to take slow, jerky steps backward.

"No, no, Lannard. Look at me," Mahrree said in her best teacher tone. "Stop this, this *ridiculous* thing you're doing! He's using you, Lannard. Just like he did when you were a boy. He's *always* used you—"

Another voice rang out. "Lannard! Stop! Behind you!"

But Lannard only stared at Mrs. Shin, the woman who had been his teacher for two years, who criticized his ideas one minute then winked her apologies the next. The teacher he complained about to Captain Thorne, who wrote down what she taught and sent it to Chairman Mal and the Administrators, who then came to arrest her for sedition against Idumea.

Mahrree could see their shared history flash in his eyes, and the man was reduced to cowering like a terrified child.

He took a few more steps backward.

She took a few more steps toward him. "Lannard, stop. Come now—"

He was completely white with terror. "*You're dead,*" he finally said as if trying to reassure himself. "You're dead, you're dead, you're dead." He continued to back up. "I didn't know he was sending letters . . . That he wrote down what I complained about . . . *You're already dead.*" His hands were still outstretched and beginning to tremble.

"No, I'm not. Stop, Lannard. Stop walking—*Lannard!*" Mahrree cried out and reached for him, but she was too late.

He'd gone too far, over the side of the portico, his arms still up in shock not realizing that he was falling, not noticing anything but his teacher from so many years ago. Miserably, her face was the last thing he saw as he fell backward onto the stones below and hit with a sickening thud.

Mahrree slapped her hand over her mouth and cautiously peered over the edge.

Several soldiers rushed to his aid. By his unnatural position on the jagged rock, Mahrree already knew what they would shout.

"He's dead! His neck's broke!"

Mahrree gulped and twisted to the bulk of the army.

They were gasping in shock and crying out in dismay. Obviously the poor, gullible man meant something to them. Many were already backing away, as if dreading the same evil was about to happen to them. At the far edges of the crowd, Mahrree could make out soldiers running—

It was *happening!*

Thorne dismounted and rushed over to see Lannard for himself, as did the gray-haired man who had previously been holding on to him. He looked up at Mahrree.

Poe!

She nearly cried out his name but was too overwhelmed to do anything but stare.

Poe stared back at her, a flurry of emotions racing across his face and his chest began to heave. But he didn't get a chance to say anything either because Thorne's head snapped up, his eyes on fire.

"Who the slag are you?!" he demanded.

This was *it*. She knew it, and she also knew the words she needed to say. Mahrree turned to face her biggest audience ever. In as loud as a voice as she could muster, she shouted, "My name is Mahrree Peto Shin! And because you have invaded Salem, *all* of you will die, just like Lannard Kroop!"

The effect was extraordinary. She had barely proclaimed her identity when the carefully formed lines began to dissolve. The sea of blue churned and tossed as men ran in a panic. She had to finish the speech that was rapidly forming in her mind before her audience was thoroughly undone. Or, rather, so she could further undo them.

"Lemuel Thorne has lied to you all these years! I never died in the forest nor did my family or the colonel! We escaped here to Salem. Perrin Shin built those towers flying the black banners. And he devised a way to keep our people safe until the Last Day. Know this— it is coming, the Last Day! Jon Offra has been warning you, and he's right! Stop this now! You cannot win!"

Thorne was fighting through the crowd of soldiers rushing to see the guide's body, who were rushing to get past the temple, who were rushing around just to rush around in a frenzy. He tried to get to the stairs but kept getting pushed back and shoved to the side. He yelled,

"She lies! She lies!" as he struggled to the stairs.

But the damage was done.

Mahrree gazed out over the vast field and did her best estimating. Hundreds. Thousands. Now tens of thousands. Yes, one third—*it had to be!*—was running away in terror of the death of their guide and the name of the one who caused it, even though she hadn't even touched poor Lannard.

That probably made it even worse.

The remaining soldiers looked hysterically around, trying to figure out what to do next in the swirling chaos.

Mahrree's chest burned in gratitude, relief, and even a touch of pride. It was done! She, the "aged," terrifying one-third of the army!

Suddenly her view was filled with Lemuel Thorne running up the stairs. He'd broken through his soldiers and now strode straight for her.

Mahrree stepped back in alarm.

Today, my darling daughter, the world has come to get you—

"Slagging Creet!" Lemuel hissed in a low voice, but Mahrree could hear him plainly over the mayhem caused by the retreating soldiers. "It *is* you!"

She swallowed hard and retreated backward until she bumped into the cold stone of the temple wall. Soldiers—large, beefy men, likely Thorne's faithful guard—followed him up the stairs and filled the portico, cutting off any possibility of escape.

She was trapped.

"Oh, I have been *waiting* for this for a *very long time*," Lemuel said, a thin, cruel smile on his lips. "Perrin was too blinded by love to do what he should have done all those years ago." He stalked toward her as Mahrree pressed her back against the stone wall. She couldn't think of anything to do, paralyzed by fear.

Lemuel drew his sword.

Mahrree couldn't even gasp.

"But today I will right a great many wrongs. Mahrree Peto Shin, this is *your* Last Day!"

The only man faster with a blade was Perrin, but only just. Lemuel raised his left arm and thrust in the sword.

Mahrree couldn't move or scream. Her chest burned again, but this time with a searing pain that took away all her strength.

The last thing she saw was Lemuel's sneer.

Then everything grew dark.

And the pain stopped.

Shem fell to his knees, his mouth hanging open, his hands gripping his head in agony.

"NO!" he cried, pulling out clumps of hair. None of the soldiers running past him in a panic noticed. They didn't even realize they were running into the trees. They were just running to get away from the woman who was supposed to be dead but who killed the guide without even touching him.

Shem didn't notice them, either. He just stared, dumbfounded, as her body fell. It happened so fast he didn't know what to do to prevent it. He hadn't even mounted on Clark 14 but stood rooted to the ground as if being held back, his mind wiped clean of any wild ideas of rescue he had entertained only moments before. He'd remained there, useless and clueless. But now there was no doubt in his mind.

Mahrree was gone. And by Lemuel's hand. Because Shem delivered her there.

The *Deliverer*.

He collapsed to the ground. "Perrin!" he gasped in sobs. "I'm so sorry! I'm so sorry! I'm so sorry!"

Versa had initially been watching with fascination. First that ridiculous 'guide' fell, then everyone started running. It was the prophecy! One-third of the soldiers were running! Many others were completely stunned. *She did it!* Mahrree Peto Shin—the *aged*—did it! Defeated one-third of the Army of Idumea!

Versa leaped to her feet and raised her hands to cheer.

Until she saw the general striding up the stairs.

"Don't you dare. Don't you dare do it. General . . ." She rushed to the edge of the trees and held on to them as she watched him draw his sword. "Oh, no, no, no, no, no . . ."

The last one came out as a whimper.

"*No!*"

Up on the hillside, Young Pere fought vainly to free himself from the tree. The moment he saw the small body come out of hiding on the portico and walk resolutely up to Guide Lannard, he knew exactly who it was and what was going to happen. He lunged and clawed and flailed and even dug frantically at the roots, but the tree held securely. There was nothing he could do to save her. Nothing but thrash against his confines and watch as Thorne walked up those stairs and pulled out his sword. Young Pere was gasping in desperation as he saw Thorne's arm rise. There was nothing, nothing, *absolutely nothing* he could do to stop it. All he could do was scream and hope she heard him.

"*MUGGAH!*"

It wasn't so bad.

Pain, then . . . it was *over*.

Just like that.

Mahrree suspected that even if the pain *had* lasted much longer, or been more excruciating, right now it wouldn't have mattered, not one bit. Just like childbirth. Nothing can compare to the agony of it, nor to the elation that follows it. All had gone dark, but now it was growing light, so bright and so quickly it took her breath away—

Immediately she knew that wasn't correct. She had no breath to take away but that was the *sensation*. Then she considered, maybe it never was her breath or her heart fluttering that she felt, but the responses of her soul that affected her body.

Everything continued to grow brighter and warmer, until suddenly she was engulfed with—

Joy! Pure joy!

"Oh, *well done*, my fantastic daughter!"

There he stood in brilliant white, smiling broadly with his arms outstretched. She would have recognized him anywhere.

"FATHER!" she cried and rushed into his arms. There were no tears to shed because she had no tears, yet the emotion of sobbing for joy remained. The feel of his soul against hers wasn't quite the same as physical bodies, but still it was a wonderful sensation. She was a teenager again wrapped up in her father's protection, and she closed her eyes in bliss.

Reality filled her.

Real reality, not the vague feelings of, "This is what I perceive as real," that plagued those limited by their minds and bodies. But a reality of depth, of breadth, of "This is how things truly are."

She was *home.*

She'd experienced that sense before, when they came to Salem and she realized Edge wasn't home but just a place where she lived for forty-seven years. But now the thoughts of her physical life felt as slim and shallow as her existence in Edge had seemed.

Because now she truly was home.

This was an old place—no, an *ancient* place. Yet vibrant and new and growing and timeless.

And so was she. Her mind erupted, rapidly filling to overflowing with so much knowledge and understanding of everything she used to know, as if her brain used to be covered by a veil which had just slipped off.

She had been permitted to forget her ancient existence for seventy-four years. That was part of her test: what would her heart choose when her mind could no longer remember what she knew?

But while she didn't feel as gray and frail as the body she had left, her spirit was eons old—timeless beyond time. How did she tolerate existing in such a rapidly aging and decaying body for so long?

When she left it, all she took were experiences and memories. And yet, that was everything. Already she missed it, her body's form and abilities. But it would resuscitate again, so that it, too, would become as ageless and timeless as her.

She squeezed her father, feeling as if the last sixty years of separation were only sixty minutes, and was nearly overcome by the sense of belonging, of returning. She didn't know how much she had wanted to be here until she finally came back.

But it wasn't *back*, so to speak. It was *forward*. Same place, but a new and improved Mahrree coming home, as if she'd been gone on a sleep-away school break for a week and had just returned. That's how brief her seventy-four years in the world had seemed: merely a week.

Her perspective was shifting, straightening itself to this real reality. She began to recognize that so many things in her life that had seemed important weren't. And then again, so many things that had felt important *were,* far more than she had anticipated. And best of all, for *most* of her life, she had gotten the distinction correct.

She had passed the test.

"You did it, Mahrree! You did it at the temple! Fantastic! I'm so proud of you!" Cephas Peto shouted.

"You saw me?" she whispered into his ear, still not wanting to let go of her father.

He felt the same way. "Of course I did! We *all* did. You were never alone at the temple, Mahrree. We've been waiting for this moment for years. There were more with you cheering you on than there were soldiers."

She opened her eyes and saw someone bouncing in excitement behind her father. She was young, also wore all white and had brown hair with curls. Mahrree laughed. There was only one person she would release her father for.

"MOTHER!"

Her father gently pushed her toward her mother.

Hycymum caught her in a big embrace. "I've missed you, Mahrree!" she cried.

"I kept making your recipes!" Mahrree yelled cheerfully.

"I know!" Hycymum yelled back, still hugging her daughter. "You actually *learned* something from me!"

Mahrree heard her father laugh and turned back to look at him properly. She'd forgotten how handsome he was. Then again, she really didn't remember such a young version of him. He might have been about twenty years old. In him she saw so much of Peto and her grandsons.

He came over and put his arms around his wife and daughter. "Been waiting so long to do this." He sighed in satisfaction as he squeezed. "Worth the wait!"

"And how long are you going to do that, Cephas?" a deep but happy voice rumbled. "Because there's a line forming, you know."

Mahrree knew that voice. She twisted and saw another handsome young man in white grinning at her. Next to him stood a beautiful young woman with her hands clasped together in anticipation.

"RELF! JORIANA!"

Cephas released her and she rushed to them. They caught her at the same time.

"Mahrree, you're the greatest soldier ever," Relf said with a chuckle. "I never saw anyone else make more than twenty thousand soldiers run in terror."

"Only the most aggravating woman in the world could have done that," Joriana said, hugging her. "I knew you had to be that way for some reason!"

Mahrree laughed and kissed them both on the cheeks.

"As you said, Relf," interrupted another merry voice, "there's a line forming . . . to embrace the most dangerous woman in the world."

Mahrree looked past her in-laws to see another favorite couple beaming at her. It was too good, just too much. But of course, that's what Paradise was.

"TABBIT! HOGAL!"

She ran to yet another two sets of waiting arms and laughed in joy as first Hogal Densal kissed her cheek, then Tabbit Densal. They were both young and radiant and dressed in white, like everyone else there.

"You!" She pointed at Hogal and grinned. "You were the one who said I was the most dangerous woman. Did you know then? How this would go?"

"No, I didn't!" Hogal laughed. "And I'm glad I didn't, because I would have been tempted to tell you. I just knew you'd do something great and terrifying. And you did—today!"

Her attention was captured by something beyond them. More people grinning and waving in welcome. Hundreds. Thousands. Hundreds of thousands.

Millions.

And she knew them, *all of them*. Neighbors. Friends. Distant relatives. People from Salem. People from Edge. People she never shared a life with on the world but knew intimately from long, long before. Her mind opened further, with millions of more faces and ideas suddenly remembered. So much was back, and none of it was overwhelming. It should have been, she considered later—such a mass of comprehension. But it settled easily onto her mind as if it always belonged there, filling her soul with knowledge, power, and joy, pure joy.

Then she saw a face she didn't expect to see. She blinked, then blinked again.

"*Calla*?! Calla? CALLA!"

Calla, younger and sweeter than Mahrree remembered, walked over to her with her arms open.

Mahrree released the Densals and took Calla instead. "Why . . . why are *you* here? Oh *no*!"

Calla smiled sadly. "Oh, *yes*. I got to see my sergeant major in action, Mahrree. And he was wonderful! Amazing!"

"So . . . so what happened?!"

"Two bowmen. Both of them terrified as Shem came to destroy them. They released their arrows and they both hit me."

Mahrree realized that even in this elevated state, she could still be surprised. "That's . . . that's . . ."

"Impossible?" Calla suggested. "Yes, it was. Those arrows were guided. It was supposed to be my last day, too."

"Shem doesn't know! Oh, Calla! First me, then you?"

"Actually, the other way around," she said. "He's going to need a lot of help soon. When the time is right, will you help me reach him?"

"Of course!" Mahrree gripped her best friend's arm. "We should go now!"

"You don't have to, not yet," Cephas told her. "Nothing more is happening in the world while we are here. We have the ability to step out of their time. Most of us stay in their time to lend assistance and feel the moments with them as they experience them so we can help them. But for special occasions such as a welcoming home, we can suspend it. No time has passed in the world since you've come back to us. Calla, as well as her father and many other ancestors trying to help those at the ancient temple site have, according to our descendants' reckoning, not even left them. They will be able to return to them without missing a single heartbeat of theirs."

Mahrree hugged Calla. "What's this going to do to Shem?"

"It's his final trial, Mahrree," Calla said, her voice trembling. "And we'll need to help him."

"I know who could," Mahrree said, searching over the familiar faces.

She didn't see him.

That struck her almost like a slap across the physical face she no longer had. There was one person missing, the most important person to her. Why didn't she see him?

"Mahrree," Cephas said gently. "I know who you're looking for."

"Why isn't he here?" she whispered, thinking she should be worried about his absence, but instead felt such peace that her physical mind would have been perplexed. "I wanted him to be here."

Hogal smiled. "Don't you remember what you made him promise?"

"To never leave Young Pere?"

"And he's been very faithful to that promise. Until today, I was his constant companion," Hogal told her. "As he stayed with Young Pere, I stayed right next to him. But after my company for *so long,*" Hogal rolled his eyes so dramatically Mahrree couldn't help but giggle at the familiarity of it, "I think he's ready for a new companion." He waggled his eyebrows.

Mahrree turned to her father. "How do I find him?"

"Whatever you think of, you'll be next to in an instant," Cephas said.

"And I can come right back?"

"We're all together all the time. You'll understand soon, it's not hard. The only thing here that's hard is watching our descendants suffer," Cephas said somberly. "But that's why we're here, to bring them comfort and nudge them in the right directions."

"Like you always nudged me," Mahrree said.

Cephas smiled. "Exactly. Someone's going to need a lot of that in the next little while. Just think of me, and I'll be there if you need me or have any questions. Soon you'll understand everything." He gave her another kiss.

Suddenly Mahrree was somewhere else, but not where she expected to be. The brilliant whiteness of her surroundings was gone, but the warmth remained.

Below her was her body, motionless on the wide stone portico at the temple. She knew she needed this last look to grasp what had occurred, although her mind felt clearer and stronger than ever.

Her lifeless body didn't strike her as tragic. Quite the contrary. She felt light and happy as she looked at the worn-out shell that had served her and now was ready for a rest. She smiled at it.

"Oh, dear. Looks like that might have hurt." She giggled softly as she knelt down and peered at the deep sword wound that penetrated her body's heart. The blood wasn't flowing but there was a large pool staining the white stone. Everything in time was paused.

She looked up and behind her to see Thorne standing like a statue and sneering down at her body. Mahrree thought she should feel rage but instead felt mildly amused. Why shouldn't she? It was turning out to be a fantastic day—the best in her life!

So to speak.

"This is not going to look good on your final report, Lemuel," she said, smirking. "Cutting down a seventy-four-year-old unarmed woman? Tsk-tsk-tsk."

She looked back at her body and analyzed it. "And when did I get to be so *old*?" She tried to touch her wrinkled face but her hand couldn't quite do it. She wasn't allowed back into her body; at least, not this version of it. She evaluated her hair but there wasn't a light brown strand left anywhere, even though just weeks ago she was sure there still had to be some somewhere—

"Mahrree."

She stopped. The word filled her soul with more heat and light and power than anything ever had. She stood up, the sensation of weeping for joy nearly overcoming her again. She turned to the voice and up on the hillside she saw him.

Tall, dressed in white, with black hair, the perfect smile, and those amazing dark eyes. His arms were open, waiting.

Perrin!

She ran her fastest off the portico and raced for the hillside. Her feet didn't touch the ground nor did the presence of hundreds of frozen soldiers impede her progress. She just flew right past, and maybe even through, them.

His smile broadened and he opened his arms wider.

"PERRIN!" she cried as she rushed into them. If she had still been in her body, it would have burst.

"MAHRREE!" he bellowed to the cosmos as he spun her around. "YES! YES! YES!"

His voice echoed everywhere and Mahrree thought the neighboring stars must have turned to see where that shout came from. She didn't want to let go of him, ever.

"Nor do I want to let go of you," he whispered in her ear. "Yes, I know what you're thinking. Oh, Mahrree!"

She laughed and kissed his neck. He put her down and took her face tenderly. He kissed her and she kissed him back. And kissed him. It was different without their bodies, but it was still bliss, pure bliss. Only after a long time did he pull away, and his grin was huge.

"Not exactly the same, I know," he said, "And there are a few more limitations for now, but eventually things will be even better than we remember."

"It's pretty good now!" She laughed and kissed him again.

He wrapped his arms around her again. "Oh Mahrree, how I've missed you."

"And I've missed you," she whispered back. But there was something odd about that sentiment, because she felt now, here in Paradise, that the dreary and depressing nearly two years she spent without

Perrin were more like barely two minutes. Dismayed, she felt almost cheated for her previous loneliness, and had she only known how swiftly all that would be swept away—

No, she had known. A small part of her had always understood that whatever misery she was enduring would seem but a small moment in retrospect. The Writings had said so, but it was as if her physical brain couldn't fathom what her spiritual mind already knew. No wonder her feelings were often in so much conflict.

But now, with the limitations of her mortal mind lifted, suddenly everything was easier. The sixty years without her father? Merely sixty minutes. Her mother, only half an hour. She could remember the sadness but marvelously no longer *felt* it. She held the memories but none of the pain.

"No wonder they called this place Paradise, right?" Perrin said, again reading her mind.

In the distance she saw them: her parents, her in-laws, the Densals, Calla, everyone else, smiling as they watched them embrace.

Cephas nodded at his son-in-law. "Then I leave her again to your care, Perrin?" Although he seemed to be a hundred paces away, his words sounded as if uttered just feet from them. He was close, always close, forever close.

Perrin nodded back. "I can take it from here, Cephas. I'll get her all caught up."

"See, Mahrree?" Cephas said to his daughter. "We're never more than a thought away."

Mahrree grinned. "We still have lots to talk about, Father."

"Yes, we do. And we will have eons to talk. But right now we have much more pressing matters," he said, suddenly turning sober, and Mahrree remembered that he used to do that: shift from jovial to solemn in a half second. "The time that remains for our descendants is very, very short, and there's a great deal for us to accomplish. We're not sitting around swapping death stories, you know." He winked, his sense of humor lightening the serious moment, another of his mannerisms that she'd forgotten. "We'll discuss whose death was the most memorable later. But I think your argument may be the most compelling, my wonderful daughter, no matter what Relf believes."

Relf's loud scoff, and everyone's chuckling, made Mahrree think this topic had been one of previous discussions.

Still sober, but now with that familiar twinkle in his eyes, Cephas the master debater continued. "While Relf was also stabbed in the heart, he slept through the entire thing and didn't even know it happened until he woke up here with Joriana. How does that even compare?"

Mahrree laughed with everyone else while Cephas remained serious, but his smiling eyes gave him away.

Then Mahrree realized that Relf and Cephas had never met in the world, but clearly there was a history here, even a friendship as Relf gestured earnestly as if he was about to take on the debate, and Joriana dramatically covered his mouth with her hand.

"I was stabbed in the heart as well, you know, Relf, and also slept through it."

"For now, our work continues," Cephas said, as if knowing that Mahrree wanted to know about her father and her in-laws' relationship, but that those details would have to wait. "And so will *your* work. Should you need me or any advice—"

"I'll just think of you," Mahrree said, already knowing.

Cephas smiled and suddenly everyone was gone.

Perrin chuckled, apparently used to such disappearances. "They love to see the reunions. I knew they'd be here watching us. One of the many joys. Your father's duty to care for you has never ended. Cephas is the patriarch of the family in which you were born. He's always seen to your safety and guidance." He took her face again. "I'm supposed to be explaining everything to you but instead I just want to stare at you!"

She looked back into his eyes, his wonderfully dark eyes that still made her go weak in the knees that would never creak again. In a way, he was every age she remembered him as. She could see all of them in his eyes, but his face was much, much younger. Smooth and not a scar left.

"Just how old are you?" she asked with a giggle.

Perrin grinned. "Millennia old! So are you. But that's not how you *see* me. Remember when you said in Idumea that you wished you could have seen me as an eighteen-year-old?" He stepped back, still holding her hands. "Here I am."

Mahrree sighed and took him in. "Mmm! Had I seen you *then*?" She shook her head in appreciation. He was perfect. Better than perfect, if that were possible. "But I get to see you *now*."

"And I can stay this way always, if you wish."

She tipped her head analytically. "Maybe we start with this, then age you a bit. Twenty-eight was very nice, and I really liked your forties. And even your white hair. Wait! I just remembered I put the lock of hair Yudit cut for me in my pocket—" She patted her sides futilely as Perrin tried not to snort.

Realizing that her behavior was absurd, she stopped. "I must have left it on my other body."

He laughed. "It's all right, I don't need my old white hair. You can see me at any age you wish."

"So why am I still seeing eighteen?"

"Because you obviously *like* eighteen."

Mahrree giggled again and glanced down at herself. She was dressed in a simple but radiant white dress and her hands were wrinkle-free. "What age am I?"

Perrin sighed in approval. "I'm guessing eighteen."

"Really?"

He grinned. "I rather like eighteen, too. But your sixties were cute as well. Silvery hair and all," he said, twisting a lock of her light brown hair.

"You said 'cute'! I didn't even know you knew that word."

Perrin laughed. "I may have said it once or twice. But we need to get back to work, my darling wife. We need to focus on our greatest duty."

"As long as I'm by your side, I'll do anything."

"And that's where you're going to stay: by my side. Mahrree, take a look around. I don't think you fully appreciate yet where you are."

She turned to the chaotic scene of tens of thousands of soldiers around her, suspended in their time, and sighed. "Lannard's dead." She turned back to Perrin. "Exactly where is he?"

"Not here. Not in Paradise with us. And that's a merciful act. His attitudes, knowledge, beliefs—all of them are exactly as they were in the world. Death doesn't change our personalities. He'd not be very comfortable in our presence, would he?"

Mahrree glanced back at his broken body sprawled in silks on the jagged stones below. "Not one bit. He seemed quite shocked to see me."

"You have *no* idea how much," Perrin chuckled mirthlessly. "His spirit has gone to the dark deserts where he will come to understand all the harm his deceit and cowardice has caused. He's made many mistakes, as we all have. But he did nothing to fix those mistakes. In fact, he frequently decided it was easier to just go with the flow instead of acting on what he knew was right. He *chose* to be manipulated and used, thinking that would remove the responsibility of his actions. He refused to do what was right because he never wanted anyone to not like him."

"Poor Lannard," Mahrree sighed. "He had such potential. I could see it sometimes, lurking in his timid eyes."

"*Everyone* has great potential, Mahrree," Perrin sighed back. "That's the real tragedy. Some fall far shorter of it than others. He still has a chance, though, but it's going to be a long battle. He can still fix things, but what would've taken him a year to resolve in the world may take him hundreds to accomplish in the dark deserts. The life we just left is the time to prepare to live with the Creator again. After, it's much harder."

Mahrree turned to say something to her husband when she saw him, standing behind Perrin.

"Young Pere!" She rushed to his side and looked at the frozen expression of horror on his face. "Oh, Perrin, *he* certainly doesn't look eighteen."

"That's because he's *nine*teen."

"He looks more like fifty," she said, trying to touch his anguished face. She could almost do it. The matter of her spirit was *almost* the right composition to touch the matter of his flesh. "He looks so awful."

Perrin put a comforting arm around her. "That's because he just watched his beloved Muggah be killed by the man who tried to claim him as his son."

Mahrree turned to Perrin. "His *son?* I have a feeling you better start at the beginning."

"It's not a happy story," he warned.

"I can see that. But I'm also fairly confident that whatever you have to tell me won't shock me to death. I'm rather past that now."

He chuckled. "Yes, I have missed you! You know he was scheming with Eltana, right? Well . . ."

" . . . and so Nelt strapped him to this tree and took off with the sword. He said he'd come to free him later, but he'll hesitate and come too late. Nelt will realize that he was tricked by us, that there are no caves, and then he'll run away before he has to face Thorne again. Lemuel will be furious to have been lied to, and will suspect it was Nelt who lied, not Young Pere. After all, he still thinks he has a chance with Jaytsy and Young Pere."

Mahrree may not have been able to be shocked to death, but she could still be flabbergasted. "Lemuel's delusional! Not in an understandable way like Jon Offra, but in a bizarre, fractured way. 'Hey, Jaytsy, I just killed your mother. That's not going to make it awkward for you to still be my queen now, is it?'"

Perrin snorted at her imitation. "Fortunately he won't get to make that little proposal."

Mahrree leaned against her husband. The entire time he explained Young Pere's exploits she had sat cradled in his arms savoring the sound of his voice, watching his face move, and enjoying the intimacy of their souls next to each other. She frequently caressed his face, tracing the edges of his square jaw, his straight nose, his soft earlobes. She ran her fingers through his black hair, all while he told her of the past many moons.

He, too, dragged a finger across her face and lips, and occasionally paused in what he was saying to clutch her desperately and kiss her passionately.

Then they'd giggle in delight at each other, he'd pick up the thread of the story again, and Mahrree would have to ponder the uglier, more worldly things that her grandson had suffered.

Often she covered her face in sorrow, flinched in alarm, shook her head in complete bewilderment, but often just stared in surprise at the next thing Young Pere did or experienced. She had a feeling Perrin left out a lot of details, especially about someone named Lolo that Young Pere 'encountered' his first nights in Edge.

"So now you know it," Perrin exhaled, stroking her hair as she laid against his chest. "*Most* of it, that is. At least enough to know what he's been through and what he's thinking now."

"I understand, and I thank you for your editing," she said, running her hand over his broad shoulder. "Whatever you do, don't ever tell the details to Lilla. I can't believe he's made it back."

Perrin sighed. "Young Pere vacillates between two worlds: the one he grew up with in Salem and the one the Refuser controls in the world. So many times he's come close to grasping on to Salem, but then is pulled away by the ideas of the world. But since he's been coming home, his grip on Salem is stronger. Except for right now."

"Yes, wanting to kill Lemuel *is* a bit of a worldly thought," she decided as she drew a line down his bulky arm.

"But his purpose for doing so has improved," Perrin said. "He doesn't want Lemuel to harm his family. Mahrree, three weeks ago as he lay on the floor above the dungeon, he was ready to die to make sure his family survives."

"That's got to count for something, right?"

Perrin smiled. "His heart's *getting* in the right place, but his pride is still too strong. What he needs most of all is the understanding that he can't control all of this. He still believes he's entirely reliant on himself and he hasn't accepted that the Creator is in charge, and that whatever He decides is what *should* happen."

"Seeing me die could do a lot in that direction," she said, staring at her grandson still poised in time.

"That's what we're hoping. Something has to break him, bring him to his knees."

Mahrree glanced at his leg. "That won't happen literally while he's bound by his *thigh* to the tree."

"That will give, in time."

"He needs to be broken like you were, doesn't he?" Mahrree said gently. They rarely spoke of his past; it was in the past. But Perrin also had a great deal of experience which he needed to draw upon to help their grandson come as far as his grandfather.

Perrin nodded sadly. "Hogal made a great deal of progress with me at Young Pere's age, but the trauma of watching you die over and over in my dreams is what got me the rest of the way. I finally had to surrender my sense of control and turn it all over to Him. I couldn't control the world or my life or even what happened in my dreams. I had to learn to rely on the Creator. Self-reliance is an illusion that makes us so confident in ourselves that we're confident we don't even need Him. Once I got over that arrogance, every trial was far easier to endure."

Mahrree snuggled closer into him, and he wrapped his arms tighter around her. "I'm sorry you had to witness my deaths—all of them. The real one wasn't that bad, actually. Being stabbed in the heart is quite quick. Makes a bit of a mess, but now that I look at it from this side, it's nothing more than a spider bite."

Perrin chuckled and kissed the top of her head. "Looked quite gruesome. Even I flinched when you hit the stone floor, although I knew you were already gone."

"Was your death harder?" she asked.

He thought for a moment. "Yes, I suppose. Physically it was painful, but it was the emotional part that was excruciating. I knew it was coming for some time, and knowing for those days that I was leaving you . . . I thought saying goodbye that last day would break my heart."

"Nearly broke mine," she murmured.

"I know. I was with you right after I went, but your heart was so tender and fragile, you couldn't feel me." He gripped her firmer as if to hug away those miserable memories, and she let him.

"But as for the pain?" he said. "Death was a sweet and welcome relief." He smiled and sighed in contentment. "Dying was . . . it was *miraculous* to have it all over: the final, great, hoped for miracle. It sounds strange, but I can't describe it any other way. To be released from all that physical and mental torment, then to arrive here and meet again all of our family and friends—oh, truly glorious! Just like today." He kissed her again, and she let him.

"You know," he continued in a more casual tone, "I *could* have gone later, but I decided to just get it over with. It was such a pleasant afternoon and evening anyway the day of my death, and everyone in Salem could come by and see my body—"

Suddenly she realized something, and she sat up to look at him properly. "So you *did* plan it that way!"

"I've always got a plan, Mahrree," he smiled slyly.

"Why didn't you tell me? That you were going to die that day?"

He tilted his head. "And what would you have done if I had told you?"

Mahrree paused, then said resignedly, "Talk you out of it. Beg you to stay."

"That's what I thought," he said as he ran his fingers through her hair, gathering it behind her. "The next day was much hotter, then the thunderstorm came. It wouldn't have been a good time to have a few thousand people in the orchard then."

She chuckled. "You're right."

"I always love it when you admit that," he murmured. Perrin nodded at Young Pere, still anguished and frozen in time. "Mahrree, I think you're ready. Once we go back to his time we'll feel things at the same rate that he does. It's best that we stay with him in order to remain focused. As you can see, it's far more enjoyable to just sit and hold each other for hours on end, but that's not our calling—"

"We've been sitting here for *hours?*"

"Closer to a full day, relatively speaking," he said, kissing her again. And once more. "If time were measured for us. But everyone has that before they get to work: the adjustment and education period. Consider it an extended midday meal break, granted by the Creator."

She giggled and sat up, then considered what he said. "When will I see Him?" she asked quietly.

Perrin's face went soft. "At the end of a thousand years all of us will kneel before Him to be judged to see who is ready to remain with Him, and who isn't. Until then, the test continues in another form. You still feel Him, right?"

Mahrree nodded. "Most intensely. And it's from Him that all this understanding comes from, right?" Her mind was clear and open, more so than it ever had been. Not only did she hear about Young Pere, she saw it—all of it—playing out in her mind as if she was with him. It seemed that so much information was hovering around her, waiting patiently for the right moments to make itself manifest to her.

Perrin smiled. "And more knowledge will flow into you as you're ready for it. You're not yet prepared to kneel in His presence, but you will be soon."

"Have you?" Mahrree whispered.

Perrin's eyes became even softer. "I have, Mahrree! I had to be here for a while, to adjust first before I could see Him, but then?" His chin trembled. "Fantastic! Glorious! Overwhelming, even in this form. And Mahrree, I *remembered* Him. He was so familiar—more familiar than my own father's face. I wasn't allowed to remember Him until then."

She thought she already knew so much, but there was still more? "Why can't I see Him now, just for a moment?"

"Because you won't want to leave His side," he told her longingly. "You'll want to sit and tell Him everything like you're five years old again and just had the most amazing adventure. It's too wonderful, Mahrree."

She could feel that it was, and couldn't speak in anticipation of that reunion. How she felt being with her parents and Perrin were already so much. But even more?

"It'll happen, very soon," he assured her. "Right now the Last Day is nearly upon us and there's so much work to do. You once said to Young Pere that I wasn't sitting on a cloud strumming some tuneless harp pretending to sing, and you're right. We don't rest—we keep working, day and night, tirelessly, to get everyone where they need to be. You just came from that life, so you're very much in tune with it. You need to stay in that realm in order to provide the best direction."

"I see that," she said, feeling nostalgia for an experience she couldn't yet remember. "I can't run home and tell Papa what I've been up to because there's still more to do."

He smiled. "That's right. But you'll feel Him, and hear Him. You're getting better at it already——" He hesitated, because Mahrree had a peculiar expression on her face.

She was remembering something—more of the veil was slipping away, revealing another memory.

"I *asked* to do this today," she said softly, astonished.

Perrin began to smile. "You remember that already?"

She barely heard him, because the image was so clear in her mind—a discussion, long, long ago. Hundreds, probably thousands of years ago—

But time wasn't measured, so that wasn't quite right. But there was a discussion—a debate! About their existence on this sphere, and how it would be—*should* be.

The Refuser had debated against them, not agreeing with the Creator how it should go. They all took sides, and more sided with the Creator than with the rebellious son.

The Refuser had left, furious that his plans were rejected, and many others followed him.

And then the debate resumed, this time about who was willing to do what, and when, and how.

The Creator had called for volunteers, needing some of them to give up something very important. To make sacrifices, willingly.

To give up the very lives that they were so eager to get.

"I *asked* to do this today," Mahrree whispered again. She couldn't quite see it yet in her memory, but she remembered going to the Creator, declaring that she wanted to make the sacrifice, wait until the right moment, do what was required to help her brothers and sisters, even if it was scary.

"And He agreed," she recalled. "I *made* Him promise me I could do this, and I insisted that He not let me forget! He sent me little reminders, didn't He? Every time I read that passage in The Writings, something prickled in my memory—something distant. I couldn't remember much at all, but those words about the aged before the Last Day . . . they always meant something. But until last night I didn't understand why. Last night, He gave me enough to remember. I had *insisted* long ago that He give me those clues!" she exclaimed. "Oh, Perrin—I prayed after you died that I could die, too. But the Creator didn't give in because He was honoring something I had asked for much, much longer ago."

Perrin smiled. "That's why I couldn't come get you after I died. I remembered then, too, that you wanted to be the means of helping others escape. Right after I came to Paradise, not only did I foresee your sacrifice today, I also remembered that conversation you had with our Creator. I was there, too. A few of us had gone with you, because you wanted us to help you remember your decision once we got to that life. Not that I ever did remember," he added apologetically.

She met his eyes. "Shem was there, with us. He was one of those who promised to help me do this. And in the end, he's the one who actually did! Oh, Perrin—he has no idea, does he? He always does the right things."

"Speaking of doing the right things," she continued, her tone shifting, "there were a lot of things I wanted to accomplish in my life." She searched the immense memory she could access, but not all of it was available yet. "I missed a few things," she murmured regretfully. "But . . . but overall, I did nearly everything." She knew inherently that once the Last Day was over she'd have the opportunity to recall all of her life, to reflect on what she did and didn't do. She was sure there was a list she'd created, and it'd manifest itself in her hands and she'd review it, remembering what she'd written so long ago: all of her goals and plans and desires for her life in her body.

But for now, her Creator wanted her to understand one thing from that list: that most important thing she wanted to accomplish.

And she had done it, today.

In her mind formed the words she's heard Cephas say when she first arrived in Paradise, but now they came from the Creator: *Well Done, My Faithful Daughter!*

She closed her eyes in satisfaction, in joy. Looking back on it, meeting Lemuel at the temple and dying really wasn't such a big sacrifice. Not one bit.

Look where it got her—home!

Perrin squeezed her. "I felt the same way," he whispered. "Everything I did, or endured, or suffered in life? Wasn't such a big deal once I came back here. Like a child who's skinned his knee and is consumed by the pain, sure that in all the world there's no bigger agony. And then, not so much later, he's off again, happily playing. Life is brief, and so is its pain."

Pain. Mahrree glanced up and saw Young Pere's face, consumed with it. In such a short time he'd forget how terrible it was, she knew.

But for the interval between then and now, he needed help. And she had insisted long ago on providing that, too.

Perrin noticed her staring at Young Pere. "If you're ready?"

Mahrree extracted herself from her husband and stood up. Perrin got up too. Cuddling and chatting endlessly would resume later; there was work to do.

As Mahrree gazed at Young Pere's agonized expression, she was more than ready to see it change. "Will he hear me?"

"I don't know," Perrin said. "He was extraordinarily in tune with me. We had hours' long conversations in the dungeon. He was even closer to you, so he should hear you. *If* he's listening."

"So it's easy to ignore us?"

"Very. Takes no effort all to stop listening. One more thing: put your hand on his chest, just above his heart."

She stepped closer and did so. Surprised to feel something so distinctly, she gasped. "What is this? It's so cold and hard."

"That's his soul," Perrin told her. "You can reach him there, but only if he wants to be reached. That's where I felt my parents touching me after they died."

Mahrree nodded. "I felt you there often, too, at the beginning."

Perrin put his hand on top of hers. "His anger has done this. There were times he was so soft and pliable. We need to get him back to that in order for him to make it on time."

"And just how much time is left?" she wondered.

Perrin looked at her.

She saw it all, *everything* that would transpire in the future.

"Wow. How'd you do that?"

He smiled. "I didn't. Already you're realizing how to properly use your mind, to let the Creator pour pure knowledge into you. You asked, *He* gave you the answer. Ready?"

She nodded and kept her hand in place, Perrin's firmly on top of hers.

Suddenly Young Pere lunged, pulling at the tree like a ferocious dog. "No! No! Muggah!" he screamed.

I'm right here, Young Pere! Feel me! It's all right! In fact, it's wonderful!

He yanked again and again at the tree, then smacked it with his arm in full fury. Nothing budged. The pain in his arm stopped his mad yanking, and he cradled his throbbing arm and sobbed.

Down at the temple, Thorne was turning around.

"SHE'S DEAD!" the general bellowed to the soldiers who remained.

Many turned to look at him. Some stopped in their running, but others continued to flee.

Thorne thrust the sword in the air. "She has no power! She's dead! Salem is still ours!"

A fraction of the remaining soldiers began to cheer, uncertainly at first, then stronger as they were joined by more voices.

Young Pere slumped against the tree in defeat. "He did it," he mumbled. "He killed her. She did nothing to him . . . She was totally defenseless. She just *let* him kill her—"

Why, Young Pere? Why did I do that?

Young Pere held his head. "Why did she do that? Puggah!"

I'M HERE, YOUNG PERE. AND SO IS SHE.

Young Pere pulled down on his face. "No, no, no . . . Oh, Creet! *He killed her!* MUGGAH! She didn't even get to know I was coming home!" He gasped and panted and lunged and finally whimpered, "Muggah!"

I knew you were coming home! I made you a sign above your bed. Young Pere, feel me! Feel me!

Young Pere held his head and sobbed.

Perrin, he can't feel me!

HE'S GRIEVING TOO DEEPLY. YOU DID THE SAME THING TO ME. SHUT ME OUT FOR HOURS AFTER I PASSED.

We don't have hours.

WE'LL GET TO HIM. KEEP AT IT. I NEED TO LEAVE FOR ONE MINUTE. I'LL BE RIGHT BACK.

"Muggah . . . Muggah . . . Muggah . . ."

Shem crawled back to the big black horse, sobbing and shaking. He reached Clark 14 and leaned against its legs. "I've failed! Oh, Perrin! I've failed!"

OH, NO YOU DIDN'T, BROTHER. YOU GAVE HER BACK TO ME! THANK YOU, SHEM! THANK YOU!

Shem pushed that away. He didn't deserve the comfort. He especially didn't deserve to feel Perrin. How could he be coming to him now, and happily? Didn't he see what just happened?

OF COURSE I SAW WHAT HAPPENED! YOU SENT HER BACK TO MY ARMS. SHEM, GO THE ANCIENT TEMPLE. THERE'S NOTHING MORE FOR YOU TO DO HERE. THANK YOU, MY BROTHER.

"Go away!" Shem waved around himself, as if trying to shoo away attacking bats. "Just go away, Perrin! I'm so sorry." He struggled to his feet, mounted Clark 14 in an awkward flop, and kicked the horse to run away from the General of Salem.

Mahrree kept holding Young Pere as he alternated between sobbing uncontrollably and flailing against the tree. She'd stopped trying to talk to him, knowing he wouldn't listen yet, but kept her hand on his chest and her arms around him.

And 'holding' him wasn't exactly accurate, either. She would describe it more as 'occupying the same space.' So desperately she wished she could reach him, help him feel the joy she was feeling, help him release the anger and realize that truly, all was well. *Better* than well.

Perrin appeared next to him and winced at his grandson. "Not much progress yet, I see." He put a hand on Young Pere's chest.

"How long will it take for him to feel us?" she asked.

"Once it took him eight moons to finally let me talk to him again."

"*Eight moons*?!"

"But Hogal and I spent a lot of wonderful days chatting, sending messages, hearing about the family—"

"You kept up?"

"Completely. We knew Meiki was expecting even before she did. It's a girl and will look just like Calla."

Mahrree closed her eyes. "Oh, poor Meiki! She was so close to Calla."

"It's going to be a terrible night up there," Perrin agreed. "You should go stay with them once we have Young Pere down for the night."

When she looked at him with hesitation, he smiled and said, "You can be back in my arms in an instant, remember that."

She grinned, but it quickly faded. "You went to see Shem, didn't you? I could feel him.''

"Yeah," he sighed.

"And how's he taking it?"

"About as good as can be expected."

Mahrree frowned. "That bad, huh?"

Perrin scoffed sadly. "Calla will definitely need your help. He actually *pushed* me away, if you can believe that. He knew I was there, he heard me thanking him for bringing you here, but he's not ready yet. For anyone."

"Poor Shem." Mahrree glanced down the hillside between Young Pere's lunges. "Perrin, is that . . . Versa Thorne?"

Perrin glanced over his shoulder to see Versa sitting on a log, weeping. "Do you realize you just looked *through* the trees to spot her?"

"Hey, I did, didn't I! Who's that with her? It looks like Joriana."

"It is. Mother's been trying to work with her, but just like Young Pere, she's come here with her own ideas and is listening for only what she wants to hear."

"And what was she planning to do?"

"Stop Lemuel."

Mahrree closed her eyes again. "The poor girl! Why isn't Druses' mother with her?"

"She's already busy working with Priscill."

"Where is she? We haven't heard anything . . ."

Perrin's sad look told her all she needed to know.

"The dark deserts," Mahrree said.

Perrin nodded. "She was on a fast horse to destruction, just as Young Pere was. Only she didn't survive it."

"Oh, Priscill! She was so young."

"She's not without hope, Mahrree. Already she's made great progress. She never understood the purpose of her life as we did, but now she's learning rapidly all that she never knew. Her grandmother is by her side constantly, as are many other relatives, waiting to escort her here when she's ready. It won't be long for her."

Mahrree looked back over at Versa, realizing there was someone else holding Versa on the other side of Joriana. "Is that . . . Shaleea Fadh?"

Perrin smiled. "The Fadhs cared for Druses and their daughters when they were young, until the Fadhs were killed. Shaleea and my mother have had *some* success in reaching Versa, but right now they're dealing with a young woman deep in mourning, and she's also feeling like a failure. She didn't reach Lemuel in time. She's been trying for days to get to him, to try to stop all of this, but we've been holding her back.

"So far, today alone, Shaleea slipped Versa past a dozen of Eltana's army members, Graeson has distracted dozens of soldiers from noticing her—"

Perrin gestured, and for the first time Mahrree noticed former General Graeson Fadh, slender and imposing in all white, standing in front of the cluster of trees where Versa sat and wept. Mahrree wasn't sure what he was doing beyond folding his arms and posing menacingly, but no fleeing soldiers even came near him. They all seemed to suddenly veer into another direction.

"—Shaleea and my mother convinced her to take a long nap on a porch so that she slept through the arrival of the army, and they even made sure she fell into an unfinished well! She got out all right, it was dry, so don't worry," he added when he saw Mahrree's alarm. "But *after* Lemuel rode by. He never noticed the hole which his horse was headed for, because once again Graeson directed the horse into a slightly different direction. We all know that Lemuel would have killed Versa without a second thought. Shaleea even nudged Shem to catch his breath by the porch where Versa was hiding, just to give Versa another chance to get away. But that's not what she wanted."

Mahrree watched Joriana and Shaleea trying to hold Versa in the same way she tried to hold Young Pere. "Will she be all right?"

"She won't be going to the ancient site alone."

Young Pere thrashed and wept.

"Can we release him?" Mahrree asked, trying to stroke his hair.

"Think about it," Perrin said. "What would happen?"

The image materialized in her mind. "He's still too angry. He'd rush down there and find a sword, but he's too inexperienced. Lemuel would win that battle within seconds. We have to wait, don't we?"

"Very good. This is why the Creator has trusted you to this duty—you'll do what's best for him, not what you want for him."

The image continued to play out in her mind. "We need to wait for him to calm down and for Lemuel to leave. That will be about another hour, once Lemuel can't find the alleged cave entrance in the temple."

Perrin looked down at the stone structure. A window smashed as a chair came flying through it. "Already they're looting it, tearing it apart, looking for some secret door. So tragic," he whispered. "The very thing that could bring them such peace they destroy with alacrity."

"Definition of the world," Mahrree whispered back. "Lemuel's in there. I think I can hear him swearing."

"Look at the portico, Mahrree. At your body."

"I've tried to avoid that." But she looked anyway. "It's Poe, isn't it?"

"He still doesn't know what to think about you. When I visited him a few weeks ago I could tell he still believed the official story. Right now he doesn't know what to do."

Poe was kneeling by Mahrree's body, which several soldiers had kicked and spit upon as they rushed into the temple. He gently pushed it up against the wall and out of the way, leaving a great red smear on the white stone.

"Ah, Poe! That's so sweet," Mahrree smiled. "Thank you. But I'm not in there, you know."

Still on his knees, Poe gazed at her body, seemingly perplexed. After a moment he glanced around to make sure no one was watching, then he kissed his fingers and touched his fingers to her cheek.

"Good man, Qualipoe Hili!" Perrin declared. "She deserves your devotion. Now do the truly brave thing and abandon Thorne."

"Come on, Poe! You can do it!" Mahrree clenched her fist, pleading. "Look at the sky, Poe! What color is it? It's not only blue, is it? Think for yourself. Question all they've tricked you to believe. See that it's not what they've told you it is. What color is the sky, Poe?"

Slowly Poe stood up, nodded respectfully to Mahrree's body, and went into the temple.

Mahrree and Perrin groaned together.

"Still too hard, Poe?" Perrin sighed. "Follow your instincts, Sergeant Major. They've always been good. Don't do what's expected; do what's right."

Mahrree smiled sadly after Poe, then recoiled as a sofa came out another window, crashing in a spray of glass.

"The temple!" Young Pere whimpered. "Salem! All of it is lost, everything." He leaned against the tree and wrapped his arms around it as if it were his mother.

Perrin and Mahrree hugged him on either side.

It's supposed to be lost, Young Pere. Mahrree told him. *Remember the prophecies? Remember the stories we told you? Salem would be lost but the people would be spared at the ancient site. The Deliverer would keep his people safe before the coming Destruction. Look around, Young Pere—Salem left. The Creator knows all of this would happen and has a plan. Everything is happening as it should. Now you need to happen as you should!*

Young Pere's sobs slowed. He sniffed and mumbled, "Happen as *I* should?"

Perrin rolled his eyes at Mahrree. *A LITTLE CONFUSINGLY PHRASED. But he heard me!*

Young Pere blinked. He was used to hearing the voice on his right side, but the last thought came from the left.

Perrin prodded Mahrree to speak.

Young Pere, listen to me. All you have to do is go west! Go straight to the ancient site.

Young Pere held his breath.

You know it's me, Young Pere! And I did know you were coming home. Jaytsy saw you escape and rushed home to tell us. Your parents know! They've gone to the temple ruins, and soon everyone there will know and will be watching for you. I'm here to help you get there. Scaring away one third of the army was only one of my callings. My most important one is to bring you home.

Young Pere sagged, pulling some of the tree down with him. "I can't go back to them. I haven't done anything good. I haven't stopped Thorne, I've only wasted all this time and caused them all this pain—"

So don't waste any more time! Don't cause any more pain. Make them happy, Young Pere! Just go!

Young Pere swallowed. "Muggah?"

Yes!

Young Pere rested his head against the tree. "I'm so sorry I failed you! Look at them, what they're doing to your body . . . This isn't right. I need to at least bury you. It's so unfair. All of Salem came to honor Puggah, but you won't even be dressed in white. No one will carry you through Salem. No one will come to your service. You won't even have one. You don't deserve this. No—NO! Someone's kicking you!"

I'm not in there, Young Pere. You want to honor me? Then listen to me. Argue with me. I've missed arguing with you, you know. You kept me on my toes. But I've gone rusty, Young Pere. Try me—you just might win. I'm arguing for you to go west, to go to our family.

You're arguing to not. Why?

Young Pere began to sob again. "Muggah, I've missed you so much, and now you're gone . . ."

Mahrree sighed at Perrin. "He thinks I'm only his imagination, doesn't he?"

Perrin smiled in sympathy. "This will be your toughest debate ever, my darling wife. You *have* to win this one."

Sergeant Beaved observed the mayhem swirling around him. He was near the front of the temple, waiting for Cloud Man and Shin to reappear as Thorne suggested they would, but it was clear that he wouldn't be finding either of them in this mess. His security team stayed close by, also anxiously watching the soldiers.

Some were running toward the temple, eager to smash something. Others were running for the trees in terror. Still more ran to the canyon behind, having been inspired by Thorne, with their swords drawn and looking for more blood to shed. But many just looked helplessly around, waiting for someone to tell them what to do.

Beaved noticed movement on the portico. Two soldiers were kicking the body of the old woman toward the edge of the wide porch. He recoiled as the blood-stained body slipped over the side and tumbled down to the stones below, to the cheers of the soldiers. He closed his eyes barely in time.

"She was his *grandmother!*" Iron hissed, having also seen what just happened. "I don't care who she was to Thorne, you just don't do that to an old woman."

Hammer, Reg, Buddy, and Pal nodded in bitter agreement.

"There are a lot of things happening today that you *just don't do*," said Teach with his fists clenched. "That temple thing is supposed to be sacred. I'm not entirely sure what that means, but I know it *doesn't* mean that you destroy it."

Snarl shrugged and looked longingly at the stone structure.

"There's one thing we're *not* going to do," Beaved decided. "Stay here any longer. All of you, follow me." He took off in a jog for the dense forest, his security team following hesitantly.

"Where are you going?" Hammer called to him.

"Shin wasn't afraid of the trees, and he's the only one I think we can trust right now," the sergeant called back. "We're following

Shin's example. He used to be an officer, you know."

A few moments later, Beaved neared the forest, having had to weave his way through masses of soldiers. He hesitated for the briefest of moments before plowing into the dense foliage. He kept going in a relatively straight direction, hoping to not lose any of his team. About thirty paces in, he stopped and turned around.

Each man had stayed with him, but now looked as if he regretted it. It was growing dark as the sun set, and the trees cast unnatural shadows all around them.

Beaved clutched one of the narrower tree trunks and shook it. "Look—wood, leaves, branches. That's all it is. Lots of them. We're not afraid of orchards, are we? Of the trees that grew around our houses? Didn't we climb them as boys? Same thing! Just lots more."

But Teach was looking at his feet. "This is what worries me; not above ground, *below* it."

"Smell the air," Beaved demanded. "None of that rotten egg sulfur smell anywhere. Nor have I seen a single hot spring or mud volcano. There are no hissing noises, nothing. Look around!"

The men did cautiously at first, then more confidently.

"It's just *trees*, isn't it?" Reg finally said.

"Yes! And no spirits of the dead soldiers, either. Never were. More lies, made up and fed to us by Thorne so we'd follow him like lost mutts. Well, no more. If we stick together, we'll be fine."

Teach folded his arms. "And where do you propose we go?"

Beaved nodded to the west. "Where Shin is going. The ancient temple site he mentioned. Maybe we'll find him on the way."

Reg squinted. "What makes you think the people up there will take us in?"

"I don't know that they will," Beaved admitted. "But I like our chances better with them than I do with him," he said, cocking his head at the temple which Thorne was ravaging. "Agreed?"

Each of the men nodded. "Agreed."

Beaved smiled, feeling a sliver of hope. "Then let's find a place to sleep here tonight. I have a feeling we'll be relatively undisturbed in the trees."

"Not even by the ghosts of dead soldiers?" Buddy asked hesitantly.

Beaved smiled broader. "Actually, if there are any, I think they'll be on our side tonight."

None of them knew it, but several voices, belonging to past

generals, chuckled just beyond their range of perception.

Very good, Sergeant.

For once, you got something right!

Bed down over there, boys. We're on duty tonight.

Deck rode in the lead with the Zenos children—Zaddick, Huldah, and Ester. Then came the rest of the Briter family; Jaytsy and Cephas in the lead, followed by Yenali, Tabbit, Banu, Atlee, and Young Shem.

Behind them rode the Shins: Hogal, Sakal, Centia, then Lilla with Morah seated in front of her, with Peto bringing up the rear.

The sun was getting lower on the horizon and Deck was relieved he was getting them to the site before sundown. It had been a very long day, and he was ready for the excitement to end.

But even before he reached the high meadow where the horses would be left, he could feel something dark and heavy sliding over the ridge and down the mountain. Something was definitely wrong.

Maybe the giveaway was the dozens of people on the ridge that noticed them and broke into a run over it, as if to announce their arrival.

Deck looked behind to Zaddick, who was visibly worried. Further down the line Deck tried to catch Jaytsy's eye, but she was saying something to Cephas behind her. Lilla and Peto were too far back to see. Deck clucked the horse to hurry. He didn't want to prolong whatever it was.

Just as he reached the meadow near the top of the route, he saw Salema come over the ridge. She stopped halfway, folded her arms, and waited. Everything about her demeanor was somber.

Deck exhaled in dread. Maybe one of the children. Or grandchildren. Salema was a midwife, so maybe it was Eraliz or Meiki with a lost baby . . .

He nodded gravely at his oldest daughter, but she didn't nod back. She just shifted her stance and dabbed at her eyes.

Deck dismounted about twenty paces away from her, and so did Zaddick.

"What's going on, Uncle Deck?" he whispered.

"I don't know, Zad."

The rest of their horses came quickly, and each person who saw

Salema waiting, as well as the now dozens of people on the ridge huddling nearby, could tell something was not right.

Jaytsy slid off her horse and rushed up the slope to her daughter. "What's wrong? I could feel it for the entire last stretch."

Salema sniffled. "In a moment. We need everyone."

Huldah and Ester jogged over to their brother Zaddick who only shrugged. Deck and Cephas helped the younger children off their horses just as Lilla and Peto arrived.

Peto was off his horse in an instant, his wife and family following. "Salema? What's wrong?"

She took a bracing breath. "Where's Papa Shem and Muggah?"

"Behind us a ways. Don't wait."

Salema began shakily. "During Shem's battle, two arrows were fired." She took another breath. "Calla was hiding in the bushes—"

That's all she got out. Lilla screamed her sister's name and ran up the ridge, with Zaddick, Huldah, and Ester right behind her.

Jaytsy covered her face with her hands. "No, no, no . . ."

Peto's chest heaved. "What happened?"

Salema's chin quivered with disbelief. "Uncle Peto, *she died*—"

Peto tore up to the ridge after his wife while Salema started to sob again. The Shin children chased after their father while Deck wrapped his arms around Salema and Jaytsy. The remaining Briter children clung to them.

It took Lilla and the Zenoses only a minute of frantic running to reach Shem's large tent. Several of his assistants were in place and waiting. As Lilla plowed to where her other sisters and family were gathered, two of the younger assistants caught her. Relf, Cambo, and Barnos were waiting for Zaddick, Huldah, and Ester. They gingerly guided them to their mother.

Boskos, standing near her head, nodded gratefully to his cousins. He stepped over to his aunt and took her gently, but Lilla tried to get around him to the body lying under the white blanket. "There was nothing we could do. When we found her she was already gone—"

"NO!" Lilla wailed and collapsed in Boskos's arms. Peto arrived just in time to lower her to the ground by Calla.

Zaddick, Ester, and Huldah reacted exactly as their aunt had, and were led by their cousins to Lek and Meiki on the other side, who held them and cried all over again.

Boskos stood by and watched while wiping his eyes, looking frequently back up the ridge. Eventually Deck, Salema, Jaytsy, and the rest of the Briters came down.

Boskos shuffled over to Deck. "Where's Papa?"

Deck shook his head. "Not here yet. All Peto would say was that Mahrree was being unreasonable again and that Shem was taking her somewhere. I suspect they're making one last search for Young Pere. Your father was planning to be back up here by dark, so he should be here soon. I'm so sorry, Bos. What can I do?"

"Help me with Papa," Boskos whispered. "Jaytsy can take care of Muggah when she arrives, but Deck, I think only you and Peto would understand since you lived in the world. When I saw Papa's eyes this morning, after he killed those men, there was something there I've never seen before."

Deck sighed. "I saw it occasionally in Perrin's eyes when someone from the world came and he started reminiscing. Terrifying."

"Papa's not going to remember that he's already taken vengeance for what happened to Mama." Boskos choked on the words, and Deck put an arm around him. "He already killed them. I'm just not sure who's going to be on duty when he gets the news: the guide or the sergeant major. The sergeant major might go looking for another sword."

"I agree," Deck murmured. "It may not help that he's currently wearing a colonel's uniform."

"He's what?"

Deck sighed heavily. "It's been a wild day, Bos. And not entirely horrible."

"Any good news, Deck? Anything at all? I could use something right now. All of us could."

Deck smiled dimly. "One glimmer of hope, Boskos. Young Pere is running free."

It was an hour later that Jaytsy, her own sobbing momentarily slowed down because she was dehydrated, explained quietly to the rest of the extended family what had happened with Lemuel Thorne at the Second Resting Station. Everyone listened, grateful to hear something new and promising.

"It seemed that Lemuel was under the impression that Young Pere was his and *my* child," she told them, wincing.

Relf frowned at his aunt. "So Young Pere's older than Lori and Jori?"

"Older than Salema." Jaytsy scrunched her face, trying to work it out. "Or maybe he *was* Salema."

The family smiled feebly at that.

Salema shivered, and Lek looked up from his spot next to his mother, his two youngest sisters still in his arms. He almost seemed amused.

"I stared Young Pere right in the eyes," Jaytsy said in a hushed tone. "And honestly, whatever he's been through, he looks older than Salema now. He's trying to come home, that much I could tell. He was trying to tell me so much, and I was trying to say so much back to him. But I knew most importantly that he had to get away. So I turned to Lemuel and said, as loudly as I could so the soldiers could hear me, 'I have seven sons. And *that* is not my son!'"

Boskos and Lek actually smiled. Meiki could only sigh.

"Then I marched back into the kitchen, with Lemuel right behind me. 'But Jaytsy!' he said, 'You just don't *remember*!'"

Cambo regarded his mother incredulously. "Don't remember having a baby with *Lemuel Thorne*?"

His sisters and female cousins shuddered at the thought.

Meiki mumbled from her prone position, "I'd have a hard time forgetting *that*."

Jaytsy smiled sympathetically at Meiki. "I don't know what happened next outside, but a moment later I heard shouting. Lemuel charged back on to the back porch, and I followed him in time to see the backside of Young Pere sprinting to the forest! Somehow the chains binding his wrists were on the ground, and only one other soldier was bothering to chase him!"

Fennic sat up excitedly. "So Young Pere got away?"

Jaytsy nodded at her grandson.

Boskos hid his face in his hands. "Thank the Creator."

"I already am," Jori started to cry and hugged her little Peto.

For a few seconds everyone had smiles on their faces.

"Which way was he running?" Briter asked.

Jaytsy bit her lip. "Southeast."

Briter's expression faded. "He's supposed to go west, right?"

Jaytsy smiled bravely. "Southeast was the fastest way to the forest. No soldiers dared follow him except for the one chasing him, and I think he's the one who helped Young Pere get away. He can still make it here, Briter," she told her seven-year-old grandson. "Because he has special help."

"What kind of help?" Nool asked his aunt.

"Puggah."

Everyone stared at Jaytsy.

She couldn't stop the tears that flowed again, but these were hopeful tears. "He was there. I could even smell him—you know, that kind of earthy-sweet smell he had? He told me what to say to give Young Pere time to escape. Puggah is running with him!"

But Briter shook his head. "I think Young Pere might be faster than Puggah."

"Oh no, Briter," Jaytsy assured him. "When Puggah was a younger man, no one was faster than him! He'll keep up, I'm sure."

No one mentioned the fact that neither Shem nor Mahrree had arrived yet. But every few minutes their tear-filled gazes shifted to the ridge, waiting.

It was a good thing Clark 14 was so sure-footed, because Shem couldn't focus on anything. He rode past fleeing soldiers and others rushing in a panic, and he didn't know if they were Salemites or people from the world because his eyes were too blurry, his mind too distraught.

Because Mahrree was dead.

Because he delivered her there. And now he had to go to the ancient site, face all her descendants and all of Salem and tell them what he did to contribute to her death.

There was only one person who could help him through the pain and horror of what he'd caused. Maybe he could tell her, then she could break it to everyone else. Then she could hold him all night, once she forgave him for the death of her best friend—

She *would* forgive him, wouldn't she? Somehow she'd be able to see why it had to happen? And then maybe she could help Shem understand—

Calla was the only thing that made him finally turn the horse to head up the trail. He wouldn't get there until well past dark, but he *would* get there, because he promised her he'd be there tonight.

But it felt like the day would never end.

Young Pere's thrashing had ceased. Exhausted, he now flopped against the tree, unable to sit because his thigh was strapped to it. The sun slid behind the mountains, and soon all would be dark and cold.

And he had nothing. No pack, no emergency rations, no candles, no matches—just him and that stupid tree.

The soldiers were leaving, running out of the temple and the canyon behind it. Some were furious they'd found nothing, others appeared to be losing confidence in Thorne, especially after he tore out of the temple screaming in fury, mounted his horse, and kicked it into a run while calling for Nelt. Other soldiers simply sat down in the slush and held their heads. Spending the night in unfamiliar territory wasn't a very comforting prospect. Young Pere knew how they felt, but still was a bit irked that no one came up the hill far enough to see him belted to a tree.

Young Pere watched as Thorne rode in an erratic line across the darkening field, trying to find Nelt who had told him about the non-existent caverns, and screeching to know where the rest of the Salemites were hiding. Killing only one of them apparently wasn't enough for Thorne.

WHAT A MESS! He heard a chuckle next to him. *CHAOS INDEED! LOSING CONTROL OF YOUR ARMY AND OFFICERS IS NOT THE BEST STRATEGY, LEMUEL. AND LOSING CONTROL OF YOUR TEMPER IS EVEN WORSE.*

Young Pere couldn't smile. Everything was dead and hopeless in him. And he couldn't sit down.

The sun was now gone and the valley was rapidly going dark.

It's not going to be a pleasant night out here for all those soldiers. They're not even trying to run to the empty houses.

NOR WILL THEY. NO ONE HAS ORDERED THEM TO. PEOPLE IN THE WORLD CAN'T DO ANYTHING ON THEIR OWN EXCEPT COPY SOMEONE ELSE. BESIDES, THEY'D HAVE TO CROSS THE RIVER, AND IN THE DARK. THEY'RE CHILDREN—TERRIFIED, DUMB CHILDREN.

So tragic. So unnecessary.

Young Pere held his breath. There *were* two of them talking, on either side of him.

Thorne's gone. Is it time yet?

YES, IT'S TIME.

Suddenly the tree holding Young Pere began to creak. He looked at it in surprise and yanked. The trunk split, then the tree collapsed completely, the band holding his leg slipping useless to the ground.

Oh, look—I did it!

He sat down on the ground in relief and heaviness. "Thank you, Puggah."

DON'T THANK ME. THAT WAS YOUR GRANDMOTHER'S DOING.

And your 'grandmother' now wants you to rest, and in the morning go west. Perrin, since when have you referred to me as 'Grandmother'?

Young Pere couldn't smile at their conversation. The thought of facing his family now, with the news that he watched Muggah die and did nothing to stop it, was too much.

He would have killed you, Young Pere.

"Muggah, I deserve death," Young Pere whispered, knowing it was only to the desperation of his grieving mind but feeling he should confess such things out loud anyway. "You have no idea what I've been doing the past seven seasons. What I've been thinking, wanting, planning—"

Oh, but I do. And you do not deserve death. You have a few things to fix, there's no debate about that, but it IS fixable, Young Pere. That's the wonderful truth—the Creator can heal you!

"Why would He want to?" Young Pere whispered.

Because He loves you! Because I love you!

"Why? Why love me?" he said to the dark. "I've done nothing to deserve it."

That's the funny thing about love—I choose who I want to love. There's nothing you can do to deserve it. From the day you were born I loved you. What did you do for me then? Nothing. You just laid there and cried and turned red and made messes in your cloths. And you know what? I still loved you immensely. Even then I would have chosen to die for you, just to let you live.

Young Pere began to weep. "I still don't know why you would."

Some day you will, Young Pere. When you cradle your first child, you will understand. But will you do something for me now?

Young Pere sniffled. "There's nothing left to do. I can't even find Thorne in the dark—"

I want you to abandon this quest of yours. This isn't your calling, Young Pere. The Creator never intended for you to reunite the world or destroy Thorne. While the ideas may have been noble, it wasn't His plan. Young Pere, are you ready to do His will for you and abandon your own?

Young Pere didn't say anything, partly because the request was so hard, and partly because he realized his imagination would never ask such a thing of him.

Someone else, however, would.

Are you afraid His will for you won't be as thrilling or exciting as yours?

Young Pere shrugged. "I don't know."

Do you think you have better ideas than the Creator?

He sighed heavily. "No, of course not."

How successful have your ideas been so far, Young Pere?

He cleared his throat. "Uh . . . not too much."

Do you know why?

"Yes," he whispered. "My goals were not His will for me."

Think this through, Young Pere: what would've happened if you'd been successful? Honestly, do you really think you would have found joy? By killing Lemuel? Taking over the army? Sounds glorious and even romantic, but is it really? What would happen after all of that?

Young Pere considered. "I'd be waiting for the next man to take me out, wouldn't I?"

Yes. It'd be a miserable life, always looking over your shoulder. You would've become as paranoid and cruel as Lemuel, while bitter soldiers around you waited for their opportunities to kill you and become the next man in charge. What a nasty pattern.

He closed his eyes and rubbed them.

You look so tired, Young Pere. So weary, my sweet boy. Did you ever have a day of peace in the world?

"No," he sighed. "Not that I remember."

Then isn't it time to let go of the world?

Young Pere let the words wash over him, some remote part of him beginning to accept that maybe it wasn't such a bad idea.

Isn't it time to try someone else's ideas for a while? The Creator has a plan for you, Young Pere. It's been revealed to me, and my sweet boy, it's wonderful!

He rubbed his face again.

Do you trust me, Young Pere?

"Yes, Muggah," he whispered. There was no one else who would call him a sweet boy. Not even his imagination.

Then will you please, for my sake, try things the Creator's way? Just for a couple of days?

Finally Young Pere smiled, ever so faintly. "A couple of days, huh? And what happens in a couple of days?"

Well, we'll just have to see, together.

Together. The offer to stay with him was too much, too kind. How could he just easily say, "All right, you win. Let's go"?

Tears dripped from his eyes as he said, "I'm so sorry, Muggah! If I could just erase the last seven seasons, I would. I'm terrified that all of this is my fault, that I caused all of this to happen, that I caused you to die—"

No, no you didn't, Young Pere! Lemuel found his way here because of Amory. And she would've eventually found her way to the world with or without you. You went along just to, what . . . I don't know, suffer? But you don't have to anymore.

And you know what, Young Pere? Even if you DID cause all of this, even if Salem's downfall and my death were directly your fault, I would still love you and want you back. I would still forgive you, because I CHOOSE to love you.

And if I feel that way about you, how must your parents feel? I promise you, your mother and father wanted nothing more than to find you today. Lilla had to be told again and again that you could find your way back to us. She knew it was the Creator's will that they leave, and so she did the Creator's will, even though she didn't want to. But it's a good thing they did, because Lemuel went to the Eztates, Young Pere, arriving only moments after they'd left. Had your mother stayed, he would have found her.

Young Pere held his head. "I know what you're trying to say, but how could they ever forgive me? I don't even want to forgive myself!"

They've already forgiven you, Young Pere. Please, promise me now that you'll go back to them. Start to make things right: make things right with the Creator, and make things right with your rector. And then be ready for a wonderful future.

Young Pere scoffed. "You make it sound so easy, Muggah."

No, it's not entirely easy. But it will be much easier than continuing to live with this grief and pain. Nothing is worse than this despair that's shoving your soul into the ground right now. Choose to give it all up to the Creator, Young Pere.

Nothing in the last seven seasons in the world had been what it initially seemed to be. But now, as Young Pere looked up at the western mountains where the first bright stars were appearing, there seemed to be nothing more clear or obvious. Suddenly, it all seemed *almost* within his reach, as if joy—real joy—just might be around the corner . . . or at least a dozen miles to the west and on top of a mountain.

"All right, Muggah. I'll consider it."

Versa slumped between the shrubs in the forest—

No, she cowered. She knew she was cowering, trying to hide from soldiers who weren't looking for her.

In fact, they were more terrified than she was, and just a few paces away from her was a soldier in his thirties, wearing a mismatched uniform, curled up on the river bank and sobbing. He hadn't noticed her, nor had any of the others who came running through, screaming about the dead old woman, screaming about the dead guide, screaming about the Last Day, whatever terror *that* was, and just screaming to scream.

But everything had fallen quiet since the sun went down. Between the tree branches she watched it, orange-red, dip below the mountain ridge where the rest of Salem had taken refuge. And not for the first time she felt the nagging dread that she should've been there already. She sighed as she hugged her knees as best as she could and estimated she had about ten miles to walk in the morning.

She readjusted her pack to rest her head on it, making sure most of her was concealed in the scratchy vegetation around her, and closed her eyes in a futile attempt to sleep.

As Clark 14 plodded carefully in the darkness, Shem was sure there had never been a longer, more horrible ride. A couple of times his downcast eyes missed the slash marks and he had to backtrack. He really wasn't bothered by losing his way. It just helped to postpone the inevitable confrontation with Mahrree's family.

A few times he thought he glimpsed torchlight up on the ridge, but shook that off. Making any fire on this side of the ancient site wasn't allowed. They didn't want to give away their position to the army below, running in panic.

As he neared, Shem saw torches, several it seemed, but he couldn't bother to worry why they were lit. His heart couldn't handle any more conflicts. It couldn't handle anything. Peto would be on top of the torch problem, and once he heard the terrible news about his mother, who Shem failed to save, one of Shem's assistants could take over securing the last of the Salemites. All of them knew what to do anyway.

Clark 14 carried him to the meadow before the ridge. The area was filled with horses and, further up, the torches. Many of them started to move, and he groaned.

They were waiting for him.

He fell off Clark 14 and went to his knees, weakened by fatigue and grief. People began to rush to him, but before they reached him, he waved his arms to keep them away. "Please, no . . . you don't understand. Something terrible has happened, please. Let me get over on my own—"

But a familiar man put an arm around him. "Shem, I'm only here to help. We've been so worried about you. I'll sit with you until you're ready." Deck motioned for the other two dozen people to go back to the site, but one of Shem's assistants stood nearby holding a torch for light.

"Can we bring you something, Guide?" the assistant asked. "You look like you could use something to eat or drink."

Shem shook his head. "No, no."

Deck looked around. "Shem," he said quietly, "I have a feeling you're doing so poorly because . . . I don't see Mahrree."

Shem's shoulders began to shake. "Deck, Deck . . . Get me Calla. I need Calla!"

Now, oddly, Deck began to tremble. "Shem, I don't even know how to begin, but . . ."

Shem knew what it meant when someone started a sentence with such words. But it couldn't be . . .

He looked into Deck's devastated eyes and read into them far more than he wanted to. "Dear Creator, *no!*"

Deck's chin trembled. "The two arrows from the bowmen, Shem. They hit Calla. I'm so sorry—"

Shem took off in a frantic, clumsy crawl up the ridge, Deck and the assistant trying to help him up, but he pushed them away. Torches lined the route, waiting for his arrival. He ran, stumbling, over the ridge and down past the ruins to the Zenos' campsite. Thousands of people were there, completely silent, lighting the area.

The first thing Shem noticed were his three sons who caught him. He was a mess of tears and sobs as they guided him to his wife's side.

He knelt beside her and looked upon her sweet, still features.

It was too much. He crumpled beside her, unable to speak. He just put his hand on her cold face and wept uncontrollably.

The rest of the Salemites slowly went back to their camps, each of them praying their guide would somehow survive the night.

Mahrree looked at Perrin.

"I feel it too," he said. "Calla needs you now."

"He hasn't even been able to tell them about me, has he? Oh, poor Shem!"

Perrin leaned over and kissed her. "Go. I have a few things to discuss alone with Young Pere anyway."

She took his arm. "Tell him. Tell Young Pere *everything*."

Her husband squirmed. "Well, some of it, maybe. I *was* thinking of—"

Mahrree cut him off before he started into genuine hemming and hawing. "Make everything you experienced at his age *mean something*. Share with him your pain and also your triumphs. He needs to see that all is not lost. That *he* isn't lost. That you once were, and then you were found."

Perrin stared at the ground pensively, almost anxiously, then finally looked up and met Mahrree's eyes. "How did I end up with you? Why did you stay with me? There were some very rough times, I know. I just never understood how you understood so much. I still don't."

She kissed him on the lips. "You're the most perfect man in the world, and I loved and adored you every day. What more do we need to understand? Now, I need to go help Calla. And you need to help your grandson. It'll be all right. I know it. I feel it. You need to talk to him."

Perrin nodded his agreement, and Mahrree vanished.

In an instant she was by Calla's side. She was sitting with Shem's head in her lap, trying to stroke his cheek, but he didn't know it. He just sobbed hoarsely.

"Oh, Calla," Mahrree whispered to her friend. "I've never seen someone so devastated."

Calla kissed his head, her hand over his heart. "He's so unreachable, Mahrree. I've never known him to be so closed."

She sat down next to Calla and tried to touch Shem's chest. It was as hard as Young Pere's had been. "Why is he refusing comfort?"

Calla smiled faintly. "I think I know why. And it has to do with you, decades ago. That's why I was hoping we could reach him together."

Baffled, Mahrree looked at Calla. "Me? What did I do?"

"Actually, *you* did nothing at all . . ."

Honri had been waiting by the still body of his sister-in-law Calla, watching for Mahrree to arrive so he could hold her and let her rage and weep and wail about the loss of her best friend.

But she didn't come over the ridge as Shem had, stumbling and sobbing, to collapse next to her. Deckett Briter was still on the other side, likely holding Mahrree up. Honri glanced at Jaytsy, still searching the dark landscape for her mother, and he knew what needed to be done.

"I'll help Deck bring her over," Honri told her softly, and nodded in assurance to Peto, who was cradling Lilla.

"Thank you," Jaytsy whispered, looking like she desperately needed her husband back.

Honri started to jog toward the string of torches heading up and over the ridge, and realized Cephas Briter was by his side, also worried about his grandmother. Honri smiled inwardly. It'd be good to have some younger muscle around to help carry Mahrree over the hill. It had been a very long day, and Honri was wearier than he wished.

Silently the two men ran, and as they came over the top, they saw a large knot of men and women, with Deck in the middle of it. Strangely, however, they were looking around, as if missing something.

Suddenly Honri felt very uneasy. As they neared, they could hear the murmurs of, "Mrs. Shin . . ."

"Professor Shin . . ."

"Mahrree . . . isn't here."

He and Cephas shared the same inquiring look and didn't stop until they'd plowed through the crowd to reach Deck. His arms weren't filled with his weeping mother-in-law, but were folded worriedly.

"Where is she?" Honri demanded, probably louder than he should have. "Where's Mahrree?!"

Deck shrugged, turning around absurdly as if he could point her out in the torchlight. "We don't know!"

"What do you mean?" snapped Honri.

"Papa?" Cephas said, his tone anxious. "Wasn't she with Uncle Shem?"

"No!" Deck said, his voice trembling. "Shem arrived alone, absolutely devastated, and he didn't even know about Calla yet—"

Honri heard no more. Furious, he raced for a horse, the biggest and most rested Clark he could find, and grabbed the reins.

"What are you doing?" another man asked, taking his arm.

"Mahrree Shin's still down there!" Honri bellowed at the Salemites now converging on him. Deck was jogging over as well, but his son Cephas was searching the horses for another rested one.

"He just . . ." Honri began, angry that his brother-in-law had failed. "Shem just—" His heart was in his throat now, and he couldn't choke out the angry words that shouldn't have been uttered anyway.

Deck, with tears streaming down his dusty face, shook his head. "Honri, no. It's too dangerous. You can't go down," he said gently. "Nor you, son," he said to Cephas. "Get off that horse."

"But, Papa—"

"GET OFF THAT HORSE!" Deck shouted, and everyone around him shrank back.

Except for Honri. "I know the ways of the world, Deck," he told him, clutching the reins. "And I—"

"I know the ways of the world, too," Deck reminded him. "I spent twenty-two years in it. A lot longer than you did. Mahrree was there even longer. She knew what she was doing. She'd be livid if any of us thought we could beat the world better than she could. No. No one is to go down in the dark, unarmed, unprepared, searching uselessly in the night. Mahrree would say no, Peto would say no, Shem would say no, and most importantly, Perrin would say no."

Honri quavered, because something in Deck's voice had changed, and in his tone he thought just for a moment that he'd heard the general of Salem.

Cephas reluctantly dismounted, struggling not to cry, and Honri let the reins fall from his hands.

Deck stepped forward and caught Honri in an embrace, reaching out to grab his son and pull him into it as well.

Salemites respectfully drifted away as the three men sobbed together, helpless.

YOUNG PERE, I'M CONCERNED ABOUT YOU. LET'S TALK.

Young Pere mouthed the last words along with the voice in his head and smiled dimly. "Knew you were going to say that. What do you want to talk about?"

THE PAST SEVEN SEASONS. WHAT YOU'VE BEEN THROUGH. WHAT YOU NEED TO DO NOW.

Young Pere sighed and looked up into the black sky. He had made himself as comfortable as possible on the cold ground, before his grandfather suggested that the sofa lying on its side outside of the temple would be far better.

He was right. Young Pere felt guilty for putting his dirty boots on the pristine cloth, but no one was going to be putting it back into the temple. Besides, Puggah reminded him, it was only for Salemites and if Young Pere didn't make a bed of the sofa, some other soldier from the world would. The torn, blood-red curtain was also an adequate blanket, which he had wrapped around himself like a cloak.

"I'm thinking about everything I need to try to fix. A lot of it I can't." He sighed in frustration. "Puggah, you and Muggah really don't want to know what your grandson has been up to."

MUGGAH'S NOT HERE. SHE'S GONE TO THE ANCIENT TEMPLE SITE TO TRY TO REACH EVERYONE ELSE. IT'S JUST YOU AND ME, AND WE CAN TALK FREELY. AND YOUNG PERE, I ALREADY KNOW IT ALL. YOU KNOW I DO. THERE'S NOTHING IN LIFE THAT'S DONE IN SECRET. NOTHING IS SHIELDED FROM US ON THIS SIDE.

Young Pere closed his eyes and groaned. "I still don't know if I can do this tomorrow. I know I promised Muggah, but the more I think about it, the worse I feel. Why don't you just leave me to rot? As desperately as I want to go home, I don't deserve to be there. I betrayed my family, lied to everyone, violated nearly every rule I had been taught to keep, and . . ."

A LOT OF YOUR PAIN STARTED WITH YOUR TIME WITH LOLO, DIDN'T IT?

Young Pere opened his eyes to the stars. "Somehow that was the worst, like pounding the last nail into the coffin. Oh, I'm sorry," he winced. "Bad comparison—"

He heard the chuckle right next to him, as if Puggah sat on the armrest next to his head. *I KNOW WHAT YOU MEAN. I WASN'T IN THERE WHEN IT HAPPENED, YOU KNOW.*

Young Pere smiled at Puggah's response, but the smile faded fast. "I still felt the smallest glimmer of light until that night. As if my betrayal of my family and Salem wasn't enough, then I had to go and be with Lolo. It was as if I smashed the last candle. I've never been able to fully crawl out of that grave. You know what I mean."

VERY PERCEPTIVE. THAT'S WHAT HAPPENED EXACTLY. I WAS WITH YOU THE ENTIRE TIME, EXCEPT THEN. I LEFT AND REFUSED TO WATCH YOU BURY YOURSELF BY SO CASUALLY PLAYING WITH THE POWER TO GIVE LIFE. IT'S ALMOST AS SERIOUS AS TRYING TO TAKE A LIFE. BUT YOU CALLED FOR ME TO COME BACK. THAT WAS THE FIRST STEP, BUT LONG AGO. NOW YOU NEED TO TAKE SOME MORE. BUT YOU CAN'T DO THIS ALONE.

Young Pere stared up at the stars, feeling their depth, feeling his grandfather, and also feeling hope. But immediately that hope disappeared. "Puggah, you just don't understand. I'm in too deep."

YOUNG PERE, I DO UNDERSTAND. FAR TOO WELL. THAT'S WHY THIS IS MY CALLING, WHY I VOLUNTEERED TO FOLLOW YOU.

"What do you mean?" Young Pere whispered.

There was a cosmic sigh. *YOU AND I ARE MORE ALIKE THAN I CARE TO ADMIT. MAYBE IT HAS TO DO WITH THE NAME. BUT YOU AND I WALKED THE SAME PATHS, JUST MANY YEARS APART.*

Young Pere sat up, keeping his red curtain wrapped around him. "Really?"

I WANT YOU TO REALIZE THAT YOUR PAST DOESN'T HAVE TO BE IN YOUR FUTURE. YOU CAN LEAVE IT BACK THERE. TURN AWAY FROM THAT LIFE, THOSE ATTITUDES, AND START NEW AGAIN.

"Do you realize what I have to *do*, Puggah?"

YES. TALK WITH YOUR RECTOR. CONFESS ALL THAT YOU DID. THAT'S THE FIRST STEP. THAT'S WHAT I DID IN EDGE FOR SEVERAL WEEKS WHEN I WAS EIGHTEEN.

Young Pere scoffed. "But my rector is my *father*, Puggah! Do you realize what I have to tell him? Everything?!"

HOGAL DENSAL WAS MUCH MORE THAN MY RECTOR, YOUNG PERE. HE WAS MY GREAT UNCLE BUT ALSO LIKE A GRANDFATHER TO ME. IT WASN'T AS PAINFUL AS YOU'RE IMAGINING. HOLDING ON TO ALL OF IT HURTS MUCH MORE THAN LETTING IT GO. LIKE GETTING A SPLINTER IN YOUR FOOT AND INSISTING ON WALKING ON IT. IT'S FAR BETTER TO JUST SIT DOWN AND LET YOUR FATHER YANK IT OUT. WHY HOLD ON TO THAT

PAIN?

Young Pere exhaled. "What will he think of me? That's my biggest fear, I suppose. That he'll never look at me the same way. That I'll always be *that* son."

I DIDN'T REALIZE YOU WERE STILL SO PRIDEFUL. YOU DON'T GIVE PETO ENOUGH CREDIT. YOU THINK HE LOVES YOU LESS BECAUSE OF WHAT YOU'VE DONE? HE DOESN'T. WHEN YOU BECOME A FATHER YOU'LL UNDERSTAND. HE ALREADY KNOWS YOU'RE HURTING. HE CAN FEEL IT, MILES AWAY. THERE'S NOTHING HE WANTS MORE THAN TO HELP YOU LEARN HOW TO GIVE THAT PAIN TO THE CREATOR. ALL OF HIS YEARS OF EXPERIENCE HAVE BEEN LEADING UP TO THIS MOMENT, SO HE CAN HELP HIS SON.

"It will just be . . . too hard."

YOU MEAN, TOO HUMBLING? TO CONFESS WHAT A FAILURE YOU WERE? YES, IT IS HUMBLING. I KNOW. I'VE BEEN THROUGH IT. I WAS BARELY A TEENAGER WHEN I REALIZED I WAS TO BE THE FUTURE HIGH GENERAL OF THE WORLD. I DECIDED THAT MEANT NOTHING SHOULD BE KEPT FROM ME. NO GLORY, NO PRIVILEGES, AND CERTAINLY NO GIRLS. I HAD A HERD FOLLOWING ME AROUND BY THE TIME I WAS SIXTEEN, JUST LIKE YOU. YES, I NOTICED YOU HAD A FLOCK OF GIRLS EYEING YOU IN SALEM. KIND OF HARD NOT TO NOTICE. BUT THE GIRLS WHO WERE TRYING TO GET MY ATTENTION WERE, SHALL WE SAY, FAR MORE WILLING THAN THE GIRLS IN SALEM. ALL I HAD TO DO WAS LOOK AT ONE OF THEM, AND SHE'D FOLLOW ME ANYWHERE AND DO ANYTHING. I WAS ON TOP OF THE WORLD, YOUNG PERE. ANYTHING I WANTED I COULD TAKE. NO ONE WOULD DENY HIGH GENERAL SHIN'S SON.

"I was trying to get that kind of status myself," Young Pere admitted.

I KNOW. AND HOW DID IT MAKE YOU FEEL TO GET IT, WHEN YOU WERE LIEUTENANT LEK THORNE? HONESTLY, NOW.

Young Pere sighed. "I was so lonely in the mansion. No one really cared about me. I even thought about finding some girls to—"

YES, I KNOW.

Young Pere winced to think his grandfather knew of his late night fantasies. "I was miserable," he whispered. "Empty. Lost."

EXACTLY. WITH ME, IT DIDN'T MATTER HOW PRETTY THE GIRL OR HOW WILLING SHE WAS, IT NEVER FELT RIGHT. BY THE TIME I WAS EIGHTEEN I WAS POSITIVELY CONTEMPTIBLE. ARROGANT. HEARTLESS. CALLOUS. AND UTTERLY MISERABLE. I COULDN'T UNDERSTAND WHY. ARMY OFFICERS ARE SUPPOSED TO BE FULL OF PRIDE! I WAS JUST STARTING EARLY. NO

ONE REALLY NOTICED HOW WRETCHED I WAS. BUT HOGAL DENSAL KNEW I WAS MISERABLE, BECAUSE THE CREATOR TOLD HIM TO BRING ME TO EDGE TO TEACH ME SOME HUMILITY. THE BOY THAT I WAS? WELL, YOUNG PERE, I HARDLY LIKE TO THINK ABOUT HIM. I RARELY DO. HE'S MOSTLY JUST A FADED MEMORY THAT I RECALL FROM TIME TO TIME, IF ONLY TO REMIND MYSELF NEVER TO BE THAT WAY AGAIN, AND TO REMEMBER TO THANK THE CREATOR FOR GIVING ME ANOTHER CHANCE. YOUNG PERE, LET HIM GIVE YOU ANOTHER CHANCE.

Young Pere sat with his mouth slightly open. It never occurred to him that nearly sixty years ago people had the same kind of troubles he did. Then again, why should anything be different?

He mulled over the last sentence of his grandfather. *He* was Perrin Shin, after all. One of the greatest men to ever live, and even declared so by the Creator's guide at his memorial service. Of course the Creator would give *Perrin Shin* another chance. He needed it, deserved it. But his grandson? Who was he? Just an inferior copy.

"I don't feel worthy."

THAT'S BECAUSE YOU'RE NOT. NO ONE IS, YOUNG PERE. BUT IF WE WAITED UNTIL WE WERE WORTHY TO APPROACH THE CREATOR, NO ONE EVER WOULD. HE CHANGES YOU TO BE WORTHY. THAT'S HIS WORK. YOU HAVE TO MAKE THE FIRST STEP TO COME TO HIM, THEN WILLINGLY DO WHATEVER HE REQUIRES. YOU STILL HAVE SO MUCH AHEAD OF YOU. SO MUCH POTENTIAL.

Young Pere scoffed quietly. "I know what you're suggesting, Puggah, but who would want someone like me? After all of this? You said when I become a father, but what kind of girl would want to marry me?"

NO ONE'S PERFECT, YOUNG PERE. EVERYONE HAS LESS-THAN-IMPRESSIVE MOMENTS. WE ALL HOPE SOMEONE WILL FORGIVE US OF THOSE MOMENTS AND LET US MOVE ON. COULD YOU LOVE A YOUNG WOMAN WHO MADE MISTAKES IN HER PAST BUT FEELS ABOUT THEM NOW THE WAY YOU FEEL ABOUT YOURS?

He pondered that. "I think . . . I think *I could.*"

THEN THERE IS SOMEONE FOR YOU, OUT THERE, WHO WILL LOVE YOU AS WELL. SHE DOESN'T NEED TO KNOW ABOUT YOUR PAST. SHE ONLY NEEDS TO KNOW ABOUT THE KIND OF MAN YOU ARE NOW AND THE KIND OF MAN YOU WANT TO BECOME.

"Puggah, can I ask . . . does Muggah know about *your* past?"

There was another cosmic sigh.

YES, SHE DOES. SHE DIDN'T KNOW ABOUT IT UNTIL LATER. I NEVER

INTENDED TO TELL HER, BUT CIRCUMSTANCES AROSE THAT, WELL, IT JUST SEEMED WISER TO LET HER UNDERSTAND.

"If I may ask . . . how did she take it?"

WELL, AFTER A VERY, <u>VERY</u> LONG PAUSE, SHE SAID THAT SOMEHOW SHE ALWAYS KNEW. SHE KNEW I WAS A VERY DIFFERENT MAN THAN I HAD STARTED OUT AS, AND THAT SHE WAS GRATEFUL FOR WHAT I HAD BECOME.

"Just one more question . . . *why* did you tell her?"

Silence.

Then finally,

YOUNG PERE, YOU SHOULD PROBABLY KNOW. IT HAS TO DO WITH THE THORNES, INTERESTINGLY ENOUGH. YOU SEE, WHEN WE WERE IN IDUMEA FOR THE DINNER—YOUR FATHER WAS ALMOST FOURTEEN, YOUR AUNT JUST TURNING FIFTEEN—MAHRREE DISCOVERED THAT I HAD BEEN IN EDGE WHEN I WAS EIGHTEEN. SHE FELT BAD ABOUT THAT, WISHING WE WOULD HAVE MET THEN, INSTEAD OF TEN YEARS LATER. I TOLD HER THAT SHE WOULDN'T HAVE LIKED ME MUCH AS AN EIGHTEEN-YEAR-OLD. THAT NIGHT AS WE WENT TO BED SHE ASKED ME WHY. SO . . . I TOLD HER. NO DETAILS, JUST GENERALITIES. ENOUGH FOR HER TO GET A CLEAR IDEA AS TO WHAT KIND OF A CONTEMPTIBLE YOUNG MAN I WAS. I WAS TO MEET THE ADMINISTRATORS IN THE MORNING, AND SHE WAS TERRIFIED ABOUT THAT, SO AT LEAST OUR BEDTIME DISCUSSION GOT HER MIND OFF OF THE ADMINISTRATORS AND ON TO SOMETHING COMPLETELY DIFFERENT.

I DON'T KNOW WHEN I'VE EVER KNOWN HER TO BE SO QUIET. I THOUGHT MAYBE SHE HAD FALLEN ASLEEP AND I'D HAVE TO GIVE HER ALL THAT AWFUL INFORMATION AGAIN WHEN SHE WOKE UP. BUT THEN SHE FINALLY SAID SHE HAD SOMEHOW ALWAYS KNOWN, BUT ALSO KNEW MY PAST WAS NOTHING SHE NEEDED TO WORRY ABOUT. I WAS A DIFFERENT MAN.

BUT A FEW DAYS LATER, WHEN WE HAD THE DINNER AND I SAW LEMUEL EYEING MY DAUGHTER, I KNEW I COULDN'T LET HAPPEN TO HER WHAT HAPPENED TO MANY GIRLS WHO LOOKED AT ME. YOU SEE, YOUNG PERE, I KNEW WHAT KIND OF A MAN LEMUEL WAS, BECAUSE I KNEW WHAT QAYIN WAS LIKE, AND WHAT LEMUEL'S MOTHER WENT THROUGH BEING MARRIED TO HIM.

The voice went quiet in Young Pere's head.

"Go on," he encouraged.

I DON'T REALLY KNOW HOW TO EXPLAIN THIS . . . YOU SEE, LEMUEL'S MOTHER VERSULA WAS ONE OF MY FOLLOWERS, SHALL WE SAY. AND OUR PATHS CROSSED MORE THAN ONCE, I'M ASHAMED TO ADMIT. OUR FAMILIES WERE ALWAYS INVOLVED WITH EACH OTHER, SINCE HER FATHER

WORKED FOR MY FATHER.

The voice paused again, trying to find the words.

Young Pere held his breath, waiting.

I WOULDN'T HAVE HAD TO TELL MY WIFE ANY OF THIS, EXCEPT THAT AFTER THE DINNER IN IDUMEA, THE NIGHT THAT LEMUEL STARTED LOOKING AT JAYTSY, MY WIFE INNOCENTLY SAID THAT MAYBE WE SHOULD GET TO KNOW THE THORNE FAMILY BETTER. THE CUSHES AND SHINS HAD BEEN FRIENDS FOR SO MANY YEARS, AFTER ALL. MAYBE WE SHOULD INVITE THEM OVER FOR DINNER A COUPLE OF NIGHTS LATER, TO LET US WATCH LEMUEL AND JAYTSY MORE CLOSELY.

"But you had to leave early, right? To bring the caravan of food to Edge. Is that why the dinner never happened?"

OH, THAT'S NOT THE ONLY REASON, YOUNG PERE. YOU SEE, VERSULA HAD MARRIED QAYIN THORNE WHEN SHE WAS SEVENTEEN. HE WAS A FEW YEARS OLDER, ALREADY GRADUATED AND AN OFFICER. BUT THE MARRIAGE WAS NOT A HAPPY ONE.

AFTER I CAME BACK FROM EDGE THAT WEEDING SEASON WHEN I WAS EIGHTEEN, I ENROLLED AT THE UNIVERSITY AND WAS LIVING IN THE DORMITORY. VERSULA HAD BEEN MARRIED FOR OVER A YEAR BY THEN, AND I HADN'T GIVEN HER A SECOND THOUGHT SINCE HER WEDDING. IN FACT, I WAS WORKING VERY HARD TO NOT THINK OF ANYTHING I SHOULDN'T DURING THAT FIRST SEASON BACK. I HAD THREE ROOMMATES WHO MADE THAT VERY DIFFICULT FOR ME. MY REPUTATION PRECEDED ME, AND MANY STUDENTS WERE HOPING I WOULD TEACH THEM A THING OR TWO ABOUT GIRLS. WHY I STAYED IN MY ROOM STUDYING WHILE THEY WENT OUT TO ROAM THE UNIVERSITY GROUNDS IN SEARCH OF COMPANY, THEY SIMPLY COULDN'T UNDERSTAND. WHAT THEY DIDN'T REALIZE IS THAT MOST OF THE TIME I WAS READING THE WRITINGS, TRYING TO REMEMBER ALL THAT HOGAL HAD TAUGHT ME, TRYING TO KEEP TO THE PATH I HAD CHOSEN.

ONE OF THOSE EVENINGS, WHEN MY ROOMMATES LEFT TO A MEAD PARTY, I HEARD A KNOCK ON MY DOOR. TO MY SURPRISE THERE STOOD VERSULA CUSH THORNE. HER EYES WERE RED WITH CRYING, AND SHE TOOK HER FINGER AND DRAGGED IT ACROSS MY FOREHEAD, ALONG THE SCAR SHE GAVE ME WHEN SHE SMACKED ME WITH A STICK WHEN WE WERE YOUNGER. SHE SAID, "I ALWAYS REGRETTED DOING THAT TO YOU. BUT AT LEAST I GAVE YOU SOME WAY TO ALWAYS REMEMBER ME." THEN SHE HANDED ME THE BIGGEST TEMPTATION OF MY NEW LIFE. SHE ASKED ME IF I COULD GIVE HER SOMETHING, SO SHE COULD ALWAYS HAVE A REMEMBRANCE OF ME IN HER LIFE.

"Oh, Puggah. Whoa. Was she meaning . . .?"

OH YES, SHE WAS MEANING . . . THAT. AND I HAD THE SAME REACTION YOU DID: WHOA. I JUST STOOD THERE, STARING AT THIS BEAUTIFUL WOMAN WHO WANTED MY 'COMFORT,' KNOWING FULL WELL MY ROOMMATES WOULDN'T BE BACK UNTIL DAWN.

Young Pere was hit with a thought that nearly knocked him breathless. Perhaps there was another reason Perrin Shin was so opposed to Lemuel Thorne trying to court Aunt Jaytsy. It was something he'd said when they were on the marking trail before Young Pere left, how when Puggah looked back to see Thorne pursuing him in the forest, that Lemuel regarded him as a father abandoning him—

"Uh, Puggah . . . I'm not sure how to ask this, but—" he swallowed hard, "—is Lemuel Thorne my *uncle?*"

The silence went on for too long.

"Oh no," Young Pere gasped. "Oh no . . . oh no . . ."

I DON'T KNOW.

Young Pere's heart must have stopped, because he felt everything else in the world go deathly still as if the cosmos themselves sighed, long and heavy.

YOUNG PERE, I SENT HER AWAY THAT NIGHT. I WAS A CHANGED MAN. I TOOK VERSULA BY THE ARMS, TOLD HER THAT WASN'T WHAT I DID ANYMORE, AND TURNED HER AWAY. JUST LIKE THAT. SLAMMED THE DOOR BEHIND HER. I WAS VERY SELF-RIGHTEOUS.

Young Pere sighed in relief but remembered. "Wait. Then . . . why did you say *you don't know.*"

Again, there was no response for far too long.

AFTER ALL THESE YEARS IT'S STILL SO HARD. I CAN'T BELIEVE I'M STRUGGLING TO GET THIS OUT, BUT . . .

"So you know how I feel about tomorrow," Young Pere said carefully.

OH, YES. FAR, FAR TOO WELL. YOU SEE, THAT NIGHT I DID SEND HER AWAY. FULL OF RESOLVE TO BE OBEDIENT AND GOOD AND SOLID, I KNEW I'D NEVER HAVE A PROBLEM AGAIN.

The quiet pauses were getting to Young Pere. "But . . ."

BUT . . . I SAW HER AGAIN. ABOUT A YEAR LATER, AT A DANCE MY MOTHER FORCED ME TO ATTEND. THEY HAD THOSE A LOT—THE WEALTHY OF IDUMEA SHOWING OFF THEIR MANSIONS BY HOSTING DANCES. QAYIN WASN'T THERE—HE WAS AT SOME FORT FOR SOMETHING. BUT VERSULA ATTENDED, AS ONE OF THE HOPING-TO-BE-ELITE OF THE CITY. SHE LOOKED MISERABLE, AND I, TRYING TO BE GALLANT, ASKED HER TO

DANCE. *IT WAS CLEAR THAT SHE WAS DEEPLY WORRIED ABOUT SOMETHING, AND I TOOK HER ASIDE TO TALK. SHE TOLD ME THAT SHE'D BEEN MARRIED FOR TWO YEARS BUT HADN'T YET CONCEIVED. QAYIN WAS GROWING ABUSIVE, BLAMING HER FOR NOT PRODUCING A SON.*

Again, silence.

I'M STILL NOT ENTIRELY SURE WHAT CAME OVER ME, WHY CRADLING HER AS SHE SOBBED STIRRED SO MUCH IN ME, AND . . . OH, YOUNG PERE. I KNEW BETTER! I KNEW SO, SO MUCH BETTER! BUT I WAS WEAK. I KNOW YOU THOUGHT ME WEAK AT TIMES, BUT YOUNG PERE—I REALLY WAS.

Breathless with dread, Young Pere whispered, "What happened?"

I KNEW ALL OF MY ROOMMATES WERE AT THE DANCE, SO I TOOK HER BACK TO MY DORM ROOM WHICH WASN'T TOO FAR AWAY SO WE COULD TALK IN PRIVATE, AND . . .

"No, Puggah."

I DIDN'T INTEND FOR ANYTHING TO HAPPEN . . . WELL, THAT'S NOT ENTIRELY TRUE. I WAS A CHANGED MAN, BUT THE WORSE PART OF ME WAS STILL THERE, SHOVED INTO A CORNER BUT NOT SECURED VERY WELL. I TOOK VERSULA TO MY DORM ROOM SO I COULD COMFORT HER, OR SO I TOLD MYSELF . . . DEEP DOWN THAT WRETCHED PART OF ME WAS HOPING SOMETHING MORE WOULD HAPPEN, THOUGH. OUR RELATIONSHIP HAD BEEN ON AGAIN, OFF AGAIN THROUGHOUT OUR TEENAGE YEARS. SHE'D STARTED SEEING QAYIN AFTER ONE OF OUR SPATS, AND I THOUGHT IT WAS ONLY TO MAKE ME JEALOUS BECAUSE I'D DO THE SAME THING TO HER WITH OTHER GIRLS. I WAS RATHER SURPRISED WHEN HE PROPOSED TO HER WHEN WE WERE SEVENTEEN, AND SHE ACCEPTED.

I'M A VERY COMPETITIVE MAN, YOUNG PERE, MUCH TO MY DETRIMENT AS YOU KNOW, AND I TOOK THAT AS A LOSS. I GUESS THAT EVENING I WAS THINKING I COULD 'WIN' AGAIN, EVEN UP THE SCORE. AND SO I HELD HER AS SHE WEPT AND TOLD HER HOW SHE DESERVED SO MUCH BETTER, AND THEN SHE BEGAN TO KISS MY NECK WHICH SHE KNEW FROM PAST EXPERIENCE UNLEASHED THAT WRETCHED PART OF ME—

"But . . . you didn't," breathed Young Pere.

I TOLD MYSELF I COULD STOP AT ANY POINT, THAT SHE NEEDED TO FEEL AFFECTION AND LOVE . . . THEN SHE REACHED MY LIPS AND KISSED ME.

Young Pere held his breath in dread.

AND NO, I DIDN'T STOP MYSELF.

Young Pere closed his eyes, squeezing out tears. "Oh, Puggah."

I'VE NEVER BEEN MORE ASHAMED OF ANYTHING ELSE IN MY ENTIRE LIFE. YOUNG PERE, THAT NIGHT AFTER YOU AND LOLO—

"Don't say it."

WASN'T GOING TO. I WAS GOING TO SKIP TO THE PART WHERE YOU WERE LAYING THERE, WISHING TO DIE. WHEN YOU WERE SICK AT HEART AND LOWER THAN THE MUD. BECAUSE—

"Because you knew. You knew exactly how I felt."

WE BOTH KNEW BETTER. WE BOTH WERE ABSOLUTELY STUPID. WE BOTH WISHED TO DIE. NO, NOT DIE; THAT'D MEAN FACING THE CREATOR. WE BOTH WANTED TO "CEASE TO EXIST."

"Oh, Puggah," Young Pere said again, aware that tears were trickling down his face, and must have been for quite some time. He wasn't sure who they were for—himself, his grandfather, or both of them.

Both of them.

"You were there that night," he recalled. "After Lolo and I—you were sitting on that rock, rocking back and forth, weren't you?"

AND GRIEVING FOR YOU, BECAUSE THEY NAMED YOU TOO ACCURATELY. I KNEW, YOUNG PERE. AND I KNOW. I KNOW HOW IT FEELS TO BETRAY YOURSELF AND THE CREATOR. TO TURN YOUR BACK ON EVERYTHING YOU KNOW IS RIGHT AND TO FEEL EVERYTHING YOU'VE HELD SO PRECIOUS SHRIVEL INSIDE.

"Yes," Young Pere whispered. "That was exactly it. What did you do?"

I BECAME SICK. BEFORE VERSULA EVEN FINISHED GETTING DRESSED, I BECAME HORRIBLY NAUSEATED AS I FINALLY REALIZED—A FEW MINUTES TOO LATE—WHAT I HAD DONE. THAT WASN'T SUPPOSED TO BE ME ANYMORE! I'D LEFT THAT ALL BEHIND ME! I'D FIXED IT ALL! I WAS FORGIVEN AND PROGRESSING, BUT I CRASHED? AGAIN!?

AS SOON AS SHE LEFT, I VOMITED, AND DID SO FOR THE REST OF THE NIGHT, TERRIFIED AT HAVING DISAPPOINTED THE CREATOR. I KNEW HIS SPIRIT AND INFLUENCE HAD LEFT ME BECAUSE EVERYTHING INSIDE OF ME HAD GONE NUMB AND DEAD. THERE WAS NO HOPE, NONE WHATSOEVER. I KNEW MY SOUL WAS LOST.

BY THE MORNING, I WAS SO EMPTY AND DEPRESSED THAT MY ROOMMATES COULDN'T GET ME UP TO BREAKFAST. ONE OF THEM BROUGHT ME SOME TOAST BEFORE HE WENT TO CLASS, BUT I COULDN'T EAT IT. I WANTED TO CEASE EXISTING. I NEEDED TO DISSOLVE AWAY. BY AFTERNOON, I WAS SO WEAK AND DESPONDENT THAT EVERYONE THOUGHT I WAS SERIOUSLY ILL. THEY SENT FOR MY FATHER, AND HE AND TWO ROOMMATES CARRIED ME TO THE INFIRMARY OF COMMAND SCHOOL. I WOULDN'T EAT. I WOULDN'T DRINK. I COULDN'T EVEN MAKE EYE

CONTACT. YOUNG PERE, IT WAS AS IF THE REFUSER HAD TAKEN ME OVER, BODY AND SOUL, AND WAS INTENT ON DRAGGING ME ALL THE WAY DOWN TO THE DARK DESERTS THAT DAY.

"Oh, Puggah," Young Pere quietly wept. "I know. I know that feeling."

YES, YOU DO. MY POOR BOY, YOU DO.

Young Pere wiped his nose on the red curtain, realizing something. "But . . . you didn't 'cease to exist.' What happened?"

MY MOTHER SAT BY MY BEDSIDE, WEEPING AND TRYING TO GET ME TO DRINK, BUT I COULDN'T. NOR COULD I BRING MYSELF TO TELL HER WHAT I'D DONE. MY PARENTS DIDN'T KNOW WHAT A DETESTABLE TEENAGER I'D BEEN, NOR DID THEY KNOW HOW FAR I'D COME WITH HOGAL. MY FATHER, NEVER ONE FOR PRAYING OR READING THE WRITINGS—AT LEAST, NOT UNTIL MUCH LATER IN LIFE—PANICKED. HE WAS SURE HIS ONLY SON WAS ABOUT TO DIE BECAUSE OF SOME STRANGE MALADY. SO HE SENT A MESSENGER TO MY UNCLE HOGAL, BEGGING HIM TO COME PRAY OVER ME.

WHEN HE TOLD ME THAT HOGAL WAS COMING, I GREW EVEN WORSE, DRY-HEAVING IN TERROR. OH, WHAT WOULD HOGAL THINK OF ME! AFTER ALL WE'D GONE THROUGH, AFTER ALL I'D TRY TO BECOME—HE'D HATE ME FOR UNDOING IT ALL, I WAS SURE. HE WAS IN HIS SEVENTIES THEN, AND WOULD HAVE TO TRAVEL ALL THE WAY TO IDUMEA JUST TO SEE WHAT A HUGE DISAPPOINTMENT I'D BECOME?

Young Pere's chin was trembling violently. "I know. I know that feeling, too."

I KNOW YOU DO. YOU SEE NOW WHY I'M HERE, RIGHT? WHY I WAS THE BEST CHOICE TO ACCOMPANY YOU?

"We're a pair of Peres," Young Pere said miserably.

BUT HERE COMES THE GOOD PART, YOUNG PERE: HOGAL CAME, FASTER THAN I THOUGHT POSSIBLE. I STILL REMEMBER SEEING HIM RUSH THROUGH THE INFIRMARY TO MY BEDSIDE. I'D BEEN ILL FOR THREE DAYS BY THEN, LOSING WEIGHT AND TOO WEAK TO MOVE. BUT I STARTED CRYING WHEN HOGAL GRIPPED MY HAND. "PRAY FOR HIM!" MY MOTHER BEGGED. "SAVE HIM, HOGAL!" BUT HOGAL KNEW WHAT WAS REALLY WRONG: THE CREATOR HAD TOLD HIM THAT MY ILLNESS WASN'T BECAUSE OF SOMETHING I ATE OR CAUGHT, BUT BECAUSE OF SOMETHING I'D DONE.

SO HOGAL, BEING THE WISEST MAN I'VE EVER KNOWN, SAID THAT WE NEEDED TO BE ALONE. HE HAD THEM PUSH MY COT INTO A PRIVATE ROOM, TOLD MY PARENTS HE NEEDED TO PRAY FOR ME, ALONE—AT THAT POINT, THEY WOULD HAVE AGREED TO ANYTHING—AND HE LOCKED THE DOOR

BEHIND HIM. THEN HE SAT DOWN AND SAID, "MY BOY—YOU MESSED UP, DIDN'T YOU?"

"I messed up, too, Puggah," Young Pere said, hugging his legs.

SEE? ALREADY YOU'RE DOING BETTER THAN I WAS. YOU CAN SAY THE WORDS—AND YOU CAN SAY THEM TO YOUR FATHER, JUST LIKE THAT. BUT I COULDN'T BECAUSE OF MY CONDITION. EVENTUALLY, SOMEHOW, I WHISPERED WHAT I DID WITH VERSULA—WITH MY FORMER GIRLFRIEND AND NOW ANOTHER MAN'S WIFE. AND YOU KNOW WHAT HOGAL DID?

Young Pere was afraid to answer, afraid to guess.

HE WEPT WITH ME. HE LAID DOWN ON THAT COT NEXT TO ME, HELD ME IN HIS ARMS AS IF I WERE A LITTLE BOY, AND JUST WEPT.

Young Pere felt the tiniest flicker of hope.

AND THEN HE SAID THE WORDS I DIDN'T DARE BELIEVE. HE SAID, "PERRIN, MY BOY—NO ONE CAN FALL SO FAR THAT THE CREATOR CAN'T PICK THEM BACK UP AGAIN."

Still Young Pere had no response, because those words did border on the unbelievable.

I KNOW. I DIDN'T BELIEVE HIM EITHER. BUT YOUNG PERE, I WANTED TO. MORE THAN ANYTHING IN THE WORLD I WANTED TO BELIEVE THAT I COULD MAYBE HAVE ONE MORE CHANCE. ONE MORE OPPORTUNITY TO PROVE MYSELF. TO FIX THINGS. TO FIGURE OUT WHY I FELL TO THAT TEMPTATION, AND TO MAKE SURE I NEVER, EVER DID IT AGAIN.

"But I don't think it'll work for me—"

STOP RIGHT THERE. THAT'S THE REFUSER, YOUNG PERE. HE WAS FIGHTING HARD IN MY HEAD, TOO. I KNOW THOSE WORDS, THOSE AWFUL, HORRIBLE WORDS: "IT WON'T WORK FOR ME. WHAT I'VE DONE IS DIFFERENT. I HAVE GONE TOO FAR. NO ONE WILL WANT ME BACK. IT'S TOO LATE FOR ME." ANY OF THAT SOUND FAMILIAR?

"All of it."

YES, I KNOW. AND I ALSO KNOW THIS: IT'S ALL A LIE, YOUNG PERE! IT'S NOT TOO MUCH TO COME BACK FROM. IT'S FIXABLE, ALL OF IT. LOOK FORWARD IN MY LIFE, YOUNG PERE. DID I FIX IT? DID I IMPROVE?

How Puggah could understand any of his words was beyond Young Pere's comprehension, because he was blubbering so hard when he said, "You're the best man I ever knew."

WELL, I THINK THAT'S A GROSS OVERSTATEMENT, BUT I APPRECIATE THE SENTIMENT. BUT REALIZE, YOUNG PERE, THAT I WASN'T TO BEGIN WITH. I WAS GIVEN ANOTHER CHANCE. YET AGAIN. AS HOGAL HELD ME, HE TOLD ME I COULD REGAIN ALL THE GROUND I'D LOST, AND LEAVE THAT FOR AN EVEN HIGHER GROUND. I WAS NOT BEYOND SAVING, AND YOUNG

PERE, IF I WASN'T BEYOND SAVING, YOU CERTAINLY AREN'T. IF WE'RE RANKING THE HORRIBLENESS OF PAST DEEDS, I THINK I'D WIN. SEE HOW MISERABLY COMPETITIVE I AM?

"So what did Uncle Hogal do with you?"

HE MADE ME DRINK SOME WATER, FIRST OF ALL. WIPED OFF MY FACE NEXT, THEN PRAYED WITH ME. THEN, HE MADE ME PRAY BY MYSELF. I NEEDED TO NOT ONLY CONFESS TO MY RECTOR HOGAL DENSAL, BUT I NEEDED TO CONFESS TO THE CREATOR, WHO ALREADY KNEW IT ALL BUT NEEDED ME TO ACKNOWLEDGE IT. AFTER THAT VERY DIFFICULT PRAYER, I ACTUALLY FELT A LITTLE BETTER. AS IF I'D BEEN SHOVED HARD OFF OF A TRAIL BUT HAD CRAWLED BACK TO FIND IT AGAIN. I HAD TO CLIMB BACK UP THAT MOUNTAIN, BUT AT LEAST I HAD THE RIGHT PATH AGAIN. THEN, HOGAL TOLD ME WE HAD SOME DIFFICULT TIMES AHEAD, ESPECIALLY IF VERSULA CONCEIVED.

Young Pere sagged back into the sofa. "I'd already forgotten about that."

WELL, I CERTAINLY DIDN'T. HOGAL AND I DISCUSSED WHAT THE CORRECT AND HONORABLE THING WOULD BE, AND IF VERSULA FOUND HERSELF EXPECTING, I WOULD PUBLICLY CONFESS WHAT HAD HAPPENED AND TAKE THE CONSEQUENCES. THAT MEANT QAYIN COULD HAVE FOUGHT ME FOR HER WITH HIS CHOICE OF WEAPON, OR ABANDONED HER AND I'D HAVE TO MARRY HER.

I WAS SICK ABOUT THAT FOR WEEKS, WAITING TO HEAR IF SOMETHING WAS HAPPENING WITH HER. I WAS SLOWLY IMPROVING HEALTH-WISE; AFTER THREE MORE DAYS I WAS ABLE TO LEAVE THE INFIRMARY AND WAS GETTING MY STRENGTH BACK. MY MOTHER BROUGHT ME HOME TO THEIR MANSION FOR ANOTHER WEEK, WITH HOGAL TENDING TO ME DAY AND NIGHT. MY PARENTS NEVER SUSPECTED I WAS ANYTHING ELSE BUT VIOLENTLY ILL. ONE DAY VERSULA CAME TO VISIT, HAVING HEARD OF HOW ILL I WAS, BUT I COULDN'T BEAR TO FACE HER.

ONCE I WAS WELL ENOUGH TO RETURN TO SCHOOL, HOGAL HEADED HOME TO EDGE, BUT NOT BEFORE MAKING ME PROMISE TO WRITE HIM EVERY DAY ABOUT WHAT I WAS THINKING, READING, PRAYING, AND DOING TO MAKE SURE NOTHING LIKE THIS EVER HAPPENED AGAIN. AND I DID. I WROTE HIM PAGES-LONG LETTERS, AND HE RESPONDED WITH JUST AS LONG OF LETTERS BACK. BY THE WAY, MY GRADES WERE DISMAL THAT SEMESTER.

Young Pere almost smiled.

THEN, THE MESSAGE I WAS FEARING FINALLY ARRIVED. IN VERSULA'S HAND WAS ONLY FOUR WORDS: "IT WORKED. THANK YOU."

Through his tears, Young Pere scoffed. "She *thanked* you?! Wait a minute—she *wanted* that to happen, didn't she?"

WE WILLINGLY FELL INTO EACH OTHER'S TRAPS, YES. AT THAT NEWS, I BECAME SICK ALL OVER AGAIN—

"Wait, wait, wait—so . . . that was Lemuel?!"

LET ME FINISH—

Young Pere was now on the edge of the sofa. "Puggah, you're killing me here—"

NOW YOU KNOW A TINY BIT OF THE AGONY I ENDURED FOR THE NEXT SEVERAL MOONS. SHE FOLLOWED UP THAT MESSAGE WITH ANOTHER, A WEEK LATER. IT SAID ONLY, "MIGHT BE HIS."

Young Pere hadn't realized he was gripping his face and pulling down on it until his eyes burned. "What's *that* supposed to mean?"

MY THOUGHTS AND HOPES EXACTLY. SHE MAY HAVE CONCEIVED QAYIN'S BABY, INSTEAD. ALL I COULD DO WAS HOPE AND PRAY.

"Hope and pray that the baby wasn't born with black hair and dark eyes?"

PRECISELY. QAYIN WAS AS FAIR AND BLOND AS VERSULA. SHE SENT ME ANOTHER MESSAGE, LATER, THAT QAYIN WAS TREATING HER BETTER THAN EVER NOW THAT SHE MIGHT BE PRESENTING HIM WITH A SON. SHE WAS GOING TO STAY WITH HIM IF EVERYTHING WORKED OUT ALL RIGHT. I WAS SLIGHTLY RELIEVED ABOUT THAT—

"So?!" Young Pere was beside himself. "It was a boy . . ."

IT WAS A BOY, AND IT WAS LEMUEL. AGAIN I WAS ILL WITH WORRY— MY POOR MOTHER THOUGHT I HAD A CHRONIC STOMACH CONDITION, LASTING NOW FOR TEN MOONS, COMING AND GOING AND MAKING ME VOMIT AND DEHYDRATE FOR DAYS AT A TIME. FINALLY, THREE DAYS AFTER THE BIRTH CAME THE MESSAGE: "I THINK IT'S HIS." FOR THE FIRST TIME IN MOONS I FELT AN ENORMOUS WEIGHT FALL FROM MY BACK, AND I COULD FINALLY BREATHE AGAIN. MY MOTHER WENT TO VISIT VERSULA TO WISH HER WELL, AND REPORTED BACK THAT THE BABY WAS BLOND LIKE HIS MOTHER AND FATHER, WITH BLUE EYES LIKE THEM AS WELL. I NEARLY FAINTED IN RELIEF.

So did Young Pere as he fell back against the sofa. "So Lemuel's not *my uncle*."

AS I SAID EARLIER, I DON'T KNOW.

Young Pere sat up again. "But he doesn't look anything like you—"

AND I HELD ON TO THAT. BACK WHEN LEMUEL WAS A TODDLER, THE THORNES WERE IN IDUMEA, AND I SURREPTITIOUSLY FOLLOWED VERSULA

AS SHE VISITED THE SHOPS SO I COULD GET A GOOD LOOK AT LEMUEL. I DIDN'T SEE ANYTHING OF ME IN HIM, AND I DECIDED HE WASN'T MY SON AFTER ALL. I ESPECIALLY HELD TO THAT WHEN HE WAS MADE MY CAPTAIN IN EDGE. I HATED HIM, YOUNG PERE. HATED HIM. HE WAS CONNIVING AND MANIPULATIVE, AND I EVEN ONCE PUNCHED HIM IN THE JAW AND KNOCKED OUT A MOLAR.

Young Pere rocked back. "Why? Why'd you hit him?"

I DIDN'T LIKE THE WAY HE WAS LOOKING AT MY DAUGHTER.

Young Pere blinked at that seeming overreaction. "Well, then, certainly a good reason for punching a man—"

THERE'S MORE TO IT THAN THAT, BUT WE DON'T NEED TO DISCUSS IT. IT WAS EASIER TO HATE HIM THINKING HE WAS QAYIN'S SON.

"Then . . . then he was. I mean, as I said, he looks nothing like you—"

NOR DOES YOUR BROTHER RELF. BLOND HAIR, BLUE EYES, GRANDPA TROVATO'S FEATURES . . . STILL MY GRANDSON, THOUGH.

"But Puggah, there are more traits involved," Young Pere told him, eager to share something that may assuage his guilt. "I remember this from my basic medicine classes at the university—"

THE ONE YOU LEFT AFTER ONLY A FEW WEEKS?

"Well, I learned enough! Dominant and recessive traits. Some are stronger than others, like your black hair and dark brown eyes. While they overrule fairer traits, they get diluted in generations. In your own children, they'd dominate. But your blood is more diluted in Relf; he has only a quarter of you. That's why he can be Grandpa Trovato, through and through—"

I STUDIED THE THEORY OF DOMINANT AND RECESSIVE TRAITS, TOO. SHORTLY AFTER RELF WAS BORN, IN FACT, BECAUSE I WAS STARTLED TO SEE HOW FAIR HE WAS—AS FAIR AS LEMUEL. I EVEN SPOKE TO PROFESSOR MENDEL ABOUT IT, CASUALLY ASKING HIM TO EXPLAIN THE THEORIES, PRETENDING I WAS MERELY CURIOUS, NOT DEEPLY WORRIED. WHILE JAYTSY CERTAINLY DEMONSTRATES MY DOMINANCE, YOUR FATHER, ON THE OTHER HAND, HAS LIGHT GRAY EYES—NEARLY BLUE—AND HIS HAIR'S LIGHTER THAN MINE. MY SO-CALLED DOMINANT TRAITS WERE OVERRULED BY CEPHAS PETO'S MORE RECESSIVE TRAITS.

Young Pere's mouth pursed into a small, anxious o.

PROFESSOR MENDEL PULLED OUT ALL KINDS OF FAMILY TRAITS CHARTS HE'D PLOTTED OF LARGE FAMILIES IN SALEM, AND TAKING MY AND MAHRREE'S TRAITS, MADE A CHART OF US. HE CHUCKLED WHEN HE POINTED OUT THAT, BECAUSE OF THE RECESSIVE TRAITS IN MY BLOOD,

THERE WAS A 25% CHANCE THAT, HAD WE BEEN ABLE TO HAVE MORE CHILDREN, I COULD'VE FATHERED A BLOND-HAIRED, BLUE-EYED CHILD.

Startled, Young Pere could only respond with, "And I'm sure you chuckled back."

WELL, I TRIED. LEMUEL MAY HAVE VERSULA'S COLORING, BUT STILL HAVE SHIN BLOOD, JUST AS MY SON PETO DEMONSTRATES CEPHAS PETO'S COLORING. THINK ABOUT IT: HOW SIMILAR TO ME IS LEMUEL? HOW AMBITIOUS, CHARISMATIC, VAIN, AND STUBBORN? I WAS THE SAME WAY, YOUNG PERE. THE SAME WAY. SO ARE YOU.

Young Pere sank deeper into the sofa. "I don't want to believe it, Puggah," he said dully.

NOR DO I. BUT YOUNG PERE, SINCE YOUR BROTHER RELF WAS BORN, THAT QUESTION PLAGUED ME ALL OVER AGAIN: COULD LEMUEL ACTUALLY BE MY SON?

"But, Puggah," Young Pere tried again, desperate to not be Lemuel Thorne's half nephew, almost as desperately as he didn't want Puggah to be his father. "Maybe you share those stubborn, ambitious traits only because of the blood of generals. Versula Cush's father was a High General. Maybe we're all similar because of something much, much further back?"

THAT'S A POSSIBILITY. I DON'T KNOW IF YOU REALIZE THIS, BUT PART OF OUR FAMILY LINE DESCENDS FROM THE FIRST GREAT GUIDE HIERUM.

"Yes, I know that—"

SO DOES THE THORNE LINE.

While surprised, Young Pere was quick to snatch at it. "See, Puggah? This could be something from way, way back, all of us challenged to see how we deal with this . . . *general pride*."

MY, HOW YOU'VE MATURED, YOUNG PERE. I'M NOT SAYING THAT FACETIOUSLY, BY THE WAY.

Young Pere smiled. "I know. Thank you. I really don't think it's *your* traits that made the world as it is right now. Is that what you worry about?"

WHEN DID YOU BECOME SO ASTUTE?

Young Pere smiled briefly. "Puggah, I remember Lemuel telling me that Qayin was a hard man; a terrible father. Lemuel thought he was much better to me, if you can believe that."

I BELIEVE HE THINKS ALL KINDS OF THINGS THAT ARE CONVENIENT FOR HIM. HMM, AGAIN, A LITTLE LIKE ME—

"Now stop that, Puggah. For once, I may be on to something. Lemuel is as he is because of how he was raised, *not* because of any traits you may have passed down if—*IF*—you happen to be his physical father. I mean, look at me and my cousin Cephas: same families, lots of the same blood and traits, but totally different kinds of boys."

There was cosmic chuckling.

THANK YOU, YOUNG PERE. YOU KNOW, YOUR GRANDMOTHER WOULD SAY SOMETHING SIMILAR EVERY TIME THESE FEARS SANK ME DOWN. MAYBE . . . MAYBE IT'S STILL MY PRIDE, DREADING THAT THE WORLD MAY FIND OUT THAT PERHAPS LEMUEL WAS MY SON, AND THAT MY SON DESTROYED THE WORLD. DISMAL LEGACY.

Young Pere chanced a smile. "Well, your *grandson*," and he pointed to himself, "was trying to do something similar. It could very well be that blood of generals."

Again there was cosmic chuckling, tinged with despair.

YES, THAT BLOOD OF GENERALS. THAT'S OUR WEAKNESS, YOUNG PERE. I FELL TO VERSULA'S TEMPTATIONS BECAUSE I WAS SO SELF-RIGHTEOUS THINKING THAT NOTHING COULD TOUCH ME. I NEEDED TO BE MORE HUMBLE, AND HUMILITY'S NOT A COURSE TAUGHT IN COMMAND SCHOOL. MY PRIDE WAS A STRUGGLE—HAS REMAINED A STRUGGLE, ACTUALLY, FOR MY ENTIRE LIFE. THAT'S WHY I COULDN'T DO ELTANA'S BIDDING AND GO DOWN INTO THE WORLD FOR HER. THAT WAS PART OF THE REASON I COULD NEVER BE HIGH GENERAL; I HAD FAR TOO MUCH SELF-RIGHTEOUS PRIDE FIGHTING TO GET OUT OF ME. ALTHOUGH I KEPT IT LOCKED UP IN A CORNER AS SECURELY AS I COULD, I ALWAYS KNEW WHERE THE KEY WAS.

"I remember you telling me that Uncle Shem was the only man who could have done it, who could have been king of the world. He really is that sincerely humble, isn't he?" Young Pere sighed. "I thought some terrible things about him over the years. I was wrong. About everything."

YES, SHEM'S THE ONLY MAN WHO COULD HAVE RULED THE WORLD PROPERLY, BECAUSE HE TAKES ORDERS NOT FROM HIS EGO BUT FROM THE CREATOR. I NEVER KNEW HIM TO TAKE AN HONOR; IT HAD TO BE FORCED UPON HIM, EVERY TIME. WE'LL HAVE TO FORCE ONE MORE UPON HIM BECAUSE HE SIMPLY DOESN'T GET IT.

ME, HOWEVER—I WOULD'VE ABUSED THAT POSITION OF HIGH GENERAL. I WOULD'VE BEEN MORE HIGH-MINDED AND ARROGANT THAN EVEN CHAIRMAN NICKO MAL, AND IF YOU KNEW THE MAN, THAT'S SAYING SOMETHING. I'D JUSTIFY MY BEHAVIOR, NO MATTER HOW DISGRACEFUL, BECAUSE I WAS BETTER THAN ANYONE ELSE. THAT'S WHAT LED ME TO BRING VERSULA TO MY DORM ROOM THAT NIGHT: I JUSTIFIED IT THAT SHE

'DESERVED' ME, THAT I WAS 'NEEDED.' I WAS JUST 'SAVING' HER, YOU KNOW. HOW NOBLE OF ME.

Young Pere scoffed quietly along with him. "I was 'noble' too. I can't even remember all the lies I told in my 'nobility.'"

THERE'S NO REAL RIGHTEOUSNESS IN SELF-RIGHTEOUSNESS, IS THERE?

"Nope."

I CAME OUT OF ALL OF THAT A TRULY DIFFERENT MAN—FINALLY CHANGED, FINALLY UNDERSTANDING HOW MY ARROGANCE COULD DESTROY ME. AND I DIDN'T SUCCUMB TO THAT TEMPTATION EVER AGAIN.

WHEN I MET MAHRREE, SEVERAL YEARS LATER, I HOPED I MIGHT BE WORTHY ENOUGH FOR SUCH A WOMAN. HOGAL EVEN SET US UP, SAYING THAT SHE'D HAVE A HUMBLING EFFECT ON ME! THE MOMENT I SAW HER— EXPECTING TO DEBATE THE OLD SCHOOL TEACHER, BUT INSTEAD FINDING THIS VIBRANT, SHARP YOUNG WOMAN—I WAS SMITTEN. WHAT I FELT FOR HER WAS NOTHING LIKE WHAT I'D FELT FOR VERSULA OR ANY OF THOSE OTHER GIRLS. IT WAS HOPE MINGLED WITH ADORATION. I WANTED NOTHING MORE THAN TO KEEP HER SAFE FROM THE WORLD AND FROM MEN LIKE WHO I USED TO BE. SO INTENSELY I WANTED HER, BUT I WASN'T GOING TO RUIN HER. NOR WAS I GOING TO RUIN MYSELF EVER AGAIN; SHE NEEDED ME—THE BEST ME. OR AT LEAST, I NEEDED HER TO NEED ME. I BEHAVED MYSELF, EVEN THOUGH IT WAS WITH SOME DIFFICULTY, TO BE SURE, BECAUSE MAHRREE IS QUITE THE—

"Uh, Puggah—you can stop right there. Please, I get the idea."

There was soft chuckling.

SORRY. BUT I BEHAVED MYSELF. I DIDN'T EVER WANT A VERSULA THORNE AGAIN.

"So you never saw Versula again?"

UNFORTUNATELY, I DID. WHEN WE HAD TO GO BACK TO IDUMEA WHEN MY FATHER WAS TRAPPED BY THE LAND TREMOR, AND THEY HELD THE DINNER. SHE WALKED RIGHT UP TO ME AT THE END OF THE DANCING, DRAGGED HER FINGER ACROSS MY FOREHEAD AGAIN, AND SAID, "I SEE YOU STILL HAVE A WAY TO REMEMBER ME. I THINK ABOUT THAT OFTEN. AND WONDER."

"Wait . . . did she think that—?"

I FELT SICK TO MY STOMACH ALL OVER AGAIN. MAYBE SHE THOUGHT LEMUEL WAS MINE AFTER ALL. MAYBE SHE THOUGHT ABOUT THAT NIGHT AT MY DORM ROOM, AND THE FACT THAT SHE STILL THOUGHT ABOUT IT OFTEN? AND WONDERED!?

SHE SAID THAT IN FRONT OF HER HUSBAND, WHO WAS GLARING AT ME,

AND I WAS WITH MY WIFE! I WAS NEVER MORE GRATEFUL TO HAVE MAHRREE BY MY SIDE. I PULLED HER CLOSE AND SAID, "MAY I PRESENT MY WIFE, MAHRREE." AND THEN THAT SAME WIFE SAID LATER THAT NIGHT AS WE GOT READY FOR BED, "MAYBE WE SHOULD GET TO KNOW THE THORNES BETTER. VERSULA SEEMS TO BE A PLEASANT ENOUGH WOMAN. I WAS THINKING WE SHOULD INVITE THEM OVER TO DINNER BEFORE WE LEAVE FOR EDGE."

Young Pere held his face. "Oh Puggah, I can't imagine what you were thinking then!"

I WAS THINKING, OH MAHRREE, IF ONLY YOU KNEW! THAT'S WHEN I DECIDED THAT MAYBE SHE SHOULD KNOW. IT WAS ANOTHER VERY LATE NIGHT. SHE LEARNED QUITE A BIT ABOUT ME ON THAT VISIT, I HAVE TO ADMIT. ALTHOUGH THE TRIP OUT OF IDUMEA THE NEXT EVENING WAS UNDER LESS THAN IDEAL CIRCUMSTANCES, I WAS NEVER SO GRATEFUL TO GO!

"So that was the last time?"

Another cosmic sigh.

NO. ABOUT A WEEK LATER, WITH SHEM AT MY SIDE, RIGHT AFTER MY PARENTS WERE KILLED, SHE CAME TO THE HOSPITAL WHERE SHEM AND I WERE STAYING UNTIL THE BURIAL. SHE WALKED RIGHT IN, HUGGED ME, AND STARTED KISSING MY NECK AGAIN, AS SHE HAD BEFORE, TRYING TO GET CLOSER TO MY MOUTH. SHE WANTED TO KNOW WHAT SHE COULD 'DO' FOR ME.

Young Pere was aghast. "In front of Uncle Shem?!"

AND IN FRONT OF HER MOTHER AS WELL!

"You're joking."

I WISH I WAS, YOUNG PERE. I MADE SHEM PROMISE TO NEVER TELL MAHRREE WHAT VERSULA DID IN THAT HOSPITAL ROOM. MAHRREE HAD JUST BARELY LEARNED ABOUT VERSULA'S AND MY PAST, AND OF THE POSSIBILITY THAT LEMUEL THORNE MIGHT NOT BE QAYIN'S SON. SHE DIDN'T NEED TO KNOW VERSULA WAS TRYING TO MAKE THE PAST THE PRESENT AGAIN.

"I imagine Uncle Shem was shocked."

NEVER KNEW A MAN'S EYES COULD BULGE OUT SO FAR FROM HIS HEAD.

Young Pere smiled feebly.

AND HE DIDN'T EVEN KNOW ABOUT THE WHOLE LEMUEL COMPLICATION. HE NEVER DID. THE VERY NEXT DAY I RODE TO EDGE WITH LEMUEL THORNE BY MY SIDE AS MY NEW CAPTAIN. YOU HAVE TO KNOW, THE MOMENT I SAW HIM AT COMMAND SCHOOL—I WENT THERE

DURING OUR VISIT TO IDUMEA BECAUSE HIS GRANDFATHER CUSH SAID HE WANTED TO MEET ME—I HATED LEMUEL. NOT FOR ANYTHING HE SAID OR DID, BUT WHAT HE MIGHT BE: THE EMBODIMENT OF ME AT MY LOWEST. THERE HE STOOD, CONFIDENT AND ARROGANT AND ALMOST DESPERATE TO IMPRESS ME, AND I HATED HIM TO HIS CORE BECAUSE HE MIGHT HAVE BEEN EVIDENCE OF MY VERY WORST SELF.

Young Pere sighed. "Oh, Puggah. I *am* sorry. I wish I'd known all of this before . . . before *everything*."

I DON'T THINK YOU WOULD HAVE APPRECIATED IT EARLIER. THIS IS NOT EXACTLY A STORY I'VE SHARED WITH MANY PEOPLE. IN FACT, YOU'RE THE ONLY ONE WHO KNOWS EVERYTHING, ASIDE FROM MAHRREE AND HOGAL DENSAL. I ALSO DIDN'T WANT LEMUEL ANYWHERE NEAR JAYTSY. NOT ONLY BECAUSE OF THE STICKY POSSIBILITY THAT HE MIGHT BE HER HALF-BROTHER, BUT BECAUSE HE WAS SUCH A MANIPULATIVE, SELFISH MAN. JUST AS I WAS WHEN I WAS YOUNG. VERSULA PUSHED FOR THE RELATIONSHIP, THOUGH. SHE MUST HAVE BEEN CONFIDENT AT THE TIME THAT LEMUEL WAS QAYIN'S.

THE LAST TIME I SAW VERSULA WAS WHEN LEMUEL HAD THE POX. SHE CAME ON THE PRETENSE OF CARING FOR HIM, BUT SHE SPENT MORE TIME CHASING ME AROUND THE FORT THAN SHE DID SITTING AT HIS BEDSIDE. SHE GAVE UP AFTER A WEEK, AND ONCE LEMUEL BEGAN TO IMPROVE SHE WENT BACK TO IDUMEA. SHE NEVER CAUGHT ME ALONE. I COULD HAVE WRITTEN A MANUAL ON THE EVASIVE TECHNIQUES I MASTERED AFTER THAT VISIT. I EVEN ONCE TOOK TO COWERING BEHIND CLARK AS SHE SEARCHED THE STABLES FOR ME, AND ANOTHER TIME SWAPPED CAPS WITH A TALL PRIVATE SO THAT SHE COULDN'T FIND ME IN THE MESS HALL. SHE FOLLOWED THAT POOR BOY FROM A DISTANCE NEARLY TO HIS BARRACKS BEFORE SHE REALIZED HE WASN'T ME—

"So," Young Pere scratched his head, truly perplexed. "Don't . . . don't you know *by now*? Couldn't . . . couldn't someone *there* tell you?" It seemed like Paradise was the place of no more secrets.

Then again, if one was forgiven of something, it was no longer remembered.

I HAVE ASKED, YOUNG PERE. AND I WAS TOLD THAT I DON'T NEED TO KNOW IF HE WAS MY SON OR NOT.

Now Young Pere was even more astonished. "But . . . why?"

BECAUSE IT DOESN'T MATTER; I SHOULD HAVE TREATED LEMUEL LIKE A SON. I SHOULD HAVE FORGOTTEN MYSELF AND MY PAST, AND FOCUSED ON GIVING HIM THE FUTURE HE NEEDED. WE ARE ALL FAMILY, YOUNG PERE. I TOOK MANY YOUNG MEN UNDER MY WING OVER THE

YEARS. NONE NEEDED THAT ATTENTION FROM ME MORE THAN LEMUEL. BUT I COULDN'T. I JUST COULDN'T. I FEEL IN MANY WAYS I CONTRIBUTED TO THE TRAGEDY THAT'S HIS LIFE. I FEEL IMMENSE REMORSE FOR IT NOW, AND I HOPE TO SOMEHOW MAKE IT UP TO HIM IN THE FUTURE, BUT HERE'S THE REALLY HARD TRUTH: I WAS FORGIVEN OF MY ACT WITH VERSULA. I FELT IT, DISTINCTLY, MANY MOONS AFTER THE FACT. IT WAS AS IF THE CREATOR REMOVED CHAINS FROM MY WRISTS AND ANKLES, AND SAID, "IT IS ENOUGH. GO FREE."

"And I know that feeling, too. Physically, at least. It's fantastic."

YES, YOU DO KNOW THAT SENSATION. BUT WHILE I WAS FORGIVEN OF MY SINS, I WASN'T FREED FROM THE CONSEQUENCES. THAT WASN'T POSSIBLE. LEMUEL WAS STILL OUT THERE, POPPING INTO MY LIFE WHEN I LEAST EXPECTED IT.

"Muggah tried to explain that, before I left," Young Pere remembered. "I told her it didn't matter what I did, that I could just repent of it later. Bones mended, wounds healed . . . But she said that wounds often left scars. She wasn't talking about your back or any of the other scars you had. She was referring to him, wasn't she? Lemuel is your scar."

YES. ONE THAT I PICKED AT SENSELESSLY. I HAVE A LOT TO TRY TO FIX ONCE HE COMES OVER HERE. IT MAY TAKE A THOUSAND YEARS, BUT I'M GOING TO TRY TO FIX IT.

Drained and astonished, Young Pere stared off into the distance, mulling over everything.

THERE'S A LOT GOING THROUGH YOUR MIND RIGHT NOW. WHAT WOULD YOU LIKE TO KNOW?

"Lots of things. But right now, I'm thinking about Muggah. How amazing she must have been for . . . understanding."

SHE IS AMAZING. I COULDN'T HAVE FOUND A MORE WONDERFUL WOMAN. THAT NIGHT IN IDUMEA, WHEN I CONFESSED TO HER ALL THAT I'D DONE AND WHAT IT MIGHT MEAN, I HELD HER TIGHT, TERRIFIED THAT IT'D BE THE LAST TIME SHE'D EVER LET ME TOUCH HER. I WAS SURE THAT SHE'D LEAVE ME, AND I WOULDN'T HAVE BLAMED HER, NOT ONE BIT. I WAS SURE THAT OLD SCAR WOULD DESTROY ALL THAT WE'D BUILT TOGETHER OVER THE YEARS.

BUT IT DIDN'T. SHE SAID SHE'D FALLEN IN LOVE WITH THE IMPROVED VERSION OF PERRIN, NOT THE OLD ONE WHICH SHE WAS CONFIDENT WAS GONE FOREVER.

Young Pere closed his eyes.

I KNOW WHAT YOU'RE WORRIED ABOUT, BUT THERE'S A WONDERFUL

WOMAN FOR YOU, TOO.

"Oh, Puggah, I'm not worthy. For any woman."

YOUNG PERE, HOW WOULD YOU DESCRIBE MY LIFE? MY MARRIAGE, MY FAMILY?

"About as good as it could get, I suppose."

EXACTLY. NOW THAT YOU KNOW WHAT KIND OF A YOUNG MAN I WAS, DID I DESERVE THAT LIFE? WAS I WORTHY OF ANY OF THAT?

Young Pere didn't want to answer.

THAT'S ALL RIGHT. I'LL ANSWER FOR YOU—NO. OF COURSE NOT. NONE OF US DESERVE WHAT THE CREATOR GIVES US. THAT'S WHY WE SAY OUR LIVES ARE GIFTS. NONE OF US DESERVE SUCH GIFTS. BUT I SPENT THE NEXT FIFTY-TWO YEARS TRYING TO BE WORTHY OF THAT TRUST HE PUT IN ME BY GIVING ME ANOTHER CHANCE. TELL ME HONESTLY, NOW THAT YOU KNOW WHAT I REALLY WAS, DO YOU THINK DIFFERENTLY OF ME?

Young Pere exhaled heavily. "Yes. Yes, I do, Puggah. And because I know exactly what you went through, and what you overcame, I now think more of you than I ever have."

He was surprised to hear a familiar chuckle. *LAYING IT ON A LITTLE THICK THERE, DON'T YOU THINK, YOUNG PERE?*

Young Pere smiled even though his chin trembled. "If only I can be half the man you were—*are* . . ."

I MADE IT THROUGH ALL OF THAT, YOUNG PERE. SO CAN YOU. I SEE NOW WHY THE CREATOR INFLUENCED YOUR PARENTS TO GIVE YOU MY NAME: FOR THIS DAY, TO LET YOU SEE WHAT YOUR FUTURE CAN STILL HOLD. YOU SAID THAT BECAUSE YOU KNOW WHAT I'VE BEEN THROUGH, YOU SEE ME DIFFERENTLY, AND NOT IN A BAD WAY. WHEN YOU GET TO SEE YOUR FATHER, YOU'LL NEED TO CONFESS TO HIM WHAT YOU'VE DONE. BUT I KNOW MY SON. HE WILL WEEP WITH YOU JUST AS HOGAL WEPT WITH ME, AND HE'LL HELP YOU FIGURE OUT HOW TO FIX IT ALL. HE ALREADY KNOWS IN HIS HEART WHAT'S HAPPENED. HE LOVES YOU MORE THAN YOU COULD EVER IMAGINE. HE WANTS TO HELP HEAL YOU. AND WHEN HE LOOKS AT YOU IN THE FUTURE, IT WILL BE WITH A BIG SMILE AND PROFOUND GRATITUDE THAT YOU CAME TO HIM, THAT YOU LET HIM HELP YOU.

"But . . . forgiveness just seems too much to ask for," Young Pere whispered.

IT'S ALREADY BEEN PAID FOR, IN WAYS WE CAN'T FULLY UNDERSTAND. IT HAPPENED AT A DIFFERENT TIME ON A DIFFERENT PLANET, BY SOMEONE WHO IS OUR SAVIOR. HE ALREADY PAID FOR ALL OF OUR SINS. HE'S ALREADY SECURED FORGIVENESS FOR US ALL. THE CREATOR IS

HOLDING THAT FORGIVENESS OUT TO YOU. IT'S YOURS, JUST WAITING. TAKE IT.

"Peto," Shem finally whispered from his prone position on the ground next to his wife.

It was well after midnight, but no one was sleeping in the Shin, Briter, or Zenos camps.

Lek was sitting next to his father's head as Shem held his wife's cold hand. He was the only one who heard the word, so Lek motioned for his uncle to come over. Boskos kept a comforting hand on his father's shoulder.

Peto left Lilla to be soothed by their daughters. "I'm right here, Shem," he said, sitting down on the ground next to him. "What can I get you?"

"It's about Mahrree," Shem whispered.

"Couldn't help but notice she wasn't with you," Peto said in a shaky voice.

There was still a vigil over the ridge, hundreds of people waiting with torches, staring into the dark, hoping. More than once Honri had started down the trail, returning a short time later shaking and frustrated, mumbling about how Perrin didn't want him to risk it.

But no one even considered asking Shem what happened. They just sat in dread and waited for hours.

Shem closed his eyes. "Just listen—I won't be able to say it twice. We went to the temple. I left her there. I hid in the trees like a coward. Thorne came. His guide . . . his guide was Lannard Kroop! Lannard walked up to the temple, Mahrree confronted him, scared Lannard to death. Literally. He backed up off the portico, fell, broke his neck, I think, on the sharp stones below. Soldiers panicked. The prophecy, Peto—she did it. She told everyone who she was. One third ran in terror of her. Fantastic. Until," Shem began to tremble despite Boskos holding him. "Until Lemuel got to her. He drew his sword . . ."

Peto was already quivering, huge tears sliding down his cheeks.

Shem finally whispered the last words. "Lemuel killed Mahrree."

Mahrree appeared at the ransacked temple in the middle of the night. She saw Perrin sitting on the sofa set up properly in the slushy snow. Now he appeared to be in his forties, the handsome colonel in white.

"This remind you of anything?" he asked with a wink. He put his leg easily up on the arm of the sofa.

She smiled at the memory of his moving her beloved sofa in Edge outside to the back garden after the first major land tremor so they'd have a safe place to sleep that night. But her thoughts quickly traveled back to more recent matters. She sat down next to him and sighed.

Perrin put his arm around her. "Not going well at the ancient site, is it?"

Mahrree rested her head against him. "No, it's terrible. Just terrible."

"I can feel them. Could you reach anyone?"

"I finally got to Jaytsy and some of the younger ones. I think Peto felt me, but he was so involved with calming Lilla. Oh Perrin, poor Lilla! She was hoarse with sobbing. I've never known her to get worked up to *silence* before. First Calla, then me . . ." She shook her head sadly. "Everyone has finally fallen asleep out of exhaustion. I held Briter for half an hour until he fell asleep. I think he realized it was me. The poor boy kept whispering, 'I'm next, Muggah. I know I'm next.' Dawn will be coming too early for them."

"I had to send Honri back a few times," Perrin told her. "He kept trying to go down to find you. We're close enough now that I could just shout and he heard me."

"Poor Honri!" Mahrree sighed, then glanced at her husband who was smirking slightly. "Nothing ever happened between us—"

"It's all right," he assured her. "And really, I wouldn't have minded. I may have been a little jealous that he was with you and I wasn't, but had you two married, I would have been fine with you two making each other happy until the end. So would have Nan."

"She told me that," Mahrree admitted. "Up at the site. She was rather sad that we never got together. Even she thought we would have been a cute couple. Her words, not mine."

Perrin chuckled and pulled her closer. He was much more sober when he asked, "And how's Shem?"

"Is there any term stronger than 'devastated'?" she whispered. "Never have I seen a man so thoroughly distraught. I don't think even *you* could reach him now. Calla and I were on either side of him for quite a while doing all we could to get him to feel comfort. At one point he felt Calla, but he was so consumed with guilt that he pushed her away, afraid to feel her. Delivering me to Thorne was one thing, but now he feels he abandoned his wife." She turned to look at him. "Perrin," she hesitated to tell him the news Calla had given her, but she felt obligated. "He had *feelings* for me when we were in Edge."

Perrin simply smiled at her shocking revelation.

Mahrree's eyes widened. "So you knew it too?"

"I could see it in his eyes. Remember, I became very skilled at reading his expressions. It was off and on for him. He could go for seasons without feeling anything, then suddenly be struck again with a desire for you. Why do you think I made it a point of kissing you in front of him so often? I wasn't just showing him the 'benefits of marriage'; I was reminding him who you truly loved."

She wilted against him. "I missed a lot of things, didn't I?"

Perrin chuckled softly and kissed her head. "But never the important things, my darling wife. That's why I wrote the letter, the one I left in my desk in Edge that I fully expected him to find if I died. In it, I told Shem that I knew he admired you from afar for all those years, and now that I was dead I wanted him to act on his desires, marry you, and take care of you and my children as if they were his. I told him that I was sure you two would be very happy together."

Mahrree blinked at him. "You put it that bluntly?"

Perrin nodded sadly. "Shem would have needed it put to him bluntly or he wouldn't have dared to do it! But I never once thought that letter would end up in Lemuel's hands. Or Genev's. I planned to burn it the day I retired from the army and the danger of my dying on duty had passed, or Shem finally married. But I never went back to my office after I resigned, if you remember.

"But in a way," he continued thoughtfully, "I realize now just how important that letter was to everything else that followed. It must have led them to create that story about you and Shem, and kept your 'traitorous behavior' in the minds of the army for all these years. Every soldier out there *knows* the history of what you supposedly did to me, and that Lemuel had you filled with arrows for it. If they hadn't, your name would have been forgotten, then hearing you shout it a few hours ago wouldn't have had any effect on them. Instead, it terrified them to know you were still alive."

Mahrree shook her head in amazement. "I'm just beginning to realize how our actions in the past affect the future. I can only imagine what horrible moments from school poor Lannard was reliving when he saw me coming for him.

"And *Shem*!" she exclaimed. "Oh, I *never knew*, but Calla knew. She said that Shem explained his feelings for me before he even asked her to marry him. But he never thought of me again, or any other woman, besides his wife. But now he feels like he was unfaithful to her at the end! While she was laying for hours in the brush, he was with me. During his wife's last moments, he wasn't there for her. I don't know if he'll ever get over that," she whispered.

Perrin sighed. "We knew Shem would be tried severely before the end. This is it."

"Forgive me, but I don't understand it!" Mahrree exclaimed, nearly angry for what was happening to him. "Shem's trial is to lose those closest to him right when he needs all of us the most?"

Perrin looked at her patiently.

"Oh," she said slowly as the Creator gently dropped another lump of understanding into her mind, along with a sense of forgiveness for her lack of understanding. She'd asked for it, after all.

"I see it now. His trial is to see if he will *take* comfort. He's always giving it and always telling others to receive it, but will he receive it himself?"

Perrin nodded. "Not only comfort, but forgiveness. Shem's never done anything truly terrible in his life, unlike some of us," he nodded to Young Pere over in the trees.

Mahrree leaned forward. "Exactly what is he doing? I noticed him when I arrived."

"He's doing some thinking."

"On his knees?"

"Best way, isn't it?"

Mahrree started to smile. "Oh, Perrin!"

"Give him some time. He has a lot to discuss with the Creator tonight. He might be there until morning."

Mahrree leaned back into his arms. "Thank goodness! So what finally got him there?"

Perrin hesitated. "Well, we had a lot to discuss ourselves."

By his demeanor, she knew what their discussion had been. "Good. I'm glad you did." Mahrree patted his arm reassuringly. "So . . . did you tell him *everything*?"

"Everything," he said.

"Even about Lemuel?"

"Yes."

She felt all his heaviness in that small word. Taking his face in her hands, she said, firmly, "He's *not*, Perrin. I've told you this before."

Reluctantly he lifted his gaze to meet her eyes, and she was surprised that after all these years, and even in Paradise, he still dragged that around, as if his soul was hunchbacked. Not even the jagged scar on his back was there anymore, but this one was, twisting him at odd angles.

"He's not yours," Mahrree insisted. "Perrin, *your son* did not murder me tonight. He didn't try to apprehend us for trial, nor did he try to frame me as a traitor all those years ago."

But the old scar itched at him again, and he started to turn away until Mahrree jerked him back. "It doesn't matter whose blood flows in his veins; he is *Qayin's* son. Raised and trained and manipulated by Qayin, *not you*. You couldn't have changed all of that in the few moons you had him in Edge. None of that matters!"

"How can you be so sure?" he whispered. "That who I was—who I was *then*, didn't create *him*, and then all of this horror now?"

"Because blood doesn't matter; decisions do!" she insisted, and saw that he didn't know how to believe her. It was time to do what she did best. "Fine, we're doing this, right now. And don't start to say there's no time to debate, because we just left time. This is important, Perrin Shin. More important at this moment than anything else going on in the world, because you can't complete your duty *to* the world until you get this right in your head!"

She knew the words weren't hers but the Creator's. And only Mahrree could deliver them.

Perrin appeared to her now merely a teenage boy, as one of her many students back in Edge meekly ready to receive her chastising but wishing for something better. The agony mixed with hope in his eyes nearly melted her.

Only nearly. Professor Shin never let her students get to her when she was in her element.

"Let's take the stance that Lemuel Thorne is, indeed, your son— No, no, no, don't turn away from me, Perrin. Look me in the eyes! That's better. Now, would you agree that for your first twenty years or so, you were exactly like Lemuel?"

His chin trembled as he nodded. Knowing that was inadequate, he said, feebly, "Yes, ma'am."

"And I agree too," Mahrree said sternly. "His vain ambition, his lack of concern for anything else but his own status . . . yes, that *was* you. But for the more than fifty years *after* that, you were much more like your son Peto Shin. Do you agree?"

Perrin began to bob his head noncommittally, but then nodded once. Again, he said, even quieter, "Yes, ma'am. I tried."

Mahrree's expression softened. "Oh, yes, you tried. And you succeeded, Perrin Shin. Oh, how you succeeded! Now, what was the difference between Young Perrin and Older Perrin?"

"Well, there was Hogal—" he began, almost timidly.

Mahrree cut him off with, "No. He assisted, but something else made that dramatic change in you. What was it?"

He looked up, his eyes slightly brighter. "The Creator."

Mahrree beamed at him as if he'd just completed a difficult math problem. "Yes. The Creator. You let Him into your soul, and then after that whole mess with Versula, you let Him *change you*, for good. There was nothing you could have done to fix any of that. You had to turn it all over to the Creator.

"But that's not everything," she told him, and his large, dark eyes stared at her with hope on the very edge of acceptance. "You *chose* to let Him in. You *wanted* to be a different man. You asked the Creator to forgive you, to change you. To make you into an excellent patriarch who loved his family and his community, and wanted nothing more than to serve them. *You*," she jabbed him in the chest, "chose this life. Do you agree with that?"

Something in his countenance shifted, and he appeared to her to be the twenty-eight-year-old captain she debated in Edge and also fell in love with. "Yes, I agree with that," he said with a cautious smile.

"As do I," she said, trying to keep her teacher-tone, but looking so deeply into his eyes was getting to her. "Perrin, I noticed that even when we were courting . . . well, it wasn't really courting . . . whatever we were doing before we were married, let's put it that way—"

Oh, he looked exactly as he did then, and she had to break away from his gaze in order to concentrate.

"Perrin, for years I felt like you were two men shoved into one body: there was the officer side of you, then the husband and father side. Frequently they were in conflict. Do you remember?"

His countenance shifted, to something more brooding. "Oh yes, I remember."

"I now understand why," she said, lifting his chin. "Perrin, right now there are two very influential men in Salem: one has been securing it for the past twenty-five years and has been up since well before dawn today trying to get the last of the Salemites to leave. The other man has been here for a much shorter time but is trying to destroy all that the first man loves. It's the Rector of Salem against the General of the World, if you will. And, Perrin," she placed a hand on his chest, "both of those men came from right here. What makes the difference between your two sons is the choices *they* make. Look at the man *you* chose to nurture. Who *you* became. What your son Peto became. It's all a choice. And whatever Lemuel decides reflects *only Lemuel*. Not you. Will you accept that?"

He was trembling so violently that she knew his answer already, but he needed to say it. He needed to hear himself say it.

"Yes," he managed. "Yes, I . . . will accept that. But Mahrree—I failed with Lemuel. I failed to raise him. Did I abandon my own son? To be raised by Qayin, of all people?! And then I had another chance when Lemuel came to the fort as my captain, but I couldn't. Oh, I just couldn't. I hated everything about him because . . . because I was afraid of him. Mahrree, I might have been able to help him then, but I couldn't get past myself. I messed it up. I can't go back and fix any of that. The state of the world right now may very well be my fault. I can't fix that!"

"No, you can't," she said simply. "Only the Creator can. Lemuel is the Creator's son, too, and I have no doubt that the Creator can heal all the wounds you've inflicted on each other over the years. In fact, the entire world can be healed. And you're right—sometimes we make such big mistakes we can't fix them. That's why the Creator sent His Son, why we have a Savior. And why you have to turn all of this over to Them. When the time is right, They will let you assist in helping Lemuel, I have no doubt. Now, General of Salem: surrender. Surrender your pride, your fear, your doubt—everything that traps you—and give it all to Them. Let Them heal and strengthen you, so you can finish what you were sent to do. You can't save yourself or Lemuel. Only the Savior can save."

She gripped his face again and kissed him, and he could barely kiss her back.

"Thank you," he whispered. "Thank you," and he collapsed in her arms.

Mahrree held him tightly as he melted into her, and she had the impression that he was having another conversation she wasn't privy to. But that was all right. The Creator was done using her and was now pouring understanding and strength directly into Perrin. There was something more he had to accomplish, but first he had to release this one last enormous regret.

"You fear you had caused all of this by fathering Lemuel then abandoning him to Qayin," Mahrree whispered as she stroked his hair, his head against her chest. "But consider this: even if you *had* raised him—even if *we* had influenced him—he might have made the same decisions. Just look at Young Pere and how easily he rejected all we gave him. We still may be in this same position because of who Lemuel wanted to be.

"All of your worry, all of your regret, led to another fear," she continued, insight filling her mind. "What your duty is at the Last Day. But you couldn't deal with that until you came to some acceptance about Lemuel. Right?"

He nodded into her shoulder.

"You have a part to play, don't you?" she guessed. Then she knew, because the Creator set into her mind her duty as well. "We all have a part."

Something changed in Perrin and suddenly he became steadier, stronger within her embrace.

"And now I see it all," he said, his voice determined and powerful. He sat up out of her hug, and Mahrree was taken aback to see him now: fierce and strong, as he appeared in his forties during the Moorland Offensive. Yet also so full of sympathy and even love.

He pulled her into his arms again, not the penitent, regretful teenage boy anymore, but the protective, commanding husband and officer.

It was Mahrree's turn to melt into him as he remained silent, and she knew he was thinking, preparing, and plotting. He held her tightly, letting their strength mingle together.

Eventually he said, "I've got it all now. I've got the plan. I do get to help save. We all do."

Mahrree knew he wasn't murmuring to her but to the entire cosmos.

His grip on her finally loosened and he kissed her tenderly.

"Are you all right again?" she asked as he pulled away. Much had shifted and rearranged in him, and now he appeared so young and innocent, yet also so old. Like an ancient general, born today.

He nodded soberly. "You're right—I couldn't see it all before because I couldn't get past Lemuel. I had to release him to Those who can actually fix all my mistakes. And now?" He surprised her by smiling. "I needed you here, to get me through one more worry. Only you could do that for me, here in Paradise. I'm so glad Lemuel killed you."

She couldn't help but snicker at that, but only briefly, because she could feel the burden that had fallen upon him. It was enormous, but he hefted it easily, confidently. He was capable of anything.

"By the way," he added, that familiar twinkle in his eye, "that wasn't so much a debate as it was a lecture."

She batted her eyelashes at him. "Of course, because you had absolutely no position for a proper debate. Any flimsy argument you could have presented would have no chance against my superior intellect and logic." She sniffed haughtily.

He burst into a grin. "Have I told you today how much I love you?"

She opened her mouth to answer, then tilted her head. "Actually, you have *not*. Not *once* since I came to Paradise!"

"Well, then," he leaned in closely, "I love you."

Her forehead met his. "And I love you, too."

"Of course you do." He sat up and sniffed haughtily himself, and she giggled. His countenance was brighter than she'd ever seen, and was much lighter as if a burden had finally been set aside, to make room for a new duty. What that was, he wasn't about to share it with her yet, because she needed to remain focused on their grandson and on—

"Shem," she reminded both of them. "We were talking about Shem, if he will accept forgiveness."

"Oh. Yes," Perrin said, and sighed. "He's so unlike me, yet he's carrying a burden even heavier than mine. A burden he didn't even have to pick up and now refuses to put down."

Mahrree felt the shift as he did, the move back into regular time. Young Pere had been frozen in the distance, but now he appeared to be breathing again, his lips silently moving. Had she been in her body, Mahrree would have felt the shift jarring. But moving in and out of time was no problem for her spirit.

"Shem never made any grave mistakes to plead forgiveness for," Perrin said, picking up where they had left off. "Not even his temptations about you, really. He beat them down every time they tormented him, and never did anything to encourage them. In many ways, he's the complete opposite of me when I was younger," he added contritely. "His knowledge of right and wrong, his sense of duty, and most of all, his devotion to me were all stronger than his attraction to you. He never acted on those temptations, even though he had plenty of opportunities."

Mahrree scrunched her face. "He did?"

"Think about it; how often was I sedated and he was in our house all night to lend assistance should you need it?"

Mahrree cringed. "Dozens."

"Remarkable man, isn't he? He had the opportunities right before him to act on his feelings, knowing I was completely incapacitated, and never once did he attempt anything, did he?"

"Never," Mahrree remembered, then she bit her lip.

Perrin tipped his head. "Mahrree? For once I'm having a hard time reading you. What is it?"

"I'm realizing now," she began slowly, "how difficult I made things for him. I frequently hugged him, especially on your worst nights. I begged him to stay, nearly every night. I was feeling . . . lonely," she confessed. "And also very, *very* vulnerable. Not only were you not in a position to protect us, but we needed protection *from* you. Shem was the only capable man who came to our rescue, besides Rector Yung," she added with a sad chuckle, remembering their old, tiny rector.

Here in Paradise, Yung was much younger, larger, and stronger.

"Had Shem, at any point, pressed his advantage . . ." She looked up at her husband. "Considering my fragile and vulnerable state, my need to feel close to a strong man . . . I have to confess that had he tried, he may have succeeded." She grimaced in apology.

But Perrin only smiled sadly. "Everyone thinks that's what happened anyway. No one realizes just how strong each of you had to be, by yourselves, to do the right thing. I'm sorry, Mahrree, that I left you so vulnerable, that both of you were put into such difficult circumstances. But I also think we all came out of it far stronger and abler than before. And with *nothing* to regret," he added significantly.

But one last thing worried Mahrree. "I kissed him goodbye yesterday. On the lips."

"I know," Perrin said steadily. "I was watching."

"But I didn't mean anything by it!" she exclaimed. "He's my brother! That's the *only* way I've seen him, for decades. I was—" Then she saw the twinkle in Perrin's eye, and she put her hands on her hips. "Is teasing allowed in Paradise?"

"Only briefly," he chuckled. "And don't worry—it didn't mean to Shem what it would have meant decades ago. Back in Edge, that brief kiss would've been exquisite torture. But last night he was merely saying goodbye to another sister."

Mahrree sank into Perrin's arms in relief.

"His heart is solely Calla's," Perrin assured her. "And that's what's going to cause him the greatest turmoil now. First he was blaming himself for your death—"

"And now he's blaming himself for Calla's," Mahrree sighed. "We both felt him. He was thinking that if only he had stopped and looked around before he left, he would've noticed her. He's thinking he missed a prompting somewhere because he was so thrilled by his success. He fears his pride got in the way of his duty."

"Right now," Perrin said bleakly, "he thinks he killed the two women who meant the most to him."

"But he didn't! Others killed us! Oh, it's so illogical."

"Grief isn't logical, Mahrree," he reminded her. "I remember a certain woman telling her best friend on the way to burying her husband that there was no purpose for her to keep living."

"I couldn't think of any then," she admitted. "Not that day. I was so sure you were going to come get me."

"And I fully intended to," Perrin said. "All of our parents greeted me when I arrived here, just as they greeted you. The very first thing I said was, 'Wait while I go get Mahrree.'"

"Really? You were coming to get me?"

He smiled. "It's not really Paradise without you, you know. But they said no. I was ready to get angry, right then and there *in Paradise,* if you can believe it! But suddenly Pax's vision unveiled in my mind, and what happened earlier this evening was precisely what I saw then. I realized you had to stay. Who was I to insist my wife be with me when she still had a fantastic prophecy to fulfill?

"I tried so hard to reach you that night," he continued, pulling her even closer. "But it was impossible. You were so closed off. I asked Tabbit Densal to try, but only Calla was hearing her. You finally felt me in the morning when you kissed that cold body before they moved it, but there wasn't any way I could explain that you couldn't come with me then because of what you had to do today."

Mahrree scoffed lightly. "It's probably for the best that we don't know the end from the beginning. From over here, everything is so clear."

"And Shem can't see anything clearly," said Perrin. "He's feeling a depth of grief that won't allow him to accept any other explanations besides the one he's chosen: he caused two women's deaths."

"He's going to have to forgive himself then, isn't he?" Mahrree said. "Even though he didn't do anything wrong."

"He was actually fulfilling prophecies, but each fulfillment cost a life close to him. Now he has to learn to accept the healing power of the Creator. It's the last lesson he has to learn. He's led so many people to that power, but never had to pull so deeply from it himself."

"You can help him do that, too," she encouraged. "You know more about that than almost anyone. Look how much progress you've made with Young Pere. And look how much you've learned just tonight."

But Perrin shrugged sadly. "Shem's not listening to me. He also never knew about my connection to Lemuel. He never knew to what depths I fell."

"But he *will* listen to his big brother when the time is right, I know it," Mahrree insisted.

"I know it, too," he said, squeezing her. "Until then?"

"Calla won't leave him," Mahrree said. "Lek and Huldah have felt her presence, and I think they've even heard her. Before I left, they were telling Shem that she was there and that she doesn't hold him responsible."

"It's ironic," Perrin mused. "For all the years Shem and I spent in the army, it's our wives who die glorious deaths in battle: Calla by arrows and you by a sword! The world really *has* become twisted."

Mahrree snorted softly. "Someday Shem will see how 'romantic' it all was. Oh Perrin, if he could just see what we see! If he could just understand, he wouldn't be so consumed with grief and guilt. How do we reach him?"

"That's the mortal trial, my darling wife," Perrin said. "To keep breathing and crawling in the dark when we can't see what's ahead of us. He has to *choose* to feel comfort. He has to call for the Creator to help him. He has to surrender like I'm learning how to. And since he can be as stubborn as I am sometimes, this may take him some time."

"Time we don't have anymore," Mahrree pointed out. She glanced over at Young Pere. "Speaking of time—do you think he'll make it?"

He shrugged. "It's up to him how quickly he progresses. There's time, but just barely enough. But Mahrree, he's already asked that we go with him in the morning. He's heading for the ancient site and he wants us to help him face his parents."

"Yes!" she cried out, then slapped her hand over her mouth. "Did he hear me?"

Perrin chuckled. "Only if you want him to hear you."

She watched her grandson praying, but he didn't move from his position.

"Of all our family, he's the one in the best position right now," Perrin told her. "Mahrree, go back up to the temple site for the night and see if anyone else can be reached. Young Pere and I will be fine here until dawn. He's finally going home."

The 35th Day of Planting

Colonel Offra and Teman gazed down upon Salem, the first light of dawn just reaching it. From their perch in a nearby canyon, they both sighed. The valley was quiet, but there was evidence that soldiers had been there. Animals were wandering, fences were broken, glass was shattered, and blankets and curtains were strewn—as if a wild party had occurred and no one had bothered to clean up.

"I feel like something happened last night," Teman said in hushed tones, although no one was around to hear him except Woodson and three other scouts, who were making their way up the slope through the brush to greet them. "Something . . . more than this."

"What was that?" Woodson asked, his voice also subdued as he reached them. "Something happened last night?" He exhaled. "I feel it, too. A great many things happened, but what, I don't know. We're the last six Salemites free in the valley, as far as I can tell. Then again, none of us have been in the valley since yesterday."

"What about Assistant Ahno?" Teman asked. "He went into the Second Resting Station with Thorne—that was observed. But have any of your men seen him come out again?"

Woodson only sighed and his three scouts said nothing.

After a moment of silence, Jon whispered, "Bravest Salemite since Perrin."

"Amen," Teman whispered, and Woodson gruffly cleared his throat.

"We'll tell his children later," Woodson said. "Because, gentlemen, it's time for us to go to the ancient site. There's nothing more for us to do here."

Offra looked longingly across Salem. "Woodson, are you sure? Nothing more I could do?"

Woodson put a hand on his shoulder. "Jon, you have been aston-ishingly helpful. I'll be honest, I had my doubts about you. I figured you'd get in my way and I'd have to rescue you. But you've con-vinced thousands of soldiers to not even enter Salem, but go back to Edge. You've put thousands more *on* edge, and I think every last one of them has heard all of the prophecies concerning the Last Day, thanks to you. Why, you're probably the most effective rector we've ever had in Salem, and you're not even a rector."

All the men smiled, even Woodson, who wasn't known to ever be lighthearted. It certainly was an unusual day if Woodson was mak-ing jokes.

"Boys," he said, his voice almost tender, "working with all of you has been an opportunity of a lifetime, and aren't we all blessed that all of this happened in our lifetimes? But as I already told the rest of the scouting corps, our job here is done. We were organized to keep the soldiers out of Salem, and now that we've failed that task en-tirely," he produced another wry smile, "it's time for us to get over to the Idumean trail before the Idumeans do. Let's go."

He turned to head west, expecting his scouts to faithfully follow him, but two didn't.

"Woodson," Jon tried again. "There's still time, right? There are soldiers who haven't yet made up their minds about everything. Maybe . . . maybe I can still reach a few more? Turn around some of those more naïve boys, those worried fathers, those women and chil-dren who are beginning to think all of this was a bad idea? Conditions up on the trail in the mountains are deteriorating rapidly. I heard one of your men talking. There's so much filth and muck, and people are losing heart . . . And *something* awful happened last night here in the valley, I feel it in my gut. I think . . . I think a few more might be willing to listen today."

Woodson turned around again, but focused on Teman. "What do you think?"

The small man shrugged. "I think it's possible—"

"No, not about Jon's idea. *About Jon*," Woodson said, tipping his head. Not worrying about tact, he asked, "Do you think Jon can han-dle staying? How stable has our colonel been?"

Jon rocked back, surprised to hear himself discussed so casually, so conspicuously. His timid, boyish part came forward and he cow-ered a little, worried.

But Teman took him by the arm. "No, Jon. That's not who you

are anymore. Who have you been the past two days? I've seen a very different man out there, one who was more focused than I've ever known, a powerful blend of Jon and Colonel Offra. Now, where is he?" He shook Jon's arm, as if trying to dislodge the correct personality from wherever it was hiding.

It worked.

Jon straightened up and squared his shoulders. In Colonel Shin's jacket, he looked even broader.

Something about that jacket, Woodson mused privately. The jacket was keeping Offra on task, lending him strength and steadiness. As if Perrin Shin was still rubbing off on him, quite literally.

"I'm stable enough, Woodson," Colonel Offra declared. "If I were any saner, I wouldn't be trying to stay and undo the army—I'd be running for the ancient site. Maybe a little instability is a good thing right now?"

Teman beamed and the other scouts snorted.

Woodson eyed him analytically. Finally he said, "It's not up to you or me but up to your friend. Teman, he can't do this alone. Are you up to staying with him, whatever he does?"

Teman continued to beam. "Absolutely, Woodson. I can play the part of hostage very well," and he put on a terrified expression as Jon grabbed the scruff of his collar.

The rest of the corps chuckled.

Woodson stepped up and shook Jon's hand. "Then we'll see you later, sometime. Teman," he took his hand, "good luck. May the Creator preserve both of you. Or take you. Frankly, I don't know what we should be hoping for right now, so let's just leave it up to Him, right? Be careful, both of you. Or don't be. I don't know. Just continue wrecking things for the army. And have fun doing it."

In the morning, Versa crawled out from under the brush and looked around in the growing dawn.

If any soldiers were around, they were long gone, fled from the trees to the fields or houses beyond. With a heaving groan, she pulled herself to her feet, using an obliging tree. Arching her back—and immediately regretting it—she chuckled ruefully.

"Whoever thinks sleeping out under the stars is romantic has never actually done it."

She retrieved her pack, slung it on her back, and untied the water flask to fill in the river. Spying a soldier downstream adding his own water to the river, she scowled and headed upstream to ensure the purest water she could find. Where the water was running the roughest over the rocks, she knelt on the bank and dipped in her flask. Once it was filled, she corked it, and—

"Oh, dear Creator," she whispered as her back tightened in a strange twinge. "No, that's not supposed to happen already, and I've told You that!"

Closing her eyes, she sat down clumsily on the bank and held her head, because maybe—just maybe—things really weren't going her way, and hadn't for quite some time.

"I can't. I can't." She looked up with new humility. "All right, dear Creator—You win this round. For once I'll admit it: I can't do this alone. I think . . . I think I *may* need some help. Just for a few hours. Just to get me to the ancient site. Please?"

When Young Pere opened his eyes it was to see the light coming over the mountains ahead of the dawn. He sat up on the sofa wet with frost and smiled at it. Even though he'd had only a few hours of sleep, he felt energy and desire unlike anything else. It told him he could do this, he could still make it, he was still needed, and most importantly, he was still *wanted*.

There was really only one route from here, the fastest and most direct: the Back Door. He needed to cross the valley first to the other side, about twelve miles, making sure he avoided the soldiers that were undoubtedly roaming it.

Then it would be over two miles up the mountain, going up the steepest part that was a rocky face, to spill out over the back side of the temple site. By that afternoon, he should be facing his family.

Still up to it, Young Pere?

"Yes, Muggah. I'm tired of the thorn in my foot. I'm ready to ask for help to get it out."

Excellent! I'm so happy!

Young Pere scoffed a chuckle. "Happy to finally see me humbled?"

Oh, Young Pere, you know what I mean.

BESIDES, Young Pere heard Puggah on the other side, *YOU HAVE*

YET TO BE COMPLETELY HUMBLED.

Young Pere cringed. "Just what do you have planned, Puggah?"

All he heard was a faint chuckle in the cosmos.

YOU BEST GET MOVING. THERE ARE DISORIENTED, HUNGRY, AND FRIGHTENED SOLDIERS EVERYWHERE.

Are you hungry? The thought was distinctly Muggah-originated.

"I'm all right for the day." He stood up and stretched. "I decided to fast until I get to the site. Not having any food makes that decision easier."

Oh, Young Pere—I'm not sure that's a good idea for today. Promise me if you find any food, you'll eat it. You'll need your strength.

"Yes, Muggah," he grinned. He was ready to do anything she asked. Before he continued, he took off his uniform jacket. "For you, Puggah," he said. He turned it inside-out and put it back on, the dull black lining already deflecting the rising sunlight.

PERFECT, YOUNG PERE. ARE YOU TAKING THE BACK DOOR?

"It's the closest."

JUST MAKE SURE YOU STAY IN THE FOREST FOR AS LONG AS POSSIBLE. MUCH LESS TRAFFIC.

"Whatever you say, Puggah."

Go to the river, Young Pere. You could . . . wash up a bit.

MAHRREE, WHAT DOES HE NEED TO WASH UP FOR? I'M SURE THEY'LL BE HAPPY TO SEE HIM IN WHATEVER CONDITION HE'S IN.

Young Pere smiled at the familiarity of the gentle bickering on either side of him.

I know, Perrin, but . . . don't you think he should go to the water anyway? Just beyond that second foot bridge? At least get a drink.

YOUNG PERE, MUGGAH WANTS YOU TO GO TO THE RIVER. I AGREE. THAT'S THE BEST ROUTE.

"Whatever you say."

He didn't see anyone else awake that early. Without officers to rouse them, he doubted any soldiers who slept in abandoned houses or barns or in the temple would be awake for some time. None of the soldiers curled up in the slush on the field showed signs of moving. He didn't even have competition for the sofa last night. No one dared come near it, as if they could tell the spirit of a general sat there, glaring.

He deliberately didn't look at the temple behind him, where his grandmother's body was. She wasn't there, anyway, but was so close that he could feel her small frame walking alongside, as if her arm was looped through his. The sensation put a permanent smile on his face and he didn't even notice the chill of the morning as he stepped into the forest by the river.

As he'd knelt last night telling the Creator all that he had done, he'd felt the hope grow. He was still loved, and although he had a lot to make right again, he was on the right trail, headed in the right direction, escorted by strength on either side. All he had to do was crawl up that mountain as Puggah had. He just hoped he had enough time.

The river, remember?

"I remember, Muggah. And yes, I'll get a drink." He picked his way through the thick foliage to where he heard the bubbling, and realized he wasn't alone.

A figure, several paces away, was kneeling to get a drink.

He stiffened with worry until he realized it wasn't a soldier but a woman. The speed with which she arose and spun to face him was truly astonishing. Almost as astonishing as the long knife brandished in her fist.

Young Pere took a protective step back but couldn't take his eyes off of the knife. Or rather, what was behind the knife: a very large, very bulging belly.

Young Pere sighed and knew why his grandparents sent him there. The brown-gray tunic and breeches the young woman wore couldn't camouflage the fact that she was expecting, and very soon. She couldn't even fully fasten her long cloak around her middle.

Young Pere immediately held up his hands. "I mean you no harm, I promise. In fact, I was wondering if you needed help."

To his surprise, she took an aggressive step toward him, firming her grip on the long knife which she held quite properly.

Young Pere knew how to take a hint. "All right then, no closer."

"Why should I trust a soldier?" she snapped.

Her voice didn't even waver. She had no fear—none at all, which made Young Pere a bit fearful of her.

With his hands still up he gestured to his jacket. "I'm not a soldier anymore. See? I turned my jacket inside out. I want nothing more to do with the Army of Idumea. I'm trying to get to safety, and I'm guessing you are too."

The woman only glared at him.

After an uncomfortable moment, he said, "I can help. I know the way to the ancient temple site."

With her gaze as sharp as her blade, she demanded, "And what do you know of the site?"

Young Pere took another step, but raised his hands higher as her knife rose as well. "I'm originally from Salem. But *you,* originally, are not."

"And what makes you so sure of that?"

He nodded to her knife. "That. It's army issued. No one in Salem makes those. You're not supposed to have that, you know. All weapons are to remain in the world. How did you get it out?"

"Easy enough. Just kept it alongside my hip," she said curtly. "Not like any Salemite scouts pat down the refugees they bring into the valley."

Young Pere couldn't help but grin.

"And why are you smiling?" she asked severely.

"I'm sorry. I had a great-great-great-something grandmother named Lorixania who also had an affinity for long blades. The story goes that she hid them all around her house and often kept one with her. I could never imagine a woman behaving that way, then today I see you and, well . . ." He tried to stifle his smile but the harder he tried, the goofier it became.

The woman's mouthed twitched. "Maybe I'm related. Haven't found much evidence of my family in Salem. It seems we're the first ones here."

Young Pere nodded to her hand. "Please, you can put that away. I promise you that I'm unarmed. No weapons are to be at the ancient site, according to Guide Gleace's vision."

The woman finally softened enough to relax her grip on the knife. "You *are* from Salem, aren't you? Who else would know Gleace's name and that they're unarmed up there? Still, I'm not entirely sure about you, but it's not like I can be too particular today."

She looked up to the sky, shrugged at it, and eyed Young Pere critically.

He couldn't help but glance up too, to see who she might be consulting with.

Clearly disappointed, she sighed. "Well, I suppose you're it, then." Expertly she flipped the knife, pulled aside her tunic, and slipped the knife into the waistband in one smooth motion.

Young Pere was duly impressed. "Don't nick your baby with that, now."

She almost smiled. "Never had an accident yet, and I've been carrying knives since I was seven." She leaned over to pick up her pack.

But Young Pere was faster. "Let me get that for you. Carrying knives since you were seven?" he asked as he slung her weighty pack over his shoulder. "You must have had a cheery childhood."

The woman scoffed and, for the first time, Young Pere noticed how young she was, likely no more than twenty. But her blue eyes seemed much older. "No, not the cheeriest. But I'm used to taking care of myself."

"But you'll let me walk with you anyway?" Young Pere gestured at the woods ahead of them. "So, things got better once you came to Salem?" he said as he led the way, the woman stepping up next to him.

She pursed her lips. "In many ways, yes. In a couple of ways, no. But then again, staying in the world wouldn't have changed that either, I'm sure. Do you know where you're going?"

"I do," he said. "The tree-marked trail doesn't start for about another twelve miles. We should make it to the trail head in a few hours, as long as you're up to it, Mrs. . . . I'm sorry, I don't know your name."

She stared straight ahead as she answered. "I'm not a wife. Not anymore. My husband abandoned me over a season ago and Guide Zenos has granted me a termination of marriage."

"I'm sorry to hear that," Young Pere said, but for a brief, shocking moment he thought that maybe he wasn't.

Fortunately that moment passed.

"So . . . what should I call you?"

She sighed heavily. "Does my name really matter?"

"Just a random designation, isn't it?" Young Pere said. "You could take any name. I know of some women who went back to their father's name—"

Her aggravated exhale told him that wasn't the best idea. "That's not much of a name, either. In fact, he's part of the reason why I'm alone right now."

"I was wondering about that. No one's supposed to go to the site unaccompanied. Especially someone expecting."

She shrugged. "I told my mother I'd join her there. She left with my sister and others from our area, but I told her I'd go with another group."

"So what happened to that group?"

"They never existed. My plan was to talk to my father, convince him to . . . well, to change his mind, I guess."

Young Pere nodded. "I noticed that not everyone went up to the ancient site, that some decided to stay and fight instead. I'm assuming your father's one without faith in the guide?"

She snorted. "Oh, I suppose you could say that. I never got a chance to talk to him, though. I always seemed to keep missing him." The annoyance in her tone returned.

They walked quietly for a few minutes until Young Pere said, "Did you see what happened at the temple last night?"

"Oh, yes," she said darkly. "So did you, I assume?"

"Yes," he whispered.

"That was astounding, wasn't it?" she said, her voice filling with admiration.

Not expecting that reaction, Young Pere glanced over at her. She was staring off in the distance, her face set and rather fierce.

"I mean, there she stood with tens of thousands of soldiers in front of her. She must have known there was no chance for her, but she did it anyway! She just . . . she just *shouted* at them, and one little old woman terrified thousands of soldiers. I thought, Dear Creator, make me that brave! Make me that willing to die so others can live!"

Young Pere eyed her, unsure of what to think, but she didn't notice.

"I met her once, Mahrree Shin. Right after the volcano erupted. We were supposed to have met her earlier but we were able to avoid it. I did not want to meet her then, I assure you.

"I ran into her quite by accident, and when I realized who she was . . . well, I was quite uneasy. But she took one look at me and embraced me. She was so kind yet so powerful. How could a woman in her seventies be so strong?" She smiled at the memory.

Then her smile faded. "And then last night that absurd guide took one look at her—he must have known her from the world and believed she was dead all these years. I was hiding in the trees and I nearly laughed when they said he had died! Did you see the reaction of the soldiers?" She finally looked at Young Pere, her eyes glowing. "She did it! She terrified them! Just like The Writings said she would. One third of the soldiers, running in a panic because of a little old lady! It was amazing."

Young Pere couldn't meet the fire in her eyes, and instead looked down at the ground. "And then she was dead," he said tonelessly.

"Yes." The energy also gone from her voice. "That *ridiculous* general walked up to her and just cut her down," she said bitterly.

"And then he gloried in it, as if he had defeated some massive bear with only his one good arm instead of a helpless great-grandmother." She watched the ground in front of her, picking her way around a log. "I knew then that there was no hope."

Something in the way she said that caught Young Pere off guard. But, not knowing what else to say, he said nothing.

They walked silently through the woods, the woman running her hand over her large belly.

"You all right?" Young Pere asked a minute later, seeing her holding herself.

"Yes," she whispered back. "It's just pulling on my muscles. By the way, I don't know your name, soldier-who's-not-a-soldier."

"Name's just a random designation, remember? Unimportant."

"Hm," she smirked.

"Tell you what," he said, "when you tell me *your* name, I'll tell you *mine*."

"Names are tricky things, aren't they?" she said evasively. "They can hold so much history. The weight of generations attached to them makes it so you can't always carry it all." She grimaced as she stepped over another log.

Young Pere stopped. "I have an idea. That shawl around your shoulders, do you really need it to keep warm?"

"No, it's my mother's. She wanted me to take it. But this baby's got me so heated up I could be standing in a blizzard and melt everything around me."

Young Pere smiled. "Understood. Then I have a better use for it. I saw my sisters and cousins do this. If I may?" He took the shawl from her shoulders, kneeled, and gingerly put his arms under her coat and around her waist to wrap it around her lower back.

"I'm sorry," he whispered as he reached around her, his face nearly up against her belly. "Here, maybe you should do this," he said anxiously, giving her the ends of the shawl and stepping back. "Now tie it under your belly. The back part should go down on your hips, um, not quite . . ."

She smiled at his nervousness and said, "Just do it for me, all right? Remember, I don't have a jealous husband."

"I know. Somehow that makes it worse," he mumbled. He thought he heard the woman quietly chuckle as he slid the shawl down on her hips to the position he'd seen his expecting sisters and cousins wear their supports. Then he tied the ends firmly under her belly.

"There. See? That should help your lateral stomach muscles hold up the weight, and give your back more support."

She nodded in appreciation. "I already feel a difference. Thank you. Ever thought of becoming a midwife?" she smirked.

"A doctor, for a time. Might look into it again."

"Well, you *almost* have a gentle touch," she said as she headed again on the faint path.

Young Pere stepped up next to her and tried to fight the blush heating his cheeks. He glanced over at her again under the pretext of making sure the support was staying, but also wanting to study her features.

Her blond hair was pulled back into a braid that ran down her back, and her face probably would have seemed gentler if her eyes were. Young Pere couldn't shake the feeling that she was familiar somehow. Her face was striking, her eyes severe. While she was vulnerable, she was also ready for a fight. Why any man would want to abandon such a combination of strength and confidence—

"So," she broke into his thoughts. "We have a ways to walk—tell me your story. I should know who I'm naively following into the forest." Her hand hovered near her hip where the long knife was concealed, and Young Pere wondered if she planned to abandon it or use it.

He scoffed lightly. "You do *not* want to hear my story, I promise. Tell me yours, then I'll see if I should tell you mine."

She scoffed back. "My story? Where to begin?"

"How about no details, just generalities? So I get an idea?"

She nodded. "All right—generalities. My family lived in the world for a couple of years in peace and luxury and security and . . . then we didn't."

"That's it?" Young Pere said when she didn't continue. "That's a little *too* general. We still have miles to go before we even get to the trail."

"All right," she sighed. "More details. Our father didn't want us after I turned three years old. My sister was almost one, and my mother had a newborn girl."

"*Three* children? In the world?"

"You can see the problem, can't you?"

"Oh, yes. How'd that happen back then? I mean—" Young Pere tried to think of a better way to phrase it, but she chuckled.

"I know what you mean. My father was hoping for a son, and his stature allowed him to bend a few rules. But he didn't get his son, so he didn't want any of us."

"That's terrible. Little girls are wonderful. Better than sons, I think. At least daughters don't take off and—" He stopped abruptly.

She glanced over at him, "Want to tell me *your* story now?"

"No. You keep going. So he didn't get a son . . ."

"Actually, my mother took us away. At that time the marriage laws in the world stated that he could remarry and have more children if his wife and daughters were dead. So, that's what my mother feared was his next step."

Astonished, Young Pere said, "You really think your father was going to try to kill you?"

She shrugged, obviously used to the idea. "Yes. And he did try. He sent men looking for us. We were hidden and protected for a few years at a southern fort, but after that commander died we were on our own. I remember clearly six different attempts on our lives when I was younger, by mysterious men dressed like Guarders, and a couple of times by soldiers."

"Soldiers?" Young Pere spluttered. "Killing a woman and three children? That's not the work of soldiers!"

"It is if that woman and those children are a direct threat to the security of the area," she said coolly.

"That's ridiculous," Young Pere said.

"Yes, it was. It also was ridiculous how often they failed. I realize now we were protected by the Creator, each and every time. He didn't want us to die."

"But for Him to let you suffer like that?" he said without thinking. "That doesn't seem fair—"

The woman stopped and caught his arm. "Seriously? Did you seriously just say that?"

Startled by the ferocity in her eyes, he said lamely, "Well, yeah, considering how—"

She put her hands on her hips. "How long have you lived in Salem?"

"Most of my life."

"And you still don't get it?"

"Get what?"

She held out her hands. "The point? The purpose of all of this?"

"Which is?"

"The Test!" she exclaimed. "I've only understood it for the past two seasons, but you've known about it your whole life and *still* have the nerve to say that the Creator is unfair? *He's* not unfair, *life* is! It's how we react to that unfairness that's part of the Test!" She rolled her eyes and looked past the trees to the sky. "I'm walking with an idiot here!" she announced loudly to the clouds. "Is this the best You could send me? *Really?*"

Stunned, Young Pere looked around at the treetops. "Are you *complaining* to someone?"

She cast him a playfully disdainful look. "I am, because He listens." She pointed upward. "I'm sure He has a reason for sending you to be my escort, but right now I'm just *not seeing it.*"

Again Young Pere couldn't fight the goofy smile that appeared on his face. "You're really something else, aren't you?"

She narrowed her eyes at him. "I looked for the meaning of my life since I was a small child, trying to understand why we had to go through what we did. When I finally learned about the Test last year, everything made sense. I was given trials, and I beat them, nearly every time! You, on the other hand, have known your whole life about this Test and yet you're completely clueless. I don't have any patience for such stupidity." She marched on, leaving him speechless.

But he had to catch up, so stumbling after her he came up with, "Whew. Wow. Please tell me what you think, because I'm not very good at reading minds," he said sarcastically. "You're a little critical, you know, and you know nothing about me—"

"I know *enough*," she spat, sneering at his uniform. "You left Salem to go to the world. The guide said they haven't had anyone in the army since he left. That means you purposely abandoned what you know was right to pursue something less. You threw away something great for just shadows." She was nearly shouting now. "You're a dog, just like my father and just like my ex-husband! And before you start protesting, realize that I'm not saying *all* men are like that, just a particularly disappointing *breed!*"

Young Pere's mouth was open so far he was surprised a bug didn't fly into it. A variety of comebacks flowed through his mind as he plowed through the bushes, but he didn't mention any of them. All he could think was, *Puggah wants me to be humbled.*

"You're right," he finally said, once he caught up to her again. She could walk pretty fast for hefting such a large belly. "I abandoned a blessed life and now I'm struggling to get it back. I regret what I did and I hope to somehow make it up to my family."

She was quiet as they walked. "That's it?" she eventually asked.

"That's it."

"Well, I'm almost impressed. I think you actually meant that."

"I do," he said.

"Then I'm sorry. You may not actually be that breed after all. You may yet be a decent dog, but it's far too soon to tell."

"Thank you. I think." Young Pere wondered why he felt again the urge to smile. "So tell me about some of those escapes. The ones you attribute to the Creator."

She cast him a challenging glance. "It *was* Him."

"I believe you. Really. So tell me."

She sighed and shifted the shawl on her hips.

"Should we walk slower?"

"No. I'm fine," she said brusquely. "One time I remember very well happened when I was nearly eight."

"When you started carrying knives?"

"Yes. This is why, too. The commander of the fort where we had lived had recently died, and the makeup of the army changed drastically. We were on our own, desperately poor and my mother was trying to find a way to support us. Somehow word got back to my father where we were. My mother had the idea to disguise us as boys. She cut our hair, got us shirts and trousers, and told our new neighbors that my littlest sister was a nephew she was caring for. My name became Darryl."

"Darryl? What kind of a name is Darryl?"

"It was a popular boys' name near Marsh where we were living," she scowled. "And I liked it. My mother had just started us in school, and we were waiting for her to pick us up at the end of the day. No one wanted their children walking home alone at that time.

"As we stood at the front steps watching the other children leave with their mothers, soldiers came from nowhere. A man in an officer's uniform marched up the walk, paused when he saw us, looked at me carefully, then walked past. But I knew it was my father. I remembered him from when I was little, over four years earlier."

Her face almost softened. "I have one very clear, very happy memory of him. He was holding me and laughing, and I was laughing too. I *loved* him. So when I looked into his face that afternoon, I remembered being with him as if it had happened yesterday. But when he looked at me, it was as if he couldn't focus."

Her jaw shifted and her features hardened. "He seemed to look right past me, almost through me. I was so hurt, and I wanted to run after him and hug his legs and beg him to remember me. Because Uncle Fadhy—he was the man who had hid us in his fort for many years—he had hugged us and tickled us and was so loving before he died. All I wanted was to feel that closeness again, and with my real father.

"But something held me back. I was holding on to my sisters' hands and had a very distinct feeling that I shouldn't move. They were only about six and five. Then I heard him talking to one of the teachers, just inside the building. He said my mother's name and mentioned three girls. The teacher said they knew no one like that but they would keep an eye out. I still remember how angry his voice was when he said, 'They're dangerous, no matter how they appear.' Then he marched out right past us and out of the school grounds. My sisters were terrified but I was furious. He claimed we were dangerous!"

She took a deep breath as her fist clenched. "We waited for a long time for our mother, but she didn't come. So I took my sisters to the market to see if she might be there. All we found were soldiers, everywhere, looking at each woman, staring at each child. Although I think every soldier noticed us, none of them *really* saw us. Except for my father. He spotted us again, and as he tried once more to evaluate me, his eyes seemed to drift as if he wasn't allowed to see us. He marched past us again, and all I wanted to do was to kick him, to hurt him somehow, like he hurt us.

"We didn't find our mother at the market or in any of the neighborhoods," she told a silent Young Pere. "She'd seen the soldiers coming and went into hiding, feeling confident that while we wouldn't be recognized, she would be.

"We wandered around the village for hours, not sure what to do. Someone gave us apples, and it wasn't until after dark that I finally found my mother, dressed in men's clothing she had stolen from someone's laundry line, and her own hair cut very short. She took our hands and whisked us away. She didn't say a word or stop until we were clear of the village. We spent the night in a barn, stealing milk from the cows and chewing on the horses' oats and the pigs' corn. We didn't go back home for days. Well, our 'home' was just an old shed then, made out of block. The barn was roomier and warmer."

Her eyes became steely as she stared in the distance. "That was the first time I realized my father didn't love me but wanted me gone.

Only years later did I understand that we represented his failure: daughters were a mistake that he needed to remove. When we finally returned to the village after the soldiers were back to their regular routines, we walked through the market and I stole a knife from a peddler as we walked by. I was pretty good at stealing things. We had no other choice. Don't worry," she interrupted herself, "Guide Zenos has heard all of this already. So has my rector. They said the Creator understood, too.

"At the time we lived in that shack with two rooms, and when my sisters went to sleep, I would practice hiding the knife in my clothes, pulling it out quickly, and slashing with it. I never actually used it on a soldier until I was fourteen, and that soldier wasn't acting under my father's orders. He was after something *else* entirely. But I changed his mind for him and took his knife, too, since it was much better quality," she added with a smug smile. "My only regret is that I didn't get to hear his explanation to the fort surgeon as to how he acquired such an *extraordinary* injury." She patted the knife secured at her hip.

Young Pere hadn't said a word as she told her story, but an awful thought had formed in his mind as she spoke.

Who else in the world would order his soldiers to chase his wife and daughters?

No. There was absolutely no way that . . .

He glanced at the woman again, assessing her profile, then turned abruptly back.

"So," she said, "you're very quiet. Did I shock you?" Her tone suggested she hoped he'd say yes.

"I guess I'm just a little preoccupied," Young Pere ventured, "with the wound you inflicted on the soldier. My mind is racing with *possibilities.*"

To his surprise, she laughed darkly. "Just don't do anything that would cause me to repeat my previous work. You *really* don't want to see *that.*"

Young Pere coughed. "Not planning on it! To be honest, you've got me just a little . . . stunned."

She smiled proudly and they walked on before he spoke again, trying to think of how to get more information to confirm his suspicions.

"Quite amazing what you went through. I think you're right—the Creator did preserve you and your sisters. It's been my experience that when someone is looking intently for someone, *everyone* looks like that person. That he didn't see or focus on you, that's the Creator's hand."

"I'm glad you see it that way," she said. "I wish my mother could have, earlier. Shortly after that incident, someone from Salem came to try to bring us here, but my mother was too skeptical. She thought it was a trap to bring us back to our father. The night the scouts came to retrieve us, we were already gone to another village.

"Then a few years later, when we were teenagers and couldn't pretend to be boys anymore, Guide Zenos sent another group of scouts to find us. This time my mother listened more carefully but still she was too fearful." She sighed. "After all those years it was hard for her to trust any man, no matter how kind and sincere he seemed to be.

"Finally last year we were sought out again, and this time my mother was ready to come to Salem. The Creator always kept His eye on us. We never starved, although we were often hungry. We never froze, although we were often cold. And when we came to Salem, it was right before the volcano erupted. We would have died where we were, I'm sure of it. We stayed at the Second Resting Station for several weeks. We ate very well, slept very well, and I felt great peace that the Creator would make up for everything I had gone through. He would make everything better."

"You really are something else, aren't you?" Young Pere said, this time more respectfully. "Do you still feel that way? Even after losing your husband?"

She massaged her neck. "Actually, I must confess I'm not too disappointed about that, or surprised. He never really understood. He seemed anxious to come to Salem but he just kept complaining once we got here. Even *before* we got here, actually. Turns out he was only using me. I'm not even sure why I married him in the first place. I guess I was just so desperate for the attention of a man—*any* man—that I accepted the first offer that came my way.

"He was different before our move," she continued. "Attentive. Kind. Then afterward he turned unpredictable. He was occasionally loving, but only when he wanted something. Otherwise, he was always agitated.

"Now I realize I should have demanded better," she said. "After seeing the quality of men here in Salem I realized that maybe, just maybe, the Creator *could* give me someone who believed in Him, and who could love me and even my baby. At least, that's what Guide

Zenos promised after he granted me the termination of marriage."

Young Pere smiled, feeling a kick in his gut as he focused on her features which were now very familiar. "You're right. You can do much better. I've never known Guide Zenos to be wrong."

It was obvious why she didn't want to tell him her maiden name. He was walking in the forest with Thorne's daughter.

Maybe even his cousin. His *half* cousin? Possibly?

How did that work, anyway?

He didn't realize he was still staring at her until she said, "Something wrong? I *did* shock you, didn't I? Come on, what is it?"

"No, no, no," he said, turning quickly back. "Not at all—"

"It's just that you keep looking at me and I'm not sure why."

"I'm just . . . just making sure the support is staying."

"*Sure* you are."

They walked in silence again for a few minutes before she broke it with, "So you're not going to tell me your story?"

Remaining focused on the terrain before them, he said, "You come off as a hero in your story. I won't in mine."

"Then can I ask you a question instead?"

He hesitated. "Uh, sure."

"Your name's Perrin, isn't it?"

He hadn't expected that and stumbled on nothing but dirt. Once he regained his footing, he dared to meet her amused gaze.

Never before had it been so hard to say the word, "Yes."

Her pace slowed to match his. "So then your last name is . . . ?"

He sighed and opened his jacket to show her his name patch.

SHIN.

Her eyebrows rose.

"I'm the only one who gave his real name when he signed up," Young Pere explained sheepishly. "And I was still a bit fogged."

There was an odd smile on her face. "There were a lot of Perrin Shins in the northern army."

"I know. I was the real thing. Well, sort of."

Her smile broadened. "Your family will be thrilled to see you. They've never stopped searching and hoping they'd find you. I only guessed at the name because of the descriptions they sent around a few days ago in case someone saw you."

That news struck Young Pere oddly, and he wasn't sure if he was happy that they told all of Salem their son might be returning, or if he should be worried that maybe they sent out the description as a warning.

The fact that Thorne's daughter suddenly seemed nervous suggested the latter; her hand was hovering near her long knife again.

She forced a chuckle. "I must confess I also recognized your features. For a while our family was your poor father's special project. Rector Shin was a regular visitor, especially when we had trouble, so I saw him quite a bit. You look a lot like him." She was trying to smile but Young Pere saw something else in her eyes.

To avoid that, he looked ahead. "I'm sorry if the name startled you."

"Why would you think your name would startle me?"

"Anyone with the last name of Thorne *would* be startled by a Shin."

Her eyes widened and she stopped. "How did you know I'm a Thorne?"

He stopped, too, a generous distance away so that she wouldn't feel threatened nor feel like pulling out her knife again. "Because I got to know General Lemuel Thorne very well. You have the same profile. Same nose, same hair coloring . . . You look a lot like your father, too."

She unconsciously touched her nose, noticed his hesitant smile, and smiled nervously back. "Can you imagine if the general and your grandfather could see us right now? Perrin Shin and Versula Thorne, walking in the forest together?"

Young Pere nearly choked. "Your name is *Versula*?" He thought he heard a faint cosmic chuckle and giggle that reminded him of his grandparents.

She shrugged. "Not the greatest name, I know. Named after my paternal grandmother. That's part of the reason my mother shortened it to Versa when I was older. That's what I go by: Versa. And you were named after your grandfather?"

"I'm sorry—I wasn't making fun of your name. I just didn't realize that . . ." He shrugged, realizing that now really wasn't the time to explain that *her* grandmother and *his* grandfather with the same names at *their* ages were—

"You're right," Young Pere held up his hands in surrender to the swirling in his mind. "Perrin Shin and Versula Thorne, walking together in the forest." He gestured to it to remind her that they hadn't been walking for the last minute. She began again, and he stepped in next to her. "But I have to tell you, I think my grandfather already knows."

OF COURSE I DO. WHY DO YOU THINK WE TOLD YOU TO GO THIS WAY?

Versa scowled at him. She seemed to be suspicious of nearly everything, and with good reason. "Why do you say that?"

"He's the one who nudged me to go to the river," Young Pere explained, sort of. "He's always had his own plans."

Versa nodded slowly, as if trying to make sense of that, and continued walking. "I wish I could've met him. I heard so many stories about him, in the world and then here in Salem. I was so disappointed to realize I missed meeting him by a year. I always wondered if he lived up to his reputation."

Young Pere smiled as he kept in step with her. "The stories didn't do him justice. I really miss him. But maybe someday, somehow, you'll meet my Puggah."

He wondered why he said that, and his thoughts drifted to what Puggah told him when he was thrown into the dungeon. He'd been slightly disappointed that Young Pere didn't die that day so that he could embrace him again, but he *had* said that the day was coming, soon enough, when he would.

Young Pere had been sure that meant he was to die soon. But he had endured the dungeon, survived getting to Salem, and even escaped Thorne and the army. Still, he couldn't help but think that somehow an end, maybe *the end*, was rapidly coming for him.

He didn't have long to dwell on that dark idea, because Versa was speaking.

"So," she said slowly, and he realized he must have been quiet for some time, lost in his thoughts. "Are you still all right with escorting me to the ancient site, knowing who I am and all?"

"Of course I am. Seems only fitting somehow, doesn't it? As if our families are meant to run into each other every generation." He didn't add, *Because we also might be the same family.* "Besides," he added gravely, "you need protection."

Versa scoffed. "I told you, I can take care of myself."

"Even with tens of thousands of soldiers looking for you?"

She again stopped in her tracks. "Why would they be looking for me?"

"You're worth one hundred slips of gold to the general," Young Pere told her, gently tugging on her arm to keep her moving. "So are your mother and sister. Each."

"Pretty good bounty, I suppose," she remarked casually. "You plan to claim it?"

He heard the apprehension in her tone. "No! Of course not! I don't want gold or anything. I just want to get back to my family and I want to take you back to yours. I just thought you should know."

She nodded slowly as if not sure if she should believe him.

"Besides," he said with a growing smile, "the bounty is *twice* as much for my father and aunt. I'm heading up there to turn the both of them in."

She chuckled, but tensely, unsure if he was joking or not.

After a few more silent minutes she said, "You rode with the general?"

Young Pere sighed. "Yes. Right after the volcano erupted. I, uh, I actually saved him, I'm sort of sorry to say now. And more than once. From the ash fall, then from the river after the mudslide."

"Really?" Versa smirked. "Tell me."

Young Pere sighed. "Well, we do have all day . . . You see, I had been in Province 8 for several seasons before even meeting him, which was apparently unusual for someone who had taken the name of Perrin Shin . . ."

The sun rose on the ancient temple site but it brought no warmth. At the base of the ridge, several strong men were digging a grave in the rocky ground.

Lek Zenos supervised quietly, holding his toddler Plump Perrin who rested his sleepy head against his father's shoulder. A few other cousins also watched in silence. The rest of the families sat in huddles around the campsites, weeping.

Mattilin Shin, sitting with her husband Relf, whispered, "M1 took on the wolves. I'm sure of it now. We shouldn't have left her!"

Peto sat on the ground by Shem, who still laid on the rocky soil, tears trickling down their weary faces.

"This is madness!" Thorne exclaimed, looking around the Second Resting Station. According to the estimates of his officers, there were only thirty thousand soldiers who made it back from the temple debacle. The rest were somewhere in the vastness of Salem.

"We need to march to the west!" Thorne bellowed. "Obviously that was the correct direction all along! Who was the slagging Zenos who said otherwise?"

Major Twigg shrugged. "We can send out men to look for the missing soldiers, then tomorrow we march west."

Thorne grunted. He looked over at Sergeant Major Hili who had never regained his color from last night. "Recommendations, Poe?"

"Whatever you want, General," he said dully.

There was one thing on Poe's mind, ever since he saw Mahrree Shin fall: It most likely was *the* slagging Zenos who spread the rumor that sent the army to find nothing in the north. If it was, he also set up Mahrree to die.

It was just like Shem.

He did it to Poe, too, years ago. Instead of going himself down to Idumea to deliver the message to the Shins that Edge was in trouble, Zenos asked Poe to do it.

Of course he said that Poe could turn down the request, but Poe knew better. He was the newest recruit, the skinniest man, and most importantly, he knew how to steal horses. Zenos had even said he'd be willing to try to go, but he wasn't sure if the messengers' horses could carry his weight. Poe really had no choice.

At the time, he was eager to do it, to prove his worth to the Shins. He and Zenos had spent several days rebuilding their bedroom while talking and reminiscing about Mahrree's After School Care. Poe had even confessed to Zenos his deepest worries, his greatest crimes, and his darkest fears about the future.

Zenos had been, or at least *seemed* to be, most understanding. He told Poe he could make a new future for himself, he could fix his past wrongs by being the best man he could in the future, and that Perrin Shin would always be there to help him.

And then Poe agreed to steal those horses all the way to Idumea.

True, he delivered the message in record time. True, he was instrumental in saving Edge. And true, he even gained a bit of fame himself with that play about the colonel.

But for his thievery, which Zenos told him he needed to stop, then asked him to do *just one more time*, he was sent away from Edge. Perrin Shin *wasn't* his commander anymore. Grasses proved to be a good fort, but Edge would have been better.

Poe couldn't get Jaytsy's words out of his mind: "My mother

always thought of you as a lost son."

If Poe had been able to stay in Edge, maybe Mahrree and Perrin would have taken him with them to Salem. He had nothing left in the world. His parents didn't care about him and the few girls he tried to love didn't reciprocate his feelings. Everything—*everything*—would have been different.

It should have been Shem Zenos who rode to Idumea, who was transferred to Grasses, or *at least* should have stood last night at the temple waiting for Lemuel Thorne.

There was no doubt in his mind—Shem Zenos was still alive. Lemuel's stories were falling apart.

And it was Shem's fault that Mahrree Shin was dead. Once again, Zenos the coward made someone else do the job he was too scared to do. Zenos and a sword might have had a chance against Lemuel Thorne. But Miss Mahrree? What were they thinking?!

Poe didn't even get to say goodbye to her. He didn't even know if she recognized him in the brief moment that their eyes met. He thought maybe she did, and if she had—

For some reason he still heard her words in his head: *What color is the sky, Poe? See that it's not what they've told you it is! What color is the sky, Poe?*

He knew the truth now: she never did betray her husband. He knew it by the way the colonel referred to her in his dream: he still loved her, deeply. She had always been faithful to Perrin, and for that Poe loved her even more.

But Shem Zenos?

Poe hated Shem Zenos.

But there was now one man he hated even more: Lemuel Thorne. The man who literally broke Mahrree Shin's heart.

"Wait, wait—I'm getting confused," Versa said. "So he knew you gave your name originally as Pere Shin, but he thought your real name was Lek Briter? Then he *changed* your name when he claimed you in front of everyone before the battle for Idumea?"

Young Pere nodded. "Yep. Started calling me Corporal Lek Thorne. A few weeks later he promoted me to Lieutenant Lek Thorne."

Versa flapped her lips in disgust. "So what was the name you had made for yourself, before he changed your name?"

Young Pere hesitated. "I'm afraid to tell you."

"Why? That bad?"

"Just about."

"I won't laugh. I promise."

"You better not." Young Pere cleared his throat. "I had changed it to Sword Master Thorne Shin."

She broke her promise. "What?" she burst out, holding the sides of her belly as she laughed. "That sounds like something an eleven-year-old would make up!"

Young Pere shook his head at her, but he knew he was smiling. Then grinning. Then finally laughing.

The sound surprised him. He hadn't heard himself laugh for much longer than he could remember. It felt wonderful.

Versa wiped her eyes. "So, tell me the story behind that. There's got to be one."

"I *did* make up that name when my brothers and cousins and I were playing 'The World' with sticks we used like swords," he confessed, "but only when my grandfather and Uncle Shem weren't around. We gave ourselves designations. I called myself the 'Sword Master of the Cosmos'."

"Oh, that's *awful*," she snickered. "How old were you?"

Young Pere blushed as he confessed, "Fourteen."

They both laughed.

Versa held her belly tighter. "Stop, stop! It's too much. I'll need to relieve myself again. *Fourteen?* I was sure you were younger."

"Just acted younger. My life at fourteen was considerably different than yours," he chuckled, and the smile stayed on his face. It had missed using those muscles. "You know, the general got pretty close to the truth. A couple of times I became confused as to who I was and who he *thought* I was. My real name was Perrin Shin, but no one believed that. And General Thorne was right—I was Perrin Shin's grandson, just not Jaytsy and Deck's—or *his*—son."

"Unbelievable. Did you ever make mistakes? Get confused?"

"Oh, yeah. One time I was pretending to see your great-grandfather Cush. I was thinking about my grandfather's uniform, the one he pulled out every year, and I remembered the brass buttons on it. I'd forgotten that uniforms no longer had brass buttons, and most of the soldiers wouldn't have known, but the older ones did. Captain Nelt hadn't told me about the buttons and he confronted me about that."

"I bet that made you nervous."

"Definitely. But fortunately he was more nervous than me. By the time we got to the Pools fort there were so many stories circulating about me no one was quite sure what to think. Some of the officers thought I was Jaytsy's son and maybe even the general's real son as well. Others thought I was the original Perrin Shin come back, some of the soldiers thought I was some kind of embodied ghost at worst, or Lemuel Thorne's long-lost nephew at best, even though he never had siblings—"

He hesitated, not so sure that was entirely true.

But Versa chuckled. "And what did you tell people you were?"

"That I was a distant relation of Deckett Briter and forgot my real name when I enlisted. Then after the general claimed me, I was his son."

Versa rolled her eyes. "And I thought I got confused when my name was Darryl."

Young Pere grinned. "I never tried passing myself off as a woman. Maybe I should've tried that as well."

Versa grinned back. "You would have been the largest, scariest woman anyone would have ever seen. Now that would have provoked a few nightmares!"

They both laughed as they walked, and Young Pere watched her out of the corner of his eye. She was watching him too.

"So," she started again, "after the battle at Pools . . . off to Idumea then?"

Young Pere nodded. "The general left the next morning to claim his mansions."

Versa was quiet for a moment, and when she spoke her voice was cold. "Sargon was a cockroach. Someone should have crushed him years ago. After he betrayed General Karna, then killed my Uncle and Aunt Fadhy—" Her voice cracked.

It took her another moment to compose herself again.

"Once the Fadhs were gone, it was the end of everything for us. All because Sargon wanted everything for himself." She cleared her throat, her tone still icy. "Rumor was that his daughters were very beautiful. Did they live up to your expectations?"

Young Pere shrugged, trying to understand her sudden change of tone. But then he understood. "I didn't go with him, Versa. I'm not that kind of a man."

"Really."

Young Pere stopped walking.

She stopped midstride and looked back at him.

"Really," he said firmly. "In fact, I headed back to Edge the next day, much to the general's disappointment. I knew what he wanted me to do in Idumea with Sargon's daughters, but as I said, I'm not that kind of a man. General Perrin Shin would never have tolerated such abuse in his ranks, and I still wanted to be a General Shin."

"Good," she whispered and continued walking again. In three quick strides Young Pere was back by her side. "But how could you be General Shin when your name was Lek Thorne?"

He shrugged again. "Lots I didn't have figured out, but assumed somehow it would all work itself out."

"But the world is never *that* convenient," Versa declared.

They continued on in silence before Young Pere found a way to break it.

"So Versa, in a way it's appropriate that I escort you to the temple site. Since I was claimed, I guess I must be your brother—" *or cousin.* "But then again, I didn't exactly accept the claiming, but Slither told me once that it wasn't necessary—"

"What stupid laws. But then again, look at who came up with them." She glanced over to him. "So, Young Pere, if I may know . . . *why* did you leave Salem in the first place?"

Young Pere sighed. "For dumb reasons. I was bored. I wanted something different to do. I told myself I left to clear my family's name, but that really wasn't true. Eltana Yordin wanted vengeance, and I felt like I was being denied something by being trapped in Salem. You know the saying, The cows are always fatter in the neighbor's field? That's what I thought. The world *had* to be better than what I had in Salem. I also wanted to feel some of the glory I thought my grandfather and uncle had experienced. The army was so . . . *romantic*, I suppose. Sounds ludicrous now, but I was a rather stupid boy. I see that now. I guess it was just all a selfish temper tantrum that I took too far."

"I'll say 'too far'," she agreed.

"You know," he decided to confess, because he needed the practice, "the strange thing is, all the time I was in world trying to get everything I wanted, I was miserable. I just realized now that the happiest I've been since I left was when I was taking care of my security team these last few days, and I think I know why: I wasn't focused on myself, I was focused on taking care of others. Making sure they had comfortable ways to sleep, teaching them about Salem's ways, keeping track that none of them got lost. I was never so happy as when I quit thinking about myself."

"Hmm," Versa said thoughtfully, "sounds like you've come up with a world-shattering way of thinking about life. Too bad there isn't an entire society like that, all devoted to helping each other, where no one is more important than someone else, and where even the man in charge doesn't employ servants but stables his own horse. Hmm . . . if only one could *find* such a place."

To be honest, he was slightly annoyed by her sarcasm after he'd just confessed what he considered was a deep and important insight to his life. But, his annoyance meant that he was being selfish once more, and grudgingly he had to admit to himself that she was right. Again.

He glanced over to see her smirking.

"So let me see if I've got this straight," she said in a critical tone coated in syrup. "You not only had a mother who loved you, but a father who actually cared for you and wasn't out to kill you."

Young Pere sighed.

"Not only that, but you had two uncles who you were very close to, as well as two aunts, and a grandfather and grandmother who tolerated your behavior no matter what foolhardy thing you did."

Young Pere nodded guiltily.

"You never dug food out of rubbish heaps—well, not more than once, that is—"

"I spent a lot more time chasing women and children away from them so I wouldn't have a mess to clean up."

Versa peered over at him. "Chasing away families like mine?"

"Yes," he said quietly. "And *again*, I apologize to you and all the families in the world that soldiers pulled a sword on."

Versa nodded once. "You also never moved houses, always had your own bed—"

"Even my own bedroom once Relf married and Barnos took his room," he supplied with a wince.

"Relf's the one I met last year, right?"

"Yes. The one who came to retrieve me."

Versa nodded. "I liked him. Very nice man. Sincere, concerned, helpful. Hard to imagine he's *your* brother. Are all of your siblings and cousins as selfless as him, willing to leave their family and home for weeks just to search for someone who didn't want to be found?"

"Pretty much, yes."

"You poor, *poor* boy," she bubbled. "How *ever* did you tolerate such a life? I can see why it simply wasn't good enough for you, why you felt the need to leave it all."

Young Pere rubbed his forehead. This wasn't exactly the kind of humbling he was expecting, but while it was painful to hear her describe him that way, it wasn't unbearable. In a strange way it actually made him feel better to get it all out. At least Versa was a good practice for what might come when he finally met his father. "I was foolish. I know."

Versa nodded. "Yes, incredibly foolish."

"Thanks for the confirmation. Just what I needed to hear."

Versa nudged him with her elbow. "But what matters is what you understand now and what you've learned. Salem's taught me that one's past stays in the past. You sound like a different man now and I dare say you may even have potential."

"Thanks, again," Young Pere said more genuinely.

"You're welcome," she said. "I suppose I was a bit quick to question the Creator's choice in sending you to escort me. You may be *adequate* after all. So tell me more about your childhood. What kind of mischief did Sword Master of the Cosmos get into?"

Young Pere groaned. They still had many miles to go.

The sun bathed the ancient temple site in cheery light, but the air was cold as Calla Trovato Zenos was lowered into the grave.

Shem couldn't speak. One of his assistants gave a sweet tribute that was relayed throughout the area. Nor could Shem bring himself to pray over her grave. He only mumbled to Lek that he felt unworthy and asked his oldest son to do it.

Lek knelt to ask protection for his mother's resting spot as the rest of the family and thousands of more Salemites listened and quietly wept.

Shem sat on the ground braced up by his daughters as the shovelfuls of gravel and rock, mixed with a little dirt, were thrown over her body shielded only by the white blanket. In all of their preparations for the Last Day, no one had ever considered someone would pass away up there. None of them had thought of bringing coffins.

When they finished the burial, Shem could do nothing else than stare at the pile of rubble.

Deck then gave a moving tribute to his mother-in-law, since neither her son nor daughter had any strength to do so. His words were also relayed throughout the tableland, to more tears and sniffles.

No one dared guess what happened to her body, left at the temple where Idumean soldiers surely wouldn't give it a respectful burial.

Relf carved that morning, as hastily but neatly as he could, a marker out wood. On it were the words:

CALLA TROVATO ZENOS 308-365

IN MEMORY OF
MAHRREE PETO SHIN 291-365

The 35th Day of Planting was going to be another very long day.

Even if Young Pere and Versa weren't so engaged in swapping tales to prove whose youth was more trouble-filled, nibbling on dried fruit and elk jerky from her pack as they walked, they still wouldn't have noticed the two figures in white just outside their field of perception who walked behind them, hand in hand, listening, smiling, and whispering to each other.

Nor would they have realized that three additional couples in white took position around them, securing a wide perimeter which no soldier dared, or even thought, to infiltrate.

That was good, because Young Pere and Versa didn't seem to notice anything beyond each other.

"You did what you were supposed to do," Jaytsy whispered to Shem as he sat by the gravelly grave.

His assistants had taken over for the day and no one was supposed to approach him except for family.

Shem didn't look at her, even though she sat right in front of him. His glazed eyes focused on nothing.

"I've felt them, Shem. Both of them," Jaytsy said earnestly. "They are well and happy and so terribly worried about you. It's not your fault. They want you to know that. It was simply their last day. *You did the right things*!"

Shem stared past her, refusing to believe any of it.

"Are you telling me you can only find another ten thousand?" Thorne roared at the officers who stood before him. "It's midday meal! Where's the rest of my army?"

The officers glanced at each other. "Many have abandoned the army, sir," one bravely explained. "The ones we spoke to are convinced Mahrree Shin is going to get them too. They're throwing down their weapons and running away when we approach."

"It's true, sir," said a colonel, his tone bitter. "They're scared and hiding in barns and sheds, waiting to die. We've heard reports of soldiers taking their own lives rather than waiting for death to come find them, and we found a few hundred that are trying to organize to return to Edge. And guess who's helping them? Jon Offra! Now, we may be able to find a few thousand more by tonight, but General, you'll be lucky if you have forty thousand to march with."

Major Twigg squinted, clearly unaccustomed to the idea of soldiers disobeying the commands of the general. "But even with the men we lost along the way, we had close to seventy thousand at the temple last night."

"Yes, we *did,*" the colonel said abruptly. "Then the long-dead Mahrree Shin suddenly appeared. Then the 'chosen guide' died. Then General Thorne killed a defenseless old woman. Then there was no secret entrance in the temple and there were no Salemites hiding in the canyon."

Thorne stepped up to him. "What are you insinuating?"

The colonel whipped off his cap and threw it on the ground. "That it's time to follow another colonel's example. I'm finding Perrin Shin!"

"He's DEAD!" Thorne shouted. "I found his grave marker myself! He died two years ago!"

Hili's head shot up in surprise.

The rest of the officers stared at the general, dumbfounded by the news and that Thorne exposed his own lie. Everything was falling apart. Everything they had believed in, been told over and over until they accepted it . . . *wasn't* true. Next thing, someone would tell them that the sky wasn't really blue.

"I don't care," the colonel said sullenly. "I'm not doing this anymore. I'll find me a nice flock of sheep somewhere. Plenty of them wandering around. Jon Offra can probably give me some directions." He turned his back on Thorne and headed for the door.

The other officers twitched, wondering if they should follow, but also half-expecting the general to run through the defecting colonel with his sword.

But Thorne seemed a little less thorny today, perhaps a little surprised himself that things weren't quite going his way. All he did was yell after the colonel. "I'll tax you so heavily that you'll be left with only one old ram!"

The colonel waved a sloppy goodbye, adding a vulgar flourish, before slamming the door behind him.

Thorne glared at the other men.

None of them moved.

"FIND THE REST OF MY ARMY!"

They filed out of the station, slowly.

Hili, the slowest of all.

Sergeant Beaved was waiting for the first complaint. His men had been relatively quiet, but the valley stretched out for miles. It was Teach who finally said it, and Beaved wasn't all surprised.

"This is going to take forever! How far away are those mountains? We're not getting any closer."

"Yes, we are, Teach," Reg said patiently. "We've probably covered six miles by now."

Snarl looked with disgust at the last of his dried rations in his hand. "I'm sick of this stuff. Let's find a house and get a decent meal."

Beaved sighed loudly. "We already agreed: we're not going to raid any houses or act like soldiers."

"Well we look like them!" Snarl pointed out. "Who's going to know?"

"We'll know!" Reg snapped at him.

Snarl blinked in surprise at Reg's sudden gumption.

"Besides," Reg said more timidly, already backing down, "there aren't any houses around here. Just this forest and these fields."

"Yeah, what's the point of this?" Pal asked, looking around. "This whole swath of land just left completely untouched, from one end of the valley to the other along the river? It looks like no one's ever disturbed it."

"It looks *natural*," Teach said with a slight shiver.

"Yes, it does," Beaved agreed. "I think I rather like it."

Teach shrugged. "They better have a full dinner waiting up there. My rations are gone."

Beaved wished he had taken a sample of that applesauce when he had the opportunity. His stomach rumbled.

Suddenly Teach gasped.

The rest of the men turned to see him gesturing feebly to the edge of the trees. They blinked, then blinked again to make sure their eyes were functioning properly.

About forty paces away was something that looked like a deer, but was much more massive than what the world was used to seeing darting through the farms. It was rubbing its antlers against a large tree trunk, as if its enormous rack was itchy.

"What is that?" Reg whispered.

Teach tried to answer. "Wa—Wa—Wa—"

Beaved frowned. "Wa?"

"Stupidest song I ever heard," Snarl snarled.

"Wapiti!" Teach finally exclaimed.

The men were duly amazed.

"Elk, right?" Hammer asked. "Shin said they were delicious, didn't he?"

"I wonder what elephants taste like," Iron said, licking his lips.

Buddy and Pal glanced around nervously in case one was sneaking up on them.

"No way to hunt it, men," Beaved said sadly. "And I feel like we're running out of time, anyway."

"I can hunt it," Snarl insisted, slowly stalking toward it.

But the elk stopped its rubbing and gave Snarl such a conscious and deliberate look that he stopped in his tracks. The elk watched him for a moment before striding purposefully along the edge of the trees past them.

Even Snarl seemed taken aback by its confidence. "Yeah, we're running out of time," he said.

Beaved started on again. "But maybe there's jerky up at the ancient temple site."

Everyone followed Beaved, but Teach still couldn't move. "He was right," he mumbled. "About wapiti . . . Salem . . . He was right. He might have been right about *everything.*"

Beaved turned around. "Every moment I'm more and more convinced Young Pere was right, Teach. Which means we better get up to that ancient site, and soon! I don't want to be on the wrong side, whenever the Last Day is."

Teach jumped a little, nodded respectfully to the bull elk still unconcerned with him, and jogged to catch up.

"You're going to have to help me," Versa said, blinking rapidly, "because I *really* want to understand this."

Young Pere had offered the explanation in the past but with poor results.

"I mean," Versa sighed, "I understand wanting to be different. But why would you think a badger would be a great pet?"

"Well, Muggah told us to write about an unusual animal as a pet, so I chose a badger because I think they're cute—"

"Cute and vicious! But then why would you get one drunk on old berries and smuggle it into your bedroom as a pet? That's the stupidest experiment I've ever heard of."

He shrugged. "I told you before—I didn't think things through very much, especially when I was twelve."

"And so it woke up earlier than you expected while you were doing your schoolwork in the eating room?" she reminded him.

"Yep," he sighed sadly. "And proceeded to stink up everything Barnos owned—he shared the bedroom with me at the time."

"I can see why *he* didn't come to retrieve you in Edge," she chuckled.

"No, Relf came because he looks the least like a Shin. Barnos favors my Shin grandparents too much."

"*Sure* that's why."

Young Pere's gait slowed, seeing things from different angles and suddenly rethinking everything he knew about himself. "I guess . . . I guess he *would* have been pretty mad at me. About a lot of things, really. I wasn't the easiest brother to live with. Relf was always the peacemaker in the family. But we're good now, Barn and me. He married and moved out before I left, so I'm sure all is forgiven . . ."

But it was a *lot* to forgive over the years of having to live with the most difficult brother in Salem, and as Young Pere reflected, he realized there was even more that his siblings and cousins had had to put up with.

Versa, who forged ahead, hadn't realized that Young Pere was trailing behind.

Nor did he, too overwhelmed with the many, many times he'd aggravated his family, caused another near-disaster, or had another mishap that required all of them to drop what they were doing and run to his rescue.

He remembered playing Bad Men, Good Men with Cephas and the boys, and recalled how often he endangered all of their lives . . . and that he truly was a 'Bad Man.'

And that Cephas was always a 'Good Man.'

He stopped walking and squeezed his eyes shut tight in regret for all the times his pride and selfishness had forced everyone to accommodate him. And how often had Cephas tried to swing things back again? How many times had Cephas proven to be the opposite of Young Pere in calm and restraint and help?

How often had Cephas been the kind of boy Young Pere should have been?

"Hey," he heard Versa call from ahead. "What's wrong? Are you coming or not?"

He opened his eyes. "Tell me, honestly: how many arrogant people have you known that you actually liked?"

She frowned at the unusual question and started back to him. "Liked? Probably none. No one *likes* an arrogant person. They may tolerate them, but *like* them? Never."

"That's what I was afraid of."

He had been the most arrogant Salemite to have ever lived. He thought he'd had admirers by the dozens, but maybe no one cared for him at all. If he hadn't been handsome and charismatic, no one would have put up with him. And those who got to know him better—like his family—saw right through his Mr. Charm persona. They knew, all too well, that he was Mr. Arrogance. And no one likes an arrogant person.

As she got closer, he confessed in a small voice, "They used to call me the Little Lieutenant in Edge because they said I strutted around like a rooster."

She must have seen the anguish in his eyes, because she didn't have a snappy comeback. Instead she said, "I have not seen you strut once today. Officers are, by nature, arrogant creatures. You're no longer an officer. You weren't even really one legitimately, either."

"Makes it worse."

She shrugged that off. "So what? That's not what you are anymore, right? You're not that haughty officer nor are you that reckless boy, right?"

His next words came out as a whisper. "But *they* don't know that anymore."

"*They* who? Oh, wait—your family?"

He nodded, embarrassed that he was revealing such things to her, but Puggah said he needed to be humbled.

"Everyone's an idiot when they're young," she declared.

Not Cephas, he thought.

When he didn't answer, she said, "It doesn't matter, Young Pere. They'll see who you are now. I heard your father speak to my mother about you a few times. He never said you were arrogant. I only heard him express his deep concern for you, and say how much he missed you. It'll be all right. Your past gets to stay in the past. That's what I've learned in Salem."

He wasn't so sure, but he knew he was wasting time in feeling sorry for himself, and only arrogant, selfish people hinder progress. That wasn't him anymore.

But he worried that it was.

"Sorry, I shouldn't be holding us up. Let's keep walking."

"Eat, Papa," Huldah said gently. "Please." She held out a wooden plate.

Salemites had been bringing food all morning, hoping to find something in their rations to tempt the guide. Ester and Huldah had filled a plate with all his favorites.

It was well past midday meal now, and still Shem didn't move, didn't drink, and certainly didn't eat.

He just stared at the pile of gravel.

Young Pere watched as Versa whipped out the knife, slashed through the thorny shrub in their way, and slipped the knife back into her waistband almost faster than Young Pere could follow the movement.

"That's amazing, in a scary sort of way," he chuckled nervously.

Versa smiled slyly and stepped through the gap she had cut. "You *should* be scared. I terrified more than one soldier when I was in the world."

Young Pere stared at her as a thought came to him.

Versa turned. "The thorns aren't bad. Just get past them."

He slipped through the gap but still stared. "Are you . . . are you the Slashing—" He didn't want to use the word that completed the title soldiers had created.

Versa narrowed her eyes. "The Slashing *what?*"

Young Pere swallowed. "Uh, there was a story that went around the forts about a girl who hung around certain entrances, willing to *entertain* soldiers on an individual basis . . ." His voice trailed off as he looked into her eyes.

They were hard and impenetrable. "Go on," she insisted.

Young Pere cleared his throat. "Supposedly she would lure men into a barn or a stand of trees in the guise of making herself available to them. Once they lowered their . . ."

He struggled to find an appropriate word.

"—*guard*, she would slash them and steal their silver and gold slips, leaving them bleeding and robbed."

Versa continued to stare back, not even blinking.

"She had an army-issued long knife, according to rumors," Young Pere said, a little anxiously. "No one ever got what they expected when they were alone with her."

Versa finally blinked. "Not what they expected but what they *deserved*. They cared nothing for the girls they used up and left. They deserved to be used back."

He took a cautious step back. "It *was* you, wasn't it?"

She looked down. "I'm not proud of it, but I had no choice. Do you know how hard it is for a single woman to find a way to support a family of four? Everything I did was to help my mother, since her husband never would. I told my mother I was working for a farmer tending his swine. In a way, it was the truth. Each of those men was a pig! But I confessed all my indiscretions to my rector when I got here, by the way," she said, looking back up at him. "But I also have to admit I would've done it again. My mother needed the money, and I hated the soldiers—everything they stood for, the man they followed, the way they thought they could abuse girls and women. I was trying to get back at my father by attacking his soldiers. I only did it eight or nine times before we moved from Coast to Midplain."

Young Pere coughed. "Eight or nine times? I heard it was hundreds! And at almost every fort! Then again, you know how soldiers like to exaggerate. They *did* say she was a beautiful blond. That wasn't really an exaggeration, though."

She gave him a small, cynical smile. "Really, now?"

Young Pere blushed. "Really," he said quietly. "And while we may not be near a barn, I do realize that we're in the trees so I promise I will stay far, far away from you."

"I think you're safe. When I told my rector at the time that I was past doing that sort of thing, he said that was good, because in my condition," Versa patted her belly, "it'd be rather difficult to lure anyone now, especially Salemites. But then he added he would've been amused to watch me try."

Young Pere grinned. "Who was your rector? Anyone I know?"

Versa raised her eyebrows. "I would think so. Peto Shin."

"Ah," Young Pere said, then didn't know what else to say.

"He was very easy to talk to," she said. "He listened to my long descriptions without any expression of surprise or dismay, as if he'd heard it all before. No judgments, no criticisms, just patient listening. And that's the father you chose to *abandon.*"

"Thank you for the reminder."

"So what was the rest of that name they called me? The Slashing what?"

"The Slashing *Sow*. I'm sorry."

Versa shook her head. "I'm not. As I said before, they were all swine so the title was fitting. To this day I still refuse to eat pork. Whenever I see a ham I feel a need to pull out my knife and stab the filthy animal!"

Young Pere couldn't help but burst out in nervous laughter.

She smiled forgivingly.

When he recovered, Young Pere said, "I'm sorry you didn't have a father to protect you."

She tossed her braid behind her. "It's not as if he would have ever come to my rescue. He encouraged that kind of behavior in his soldiers."

Young Pere guiltily remembered the daughters of Sargon and what the general had wanted him to do with them.

She seemed to read his mind. "Had he heard how I got my long knife in the first place, he likely would have berated the soldier for his failure, not his attempt. The general is selfish and brutal, and because he has power, his behavior is tolerated. Venerated, even."

He nodded in sad agreement.

"How long did it take you to notice?" she asked.

"Notice what?"

"That he wasn't the inspired and brilliant leader he's proclaimed himself to be?"

"Several moons," he confessed. "I was sucked in by the stories myself until I *became* one of those stories, and had to realize all of it was fake, even down to his general's uniform."

"Well done," Versa said, to his astonishment. "Most of the world will never notice the holes in his stories because their imaginations fill them in. They allow him to lead because they're thinking, 'If *he* can get away with this, then I can, too.' Every once in a while someone steps back and thinks, 'This is *wrong*.' Not that they have any power to fix any of it, but I like to believe there's some hope for them."

"So is there any hope for me?"

Versa evaluated him critically as they slogged through a slushy patch. "It's *all* up to you."

Eventually Young Pere said, "May I ask you a question?"

"Let me hear it first, then I'll decide if I'll answer."

"I was wondering, where's your husband now?"

"Not anywhere near here, I'm sure. Then again, maybe he is," she wrinkled her nose. "He may have come back with the army."

"Wait—he *left* Salem?"

"Yes. He went back to the world with my youngest sister."

"But no one's supposed to go back to the world," Young Pere said, alarmed.

"Guide Zenos chased him all the way back to the canyon before Edge a few moons ago."

Suddenly a memory came back to Young Pere. A man and a girl, found in the forest above Edge. He closed his eyes and stopped walking. "May I ask his name?"

"Anoki Kiah," she said, not noticing he wasn't following.

Young Pere had mouthed the words with her. "Lieutenant Kiah!"

he breathed. "Now that makes sense—"

"Lieutenant!" Versa exclaimed and stopped, realizing she was alone. "He was never an officer! Oh, why am I surprised? Nothing he ever said was true. He might as well been in the amphitheater for all the acting he ever did. He and his brother—"

Young Pere had started walking to her but stopped again. "His brother?"

She continued on. "Called himself Lick. Pretended to be a captain. Are you ever coming or am I walking to the ancient site alone after all?"

Young Pere shook his head in amazement. "Lick! The last word he said when the general killed him was, 'Salem'."

Versa rolled her eyes. "The general killed Lick? That figures. He killed the uncle of his unborn grandchild. You know, in Salem that would be a tragedy. But it's just another day in the life of the Thornes. Wait!" She grabbed his arm. "Do you know what happened to my sister Priscill? No one's heard from her since she ran back to the world with Anoki."

He hesitated. "I saw her briefly when they pulled her and Kiah from the forest. But after that?" He shrugged.

Yes, he was lying. Even though last night when he was on his knees he asked the Creator to help him be honest in everything, he chose to lie. But there had been so much death already and, Young Pere worried, more to come. He needed Versa to be solid and steady on the rock face that afternoon. She'd be angry with him later for not telling her that Priscill died from the herbs, but by then they'd be at the temple site where she could grieve safely.

"Guide Zenos doesn't know either," Versa said flatly. "Priscill was barely sixteen, and running away with a married man ten years her senior? Well, what do you think about my family now? We just get more deplorable by the hour, don't we?"

The words, *It might not be only your family*, formed in his head.

Young Pere watched her belly and wondered if he should tell her that Priscill tried to talk to their father at the mansion. Her sobbing as Thorne sent her away was vivid in his mind.

His cousin, perhaps, sobbing as she was sent away . . .

"I, I don't know what to say. Lick is the uncle of your baby? Kiah the father?"

She shrugged that off. "She'll never meet them, fortunately. They'll have no influence in her life. I'll remind my baby that her heritage doesn't determine her actions. I like to think I'm proof of that."

She turned to walk on, leaving Young Pere to jog to catch up to her. "Do you know how Lick knew about Salem?" he asked. "I could never piece that together."

"Your father and I figured out a few things," Versa told him. "A very kind and inspired man, your father is." She glanced accusingly at him.

"I know, I know. So what did you figure out?"

"Ever hear about someone called Walickiah?"

"Sounds vaguely familiar," he said. "From a while ago?"

"He was a Guarder," Versa told him. "Sent years ago to Edge to kill your father and aunt when they were small children. Zenos caught on, though, lured him to the forest, and had him abducted. Interestingly, he was the only Guarder who chose to try a life in Salem and didn't kill himself."

"I think I remember the story now," Young Pere said. "Wasn't he here for a while, then disappeared?"

"He grew disaffected after a few years, then suddenly one day he was gone. Salem looked all over for him, assumed he died trying to reach the world, and that was that.

"But he made it to Scrub," Versa continued. "Anoki told me about his father, how he always talked of two secret groups in the world, one of them ready to kill him if he revealed them, and another which would steal him away. His wife married him out of pity, and his sons were always embarrassed by his paranoia. But after he died, they began to feel they needed to vindicate him.

"Both Lick and Anoki tried the army and law enforcement, looking for evidence of secret groups. They knew the name of Salem from their father, and for years they looked for some way to find it, to prove their father wasn't the village idiot. When they found us, they assumed Salem would try to steal us away from the world, as their father said Salemites did. Sure enough, Salem did take us away, along with one of Walickiah's sons."

"Whoa," Young Pere exhaled. "Lick told the general about Salem. I'm sure of it. And Kiah's still down there, somewhere."

"Yes," Versa sighed heavily. "They knew the secret of Salem but it didn't do them any good, did it? Lick is dead and one of Salem's own told the general how to get here."

Young Pere picked up on her accusation. "It wasn't me," he

insisted. "I never revealed Salem. I was ready to die first."

Versa regarded him blankly. "Then who told him?"

"Amory. And yes, she is—*was*—a Salemite. She became his latest mistress and she planned to be his queen. She told him about Salem. But he killed her in the canyon before the last wall."

Versa's mouth turned up into a vague smile, as if Young Pere had just passed some kind of test. He suspected he'd been tested several times that day already. "Glad to hear it. That it wasn't you, that is. Not that he killed her. But as I said—just another day in the life of the Thornes."

She placed her hand on her hip where the long knife was secured. "Yes, just another day. . . Now, you keep giving the right answers or it'll be *your last day*, Shin."

Young Pere chuckled, but Versa gave him a deliberate look that stopped him.

There were moments when she favored the general a little *too* much.

"Maybe by dinner time, General," Major Twigg said in a conciliatory manner. "Maybe more soldiers will be willing to come back."

"Why should they?" A lieutenant colonel said, sliding an empty plate on the large table, carefully so as to not disturb any of the plans spread out in the middle of it. He belched happily and patted his belly. "Haven't had such a filling meal since Deceit blew! Hey," he said as an idea occurred to him, and he turned to the other fifteen men who had joined Thorne for their meal. "It would've been decent of these Salemites to have offered us some of their surplus. I heard there are massive storehouses bursting with grain! They could have shared with us, you know."

Poe Hili, sitting dully at the end of the table, perked up, and he watched General Thorne for a response. It likely was these very Salemites who had come down several moons ago, causing the tree fall above Edge in order to offer a way to save them all.

But feeding the world didn't fit into Lemuel Thorne's plans, and Poe watched him steadily as he concentrated on the sketched maps before him. The comment wasn't going to be acknowledged, nor would it be admitted that such an offer had once been made.

Poe glanced at Twigg to see if he'd put it together. The spindly man shifted uncomfortably in his chair, picking at the food offered freely to him last year.

"If every kitchen in these houses is similarly stocked," said a major, licking his fingers, "what's to bring the soldiers back for dried rations and a bedroll in the cold? There are beds enough in these empty houses for everyone."

The men were exchanging jars, no longer concerned about tomorrow's attack but commenting to each other on the wonders of smashed apples and strawberry sauce which they sopped up with hard bread.

Hili stared blankly at a large bowl of mixed nuts on the table.

"Poe," the general said. "Recommendations."

He shrugged. "Whatever you want to do, General. Salem seems to be yours."

"The soldiers seem to think so, too," said a captain. "I saw one man and his woman selecting their house already. There was another couple arguing with someone else over a larger house west of here."

Another major held out his hands. "Arguing? There's plenty out there! They could have two houses each if they move fast enough."

Poe sighed. "They'll never be satisfied."

Each man at the table looked at him.

"They can find the biggest house and still look over the entire valley and imagine they were cheated. They won't even pay for it, they'll just take it. Like the food, like the animals—but none of it will be enough," Poe said in disgust. "They're insatiable. Just like after the first pox outbreak decades ago. Every village was fighting for the possessions of the dead. We don't even have the decency to wait until these people are dead. We're robbing them now."

"Spoils of war," one captain insisted. "We deserve—"

"We deserve NOTHING, Captain!" Poe exploded, tired of pretending he agreed with any of this. "*How* have we deserved *anything?* Invading? Killing? That somehow makes us *worthy?* All we do is take! When is it enough?" He threw his plate on the table, scattering the pages. "I've had ENOUGH!"

"Yes, you have, Hili!" said Thorne brusquely.

But Poe didn't care. He stood up and strode out of the station, ignoring the shouts of General Thorne to return. He trotted down the stairs and over to the barn, noticing the sky.

It was blue. With white, he told himself. Blue *with white*. Don't ignore the white.

Inside the barn he lay down on the straw like an animal. He spent the next hour arguing with himself about the nature of the sky. It was much simpler when he was six.

What color is the sky, Poe? See that it's not what they've told you it is! What color is the sky, Poe?

Yes, the sky was blue. Occasionally.

But maybe the blue was just an illusion, and the sky really was black, with stars in it all the time except when the sun came up and outshined everything else, demanding all the attention, changing what everyone saw, casting shadows and illuminating crevices and altering everyone's perceptions.

Maybe that was the whole problem, Poe considered.

Everyone *sees* the blue, but the blue's not real. What the sky was doing every minute of every day and night, *that* was what was critical to observe.

And no one, *no one in the entire world*, bothered to see what the sky was really doing.

She tried to teach him that when he was six. He was more stupid now than when he was a small child.

Poe held his head and wept like that child.

"How long will he keep this up?" Lilla whispered to Peto, seeing Shem staring listlessly. "He hasn't moved in hours."

"I don't know."

She covered her face with her hands, and Peto put an arm around her. "I know how he feels, and it's too much, Peto," she whimpered. "It's the worst maggoty day ever. Moldy fruit and rancid vegetables and weevils infesting the wheat. I just want to lay down and never get back up again."

"Shh," he said, stroking her hair. "Morah and Centia are already sure that's what's going to happen next. Everyone's so heavy right now. We need to be careful what we say in front of them."

"Why, Peto?" Lilla sobbed softly. "Why so much? Why now? Why us?"

"I don't know. I don't know anything, anymore," he confessed. "We didn't do anything wrong, I'm sure. We're not being punished. Calla wasn't punished, nor was my mother—"

"It sure feels like it!"

"Shh, I know, I know." He sighed and kissed her head. "Sometimes bad things just happen. Do we lose our faith when tragedy strikes? Seems to me that's when we need it the most."

Lilla went limp in his arms. "I still have faith, just no joy left. I remember how I tried to comfort you after Perrin died."

"I do too."

"Well, I was wrong then. As heartless and wrong as jam on trout," she said, with uncharacteristic bitterness. "There's no reason for joy, no reason to continue until the Last Day. It's all over for me. Just make it all end now. And where is he?" she wailed softly.

Peto knew who she was whimpering about.

"He could have made it by now!"

"He may have been trapped in the forests somewhere," Peto said, trying to console himself as much as her. "Maybe he was unable to get around the army until they moved. He might've gone north instead to go around the temple, then head to the west. If he did, that's fifteen miles altogether, Lilla. He may have even seen what happened to my mother." He choked on the words. "If he did, how it's affecting him is anyone's guess. He may be sitting stunned, just like Shem."

"He won't make it, Peto," Lilla muttered hopelessly. "There's no protection for us. There's no special help. Young Pere will die alone and surrounded by evil, just like his grandmother and aunt."

"You don't know that," Peto said, rocking his wife. "We don't know anything."

"That's the worst part, Peto."

Versa was hunched over, gripping her sides in agony, while tears streamed down her face.

Young Pere stood patiently next to her. "Do we need to find another shrub for you to squat behind?"

Versa shook her head and gasped.

"Or . . . is it too late for that?" he asked tactfully.

She burst out into another round of laughter and clutched the shawl support that was slipping down her hips. "No!" she panted as she caught her breath. "Not yet! But I don't think I can take any more." With Young Pere's help, she finally righted herself.

Young Pere was grinning as he kept his hand on her arm to stabilize her. "Now, if only my *family* had reacted to my jumping off the school building the way you just did—"

"I mean," she said, wiping her eyes, "it's just so *ridiculous*! 'Oh, I'm as light as a bird and built like one too—I'm going to *fly*.' I can just see you trying to flap your pathetic little blanket wings. Did you have absolutely *no sense* at all?"

Muggah had said something like that, and it had made him furious at the time. Now he found himself grinning as he heard the same sentiment.

"No, I guess I didn't. And I think I forgot to flap my arms. That might have been part of the problem," he contemplated. "But I like to believe I've learned a few things in the past two years."

"Wait, wait—" Versa gasped. "You weren't a *child* when you did this? How old *were* you?"

Young Pere braced himself and said, "Almost eighteen."

She howled again. "I *AM* walking with an idiot!"

He grinned. "I'll go find you a secluded shrub."

"If you give them the night in the houses," began the major, "I have another seven hundred men who'll join you in the morning. Not at the crack of dawn, though."

It was after midday meal, and Thorne was furious.

Major Twigg added the number to the tally. "That'd be an even forty-five thousand, sir."

The major bringing the news had even more. "And the lieutenant colonel said he found another four hundred that took over a section of houses on the eastern side. They'll agree to come if they're assured they can keep their houses."

"Forty-five thousand, four hundred," Twigg said encouragingly.

A captain squirmed. "That group of two thousand organizing near here? Uh, they're following Colonel Offra and some old little man back up the canyon. They laughed at me when I asked if they didn't rather want to join us for glory and honor in battle—"

Another lieutenant colonel cleared his throat. "But I located another two thousand sir, in a massive building filled with all kinds of clothing, furniture, tools—you name it. They want assurances they can keep everything they can carry."

"Carry *west?*" Thorne finally spoke, bristling with rage. "On our attack?"

The officer shrugged. "Apparently."

"*Would be* forty-seven thousand, four hundred," Twigg pointed out.

Thorne steamed. Now he was negotiating with soldiers for their services. And he was losing.

"I can't believe your grandfather survived so much, only to die from an infection from a stick! I can understand why you were so upset about his passing," Versa remarked as they made their way through a meadow. The grasses were just starting to come up out of the slush. "Your inability to cope with your grief likely contributed to your stupidity."

"Wow," Young Pere said, "that almost sounded compassionate."

"Guide Zenos said I needed to work on developing empathy toward men," she said with mock haughtiness. "Just practicing."

Young Pere chuckled.

"I still remember the first time I heard the name of Perrin Shin," Versa said with a small smile.

"Is that good or bad?" Young Pere asked.

"Good, I promise. I was maybe four years old." She squinted, trying to remember. "We were living with Uncle and Aunt Fadhy at the time. General Fadh," she clarified. "After he took over the fort at Marsh, he built a house in the compound for his wife. When my mother ran away from Edge with the three of us, the Fadhs took us in. Uncle Fadhy even added two bedrooms for us, and put up a tall fence around the back garden of the house. We had a small yard to play in, right there in the middle of the fort, with a barricade fence and the outer fort wall to protect us."

"Sounds a little crowded," Young Pere decided.

"Oh, no," Versa sighed with a smile. "It was wonderful! True, we never left the house and yard for those four years; in fact, I don't think that more than a few soldiers ever knew we were there. Uncle Fadhy had passed us off as his wife's cousins or something. But no one could see us because we're so pale and the Fadhs were so dark, it would've been obvious we weren't related."

She chuckled.

"But they took such good care of us. Uncle Fadhy always came home for midday meal to play for a few minutes, then each evening he'd tell us stories and even wrestle with us. He taught me some moves that I used later to get out of bad situations. He wanted us to be safe," she added heavily. "Aunt Fadhy was like a second mother to me, letting me cook in the kitchen with her and sewing us clothing. They wanted to have children of their own but never could," she said sadly. "But for their last years, they had three blond daughters."

"So when did you hear the name of Perrin Shin?" Young Pere reminded her.

"I'm getting to that!" she snapped, annoyed that he interrupted her happy memory. "One day we had a visitor who was allowed to come into the back part of the house to see us. He was another commander, shorter and lighter skinned than the Fadhs, but his face was harder, rougher. I remember the look in his eyes when he saw the three of us. I couldn't tell if he was angry or sad, because he seemed to be both. He was carrying a large crate and he put it down on the floor in front of us. When he opened the lid, it was the greatest day. There were dolls!"

Versa laughed quietly at the recollection.

"I didn't even know those existed until that day. One for each of us, made from soft cloth and yarn hair, and with beautifully stitched faces. There were even changes of clothes for the dolls. Mine had a skirt made of silk. That was the first time I ever touched silk, and it was just for me.

"Under the dolls were books. Simple ones to start learning to read, and another one filled with easy math problems. They were so we could start learning at home without having to go to the schools. My mother wept. I didn't understand why she did that at the time. I thought they were lovely gifts! But my mother was weeping out of gratitude, I realized later. Someone else in a uniform was worried about her and her children. She thanked the commander, but he just shook his head and said something like, 'The dolls were made by my wife, and the books were easy to come by in the south. I'm just doing what Perrin Shin would have done. Every good thing I learned, I learned from Perrin Shin.'"

"Who was that commander?" Young Pere asked.

"His name was Brillen Karna," said Versa reverently. "Your grandfather's first lieutenant, I found out later."

"He served with him for over fifteen years, if I remember correctly," Young Pere added.

"He came two more times while we were living with the Fadhs,"

Versa recalled. "Once he brought more clothes for our dolls, and clothes for us. He also brought more books, and once he had a small crate full of sweets and candy. He kept saying it was his wife's doing, and Perrin Shin's—whoever that man was—but still I hugged General Karna to thank him. It was obvious he wasn't used to small children hugging him, and he stiffened up each time I did it. But the last time I saw him, his eyes were filled with tears as if he knew he'd never see us again.

"The world was getting worse, then," her voice diminished to a whisper. "The end *was* coming, for both of those dear generals and their kind, generous wives. My Aunt Fadhy—she taught me to read and helped me learn to add and subtract. She was such a good friend to my mother, and I'd hear them laughing as if they were truly sisters. Aunt Fadhy fed us all, dressed us, and loved us as if we were really her own.

Her tone shifted as she said, "And *then* Sargon's army came."

She hesitated, and Young Pere remained silent. He'd learned this part of history in his training. Sargon had brought his army up to join with Fadh's as a pretext to fighting off Snyd, who was in charge of the western factions. Only now did Young Pere remember that General Snyd had been Versa's mother's uncle. Who Versa's mother felt she could trust in those days must have been quite perplexing.

But Sargon instead killed Fadh in the heat of battle—no one believed it was an accident—and the next day Fadh's wife was running from the fort when she was cut down by Sargon's men. Versa and her mother and sisters must have still been hiding in the compound.

Young Pere realized why Versa so hated Sargon.

"When we escaped from the fort," Versa started again somberly, "it was in such a hurry that we had to leave behind the dolls and books. I wondered frequently who Perrin Shin was, and if maybe he couldn't find us or send us help."

Young Pere didn't know what to say. Finally he came up with, "I'm sorry no one else came."

"Ah, but they did," she smiled. "Otherwise I wouldn't be in Salem now, or walking with *Perrin Shin* himself," she nodded to Young Pere. "Somehow, I have a feeling he sent you as well. When I was younger, I thought of this mysterious Perrin Shin as some sort of distant grandfather who knew we were hurting and wanted to help us."

Young Pere swallowed at the veracity of that thought. Some sort of *distant grandfather* . . .

"But later, once I understood about the Creator," Versa continued, "I realized that's who I was really longing for: an eternal Father who always kept His eye on us. And He did," she said quietly. "And He is right now."

"I almost feel like we're spying on them," Mahrree said in a low voice to her husband. They walked, hand in hand, several paces behind Young Pere and Versa, smiling as they listened to the two of them talking. "Kind of like what we did to Jaytsy and Deck when they were courting. I almost feel a little guilty."

Perrin smiled. "This isn't spying. This is *guarding*. We're Guarders, after all." He gestured to those ahead of them.

Versa had no idea that on her left were the Fadhs, smiling in remembrance of when they had three blond little girls, or that to the right of Young Pere were the Karnas, chuckling that Brillen was so uncomfortable with little girls hugging him.

Ahead were another set of Shins, an imposing general named Relf and his wife Joriana, arm-in-arm, completing the bubble that enclosed Versa and Young Pere and repelled soldiers so that none of them even dared to think to get within fifty paces.

"So," Mahrree elbowed her husband gently, "you admit we were spying on Jaytsy and Deck all those years ago?"

Perrin sighed. "Yes, I have to confess we *were* spying then. But this is different—we're supposed to be here watching and directing the protection."

Mahrree grinned. "I like this complete honesty of yours. All kinds of things I can ask you about now and the law of Paradise won't let you evade the truth," she chuckled. "So, tell me, you're not enjoying this *just* a little bit? Tailing our grandson, watching him watching her, watching her watching him?"

Perrin smiled uneasily. He knew he couldn't dance around this one. As if he ever danced. "Paradise is supposed to be a place of joy. Of course I'm allowed to *enjoy* this a bit. After what we've been through in the last seven seasons, I think we've earned this lovely stroll." He put his arm around Mahrree and pulled her closer.

She rested her head against him. "Just so that you finally admit you *were* spying on Jaytsy and Deck."

Perrin growled.

"What in the world?" Versa said. "Or rather, in Salem?" and she paused to squint between the trees.

Young Pere halted next to her and tensed when he saw the soldier on the other side of the trees forty paces away. He wondered if he could slip Versa's long knife from her hip quickly enough, until he realized the soldier wasn't interested in them.

"What is he carrying?"

"From what I can tell," Versa tilted her head, "three hammers, a few fire starters, something incredibly heavy in a bag . . . I'd say he's trying to become the first traveling blacksmith! I wonder where he stowed his anvil?"

Young Pere chuckled. "And he's in a hurry."

Versa nodded. "No doubt he's intending to take all of that back to the world to start his own blacksmithing business."

"So you really think he's going to take all of that over the mountains?"

"Of course not," said Versa. "Look at his gut. He's already panting from all that weight. No, I predict that he'll drop all of that in about a quarter of a mile, realize that yarn is much lighter, and decide that knitting is a very acceptable craft for a man of his belly."

Young Pere was snorting so much he had to wipe his nose. Sure enough, the portly soldier was already slowing down, huffing and reevaluating if he really needed so many hammers. He dropped one, shrugged at it, and continued on his lumbering jog south.

Young Pere just laughed. It felt so good and he wished Versa would say something else caustic, even if it were aimed at him, just to give him more reasons to laugh.

She grinned at him. "Anyone ever tell you your laugh sounds like bells?"

"Well, sort of," he said.

"That's because you're a ding-a-ling."

Young Pere laughed again.

Beaved automatically drew his sword as the man bounded from

the trees, headed straight for them.

The rest of his team pulled their weapons too.

"I promise I mean no harm!" Cloud Man shouted as he raised his hands and stopped. "I'm so glad I found you! I don't know what happened, but I was looking at these clouds, and then—"

Beaved scoffed. "No *harm?* You're a slagging assassin!"

Cloud Man halted, stunned. "I'm a . . . a what? Why, who would say such terrible things about—"

"General Thorne told me," Beaved tilted his head. "*Lieutenant Nelt.*"

The innocent gleam in Nelt's eye vanished. "Oh. I see." His tone changed completely. "Look, I'm not an assassin, well, not an official one. I never took the oaths or completed the training—"

"Then you're a traitor!" Buddy shouted, his arm trembling as he held his sword outstretched. "That's worse!"

Nelt sighed, not at all convinced that the pimply-faced boy could harm him. Nor could his Pal, cowering bravely behind him. "I know, and you're right. But look, I'm here now and I'm not with Thorne. Doesn't that mean something?"

Teach folded his arms, his long knife still clutched in his fist. "According to the assassin's code, that means you're looking for the next best opportunity. And we're it? You *must* be desperate."

Reg glanced at Teach. "How do you know about the assassin's code?"

"I'm a teacher," he said easily. "I know a little about everything." After a pause he added in a whisper, "And I couldn't pass their final tests."

Reg's eyes widened with new respect and worry.

"I'll take care of our Cloudy Nelt," Hammer offered, cracking his knuckles. "No one else needs to be bloodied." He took a few steps and Nelt retreated, waving his arms.

"No, no! I promise, *no one* needs to be bloodied!"

"What about Shin?" Beaved barked. "Where's his body? How soon after you freed him did you kill him?"

"He's not dead!" Nelt exclaimed. "In fact, that's what I've been trying to do—keep him alive! I secured him to a tree last night to keep him from attacking Thorne. Shin was ready to kill him."

"So was I!" Iron said.

Snarl snarled.

Nelt waved his arms again as if to fend them off. "And so am I, I promise. You don't kill unarmed great-grandmothers, no matter what their names. I gave Thorne the slip, then went back late last night to find Shin. The tree he was secured to was broken. I've been looking for him all day, and I think I've seen him, on his way to the western mountains. He's walking with a Salemite woman, someone who seems to know him—maybe a sister or a cousin. Look at me," Nelt said. "No sword. And look here—" He started to open his jacket, and each of the men tightened his grip on their weapons.

Nelt gestured to the inside of his empty jacket. "I threw my small crossbow into the river along with everything else. I come to you willingly, unarmed, begging your forgiveness, and wanting to help Shin. Pat me down if you need to. I want nothing more to do with Thorne or any of this. I just want to find Shin, apologize, and get to safety. Just like all of you."

"Why didn't you go to Shin now?" Beaved said.

Nelt swallowed. "I don't think he'd want to see me just now."

Iron cracked his knuckles. "I wonder why?"

"No, I mean Shin was actually *laughing* with that woman he was walking with. I don't remember ever hearing him laugh."

"Not been much to laugh about lately," Teach reminded him.

"I know, I know," Nelt nodded. "And it didn't seem right to interrupt that. But we can find him again, I'm confident. Please—I regret deceiving you and Shin, but I don't regret preserving his life. Eventually he'll see that was the best thing to do and he'll forgive me. I'm sure of it. Can *you* forgive me?"

Beaved evaluated him and finally sighed. "We'll think about it. Hammer, Iron. Pat him down first." He smiled slyly. "And do a *very thorough* job of it."

Nelt gulped.

By the time they reached the field before the trail head, Versa knew nearly every story about Young Pere's mischievous childhood and his experiences in the world.

Almost every worldly experience.

Young Pere had watched her every time he explained how he was stupid, foolish, or downright reckless. Each time she nodded, labeled the action, then gave him an almost forgiving smile.

"So I suppose it's a miracle you haven't needed a doctor while we've been walking," she remarked. "No wonder you know so much medically."

"Maybe today's just a day of miracles for us. I haven't even had the *urge* to climb a tree or start a fire."

"Maybe you're just growing up?" she suggested.

He looked at her in mock dismay. "Me become *an adult*? My, my, will the miracles never cease?" he said with a grand gesture. "So often my family thought they'd never see me reach maturity."

"'Maturity' and 'growing up' are two different things," Versa pointed out. "I think you still have a ways to go to be considered 'mature.'"

Young Pere chuckled. "Yeah, you're definitely something else, Versa. I still haven't figured out just what, exactly, but I suggest we rest here for a time." He pointed to some fallen logs. "The trail head is just beyond that field in front of us, and it might be best for you to eat before we continue on. It's only mid-afternoon, but now's as good as time as any for dinner."

"What makes you think I still have something to eat?" Versa sat down on a log and propped her feet up on another one.

"You're an expecting woman. I've never met an expecting woman who doesn't travel with a pack full of food."

Versa squinted at him. "Sure you never posed as an expecting woman before?" She took her pack from him, opened it, and smiled as she pulled out bread and dried fruit. She held some out to Young Pere.

"I'm fine until we reach the site," he waved it off. "You need it."

"I have plenty," she insisted. "And you're right—I've packed enough for days."

"Have you really?"

She chuckled. "Yes! Please, eat. I even restocked at a house yesterday. I may need your strength as well if I get too tired. You won't do me any good if you're light-headed with hunger."

Young Pere sighed and reluctantly took what she offered. "Thank you."

"Besides," she said, "we should be able to restock at the emergency shelter on the trail if we need to, right?"

He frowned as he took a bite of bread, wondering if he should give it back. "We never had an emergency shelter on that route. We kind of neglected it. It was just an afterthought route. Do you want this back?" He held out the bread.

Versa gave him a slightly pained smile. "Not at all. I have enough, see?" She opened the pack to show him several more items wrapped in cloth and tied with string. "We'll be fine for another day and a half. But we'll be at the ancient site well before then, right?"

"If all goes well and we have no delays, we should be there to-night," he said, taking another bite.

"Tonight would be good," she sighed. "If I weren't so out of shape we could have made much faster time. Before the baby, I could have run half this distance. Instead, I've been waddling like a goose and panting like a dog, and it just seems to be getting worse. I'm sorry."

"We're fine," he assured her. "We have plenty of time. The only thing I'm worried about is you. It's been quite a distance to go for a woman in your condition."

Versa turned a little pink when he said that he was worried about her, and she became interested in a handful of raisins.

After a while she said, "I've been thinking about what I said to you when we first met. About your grandmother. I realize now that must have sounded jarring, my talking about the way she went."

"That's all right," he said. "You didn't know then that she was my grandmother."

"I really did admire her, you know. And she was wonderful when I met her. It's just that the stupid general—"

"I've noticed that you always call him 'the general,'" Young Pere interrupted.

She glared at him. "Did *you* ever want to call him 'father'?"

"No." He chuckled bitterly. "You're right. You know, Versa, you remind me of my Muggah. She always said exactly what she thought, and she didn't care how others took it. She only wanted to say what she was sure was right, even if she was wrong, which really wasn't that often now that I think about it."

Versa chewed on a dried apple. "I'm not sure, is that supposed to be a compliment?"

"Yes, it is. Although many times today you have . . . well, let's just say you have a *humbling* way about you."

Versa chuckled. "Well then, I thank you, and I'm sorry for the other times. I'm supposed to be working on that. I've been told I can be too critical," she added quietly.

They ate in silence until Versa offered, "My mother always called me 'the general.' My sisters said it was because I was so bossy and always took charge, but my mother usually called me that in a pleased sort of way. I think many times I helped carry her burdens because I refused to give up and didn't have patience for anyone who did."

"I can see that," he said. "I would've loved to have seen you take on General Thorne. You just might have won him over, if you had the opportunity."

Versa took another piece of dried apple and eyed it suspiciously as if it were her father. "I doubt he even would've spoken to me. Last night I finally had a whole speech prepared in my mind, but I knew the Creator didn't want me to see him. I was always a few steps behind him, never able to catch up, or trapped by a *stupid well*—"

Young Pere's eyebrow furrowed, wondering what that meant.

She didn't elaborate. "It's all right, though. I see now how everything has happened as it should. I feel some regret that I didn't listen more carefully, and now I'm burdening you with getting me to safety."

"You're no burden," Young Pere told her. "And I'll get you there, I promise."

But he wasn't so sure how to fulfill that promise. As he scanned the terrain, looking for the best way to cross, he couldn't help but notice several soldiers in the field, looking lost and nervous, and all of them still armed.

He sighed a prayer, asking for ideas as he watched soldiers eyeing each other for food or worse.

"They won't see us," Versa broke into his thoughts.

"What?" he asked turning back to look at her. His chest tightened again, as it had several times that day when he looked into her clear blue eyes. Somehow they had gentled over the past few hours, softening her entire face.

"The soldiers. I know you're worried. It's about one hundred paces to the trail head, right? Trust me, they won't see us."

Young Pere sat down across from her on another log. "We're not exactly inconspicuous," he said, nodding at her belly.

She rolled her eyes, reminding him that he was an idiot. "Don't you remember what I told you? How often soldiers missed seeing us? Don't you have any faith?"

"I do. I have faith."

"Then ask for a miracle!" she insisted.

"I have been," he said. "That no one's bothered us the past several hours is a miracle."

"I agree. So why should the miracles stop now?"

"It's not that I don't think we won't be helped," he tried to explain his thoughts which hadn't figured themselves out yet. "It's just that I also know the Creator expects us to do our part. I'm looking for ways He would want me to act to get you to safety. To be honest, I'm not so sure any miracles we experience are for me. They are for you, *Versula Thorne*."

Versa squinted at him. "For me? No, no they are for you, *Perrin Shin*. Do you have any idea how many people have been praying for you?"

Young Pere guiltily looked down at his hands, but lifted his gaze to Versa's belly. "I know who the miracles are for." He gestured to her stomach.

Versa ran a hand over it and readjusted the shawl. "I think you're right. And the greatest miracle is still to come—finding her a father who can love her." She sighed and stared off at the mountain they'd soon have to scale. "I want to find a man like Guide Zenos. He's been so good to me and my family. He's treated us like we're his. I finally know what a father is *supposed* to be like. I want her to have someone like him. Or like your father," she added with a slight blush. "For the same reasons."

Young Pere smiled gently. "You think it's a girl?"

Versa shrugged. "With my mother's history, what else could it be?"

Young Pere chuckled, and he watched her belly shift. Knowing it was an awkward question, but still intrigued, he said, "May I?"

Versa hesitated before nodding.

He gently placed his hand on her belly, the baby slowly shifting underneath his touch. "She's active—that's a good sign."

But Versa grimaced. "So I've been told. But right now it feels like she's trying to kick her way out through my back."

Young Pere patted her belly until the baby's rolling slowed.

Versa laughed quietly. "I think she actually feels you patting her."

"My uncle Shem would do that," Young Pere explained. "So often the unborn babies in our families would become active when he was around. I think they could feel who he was and were excited to be around the Creator's guide. Then he'd pat them and say, 'Give your poor mother a rest, will you?'"

Versa smiled and watched Young Pere's hand continue to pat her belly until the baby was still again.

She placed her hand on top of his. "Thank you," she whispered.

"As I was kneeling by the river this morning, I wasn't just getting a drink. I was pleading for help. I had no idea what to do next."

Young Pere stared at her hand on top of his. She slid it off, and he, feeling embarrassment at his forwardness, and her forwardness, and forwardness in general, quickly withdrew his hand from her belly as if it were on fire.

He sat back, well out of touching distance, before he dared to look up into her face which struck him as more beautiful every time he gazed at her. Still, he thought he sounded quite casual as he said, "It's been my pleasure. Besides, it feels right to be around expecting women again. I've missed seeing children and families."

Versa turned pink again and looked down.

Young Pere touched her foot to get her attention. "Tell you what—I'll help you with the next miracle when we get to the site."

Versa frowned. "Next miracle?"

"Yes. Finding you the most wonderful husband and father Salem can offer."

Versa tilted her head. "Oh *really*?"

Young Pere nodded, trying to understand why his cheeks were growing hot and red. "You should have someone who can really appreciate you. I already have someone in mind."

Now Versa was blushing. "Who?"

"My cousin Cephas Briter," he said. "There's no one more faithful or strong than him."

Because maybe she *wasn't* his half-cousin, but even if she were, that'd still be all right, wouldn't it? He knew of a few cousins in Salem who had married, and their children were healthy and fine, and Versa might be only a *half* cousin—

She was staring blankly at him, and he realized he needed a stronger pitch. "Cephas was always the man I should've been. Everything I should've done, he did. He's the perfect son: sober, thoughtful, and the best example. And," he sighed heavily, "I'm going to have to confess all of that to him when I finally see him again. He'd be perfect for you." When he saw Versa's knitted eyebrows, he added, "And I've been told he's even better looking than me."

Versa snorted a laugh.

Young Pere grinned.

"I guess I haven't humbled you completely yet. Yes, I know who Cephas is. He accompanied your father a few times. He favors your uncle—"

Young Pere had to remind himself she was referring to Deck.

"—but with more hair. I supposed he is rather handsome," she said thoughtfully. "Although on the quiet side, so I'd always get my say in. But what makes you think he's still available?"

And somehow that simple question knocked Young Pere like a timber upside his head, and thousands of previously unconsidered thoughts piled on top of him like an avalanche.

"I hadn't thought of that," he whispered. "He could already be married. It *has* been almost two years, after all. Wow. I hadn't—"

He hadn't considered *anything*, he had to admit to himself. Earlier he was struck with the idea that he'd been the most detestable Shin in Salem. While he hoped that wasn't the case anymore, he had to face the fact that *no one* would be the same as they were.

"You know, a lot may have changed," he mused out loud. "Little kids growing bigger. Morah would be nine years old now. My sister Hycy married right before I left. What if she's a mother now? I missed it! And my cousin Salema was just as big as you when I took off—I don't even know what kind of baby she had. It's probably already walking and talking. She was really hoping for a girl. She already had two boys—"

He broke off his rambling to cover his face with his hands.

Versa sat in silence, waiting.

When Young Pere composed himself again, he whispered, "Relf asked me last year if I wanted to know about the new romances. Maybe he was talking about Cephas. Or Zaddick finally found someone who could put up with him. *I missed it all.*"

That last realization bubbled up around him like a suffocating river, trying to swallow him up, smothering him with despair—

The hand squeezing his arm caused him to open his eyes.

Versa was kneeling in front of him. "It doesn't matter, Young Pere," she whispered earnestly. "You can fix it. You can get to know everyone again. You can't dwell on what's lost. I know because I've tried. All you can do is look to the future and think about how great it'll be."

Young Pere felt his eyes dribbling tears and he clumsily wiped them. Versa was fishing a gray cloth out of her bag, but he tried to dry his face before she could hand it to him. "You're right, you're right," he sniffed. "You know, I think I've said that a lot today."

Versa ventured a smile. "That I'm right? I've noticed that, too. Those are a woman's favorite words, you know."

Young Pere couldn't help but scoff a chuckle as she wiped away a stray tear he missed. No matter what she said, she had a way of making him want to laugh. "And here I thought that a woman's favorite words were, 'I love you.'"

Versa pretended to ponder that, but Young Pere noticed her cheeks growing pink again.

"*I love you* is good," she decided, "but *You're right*, might be even better. You know, Young Pere, you already have the makings of a—"

His chest tightened again as she looked up into his eyes, and this time the blush in her cheeks was unmistakable. She must have felt it, because she quickly backed away and sat down on her log again.

But Young Pere wasn't about to let her off that easy. "I'm sorry, what were you saying? I have the makings of a what?"

Versa pursed her lips, her eyes narrowing, but her cheeks nearly glowing red. "I'll tell you later. Maybe." She repositioned herself.

While Young Pere wanted to continue the line of teasing—or maybe even flirting, he wasn't sure what was happening between them—he couldn't help but notice her discomfort. He'd been around too many expecting women in his family. "How often are you feeling that?"

"Feeling what?"

"The pain."

Versa stared at him. "I know what you're suggesting, but it's a constant pain. All of this has been a little much today, as you might imagine, and it's catching up to me now. That's all."

"Are you sure? *Absolutely* sure?"

"Yes. Besides, it's in my back."

Young Pere sighed. "That's where birthing pains often start. If the pains increase and decrease at regular intervals, you need to tell me." When she only examined her chunk of bread again, he prodded her with, "So when do you think you're due?"

Versa shrugged, nibbling on a crust. "It doesn't matter. We're going in the right direction, correct?"

He knew an avoidance answer when he heard it. He practically invented them. "Versa," he repeated, leaning toward her. "*When?*"

"I have plenty of time," she met his eyes. "Several weeks still."

Young Pere leaned back against a tree and sighed in relief. "You don't really look too big, either," he said diplomatically, "but still your belly could get in the way. That route, right there? The Back

Door? It's not going to be easy. We could take an easier route, but that would be another half day's walk through the forest to get there, and I don't want to risk you suddenly *doing* something."

"I've heard about the Back Door. It's supposed to be the fastest way. I'm not birthing here," she insisted. "I promise."

While she looked him solidly in the eyes, he could tell she was keeping something back. He kneeled in front of her and put his hands on her belly again. "It's not exactly up to you, you know. Nature has a way of doing things when it's ready. I noticed earlier—" and he gently pressed on her bulge, "you're very tight."

"I've always been in excellent shape, so of course it's tight!" she exclaimed.

"I mean, firm," he said. "*Birthing pain* firm."

"And how would you know?!"

"I always felt my sisters' and cousins' bellies when they were expecting," he said, still holding her. "Kind of a weird family tradition to see whose touch the baby responds to. The women in our family would get desperate near the end of their terms. My aunt Calla could put her hands on someone's belly, and if it was a girl it would be born the next day. But it didn't work for boys. So, beginning with my cousin Salema's first expecting, each of the men would put their hands on the expecting mother's belly, trying to convince the baby it was time to be born. My sister Jori's son was born the night after I held her belly, but I could feel her belly was already tightening. Still, everyone in the family thought maybe I had something to do with it, so I became an official belly holder." He smiled faintly at the tradition he'd forgotten about.

But Versa raised her eyebrows at him and glanced down at his hands. "If they were right, then maybe you better *stop touching me!*"

He hadn't realize he was still holding her belly, and his hands flew off it. "I'm sorry! I didn't mean—"

She caught his arm and smiled forgivingly. "I promise, I'll tell you if I feel anything. In the meantime, I'm still in good condition and I can handle anything that's coming our way. Tell me more about the route so I can prepare."

Young Pere sat back down again, still a little surprised at himself for holding her so long. He shook out his shoulders and turned to point to the field. "After we cross that, we enter between the two trees that are slashed like bear claw markings."

"I think I see it," Versa nodded. "And then?"

Young Pere squinted. "Yes, you can see it, can't you? We hadn't marked that one since I was probably twelve. They must have marked it again after I left."

And, not for the first time that day, he felt a wave of hope.

"Then we follow the markings on the trees for about two miles. It's a gentle climb all the way to a river. We cross the river, and that's where the fun begins. We climb up a steep trail for a couple hundred paces, then it's up a rock face for about another two hundred paces. There are grassy parts on either side of the rock, but it's too steep an incline to climb without slipping. I know—we've tried. The rock goes all the way to the top of the mountain—it dips down there as a kind of saddle—but it leads right to the temple site. Once you're at the saddle it's a nice little stroll from the top of the mountain through the trees for a few dozen paces, and you're there."

"Doesn't sound too bad, *mostly*," Versa said, looking across the field. "Tell me more about the rock face."

Young Pere sighed. "That's what I'm worried about for you. It's rather steep, but if you keep leaning forward, you can pretty much just crawl up it. There are a lot of natural hand holds. I even did it back when I was six or seven. Just a little difficult to balance at times."

Versa stared up at the mountain challenging her. "I am forward-heavy right now," she acknowledged. "Let's just do it. It seems like the most logical way to go."

"Are you sure?" Young Pere asked, trying to read her face.

She looked over at him. "Will you help me?"

He smiled broader than he meant to. "Absolutely."

"Then I'm sure I can make it. And we should probably go now," she said, struggling to stand up.

Young Pere got to his feet, took her arms, and pulled her up.

"I can get up myself," she said as she looked up into his face. He knew he was standing a little too closely but he didn't feel like stepping back yet.

"But thank you anyway," she added.

"You're not used to someone trying to take care of you, are you?" Young Pere said softly, aware that he was still holding her arms on the pretext of making sure she didn't topple over.

Versa shifted her gaze to the west. "Any plans for crossing the field, or do we just start walking?"

Feeling the same embarrassment as before, Young Pere released her arms and turned to look at the field. Filled with confidence he was sure was given him by the General of Salem, he announced, "It's all right. We can do this." He picked up her bag and eagerly slung it over his shoulder. "Let's go." Gripping her hand, he pulled her out of the shelter of the forest and into the field.

They walked as quickly as they could straight through the field to the marked trees. Young Pere firmed his grasp on Versa's hand as two soldiers looked at their direction, then, suddenly distracted, turned to go another way. It happened again and again, soldiers noticing them, soldiers abruptly turning away.

Versa stumbled a bit but did her best to keep up. When she tripped again, Young Pere stepped closer and wrapped an arm around her back.

"We could just go a little slower," she panted.

"No. No, we can't. Come on, we're almost there."

"Young Pere, I just can't move that fast—"

"Yes, you can," he insisted, feeling an urgent need to get her out of sight of the soldiers. "Keep going!" He rushed her to the trees with the slashes and nearly dragged her in between them. He didn't stop until they were deep in a thicket of trees.

"I need a minute, Young Pere," Versa panted. "Let me sit!"

He looked around and, satisfied they weren't followed, directed her to a stump where she sat down hard, holding her belly and breathing heavily.

Young Pere continued to scan the trees. "Sorry about that. You all right?" he asked her, not looking back but watching the field to make sure no one was coming in after them.

"Yeah, I'm fine. See anything out there?"

"Yes," he said. "About a dozen soldiers, maybe more, and they're looking for something. I'd guess the houses around here have already been raided or they don't know where to go. Versa, I hate to say it, but we need to move and move quickly. I'm feeling a bit anxious." He turned to look back at her.

Her face was calm as she nodded. "Well then, let's get going!"

Young Pere took her by the arms and pulled her up. "Sure you're all right?"

"Yes. Now, we're looking for the next slashes, right?" she said, stepping in front of him and walking.

"Yes," he fell in behind her. "Thirty paces northwest. I'm not sure how many paces we ran into here, but we should see the next markings relatively soon."

"I want to find them," she said. "How about I lead and you stay behind me? You can hear if anything is following us, and I can practice my tree deciphering skills."

Young Pere shrugged. "You're the general."

She glanced behind her with a scowl and Young Pere chuckled. She marched on into the woods, counting.

"It's going to have to be enough, General," Major Twigg looked out at the fields beyond the station, just in case someone else with a message showed up. But all was quiet that late afternoon. "We have almost fifty thousand committed to follow you tomorrow morning."

Thorne stared, his voice unnaturally calm as he considered the reduction in his forces by one-third. "Where's Hili?"

"Barn, sir. Do you want him?"

Thorne shook his head. "Poe used to be close to Mahrree Shin. I think all that he remembers right now is his former teacher. He needs time to remember her as a traitor to the Administrators. He also helped Kroop on occasion. I suppose he thought of him as a friend or something."

Twigg realized that was the first time Thorne, or anyone for that matter, had even mentioned Lannard Kroop. As soon as he had died yesterday, he'd been forgotten.

Twigg also realized then that no one had bothered to recover his body to give it a proper burial. The guide of the Creator wasn't important enough, apparently.

"Hili may be troubled about losing the foolish man," Thorne was saying, "even though Lannard deserved what he got. Let Hili pout tonight in the barn. By tomorrow morning, he'll be mine again."

Shem finally moved.

He hadn't had anything to eat or drink all day, but now at dinner time he finally looked away from the wooden grave marker and beckoned to his assistant who had kept a constant vigil by his side.

The man squatted next to him. "Yes, Guide?"

"Choruk, you're in charge now," Shem whispered. "You've served the next longest. You'll need another assistant, probably two until we hear back on what happened to Ahno. Under different circumstances, I'd recommend Peto Shin as a new assistant, but he's needed by his family right now. Find other solid men of faith, make your selection, pray about your decisions, then tell the other assistants to come here. I'll formally grant you the power of guide. It's only until the Deliverer comes, anyway."

Choruk sat by Shem and put a brotherly arm around him. "Don't worry about the Deliverer just yet. And handing over being a guide? That's never been done before, Guide Zenos. The Creator established His successor procedure with Guide Hierum, and there's no successor for you until you die."

Shem stared at the grave marker. "I am dead. He just forgot to shut down my body."

Choruk squeezed him. "The Creator forgets nothing, Guide."

"I'm not worthy of that title," he whispered.

"Obviously you are, because you're still here, Shem."

His shoulders began to heave.

"You're still Guide, Shem. The Creator has chosen you to do great things, including defending your people with the sword and distracting the army to give our people more time. The scouts estimated that one-third of the army has now abandoned Thorne, just as the prophecies said. Two lives were lost, but thousands more were saved because of you.

"I knew both Mahrree and Calla," Choruk continued. "They would readily give up their lives to make sure others survived. Mahrree knew exactly what she was doing at the temple, I'm sure of it. Calla chose to follow you here. No one forced either of those women. It was the Creator who took them, Shem. Not you. You were merely an instrument for Him to work through, as you always have been, as you must continue to be. I'll continue to direct the others while you are indisposed, but I'm not the guide. You are, Shem Zenos. I know it with all that I am."

Choruk embraced the guide who sat unresponsive, then stood up and took his position again standing by his side.

"Not too bad," Young Pere said as Versa pointed out another

hashed tree in the distance. "You've spotted all five so far."

"It's rather fun." She smiled with another cringe Young Pere couldn't see. She pressed her lips together tightly and took long, quiet, deep breathes deliberately through her nose, counting as she walked.

The reports came in sporadically all day at the ancient site. Peto was able to join the assistants occasionally to get updates, but all he could do was acknowledge the news with a weak nod. When he returned to the families trying to buoy each other up, he wondered why he bothered to do anything that day.

The reports delivered by Woodson's scouts leaving the valley were grim. Thousands of Salemites had been killed, including women and children, their corpses strewn in the farms and lands where they fell.

Hundreds were taken prisoner and questioned, tied up and under armed guard. A couple thousand were still trying to escape, taking the southern Idumean trail. Some soldiers sitting near the canyon, with a newly acquired taste for blood, massacred many. A few escaped and were on their way to the ancient site.

There were a couple hundred of Eltana's failed army attempting to take the Lower Middle route by the Eztates, and a few others had made it even further north to the Upper Middle Route. They'd seen the devastation of the Army of Idumea and had finally come to their senses, running away only minutes before soldiers invaded their homes. Houses were looted, animals were slaughtered, and storehouses were raided. Salem was being ravaged.

And Peto was helpless.

At dinner, Cephas Briter joined his uncle in receiving updates.

"We have to help!" he insisted. "We need to go down and—"

"Become targets ourselves?" Peto said. "Too risky, Cephas."

"I'll do it, Uncle Peto! I volunteer—"

"NO!" Peto shouted, with the most energy he'd felt all day. "No more death for this family! No one goes down. We wait and we watch, but they delayed their coming to us. We can only pray for them now."

"Let me find Young Pere, then," Cephas begged. "I might be able to—"

Peto closed his eyes, feeling as if the day would shove him into the ground like a tent stake. "We wait and we watch," he repeated drearily, "but he delayed his coming to us. We can only pray for him now. Go sit with your mother. She doesn't need to mourn for another person, Cephas."

Jon Offra and Teman waved farewell to the tail end of the Idumeans heading back to the world. By the time their group had reached the glacial fort, the ranks of retreaters had swollen to over five thousand. Women and children, some who had just barely arrived, were following them back, too, after hearing the horror stories about the demise of Guide Lannard and the shocking appearance—and subsequent death—of Mrs. Shin.

While Jon and Teman were heartened to see so many come to their senses and leave before the Last Day, they were equally discouraged to see so many more from the world still intent on invading Salem. They didn't believe the reports, even as retreating soldiers shouted at them to turn around, because they wouldn't believe anything except their own desires.

Jon had also tried to dissuade them, but Teman held him back. "If they don't want to listen, no words you say will change their minds. Let's help these back to the world instead. We can save only those who want to be saved."

They went no further than the glacial fort, Jon possessed with the odd feeling that Perrin's jacket didn't want to get any closer to the world. He obeyed it. They gave clear instructions to those heading down the mountain, and shook the hands of hundreds of grateful, and trembling, soldiers.

Jon sighed and glanced at the sky. "Getting dark, soon. Not sure we have time to find any other stragglers."

"I don't think we have time for anything else," Teman agreed, his voice so filled with such finality that Jon looked down at him.

"What do you mean?"

"It's time," Teman said heavily. "The end, of everything. We've done all that we possibly can. Now it's time for us to head back."

"Back? Where?"

"The site, Jon. The ancient site. It's going to be happening very soon—I feel it—and we need to get to safety."

Jon sagged onto a felled log. "Teman?" he said in a small voice. "Can I confess something?"

It was the first time in days that Teman had heard his dull child-like tone. That aspect of him had been gone for a while, but apparently it had just been hiding behind the colonel.

"I'm scared. What if I haven't done enough? What if the Creator says I'm not ready? What if I'm not allowed to be there—"

Teman dropped to his knees and took Jon's face as if he were seven years old. "Jon, do you want to serve the Creator? What does your heart want?"

"To be good enough," he whispered. "But I'm not yet—"

Teman shook his head rapidly. "You don't need to be! That's the glorious part! The Creator asks only for our hearts to be willing to try, and He'll do all the rest. None of us are 'good enough,' whatever we think that means. His entire purpose is to get us the rest of the way there. Everything you've done these past many days—many weeks!—have demonstrated your desire to help and serve. Jon, you're as good as you can be, and that's good enough."

Jon smiled tenuously, hopefully. Then it grew stronger, and something passed across his face that Teman knew meant another aspect of him had shifted. "For some reason I believe you. Maybe it's just hope that makes me believe you, and strangely, I think that may be enough. I have an idea. There's really only one way from here to get to the ancient site, right? The Idumean trail?"

Teman released Jon's face. "You mean, the trail which the army of Idumea will take?"

Jon waggled his eyebrows. "That's the very one. We have time to do one more thing, right?"

"And that would be . . .?"

"Join the army!"

"Nelt, are you sure he went in here?" Beaved asked, eyeing the dense woods.

"Positive. Here, look at this." Nelt tried to raise his arm but it was too swollen. There hadn't been any bloodshed, but there was a great deal of bruising that occurred before Hammer and Iron finally agreed Nelt wasn't armed. And if he was, he would struggle mightily to retrieve his weapon.

Nelt nodded instead to bear claw marks on the trees.

"Very aggressive animals around here," Teach said nervously. "Those bear scratches are rather deep."

"They are," Nelt agreed. "A little *too* deep and even. I once saw a bear at the edge of the trees beyond Sands, scratching a tree. This looks a lot like bear markings but not *entirely*. It's a human-made code. Look at the tree over there," he said cocking his head to it, and immediately regretting the action as his neck muscles ached.

The two blacksmiths had been very thorough in their search.

"The markings roughly match the one on this tree. I saw Shin and the woman rush over here, and this was the way they came. Between these marked trees."

"What does the code mean?" Buddy wondered.

Nelt almost shrugged, catching himself just before he caused himself more injury. "I can't decipher it, and I don't think we have time to figure it out. But I know a little about tracking. We can follow them, I'm sure."

Beaved sighed. "Might as well let you try."

Versa hadn't noticed anything out of the ordinary, but Young Pere did. He stepped up and caught her by the shoulder.

"Quiet!" He pulled her to a stop.

She heard the noise, too. Someone was behind a boulder ahead on the trail, about twenty paces.

Without a word, Young Pere patted Versa's hip until he found the long knife. Her face flushed as his hand pushed past her coat and slipped under her tunic to grasp the handle. Then he slowly slid the knife out as Versa held her breath. His grip on her shoulder tightened as he held the knife up in the direction of the boulder.

"Show yourself!" he demanded.

"Let her go!" cried a young voice from behind the stony shield. "Let her go, or . . . I'll hit you with a rock!"

Young Pere frowned. "How old are you?"

"Let her go!"

Versa pulled Young Pere's hand off her shoulder. "I'm not his prisoner, he's my companion. Do you need help?"

The voice behind the boulder went silent.

Young Pere lowered the knife. "Are you trying to reach the ancient temple?"

"Yes!" whimpered a frightened voice.

Versa went to take her knife back from Young Pere, but he slipped it into his waistband instead. Ignoring her attempt to retrieve it, he strode to the boulder, Versa following close behind.

Behind the rock they found a boy of about twelve and a girl maybe fourteen, cowering together, each holding a jagged rock as a crude weapon. Warily they stood up, eyeing Young Pere.

The girl squinted her dark brown eyes and tipped her head. "Wait, aren't you one of Rector Shin's sons?"

Young Pere admitted, a bit reluctantly, "I am. Do I know you?"

"We're the Rescatars!" She nodded eagerly and elbowed her brother. "Luis, we know him!" Turning back to Young Pere, who had no idea who the Rescatars were, she said, "We live near the Trovatos in Norden. East of your grandmother's house? I saw you a few times when you came up to visit."

Young Pere nodded as if the girl looked familiar. Knowing enough about females he said, "You've certainly grown up. I didn't recognize you as such a young woman."

She beamed, and Young Pere thought he heard Versa scoff quietly behind him.

That's when he remembered he'd told Versa his *How to Make Girls Swoon in 5 Easy Steps*, and had just demonstrated step 1: vague flattery and a flirtatious smile. He'd tell Versa later that he was just trying to put the trembling girl at ease. Really.

"Why are you on this route?" he asked Miss Rescatar. "You should have taken the Norden route. Where are your parents?"

The boy Luis squirmed and the girl said, "They're hurt. We're down here because my papa wanted to try to convince his brother to join us. He didn't want to go to the ancient site and wanted to defend his house instead." Her voice quavered. "He didn't believe Guide Zenos, but now it's too late. Mama told Papa we had to leave when the soldiers were coming, and we did, just before . . . they went into my uncle's house. We were watching from the forest. We saw them drag my uncle, and—" She stopped, unable to continue.

Versa put a comforting arm around her and she rested her head on Versa's shoulder.

"You said your parents are hurt?" Versa asked kindly. "What happened? Where are they?"

"Back there, in a clearing," Luis answered, his chin trembling angrily. "Some of the soldiers came running into the forest looking for food. We had some and gave it to them, but then they *still* pushed down Mama and cut Papa." His eyes hard and bitter. "We gave them everything we had, and still they were mean!"

Salemites knew nothing of unfairness, Young Pere thought, not to mention mindless brutality.

"They can't go on," Luis said. "They wanted us to go, but Febe and I—" and he, too, lost his voice.

Young Pere rubbed his forehead.

YOU CAN FIX THIS, YOUNG PERE. YOU CAN GET THEM THERE. IT MAY NOT BE TONIGHT, BUT YOU STILL HAVE TIME.

Young Pere looked to Versa, mostly worried about her. But she was already glaring at him with an expression that said, Don't you *dare* think about not helping them!

"Take us to your parents," Young Pere said to Febe.

She smiled in gratitude and took off past the trail and down a small ravine, her brother close behind.

Versa held her belly as she tried to keep up with their excited pace, and Young Pere followed closely, hoping to catch her if she stumbled. About thirty paces off the path they saw a slight movement behind several felled trees.

"Mama! Papa! We've found help!" Luis called.

"No!" came a cry from behind the logs. "We told you to leave!"

"Well we're not obeying," Febe said as she bounded to them.

"Ah, the evil influence of the world is already here," Versa murmured. "Teaching teenage girls to disobey their parents."

Young Pere sucked in his breath when he saw two more boys come out of hiding by the logs. One looked to be about nine and the other around eight. They each held sticks they probably thought would be effective and stared in fright at Young Pere's inside-out jacket and uniform pants.

"It's all right," he assured them as he walked to the other side of the logs. "I'm not with the army anymore. Where are your parents?" But already he saw them.

Versa gasped when she joined him.

Huddled next to each other in the dried leaves were their mother and father. Mrs. Rescatar had a growing black eye and an obviously broken arm. Mr. Rescatar, lying next to her, was drenched in blood from several stab wounds to his torso.

"Oh, I shouldn't have quit taking medical classes," Young Pere muttered as he knelt beside them.

But Mrs. Rescatar, who looked vaguely familiar, stared in surprise. "No—no, it can't be, can it? Are you . . . are you Young Perrin Shin?"

He gave her a dismal smile as he examined her broken arm. "Yes, I am, Mrs. Rescatar. Normally I'd say, 'Good to see you, too,' but that doesn't seem appropriate right now." Realizing he'd have to fashion some kind of splint for her arm, he turned his attention next to Mr. Rescatar, who he remembered chatting with his father and grandfather a few times.

"Young Pere," Mr. Rescatar said raspily, "you are an answer to prayer, you know that?"

He gingerly unbuttoned Mr. Rescatar's reddening shirt. "Now I'm wondering just what kind of prayer you offered that would bring someone like me to you. Versa?" he called over his shoulder. "Give me some of those cloth wrappings you had in your bag. I need to see what we're dealing with."

Versa, her hand over her mouth in horror, took the pack off Young Pere's shoulder.

"You should go to the emergency shelter and get the medical kit," Mrs. Rescatar said to Young Pere. "The children tried once but they became too frightened to go alone."

Young Pere frowned apologetically. "We never had an emergency shelter on this trail."

Mr. Rescatar caught his hand. "Yes, there is," he whispered. "I know—we stocked it a year and a half ago. That's why I knew we could do the Back Door, because we did it then."

Young Pere sat back on his heels. "There's a shelter here? Since when?"

"Since you left."

Young Pere closed his eyes briefly, unsure of how to interpret that answer. "But we never put medical kits in them."

"Yes, we did," Mrs. Rescatar said. "Every shelter now has a medical bag and supplies."

It was the sudden rush of protection, the feeling of being surrounded by help, that startled him. But only for a moment, because there was work to do.

"Then I better go find it," he decided. "Versa, stay here and start wiping the blood so I can see his wounds. Mrs. Rescatar, can your oldest son help me find the emergency site?"

Luis was already nodding.

"Then let's go, Luis," Young Pere said, pulling out Versa's knife for protection. "Is it on the trail?"

"Yep, come on!" and Luis started back up the ravine.

Young Pere put a hand on Versa's shoulder. "You all right for a few minutes if I leave?"

Versa nodded, a cloth in her hand as she bit her lip, unsure of where to start on Mr. Rescatar. "Of course I am. Go, go. But please be careful, Young Pere."

"Don't worry about me—I'm *maturing* every minute." He gave her a quick wink and turned to follow Luis who was already back up at the trail.

Mrs. Rescatar noticed that Versa's gaze followed him, even after he'd vanished from view.

"He does seem to be maturing," Mrs. Rescatar said as Versa met her eyes. "I remember him from a couple of years ago, and I remember the many stories his grandmother told me about his exploits. I can tell that's not the same boy. *Man*," she amended.

Versa went pink. "No, he's not. He's not at all." She cleared her throat and tried to suppress a smile. "Well, Mr. Rescatar, you have my sympathies. I'm not known for my tenderness, but I'm the one holding a wiping cloth, so . . ."

Back up on the trail, Luis soon found the route and Young Pere followed. They ran another five hundred paces or so to where an outcropping of rock hugged a slope in the forest.

"Over here," Luis called and darted to the side of it.

Young Pere grinned as he noticed the beaver-chewed logs no beaver ever chewed, pointing in the correct direction. He had never noticed the outcropping of rock before on their other trips and wondered how long it had been there. The boy vanished into a slit in the rock and Young Pere followed.

Inside, he smiled at the collection of crates of food.

"We should take some food with us," he said to Luis. "I don't think we'll be making it to the site tonight."

Luis opened the crate closest to him. He grabbed a large empty bag off of the top of another crate and started filling it with small wooden boxes labeled jerky, dried fruit, nuts, crackers.

Young Pere, looking for the medical kit, paused to watch him. "Since when did we start stocking these with leather bags?"

"Since the last time we filled the emergency caves," Luis said casually. "Just in case someone needed to carry a lot of things to someone else."

"Makes sense." Young Pere found another bag next to what he was looking for. "Ah, the kit! And it's a big one, too." He inspected the kit and pulled out the first item on top, a large brown bottle.

"Oh, Puggah, Boskos," he whispered as he stared at the label. "The numbing agent. Bos, I'm not sure I can do this."

SO WHY DID YOU PRACTICE ON ME? DON'T YOU THINK THERE'S A REASON FOR EVERYTHING? BESIDES, YOUR STITCHES DIDN'T BOTHER ME AS MUCH AS BOSKOS' DID. YOU DID A GOOD JOB; IT JUST WASN'T MEANT TO BE.

Young Pere smiled briefly, shoved the bottle back into the bag, and slung it over his shoulder. "Now," he looked around the tightly packed cave and asked, "did anyone happen to stock net litters?" knowing full well the answer was, No.

"Like those?" Luis said, pausing in his rush to pack food, and pointing to a tangle of nets by the entrance.

"Since when did . . . ?" Young Pere pulled one off the natural knob on the stone, but the second one behind was tangled with it. Young Pere tried to pull them apart, then decided to shove them both into the bag. Versa and Febe would need something to occupy them while Young Pere tried to do something he did only once, and nearly two years ago.

Young Pere nudged Luis who was trying to shove one more box of elk jerky into the bulging bag. "I think you have enough. I know twelve year-old boys can eat forever, but we'll never eat all of that. We need to get back to your parents before it's dark."

Luis nodded, gave the jerky one more shove, and tied the remaining ends of the bag together. He and Young Pere started to slip out of the cave when Young Pere's foot kicked something.

"Now I *know* we didn't stock pots in these things!" he declared. "What's the point?"

Luis shrugged. "All I remember is that it was with the crates when we were loading the wagon at the storehouse. They said to take it."

Young Pere scoffed at it, then thought again. "Actually, this *would* be good if we could find a source of water. We can heat up some water to properly clean your father's wounds." He put the heavy iron pot on Luis's head like a hat. "There you go. Bring it back to him."

"We already found water," Luis said, sagging a little and peeking out from the rim that sat just above his eyes. "That's why we dragged Papa to the logs. There's a spring down there."

It was just too much, Young Pere thought. If only he could've had a medical assistant—or better yet, Doctor Toon float down from the treetops to take over—it would've been perfect.

Except for . . . "I can think of only a few more things we might need," he told Luis. "And I have a feeling somehow those will come to us as well."

They jogged back down the route to the large boulder. Along the way Young Pere tried to remember how to do the stitches and what he should do if he noticed damage deeper in Mr. Rescatar's body. In the pack there was also a bottle of Pain Tea. Should he give it to Mr. Rescatar before or after?

Then he thought of the times he had a broken arm set and wished now he'd watched more closely instead of letting his mother cover his eyes.

He jogged, trying to envision procedures from the other side of the wounds, until a voice came seemingly out of nowhere.

"And where do you think *you're* going?"

It was a soldier, with his sword drawn.

Young Pere stopped in amazement but Luis panicked.

"RUN!" he screamed.

Another soldier appeared from behind a tree and caught him. Luis thrashed violently but ineffectively as the brawny blond man held him tight.

"No, no, no!" Young Pere said. "It's all right . . . I think. Hammer? Put him down."

"Gladly," Hammer said, dropping the kicking boy. "Shin, we've been looking for you."

Luis pushed the pot back on his head and gazed nervously up at the massive man who had captured him.

Young Pere looked over at Iron who sheathed his sword and grinned at him. "How many of you are there?"

"Enough!" Buddy said, coming out from behind a tree with a

smile of relief on his face. "Am I glad to see you. The forest still makes me nervous."

From up in a stand of trees and voice came down to them. "Told you he was coming. I could see him a mile off." Snarl dropped from the tree.

"Even though I wasn't a mile away?" Young Pere asked. "So why are you all here?"

"Because we believe you," Sergeant Beaved said, coming up the trail to shake Young Pere's hand. "I'm sorry about your grandmother. That wasn't right. None of us want to be part of this anymore. You've been right about everything. We're yours to command."

Young Pere nodded. "Thank you, but I won't be commanding anyone. Just giving suggestions. And I can use your help. We've got injured, just down there."

"I know," Beaved said, gesturing to the ravine. The men and Luis began to walk down into it. "Teach, Reg, Pal and—" That's as far as Beaved got.

Young Pere's eyes flashed in fury when he saw Nelt walking up to meet them. "YOU!"

"No, wait!" Nelt cried as he held up his hands, but Young Pere was already charging at him. He tackled him into a pile of wet leaves and Nelt landed with a grunt. Before Young Pere could punch him in the face, Reg was pulling him off.

"You don't understand who he is!" Young Pere said, thrashing. "This is—"

"A spy and an assassin, we know," Beaved said, running down to them. "Take a good look at him, Shin. Tell me, doesn't he look roughed up already?"

Panting, Young Pere looked at the former Cloud Man. He was holding his arms at odd angles, as if in pain. His dark skin was bruised and an eye was partially swollen shut.

"Young Pere," he said between anxious breaths, "if Hammer and Iron offer to give you a full body massage, I wouldn't recommend it. I'm here to apologize and to offer my services. I'm completely unarmed. I'm sorry about deceiving you. But I did it to save your life, remember? Thorne would've killed you at the temple, and you know it. Now . . . save mine?"

Young Pere wanted to feel anger, but he couldn't find it. It wasn't anywhere in him. Part of him actually wanted to forgive Cloud Man. He *had* kept him quite entertained.

Young Pere nodded reluctantly. "But I'm watching you, every moment."

"You and everyone else," Nelt smiled tightly. "Thanks."

Young Pere offered a hand to Nelt. He got up with considerable grunting, and Hammer and Iron exchanged satisfied looks.

"What's with the jacket?" Nelt asked Young Pere.

"It's inside out. And I recommend you do the same. The Salemites on the mountain will recognize it as a sign of rejecting the army." He nodded to the rest of the security team that appeared from behind the fallen logs. Pal and Teach smiled when they saw him.

Versa came out from behind a tree and sighed in relief.

He walked over to her, feeling guilty for having left her so exposed, and suppressed the urge to embrace her in apology. Instead he patted her shoulder in a brotherly way. "Sorry if they startled you. Are you all right?"

She nodded and patted him back just as awkwardly. "They arrived shortly after you left. Said they knew you. I felt like I could trust them, but I wasn't sure."

"This is my security team that I told you about," he said in an undertone. "I can trust them about as much as anyone. They're *mostly* good men. But," he added in a whisper, "I'll keep an eye out for them."

Versa smiled.

Young Pere felt his chest constrict and he had to turn away.

"Is she a relative?" Beaved asked, nodding to Versa.

Young Pere thought quickly. "Uh, yeah. A distant sister. I mean, *cousin*. Versa. Cousin Versa Trovato." He wrapped an arm around her clumsily and pulled her close.

Versa waved just as uncomfortably. "Hi. Surprised to find him, as you might imagine. But so glad I did!" She patted his chest in what she likely thought seemed a familial way.

Beaved squinted suspiciously at each of them.

"Yeah," Young Pere smiled nervously. "What are the odds? Well, my little friend here," he said, releasing Versa and gesturing to Luis in order to change the subject, "has something in his pack that ought to interest all of you."

Luis looked anxiously at the soldiers surrounding him and took the bag that was slung over his shoulder. He opened it up and dumped the boxes on the ground.

The security team shouted in surprise as they read the labels and dove at the boxes like starved dogs around a discarded bone.

"Dried apples?" Teach exclaimed as he opened one of the small crates.

"And dried peaches, raisins, nuts, crackers, and this," Young Pere picked up a box full of dark strips, "is jerky, Teach. Wapiti, or *elk* jerky."

Teach, now on his knees grabbing at items as quickly as he could with the rest of the security team, looked up into Young Pere's eyes. He took one of the strips of jerky Young Pere held out.

"I believe you, Young Pere," he said reverently. "We saw a wapiti. I believe you about *everything.*"

"Mumph thoo," Reg garbled with a mouthful of walnuts. He gestured to Young Pere who grinned and handed him a big strip of jerky.

"I'm assuming he said, 'Me too,'" Beaved said as he took the box out of Young Pere's hands to distribute to the other soldiers. "I think we're all believers right now."

Luis looked accusingly at Young Pere as he saw the men clawing open crates. "And you thought we had too much!"

Young Pere chuckled. "Keep them under control, *soldier*, while I get to work on your father."

The boy saluted with the wrong hand and Young Pere winked.

His two younger brothers peeked through the logs at the ravenous men, and scrunched just a little lower.

Behind the logs, Young Pere knelt by Mr. Rescatar and waved over their daughter. "Take the pot your brother brought and fill it with water, please. Bring it back to me so I can start washing off this blood."

Febe nodded and rushed over to the spring that bubbled nearby.

"Versa," Young Pere called to her. "Ask Beaved to build a small fire. I'd feel better about heating some water to clean these wounds properly. We don't need infection setting in."

Versa nodded and went to speak to Beaved while Young Pere quickly emptied the medical kit and laid everything out neatly on a cloth on the ground.

"So," Mrs. Rescatar began, understandably nervous, "you know what to do with all of this?" She eyed the supplies.

"Most of them, yes." He picked up a roll of thick cloths, took one off, and dipped a corner in the pot of water the girl had just placed in front of him. "Get some more cloth and help me wipe up your father. Get it wet first. That's right."

"We wouldn't let her work on him. Versa?" Mrs. Rescatar explained as Young Pere began to wipe the dried blood. "We didn't want her using the changing cloths for this."

Young Pere looked up from his work on Mr. Rescatar's belly. "The what?"

"The new changing cloths. From the looks of things, she'll be needing those in the next few days and we didn't want her putting them on her baby, still stained with blood."

Young Pere swallowed hard and continued to wipe around a stab wound. That one would take only four stitches.

"Changing cloths," he whispered, remembering how all the food was wrapped in thick beige and gray cloth. He hadn't recognized the cloth or remembered what it was traditionally used for. The strings, used to secure the changing cloth around the baby's middle, should have been the giveaway.

Versa came over to check on his progress. "They're starting a fire right now, Young Pere. Is that the pot you need heated up?"

Young Pere looked up and evaluated her critically. "Yes, in a moment. We'll be done wiping here soon, then we can start heating the water. How are you are doing, anyway?"

Her smile was immediate and eager, which concerned him. "I'm fine! Do you need anything to eat? There's plenty. I just gave some rations to the little boys."

"No. Not right now. But Versa, if you—" He nodded to her belly.

She cocked her head at him inquisitively.

Deciding that she didn't seem to be in any kind of pain or distress, Young Pere went back to cleaning. Versa watched him work for a moment, shuddered, and made her way back to the fire.

"Mr. Rescatar, from what I can see you have four stab wounds," Young Pere said, gently wiping his torso with his daughter. "Does that seem right?"

He nodded slowly. "That's what I remember. How bad do you think it is?"

"Actually, I think it's not as bad as it appears," he said, gingerly cutting away Mr. Rescatar's shirt. "Two stabs seem to have hit the region of your liver. That's why there was so much blood. The third cut isn't very deep, and the fourth, well, it goes in about an inch and I'm not really sure what's in that area. I didn't get that far in my anatomy class. Whatever's below the liver, I guess," he said lamely.

Mrs. Rescatar smiled worriedly at his dismal diagnostic attempts.

"So what do we do for him?"

"I can stitch him up. I've done it before and I have the right brown stuff to numb the flesh, and Pain Tea for later."

"Brown stuff?" she asked.

"Numbing agent," he remembered the name. "My favorite bottle in the medical bags. After that, we let him rest. But Mrs. Rescatar, while we wait for the water to boil, I should take care of you." He handed the pot to their daughter and nodded for her to get more water in it.

Mrs. Rescatar closed her eyes. "That's what I was afraid of. Can't you just wrap my arm or something?"

"I've been thinking about that, and no. I feel distinctly that we should try to set it. From experience I know it will actually hurt less once it's set and secured. But I promise we'll give it only one try, all right? And there's plenty of Pain Tea."

Mrs. Rescatar sighed. "I know you're right," her voice quavered. "I just don't like the idea."

"To be honest," he said, pulling out a long bandage, "I don't either." Realizing that his complete honesty probably wasn't too comforting at that moment, he busied himself picking up several sticks. He crouched next to her, measuring the sticks against her arm until he found three that were similar in length.

"Why don't you lie down, Mrs. Rescatar. You're losing color. Mrs. Rescatar? Uh-oh—"

She slumped unconscious against the log.

"Now's your chance," Mr. Rescatar whispered urgently. "Do it quick, Young Pere. She'll be out for only a minute. Broken bones always make her faint."

Young Pere said a silent prayer that consisted of, *Help me not to mess this up*, took her arm, and with a quick yank and twist, lined up the bone relatively straight. He blinked in amazement that it worked, laid the sticks around her arm as braces, and was just starting to wrap it when Mrs. Rescatar began to stir.

"Just do it," she whispered. "Just do it . . ."

Young Pere grinned as he tied the bands securing the sticks to her arm. "Already did, Mrs. Rescatar! And I didn't even have to plank you."

"Plank me?"

Young Pere chuckled as he continued to wrap and tie her arm, pleased with his success. "I can't wait to see Boskos' face when—"

He stopped and gulped, thinking about seeing his cousin later.

He finished in silence, staying focused on the tasks at hand. After he helped Mrs. Rescatar lie down more comfortably on the ground, he fashioned her a sling out of another bandage. Then he gave her a dose of Pain Tea, along with an extra swig because why not, and he walked over to the fire to check on the water's progress.

Versa was sitting on a log near the flames while the soldiers finished eating.

"How's Mrs. Rescatar doing?" she asked. "I didn't hear her scream. I was kind of expecting that."

Young Pere squatted next to her. "She passed out just at the thought of the setting, which made my job much easier. I think I did a fair job, too. But my cousin can fix her tomorrow, if necessary."

"Tomorrow?" Her voice was pitched higher than normal.

"There's no way we can get them up tonight," he explained. "The sun will be going down soon, and that rock face is impossible in the dark. But we should be all right." He nodded to his security team and whispered, "We've fed them, so they should be as loyal as dogs. By morning the soldiers will be rested and the Rescatars will be stronger and better able to handle what's ahead of them. Mrs. Rescatar might be able to do the climb with some help, but we're going to have to carry Mr. Rescatar."

"Of course, of course," Versa murmured. "Tomorrow morning will be better." She stared into the fire.

"Hey," he gently shook her shoulder. "Something wrong?"

She managed a smile. "No, nothing really. I'm just a little anxious, I guess."

His eyebrows rose. "You? Anxious? *The Slashing Sow?*" he whispered mischievously. "I'd think you'd make a mountain lion nervous before he sent *you* running for cover."

Her smile became wooden. "Silly, I know. Look, your water's boiling. Best get back to Mr. Rescatar. Do you need any help?"

Young Pere used his sleeve to protect his hand while he grasped the handle. "No, I've got it. Unless you *want* to help?"

"No, that's all right," she chuckled nervously. "I'd rather just stay by the fire and watch those little boys stare at the soldiers. Quite entertaining."

Young Pere nodded, turned away, and missed seeing her wince and press her lips together.

Poe Hili hadn't intended on leaving the barn, ever, but the timid sergeant sidling up to the Second Resting Station intrigued him. Suddenly he remembered where he knew him from.

"Sergeant, where have you been? We sent you to check the other canyon at that first wall we came to days ago. Where are the rest of your men? Weren't there fourteen with you?"

The sergeant was shaking. "Sergeant Major, sir—I have some unbelievable news, sir. I . . . I've just come from there," he gestured to the southernmost canyon in the west. "The soldiers told me this was the command center, and, and . . ."

Poe sighed, realizing getting to the 'unbelievable news' from this jittery man might take some time. "Make your report to Thorne," he said shortly.

"Sir, please come with me?" the sergeant pleaded pitifully. "I can't face . . . I can't face another, another . . ."

Poe groaned with annoyance and took the man by the arm. He marched him up the front porch stairs and into the large gathering room. Thorne was gazing out the western windows, gesturing with some papers held in his left hand.

"General, this man who left us at the first wall with fifty men is *finally* here to make a report."

Thorne didn't even glance at them. "Take it yourself, Hili."

The sergeant cleared his throat. "I was specifically told to give the message to you, sir."

That turned Thorne around. "And who told you that?"

The sergeant glanced at the officers now all watching him. "Sir, in private please? I think you'd prefer that?"

Thorne threw down his papers and pointed at the study. The sergeant and Poe went in first, and Thorne slammed the door behind them.

"You have one minute. What's this all-important message?"

The sergeant tried to get to the point without dithering but his eyes were full of terror. "He said, he said, he said . . . to not go to his mountain. There were Salemites there, everywhere."

Thorne's eyes grew large. "Where?"

The sergeant gestured in the direction of the canyon. "West, then to the north. The canyon ends and there is a large valley, then a cliff. At the top of the cliff is a massive flat space, bordered by mountain peaks. Could hold tens of thousands of people. Several thousand were already there when we arrived."

"We?" Poe said. "You and who else?"

The sergeant looked down at his hands. "My fourteen soldiers."

"Where are they now?"

"Dead, sir."

"Dead?" Thorne repeated. "How?"

"Killed by a man who . . . took my sword."

Thorne scoffed. "Figures."

The sergeant cleared his throat, still studying his hands. "He has a message, sir. He said to tell you that it was his mountain and his people, and that anyone who tries to go there will be killed."

Thorne sniffed at that. "Rather bold claim."

"He *alone* killed my soldiers," the sergeant said, looking up at Thorne. "Behind him stood a line of young men taller and stronger than anything I had, armed with only sticks. They didn't even have to help . . . the *man.*"

Poe was intrigued. "Did this man identify himself?"

The sergeant hesitated before nodding.

Thorne was losing patience. "Well, who was it?!"

"Sergeant Major Shem Zenos."

Neither Poe nor Thorne could move for nearly a minute, staring in disbelief. It was obvious why the sergeant struggled to relay his message.

Finally Thorne spoke. "It's a lie."

But the sergeant didn't think so. "The man must have been in his sixties, and he definitely knew how to handle a sword. Said Perrin Shin himself trained him."

Poe covered his face with his hands. Here was proof—absolute proof—of his suspicions about Zenos. He *did* deliver Miss Mahrree to be executed last night!

Poe would take no more.

"You said you killed him yourself, Lemuel!"

"Shut up, Poe!" Thorne shouted. He ran his hand roughly through his hair and turned to the sergeant. "Did you speak to anyone? Tell anyone else about this . . . this imposter?"

The sergeant shook his head. "No, not at all sir."

"Because that's what he is, *an imposter.* Shem Zenos *is* dead," Thorne turned to his sergeant major. "I guarantee that, Poe!"

"*Of course* you do, General," Poe simpered back.

Thorne glared at him.

Poe glared back. He wouldn't back down. Never again.

"Take him," Thorne said, gesturing to the sergeant. "He's your new responsibility. See that he speaks to no one and that no one else hears about this *imposter*. Understood?"

"*Of course*, General." He prodded the sergeant out the door, took his elbow, and directed him to the barn. He didn't release the man until they were in a quiet stall.

"Tell me," Poe asked in a low voice, "was it really him?"

The sergeant shrugged. "Never met him before, but I don't know how any other Salemite would have such ability."

Poe shook his head, a lingering—or maybe hopeful—doubt remaining. "They had lots of people infiltrating the world for many years. It could easily be someone else just pretending. Did he give you any other evidence of his identity?"

The sergeant thought about that. "No, sir. He just *felt* powerful."

Poe was afraid of that. Zenos always had a presence about him.

But this sergeant, lost for days in unfamiliar land, was likely easily ruffled . . .

"Thorne's probably right. You were terrified by an imposter. But if you reveal what I'm about to tell you, I'll deny it: after dark, you run away. Get as far away from here as possible and tell no one what you told me, all right? Otherwise, I have no doubt Thorne will be looking for you, and it won't be to give you a medal."

"Where should I go?"

"Anywhere but here."

"And that, Febe," Young Pere said to the Rescatars' daughter as she hovered near him, "is how we close a wound." He cut the string and readied the needle for the next stitch.

"That's really quite amazing," Febe said. "Just like sewing cloth, but with oozing bits."

Young Pere chuckled but her father moaned. "Pain?" he asked.

"No," Mr. Rescatar said, "not from my belly but from listening to my daughter. Really, Febe, I don't need descriptions right now."

She smiled apologetically and squeezed her father's hand.

Mrs. Rescatar leaned over from her prone position to watch the next stitch, the pain tea already making her more comfortable. "You really seem to know what you are doing."

"I've seen it done a lot, experienced it myself on many occasions," Young Pere explained, "and I even practiced once on a real person."

Mrs. Rescatar smiled. "Who was the lucky victim?"

Young Pere swallowed and completed another stitch. "My grandfather, General Shin. Right before he passed."

Mrs. Rescatar sighed. "Oh, I'm sorry. I didn't realize—"

"It's all right," he said, flashing a brief smile before beginning the next stitch. "He said I did a good job. It just wasn't meant to be."

"Your family will be thrilled to see you, you know," Mrs. Rescatar assured him. "I'm looking forward to watching their reaction when you come walking out of the woods to the site. Lilla will most likely explode in joy! They'll hear her all the way in Edge."

"We'll see," was all he said.

"Young Pere," Mr. Rescatar whispered, "don't underestimate them."

He examined the next stab wound.

An hour later, Mrs. Rescatar was sitting up with her arm secured in the sling and Mr. Rescatar's torso was carefully wrapped in bandages. Febe had the privilege of completing the last three stitches. Young Pere put away the medical supplies as Febe helped her mother over to the fire to get something to eat.

"Thank you again, Young Pere," Mr. Rescatar said as he checked one of the bandages. "Without you, I'm not sure what condition our family would be in tonight. I hate to think about it, but now I don't have to. Your parents will be very impressed."

Young Pere smiled hesitantly. "It's I who should thank you, Mr. Rescatar. I think they may be more willing to take me back if they see I've done some good along the way. After all this time . . . Well, you just might be my way back home."

"No, Young Pere. You are your own way home."

"We'll see," he mumbled again. "Your son said there are blankets at the emergency cave? I've sent a few men up there to get them. It's going to get cold tonight, and we need to keep you and your wife warm and rested. We should move you to the fire before we put it out for the night. Beaved?" Young Pere waved him over. "Give me a hand?"

"Sure, Shin. You're finished? Good timing. You really should know that . . ." Beaved's voice trailed off as he reached down to pick up Mr. Rescatar's feet.

Young Pere picked him up under his arms, glad that the man was slender and lightweight. "What, Beaved?" he grunted as the two of them hefted Mr. Rescatar.

"You'll see in a moment," Beaved said as they carried Mr. Rescatar to the fire.

They gently laid him on the brushed dirt and Young Pere put the medical kit under Mr. Rescatar' head as a crude pillow.

He stood back up. "So what should I know, Beaved?"

Beaved pointed at Versa.

She was trembling as she sat by the fire. "I'm so sorry, Young Pere! I'm so sorry!"

He hadn't noticed until then that the rest of his security team sat on the opposite side of the fire, twitching, bouncing their legs, massaging their hands, and watching her intently as if she might explode at any moment.

Young Pere rushed over and kneeled in front of her. "Sorry about what? Versa, what's wrong? You're shaking!"

Her face contorted and she began to breathe heavily. Gripping his hand, she squeezed it as she tried to control her breathing.

"Oh no, no, no, no," Young Pere whispered in rhythm to her breathing. Stitches and broken bones were one thing, but this was something he'd never experienced firsthand.

Mrs. Rescatar was wincing in empathy. "Those pains were only two minutes apart, Versa. Young Pere, better get that bag again. She said her waters gushed about half an hour ago."

"What?! No, no, no," Young Pere whispered again, taking Versa's hands in his. "No, if you can wait until morning—"

"Young Pere!" Mrs. Rescatar exclaimed. "The baby's coming now!"

"Two minutes apart?" Mr. Rescatar said hoarsely. "Get her to the logs! Febe, take this bag here and start getting out whatever bandages are still clean."

Young Pere stared at Versa as the pain faded. "But you said—"

"I lied!" she whimpered. "Well, I didn't know, really. It was just back twinges but then they kept coming. I felt the first twinge by the river this morning. They were so far apart I was sure I had time. The midwives said first babies can take a whole day or even two to come—" Her voice grew shriller and more panicked, "—and we would have been up there on the mountain by now—that's what you said! We'd be there *by now*! And the pains weren't really noticeable until the last hour or two, but you were right earlier when you were holding me. You felt my belly tighten. And, and—"

Tears spilling down her cheeks startled Young Pere into action. He stood up and gently pulled her up, too. She was markedly different than the defiant, critical woman he'd spent the day with. He put a supporting arm around her and walked her gingerly to the logs which would provide meager shelter.

Mrs. Rescatar struggled to her feet with the aid of Luis, while Febe retrieved the bag from her father.

"I thought you had a few more weeks," Young Pere said as if that would change anything.

"Well it's all guesswork, isn't it?" She sobbed. "The midwife I saw last week said my body was preparing but it could still be weeks. That's what she said—weeks! Or days, who knows. I didn't tell anyone, though. My mother would've never left me if she knew."

Young Pere laid her down as Febe joined them with the bag. Mrs. Rescatar sat clumsily down next to Versa as her son ran back to the safety of the fire.

Young Pere kneeled next to Versa on her other side. She was already breathing heavily again. "Versa, I don't know how to do this. I mean, I've helped Uncle Deck with the cattle on occasion and watched the barn cats give birth, but this—"

Mrs. Rescatar put a steadying hand on Versa's shoulder as she breathed slowly through the next pain. "I've been through it four times and helped with my sister twice. I can talk you both through this." She looked up at Young Pere. "She'll be all right. If she's been walking all day and having pains, then she's probably strong enough to do this."

A quality in her voice didn't sound as confident as her words. Salemites were terrible liars.

"And so are you," she said to Young Pere. "This is what being a husband is all about."

Young Pere gulped as Versa gripped his hand for support.

"But I'm not her husband," he whispered to Mrs. Rescatar.

Her mouth formed a small, embarrassed o. "Oh, of course. I understand a bit about the ways of the world. Your father can have the privilege of fixing that up at the site tomorrow. What's important is that you're here for her and your baby—"

Young Pere was shaking his head, partly because of what Mrs.

Rescatar said, partly because of the ferocity with which Versa was squeezing his hand.

"I'm not the father, either," he whispered.

Mrs. Rescatar's eyebrows furrowed. "You're not . . . *with* her? I heard that many women followed their men here, I saw lots of them, so I assumed . . ." She babbled, searching the ground for the right thing to say and not finding it anywhere. "You two just seem so natural together, and despite what you said to those soldiers I *know* she's not a Trovato cousin—"

Versa cried out. "Something's happening!"

"I just met her this morning!" Young Pere whispered in a panic.

"Young Pere, help me! I need to push!"

"Don't! Don't! Pant through it!" Mrs. Rescatar said, and panted herself to demonstrate.

Febe, standing nearby, also panted as if it were a group activity.

Young Pere recoiled and watched as Versa panted until the pain subsided. Soon her fast breathing relaxed, and she closed her eyes.

"Well, Young Pere," Mrs. Rescatar said, looking at him with determination, "you're the only able-bodied person right now and she obviously wants you to help her. Febe, help Versa with her breeches—"

"Whoa!" Young Pere scrambled out of Versa's grip and shut his eyes. "No, no, no—"

"Young Pere!" Versa pleaded as Febe helped her undress. "Please, help me! Don't leave me! Don't be that breed! *Please!*"

Come on, Young Pere! This is why you're here. This is the right thing to do. It's not inappropriate. This is necessary! Go on.

The voice was clearly Muggah's. Puggah was probably sitting on the other side of the fire with the nervous soldiers, holding his head and rocking back and forth as he always did when a woman in the family was having birthing pains.

Young Pere took a deep breath and crawled back to Versa whose attire was now significantly altered. He focused only on her face and gripped her hand.

"I'm here, I'm here. I won't leave you." To Mrs. Rescatar he said, "What do I do now?"

She looked around urgently. "What's the best way to do this? No birthing stools, obviously . . . no place to hang a birthing rope. If we ask a couple more soldiers, we'll have enough help for the squatting position—"

"No! No!" Versa whimpered. "Only Young Pere."

"That greatly limits your options, Versa," Mrs. Rescatar warned.

"And I don't want anyone watching!"

"Don't worry," Young Pere grimaced. "I can guarantee no one at the fire wants to witness this." He didn't add, *Myself included.*

"Well, that leaves you lying on your back," Mrs. Rescatar fretted. "Most difficult position for you, it's hardly ideal—"

"Mama," Febe said timidly, "nothing seems ideal right now."

"True," Mrs. Rescatar sighed and cradled her broken arm, looking around for a strategy. "How best to do this . . . Dear Creator, we need ideas—"

Luis called from a safe distance. "Mama, Papa says, 'Try feet on chest.'"

Young Pere frowned. "How is she supposed to put her feet on her chest?"

"*Your* chest," Mrs. Rescatar said. "That's right—we did that with our last one when he was coming too fast and it was just the two of us. It's harder on the mother but easier on the catcher, so you can see what's going on."

Young Pere's eyes bulged.

"Right there, Young Pere. Kneel in front of her."

"What?!"

Versa cried out again. "I need to push!"

"NOW!" Mrs. Rescatar ordered.

Young Pere scrambled to his position and Versa firmly planted her bare feet on his chest. Young Pere went pale.

"Grab her arms!" Mrs. Rescatar said as Versa reached up to him. "She braces her feet against you and pulls on your arms."

Young Pere's mind went mercifully blank as he tried to focus on Versa's face and she gripped his arms.

"Febe!" Mrs. Rescatar pointed at her daughter who looked desperate for some way to help. "Support her from the back. Push her up to a sitting position. That's it. Now Versa, push against the pressure!"

Young Pere closed his eyes and nearly lost his balance as Versa pushed against his chest and pulled on his arms with shocking strength. He was sure there would be bruises in the shape of feet on his chest later.

"Push push push push—good! Don't forget to breathe . . . and push push push . . ."

Young Pere peeked briefly to see if it was over, but there was no baby yet by his knees.

"One more Versa?" Mrs. Rescatar asked.

"No, no," she gasped.

"Breathe slower, Versa. You can rest for a minute. Slower."

"Young Pere," Versa panted. "What do you see?"

"Nothing!" he said, his eyes still closed.

"Well *look!*"

"No!"

Mrs. Rescatar chuckled. "Versa, the head is very low down. You're doing wonderfully. This baby's been making her way down all afternoon, hasn't she? You're one tough mother. Tell us when you feel a pain again so we can support you. I think maybe five more cycles and you'll be a mama."

"Five *more*?!" Young Pere whimpered.

"Hey!" Versa snapped, "I'm the one doing the work!"

"I know, I know," he assured her. He twisted his head and looked behind him. "Where are they with the blankets?"

"Oh no, another one," Versa whispered. She took a deep breath as Young Pere closed his eyes again.

"That's it, Versa!" Mrs. Rescatar encouraged as Young Pere firmed his grip on her arms. "Push push push. Pull on his arms to balance yourself . . . Remember to breathe . . . keep going . . . push push push—"

Young Pere couldn't squeeze his eyes shut any harder but he tried. Versa's pushing and pulling on his body was a remarkably bizarre sensation, and he tried not to think what it was accomplishing.

Versa suddenly released his arms. "I can't, I can't, I can't," she panted. "I'm too tired, I'm too tired."

Young Pere opened his eyes. "Versa! There's no stopping now! You're . . ." he gestured to her lower half that he was ignoring.

She shook her head in despair. "I'm so tired, Young Pere. This day was just too much . . . I can't do it . . . I'm so weak." Tears leaked from her eyes and she moaned in pain.

Mrs. Rescatar grabbed Young Pere's arm and whispered in his ear. "She told me she walked twelve miles today. She shouldn't have!"

"That's not my fault. I didn't know!" he whispered frantically back.

"This just isn't the right time or place," Versa announced, her chin trembling in panic. "No midwives, the air's so cold, there might be other soldiers coming . . . so much can go wrong in the next few minutes." Her entire body began to shake in pain and terror. "No—I'm just not going to do this right now," she declared, as if she was in control of anything.

Young Pere's mouth dropped open at her misplaced determination.

Mrs. Rescatar grabbed his arm again and whispered urgently in his ear. "It's not uncommon for women to panic at some point in birthing. And she actually has plenty to worry about: this *is* hardly the best time or place! But Young Pere, there's no option. If she doesn't push, they'll both perish."

Stunned at that news, Young Pere stared at Mrs. Rescatar.

She nodded gravely.

He licked his lips, took a deep breath and—it was necessary, it was necessary, he reminded himself—looked down.

"Nope! I want to see this baby, Versa. So far I see the top of her head! I think she has blond hair, Versa. Nothing sadder than a bald baby, my Grandma Trovato always says. But not this one. Come on, Versa! Let's see the rest of her! You can do this." He grabbed her arm to pull her upright.

But she was as floppy as a rag doll as she sobbed, her eyes still wide with worry. "I can't, I can't, I can't!" She shut her eyes, squeezing more tears down her pale cheeks.

Young Pere held her up the best he could, but he had no idea what to say next. Her fear was beginning to transfer to him. The midwives had all kinds of strategies for dealing with every problem, but he knew very little beyond the basics. Before he could send up another prayer of pleading—he'd thought several in the past hour already—he heard a familiar voice in his mind: Muggah.

Young Pere, appeal to her toughness. Get her angry! She's strongest when she's angry.

"Versula Thorne!" he barked.

She opened her eyes and glared at him for using the full name she hated. The terror was gone, replaced by fury.

"You *will* get this baby out tonight," Young Pere commanded, "or I will tell everyone on the mountain how you were *too weak*."

It wasn't enough. She closed her eyes and sobbed again. "But I am, I am, I am—"

Young Pere leaned over her and held her face. "No, you're not. *He* made you strong! He forced you to be tough."

Her blue eyes opened again, and Young Pere saw she wanted to believe him.

"Now, let's get the ultimate revenge, Versa. Make Lemuel a *grandfather*, and to a *GIRL!*"

He couldn't tell if she was laughing or sobbing. She seemed to be doing both as she gasped. A new pain was coming.

Young Pere resumed his position and gripped her arms. She put her feet back on his chest, partly hesitant, partly insistent.

"Come on, Versa! He still thinks he's a young man but we both know better! His hair's going gray and he doesn't like it."

Versa took a deep breath and started to push.

"That's it! Make him suffer! Turn him into a *Grandpy*! He told me just last year he couldn't imagine becoming a grandfather for many more years. Well, let's imagine the look on his face when— pushpushpushpush—he hears he's *old*!"

She gasped, scoffed a laugh, and took another breath.

"Yes! Keep going! You're doing it, Versa. He can't fight it. He can't win. He's not going to get me as a son, and instead you're going to make sure he becomes a grandfather. To another girl! We can do this to him, Versa! Pushpushpush! I see part of a face! It's all smushed up and wrinkled and looks like his scowl when the cook's made stew with carrots in it!"

Versa gasped a laugh and released his arms.

"Versa, don't quit! Not now!" Young Pere said, grabbing her arms again.

Her face contorted with intense discomfort. "Pain's faded. Have to wait . . . for the next one," she panted.

Young Pere looked at Mrs. Rescatar.

"This should be the last one," she assured him. "You're both doing wonderfully."

Young Pere grinned and hurriedly wrenched off his jacket.

"What are . . . you doing?" Versa gasped between breaths.

"No blankets yet. The baby needs to be wrapped up."

"In your . . . uniform?"

"What else? Ultimate insult," Young Pere declared. "*He* gave this to me when we were in Pools."

Versa smiled weakly then took another breath. She put her bare feet back up on his chest, marking his thin graying undershirt with two dirt imprints.

"This is it, Versa!" Young Pere took her arms again as she pulled and pushed, "Go, go, go—she's coming! Remember, this is all his fault you're stuck here in the trees surrounded by soldiers and with me as your midwife. Make him suffer, Versa! Do it! Do it!"

Versa peered at him through her squished face and took another breath.

"You've got it! Pushpushpush. She's turning, Versa! There's a shoulder—"

"Catch the baby!" Mrs. Rescatar cried.

Young Pere released Versa's arms and caught the baby as it slipped on to his jacket. He quickly wrapped it up as the newborn coughed and spluttered, then—to Young Pere's enormous relief—cried out.

Young Pere's face was so wet with worry he could barely focus on the baby he cradled. "You did it, Versa!"

"Did we get our revenge?" she panted as Febe helped her lay down on the ground. "Is it a girl?"

Young Pere opened his jacket and peeked. He started to laugh as worried tears finally released from his eyes. "It's a girl! Take *that*, Grandpy Thorne."

Versa closed her eyes and laughed and cried in relief.

"The cord," Mrs. Rescatar reminded him. "Lay the baby down, Young Pere. We need to tie off the cord." Her daughter was already handing him some string from the earlier stitching job. "We need something to cut the cord with," she said, looking around.

Young Pere laid the baby on the ground and pulled the long knife out from his waistband. He showed it to Versa.

She laughed softly. "That's why I brought it! Febe, in my bag are baby blankets and changing cloths. Please bring them to Young Pere."

"How much did you bring?" he asked, his hands fumbling with the string as he tried to tie off the cord of the squirming newborn. Mrs. Rescatar winced as he held the knife to the baby, his hand trembling. He sliced through the cord—and nothing else—successfully. Mrs. Rescatar relaxed only after he put the knife back into his waistband.

"The bag is mostly full," Versa said, trying to sit up a little to see her daughter.

Young Pere now had the bag and was dumping out its contents. "Yep—it's mostly changing cloths and blankets in here. You knew you'd deliver, didn't you?" he said, quickly putting a changing cloth on the baby and swaddling her tightly in a soft, cotton blanket.

Versa nodded guiltily, her face wet with tears and perspiration. "You're pretty good at that," she smiled. "You'll have to teach me. I've never put a cloth on a baby before."

Young Pere looked up at her. "Really?"

She nodded sheepishly. "Guess I better keep you around. You're proving to be rather handy. Setting arms, stitching wounds, now midwifery—"

"*I'll* take care of the feeding lessons, though," Mrs. Rescatar suggested.

Young Pere nodded vigorously in agreement and scooped up the baby. Using another cloth Mrs. Rescatar gave him, he wiped the newborn's face clean. "We'll finish washing you when we have warm water again," he said softly to the crying baby.

"So," Versa strained to see her daughter, "what does she look like?"

Young Pere sighed. He'd never understood before what people saw in newborns. He'd seen dozens and they all looked misshapen and beat up. And a season later they looked nothing as they had, which he always thought was fortunate. When someone in their family gave birth, he'd look at the newborn, shrug at it, then pass it along to the next family member waiting to hold it.

But not today.

His vision blurred as he gazed at the tiny baby trying to open her eyes and twisting her neck. He instinctively kissed her cheek that was so soft it felt almost as if it wasn't there.

"She's absolutely beautiful, Versa. Just like you."

Versa smiled as Young Pere scooted over to her. He laid the baby in her arms and Versa kissed her head. She looked up at Young Pere with the softest eyes he'd ever seen.

"Thank you," she whispered. "I'm glad you were the first man to hold her. I'd been hoping it'd be Guide Zenos, but given the circumstances, you're not a bad second choice."

Startled, Young Pere sat back on his heels. The Salem birthing tradition. Men always held the babies first—grandfathers, uncles, husbands—to feel of their duty in protecting and guiding the child. And for practical reasons, too. Someone had to take care of the baby while they finished with the mother.

He wasn't sure how to interpret what Versa said.

But she was examining her newborn, smiling softly and studying her face, so she missed Young Pere's rapid blinking. He was just turning to get up to leave her alone with her baby when he felt Mrs. Rescatar touch his arm.

"We need to finish up here and I can't quite help her. But I'll tell you what to do."

Young Pere nodded and got back to his position.

"Shin?" he heard Beaved call from the other side of the logs. "Everything all right? We heard a baby crying."

Young Pere nodded at Versa, but she didn't notice. She was smoothing her baby's matted hair and gently touched her nose. Young Pere felt a lump build in his throat, but he smiled as he watched her.

"Perfect, Beaved," he called back. "It's a daughter."

Peto hadn't noticed her before.

He hadn't really noticed anything that day—that long, terrible day filled with holding weeping children and grandchildren, and trying to pretend he was still securing Salem.

But after dinner he felt a need to get up and do something, *anything else*, besides sitting and weeping. He wandered over to the ancient site to try to clear his head and watch the sunset, and that's when he saw her.

"Druses?"

Druses Thorne looked back at him with a miserable smile. A man stood next to her with his arm around her.

"Hello, Rector," Druses said bleakly. "I'm so sorry about—"

Peto held up his hand to stop her. "I know, and I thank you. But I don't think I've met your companion."

She blushed lightly. "This is Creer. He brought me and Delia here with his family."

Peto produced a real smile as he shook Creer's hand. "I'm glad to see Druses made a *friend*."

Creer smiled and turned slightly pink.

Peto's smile grew. "And how's Versa?"

Druses and Creer's smiles vanished, and Druses started wringing her hands. "Rector, I don't *know*."

Peto's smile fell too. "What do you mean, *you don't know*?"

Creer firmed his grip on Druses. "We expected her two days ago," he said. "She still hasn't arrived. She was going to travel with a young man and his family and meet us here."

Peto closed his eyes briefly. "No she wasn't. She lied. Creer, how much do you know about Versa Thorne?"

"Not much."

Druses started to weep. "Oh you don't think she'd really—"

"Oh, yes I do!" Peto said hotly. "If anyone thought they could stop all of this, it'd be Versa! And with a bounty on her head—"

Creer's eyes flashed with warning. "You're not *helping* things, Rector Shin."

Peto held up his hands in surrender. "You're right, I'm sorry. I'm not thinking very well today. I'm just a little on edge. Druses, if it makes you feel any better, my son's out there, too. My sister saw Young Pere escape from Lemuel and run to the eastern mountains."

Druses frowned. "The *eastern* mountains?"

Peto nodded sadly. "I know *exactly* how you feel right now, I really do. I keep closing my eyes trying to feel where he might be, and sometimes I think he's so close I could just jog down the mountain and find him. But we have to trust they are in the Creator's hands. And Druses, His hands are the best there are."

Druses nodded grudgingly. "I just really wanted to be a grandma, Peto," she said, tears filling her eyes. "I can't tell you how much I was looking forward to that. A little while ago I thought I heard a newborn crying and I turned around hoping to see her walking to me with an infant in her arms, but—"

Peto was tempted to embrace her, but Creer was doing his duty. He wrapped Druses into him and kissed the top of her head.

Now Peto's eyes filled with tears. Druses had *more* than a friend. There were still miracles to be handed out.

"Don't give up, Druses," Creer said quietly. "Whatever it takes, we'll get her back. My boys and I will find her. If Lemuel's holding her, I'll get her back. I promise you."

Peto patted Creer on the back and wandered back to his camp.

Shem was sitting up, picking at a plateful of food only because Meiki said she wouldn't eat unless her father did. She poked at the selections as ploddingly as Shem.

Peto sat on the ground next to him. "I just talked to Druses."

Shem merely nodded.

"Shem, she has a boyfriend. *Man*friend. Uh . . . ." Peto tried to think of the right word.

Shem's eyes brightened ever so slightly. "Druses has found someone? She's being taken care of?"

"By someone who already has sons, it sounds like."

Shem smiled faintly.

"And he certainly looks like he was in love," Peto said.

"But is Druses in love?"

"She looked quite comfortable in his arms." Peto didn't see the need to tell him that Versa was missing.

Shem blinked and looked at Peto. "Druses is in *love*."

Peto tried to smile. "You know what this means? Miracles are still being handed out, Shem. We just have to find the right line."

There were eight blankets, and although they were large and heavy, Young Pere worried they wouldn't be enough.

The security team would be fine sharing two blankets among them, but keeping the wounded and weak warm was his biggest concern. They laid the third blanket out by the fire for Mr. and Mrs. Rescatar and covered them with the fourth, then laid out the fifth for Versa and her baby and covered them with the sixth. The last two would be for the four Rescatar children to wrap themselves together for the night.

The soldiers still wore their jackets, but Young Pere had only his thin white—well, not white anymore—sleeveless undershirt. The sun had set, and he could see his breath in the glow of the fire, but blessedly didn't feel any cold.

He crouched by the flames and huddled over the baby, gently cleaning her with the warm water and a soft bandage. Versa lay next to him, watching.

"Maybe you didn't succeed in taking over the world," she said quietly, her critical tone returning, "but you seem to be doing everything else right tonight."

Young Pere shrugged. "Puggah told me a few years ago this kind of training would come in handy."

"What?" Versa wrinkled her nose.

"What's a Puggah?" asked Mr. Rescatar who was lying on the other side of the fire. The Pain Tea had taken affect and he was much more comfortable, as was his wife who sat next to him.

"'Puggah' is the grandchildren's name for my grandfather

Perrin," Young Pere explained as he wiped under the baby's arms. "You remember Relf, right?" he said to Versa. "When his wife Mattilin had their son Grunick, she became very ill afterward. My mother moved her into Relf's old bedroom, which meant Barnos had to move back in with me, and Mattilin's mother came to stay with us. For two weeks Mattilin fought a fever. The doctors and midwives thought she might not make it," he explained as he worked.

He sent up another thought of gratitude that by tomorrow they'd be on top of the mountain. In case anything else should happen with Versa, there'd be plenty of skilled help soon.

"Relf, my mother, and her mother cared for Mattilin and helped her feed Grunick. But Puggah would stand outside the room, waiting to burp the baby and put him to sleep."

Young Pere smiled as he turned over the baby to clean her back, and she wailed softly. "I'm trying to go fast, little one," he assured her. "Puggah always claimed babies slept deeper and longer in his arms since they knew nothing from the world could harm them there."

He cleared his throat of unexpected emotion and kept his eyes down. He knew he had a captive audience in the form of the Rescatar family and a few of his security team, and he didn't want any of them to see the wetness in his eyes, especially Versa.

He rolled the wriggling baby onto her back, covered her top half with a cloth to keep her warm, and continued to wash her stick-like legs with a new bandage.

"But what the family didn't realize," he continued, "is that Puggah would bring tiny Grunick into my bedroom with changing cloths in hand. He told Barnos and me that he was going to make real men out of us by teaching us to care for a newborn. Puggah turned it into a race to see which of us could change Grunick the fastest. And no Shin can turn down the challenge of a race."

"I remember the general being a clever man," Mr. Rescatar said.

"We even had to bathe Grunick, too, just like this," Young Pere grinned. "At the time I couldn't have imagined how that would've come in handy."

"So who won the changing contests?" Versa asked.

"Me, of course." Young Pere said off-handedly. "Otherwise I wouldn't be telling the story. Follow the steps," he announced as he laid the now-clean baby into position. "Remove—take off the old changing cloth, which we'll have in a couple of hours. Wipe—get every little bit of you-know-what off, or you'll have one unhappy baby. I think we've accomplished that. Place—put the changing cloth under the baby." He demonstrated the placement, putting the bulk of the cloth between her legs, the rest going up her back and her belly, overlapping her tiny body. "For baby boys, stay out of watering range. Thank you, Versa, for having a girl. They only dribble."

The Rescatars' sons looked at each other with confused expressions while Febe giggled into her hand.

"Secure—tie the string securely around the waist, but not too tight or baby will be upset. Then, most important: swaddle." He took the long, thick cloth the newborn had been laying on and wrapped it snugly around her. "And now, hopefully she'll be content for about two hours until we need to do it all over again." He proudly held up the wrapped package as if she were a gift on display.

Versa chuckled and pretended to applaud as Young Pere tucked the baby into one arm and, with his free hand, sorted through the extra cloths for a knitted cap he'd spied in there earlier.

"Well, well," Mr. Rescatar said, "you make an excellent father, Young Pere."

His wife made a choking noise and leaned over to whisper something in her husband's ear.

Young Pere purposely took a long time adjusting the cap on the baby's head to avoid seeing the expression on Versa's face at the mistake.

"Ah. Um," Mr. Rescatar said to his wife's whispers. "I see. Sorry. You two just seem so *together* that I just assumed—"

"Stop, dear," Mrs. Rescatar said out loud. "You're only making it worse. I already did that."

Versa laughed quietly, much to Young Pere's relief. "It's all right. I *had* a husband, but he left me. Young Pere was just an answer to prayer."

He knew his face was fully red as he finally secured the cap. Versa's words hit him strangely. Not that he didn't appreciate being an answer to a prayer. In fact, it filled him with unexpected warmth. The Creator trusted him again, so much so that He was directing Young Pere to help others.

It was just that Young Pere felt maybe his efforts that day might have made Versa think of him as something a little bit *more.*

But apparently not.

He placed the swaddled baby back into his jacket and tied the sleeves together to bundle her.

"No, Young Pere," Versa said when she saw what he was doing. "You'll need your jacket to keep warm tonight."

He shook his head as he placed the baby next to her again. "I'll be fine. She needs to keep warm. That wool is just the right thing. Besides, the jacket came from her grandfather," he whispered. "Might be the only thing she ever gets from him."

Versa sighed. "I don't want to see it that way. I'd rather remember that it came from you."

Young Pere smiled inwardly. Maybe he *was* a little more.

He patted her on the arm. "I need to go check on the soldiers. Mrs. Rescatar can give the two of you that feeding lesson. Let me know if you need anything," he said and got up.

As he headed for Beaved circling their camp, he missed hearing Versa whisper to her baby, "I know what we need, but he just walked away."

Young Pere scanned the darkening area with Beaved.

"We'll keep watch in two shifts," the sergeant told him. "I'm sending Teach, Buddy, Iron, and Pal to nap right now, then we'll trade halfway through the night. Nelt is posted beyond us there."

Beaved nodded to Nelt who sat a little ways off at the logs where Young Pere's surgery area had been. Still unarmed, he was holding a chunk of icy snow to his swollen eye.

"Hammer's up at the trail area, Reg is beyond him about twenty paces, and Snarl is circling, looking for any signs of disturbance."

Young Pere nodded as he saw the first four former soldiers make their way to the fire and lay down on the side opposite of the Rescatar family and Versa.

"Have you seen or heard anything?" Young Pere asked.

"Not yet," Beaved said. "But I think we should put out the fire. It could draw attention."

"I agree. I just hope they stay warm enough tonight."

"Tell them to huddle close together and they should be all right," Beaved said. In a lower voice he added, "And I think you should stay with your *cousin*. We already discussed it. Don't take a shift tonight but keep her and that baby warm. She seems to have taken a *liking* to you."

Young Pere knew he was turning red and started inventing. "Uh, you see, when we were younger—"

"Don't even try, Shin. We all heard you," Beaved elbowed him. "Kind of impossible to *not* have heard what was going on just twenty paces away when someone's giving birth! Some of those *sounds*," he shuddered in remembering, "I'm not going to get to sleep tonight. Young Pere—*that's Thorne's daughter*."

Young Pere rubbed his forehead. "We've got to keep her safe, Beaved. Whatever it takes. I don't think Thorne cared one bit that her sister died. This is his oldest daughter and his *granddaughter*. I can't even imagine what Thorne would do to them."

"I know," Beaved agreed. "We discussed that too. None of us want to see them taken. We'll keep her safe, and you stay by her side."

"Look, I can take a shift. I don't mind doing my part—"

"Just take care of them by the fire. If anyone starts bleeding or oozing or *whatever*," he shivered again, "that's your part."

Young Pere slapped him on the back. "Let me know if you hear anything. I still have a long knife."

He spent the next half hour walking quietly in a large perimeter surveying the shadowy forest, listening for footsteps, making sure there was nothing more he could do to secure the camp.

He tried not to think about his family just up the mountain from him, or about the news he'd have to deliver about Muggah and General Thorne.

He also tried not to think about Versa lying by the fire with her baby, and he tried not to wonder why he was so eager to get back to her.

Instead he stared deep into the woods trying to think what more General Shin would do. Several times he felt the assurance from Puggah that all would be well for the night, but still he felt he should do his part.

He smiled into the dark when he heard, *BY THE WAY, EXCELLENT JOB WITH THE BABY DELIVERY. THAT'S ONE THING I NEVER COULD HAVE DONE. YOU'VE GOT ONE UP ON ME, YOUNG PERE.*

At one point he saw Snarl walking quietly away, examining the trees. He nodded once at Young Pere, and Young Pere nodded back. The man made him edgy. He felt he shouldn't trust him, but there wasn't much choice right now. Satisfied that Snarl wasn't going any further, Young Pere finally made his way back to the fire.

Versa was sitting up on the blanket, patting the thick bundle of blankets and uniform that concealed her tiny newborn.

Young Pere's chest burned when he saw her, and her face lit up when she saw him.

"I was getting worried about you," Versa said. "I mean, *the baby's* going to need her cloth changed soon, and since you're such the expert . . ."

She needed a baby changer. That was all.

He sat down on the blanket next to her. "Staying warm?"

"Yes, and the baby feels warm too," she said as the baby burped. Versa sighed in relief. "One burp down, thousands more to go."

"Sounds like a successful feeding," he said. "What's her name?"

"I don't know yet," Versa sighed as she lowered the baby to look into her face. The newborn was drifting off to sleep. "I've had a hard time thinking about that. I was hoping something would just seem right when I saw her. But nothing yet. I guess I need to just stare at her for a while."

"You'll have plenty of time for that tomorrow." He looked over to the Rescatars. Febe was wrapped in a blanket with her youngest brother, and the two other boys shared the last blanket. They sat on either side of their parents who lay by the fire.

"Everyone warm there?" he asked.

They nodded.

He glanced over at the rest of his security team across the fire making themselves as comfortable as possible using the empty bags as pillows.

They nodded as well, except for Teach who was already snoring.

"Then I hate to say it, but we need to douse the fire. We don't need to attract the attention of anyone else looking to do harm."

He glanced over at the Rescatars who nodded in agreement.

"As soon as it's light, we'll head up the trail, cross the river, and climb up to the temple site. So don't worry," he smiled at their concerned faces, "we'll be to safety very soon."

He stood up and put out the fire with the last of the water in the pot, plunging the forest around them into near total darkness.

"Young Pere," Versa whispered.

He crouched next to her.

"Please stay by my side tonight. I'm a little uneasy, probably because you still have my knife."

"Sure. I'll sit right here."

"No, you'll get cold. Lie down next to me and share the blanket. We'll stay warmer."

"Uh, Versa, that's not entirely appropriate—"

Versa scoffed quietly. "Don't flatter yourself, Shin! I gave birth not even two hours ago and I assure you the *last* thing on my mind is anything inappropriate. I'm just being practical. You're not wearing a jacket so you'll give off more heat, and you can help warm the baby and me. Now get down here and lie next to me!"

He hoped she couldn't see him grinning in the dark. "You're the general," he whispered as he lay down stiffly beside her and adjusted the blanket over him.

She jabbed him in the ribs with her finger.

"Ow!"

"You can expect that every time you call me Versula Thorne or 'the general,'" she whispered angrily. Then he felt a kiss on his stubbly cheek. "But thank you for being so good to me today."

He chuckled quietly, hoping it would mask his surprise at her kiss. "You're welcome. I still can't believe you did that, out here. I can't imagine how you're feeling right now. *I'm* exhausted." He stared up at the stars, trying to concentrate on them rather than the fact that Versa was lying so close to him.

"Actually, Young Pere, I feel like I could climb that mountain all by myself!" she whispered. "I doubt I'll sleep at all."

"One of my sisters felt like that, right after her son was first born. Lori had so much energy that she snuck out of her bed a couple hours later to go weed the garden. A while later her husband Sam found her and had to carry her back into the house because she had fainted. She stayed in bed for four days after that, too tired to move. The feeling will pass—trust me," he whispered. "How's she doing?" He reached over to pat the baby resting on Versa's chest.

"Good, I suppose. I'm really not sure. Mrs. Rescatar said she's acting healthy, eating and squirming, but I'm so new at this. I've never been around newborns for more than five minutes. I was told I would have a lot of help."

"I can help a little. Here, hand her over. Let me make sure she's warm enough."

Versa placed the baby on his chest, and Young Pere tucked a finger into his jacket to gauge the temperature.

"She feels good," he said. "How about I hold her for the night so you can rest? Between my chest and the blanket she should stay warm."

He felt Versa slide in closer. "I don't know about that. You're a bit cold." She pulled the blanket up to cover his exposed bare shoulder. "And I need you rested for tomorrow."

Her closeness took his breath away. But she did have a point. She was just being practical. So should he.

"Come here," he whispered. He slid his free arm under her neck and pulled her right next to his body. "Just to keep warm," he explained.

"Of course," she whispered breathlessly as she huddled into him. "For warmth. And now I sort of have a pillow." She repositioned her face on his shoulder a few times. "You'd think something *so broad* might be more comfortable."

She moved her head down to his chest.

"Just to be closer to my daughter," she explained. "So I can hear her breathing. Not that *this,*" she said, trying to find a good position on his chest, "is any softer. You're rather . . . firm."

He felt his heart rate increasing, and she was in the exact position to hear it.

"So," he tried to whisper casually, "I thought motherhood would soften you, but I guess not. Now you're criticizing the sleeping conditions?"

"Not at all!" she said quickly, and patted his side in what she may have thought was a cousin-ish manner. "I . . . I was just making an observation." Her hand stopped patting but stayed on his waist.

He noticed.

"Of course." Young Pere smiled. He gripped her shoulder to hold her securely. "Go to sleep, Versa. Tomorrow's a big day. I'll keep watch."

He didn't know how long he lay there, but the idea of sleep was laughable. Last night he spent the evening talking to Puggah, alone and worried but ready to do what needed to be done. He spent the rest of the night on his knees, pleading for forgiveness and strength.

Tonight he lay with Thorne's oldest daughter in one arm and her newborn baby cradled in the other. How so much could change in a mere twenty-four hours was extraordinary.

He spent hours staring at the stars, replaying their conversations and wondering why he felt such a need to protect her. He barely knew her, but then again that wasn't really true. He couldn't think of another woman he had shared so much with before, or who had shared so much with him. It felt more like half a season had passed rather than only one day.

Maybe it was the possibility that she might be his half cousin, and that he should take care of family. Perhaps it was instinct, a sense of duty that he felt the need to hold them both tightly as the air chilled around them. Maybe he *was* growing up, even maturing.

Then again, it had been an extraordinary week. Under extreme stress, people often cling to others they normally wouldn't. If he met her casually in Salem, he would've been put off by her direct and disparaging manner. She wasn't his type—she'd never go weak at the knees at the mere sight of him.

But maybe that wasn't his type anymore. She was smart and strong and funny in a biting way—

He sighed.

Had she passed him in Salem, she would've been disappointed by his flippancy and selfishness. There was nothing more to her wanting to be close to him besides practicality. Circumstances threw them together, that was all.

That and Puggah. And maybe Muggah.

He didn't feel them near right now, but he didn't need them. It was as if he could sense the security of the temple site above them sliding down the mountain to cover them. He was almost there, and he wasn't coming alone.

He smiled as he held Versa and the baby firmly. He was right where he needed to be.

Snarl crept down the mountainside, watching the trees and deciphering the slashes. It wasn't difficult to move in the dark. He was used to it. If there was a school in thieving, he'd be the director.

But his petty thieving days were about to come to an end. At first he was hoping for the off chance of finding a Shin to claim the two hundred gold slips. But now his future was set.

Thorne's daughter *and* his granddaughter. Thorne would undoubtedly pay two hundred for them, and probably even more for information about how to find everyone else.

Snarl had seen two of his former associates sitting along the tree line when the security team entered the forest. A glance was all they needed to know that Snarl was on to something promising.

Now it was more than just promising, it was a *solid gold* guarantee. He just needed to get them the word, and Snarl would be on his way to becoming the richest man in the world and Salem.

Lilla sat on her bedroll and looked out over the dark camp. Everyone else was sleeping or pretending to be.

She sighed.

Sometimes it seemed he was so close, *so close*. Maybe it was because her sister and mother-in-law were gone, but Lilla couldn't help but feel that Young Pere was almost around the corner.

She sat awake for an hour trying to imagine all the corners there were. When the sun was up, she'd go looking around each one.

Shem laid on his bedroll staring at the stars. His two youngest daughters slept on either side, curled up next to him to give comfort or try to draw some from him. They left their tent empty. Everything in there had been prepared by Calla just before they came up, and he couldn't bear to look at any of it.

He listened to the rhythmic breathing of his girls and tried to ignore the constant pleading in his mind.

Shemmy, it's not your fault.
Shemmy, I love and forgive you.
Shemmy, it's not your fault . . .

The sky was black, with white stars. Not blue in any way.

Poe Hili lay on the straw in the barn listing everything he hated. He hated sleeping in the straw. He hated feeling itchy. He hated that he was so far away from his comfortable bed in Edge. He hated Zenos. He hated Thorne.

And now he was beginning to hate himself.

Lemuel Thorne tried to get comfortable on the large soft bed of the second level of the Second Resting Station.

The sheets were cotton, not silk; the first thing that would need to be changed.

And he hadn't seen any mansions in Salem. Several large houses, yes, but nothing mansion-like except this deceptive barn. Something else that would need changing.

He also hadn't yet been by to burn the Eztates, but he would get to that after the slaughter of the Salemites. He wanted to go through the houses first to see what else they brought with them from the world that would be useful in his new mansion.

There *was* an arena, which would be used for his first victory speech—

He thrashed in the large bed and tried for another position.

There was no mead here, either. Nor gold, at least not yet. No shops, no money holders . . .

What was the appeal of this place, anyway?! So many things to change . . .

When Lemuel was finally quiet, his mind was haunted with visions of Perrin Shin in a general's uniform. He stood with his arms folded and that one menacing eyebrow, arched.

Behind him stood *her*, with her head tilted in that annoying and admonishing manner all teachers possessed that indicated, *Now you've gone and done it.*

Lemuel tried again for another position.

It was impossible to sleep this far north.

The 36ᵗʰ Day of Planting

When the baby stirred after midnight needing to be fed, Young Pere reluctantly handed her back to Versa but made himself useful by taking care of changing her cloths in the dark when she finished. Mrs. Rescatar, in the meantime, gingerly led Versa to the privacy of some trees to 'take care of things' that Young Pere didn't want to think about.

Fortunately, Young Pere thought to himself as he fumbled in the dark with the baby, he had practiced changing Grunick blindfolded just to prove to Barnos that he could.

He continued to keep the baby on his chest, even after her second nighttime feeding and changing where both Versa and Young Pere were more quickly successful than the first time. He considered they might be experts by dawn.

He listened to the baby's tiny breaths as Versa remained snuggled close to him with her head on his chest and her hand on her daughter. If his arms were as secure against the world as his grandfather's, he didn't know. But it was the safest place he could think of for them.

He drifted in and out of a restless sleep, looking to the east every time he woke, waiting for the first light when he could finally get everyone to safety.

That he actually fell into a deep sleep was almost as alarming as looking up into Beaved's face above him in the first faint light of dawn.

"Shin, soldiers have been spotted down the trail. We may not have much time!"

Young Pere rubbed his eyes, trying to understand the message, and he slid the baby on to Versa.

"What's wrong?" she asked as he crawled out of the blanket.

"Nothing, you're fine. Just keep her warm." He gave her a quick smile.

"You're lying."

"You're right, again," he said, pulling on his boots. "As soon as I know what we're doing, I'll come tell you." And he bounded off to follow Beaved.

Versa looked around for an idea of what to do next.

Some of the other soldiers were getting up hastily and following Young Pere. The dumpy one they called Teach remained at the campsite with his long knife drawn and looking in the direction of the trail wearing an expression that said, *Please don't make me use this.* The bruised one called Nelt stood behind him and readjusted Teach's grip on the knife.

Well, there was nothing else to do, was there?

Versa glanced over at Mrs. Rescatar who was struggling to sit up. She could just make her out in the dim light of the early morning. The rest of her family was waking, too.

"I can get up now on my own, right?" Versa asked Mrs. Rescatar.

Mrs. Rescatar looked dubious. "Do you feel up to it?"

"I've got a mountain to climb," she said with determination, getting to her feet. She felt weak—weaker than she'd been in a long time, but she was up. Plus, she'd lost a lot of weight last night which would make her even more capable that morning. "See? I've got this. Febe, sit with the baby, please." Versa steadied herself, took up her pack, and headed for the dense trees.

"Take it slow, Versa!" Mrs. Rescatar called after her.

In the seclusion of the trees, she held on to steadying branches as she relieved herself, then evaluated 'things' as Mrs. Rescatar had tried futilely to do twice in the dark. Not sure if the amount of bleeding she discovered was normal or not, she sighed. It'd do no good to ask Mrs. Rescatar, either. It wasn't as if Versa could rest for a few more days before climbing.

"There's simply no other options. I just need to get to the midwives. I need to get to the top . . ."

Young Pere came running back before she returned. His eyes grew large when he found Febe holding the baby.

"Where is she?!" he shouted the whisper, trying to fight down his panic. "We need to leave!"

Versa came out from behind the trees, pale but resolute. "Just making myself presentable, Young Pere." She strode to the cold fire, put the pack on her back, and bent down to take the baby out of Febe's arms. "Ready."

He put his hands on his waist. "You have *got* to be kidding me." He turned to Mrs. Rescatar. "She can't climb the mountain, can she?"

Versa stepped up to him, grabbed his undershirt, and said, "I'm going. Are you going to show me the way or do I have to do it myself?"

Mrs. Rescatar shrugged. "She might be able to do *some* of it. I don't know how else to get her up the rock face but for her to climb it."

"There's no other option," Versa insisted. "Get the soldiers and let's get Mr. Rescatar up!"

Young Pere turned to the nets on the ground and pointed. "There *is* another option. We'll carry you and Mr. Rescatar. We already found sturdy logs last night. You're not walking, Versa. Especially carrying her." He gently pulled the baby out of her arms.

"I'm *fine*, Young Pere!" Versa said, her stance a little wobbly. "I feel well enough to climb that mountain and go horseback riding this afternoon."

"Ha!" Young Pere barked. "I'd like to see *that*. Tell you what, I'll take you riding myself, just so I can watch you pass out. But to make sure you're up for that, you're riding first in a net litter. We have two."

Young Pere picked up the two nets and handed them to Nelt, Hammer, and Reg, who quickly readied them on the poles.

Versa stepped dangerously close to Young Pere, a fierce look in her eyes. "I am *not* going to burden anyone with carrying me."

He took half a step closer as well. Only the baby he held was between them. "You wanted miracles, right? Well they're right there, in reversed jackets, fed and rested and ready to carry you. Now, if you don't get in that litter, I'll leave you here! It's the best way, and you know *I'm right*, Versa."

Beaved came jogging back with Iron and Pal, who joined in helping get the nets on the poles.

"We've distracted that last group," Beaved told Young Pere, "but soldiers are starting to enter the forest looking for food. We're running out of time."

Mrs. Rescatar struggled to get up, and two of her sons helped their father stand up. Mr. Rescatar smiled bravely, then began to collapse. The effects of the Pain Tea had their limits.

But already one of the net slings was ready. Soon he was secured in a litter supported on the sturdy shoulders of Iron and Hammer, while Pal and Nelt hurriedly readied the other sling.

Young Pere raised an eyebrow at Versa. His glare was most effective, but he couldn't hold it much longer. Her standing so close and staring up into his eyes was starting to make his head sway. Fortunately for him, she backed down first.

Versa sighed, nodded, then reluctantly got into the other net supported by Buddy and Reg.

General Thorne nodded to his horn signaler. "Sound the call. We leave in twenty minutes. We have Salemites to find."

The other officers in the large gathering room glanced at each other, hoping their predictions of the numbers of soldiers willing to join Thorne again was correct. It would probably be less than fifty thousand.

They traveled as silently as possible, the baby mercifully sleeping and tucked securely in Young Pere's arm as he jogged ahead on the trail, rapidly deciphering the markings so that no one had to pause in their travels.

Time was of the essence. Young Pere could feel General Shin urging him on. The Rescatars' sons were strung behind him at intervals, quietly calling directions to their family and the soldiers carrying the litters. They passed the emergency shelter and trotted through a muddy meadow, then back through the cover of the trees.

Eventually Young Pere heard the sound of the river. Through the trees he could make out the rock face ahead of them. His heart skipped as he remembered the times he climbed up it happily with his brothers and cousins.

Today would be very different.

The sun was cresting over the mountains, bathing the rock face in sunshine. He felt a pressing need to move faster and jogged up to the river.

And his heart sank.

It was deep. And swift. And thirty paces across.

"Oh, baby," he whispered to her, giving her a kiss of comfort that he needed more than she did. "This isn't good. It was never running like this in Weeding Season. Must be chest high."

He heard the Rescatars' sons catching up to him.

"The river! Look how big it is!" the youngest boy, called Silvo, said excitedly.

His older brothers looked at Young Pere with less enthusiasm.

"I can't swim," the middle boy named Vito confessed.

Silvo nodded guiltily too.

Young Pere rubbed his forehead. "How did I know you were going to say that."

Nelt and Teach arrived next, catching up with the little boys they were supposed to be watching.

"We need to cross *that*? It must be freezing!" Teach whined.

Nelt shook his head slowly. "Even the lightest of cloudy thoughts won't work here, Young Pere."

Beaved came next, he and Reg now carrying Versa between them. Beaved let out a low whistle. "Shin, uh . . . any great ideas for crossing this? Please don't say knocking down trees and walking across them."

Mr. Rescatar called from the net he was carried in as Hammer and Iron brought him to the river. "Running high?"

Young Pere nodded soberly.

"Then go to the rock crossing."

"Rock crossing?" Young Pere asked.

The rest of the group now made it to the river, Buddy and Pal escorting Mrs. Rescatar and her daughter, and Snarl bringing up the rear, keeping an eye out for any movements behind them.

Mr. Rescatar pointed up the river. "About two hundred paces that way. There was a landslide a couple years ago, and it threw rock all along the bottom. It shouldn't be deeper than your knees. We just wade across."

Young Pere shrugged hopefully and started up the river, the others following. He soon saw what Mr. Rescatar was talking about, and although the water wasn't as deep it was certainly swift.

He and Beaved exchanged solemn glances before turning to their group.

"Each of the soldiers should help one of the younger children," Young Pere decided. "Hammer and Iron, you carry Mr. Rescatar across. I doubt even this current can knock you two down. I'll bring Versa over myself, but I need someone to help me."

Versa tried to get out of the sling. "No, I can walk this."

"Definitely not!" Young Pere marched over to push her back in. "There's no way you can handle that."

"Young Pere, it's not deep. I can do this—"

"Versa, *no!*"

Surprised at his insistence, she obediently sat back in the sling.

"There's something else," he said to the soldiers. "No weapons are allowed up at the ancient site."

Beaved's jaw dropped. "Are you serious? No one there is armed? Shin, we're walking into a trap!"

Young Pere sighed. "Beaved, have I been wrong yet?"

"We saw wapiti yesterday," Teach admitted. "You haven't been wrong yet."

Young Pere smiled at his show of faith. "I know this sounds unbelievable, but there's a plan of sorts. We'll be safe up there, but we have to honor what the guide has decreed. No weapons. We can't rely on ourselves. This is a test to see if we'll rely on the Creator alone."

Reg was already unbuckling his sheath. "Nothing good has happened to me since I put this on last year, and I did it voluntarily. I'm ready to leave it behind."

Hammer and Iron drew their swords and tossed them to the river bank.

Teach threw his long knife as far as he could, which meant it clattered only a few paces away from him.

Buddy and Pal dropped their swords easily.

Snarl hesitated, but then unsheathed his sword and dropped it, but not without a glare at Young Pere.

Nelt raised his empty hands. "The other river already has my offerings."

Beaved regarded Young Pere with apprehension, his hand still on his hilt, but Young Pere was looking at Versa.

"No weapons, Versa."

"What are you talking about?" she asked innocently.

"The knife? You lifted it from me sometime during the night.

Probably during that last feeding. It needs to stay here. The cord's been cut."

Versa sighed, twisted in the net litter, and retrieved the long knife from the waistband of her breeches.

"Trust Shem," he said gently. "I do."

He took the knife from her, brought it to the bank, and thrust it in the dirt, blade down. Only the handle remained above ground.

Reg waved for Nelt to take the net litter from him. He took his sword and stabbed it into the ground next to the long knife, then took Hammer's and Iron's swords and plunged them into the bank.

The other soldiers followed suit, Teach retrieving his long knife to join it with the others, until eight handles stood in the dirt along the bank.

But Beaved still kept his hand on his hilt. Eventually he sighed and slipped his sword out of the sheath. Young Pere took his position at the net sling in front of Versa so Beaved could shove his sword into the bank.

He nodded worriedly at Young Pere. "I'll go first," Beaved said, turning to the river, "to see how bad it is. I always preferred just running through anyway."

He stepped into the water.

"First," he called back, "it's cold!"

"Then move quickly," Young Pere told him. "It'll get harder to move the colder you get."

Beaved was already pushing against the knee-high water as fast as he could. Once his footing slipped but he righted himself and continued across the river. At the other side he turned and waved.

"It's not too bad," he called, "but the current's strong and some rocks are slick."

Young Pere turned to Versa in the sling. Bracing the pole on his shoulder, he handed her the newborn. "Hold on to her tightly. If we should slip, keep her head above the water."

Versa's eyes grew big and she kissed her baby.

Reg went back to take the other side again, but Nelt shook his head. "It's the least I can do to get them away from the general."

"You sure you're up to it?" Young Pere asked, concerned about his bruises and slightly worried about his loyalty.

Nelt smiled. "When you have a big brother like mine toughening you up each week, a little patting by Hammer and Iron is nothing." He hefted the net litter with his arms to show he was capable. Young

Pere pretended to not see his eye twitching.

Together they started for the river, Young Pere in the lead. As he stepped into the water he prayed earnestly that neither he nor Nelt would stumble.

TO THE RIGHT. STRAIGHT AHEAD. NOW TAKE A LONGER STEP. WATCH YOUR FOOTING. GOOD, NOW A SHORTER STRIDE . . .

He glanced behind him to make sure Versa remained above the rushing water that was rapidly chilling his legs. The river occasionally splashed her, but she sat several inches above it, anxiously watching the water rush under her as she held her daughter as high as she dared.

Nelt bit his lip as he took his steps.

Young Pere focused on the bank. Just a few more feet . . . another tricky step . . . and—

He grinned as he reached the bank and sighed in relief as his boots hit the dry gravel, Versa and Nelt right behind.

Across the river, the three Rescatar boys cheered.

Young Pere spun around. "Hush!" he called across the river. "If someone's following, you just gave away our position!"

The boys flinched and shrank apologetically.

He nodded in forgiveness and called to Iron and Hammer. "Try to follow the route we took. And watch your footing—the rocks are slippery."

Mrs. Rescatar, Febe, the three boys, Teach, Pal, Reg, Buddy, and Snarl waited on the bank and watched nervously as Iron and Hammer stepped into the cold swift water, swinging Mr. Rescatar between them. Twice they each slipped but never fell into the rushing water. Soon they were on the other side as well.

That time the boys jumped up and down silently, fists pumping the air.

"Now, Reg, stay upriver of Mrs. Rescatar. You can help break the current for her," Young Pere called.

Reg nodded, put a protective arm around Mrs. Rescatar, and began to walk her out. Febe stood on her mother's other side next to her broken arm. When they were halfway across the river, Young Pere nodded to Teach, Pal, Buddy and Snarl. "Space the boys between the four of you. Reg breaking the current is working well, so Pal, take the first position upstream. Then Vito," he pointed to the nine-year-old. "And—"

"I won't need help!" Luis announced. "I've done this before." He started out into the river . . .

. . . and immediately went under the water.

"No!" Teach shouted. He lunged into the river and caught the boy before the current swept him away to deeper sections. Luis and Teach quickly righted themselves, the boy gasping and shuddering. Teach maintained a firm hold on his jacket collar despite shivering from the cold himself.

Mrs. Rescatar, now safely on the other side of the river, held her face with her good hand. "Stay together!" she cried, horrified.

Teach, soaking wet, dragged the twelve-year-old with surprising gumption across the river. Luis scrambled to his mother and Teach panted up the bank.

Young Pere grinned. "Well done, Teach!"

Teach waved it off. "It was nothing. I always had twelve-year-olds trying to escape my classroom. Just the instinct to grab them and yank them back."

"I'm still impressed, Teach," Young Pere chuckled as Teach flopped, exhausted, on the bank. "All right, two boys left. Pal, still take the upstream position. Then Vito, Buddy, Silvo, and Snarl. Keep a hold on their arms, men. Little boys are obviously slippery things."

Together the five of them headed into the river.

Young Pere held his breath as they slowly trudged along, little Silvo growing white, either with terror or cold or both. Young Pere knew exactly what was about to happen, but there was nothing he could do except to think, belatedly, *I should've carried him piggy-back—*

The eight-year-old slipped out of the grip of Buddy and Snarl, and was gone.

"Silvo!" Mrs. Rescatar cried, but Young Pere was already in action. He dropped the pole holding Versa's net litter, hoping her fall to the ground wasn't too far, and charged into the river. At first it didn't feel as cold, but quickly he was beyond the rock slide, and the ground gave way under his feet, plunging his body into chest high, freezing water.

He saw the boy's head bob down river from him, and he swam his fastest to where he thought Silvo would be in a moment, praying he could kick faster than the current could sweep the boy. He reached out, felt something cloth-like, and grabbed it.

"Got you!" Young Pere shouted as he held up a startled, coughing child. He tucked Silvo securely under his arm and fought the current back to the bank.

Febe and four soldiers were running downstream to meet them, and so was Versa, carrying the baby and jogging awkwardly.

"He's fine," Young Pere called to them as he lumbered to the bank, a terrified Silvo clinging to him. "All of you, get to the rock face NOW! We're losing time."

Up river, Mrs. Rescatar cried out in relief, and Hammer and Iron started with Mr. Rescatar for the slope that led to the rock face.

Febe waded into the river to retrieve her youngest brother, and Young Pere crawled up after her and collapsed in chilled exhaustion, his muscles seizing from the cold.

"Young Pere!" Versa called. "Are you all right?"

"Yes, I'm fine." He struggled to his feet. "Versa, you shouldn't be here. I told you to go—"

"Shin!" Beaved cut him off. "We've got trouble!"

Young Pere twisted to see two soldiers emerge from the forest, their swords brandished.

Versa screamed his thoughts. "NO!"

Febe and Silvo took off running for the rock face, with Buddy, Pal, Teach, Snarl, and Reg following and glancing worriedly behind them.

But Beaved stared across the river, his eyes darting around as if looking for some strategy.

"Beaved, get Versa and the baby up there!" Young Pere told him, wiping water from his face. "Now! I'll take care of these soldiers."

"But Shin, you're not armed—"

"Go! I can distract them. Get her up with the others. And that's an order, sergeant!"

"Young Pere!" Versa screamed. But Beaved, used to officers ordering him around—even former officers who never really earned the ranking—grabbed her arm and pulled her into a jog to the slope.

Young Pere ignored her shouts. She needed to get away as quickly as possible. If he acknowledged her, she might come back to him and—

He watched instead as the men plunged into the river and fought against the current of the deep water. If the soldiers had crossed higher upstream at the rock slide, they would've been able to move quickly. But now they were struggling against the freezing water, and Young Pere knew exactly how their muscles would be stiffening.

"Good. Just wash them away, just wash them away," he

whispered.

THE RIVER WON'T, YOUNG PERE. BUT THE COLD WILL GIVE YOU TIME.

In the early morning light, Shem sat outside his tent, trying to breathe, trying to think, trying to clear his mind of the vision of his still and cold Calla.

He closed his eyes because there was something he had to do. He'd awoken with a clear impression that he had to get up and get moving. But why, he didn't know.

Dear Creator, now what? Now what—

Startled, Shem opened his eyes.

The scene that flashed into his mind was so distinct and unexpected that it couldn't have been his imagination. He filled his lungs and tried again to discern the image.

It came again with forceful clarity.

Shem leaped to his feet and looked around. People were just beginning to stir around their campsites, and none of the exit points of the routes were active.

Not yet, at least.

"PETO!" Shem bellowed, not caring who he awoke. "PETO!"

He jogged to the Shins' nearby campsite, hopping between bodies and hurtling a cold campfire. "Cephas! The routes!"

Peto got up from his bedroll, rubbing his eyes. "Shem? Shem what's wrong?"

Cephas stumbled over to them from the adjoining Briters' site.

"Peto, Cephas, we have refugees coming."

Peto and Cephas spun to the lookout posts at the tops of the trees. None of the scouts perched there were signaling the arrival of newcomers.

"Where, Uncle Shem?" Cephas asked.

Shem closed his eyes. "The Back Door!"

"What?" Peto cried. Now nearly everyone was awake around the campsites. "No one's come up on the Back Door."

Shem pointed at Lek. "Find your brother Boskos and tell him to get his bag—there's wounded!"

"Papa, he's already helping—"

But Shem was off and running.

"What now, Puggah?" Young Pere whispered, glancing over his shoulder at the mountain behind him.

Already Hammer and Iron had made it up the slope and were at the rock face, helping Mr. Rescatar out of the net. Reg and Nelt were both with Mrs. Rescatar, pointing up at the rock face and trying to figure out the best routes for the injured to take.

Pal and Buddy were closing in, jogging up the slope with Silvo and Vito, with Febe behind. Teach was next, with Luis, and Snarl was loping ahead of them all, racing to the rock face.

Bringing up the rear was Versa, jogging clumsily with the baby while Beaved pulled her along up the hill as quickly as she could move.

Satisfied they were all safely away, each with soldiers to assist them, Young Pere turned back at the river.

YOU WAIT. CONSERVE YOUR STRENGTH. ONE WILL REACH YOU FIRST. YOU'LL NEED TO DISARM HIM. TAKE HIS SWORD, THEN I'LL HELP YOU DO THE REST.

Young Pere watched anxiously as the two soldiers slowly forded the river. One was nearing the bank but lost his footing. "He's tiring, isn't he?"

YES. THE LONGER HE'S IN THE COLD WATER, THE WEAKER HE'LL BE WHEN HE REACHES YOU. TAKE ADVANTAGE OF THAT. JUST GET HIS SWORD.

"I'm a little weak myself, Puggah." Young Pere looked behind him again. "Haven't slept well in days, just a little wet and cold here."

He saw Versa nearing the rock face, the baby clutched in her arms. Beaved was now dragging little Silvo, cold and terrified.

"Go," Young Pere whispered in Versa's direction, "Go!"

She glanced back as if she heard him from several hundred paces away.

He gestured urgently for her to keep moving, and she nodded. To his surprise, she started to ably climb the rock face while clutching her baby, catching up to Mrs. Rescatar who was gaining on her husband.

But poor Mr. Rescatar, hopelessly weak and slow, had Hammer and Iron on either side of him hefting him gingerly over the rocks he couldn't manage.

An angry shout from the river spun Young Pere back around. The first soldier was crawling on to the bank, exhausted but furious as he swore in frustration.

DON'T LET HIM REST. GET THE SWORD. NOW!

Without a word, Young Pere charged at the soldier. The man struggled to get to his feet, but Young Pere kicked him in the face. The soldier fell backward, dropping his sword on the bank, and splashed into the river, unconscious, while Young Pere snatched up the sword and stood on the bank. The current swiftly carried the soldier away.

WELL DONE, YOUNG PERE! NOW GET READY FOR THE REST.

"The rest? I see only one more—"

NO, YOUNG PERE. YOU'VE BEEN TRACKED. LOOK TO THE FOREST.

"Oh, Puggah, no . . ."

Versa ignored the cramping in her gut as she continued up the rock face. She kept her baby securely in her left arm and leaned forward to pull up with her right. Murmuring in frustration that she didn't have time to wrap the baby to her body, she'd already passed Mrs. Rescatar and her helpers who encouraged her to keep going, and was now gaining on Febe and Vito who were making quick progress scrambling up the rock.

"When you get to the top," she called up to Febe, "run to the site and get Guide Zenos. Your father's going to need more help."

"I'll get there," called Snarl. He left the side of Mrs. Rescatar and scaled the rock as if he were a spider.

"What about you?" Febe called down to Versa.

Versa considered how convenient it was that the intense cramping kept her bending forward. "I'm fine, I'm fine," she lied. "But we need to hurry."

Mrs. Rescatar screaming below caused Versa to look to the river. She saw the clash of blades before she heard it.

"No, Young Pere!" she whimpered. Beyond the river in the forest she spied the rest. "Oh, come on! That's not fair!"

Soldiers, at least two dozen, were pouring out of the trees. Most hesitated as they saw the swift water.

Keep climbing, Versa. There's nothing you can do to help him. Don't make him worry about you. Turn around.

But Versa was transfixed, staring in horror mixed with pride as an attacking soldier collapsed in front of Young Pere in his own pool of blood.

"He got one! Young Pere did it!"

Another soldier was struggling out of the freezing water and lumbering at Young Pere. Another swipe and he, too, fell back into the river.

See? He's all right. Keep going, Versa! Get yourself and the baby to safety. You don't have much time. Climb!

"Beaved!" Nelt shouted down at the staff sergeant. He was prodding little Silvo up to Nelt who was balanced a few paces higher on the rock. "We have to help Shin!"

Beaved twisted and gaped as another bleeding soldier fell into the water. "Well, he's got a sword," Beaved said uncertainly, and glanced back up the rock where Versa and the Rescatar family were making progress, but not fast enough. "We've got to stay and help the family, Nelt. Shin ordered—"

"I'M ORDERING!" Nelt bellowed. "I'm a *real* lieutenant; he was just given that title! And I say we get back down and help him!"

Beaved twisted back and forth, unsure of what to do, people on either side of him needing assistance.

"These people are helpless!" Nelt told the sergeant. "We have to be the next line of defense."

"And that's what we do," Beaved declared, suddenly struck with an idea. "We hang back, in case any soldiers get past Shin and make it up to this rock face. We fight them off from here."

Nelt bobbed his head. "All right, all right—we can help the Rescatars climb, but we stay at the end as the next line. Wish I had a blade, though," he said longingly as he noticed another abandoned sword near Shin.

"Boys," came a weak voice above them on the slope. It was Mr. Rescatar. "You're surrounded by weapons," and Iron released his arm so that he could gesture around them.

"The rocks?" Nelt asked, unconvinced.

But Beaved was already loosening a kickball-sized stone. "I could heave this a decent distance. Come on, Nelt. You should be able to improvise. You were training to be an assassin, after all—"

Mr. Rescatar, who had been struggling over a rock with

Hammer's and Iron's help, tried to turn around again when he heard the word. "You're an assassin?!" he cried down feebly.

His son Silvo had now reached Nelt and was gripping his hand, looking for comfort. Hearing the alarm in his father's voice, Silvo looked up at Nelt with wide eyes. "What's that mean?"

Nelt sighed and squeezed his hand. "It means I now work for you and your family. Start climbing up to your father." Nelt nodded reassuringly to Mr. Rescatar, but the father's eyes were still big with worry.

Nelt and Beaved made their way up a few more paces where a natural cache of smaller stones sat as if ready for that moment, and they started adding to the pile.

Young Pere stared in surprise as another man fell into the river, bleeding profusely.

"How did I—"

YOU DIDN'T DO IT ALL BY YOURSELF, YOUNG PERE.

He knew that was true. Someone as unskilled with a sword as he was shouldn't have been able to take out each man so swiftly and even elegantly. One strike, maybe two, and so far each of his attackers had fallen in the river or on the muddy banks. It was Puggah, all of it. He took what little skill Young Pere had and magnified it by fifty.

Young Pere made the mistake of glancing across the river. "Puggah, Puggah—there's too many!"

STEADY, YOUNG PERE. FOCUS. THIS IS WHY YOU'RE HERE. I'LL GUIDE YOUR ARM AGAIN, GIVE THE OTHERS A CHANCE TO ESCAPE. YOU WON'T NEED TO HOLD THEM OFF TOO LONG. JUST WORRY ABOUT THE NEXT FEW MEN.

He steadied the sword as the next man tried to climb out of the river. That's when a thought came to his mind, a certain conclusion.

"Puggah? Puggah, is this . . . is this the last day for me?"

DOES IT MATTER IF IT IS, YOUNG PERE?

Feeling suddenly hot and heavy, Young Pere decided, "No. No, it doesn't matter. I didn't get to see Papa or confess to him what I've done, but I'm going in the right direction, finally. I just took too long to get here. It's my fault, I know. But she's on the mountain. She should be safe soon. So will the baby. Puggah," his voice quavered, "just make sure she meets Cephas, all right?"

One of the soldiers from the river was righting himself, looking unnaturally large as he dripped river water like a swampy creature.

"Make sure he knows how amazing she is?" Tears stung Young Pere's eyes. "Just make sure she's happy, somehow."

SHE'LL BE HAPPY, YOUNG PERE.

"Stay with me please, all right, Puggah?"

The soldier began to stomp toward him.

THAT'S WHY I'M HERE, YOUNG PERE, UNTIL THE VERY END. YOU AND ME, TOGETHER. BRACE YOURSELF.

"Back Door!" Shem shouted as he, Peto, Cephas, and now several more men up for the morning joined them in a race to the middle route that no one had attempted to take. Shem broke into a full run, darting around cold fires and rushing past sleeping bodies and tents.

Peto struggled to keep up with him. "Shem, why are we in such a hurry?"

"Not sure, Peto," Shem panted, "but we need to get there now!"

Versa was nearing the top. It was only about twenty more paces, but the rock seemed sharper, steeper, and more impossible to climb.

Febe and Vito were almost there as well.

Versa could barely move for pain, but she wasn't about to quit, not this close. It wasn't about her; it was about her daughter. Although Versa was barely crawling, they'd make it, she was sure.

She glanced down again as she heard more swords clanging, and gasped as she saw Young Pere battling two men. He went down, the lower half of his undershirt turning red.

"No!" she whimpered. "Dear Creator, you can't take him! Please, let me keep him!"

Young Pere struggled back to his feet and one of the soldiers went down, then the other. A third was coming for him.

Versa, go! You're almost there! Get him help!

She turned, ignored her cramping, and tried to go over the next rock, but she was growing weaker. Clutching her infant who was feeling heavier every moment, she looked up and sighed in relief.

Snarl had reached the top and was looking down at her.

True to form, he snarled and pulled a long knife from his boot.

Young Pere struggled to get upright. He thought he should be feeling more pain for having been hit in the face like that, but instead he only felt confused. There was blood on his undershirt, but wasn't sure where it came from. Maybe from the dead soldier lying at his feet.

Yet, maybe he *was* hit harder than he realized, because he was inexplicably flagging. But he couldn't stop. There were soldiers, and water, and blades, and bizarrely a few stray rocks flying from behind him, occasionally hitting the soldiers with only distracting force.

"You call that a decent throw?" Nelt cried as Beaved threw a rock that didn't even roll all the way to the attacking soldiers.

"It was a big rock. And heavy," Beaved said, as Nelt hurled another smaller stone at a soldier. By the time it reached him, it merely bounced off his shoulder doing no more damage than dirtying his wet uniform.

"Just keep chucking rocks," Nelt insisted. "Draw away their attention from Shin. Maybe one of them will come up here where we can hit them with something bigger! Why the slagging Creet did I throw away my crossbow?"

Young Pere shook his head to try to clear it, but that only resulted in him growing dizzy. Maybe if he were more balanced, went the stray thought through his head.

He stooped to pick up a fallen soldier's sword in his other hand. While he now had an equal weight in each clenched fist, the color in the world was now unbalanced, everything turning shades of gray—

"Oh, I know what *this* means," he garbled, trying to focus on the next soldier hulking up to him, strangely—but fortunately—in slow motion. "Puggah, I'm going down. Are they safe yet?"

NOT QUITE. HANG ON, YOUNG PERE.

He gripped the hilts tighter until he realized that wasn't what Puggah meant by 'hanging on'. He was referring to something . . . bigger. Deeper.

But what that was, Young Pere couldn't fathom, because his stomach began to heave, and too many experiences told him he had only moments left of consciousness.

"You have to do it, Puggah. Can you do it? Help me until they're safe?"

OF COURSE.

Snarl, standing at the top of the rock face, leered down at Versa who had frozen in terror on the rocks.

"You're his daughter, aren't you? I heard Shin call you Versula Thorne last night. Did you know there's a reward for you? I imagine it will be doubled if I bring in the baby, too."

Febe cowered on the rock below Versa, pulling Vito closer to her.

"You've nowhere to go," Snarl said, beckoning to Versa. "Come up here, and I'll assure your safety from my associates below. You see, they suspect the reward is for you dead or alive. I'm confident there's more gold if you're alive, but some of them down there don't have a problem with half the gold for you dead. Come up here and I promise you'll live, and so will the baby. But my friends down there—and trust me, they'll be here soon because Shin's getting weaker by the minute—they won't give you such an offer. Now, *Versula Thorne*, climb!"

Do it, Versa. It's all right. Help is coming!

Versa cringed in pain and tried to get over the next rock.

"Don't!" Febe shouted.

"It's all right," Versa said calmly. "You stay there. It'll be all right somehow. We'll get help from above." She looked up and saw Snarl's smug smile.

"That's right, keep coming up," Snarl said. "I might even give you some of the reward."

"Lilla, where are you going?" Jaytsy asked as her sister-in-law grabbed another emergency bag.

The rest of the family was now up and wondering if they should help at the Back Door or try to start breakfast.

Lek had just returned with Boskos, who had been helping an older man who was suffering from chest pains. He rummaged frantically around his sleeping children to find his medical bag.

"I'm going to the Back Door," Lilla said as she slung the pack on her shoulder. "And no, Jaytsy—I don't know why. I just feel the need to do something. Anything. I can't sit here and weep anymore."

Lek nodded in agreement. "I'll go with you, Aunt Lilla. Boskos might need help doing . . . *something*," he finished lamely.

Salema gave her husband a sad smile. "Go ahead, Sweety. I'll stay with the children."

"Got it," Boskos announced as he held up the bag. "Come on!"

Lek and Boskos started to jog with their aunt Lilla to the Back Door.

Shem and Peto rushed through the trees to the saddle of the Back Door route, until Shem stopped abruptly. There stood a soldier, his jacket inside-out and his back to them, about thirty paces ahead. He was peering over the rock face.

Peto nearly crashed into Shem. Shem put his finger to his lips and closed his eyes. A second later he opened them and looked up.

"Really?" he asked the sky. "All right, then."

He took off in another run straight for the man. The soldier turned when he heard the footsteps of Shem crunching the old leaves, as well as the footsteps of three dozen more Salemites as they ran to the summit.

But Peto noticed the glint of metal in the soldier's hand.

"Shem!" he shouted. "Knife!"

But Shem kept running, and the soldier crouched, ready to leap.

A few paces before reaching the soldier, Shem dropped into a slide along the dry pine needles, kicking the startled soldier hard in the shins. The soldier fell to the ground then tumbled over the rock face.

"No!" Peto cried and ran to the edge of the cliff. He dropped to his knees and looked over to see the soldier's body bouncing limply down the rock.

Shem scrambled over to see as well.

Several startled faces looked up at them.

"Rector Shin!" Versa whimpered. "Guide Zenos! We need help."

"Versa?!" Peto cried in surprise as she tried to get over a large rock in her way.

Shem leaped to his feet and shouted to the men following them. "Get a midwife and doctors! We have injured coming in!"

Young Pere felt power unlike anything else. Like a rag doll in the hands of a lively child, he moved and twisted and thrust in ways he'd never done before.

Another soldier rushed him and before he knew what was happening, he took two quick steps and plunged the sword into the man's chest.

He felt himself spinning and catching another soldier off-guard, knocking him into the fast current of the river.

Turning again, he stabbed into another man's gut, then with that sword still stuck, jabbed another man in the chest with the other sword. Simultaneously, he withdrew both swords and thrust them in different angles, catching two more soldiers he didn't even know were there.

He had no idea what he was going to do next, because he knew it wasn't him doing anything at all.

Nelt and Beaved had stopped chucking rocks and stared, open-mouthed, at the most astonishing swordsman they'd ever seen.

Cephas had reached the edge of the rock face only a second after his uncles, and he saw Versa.

"Wait! Let me help you!" He pushed past his uncles and rapidly crawled down the last fifteen paces Versa needed to cover, Peto right behind him.

Cephas gingerly took the baby from her arm. "This looks like a soldier's jacket," he said.

"It is," she gasped, her cramping increasing. She tried to say something else but a wave of pain overcame her.

"Cephas, give me the baby!" Peto said, now positioned on the rocks just above his nephew. Cephas handed up the baby, then grabbed Versa's arm. She was turning as gray as the rock around her.

Shem was already sliding down to reach Versa's other side. He caught her other arm just as she went limp and her eyes closed.

"Versa!" Shem shouted, shaking her gently.

"She had the baby just last night," Febe called up to them. "She shouldn't be doing this!"

"Oh, Versa," Shem muttered sadly as he and Cephas cautiously hefted themselves and Versa over the rock.

Several men reaching over the edge helped by grabbing her shoulders to drag her to the top.

Shem was next to her as soon as they laid her down, unconscious. He grasped her face but had the sickly feeling that she wasn't about to wake up anytime soon.

"Get her back to the camp!" he bellowed to the dozens of men assembled at the summit. "Get her help!"

A few men rushed over and two picked her up, one at her shoulders, the other at her legs.

"And the baby!" Peto called.

Another man retrieved the newborn, and together they carefully jogged to the temple site.

"We need help getting the others up here!" Peto ordered, but a dozen men were already working their ways down the rock face to give assistance to those struggling.

Cephas looked down to the river to see if there were any more refugees in need of help, and his eyes bulged.

"Uncle Peto!" he pointed, "Look down by the river!"

Shem squinted into the distance. "PETO!"

Lek, Lilla, and Boskos were halfway through the forest to the summit of the Back Door, close enough to see a growing crowd of

Salemites looking over the edge, when they met the men rushing back carrying an unconscious Versa.

"Oh no!" Lilla cried when she saw her, and noticed the third man jogging to them with the baby. "Lek, run and get Salema!" she ordered as she took the newborn from the man.

"There's a storage tent behind us a few paces," Boskos said urgently. "Bring her there—she shouldn't be jostled so much!"

SHE'S SAFE, YOUNG PERE. CEPHAS REACHED HER AND HELPED PULL HER UP.

Young Pere swung and caught another soldier, slashing across his chest but not disabling him. The last four were struggling to pull themselves out of the river.

Young Pere felt his strength seeping out of him, and he began to suspect the blood on his undershirt was actually his.

"Puggah, it's too much. Even with you. My body can't go on."

I KNOW, YOUNG PERE. IT'S ALMOST OVER.

"Peto!" Shem cried. "It's him! It's Young Pere!"

Peto stared, not daring to believe. "Are you sure?"

"Look how tall he is! Peto, he's come *home*!"

Lilla turned to see Salema already running toward them.

"I just had a feeling . . ." Salema's voice trailed off when she realized the situation. "Lay her down!" she ordered the men already carrying Versa to the tent.

They set Versa down among the piles of extra blankets and stepped out to allow the others to get to work.

Boskos started examining Versa for signs of injury while Salema carefully pressed on her belly.

Lilla laid the baby down on a short pile of blankets to remove the dark covering on her, while Lek stood at the tent flap wondering what he could do.

The soldier Young Pere wounded was now hunched over in pain, but still intent on charging him with his last energy. Young Pere tried to repel his advance, but the soldier's sword caught Young Pere across the arm. He dropped that sword as all strength left his arm.

"Not yet," he whispered, and swung weakly at his attacker with his other arm, catching his throat. The man went down.

"She's lost a lot of blood," Boskos said soberly as he lifted Versa's eyelids.

"Bos, it's bad," Salema whispered, feeling around Versa's belly. "This bulge isn't right, and yes—she's bleeding far too heavily. She must have just birthed—"

A piercing scream from Lilla spun them both around.

Lek fell to his knees next to his aunt who had removed the dark wrapping from the baby. "Lilla, is it the baby?"

But Lilla wasn't looking at the startled newborn. She was holding up the uniform jacket which she immediately turned right side out and held up the label for them to see.

SHIN.

"Lek, give me your arm!" Lilla demanded.

She held the sleeve up to his arm and it ran several inches past his wrist.

"IT'S HIS!" she cried out. "It *has* to be! No one has arms this long! PETO!"

Lek was already standing up and pulling Lilla to her feet. "At the Back Door, Lilla—just keep running to the edge. You'll be there in ten seconds. I'll get everyone else!"

Another soldier, cold and stiff from the river, now staggered toward Young Pere.

He ducked as the soldier neared him, but the man still slashed him across the belly, then cut into his other arm.

Young Pere fell to his knees, barely able to hold the remaining sword. His arms felt like they were on fire.

"Puggah, it's over. There's nothing more we can do," he whispered.

Shem and Peto exchanged horrified glances.

They looked at the rock face below them, then at each other again, took several steps back and to the side, and ran.

"Peto! Shem!" Cephas cried as his uncles leaped off the cliff to the wet, snowy grasses on the steep slope.

But all they heard as they jumped was Lilla's scream.

Nelt threw down his rock. "This is stupid! We gotta help Young Pere—" But he watched in astonishment as two men sailed off the cliff. Beaved turned just in time to see them hit the sloping grasses far below, tumble down the hillside a ways, then leap to their feet.

IT'S ALL RIGHT, BOYS; THEY'VE GOT THIS.

In awe, Nelt and Beaved both said, "They've got this . . ."

The soldier, still weak from the cold water, lunged one more time at Young Pere. His sword stabbed feebly into Young Pere's side, then fell out as he crumpled in exhaustion next to Young Pere.

Young Pere gasped a sob as he saw three more men coming slowly for him. He fell on his chest into the wet ground, his strength gone.

"Puggah!"

YOUNG PERE, LOOK UP. TO THE ROCK FACE.

He tried to focus, but he could barely move his eyes. Everything was losing color. "Muggah," he whispered.

Look up, Young Pere. To the side of the rock face.

"I can't." Something warm and wet leaked down his face.

Yes, you can, Young Pere. See who's coming to help you.

In the blur he saw two figures flying off the summit, the way he had always wanted to but never did. They hit the grasses far below, tumbled and rolled, then righted themselves and ran straight for him.

One of the men shouted, "Here! Here!"

Young Pere trembled as he recognized the voice of Shem Zenos. He tried to push himself up but it was no use. He heard the remaining three soldiers jog past him to the familiar figures now rushing to his aid.

Shem stooped, picked up one of the dropped swords, and swiftly dispatched one soldier, then another, while the other man came directly to Young Pere.

He tried to push himself up again but instead was lifted quickly off the ground.

"*Young Pere*! Thank the Creator!" Peto cried as he wrapped his arms around his son and collapsed into the mud with him. He kissed Young Pere's head and held him firmly. "We'll get you to safety, son. You've come home. I can't believe it! *You're home*!" Peto wept, kissing him again and again.

Young Pere felt as if he were five years old, cradled in the safety of his father's arms. He felt like sobbing like a five-year-old, too.

"Papa, I'm so sorry," he whispered as Peto brushed his wet hair and the tears off his face. "I'm so sorry." He could barely keep his eyes open, but he could see his father frantically wiping off blood.

He was vaguely aware of Shem taking out the last soldier, his body splashing into the river, then blurry Shem stopped at another groaning soldier on the ground and stabbed him.

With his ear up against his father's chest, Young Pere felt Peto's words as much as he heard him. "Any more, Shem?"

"Not that I can see. How many were there?"

"Don't know," Young Pere said feebly. "So sorry, Papa . . . Uncle Shem."

"It's all right," Peto assured him, rocking him again. "No way you could have known you were followed. It's all right."

"No, Papa. Sorry for—" He was fading. There was so much to tell him, but it wasn't going to happen. He knew that now.

His father did too. "Shh, it's all right. Everything's fine now!" Peto said, almost convincingly. "Don't talk. Just hang on, Young Pere. We'll get you up the mountain."

A shadow came over him as Shem knelt on the other side.

"Oh, Young Pere," he said, kissing him on the head. He wrenched off his jacket and wrapped it around Young Pere's middle, tying it securely. "Just stay with us. Help will be here soon."

There was so much to say—hours' worth—but Young Pere felt he had just minutes left. Something was wrong around his belly, he could tell. Life was draining out of him like a leaking bucket, even with Uncle Shem's jacket wrapped around him to staunch the flow. Dimly he saw his uncle close his eyes in prayer.

So much to say to Shem, too. So much still to do, but . . .

Young Pere's eyes closed as the sound of the rushing river faded away.

Up at the summit, Lilla and Jaytsy held each other as Deck and their sons and nephews leapt over the edge and rolled their way to the river down below.

Lilla wept as she watched her bloodied son being rocked like a baby in the arms of her husband.

The entire Shin, Briter, and Zenos families, except for Boskos and Salema who were still tending to Versa and her baby, were either standing on the summit holding their breath or tumbling down the grassy hill to the river.

YOUNG PERE, LOOK, JUST ONE MORE TIME. THE ROCK FACE. THEY'RE ALL COMING. EVERYONE. FOR YOU.

He struggled to open his eyes. At the summit more shapes leapt from the edge. Somehow he knew who the blurs were.

That was all he needed to see. Why they'd be coming to help him, he didn't know. But there they were anyway, hurrying to his aid, in spite of everything.

It was enough.

He couldn't have asked for a better last view. Somewhere, at the top of the mountain, he was sure his mother was standing. She would see him. At least she'd know he tried to come home.

He trembled, despite his father's firm grip on him, as he recognized Uncle Deck, Relf, Cephas, Zaddick, then many more bodies closing in.

Then everything grew darker.

The pain stopped.

There was only blissful peace.

Puggah! Muggah! Thank you. Thank you for helping me get this far.

The Rescatars and the rest of the soldiers, helped by more Salemites than were necessary, slowly made their way to the temple ruin where doctors were rushing to help. The two soldiers near the bottom of the rock face, one of them still clutching a rock, reluctantly turned and started to climb up the face.

But at the summit, more people were gathering.

Lori and Jori put their arms around their mother as she clutched the uniform to her chest. Down by the river, some of the boys had picked up one of the abandoned net litters and were bringing it over to the huddle of Peto, Shem, and Young Pere. Older cousins tested the strength of the discarded poles to use as supports, then laid out the litter. There was a great deal of motion around the men as they made adjustments.

Lilla gasped and sobbed when she saw them scoop up Young Pere, who was far too limp, and set him gently in the net.

"I'm sure he's fine, Mama," Lori said in an uncertain tone. "Just unconscious. That's how he always is when they bring him home." She tightened her grip on her mother as Jori began to weep.

Jaytsy's daughters clustered around her as the men began to carry Young Pere up the hill, with Peto in the lead holding the front of the support pole. Shem remained by the riverbank, kneeling in prayer.

"Oh, no," Jaytsy moaned when she saw him there alone. Some of her daughters began to cry.

"He's always praying, Mama," Sewzi sobbed. "That's just how *he* always is."

Young Pere stood between his grandparents, their arms around each other, watching the procession of men and boys gingerly carrying his body up the slope.

"Are you ready, Young Pere?" Perrin asked.

"It's not going to be easy," Mahrree warned him. "It may be one of the most difficult things you've ever done."

"I know," Young Pere whispered, his eyes on his father who was at the lead of the net litter. "I've done a few difficult and painful things in the recent past. I know I can do this too. I *have* to."

"I know you can, too." Mahrree kissed him on the cheek. "I'm very proud of how far you've come! Remember, you won't be alone."

Young Pere smiled. "Thank you, Muggah. And Puggah. I never would have made it this far without the two of you. At least we got to the mountain."

"Yes, you did," Perrin said, embracing him again. "And now, Young Pere, you can't stay with us anymore. It's not where you belong. I'm afraid it's time for you to go."

Young Pere nodded. "I'm ready."

At the summit, more and more Salemites gathered, talking in hushed tones, trying to piece together what had happened from the details the refugees were providing.

"First he found Versa Kiah . . ."

"That's too much blood. He looks very still . . ."

"He's too far away to see anything . . ."

"How much more can that family take in three days?"

Jaytsy wished they would speak more softly, even though they were whispering.

Despite the hundreds of people now standing at the summit and filling the forest on the edges, watching the men climb up the rock face while trying to keep Young Pere steady, there was silence. Even the smallest grandchildren waited quietly, watching the men climb.

Jaytsy shoved out of her mind the thought that it was a reverent funeral procession—

Not yet. *Not yet.*

Shem finally got off his knees, picked up the last of the swords on the bank, and threw them in the river. Then he jogged up the trail, ignoring the bodies of the dead soldiers, to join the family climbing the rock face. He worked his way up to Peto and seemed to try to take over carrying Young Pere, but Peto shook his head and continued climbing, holding the front of the pole.

Relf, at the back, wouldn't relinquish his hold of the pole either. Frequently brothers and cousins took turns reaching over to support the middle section, with several additional hands joining in to help lift Young Pere over the rockier sections.

Several men at the summit pointed at the rock face and quietly called down suggestions for moving Young Pere more rapidly.

Another person arrived between Jaytsy and Lilla.

"Is it him? Really?!" Boskos said excitedly. When he realized how somber everyone was, his smile faded. "What happened?" he whispered to his sister.

"Soldiers. He was fighting them," Huldah whispered. "They stabbed him, Bos. Slashed him a few times, too." She began to weep as he put an arm around her. "Papa finished them off."

Boskos looked at Lilla who was trembling and hugging the jacket. "I'll get working on him as soon as he's here, Aunt Lilla."

She nodded, not taking her eyes off Young Pere.

Salema came trotting down to them and stood next to her brother-in-law, hopeful at first, until she saw everyone. "Oh, no."

Jaytsy shook her head at her. It was too soon to know.

"The baby's well," Salema tried to say brightly. "Beautiful little girl. Versa's regained consciousness. They've gone to find her mother and sister. They're carrying her to the midwives' tents. She's hemorrhaging, though, but I think it will be under control as long as she doesn't move for a few days."

"Good," Lilla managed to whisper.

"Aunt Lilla," Salema said softly, "Young Pere brought her here. He even helped her birth the baby last night. Caught her in that jacket. Versa wanted you to know he was wonderful to her."

Lilla nodded, tears drenching her face.

The climbing men and boys were nearly to the top, and those on the summit could see Young Pere more clearly now. But he was almost unrecognizable, his face swelling and blood dripping from his torso, despite Shem's jacket—now soaked red—tied around him.

It was all Lilla could take. "Young Pere!" she cried, as if hearing her voice would wake him. She started for the rock face, but Boskos held her back.

"They'll be up in a minute, Aunt Lilla. Just wait another moment."

Peto soon appeared at the top, holding the pole over his head to keep Young Pere from bumping on the rock. Lilla rushed over as the men at the summit caught hold of the litter and brought him the rest of the way up. Lilla could hardly wait for them to lay him on the ground.

"Young Pere!" she wailed, kneeling next to him and grabbing his hand. "Please, Young Pere! You're home!"

Peto knelt behind his wife, holding her shoulders as she pleaded with their very still son.

Boskos knelt on the other side, feeling Young Pere's wrist for his pulse. Everyone at the summit held their breath as he grasped his wrist again and again, searching. Not finding anything, he tried Young Pere's throat.

After a moment Boskos' shoulders sagged. "It's faint, but he's still with us!" Everyone exhaled in unison as Boskos quickly checked Young Pere's unresponsive eyes.

"His hand!" Lilla cried. "I felt his hand move!"

Boskos scrambled to his feet. "Let's get him to the surgery tents. Lilla, let go of him!"

She stood up as her sons and nephews grabbed the pole and took off running with Young Pere to the surgery area, Boskos sprinting in the lead. But Peto stayed on his knees, weeping quietly into his bloody hands. Lilla kneeled in front of him to wrap her arms around him while sobbing hysterically.

But something caught Jaytsy's eye. Everyone was now rushing back to the temple ruin to follow Young Pere's progress, but Jaytsy stared at something just beyond Peto and Lilla.

Shem, standing next to them, noticed Jaytsy's face began to lighten. He looked around trying to see what she saw.

As the crowd flowed away, Jaytsy began to grin and weep simultaneously. "*You did it!*" she cried softly to the air behind her brother and sister-in-law.

Shem stared at Jaytsy in confusion, but she continued to look just beyond him, her face almost glowing.

"I knew you would! You brought him home! Mother, you came here with *both* of them, just as you said you would!"

Perrin and Mahrree, arm in arm, grinned at their daughter before they faded from her view.

Boskos raced ahead of his brothers and cousins to the makeshift surgery tent the doctors had established near the temple ruin. So far they had set a couple of broken bones and done a few stitches, but nothing more serious until that morning.

When Boskos arrived, the Rescatars were being examined by two more doctors. He grabbed a kit and pointed at an apprentice. "Get ready—lots of blood to wipe off. We need to find all of his wounds."

Mrs. Rescatar sat up from her cot. "Is it Young Pere? How bad is he?"

"Bad enough," Boskos said quietly as he washed his hands in a bucket of water, then quickly dipped them into another bucket with a cleansing mixture that made his hands feel like they were on fire. He shook them out just as his brothers and cousins jogged to the surgery area. They laid the net litter down, swiftly extracted Young Pere, and carried him to a table.

Two more doctors stepped over with wet cloths, while a third came with a knife to cut off his clothing.

"Everyone out!" called Doctor Toon, who had been helping the Rescatars. "We'll let you know as soon as we know. Mr. Briter," he said, taking Deck's arm as he led him out, "do your best to occupy Peto and Lilla, all right? This may take some time."

Deck nodded. "All right, but who's going to occupy me?"

Some of the assistants dropped the tent flaps, and two more experienced doctors went to work on Young Pere's torso. Boskos took a cloth and started wiping Young Pere's head to determine if the blood splattered there was his or someone else's.

"Oh, you're a real mess, Young Pere," he murmured, relieved that, for the moment, none of the blood seemed to be his, except from a minor split on his forehead. "Going to be worse around your gut, I'm afraid—"

The whispered, "Bos?" startled him.

Boskos caught his cousin's face. "Young Pere! Yes, it's me. And no, I'm not just an assistant anymore. Oh, it's so good to see you!" He grinned as Young Pere fought to open his eyes and got no more than a slit. "Although," Boskos added, "I think I'm always finding you like this, horizontal and injured."

Young Pere was almost able to form a smile, but it dissolved. "Bos . . . tell Shem," he struggled to whisper the words, "that I . . . didn't reveal Salem. And . . . I'm so sorry . . . for everything—"

"No need, no need. Everything's going to be fine now—"

"Bos," Young Pere said as urgently as his frail condition would allow, "It's Muggah . . . Thorne—"

"We know," Boskos interrupted softly. "Papa saw what happened." He didn't think now was the time to tell him about Calla.

"Bos, tell them . . . it was because of her. She . . . got me here. And Puggah. Puggah's never left my side . . . They both brought me—"

"Shh. It's enough, Young Pere. You can tell everyone later."

Young Pere tried to shake his head, a tear slipping from his eye down to his ear, leaving a clean track in the drying blood. "I know it's bad. It's too much . . . you can't fix this—"

"Don't say that!" Boskos held his cousin's face firmly. "We're not letting you go that easily. We just got you back. We can heal you!"

"Dr. Zenos," said one of the doctors grimly. He gestured to something on Young Pere's torso.

Boskos winced but made sure his expression was optimistic when he turned back to his cousin. "Young Pere, we're going to sedate you now. We need to fix you up, all right?"

"It's too much—"

Boskos kissed his forehead. "You'll be fine, Young Pere. We can heal you."

"It's all right . . . if you can't. I'll be all right. Tell Mama that. And that I tried. And please, just tell everyone . . . I'm sorry . . ." he mumbled as he drifted into darkness.

"Lilla, if he wasn't still alive they would have come out and told us by now."

Peto was rocking his wife as they sat on a log across from the surgery tent, staring intently at the main opening where the flaps remained down.

"The longer they're in there, the better the news, right?"

She continued to weep, not noticing the hundreds of people walking to the surgery tent and quietly asking for any news.

Shem was hunched on another log, his head bent, rocking silently as Ester and Huldah sat on either side of him, each with a hand on his back.

Jaytsy and Deck positioned themselves on either side of Peto and Lilla. Already they had to jump up twice to catch Lilla as she made a break for the tent. Now Deck sat by Lilla, a heavy hand on her shoulder, as Jaytsy leaned against her brother who comforted his wife.

The rest of the family paced quietly, sat down near their parents, or spoke to those who came to inquire about Young Pere. They had waited for well over an hour, although it felt much longer than that.

When Boskos came out of the tent everyone stood up. He walked to Peto and Lilla with the expression that all the doctors had practiced—hopefulness, no matter what the prognosis. The doctors had been wrong on many occasions, because the Creator was the real healer who decided when someone survived or went Home.

"He had several gashes and lost a lot of blood," Boskos explained. "He also had—" he started to gesture to his own gut when he noticed his father shaking his head.

Lilla didn't need that much detail.

Boskos put on a small smile. "Everything's back where it belongs. We've stitched him up and think he has a chance—"

"He's going to make it?!" Lilla squealed.

Boskos put his hands on her shoulders. "We *think* so, we *think* so. We'll know more if—*when*—he wakes up. When someone loses that much blood—"

But his aunt and uncle didn't hear any more. Peto kissed Lilla on the cheek and she caught him in a rib crushing embrace.

"Can I see him? Sit with him?" she begged.

"I don't see how I can say no. But just you and Uncle Peto. And Papa," Boskos nodded at his father. He turned to the rest of the family. "As soon as we know something I'll come tell you."

Lilla and Peto were already racing to the tent. They ducked inside where Young Pere, wiped clean with his bare arms and torso wrapped tightly in bandages, lay motionless on a cot.

Solemnly, they sat down on log stools on either side of him.

"Young Pere!" Lilla whimpered. "It really is you! I can't believe it." She kissed his bruised cheek as gently as possible.

Dr. Toon wandered over to them, wiping his hands on a thick cloth. "He does have a remarkable way of coming back, doesn't he? I've lost track how many times I've worked on him. But I'm grateful I had the opportunity to do so today. He did a good job on the Rescatars for us. He set Mrs. Rescatar's arm as well as I could have."

Peto nodded, but Lilla didn't take her eyes off her son.

"Lilla?"

Mrs. Rescatar sat down next to her, her arm in fresh bandages and a new sling.

"This wasn't exactly the kind of arrival we were expecting. And Young Pere was nervous as to how you would react to seeing him again. He told my husband last night that he thought you'd be more willing to welcome him back if he brought others with him."

Lilla turned to her. "How could he think we wouldn't want him back? Oh, Young Pere!" She kissed his hand.

"That's what we told him: to not underestimate you. Lilla, Peto— I only saw him a few times before he left Salem, but this young man here is not the same boy I remember strutting around Norden. He was concerned, selfless, and very attentive to Versa and our family. I don't know what he's been through in the world, but you're going to be impressed by who he is today. I certainly am."

"Thank you," Peto whispered. "I just hope we get to see who he is now."

Shem came into the tent after Mrs. Rescatar had gone back to her husband's side, and smiled painfully at his nephew.

"Well," he whispered, running a hand through Young Pere's hair to smooth it back, "he looks better than an hour and a half ago. His hair's rather long for someone in the army, but if he spent the last several weeks locked up as we assumed, I guess that's why he's looking shaggy now. I am interested, though, to hear the story about these ears," he said as he ran a finger over the ragged tops of his ears. "Taggings, it looks like. Usually only vial heads allow someone to jab broken glass into their ears, but he seemed to avoid getting branded," he observed, looking over those parts of his body that weren't wrapped in bandages. He leaned over and kissed Young Pere on the forehead. "I'm going to see Versa, let her know. I'll be back later."

Peto and Lilla didn't look up but just nodded, both holding a hand of Young Pere and staring at his battered face.

Shem stepped out of the tent, told the waiting crowd Young Pere was still unconscious, and started off for the midwives' tents. They had moved Versa there not long ago, and he knew exactly what he needed to help soothe his soul. As he neared the row of small tents, one of the midwives came out.

"Guide Zenos, I have someone who wants to see you, if you have time."

"Versa?"

"Yes. She's been asking for you. Are you up to it?"

"Of course. Is she up to seeing me?"

"Now's a good time. Her mother and sister just left to get their things. They're going to camp here tonight."

Shem slipped into Versa's tent. "Hello, Salem's newest mama," he whispered. "How are you?"

"Guide Zenos!" Versa beamed from her cot and tried to sit up.

"No, no—none of that," Shem said, coming over to her. "You're not supposed to move for a long time. You did a lot of damage to yourself from what I heard, but at least you're not that sickly shade of gray anymore. You're just extremely pale." He sat down on a stump next to her and peered over to the bundle in her arms. "I'm so proud of you, Versa. You know how women love to tell birth stories? Well, I doubt anyone can top yours. Well done!"

To his surprise, she became teary-eyed. "Thank you," she whispered. "It wasn't like *anything* I expected it would be."

"It never is."

"Guide, how is he? Young Pere?"

Shem blew out heavily and leaned forward. "They have hope that he'll be all right."

"But you don't?"

Shem looked down at the ground. "It's been a very difficult past few days, Versa. Seeing you with the baby reminded me there are still miracles to be handed out. I'm just not sure if any are for our family."

Versa touched his hand. "What's happened? What's wrong?"

He looked up at her with a sad smile. "Nothing, nothing at all. Because you have a beautiful little girl," he said, leaning over to look at the baby again. "Who does she look like?"

Versa slid the newborn over to him. "You tell me. Besides, I was really hoping you'd be one to hold her."

"There's nothing I'd like to do more right now." He took the baby and positioned her for inspection. "I know who she looks like."

Versa sighed. "Young Pere suggested the same thing. He told me he spent a lot of time with the general."

Shem's eyebrows went up. "Really? I'd love to hear the story if . . ." He stopped, deciding it best not to finish the thought. He smiled at the baby. "On her, those features really work. Just like they do on you, Versa. Beautiful!"

He leaned back and placed Lemuel Thorne's granddaughter on

his chest.

"Versa," he said quietly as he began to pat the newborn. "Why don't you take a nap? Let a grandpa watch her. I've put one of my assistants in charge for the day. We both could use a quiet hour, don't you think?"

An hour and a half later, Shem came out of the tent helping a weakened Versa into a small cart. She wanted to see Young Pere for herself, despite her mother's protests that she needed to rest. But Versa insisted she couldn't sleep, no matter how hard she tried, until she was sure Young Pere had a chance to make it.

Druses placed the baby in her daughter's arms and Shem carefully pulled the cart to the surgery tent where Boskos was standing as if on guard.

Shem raised an eyebrow at his son.

Boskos shook his head. "But it's a good sign," he said. "His heart rate is stronger, and the more he sleeps, the more he recovers."

"Really?" Shem said, unconvinced.

Boskos shrugged. "It's one theory." He turned to the cart. "Versa, how are you doing?"

"I'll be better once I see him."

"Then let's get you better," Boskos said, helping her out of the cart while Shem took the baby.

They walked her slowly into the tent.

Peto saw her, stood up, and gave her a gentle hug.

"You're tougher than your father will ever hope to be, you know that?" he said as he helped her sit down on his log stump.

Lilla reached across Young Pere and took Versa's hand. "I may have startled your poor baby. When I saw the name SHIN on the jacket as I unwrapped your daughter, I might have yelled *a little*."

Peto scoffed quietly. "That's not what we heard! And we heard you all the way to the summit."

Lilla blushed. "She's all right, isn't she?" She glanced over at Shem who was still holding the baby, and he nodded. "I was a little excited."

Versa beamed forgivingly. "I only wish I was conscious when you saw the jacket. I can imagine your reaction."

Lilla smiled back and watched as Versa tenderly touched Young

Pere's face, her eyes growing weepy.

"You should know he was so good to me," she whispered as she pushed away some of his hair. "We walked together all day yesterday, talking, laughing, telling each other our stories . . ." Her voice drifted off as she twisted a lock of his hair around her finger.

Peto blinked in astonishment.

"I hadn't laughed like that in *forever*," Versa sighed. "He was *so sweet*."

Peto and Shem exchanged stunned looks.

Lilla watched Versa closely.

Boskos, standing at the end of the cot, suppressed a smile.

"I lied to him about being ready to birth," Versa said, smiling at the memory. "You should've seen his face when he finally realized the baby was coming. Pure horror!" She chuckled sadly and touched his arm. "But he stayed with me. Talked me through it. *Yelled* me through it, actually. Even caught her in his jacket. I couldn't have done it without him. I think I gave him that bruise when I was gripping him." She gingerly outlined the purple spot on his bicep.

Shem's eyebrows went up.

So did Lilla's.

Peto squinted.

Boskos put his hand in front of his mouth to hide his grin.

"So . . ." Lilla said softly. "Tell me about the baby's birth. Seems to be quite a story."

"And so it begins," Shem said. "I'll wait outside until Versa's ready to go back." He handed the baby to Lilla, stepped out of the tent, shook his head at everyone else to tell them Young Pere was still unconscious, and headed for a quiet stand of trees.

Shem could block everything out while he helped someone else. But the feeling had been so strong in the tent that he had to get away from it. He didn't deserve to feel it, to feel *them*. All of them were there—he knew it. And they were all trying to reach him.

He was so unworthy. Didn't they know what he did? How he betrayed all of them? The two women he loved more than any others, both felled because of his actions.

He couldn't think anymore. He paced in the stand of trees trying to empty his mind. Even sitting with the baby earlier hadn't healed the hole he gouged in his own chest. Instead, the idea of Lemuel Thorne's legacy continuing while Mahrree Shin and Calla Zenos were gone seemed to disrupt the balance of the world.

As he paced he felt again the presence of someone very strong nearby, someone he hadn't felt in almost two years. But he was too much, too powerful. Shem pushed him away, wishing he could explain why no one should be coming to him. Why the Creator hadn't replaced him yet as guide, or sent the Deliverer, Shem just didn't understand. Surely there were better men than him. He had able assistants and capable rectors.

He was relieved when he saw the tent flap open a few minutes later, Boskos and Peto both supporting a very pale Versa.

He pulled Versa in the small wagon back to her tent, focused intently on the contours of the ground and avoiding anything that might bump the fragile new mother who limply cradled her newborn.

A few minutes later, as he and Druses laid her down on the cot, Versa said wearily, "Guide Zenos, I haven't seen your wife yet. Tell Mrs. Zenos I want her to hold the baby. She was predicting she would have blond hair. Tell her she was right." She closed her eyes in exhaustion.

Druses gripped Shem's arm in sympathy as he merely nodded. "I sure will, Versa. Get some rest now."

He kissed the newborn, handed her to Druses, and left.

Peto didn't know how long they sat there. He didn't care. All he could think was, My boy is home. *My boy is home!*

By the wretchedly happy look on Lilla's face she was thinking the same thing. She kept brushing aside his hair, touching his scarred ears, wiping away dirt that wasn't there, and kissing his hand.

"Come on, Young Pere," she'd whisper. *"Come on!"*

"He's changed," Peto decided. "I could see it in the few moments I saw his eyes. And according to Versa, he's changed a lot."

"The village of Pools was far away, right?" Lilla asked as she rubbed her son's hand.

"Pretty far. He spent all that time in the army but he rejected it, Lilla. Just like Shem, just like my father. He turned that jacket inside out." Peto didn't say it out loud, but he hoped it was enough. Young Pere had been on the right path, headed in the right direction . . . he just didn't make it in time.

Or maybe—

"Tell me again what he said when you got to him," Lilla said.

"Everything. Every last detail."

"The first thing he said was, 'Papa, I'm so sorry . . .'"

After Peto told her again of every detail he could remember of their conscious son, Lilla sighed. "I wish I could hear him again. Just . . . anything from him."

"I do too," Peto said, wiping away a tear. His wife didn't even bother to wipe hers but just let them slide down her face.

"This wasn't how it was supposed to be," Peto eventually whispered as he gazed at his son. "I was supposed to walk out of the house one evening, glance down the road, and see him strolling along it, a bit sheepishly perhaps, but with that sly grin of his that says, *Can't stay mad at me forever.*"

Lilla smiled miserably and nodded.

"I would've started running," Peto continued. "And shouting and yelling for everyone, and I would've run straight for him. He would've stopped and braced himself, a bit worried as to what I would do, and a little embarrassed as well. Then I'd hug him. Just hug him, and hold him until you got there, Lilla, to make sure he couldn't get away again."

"I like that," she sniffled. "I always pictured that we were at dinner, and his chair's empty as usual. And then the door would open, and he'd peek in as if nothing at all had happened, and say, 'Sorry I'm late for dinner, but I could smell your biscuits, Mama, and I couldn't stay away.'"

Peto chuckled softly and reached across his son to hold his wife's free hand.

She squeezed it back. "Then, after all the excitement, I'd stay up all night baking. Biscuits and cookies and Grandma Hycymum's cake, and when he woke up in the morning, I'd have all of it all around his bed so that he'd have to eat his way out of there."

"And never run away again," Peto added in a whisper.

"And never run away again," Lilla agreed softly. "I can't even bake for him here. Got some preserves, but—"

"It's all right," Peto assured her. "I can't really hold him, either, without hurting him more."

"But you *did* get to hold him," she reminded him, ignoring the dried blood splotching his jacket, shirt, and trousers. "You held him. He knew it. I'm a little jealous," she confessed and sniffled again.

"You've got his hand now," he reminded her.

She nodded and kissed her son's hand. And again. And one more time, just in case the first two didn't take.

"Is it wrong," she said, "to be looking at this cot and plotting ways of tying him to it?"

They chuckled quietly together.

Peto surreptitiously made sure there wasn't any rope around, just in case. "I was going to tell him I loved him when I first saw him. But I don't think I did. That was going to be the first thing I said. I was just too surprised. But I did thank him for coming home. That was going to be the second thing—"

"Did you feel that?" interrupted Lilla urgently. "His hand? Did he move that hand? I'm sure he moved this one. Boskos!"

"Lilla, Lilla," Peto tried to soothe her. "I didn't feel anything. He may have just spasmed and—"

A soft grunt stopped him.

Peto and Lilla stared at each other.

"*Boskos!*" Peto cried. "Bos, come here!"

The tent flap moved and Boskos rushed over to them. "What's he doing?"

"He grunted!" Lilla stood up. "Young Pere! Come on, *please!*"

"Aunt Lilla," Boskos said quietly, "he's just *right there*, you don't have to shout—"

"Yes, she does," came the faint whisper. "Only way I hear my mama."

No one outside the tent needed to ask what was happening. They heard Lilla's scream of, "HE'S BACK!" as it carried outside and far beyond, probably even to the valley floor below.

Inside the tent, Lilla was reduced to a sobbing mess as she fell on Young Pere's chest. "I've missed you so much! I love you! Thank you for coming home! Oh, Young Pere!"

Peto couldn't help but laugh as he cried. There was no room for him to hug his son because his wife was taking every inch she could.

"His stitches!" Boskos tried to pull her back. "Aunt Lilla, be careful. All right, all right, back off him a little!"

"It's all right, Bos," Young Pere whispered as his mother slapped wet, happy kisses on his bruised face again and again. "I'll take my punishment."

Peto gripped his hand and Young Pere peered at him through the slits of his eyes.

"Thank you, Papa," he whispered. "Quite a jump."

Peto kissed his hand, the only part of him he could reach as Lilla continued to smother him. "Anything for you. I love you, Young Pere," he remembered to add. "You should try the jump sometime. You're now the only one who hasn't. But not today."

Young Pere's smile was fragile. "That's all right, Papa. I have no more desire to fly. Ever."

Peto exhaled in relief.

"I insist on one minute!" Boskos said, gently pulling his aunt off Young Pere. "Here, hold this," he said to her, giving her Young Pere's free hand. "Mind the stitching in his arm." He grinned as he leaned over his cousin's face. "Young Pere, you know the questions." He looked into each eye. "Well?"

"Ribs all right," he whispered, "shoulders intact, no other broken bones. I can feel everything . . . and it still moves. Sort of." He tried to smile. "Just slashes to my arms and gut, I think. Very weak, like I lost a lot of blood. And . . . I got smacked in the head."

Boskos nodded. "Sounds about right. Bruising on your chest, though," he gestured to the bare spots not covered by bandages.

"Shaped like feet?" Young Pere suggested.

Boskos tilted his head. "Now that I look at them, yes. Versa?"

"Tell me, Bos . . . there are other positions for that, right?"

Peto laughed with Boskos while Lilla sniffled.

"In an emergency, it's as good as any other. So you want to become a midwife?" Boskos asked as he pulled up a bandage and checked some of the stitches. "Salema's fully trained and ready for an assistant."

"Thank you . . . but no," Young Pere whispered.

Boskos grinned as he readjusted the bandages and patted his cousin's face. "All right, Lilla. He's all yours again. Just be gentle," and he stepped back.

"I'm always gentle!" she cried as she fell on Young Pere's chest again.

Young Pere flinched a smile.

The tent flap moved again. Relf stood there with Morah and many more bodies pressing behind them.

"Can we see him?" Relf asked.

Young Pere's chest began to heave as tears leaked out his eyes. "Only if they really want to," he whispered.

Peto kissed Young Pere's forehead. "Do you have any doubt?"

"A little," Young Pere's voice quivered. "I've done nothing but hurt them."

"Then let's dispel all doubt, Young Pere," Peto said. "We've always wanted you back, in any condition, in any situation. We've never stopped loving you. Let them show you."

Young Pere's chin trembled and he nodded.

Peto grinned and turned to the open tent flap. "Just be gentle with him."

A moment later the tent was packed, swarming with bodies trying to hug, kiss, or just touch Young Pere.

Boskos stood on the outside of the happy mob, a look of concern on his face.

Dr. Toon joined him.

"We have plenty of the numbing agent, right?" he asked Dr. Toon. "And a strong brew of the pain tea?"

"Yes, Boskos. We already gave him a dose. Why?"

"Because we're going to have to redo all those stitches. We don't do 'gentle' in our family very well."

Shem had been walking to the furthest edges of the sheltered valley, trying to find ways to be useful and block every other thought.

He'd been hoping someone needed help locating a child, or setting up a tent, or collecting firewood. But no one wanted to bother the guide except to give him a hug or pat his back. Even the soldiers who had come up with Young Pere had been taken care of by one of Shem's assistants, given a campsite and food and water, and an explanation of what they thought may be happening next. Shem didn't bother to introduce himself; their inside-out jackets jarred him in the strangest of ways.

He was considering going back to Versa's tent, the only person who didn't know about Calla, when the news spread out to the back reaches of the tableland: Young Perrin Shin had returned, injured as usual, but was now speaking. There were still miracles.

When someone jogged up to him to give him the news, Shem sat down heavily on a log and held his head.

Young Pere was going to make it. One fewer death this week. Another hasty burial that didn't have to happen. He had considered the spot next to Calla for Young Pere. But now?

The Creator had thought of them.

For as much relief as he felt about Young Pere, somehow it

seemed to increase his grief for Calla. If only Calla could have been spared, too.

Shem felt several people put their hands on his back, heard a few comments of, "We're so happy for you, Guide!" and "Isn't this wonderful about your nephew?"

Nodding, he still looked at the ground trying to sort out his emotions. He couldn't continue being so absorbed in his own heartache, but he also didn't know how to break out of it.

He needed to be ready to address the army that would soon be filing into the valley below because, for now, he was still the guide. During the past hour he'd been explaining to the Creator why someone else should be called, but the answer always came back.

You Are The One I Have Chosen.

But it couldn't be for long. The Deliverer had to arrive at any moment. Mahrree had said she thought Shem was the Deliverer, but more and more Shem didn't.

Neither did a few Salemites, according to some quiet conversations he heard as he walked earlier.

"So tragic what happened . . ."

"Why? Why to him?"

"He can't be the Deliverer, or else he would have been able to save Mrs. Zenos and Mrs. Shin . . ."

That was the comment that echoed in his mind. "He can't be the Deliverer . . . He can't be the Deliverer . . ." But he had to shelve everything—his sorrow, his frustrations, his confusion—until the Deliverer arrived. But it was so impossible.

After about the fortieth pat on his back, Shem stood up, gave a faded version of The Dinner smile to everyone around him, and started jogging back to the surgery tent.

There was something he could do. Versa needed to see Young Pere, and Shem needed to see them together again. At least watching whatever was happening between them was a sweet distraction.

He didn't stop weaving through people, and didn't even slow down as he jogged by the surgery tent where he heard only happy laughter and loud conversations, until he reached the midwives' tents. He peeked into Versa's tent and found her awake.

"Versa, did you hear the news?"

She nodded, her eyes red. "It's so terrible! I can't believe it!"

Not sure what she was talking about, and not wanting to deal with any further problems at the moment, Shem stepped in and went down on one knee next to her. "Young Pere's *all right*, Versa! He's awake. I just passed the surgery tent and heard a lot of laughter coming from it."

She struggled to sit up. "He's all right? Can I see him?"

"That's why I'm here—to bring you to him. What did you think I was talking about?"

Her chin wobbled. "I just heard about Mrs. Zenos from my mother. She went to go get me a kerchief," she explained as she sniffed loudly. "I'm so sorry! I could tell something was wrong but I never would have imagined—"

Well, it was only a matter of time. He couldn't get five minutes' respite from the grief. At least the baby didn't know.

"Thank you," he whispered, knowing that a response was required, no matter how dismal. "But I suppose there are still a couple of miracles left for us." He wiped his face, intent on finding something else to think about. "Come—let's go see the latest miracle. I have a feeling he may want to see you."

He scooped up Versa, baby included, carried her to the cart, and carefully set her down. Then he pulled her back over to the surgery tent that was still swarming with family.

Salema and Lek were next to Young Pere's head, holding Plump Perrin who was trying to reach a bandage.

Hycy was on the other side, holding her son in one arm, and keeping her other hand on her younger brother.

Lori was just stepping away, balancing her twin daughters who had just met their uncle.

There wasn't a spare inch next to Young Pere's cot that wasn't filled with a family member eager to tell him something else that had happened in the last seven seasons.

Shem gingerly escorted Versa into the tent, one arm holding her up, his other cradling the baby. Salema sent Versa a look of concern, but she noticed only Young Pere.

From his prone position he didn't notice her until the family made way for her to stand next to his head. He was listening to his younger brothers Nool and Kew explain what happened between Shem and the sergeant a few days ago when the movement of Versa caught his eye. His face lit up, but instantly darkened with worry.

"Versa! How are you?" he whispered weakly.

"I'm all right," she whispered back. "I wanted to see you, make sure you're really going to make it."

Young Pere realized Shem was holding her upright. "What happened? Did you fall?"

"No," she said, putting her hand on top of his. "Just snuck out to weed the garden. *You* were right, for once. Wasn't a good idea." She squeezed his hand with whatever little strength she had.

Young Pere turned his hand to feebly squeeze hers back. "And the baby?"

Versa released his hand and turned to Shem who had been trying to be invisible behind her. He hadn't spoken to Young Pere yet, preferring instead to be the errand boy rather than the guide, but he managed a smile for his nephew and held up the baby.

Young Pere gestured weakly for Shem to give him the newborn, and Shem laid her on his chest. Young Pere closed his eyes and lifted a bandaged arm to place on top of her. "She feels the same," he said, smiling. "So we did everything all right?"

Versa looked to Salema.

"You amazed me, Young Pere," Salema admitted, realizing that with his eyes closed he couldn't see her nodding in approval. "I nearly passed out as an assistant the first time I helped with a birthing, but there you were in the middle of the forest, and even tied off the cord *and* washed the baby? I am *almost* impressed."

Young Pere's smile widened. "Rare that I get a compliment from Salema," he muttered, and Salema chuckled and patted his shoulder.

Versa grinned. "I guess that means we got everything right."

"Except for . . . the hiking trip this morning?" he asked, his eyes still shut.

"Yes," Versa snickered. "The horseback riding we planned for this afternoon should probably wait until the evening."

Lek frowned at Salema. "Horseback riding?" he whispered.

Salema shrugged. "Even if she weren't bleeding so heavily I wouldn't recommend it."

Young Pere heard their whispered exchange. He opened his eyes and slowly winked at Versa, who was chuckling.

Shem saw it.

His chest tightened as he recognized the look—Perrin's wink in his grandson. He felt the presence again, but it was too much to ask for, too much to hope for. There was too much heaviness in his head to make room for anything else.

"Versa," Shem said softly, "we really should get you back. You shouldn't be on your feet and already I've brought you out twice."

"He's right," Salema said, raising her eyebrows in admonishment at both her father-in-law and Versa.

Versa nodded wearily, and Salema helped to take the baby off of Young Pere's chest.

"Thank you," Versa whispered as she squeezed Young Pere's hand again.

Young Pere nodded, his voice giving out on him. "Go rest, Versa. You're safe . . . now. Tonight I'll start . . . working on that arrangement we discussed. I promise." He winked at her again, so slowly that his eye struggled to open fully again.

Versa nodded back, her eyes swimming.

Shem knew better than to ask what kind of arrangement Young Pere was talking about as he carefully led Versa away, but he had a suspicion.

Druses wasn't the only Thorne woman falling in love.

The soldiers were massed, later than General Thorne wanted.

Several hours later.

It seemed many in the army believed they earned sleeping in and taking a leisurely breakfast in their new houses. By midday meal they began to return to the large staging area in the south, many riding horses and mules they had found, others bragging about their new herds and flocks, and a few complaining that there didn't seem to be a drop of mead anywhere in the wretched valley.

Twigg did a final tabulation after midday meal, watching from the south-facing window. Forty nine thousand, eight hundred.

"It'll have to be enough," Thorne grumbled as he stood next to him. "How many Salemites can there be anyway, holed up on top of a cliff?" He nodded to his messengers with the horns. "Sound preparation for forward progress. We're heading for the canyon now."

The horns blasted and Thorne looked around the large gathering room one more time. The officers were filing out of the doors, but he still hadn't seen one particular man that morning at breakfast or at midday meal. He had expected he would show up by now, but his extended insubordination was surprising.

Thorne put his cap on and started out the front door and down the stairs of the porch. He stopped halfway and saw who he was waiting for.

"Knew you wouldn't be able to stay away, Poe. You have to see the action, don't you? You're a soldier first, Hili. That's why you're my sergeant major. That's why you came back to the army two years ago, that's why you're here now."

Hili, standing at nothing near attention, merely said, "Whatever you say."

Thorne smiled thinly. "Then I say get a horse and get to the front of the line, Hili! We've got our greatest victory ahead of us!"

"Just one thing," Hili said, still not moving. "You *did* kill him, right?"

Thorne stiffened. "I killed Shem Zenos, Poe. Now find a horse."

By midday meal Peto felt so revived that he wanted to run across the entire tableland shouting with joy. One part of him was still heavier than the largest boulders, weighted down by the loss of his mother and sister-in-law, but another part of him felt as if it could fly. His son was home!

But instead of flying he did the next best thing: he returned to securing Salem. He knew he needed to, late in the morning, as he watched his family smother his son in kisses and hugs.

He'd stepped outside of the surgery tent, the flaps having been lifted to allow the extended Shin family more room to swarm a weak and emotional Young Pere.

Peto wore a perpetual grin which only expanded when he suddenly felt a presence next to him so powerful that his eyes teared up all over again. Peto could even smell him, earthy sweet.

SORRY HE'S IN SUCH POOR CONDITION, PETO. BUT HE'S HERE.

"Thanks to you, Father!" Peto whispered, not caring if anyone saw him grinning and seemingly talking to himself. "I'm so glad you're both back."

AND THANKS TO YOUR MOTHER. I COULD NEVER SEEM TO FINISH ANY JOB WITHOUT HER HELP.

"Tell her thank you! Where is she?"

IN THE MIDDLE OF THAT MESS OF FAMILY SOMEWHERE, HAVING THE TIME OF HER LIFE. SO TO SPEAK.

Peto chuckled.

BY THE WAY, RECTOR SHIN, IT'S TIME TO GET BACK TO WORK. THE ARMY'S MOVING TO THE CANYON. THEY'LL BE VISIBLE IN THE VALLEY IN

LESS THAN AN HOUR. GET SOME PEOPLE TO THE EDGE OF THE CLIFF, COUNTING. YOU KNOW HOW MANY THERE WILL BE.

"Around fifty thousand," Peto whispered.

THAT'S RIGHT. COUNT TO GAUGE THEIR RATE OF PROGRESS, AND SEND SOME SCOUTS DOWN THE ROUTES TO FIND STRAGGLERS, BUT ONLY AS FAR AS THE RIVERS. SOME OF THE DESERTED SOLDIERS ARE SWARMING THESE MOUNTAINS. MANY ARE STILL TERRIFIED, SOME ARE BLOOD-THIRSTY, AND SOME ARE JUST BORED. A WEAPON IN THE HANDS OF ANY OF THEM IS DANGEROUS. BUT THEY WON'T CROSS THE RIVERS; THEY THINK THEY'RE TOO COLD. THERE ARE ONLY A HANDFUL OF REMAINING SALEMITES COMING UP ON THE ROUTES. SEND THEM HELP.

Peto nodded again. "Of course, Father. And *then* what?"

AND THEN SOMEHOW I'VE GOT TO GET THROUGH THAT THICK SKULL OF SHEM'S! I GAVE HIM QUITE A LECTURE EARLY THIS MORNING ABOUT DOING HIS DUTY. HE SLEPT THROUGH ALL OF IT, BUT I THINK HE RECEIVED THE MESSAGE AT SOME LEVEL OF CONSCIOUSNESS, OTHERWISE HE WOULDN'T HAVE RECOGNIZED THE PROMPTING TO GO TO THE BACK DOOR.

"You know what I'm asking, Father. The Last Day?"

Silence.

"Father?"

No answer.

"General? I asked you a question!"

Peto could still feel him but no longer heard him. The feeling, as well as his scent, slowly faded. Peto chuckled to himself. His father was always such a tease.

He noticed eight men in reversed army jackets apprehensively making their way over to the surgery, tentative smiles on their faces.

"Sounds like he's going to make it?" one of them asked Peto, hearing the laughter and squeals coming from the tent.

Peto grinned. "If he survives the family mauling, I'd say he has a very good chance. I want to thank you for bringing him here."

One of the men, his dark face bruised, shook his head. "He brought *us* here. He started by luring us with ridiculous stories about the existence of elephants and a perfect life in Salem."

Peto sighed in mock sadness. "Have to travel many weeks before you see elephants. But they're there, I promise. Just like a perfect life in Salem has always been here."

The first soldier held out his hand. "Staff Sergeant Beaved, sir. This is my security team. We were in charge of keeping Shin under control."

Peto chuckled as he shook his hand. "Quite a task! I know—I tried for eighteen years to keep him under control, with little success."

The bruised man squinted at him. "Are you, are you his *father*?"

"I am. Peto Shin. I'm his *real* father."

Several of the soldiers looked at each other with surprised expressions.

The bruised man rolled his eyes. "*Peto* Shin," he scoffed, amused. "Thorne imagined all kinds of things, but I don't think he ever imagined that *Peto Shin* survived, married, and had children."

A soldier close to Peto's age, and with a thick belly, held up his hands. "Did you say, *eighteen* years?"

"He's nineteen and a half now," Peto told him.

A younger soldier elbowed the fatter one. "That's what he was *telling* us. He's not twenty-eight, Jaytsy was never his mother, and Thorne certainly wasn't his father!"

Peto bristled. "No, thank goodness. My sister told us all about Thorne's version after she came back from the Second Resting Station."

"She made it back safely, then?" the sergeant asked.

"Very," Peto smiled.

"So," asked another soldier, "who's his mother?"

Peto motioned to the crowd at the tent. "See, or rather *hear*, that woman there on the stool?"

"Is she laughing or crying?" Beaved asked.

"Both," Peto grinned. "That's his mother."

"Same loud mouth," the bruised man observed.

Peto chuckled. It was so easy to laugh today, unlike yesterday.

He turned back to the soldiers. "Have you found a place to sleep for the night? We have extra bedrolls and supplies, and a doctor can look at your bruising." He gestured to the young man with a partially swollen eye.

"Already has, sir," the sergeant said. "Nelt, here, will live. And we've got a tent set up, too, toward the back. Someone who called himself an assistant thought it best that we stay as far away from the cliff side as possible."

"What exactly is an 'assistant'?" another one of the soldiers asked.

"Assistants to the Guide," Peto explained. "He has twelve. Eleven are here, and each has been given a duty to watch over different areas.

All problems and concerns are handled by them, unless something more serious arises. Then the question is presented to the guide. A *real* guide, not Lannard Kroop!" Peto shuddered slightly. "I knew him in school. He was in a different class, but *everyone* knew of Lannard Kroop."

"As did your mother," the bruised man called Nelt said somberly. "I'm so sorry about that. We all are," he gestured to the men behind him. "That was the last thing we could bear to watch Thorne do. We knew then we had to desert."

"Thank you," Peto said. "You did the right thing. You'll be safe here, all of you. As you saw earlier with that other soldier who fell, no one can come here with malicious intents and survive."

"I've been wondering about that," said one of the massive soldiers. "Who was it that knocked him down? I could tell Snarl's neck was broken before he even finished rolling down to us."

"The guide," Peto said. "The *real* guide."

The soldiers were taken aback.

"Aren't guides supposed to be gentle and loving and give blessings and all that?" asked one of the younger men.

"Yes," Peto said, "yes, they are. They're also supposed to protect and defend the Creator's people until the Last Day."

The bruised man leaned forward as an idea came to him. "*You* survived, so did your sister, your mother, your father . . . is the guide, is the guide . . .?" He couldn't bring himself to say it.

The rest of the soldiers looked at him, waiting.

Peto paused just long enough to get their full attention. Then he relished their looks of shock as he said, "Our guide is Sergeant Major Shem Zenos."

It took several minutes for them to recover. Peto chuckled the entire time.

Finally Nelt asked reverently, "Where is he now?"

Peto gestured to the vast tableland. "Somewhere out there again, walking." More quietly he said, "His wife also died, the same day as my mother. It's been a difficult few days, losing both of them. They were all the very best of friends."

The other massive soldier finally shook his head, coming out of his amazement. "Slagging Zenoses—the slagging Zenos *survived*!"

Peto smiled patiently. "You're welcome to stay with us. Salem has always been a place of refuge for those tired of fighting the world. Has been since the very beginning. But we have a few rules you need to follow to stay with us. One of those is respect for all people, so no profanity of any kind is allowed. Shem Zenos has always been the most selfless and perfect man he could be, and his name should never be used so coarsely."

The soldier nodded in embarrassment. "Creet, I'm sorry," he mumbled.

Peto nodded back. "It's all right. It might take you a little while to adjust, but just keep trying. And by the way, the same thing goes for the Creator's name, in all its variations. It's all right—you'll get it figured out. Salemites are patient and forgiving. We Shins have been here for almost three decades and they still haven't sent us away."

General Thorne was riding at the head of the army, looking behind every bend for the valley that was supposed to be there. This canyon was by far the easiest to travel. The slope was almost non-existent, the floor was broad and wide with only a trickle of a stream, so the soldiers could ride five across, or march eight abreast, easily. Their progress was swift that early afternoon. It was less than an hour after they entered the canyon that it suddenly opened out on to a long, quiet valley.

Thorne stopped his horse and surveyed the area.

"What a waste. Look at this fertile flat plain, and not a single structure or farm anywhere! These stupid Salemites passed up the ideal place to erect a village." A smile began to grow on his face. "But that's what I'll do first. This valley will become one of the most beautiful, glorious villages ever known. And it will be called . . . Thorneville."

Major Twigg looked at the valley from atop his mount and shrugged. "I suppose this area has potential."

Thorne glanced over at Hili. "You've been very quiet, Sergeant Major. Tell me what you think of this valley? The name for it?"

"Whatever you want, General," Hili said dully. "I just do my duty to you."

"I'm asking your opinion, Poe. As a friend." The general choked a little on the last word.

Hili sent him a brittle glare. "I didn't know being your 'friend' was one of my duties."

Thorne waited for a better response.

So Hili looked at the valley. "Should I begin by leading my division out there, sir? Or do you wish to choose the location of your vacation home first?"

"Watch it, Hili. You're getting on my last nerves."

Hili only stared listlessly out at the valley.

Thorne kicked the sides of his horse and led the army out.

Poe looked up into the sky and tried to discern what color it was. It was blue, with some white, and gray in the distance. There was a storm coming, he was sure.

He just didn't know what to do about it.

Jon Offra and his timid companion were spotted by three colonels, two lieutenant colonels, four majors, five captains, and six lieutenants. None of them said a word but eyed Offra warily as he sauntered through the ranks of men. Further up and closer to Thorne were his most loyal men. But back here, where soldiers walked slower and resented more, grumbling about leaving their new homes and fields and herds, Offra was safe.

And so he talked. Or rather, sang.

"Strolling to our deaths, strolling to our deaths, yes we are, we're strolling, strolling to our deaths . . . The Last Day is coming, the Last Day is coming, only those who want to die will stroll to their deaths."

It was his inane grin that put most men off. Then the way he'd trot up the slope a bit for a better view and sing another verse of his made-up song.

Occasionally an officer would approach him, intent on giving him a good tongue-lashing, but there was still something haunting in Offra's eyes. And then they'd remember that Colonel Offra outranked all of them, so what, exactly, were they to do about that?

And then there was the jacket he wore. Something about that jacket with the old-fashioned brass buttons which said, *Don't think about it, boys.*

Silent and fidgeting, the officers would march off, making sure they didn't appear to be "strolling."

Many soldiers—or rather, men pretending to be soldiers—looked up at Offra, apologetic and apprehensive.

" . . . Strolling to our deaths, yes we are, we're strolling . . ."

Occasionally one or two would turn around and start jogging the opposite way out of the canyon, forcing their ways through the crowds or trying to get to a side to escape. Offra would salute them away and applaud for a few seconds, still singing, "Last Day is coming, Last Day is coming . . ."

Behind him, observing the crowds and occasionally nudging Offra to continue moving when a more threatening soldier closed in on them was a small man, far older than fifty, in plain clothes. He might have been a Salemite, but to many of the soldiers he seemed more like a bear tamer, keeping his pet on a close leash, but willing to release him should the situation warrant it.

And so the army of Idumea strolled—*walked*—up the wide canyon, west, then north, being serenaded by the same voice that a few nights ago had told them all about the Last Day and that they were all going to die.

Privately, a lot of them were beginning to believe it. They just didn't know what to do about it.

Jothan Hifadhi, studying the edge of the canyon, noticed the first horsemen come into the valley. He'd predicted when they'd arrive, and had he started a countdown, he would have said "one" just as the first sword glint appeared. He picked up one of the spyglasses and focused in on the glints, then he snapped his fingers, never taking his eyes off the valley.

Immediately several young women were at his side: his great-granddaughter Cabbish and a few of Perrin's granddaughters.

"There they are," he pointed in the distance. "Who's keeping tally first?"

"That would be me, sir. My name's Tabbit Briter." She sat down and took up another spy glass.

"Remember, in tens," Jothan said. "Recorders?"

Two more teenage girls sat down.

"Hello again, sir. Kanthi here, Hycy's sister, and this is my cousin Banu Briter." They readied their paper and charcoal.

Jothan never once took his eyes off the distant valley. "Good, good. Count so far, Tabbit?"

"Forty. Eighty. One hundred . . ."

Her sister and cousin listened and made a tally mark for the first one hundred soldiers.

"Good, very good," Jothan said. "My count too. Keep going. Record her numbers."

"Thirty. Fifty. Sixty. Eighty . . ."

Cabbish sat down next to her great grandfather and took up the other spyglass. "I'm taking next count."

Jothan nodded. "Practice now."

" . . . forty. Sixty. Eighty. Ninety . . ." Tabbit continued.

"How did you used to do this without a spyglass, Grandpa?" Cabbish asked.

Jothan chuckled his low laugh. "Years of practice, my dear. Choose a point in the terrain and count as they pass it. Notice the lines stay relatively straight. Assume the army is organized as it comes in."

Cabbish watched for a moment, listening to Tabbit call out numbers.

" . . . thirty, fifty, sixty, eighty, hundred . . ."

"Got it," Cabbish said, bobbing her head in cadence with the counting. When Tabbit tired, she'd be ready.

"Good," Jothan said, standing up. "Keep count in twenties, though, so you don't lost track. I have a report to make."

He strolled over to the Shin campsite where Peto had just returned after seeing off another group of scouts heading down the trails to look for any remaining Salemites.

"Rector Shin, I am here to report that the first of the soldiers have arrived. The Army of Idumea is coming."

Peto took a deep breath and released it. "So this is it, Jothan? Whew. Hmm." He scratched his chin. "Waited for decades to hear that, and somehow I expected those words to knock me over or something, but . . ." He shrugged. "With so much going on the past few days, word that the army is coming seems rather anti-climactic. 'Here comes the invasion. By the way, what's for dinner?'"

Jothan chuckled, pleased to see Peto Shin joking again.

"Well, we're getting ready," Peto said more soberly. "Counters in place?"

Jothan smiled. "I always thought girls were much more particular about such details than boys. Fine selection of young women there."

"The next shift will be there in an hour to relieve them." Peto paused. "I need to tell him, don't I? Last I heard he was wandering near the temple ruins."

Jothan patted Peto's shoulder. "He'll be ready. He's always been a man of deep feeling with a tremendous sense of duty. When he needs to be, he'll be ready."

"Thanks, Jothan. Go back to supervising the girls. Your eyes can still see more than all of them."

Peto jogged the short distance to the ancient site, still swarming with people meeting their families and sharing news.

Shem stood off a little ways near some trees, smiling dimly as a little boy was telling him something undoubtedly very important.

As Peto neared he heard, "—so that's how I got the red bedroll!"

Shem nodded. "And the red one is important because . . ."

"Skunks hate red."

"I had no idea."

The little boy waved that off. "Most people don't. I just figured it out myself. That's why I think the *next time* we do this—"

Shem recoiled slightly at his words.

"—everyone has red bedrolls. Then I won't have to fight with my sister over who gets it, and neither of us would be in trouble right now."

"I see the advantages to that."

Shem was extraordinary. Peto couldn't think of another man who, faced with as many concerns and grief as he had right now, would spend a few minutes discussing the merits of bedroll colors with a child.

"Do you want to hear the story of how I learned that skunks hate red?" he asked eagerly.

Peto stepped up to them. "I, for one, would *love* to hear that story, but I'm afraid I need to take the guide for a few minutes."

The boy shrugged. "I'll just find you later then, Guide."

Shem waved as the boy ran off, then obediently turned and followed Peto. "What's up?" he said dully.

"You'll see in just a moment. Right over here."

"We're heading to the cliff, aren't we?"

"Not a lot of other places for us to go up here, Shem."

They stopped at the cliff a short distance away and looked out at the valley.

Shem sighed. "They're coming."

"They are," Peto said. "Somewhere down there is Lemuel and Poe."

They watched in silence and listened to the counting nearby. "Forty. Sixty. Eighty. Hundred. Twenty. Forty . . ."

"Keep counting, girls," Shem said to them. "We know how many are coming. Just want to keep track of their progress."

Peto sighed. "Ah, Shem. I just remembered something."

"What?"

"Years ago, when we were first here with Father and Guide Gleace. We stood almost at the same spot, remember?"

Shem blinked back tears. "I remember," he whispered. "I wanted to be an old, gray grandfather. I was going to say to my grandchildren, 'Start counting! I know how many there'll be!'"

Peto gave him a pained smile as Shem continued to watch the distant glints of sunlight on swords. "Was funnier then, wasn't it?"

Shem shrugged.

"Thinking about you as an old gray grandfather, I mean," Peto clarified. "Here you are," he choked.

"You're going gray too, Peto."

"It's just *starting* to go gray, Shem."

He cleared his throat. "Sounded a lot like Perrin there, Peto."

"He's back, and up here. He told me the soldiers would be coming and he told me to send the scouts down the trails looking for stragglers. Already they've found eighty more people, a few from Eltana's army. The rest will be here by dinner time."

"Good . . . good."

"Shem, feel him?"

The guide shook his head. "Don't need to, Peto. He's speaking to you, and soon the Deliverer will arrive and—"

"Shem, you *are* the Deliverer. You delivered all of us here!"

"I *delivered* your mother to Lemuel Thorne, Peto."

"You also *delivered* my son from certain death! Those last three soldiers would have killed him. No other man here could have used the sword to save him, Sergeant Major."

The guide cleared his throat again roughly and patted his brother-in-law on the back. "Going to go back now. Tell the assistants the news. See if anyone wants to make a case for green bedrolls next."

And he walked away.

Young Pere slept most of the afternoon while nearly everyone else crowded to the cliff side to witness for themselves that the army was indeed coming. At the news, Young Pere only nodded and closed his eyes in fatigue. Boskos said he'd need all the rest he could get after the family mobbing and the visit from his former security team.

Lilla stayed by his side all afternoon and begged Boskos to let her take him back to their camp for the night. Boskos would be close enough to help should they need anything.

By dinner Young Pere woke to eat a little, then rested again until late evening. Just as the little ones were going to bed, Young Pere felt ready to get up, and there was one person he wanted to talk to.

"Shem said we won't be disturbed in his tent," Peto told him as he slowly led him to the tent. "No one's come in here since it was set up."

"Papa, does Uncle Shem have a problem with me? He hasn't spoken to me since you found me this morning. I know I have a lot to apologize for, but he won't even look at me." Young Pere had tried, a few times, to catch Uncle Shem's attention, but it was as if he deliberately refused to look him in the eyes. Shem had never purposely avoided him before—avoided anyone before, as far as Young Pere knew—and it concerned him, deeply.

Peto smiled sadly. "It's been a horrible few days for him. Someone told you about Calla, right?"

"I can't believe it. I really can't. Of everything else, then . . . Aunt Calla?" He sniffled, his eyes bubbling again with tears for his aunt who had never been anything but patient and kind, and frequently gave Young Pere hugs and would whisper, "Just so you know I'll always love you, no matter what you do. If ever you need anything, you can always come to me. Always."

No one ever knew she'd catch him alone and pat his cheek after yet another one of his misadventures and say, "Doing all right? Need a friend? Need some pie?" She always seemed to know when he'd had another falling out with his father or Puggah or Muggah. She was always there.

Today, he knew what he'd say to her when she finally came by to visit him. "I don't need any pie, Aunt Calla, but I could use a hug. Thanks for always being my friend."

But she never came.

When he finally learned why, from Hycy—she said no one had wanted to tell him, but since he was asking, he should know—he lost the last of his strength.

Because he never got to thank her.

"So you understand," Peto said quietly, breaking into his

thoughts. "Shem's dealing with a lot right now, but he *is* very relieved to see you, don't worry. You're the only reason he got up and got moving this morning. He just can't work through everything yet. He'll get to you when he's more himself again."

They'd reached Shem's tent and Peto helped lower Young Pere to one of the squared off logs that served as low seating in the large tent.

"Are you sure you don't want to lie down? You're still so pale."

"No, Papa. I'll be all right," he said, reclining on the numerous blankets his mother had piled up around the log to support him. "I want to be sitting up. Well, sort of," he gestured lamely to his propped up position. "I kind of had an image of how this would go. Boskos just gave me another dose of the Pain Tea. I think they improved the strength because I feel pretty good right now. But if I become dizzy, I'll lie down. I promise."

Peto sat down across from him on the other log, a lantern between them providing light. "Then I'll trust you to do so." He sighed in contentment as he looked at his son. "I still can't believe you're here! I've dreamed about this day so many times, and *here you are*!"

Young Pere smiled hesitantly. "Just don't hug me, all right? Not until I heal a little more?"

Peto chuckled. "I'm sorry about the mob earlier. Even if you weren't hurt before, you would be now. Half your internal injuries probably came from your mother alone."

Young Pere laughed softly and immediately grabbed his sides in pain. "I shouldn't do that."

Peto winced in sympathy. "Need more of the brown stuff?"

"Only works on the outside, not the inside. And the tea hasn't taken its full affect, yet. I'll be all right. I've done this before."

"Young Pere, sword wounds are different than getting impaled on a tree. It'll take more than a few days. I still remember watching Puggah trying to recover when I was little. You may not realize it, but you looked so much like him down there by the river. For a moment I fully expected to see him there, wielding the swords."

"He was, Papa," Young Pere said reverently. "I didn't know any of those moves. It was as if he stepped into my body and took over until you and Uncle Shem arrived. You *were* watching General Shin in action again. And Papa, he and Muggah both brought me home."

"I know," Peto whispered. "Jaytsy saw them together at the summit, just for a moment."

"And I was with them, Papa," Young Pere said, surprised that the memory was so sharp. "For probably less than a minute, but it wasn't my time yet to go. They said I had to come back, and they helped me get back to my body. They're still here, somewhere on the mountain. I feel them from time to time."

Peto smiled. "My father spoke to me. He's still acting as general, still completing his calling."

"I never understood that before," Young Pere said. "They really *do* keep going. Death isn't the end, just a change. Don't take this the wrong way, Papa, but I really wouldn't have minded if I *didn't* make it. I would have been just fine. I had a small glimpse of Paradise, and it was . . . Paradise!"

His father grinned. "I'm glad you finally understand. But I'm glad you were able to come back to us, for your mother especially. I suppose there's more for you to do on this side still."

Young Pere nodded. "I'm not sure why else I'm here, but I think a lot of it is for me to start making things right again."

"I think so, too," said Peto encouragingly.

Young Pere sighed, not sure how to begin all he needed to lay before his father. He blurted out the first thing that came to his mind.

"I never drew blood with my sword, not without Puggah. I wanted to. I tried to. I had the opportunity to, but never once in the world did I ever bloody it. And now I'm glad I didn't. It was only when I came home that I used a sword, and that was to defend those with me."

"That's the only way to use it, Young Pere. I'm glad you're not burdened with any guilt of misusing a sword."

Young Pere shrugged. "Does poking an ornery mule with the tip of it count as misuse?"

Peto chuckled. "Not in my book."

Young Pere smiled but it soon faded. "I guess a lot of it started with Mrs. Yordin. I haven't seen her here, yet. I'm assuming she's pretty disappointed with me."

Peto rubbed his chin. "I wouldn't know. She didn't come to the site. She thought it was wrong for Salem to not fight back. She actually organized her own army."

Young Pere closed his eyes. "That was her doing? I saw part of the attack. Very few Salemites survived it. How could she not trust Shem?"

"Perhaps in the same ways you didn't trust him?" Peto suggested.

Young Pere opened his eyes. "Shem knew so much more than I

ever realized. He knows everything, but had good reasons for not sharing it all. And I always thought he was so clueless."

"Mrs. Yordin didn't have enough faith to join us completely," Peto said. "Her heart was too much in the world still. That's why she brought her husband's jacket with her. And because she couldn't leave that behind, she was never able to fully commit to life here."

Young Pere squinted, confused. "But I brought that jacket back to the world."

"She was expecting it to return to her. When you took that jacket to Edge, her heart went with it."

Young Pere sighed. "I can see that. I suppose it's fitting that I lost it to Amory."

At her name, Peto tensed. "Do you know what happened to her?"

"Lemuel stabbed her," Young Pere said quietly. "Before the very last wall. She thought she was going to be his queen here."

Peto shrugged sadly. "We suspected as much. Her husband has remarried, by the way, to a widow with two young boys. He and his three daughters are happier than they've ever been, but he was wondering . . . I'll bring him the news tomorrow."

Then Peto looked down at his hands. "Eltana Yordin wasn't the only one who struggled to leave the world behind. Your grandfather did the same thing."

"But, I thought he was *supposed* to bring his jacket."

Peto looked up. "He was. The jacket wasn't the problem. It was his long knife."

Young Pere's eyebrows rose. "He smuggled one here too?"

Peto frowned. "Who else did that?"

"Versa."

"Why am I not surprised?" Peto threw his hands in the air. "But she doesn't still have it, does she?"

"No. She pulled it on me when I first found her, but I convinced her to leave it at the river with the swords."

"Good," said Peto. "Things will be easier for her now. If your grandfather had left his in Edge as he was instructed, we all would have slept better."

"Really? You think that was his problem?"

Peto sighed. "Father didn't fully trust Jothan when we left Edge, and he doubted Shem a little as well. He'd just found out Shem had been lying to us for all those years, after all. He told me he trusted him, but the former officer in him couldn't imagine going unarmed to Salem. I'm not sure where he had his knife—it was usually on his hip—and to my and Shem's knowledge, he never used it in the forest when we were escaping. Once we came to Salem there was no need for it, either. He burdened himself with that remnant of the world unnecessarily. I found it in the bottom drawer of his desk shortly before you left. Muggah decided to keep it next to the bed to remember him by."

Young Pere frowned. "Kind of an odd way to remember him."

"That's what I told her," Peto chuckled. "It didn't stay there, though. Early the next morning I happened to look outside when I got up, and saw her standing by Father's grave. Deck was there, digging. I went out to see what was going on. They were burying the knife. She didn't want anyone to know it was there, so that none of her grandsons would dig it up out of curiosity."

Young Pere smiled faintly. "Good idea. If I knew it was there I probably would have tried to take it with me."

Peto smiled back. "Deck pushed it in pretty deep, and we covered it up. When I walked Muggah back to the house, I asked what that was all about. She looked absolutely exhausted. All she said was, 'Peto, I now know exactly what your father went through when he relived the world in his dreams.' When I told Shem about it, he didn't seem surprised. He had a feeling Father had brought something of the world with him to Salem which was causing his sleeping problems, but Father was too stubborn to admit anything."

Young Pere nodded. "It felt odd seeing so many weapons in the valley. Once I even held a sword, near the temple, but it felt all wrong. Something just didn't feel right about weapons in a land that was supposed to be peaceful."

"Very good, Young Pere. See? You do belong in Salem," Peto smiled.

"But Papa," Young Pere said slyly, "*you* didn't belong in the world, yet you were *there*, weren't you? The tree fall?"

Peto grinned. "My night to play Guarder!"

"But *why* were you there?" Young Pere finally got to ask the question he'd been wondering about ever since that night.

"Believe it or not," Peto said with his own sly smile, "to offer our food reserves to the world."

Young Pere's jaw went slack. "I don't believe it."

"Told you," Peto chuckled. "I slipped into the command tower early in the morning, anonymously, and told your major we had enough reserves to feed the world for a year, but they had to give me soldiers to pick it up. He sent the message to Thorne, who thought it was a trap of some kind, and rejected it. I was in the fort that next evening to get Thorne's response. But with everyone waiting for me, probably to apprehend me—"

Young Pere nodded at that assumption.

"—we had to create some kind of distraction to make everyone forget about looking for a sergeant major. No one expected a colonel and an avalanche of trees, right?"

"Absolutely not!" Young Pere grinned.

"So how did the fort react?" Peto asked eagerly. "I've always wondered."

Young Pere began to laugh, holding his side. "Total panic, Papa! It was fantastic. You completely undid Major Twigg—he was jittery for days—and all of Edge was sure the Guarders had returned. I even overheard one man say he was now positive the Shins were alive in the forests!"

Peto puffed up his chest. "And he was right!"

"And I was so proud!"

"So you knew it was me?"

Young Pere sighed. "Not until it was too late. I overheard them talking that night in the command tower about someone having access to both a sergeant major's *and* a colonel's uniform. There was only one man I could think of who would have both. Later I realized I heard your voice as you were shouting."

"I saw you, too," Peto told him. "As I ran past you just as the trees were coming down, I knew immediately it was you. I nearly gave up the entire plan just to grab you and drag you home."

Young Pere looked down and adjusted a bandage. "I wish you could have. Knowing my state of mind at the time, though, I would have been overjoyed to see you but still convinced I could unite Idumea and Salem."

Peto sat back and stared, his son still not raising his head to meet his eyes. "So *that's* what you were trying to do? Unify the world, the *whole* world? And now General Thorne's trying to do that."

Young Pere looked up. "I wanted to be the next General Shin. As you can tell, I kind of fell short of that goal. Did you know there's a dungeon at the fort in Edge? Under the command tower? I do. Chained up in there, I began to finally realize that maybe this *wasn't* such a good idea after all."

To Young Pere's surprise, his father grinned. "Well, good! I'm so glad you failed. I'm proud of your failure."

Young Pere chuckled and readjusted his position.

"Sure you don't want to lie down, son? You'll be much more comfortable."

Young Pere stopped shifting when he heard his father say 'son,' and couldn't conceal the emotion that flooded him.

Peto noticed and leaned forward, worried. "Young Pere, what's wrong? Are you all right, son? Did you pull some stitches?"

Young Pere shook his head and bit his lip to stop its quivering. "It's just that . . . I heard the word 'son' a lot in the world, but it never sounded right. Not until you said it. The general called me that more times than I care to remember, and each time I wanted to punch him."

Peto's eyebrows went up. "General *Thorne*?"

Young Pere winced and nodded.

His father straightened his back and his eyes hardened. "Let me get this straight: Lemuel Thorne had the nerve to call MY boy 'son'?"

Young Pere nodded again, surprised to see how angry his father had become at that news. It was probably a good thing he didn't know that Lemuel Thorne may also be his half-brother. "Thorne did a lot more than that."

Just as quickly, Peto softened again and took a rolled up blanket from the pile of extras. He leaned forward and carefully slid it under Young Pere's arm to give him extra support. "So why don't you tell me everything that happened down there, *son*," he added with a big smile. "Start at the beginning."

Young Pere took a breath.

Jon Offra was finally relaxing in his bedroll, the weariness of the day catching up to him. Teman, next to him, was already softly snoring. Jon rolled over to avoid a tree root jabbing his back, only to find himself face-to-face with a young, terrified face.

"Can I help you?" he whispered.

The boy, maybe sixteen, but considered old enough to be conscripted into Thorne's army, was only inches away and holding his breath. "Sir? You're the one, right? The one who keeps telling us we're going to die?"

"That would be me."

The young man, who seemingly had crawled over to Jon, glanced around. "Sir, you're, you're, you're camping in the middle of the army!"

Jon snorted softly. "I never retired from the army, boy. I'm a colonel and with more experience than anyone out here. I can camp wherever I please."

"Oh. I didn't know that. Seems a little . . . dangerous, though, doesn't it? I mean, they don't like you. They keep talking about you."

"*They* is very powerful, isn't *they*? But if we're all going to die at the Last Day, what does it matter?"

"You really believe that, sir?"

"Of course I do. Why would I be out here trying to warn you all otherwise? Now, be sensible and at first light, head back south. Get out of here."

"But General Thorne will—"

"—Not care about a boy like you. Trust me. He cares for none of you. You're merely tools. As valuable as a nail, and as expendable as one, too. Don't let him rule your life or make your choices. Walk away."

The boy pondered that. "All right," he whispered, and sat up, careful not to bother the man sleeping behind him. Jon had settled in the middle of a thousand men, eating their rations and not giving any explanation as to who he was, or why there was an old Salemite with him. He just glanced around as night fell and made himself at home.

The boy leaned close again. "Sir? I want to leave."

"Good. Do so, and let me sleep."

"But, sir—you said I should make my own choices and then told me to walk away. But if I walk away, am I not following *your* orders then, instead of Thorne's? How do I choose for myself?"

Jon sighed. "Boy, do what you want. Do what makes sense. Forget everything I said you should do. Yes, including that. Sleep, then in the morning head home and forget any of this happened. I know I wish I could."

The boy hesitated, then said, "Yes, sir," and crawled away.

"How long have they been in there?" Jaytsy murmured to Deck as they sat together by the fire. Nearly everyone on the tableland had gone to sleep, but few adults in the Shin-Briter-Zenos camps felt like closing their eyes. Most of them lay with their families trying to sleep, but Jaytsy and Deck weren't even pretending as they waited by the small fire across from Shem's tent.

Deck shrugged. "Maybe close to three hours?" He glanced up at the sky. "Well past midnight now."

"If Lilla keeps pacing in front of Shem's tent, there'll be a rut in the ground," Jaytsy whispered.

"You can't get her to sit down?"

Jaytsy shook her head. "I think she's afraid to go further than ten paces from him. As if he'll vanish again."

"Do we know yet if he saw what happened to Mahrree?" Deck asked.

Jaytsy sniffled. "Boskos said he was mumbling about it as he went under. He saw it all. But somehow she got to him. She reached him again, Deck. I think she knew exactly what she was doing."

Deck kissed her wet cheek and put an arm around her. "Somehow I knew they would do it. I can't even begin to imagine what else Young Pere experienced. He looked so worn, almost broken. Cephas was stunned to see the changes in him. Now everyone knows Young Pere wasn't out on a casual camping trip for almost two years."

"I'll just need to see the look on Peto's face," Jaytsy said, "when he finally comes out of the tent to know just how bad it was. Sometimes I was so mad at him, Deck," she whispered. "So angry at my nephew for making his parents mourn and for hurting my mother. I hate to admit it, but there were times I hoped he was suffering down there. Then I'd have to spend the next week repenting of my *lovely* attitude. But seeing him . . . Did you notice the look in his eyes, Deck? Even at the Second Resting Station I could see it. The boy certainly suffered. Much more than I wished for him."

Deck was about to respond when they both saw the tent flap move. Jaytsy and Deck stood up.

Lilla rushed over just as Peto was helping Young Pere out. He was doubled over like an old man, but looked up at his mother and smiled. His eyes were visibly brighter and his face more relaxed, in spite of his obvious discomfort. She put a supporting arm around him and kissed his hanging head.

"Does this mean you're going to tuck me in tonight, Mama?" Young Pere whispered.

"Every night until you're fifty years old!" she tried to say quietly, but nothing ever came out of Lilla quietly.

Young Pere grinned, glanced over at Jaytsy and Deck, gave them a nod goodnight, and let his mother lead him to where the rest of the family was camped.

Jaytsy eyed her brother who was slowly ambling over to the smaller fire, watching his feet as he went. She put her arm around his shoulders. "Are you holding up all right?"

Peto sighed heavily, but was smiling when he finally looked up at his sister and brother-in-law. Jaytsy had never seen his eyes so red. Not even when their parents died. It *had* been bad.

"Of course," he said, his jaw trembling. "Best day of my life. My son's home."

From a thicket of trees, Shem spied on the Shins in front of his now-vacant tent. He wouldn't go in there. Not without Calla.

The scene before him helped soften the blows to his heart. Lilla led Young Pere to the cot Boskos had set up for him by the big fire which would blaze all night to keep him warm. She helped Young Pere lay down and covered him in too many blankets, but he didn't protest. She kissed him, then kissed him again, and smoothed down his hair before joining her husband at the smaller fire.

Shem watched as Peto paused in his conversation with Jaytsy and Deck to hold his arms out to his wife. She rushed into them, weeping.

She asked Peto something, and Peto nodded gravely. Lilla, Jaytsy, and Deck all seemed to groan.

Lilla asked something else, and again Peto nodded. The other three shook their heads sadly.

Lilla said something else, Peto smiled, and the four of them came together for a combined embrace.

Shem knew it was a message, a sign of hope. Nothing could've been more astonishing than Young Pere's return that morning. And the manner of his return was also stunning, because it wasn't Young Pere fighting. No other man Shem had watched in his many years in the army moved quite like Perrin when he held a sword. No one could ever match his speed and ability, not even his grandson. General Shin had taken over those swords to save his grandson, the soldiers, the Rescatars, and one new mother and her baby.

Shem found himself almost smiling as he thought about Versa and her daughter. Nothing was sweeter than watching Versa gaze at her baby on Young Pere's chest. That's when he knew. Everyone must have known, if they were watching. Shem just hoped there would still be enough time for them.

From the cover of the trees he watched as Peto lay down on one side of Young Pere, and Lilla on the other side. She reached up and placed a hand on Young Pere's shoulder. She wouldn't be letting go of him for weeks—if there *were* weeks. Between the doting of Lilla and Versa, Young Pere wouldn't have a moment of solitude for a very long time. That was probably just as well.

Shem looked around for a private spot. Among more than eighty thousand people, that was rather difficult to do. Still, it was amazingly quiet. Even the littlest children were terrified but exhausted enough to sleep.

The entire mood at the tableland had shifted when the Salemites saw the soldiers coming. Suddenly it was all real. Everyone had rushed to the edge to see the army march in, then retreated to their campsites and exchanged looks of trepidation.

They spent the rest of the evening soberly, talking in hushed tones, occasionally weeping, sometimes quietly singing, but everyone worrying. Shem knew many adults weren't sleeping but were running questions over in their minds to which he had no answers.

"How much longer, Guide?"

"What happens next?"

"What *exactly* does the Last Day mean?"

"Is it the end of *everything?*"

"Guide, will there even *be* a tomorrow night?"

"Do we all just . . . *die?*"

Shem had just shrugged helplessly at each question and gave the same answer: "The Creator will provide for us, somehow."

The Deliverer would have much better answers when he finally arrived.

Now, as Shem looked over the quiet tableland, there was only the sound of distant baby cries here and there, and down in the valley were the dim sounds of thousands of soldiers sharpening swords, singing crude songs, and occasionally shouting. By the time dark had fallen, the count was at forty-five thousand, six hundred, with more soldiers still coming in. The valley was nearly full.

Fortunately very few of the soldiers' noises traveled up to the site, another thing for which Shem was grateful. But as for tomorrow? He had the same questions as his people. He was surrounded by tens of thousands of people, but no one could help him. Just when he needed the support of his wife and best friends, they were taken from him. And it was all his fault. It was his test. His own perfectly calculated, horrible test, which he was failing.

He'd never understood what people meant when they said they 'lost faith.' He'd never had a day in his life when he didn't believe in the Creator. But tonight he knew what people meant. He believed the Creator, he just didn't believe *in himself* to recognize His promptings. Maybe he'd been acting all these years on his desires, not the Creator's.

Like so many others in Salem, Shem Zenos had lost faith in the guide. He just couldn't see how it could end well. There was no way—

SHEM, SHEM—ENOUGH ALREADY! WILL YOU FINALLY HEAR ME?

Shem startled and looked around, but no one was near.

COME ON, SHEM! YOU KNOW MY VOICE. YOU'VE HEARD IT SO OFTEN.

"Perrin," Shem finally acknowledged him with equal parts of joy and dread. "I know it's you, but I can't, I can't . . . Do you have *any idea* what I've—"

YOU ARE ONE HARD MAN TO REACH. I'VE BEEN TRYING ALL DAY, AND CALLA'S BEEN BY YOUR SIDE EVERY MOMENT, BUT YOU WON'T FEEL HER EITHER. WHY ARE YOU DOING THIS TO YOURSELF?

He couldn't hold back his tears. "Why would she want to be near me? Tell her I'm sorry. I'm so sorry. I should have looked for her, she should have been first in my mind, but instead I took Mahrree . . . Perrin, and I'm so sorry about that as well. I just *left* her there, like a coward, to face Lemuel alone. I should have—"

SHEM, I KNOW WHAT YOU DID. I SAW IT ALL. YOU GAVE ME BACK MY WIFE! SHE FULFILLED THE PROPHECY BECAUSE YOU BROUGHT HER THERE. SHE'S BEEN BY MY SIDE ALMOST CONSTANTLY SINCE THEN. I'M NOT ANGRY WITH YOU. IN FACT, I WISH YOU COULD'VE DONE IT SOONER. AND SHEM, YOUR WIFE CERTAINLY ISN'T ANGRY WITH YOU, EITHER. IS THAT WHY YOU WON'T LISTEN TO HER? DO YOU KNOW WHY CALLA WAS UP HERE? WHY SHE DIED?

He didn't move, waiting to hear the worst Perrin could reveal.

SHE WANTED TO SEE HER SERGEANT MAJOR IN ACTION, SHEM. AND SHE DID, AND SHE WAS VERY IMPRESSED.

He didn't know how to respond to that.

DO YOU KNOW WHY ELSE SHE FOLLOWED YOU? BECAUSE SHE WAS SUPPOSED TO, BECAUSE IT WAS HER LAST DAY—AS IT WAS ALWAYS MEANT

TO BE. AND ONLY BY LEAVING ALL THOSE WHO PROTECTED AND LOVED HER SO WELL COULD THE CREATOR TAKE HER HOME. YOU DID NOTHING WRONG, SHEM. YOU NEVER HAVE. EVERYTHING HAS HAPPENED PRECISELY AS IT SHOULD, BECAUSE YOU HAVE ALWAYS LISTENED AND OBEYED.

He held his head in his hands, not daring to believe Perrin but also knowing he would never lie to him.

SHEM, YOU'RE RIGHT—THIS IS PART OF YOUR TEST. BUT YOU ARE NOT ALONE. WE ARE ALL HERE TO HELP YOU. WE'VE BEEN TRYING TO HELP YOU, BUT YOU'VE JUST BEEN SO STUBBORN! YES, YOU DID SOMETHING TERRIBLE, AND YOU WERE SUPPOSED TO. YOU KILLED FOURTEEN MEN AND LET TWO WOMEN DIE, ALL IN ONE DAY. BUT IT WAS NECESSARY FOR THOSE THINGS TO HAPPEN.

YOU'RE NOT GUILTY OF ANY WRONG-DOING. YOU'RE NOT LIKE THOSE MEN. THE CREATOR'S HAND OF MERCY IS EXTENDED TO YOU.

EVEN WHEN WE'RE COMPLETELY OBEDIENT, TERRIBLE THINGS CAN HAPPEN. THAT'S PART OF LIFE. YOU MUST FORGIVE YOURSELF, RELEASE THAT GUILT. YOU NEED TO GET OVER IT, AND QUICKLY! TIME IS RAPIDLY RUNNING OUT, AND EVERYONE ON YOUR SIDE AND ON MY SIDE IS COUNTING ON YOU. SHEM, LIKE IT OR NOT, BELIEVE IT OR NOT, YOU ARE THE DELIVERER. YOU MUST ACCEPT THE TRUTH OF THAT! AND ACCEPT OUR HELP!

The words hit Shem so forcefully that they nearly knocked him off his log.

THAT HAS ALWAYS BEEN YOUR FINAL CALLING. AND YOU WILL DO ALL THAT YOU SHOULD, WE HAVE NO DOUBT. YOU'VE ALWAYS DONE THE CREATOR'S WILL. THAT'S WHY HE GAVE YOU THIS CALLING. YOU ARE STILL FAITHFUL AND PURE. SHEM, WHAT DID PAX'S PROPHECY SAY ABOUT THE LAST DAY?

He wiped the tears off his face and obediently whispered, "'On the Last Day, those who have no power shall discover the greatest power is all around them,'" he recited.

A tiny flame of hope lit inside him.

There *was* great power all around him. It was undeniable, and those who surrounded him were intensely familiar. He didn't push them away this time. They grew stronger, warmer, and he burned with their presence.

Then joy, pure joy, filled his body.

They *were* fine. All three of them: Perrin, Mahrree, and especially Calla. Shem felt the sensation of her kissing his cheek as she did so many times before, and he wouldn't have been surprised to know her arms were wrapped around him.

He closed his eyes in the intensity of the sensation, of her constant love and worry for him. Death didn't change her. She was still there loving him, pushing him on, holding him up.

He smiled and sobbed the next line. "'On the Last Day, those who stayed true to The Plan will be delivered as the Destroyer comes.'"

Do you have any power, Shem? Any weapons?

"No, Perrin," he whispered, still feeling hope in spite of his answer.

Do you have a Deliverer?

Shem swallowed hard. "I guess so." He felt Calla even closer, as if she occupied the same space as he did.

Not 'I guess so.' He heard Perrin chastise him. *You do! Now, do you have a Destroyer?*

"Not yet."

What's the last line of the prophecy, Shem?

"'I have created this Test, I have given this Plan, and I will reward my faithful children.'"

Whose Test and Plan is this, Shem?

"The Creator's."

And is He going to reward the faithful with a solution?

"That's what I've been waiting for, Perrin."

Will you accept the Creator's solution and the comfort He is sending you? The 'comfort' is me, by the way, in case you haven't figured that out yet. Calla and Mahrree are here only to tag along.

Shem snorted. It was the closest sound to a laugh he had made in days. "Yes, Perrin. I'm tired of grieving. I want to accept forgiveness, I want to lose my guilt, and I *want* to feel comfort. Even if it is just *you.*"

The cosmos chuckled.

Well, Shem, the Creator and I have been discussing things. And Shem, we have a plan . . .

For the first time in days, Shem smiled.

The 37th Day of Planting

It was well before dawn when Peto woke up.

Immediately he put his hand up on Young Pere's chest and sighed when he felt his son's warm body and steady heartbeat. He sat up and saw in the dim light of the coming morning that Lilla was still on the other side of their sleeping son, her hand on his arm.

No matter what was coming, *Young Pere was home.*

Last night, when the two of them went into Shem's tent, there was dark heaviness that seemed determined to drag his son below the ground. Never before had Peto felt such a terrible and focused power. As Young Pere tried to tell his father about leaving Salem, it seemed as if the Refuser himself was there, trying one last time to keep Young Pere in his grasp.

But Young Pere was resolved to beat it, and he had his father's help. Not until they prayed for the strength of the Creator did the darkness finally vanish and Young Pere found himself able to lay before his father all that had happened.

Peto wept along with him, overwhelmed by the guilt, grief, and fear his son had to endure.

But now it was over, a memory which could no longer hurt him but instead serve as a reminder of just how far he'd come and how completely the Creator was healing him.

By the time Young Pere left Shem's tent last night, there was lightness and joy in his eyes that was unlike anything Peto had ever seen before in someone he had counseled. Even now a profound peace rested on his sleeping form.

Young Pere was going to be just fine. *Better* than 'just fine,' Peto was sure.

He got up quietly and picked his way around the family sleeping on the ground. Worried about the guide, he walked over to Shem's tent but stopped before he lifted the flap.

A figure standing high on top of one of the temple's ruined walls caught his attention. He made his way over to the wall and looked up, blinking in surprise.

"Shem?" he called up in a whisper. "What is it?"

Shem looked down at Peto, and even though the jagged wall was over ten feet high where Shem stood, putting Shem's eyes more than sixteen feet away from him, Peto could see his resolve. "Rector, we need to be ready today."

Peto's mouth went dry but he managed to say, "Of course, Guide. Ready for what?"

Guide Zenos studied him for a moment, and Peto could feel something different about him. This was no longer simply Shem. This was, most definitely, the Deliverer. Confident, powerful, and wholly pure, as if the Creator Himself was conducting Guide Zenos, just as General Shin had conducted Young Pere and his sword the morning before.

Without a word, Guide Zenos shifted his gaze to survey the valley filled with fifty thousand soldiers beginning to awake.

Peto understood. There were no more soldiers pouring into the valley. Everyone was there.

"Rector Shin," Guide Zenos said, his voice resonating with additional layers, "it's time to wake up the Salemites. Idumea is here."

Then he said the words that made Peto's neck hair prickle.

"It's the Last Day."

An hour later as the sun crept over the peaks, the vast tableland was a bustle of activity. The guide's assistants had awakened all the people in their sections with the instructions to eat quickly and be ready to follow the directions of the guide.

The tension in the air was tangible but no one was in a panic. Parents took care of little children, grandparents helped as they could, older children and single adults folded blankets and straightened up campsites although why, they weren't sure. Everyone glanced nervously at each other as they tried to swallow down their breakfasts of dried fruits and hard breads, wondering what would be coming next.

Guide Zenos remained standing alone on the wall of the temple ruin in sight of all the Salemites, and with a clear view of what was happening below him in the valley. Frequently Salemites looked up to him for reassurance as the guide observed the soldiers in the valley finishing their rations and forming ranks.

Zenos's fierce and determined demeanor was such that not even his children dared interrupt his focus. Only Peto could break into his concentration enough to get his attention.

"Guide?" he called up to him. "All the assistants have reported. Everyone has eaten so . . . what do you wish for us to do now?"

Guide Zenos pulled his eyes away from the valley and looked down at Peto. "Rector Shin, I want everyone behind the temple ruins. There are a few hundred in front, including our families, but the area needs to be cleared. I want the children far away. What's coming is not meant for their eyes. We have less than an hour, but if they stay behind the temple, they'll be safe."

Peto nodded gravely at the guide's severe expression. He glanced at Cephas who was writing down his words. Two of the assistants stood nearby as well, also writing down the instructions.

"Four copies, each of you," Peto said, "to distribute to the other assistants. Cephas, find a horse and ride the message to the back. Tell them to please make room, if they can. We don't have a lot of time."

Peto turned back to the guide as the men around him scrambled and started issuing orders. "The word's going out, Guide."

Zenos nodded. "Rector Shin, as for the instruction I just gave, it doesn't apply to the descendants of Perrin Shin or Shem Zenos."

"What?" Peto asked, startled. He looked behind him to see Jaytsy, Deck, Lilla, and several of the children coming to join him. "Are we supposed to stay in *front* of the site?"

"Only those who want to, Peto."

Peto looked at his wife and shrugged.

The rest of the family shrugged back.

Peto turned back to Guide Zenos. "Why?"

"I'm not entirely sure," he said, his tentative answer sounding more like his old self, "but some of you may want a front row seat. Lemuel will be coming."

"Then I want him to see me!" Young Pere called weakly, hunched and hobbling over with Relf's help.

Boskos followed, shaking his head. "Young Pere, I just told you to not even *try to sit up* for a few days! Obviously you haven't changed much," he muttered as he came to support Young Pere's other side. "I knew I gave you too much Pain Tea."

But Young Pere wasn't listening to his cousin's reprimands as he lumbered to the ruin. "I want General Thorne to see me standing with you, Guide!"

Relf nodded to his father. "I'll stay with him, Papa, and send my family behind the ruin."

"I'll stay, too," Peto decided. "I want Lemuel to see Young Pere already has a father."

"Then I'm staying too!" Lilla insisted. "Let him see who his mother really is."

"And I'll stay as well," Jaytsy said.

But Shem was shaking his head. "Lilla, Jaytsy, I don't know that you really want to see this—"

"I'll stay with them, Guide," Deck offered. "I can take them away if necessary. I want to see Thorne, too. Let him realize I'm still around."

By now the entire Shin, Briter, and Zenos families had gathered at the front of the temple, as the hundreds of people who camped in front of it were hastily moving behind.

"Well, I don't want to see *anything*," Kanthi Shin said nervously. "I can take some of the little ones with me."

"Good," Salema said firmly to her cousin, handing her Plump Perrin. "Take my three boys. I want to stay. Lek?"

Lek shook his head but said, "And . . . I'm staying with you."

Boskos turned to his wife. "Take the children and get to the back of the valley with Kanthi. I may be needed up here."

"No," Noria said. "Please, Bos, isn't there someplace we can hide with the children but still watch? Uncle Peto?"

Peto searched the area and saw a spot several dozen paces away. "Up there. That pile of rock on the slope. There are enough concealing shrubs and trees you can stay up there but keep the little ones sheltered."

Jori nodded. "That's where I'll go with Con and the children." She looked expectantly at her sister.

Lori, always the braver one, said, "I want to stay. Take my four, please?"

"I'll help," Morah Shin offered. "I don't want to be here!"

Jori's husband Con tipped his head to his brother Sam. "I'll go help with the women and children. Who else is coming with us to the rocks?"

Meiki's husband Clyde raised his hand. "I'll help you." Meiki clutched his spindly arm, eager to follow.

Five minutes later, more than half of the Shin and Zenos descendants over age twelve stood at the temple ruins on the long and wide cracked stone that led to the wall where Shem stood.

The men insisted the women and teenaged children take the top step next to the remnants of the wall and columns, while the husbands and brothers stood in front of them on the second step, with two more empty steps below.

Against the broken wall stood Salema, Jaytsy, Lilla, Lori, Hycy, Sewzi, Hogal, Kew, and Nool. In front of them were Lek, Boskos, Zaddick, Deck, Young Pere, Peto, Sam, Wes, Relf, Cambo, Bubba, Holling, Viddrow, and Barnos.

They watched anxiously as the rest of the children followed Con and Jori up to the collection of rock and shrubs that Peto prayed would be big enough to shelter them all. There were too many gaps for innocent eyes to see whatever carnage may be coming, and Peto prayed silently that something else could help shield them.

All around them, people continued to scurry to the valley behind, leaving the land in front of the ancient temple empty to the edge of the cliff, except for abandoned tents and blankets.

Relf jogged over to one of the empty camps and brought back an armful of bedrolls.

"Here, Young Pere," he said, laying them on the wide stone steps. "You should sit down."

Boskos said, "You should *lie* down. You look as good as can be expected but I don't want you on your feet. You've lost so much blood. If you insist on being here you need to be resting."

"No," Young Pere said, "I need to stand. I want to be ready."

Peto put his hand on his shoulder and Young Pere nearly crumpled under the pressure. "Sit for now, son, then I promise we'll stand you up for . . . whatever."

Young Pere began to nod when a movement behind his father caught his eye. "Versa?"

She was struggling to make her way against the tide of people leaving the ruins, the baby tucked in her arm as she pushed through the crowd.

Guide Zenos noticed her. "Versa, you're the *last* person Lemuel should see," he declared, "and the *second* to last person who should be on her feet!"

Versa nodded apologetically. "I know, Guide."

"And where are your mother and sister?" he asked sharply.

She shrugged guiltily but without any intention of backing down. "Lost somewhere back there. But Creer knows I'm here. He'll explain it to my mother. Please, Guide, just let me sit over there with the others?" She gestured to the rock outcropping. "I'll stay out of the way."

Up until that point, Young Pere's vision was going gray again, knowing that he had pushed his injured body too far trying to get to the ancient site. While he wasn't feeling much pain, it was obvious he had no strength.

But he had to be at the ancient temple. It felt important.

Dizzy and swaying, he was on the verge of collapse until he heard Versa's request to stay nearby and watch.

"No!" he exclaimed, and from somewhere deep he yanked up enough grit to struggle down the large stone steps and hobble painfully over to her. Peto caught up to him and stepped under his arm to support him as he reached her.

"I want you as far away from here as possible!" he croaked at Versa. "Take the baby and go!"

But she didn't budge. "I want to watch. I want to see my father, but I promise he won't see me."

"Versa," Young Pere began, then looked over at his father still standing next to him, holding him up. "Um, Papa could you . . . ?"

Immediately he understood. "Uh, hold on," Peto said. He turned his back to the two of them, then patted his shoulder to signal for Young Pere to support himself there. "I'm officially no longer here."

"Thank you, Papa," Young Pere said, bracing himself on his father who was rock solid.

Versa smiled gratefully at Peto's back.

"Versa," Young Pere began again in an urgent whisper, "please, just go. I'll feel so much better if I know you're out of danger."

"And I'll feel so much better seeing *you*," she whispered back. "You made me a promise, remember? I expect you to fulfill it. I'm going to watch to make sure you survive to do so!"

His chest constricted, but not because of any pain or injuries. She was referring to his promise to find her the best husband Salem had to offer. But this seemed a strange time to bring all of that up.

"Versa, this might take some time which I don't think we have anymore. I just found out Cephas is already courting someone. But there's Zaddick—"

"I don't want your cousins, Young Pere, or any of your brothers." She gripped his arm where there were no bandages. "I already know what I want, and I want *you!*" She blushed. "And that's what *you* want, too."

Young Pere blinked at her in disbelief, unsure that he'd heard her correctly. Did she mean—

Versa smiled shyly. "You know I'm right," she whispered, "and you already know those are my favorite words. Please, Young Pere, let me stay *with you*."

He sighed and ran a finger tenderly over the baby's head, smoothing down her fine blond hair while she slept. He understood. Versa felt vulnerable, and was probably the most defenseless Salemite there, next to him. She was desperate to feel protected, and in her own compromised condition didn't seem to realize he wasn't exactly in a position to help her again.

But his family was strong, his brothers and cousins powerful, and they could shield her from the approaching army. That's what she really desired: the guide, the rector, his family—not him.

Besides, no matter what *he* wanted, he had to be honest: he and Versa together? It'd never work.

Still she stared into his eyes, pitifully hopeful.

"Versa, you know a lot about me, but you don't know everything. Maybe if we had more time—"

"I know enough" she said, firming her grip on his arm. "I've seen enough. I don't care who you used to be. I care only about who you are today. And what I see today," her voice became low and earnest, "is a man willing to sacrifice even his life to protect those he cares for. You're the best man the world *or* Salem can offer me. And I refuse to run away and leave you here. That's not my way."

Young Pere chuckled softly and looked into her blue eyes. "No, that's definitely not your way. Versa, believe me, there's *nothing* I want more than you and the baby, but—"

That's when Peto noticed that the conversation behind him—the one that he was trying politely to ignore—had gone silent.

The rest of the family had moved away as best they could along the rock steps just above Young Pere and Versa to try to give them some privacy, but they could still hear snippets of their quiet conversation, especially now that the crowd was fully behind the temple.

Many of the family now turned around to see why they had stopped talking.

Peto saw Jaytsy's eyebrows go up and Lilla's jaw drop. Relf and Boskos broke into grins. The rest of Young Pere's siblings and cousins wore expressions that ranged from stunned to amused.

Peto mouthed to his family, *"Are they kissing?"*

They nodded back and turned away with smiles, except for Lilla who continued to stare.

"Lilla!" Peto whispered sharply at her.

Lilla shook herself a little and finally shifted her gaze elsewhere.

Peto felt the weight on his shoulder increase as Young Pere's position shifted, and the silence behind him continue for longer than he expected for a first kiss.

Maybe it wasn't a *first* kiss.

For lack of something better to do, Peto glanced up at Shem who, for the first time in days, had a real smile on his face as he shifted his gaze to spy on the couple.

Shem winked at Peto, and Peto winked back.

Finally, Peto heard words behind him again.

"Ah, Versa, I know it's useless to fight you. You're just tougher than me," Young Pere whispered.

She giggled.

"If Uncle Shem says it's all right, go up to the rocks with the others. But please, Versa, be careful." Young Pere cupped her face. "And take good care of *our* little girl."

Peto turned his head subtly to watch Versa from the corner of his eye.

Her eyes were filling with tears, and she looked up to the wall to see Shem's response.

He nodded to her.

She beamed back at Young Pere. "Stay low, all right, Young Pere? I heard the general tends to swing high, and I couldn't bear to lose you already."

Young Pere caught her again in a quick kiss then released her to kiss the baby on the head. "Don't worry. I'll stay low. And Versa?" he whispered, "I would never leave you."

"I know," she whispered back. "You're a breed all your own." She kissed him one last time.

When she finally pulled away, Young Pere said, "I'll get someone to walk you over to the family. As you can tell, I'm not exactly in shape to do it myself, and I'm not sure Papa can ignore us much longer, although he's been shockingly quiet for the past few minutes."

Peto snorted softly and tried not to chuckle for fear he'd throw Young Pere off balance.

Next to Peto's ear, Young Pere called out, "Relf?" Leaning heavily on his father, he pivoted to see if his oldest brother could come help Versa, but he stopped short when he realized all of his family on the stone stairs was watching.

And *had* been watching.

A few of his cousins snorted.

Peto twisted to put his arm around his son, and to send warning glares to everyone else.

But no one was looking at Peto; they were all staring at Versa and Young Pere.

Peto felt Young Pere grow weaker, realizing that everyone—including his mother—had just witnessed him kissing Versula Thorne three times.

"Uhhh," was all Young Pere could utter, until his mother began to smirk. "Yeah," he said, understanding he had some explaining to do about just how well he knew Versa. "Uh Relf? Would you please help Versa to the rocks?"

Relf grinned. "Of course," he said, already walking over to them. "After all, I told Versa the day I met her that we were practically *family.*"

Versa smiled, and Peto remembered that Relf had reassured the Thornes at the First Resting Station where he had volunteered to escort them to Salem.

But for some reason Young Pere stared at Relf, looking quite startled. "You told her *what*?"

"I'll explain it later," Relf said. He took Versa's pack and the baby and led her to the rock outcropping.

The rest of the Shin-Briter-Zenos families had just secured themselves among the rocks and shrubs when they looked over to the temple ruin in time to see Versa and Young Pere kissing. Now every sibling, cousin, niece and nephew of Young Pere stared in amazement as Relf carefully guided a frail Versa across the terrain to the sheltered area.

"I don't think Versa's going to be interested in Zaddick," Tabbit Briter whispered to Banu as they noticed their cousin Young Pere was watching Versa's progress.

Banu giggled. "Exactly *when* did he meet her? Wasn't it just two days ago?"

"It was!" their cousin Jori answered, shaking her head but smiling.

"What in the world could have happened in just *two days*?" Con whispered to his wife. "I know Shins move quickly, but that's *got* to be record time."

She elbowed him.

Versa grew redder as she neared the family whose smiles grew wider as she approached.

Jori kept shaking her head and held out her hands to take the baby from Relf as Versa struggled up to a crevice next to her. Con pulled her up the rest of the way and Clyde took her pack from Relf.

"I know my little brother has a great many stories to tell us all someday," Jori said, sniffing the newborn baby, "but already I think this will be the *most interesting one*." She gave Versa a deliberate look.

Versa smiled apprehensively.

Jori leaned toward her. "So you better tell me your version *first* so I'll know the truth and can later correct Young Pere's explanation of what just went on over there."

Versa relaxed and laughed along with the rest of the family.

Young Pere didn't know what was being said over at the rock outcropping, but seeing Versa laughing and now situated by his sister Jori who was cradling the newborn, he was satisfied Versa was safe. He was grateful for the few minutes watching her afforded him so he could try to recover from the realization that his *entire family* had just watched him kiss Versa Thorne, *three times*.

Young Pere slowly turned to his father, who was trying unsuccessfully not to smirk.

"Uh, I suppose I should explain," Young Pere said in a low voice that grew faster as he spoke. "You see, I did help her birth the baby, but before that we spent all morning and afternoon walking and talking, and then I stayed by her side for the evening and *night*—it was all innocent; we were just being practical because it was cold and she and the baby needed to be kept warm—and everything I told you last night I practiced on her first. Well, *almost everything*. Some things I didn't feel like sharing with *her*, as I'm sure you can imagine—"

"Young Pere, it's all right," Peto said, cutting off his nervous rambling. He lead him slowly up the stone stairs and back to the blankets. The family grinned and occasionally giggled in his direction.

"I've gotten to know Versa quite well myself," Peto told him privately. "Maybe even better than you. I was there the day her former husband Anoki left with her sister Priscill. As I sat with her, I wondered who could ever make her smile again. I never expected her to trust another man, and I *never* would've thought *you* would actually make her giggle. She giggled, right? I wasn't just imagining that?"

Young Pere blushed.

"Don't worry, I approve completely," Peto assured him. "It's rather sudden, and we haven't been exactly encouraging such last minute attachments, but according to what I didn't mean to overhear you suggesting to her, I suppose she *does* belong over there with the rest of the family."

The stray thought that Versa may have been family all along—Puggah's granddaughter—drifted through Young Pere's mind, but no one else knew that, no one else *needed* to know that possibility, and besides, she was only a *half* cousin, *maybe*, so it could work—

No, Young Pere had to be honest, with himself and everyone else. He was right earlier; it wouldn't work.

"Papa, she doesn't know what she wants," he whispered miserably. "She's too emotional to think clearly. She just had a baby, and I delivered it and then I helped her escape? *Of course* she's going to think she loves me."

Peto turned to him. "What are you saying?" he whispered. "Young Pere, you *can't* do that to her! You just told her—"

"I know what I said," Young Pere cut him off calmly. "And I meant it. I would never leave her. She's . . . she's an amazing woman, Papa. The way she thinks and feels, what she went through . . . I could be fascinated with her for the rest of my life and a thousand years beyond.

"But Papa," he continued, "when she gets to know me better she'll realize she's settling for less, again. *She'll* want to leave *me*. I don't know what's going to happen after today, but she has a little girl who's going to need a father. And I'm going to find her that perfect man. Zaddick still hasn't found the right woman, has he?" He whispered so that his cousins and siblings couldn't overhear, although a few were leaning ludicrously to listen in. "I think I now know why," he said as Peto lowered him down to the blanket spread out on the stone stairs.

He lay down with a grimace, closed his eyes, and covered them with his arm.

"Zaddick always wanted someone with a little more spice and kick," Young Pere whispered to his father, who hovered to hear him. "That's definitely Versa. And she really admires Uncle Shem. I remember Muggah saying Zaddick's a lot like Shem when he was younger, and Shem would be the grandfather of the baby. Versa would like that. I just can't let her be disappointed again, Papa."

Peto smiled down upon his son. "She won't be, Young Pere," he whispered. "She won't be this time."

A few minutes later Cephas returned with the news that there was enough room for everyone behind the temple site. He was dismayed to see his family in front of it.

"Really," he said to his mother, "you don't have to stay here."

"We know," Jaytsy assured him. "Shem said we would want to be here. We want General Thorne to see us. Maybe if he finally sees the truth, he'll end this more peaceably."

Cephas nodded in reluctant agreement and saw his cousin Barnos gesturing for him to stand next to him. But Cephas also noticed Young Pere on the ground, his arm still covering his eyes.

He crouched next to him. "Young Pere, you don't have to be here. I know of a safe place by the trees. Let me take you there."

Young Pere let his arm fall off his face and he looked at his cousin. "Trying to get rid of me already?"

Cephas groaned. "No, no, no Young Pere! That's not what I meant at all! Believe me, I—"

Young Pere chuckled and caught his cousin's arm. "I know. I'm just teasing you, I'm sorry. I should have been more like you, in so many ways. You've always been the best example. But there's one thing you lack, Cephas: *a sense of humor*."

Cephas relaxed and smiled at his cousin. "Then you better not get hurt anymore so you can lecture *me* on that."

He squeezed his cousin's hand and went to join Barnos, who whispered something into his ear.

Cephas's eyes grew large and he slapped a hand over his mouth. He automatically looked over at the rock outcropping, although Barnos frantically grabbing his arm made it obvious that he had just told him to *not* stare at Versa Thorne. He was about to say something admonishing to Cephas when something even more intriguing caught his attention.

Everyone heard the three sharp horn blasts that came from the valley below.

They looked to Young Pere for an explanation.

He struggled to sit up.

"Attention. That's the signal to look to the middle of the field. The general's going to address the soldiers before the attack."

"I don't think so," Cambo said, watching Shem on the wall.

Guide Zenos was studying the formation of the soldiers below him. He waited for the right moment then, in a booming voice, bellowed, "Lemuel Thorne!"

His voice carried down to the valley, but was lost in the scuffle of thousands of men turning to the general whose aide just blew the horn.

The guide waited for a moment before shouting again. "Lemuel Thorne!"

Down in the valley, General Thorne, astride his horse to be more visible, thought he heard a sound in the distance, but he ignored it. The second time he heard it again more distinctly because the men were quieting.

It sounded like . . .

But he brushed it off.

He pivoted his mount in place to make sure he had the attention of all his men. Then he opened his mouth to speak—

"*Captain* Lemuel Thorne!"

While it wasn't loud, it was very distinct.

The general slowly, defiantly, turned around to face the cliff side where the voice drifted down to him. His shoulder twitched.

Every man around him fell silent, straining to listen.

"*Captain* Lemuel Thorne! I know you can hear me. Answer me!"

General Thorne glared before shouting back, "There's no *Captain* Thorne here! Identify yourself!"

"According to the rules of the Army of Idumea," came back the voice, thin but clear, "you were never promoted out of captaincy. Only a higher ranking officer can promote you. You, therefore, are still only a captain, Lemuel!"

Several of the soldiers muttered to each other, but stopped as the general looked quickly around before answering. "Whoever you are, I *AM* the Army of Idumea! Those rules changed, years ago. Now identify yourself!"

"That's not the way you address your superiors, Captain."

Something in Lemuel's face changed slightly.

"Who are you?" he demanded. "I know Perrin Shin is dead. I spat on the boulder marking his grave. There's no one else here greater than me!"

"Lemuel," the voice rang down, condescendingly, "I still have more years of experience. Therefore, in a battle I have seniority. And, in case you've forgotten, I never turned in my resignation or picked up my last pay. Did you bring it with you?"

In spite of themselves, several soldiers sniggered nervously. They were quickly silenced by glares, slaps, or in a few cases, a well-placed fist.

Poe Hili, standing next to Thorne's horse, put the clues together, and it made his eyes bulge.

General Thorne's chest began to heave.

"You know who I am, Lemuel," came the voice even louder. "Tell your soldiers who you're facing in battle today. They deserve to know the truth, Captain!"

Hili reached up and grabbed Thorne's good arm. "General, I know that voice! I spent many nights as a young man rebuilding a bedroom with *that voice*! You promised me that you—"

"Shut up, Poe!" Thorne snapped. He turned back to the cliff. "It doesn't matter who you are, because you won't live to see midday meal. This is *your* last chance: surrender now and it'll be easier on your women and children!"

"Lemuel, *Lemuel*," the voice carried down in a simpering manner. "Are you *really afraid* to tell your soldiers who I am? Don't they deserve to decide for themselves if they want to fight me? I already told your sergeant who came up here with fourteen men, but went back alone. But if he didn't give you the message, I will. My name is Sergeant Major Shem Zenos—"

Up at the temple ruin, they could hear the gasps from the valley below as fifty thousand soldiers caught their breath in unison.

Peto chuckled, Boskos and Zaddick grinned, and Lek shook his head. Lilla and Jaytsy smiled, and Young Pere struggled to his feet to look down at the valley where soldiers were frozen momentarily in shock.

Above the family on the stone steps, Shem continued to bellow.

"—and this is MY mountain and my people. Whoever comes here will die, Lemuel! But if your soldiers choose not to fight, I will guarantee their safety."

Down below, General Thorne couldn't deny anything anymore, especially with Hili gasping so rapidly next to him that he risked losing consciousness.

"He's alive! He's alive! He's alive," Poe panted. "You *slagging liar*, Lemuel! He's *ALIVE!*"

Thorne bent over and slapped him hard, knocking him to the ground.

"Enough from you, Poe! He won't be alive at the end of the day, *I guarantee that.*" Thorne turned back to the cliff. There was no choice, but there was still the opportunity to prevail, and with a full audience to witness his triumph.

He took a deep breath. "Shem!"

The soldiers stared at each other in astonishment. It was true. Even the general admitted his identity.

Sergeant Major Shem Zenos never died in the forest. He made it out, just as the entire Shin family had.

Thorne knew to salvage the moment. "You were lucky years ago to *narrowly* slip past me, but today your luck runs out! I will kill you myself and you can bet your last pay on that!"

A few soldiers laughed in agreement, but many others began to back away from the general. To know the Shin family had escaped years ago was one thing, but to realize their general, who had so often bragged about beheading Zenos but in reality had never done so, was something entirely different. Even his most devoted soldiers looked at the general with suspicion.

Major Twigg blinked in surprise, then blinked again as if none of the words he had been hearing were in an order he understood.

Poe, still sitting on the ground, held his head and muttered something under his breath about the color of the sky.

On the edges of the fields a few soldiers dropped their swords and ran into the trees.

"Lemuel, Lemuel," came down the voice again. "You cannot win.

This is the Last Day. Your men should know that. Jon Offra told them enough times. The battle that will be fought today will be the Creator's, and no one unworthy will survive it. Soldiers of the world! Abandon your weapons and go to the forests. I see a few have already done that. Follow them! You'll be safe there if you choose not to fight! You don't have to fight with the captain. He's done nothing but lie to you for the last twenty-seven years. I know—I've been watching. You cannot win."

"Lies?!" Thorne bellowed back, aware that some soldiers were now drifting toward the forest. Out of the corner of his eye he saw a few more run to the trees. "Shall we discuss *your* lies, Sergeant Major? You lied to the world for seventeen years! You were a Guarder all the time. Will your people up there still follow you as their leader when they know how *lecherous* you were while you were in the world? Oh, but wait! You haven't *told* them about Mahrree Shin, have you? Well I have the proof, Shem. I found *the letter*. Even Perrin knew of your feelings for her."

Back up on the cliff side, Peto and Jaytsy closed their eyes and groaned. Lek, Boskos, and Zaddick looked up at their father, nervous.

But Guide Zenos remained unmoved, listening to Thorne shout his accusations.

"I'd pull out the letter often to read to the men, Zenos!" Thorne taunted at the top of his lungs. "Great entertainment for those long rainy nights in Edge. Do you know what he said? Shall I tell all your people? Perrin said he knew you admired her from afar, Shem," the general sneered. "Even *he* saw it, just like I saw it! You had feelings for her, and Perrin wrote that when he was dead he wanted you to act on those feelings. You always loved her, didn't you? Another man's wife? Well guess what, Shem—I killed her! In front of all these soldiers as witnesses. The job the colonel should have done years ago but was too cowardly to do, I finally finished for him. And I still owe the colonel one more act of revenge, Shem. So today, I'm going to kill you too!"

"No!" a new voice rang down to the valley from the cliff side, but thin and hoarse. "He never did anything wrong! You're twisting the truth, General! Like you always did! Nothing you've ever said was true! You made up the stories!"

General Thorne scowled. "Who is that?"

On the temple wall, Guide Zenos shifted his gaze from the distant figure of Thorne to glare down at Young Pere.

His father was holding him back from rushing to the edge of the cliff. But because of Young Pere's weakened condition, even his nephew Ensio could have done the job. Already Young Pere was slumping but desperately trying to stay upright.

"Young Perrin!" Guide Zenos snapped.

His nephew looked up at him with loyal fury in his eyes.

"Young Pere," Shem's voice was calmer, "I appreciate the show of confidence, but I can handle a thorn. I pull it out and go on my way."

He turned back to the valley.

"Lemuel!" he yelled. "That's my nephew, Young Perrin Shin. The man who would never call you father, or so I was told last night by a *real* general. His real father, Peto Shin, is holding him back right now or he'd be down there to kill you himself." Shem winked at Young Pere. "This is your last warning, Lemuel. Surrender now or face the Creator."

Thorne shook his head. "Shem! Enough! Come down here and face me."

"No. The highest authority demands that you surrender now, Lemuel, or face your destruction."

"Shem, you are NOT the highest authority here!" Thorne yelled, drawing his sword and holding it high. "I am!"

"You're wrong, Thorne," Guide Zenos shouted down. "Neither of us is. But there is one here who is. Meet your Destruction."

Thorne scoffed in disgust and was just about to kick his heels into his horse when he noticed the sound. It was low and rumbling, and seemed to come from all around them.

Hili grabbed at his leg. "General! Put away the sword! The Last Day. It's true. It's all true. We're all going to die!"

Thorne kicked him off. "Hili, shut up already! The Last Day was just more of Offra's lies. And if I could find the stupid, insane man now, I'd prove to you that—" He stopped short when he heard the rumbling grow louder.

"Land tremor!" someone shouted.

"The volcano!" other men cried out.

Thorne spun his horse around to discern the origin of the sound.

Up on the temple site, they heard the noise as well. It felt like a calmer version of the steady land tremor that had awoken all of Salem three seasons ago. Behind the ruins, many people began to scream, but up on the sloping rock face to the side of the temple site, one of the descendants of the Shins and Zenoses grinned.

"Briter!" five-year-old Fennic said excitedly to his brother. "The rumbling! It sounds like Puggah singing! Remember?"

Seven-year-old Briter shook his head. "Not quite, Fenn," he said, his eyes growing large as he crouched behind a thick bush. "Not quite."

His fourteen-year-old aunt Banu wrapped her arms around the two boys and cowered with them.

At the temple site, Peto and Deck exchanged worried glances as the rumbling grew louder. The men turned to look at their wives behind them, their eyes huge with fear as they glanced around. Lek bravely stepped up and back to Salema to shield her, but from what he wasn't sure.

The rumbling grew louder until the ground began to tremble steadily under their feet. Young Pere grabbed Peto for support and Deck caught his other arm.

Peto twisted to look at Shem behind him, worried that he was about to fall, and gasped. "Look!"

Guide Zenos remained on the ruined wall, but the shaking wasn't disturbing his balance. Next to him, an intense point of light began to grow as if another sun was developing right next to him. The light rapidly increased in size until it became the form of a man who stood nearly as tall as Shem.

Everyone around the temple site gasped in surprise.

Shem didn't move but seemed aware of the presence beside him. The man appeared to be in his early twenties and wore a plain but bright white shirt and trousers. He put a hand solidly on Guide Zenos's shoulder and looked out over the valley with him. Other lights began to form behind him and to the left of him.

Now all of the families behind the temple stared in amazement as several more bright lights formed around Shem and grew to take distinct male shapes. One of the bright men's features became immediately recognizable.

"Guide Gleace!" Peto gasped.

"It is!" Jaytsy cried.

The man who had Guide Gleace's face, but a much younger version of it, heard them and looked down with a broad smile. "Peto, didn't I promise you would see The Day?" They felt his voice as much as they heard it.

Peto's knees grew weak and he struggled to stay upright to support Young Pere, who also lost all strength.

Lek was already on the ground with his wife leaning against him, staring up in amazement as the spirits—

No.

No, they were too bright and tangible to be *just* spirits, and they were definitely something more than mere people.

Each one was solid, a guide of the Creator, coming to stand around the last guide. It didn't seem to matter that there was no floor or support under them.

Shouts of surprise arose from behind the temple site as everyone recognized who was coming to their aid.

"Papa, what's happening?" Young Pere gasped as the ground continued to rumble.

Peto looked around him quickly, seeing the startled looks of his children, nieces, and nephews.

"It's *really* the Last Day," he whispered in awe. "No one will miss it."

He looked behind him at Lilla, who was weeping with Jaytsy.

A new understanding filled him to near bursting. "Lilla, Jaytsy, Deck, everyone!" he cried. "*No one* will miss it!" He looked wildly around and saw more lights forming.

They began on both sides of the temple and rushed away from it, blinking on by the hundreds, thousands, now hundreds of thousands, even more than a million across the mountain tops. They encircled the entire valley until the lights met at the far southern end only moments later.

The cries of joy and excitement erupting up on the ancient site were instead shouts of terror in the valley as the soldiers looked up on the mountain tops and saw each light developing into a distinct man or woman. The personages flashed into existence until the entire valley was ringed in a white, fiery glow.

Peto, barely able to breathe, turned to his wife and sister. A form between them was taking shape.

"Mother!" Jaytsy cried and everyone spun to see Mahrree grinning at them. She wore a white dress and her light brown hair flowed around her shoulders. She was certainly not the grandmother her grandchildren remembered, appearing instead to be their age as she took her daughter and daughter-in-law's hands.

"Keep watching—you haven't seen anything yet!" she told them, her voice young and powerful. She squeezed their hands and nodded at Deck and Peto in front of them.

Another light developed, and Peto held his breath in anticipation. But the man who appeared in front of him wasn't his father. Instead, it was a young man with pale eyes just like his and hair to match.

He smiled at Peto and took his hand. "Finally I get to shake my grandson's hand!" He looked up at Jaytsy and beamed at her.

Peto could barely get out the words, "Grandfather Cephas?!" when he saw two more lights appearing around Deck.

Already Jaytsy was sobbing as Deck's parents appeared on either side of him. They caught him as he collapsed in astonishment and grinned at each other as they pushed him upright.

"When this is over, Deckett," his mother Sewzi said, kissing his cheek as his father Cambozola gripped his arm, "we want to meet each of our grandchildren and great-grandchildren!"

"Especially that one," Cambozola pointed at his startled grandson Cambo. "What kind of nickname is that—Cambo? Bozola would have been much better." To his son, he said, "They call you Deck now? Did some cow knock your 'ett' off?" He grinned at his joke.

Jaytsy snorted, remembering how loud and boisterous her father-in-law could be, and how stunned her grandchildren would be to learn that. Deck was speechless as he stared at his parents, tears of joy building in his eyes.

What was happening in front of the temple was occurring in the valley behind as well. Cries of joy and surprise rose up as ancestors appeared in front, around, and behind each person, hugging them, holding them, and picking them up off the ground.

Peto, now clinging to his Grandfather Cephas who easily held him up, saw Hycymum Peto patting the cheek of a very startled Hycy Hifadhi.

"You even look a little like me!" she exclaimed.

Hycy nodded slowly as she looked at her namesake, tears streaming down her face.

Peto looked back up to Shem, biting his lip in anticipation, hoping to see who might be there. Lilla looked up as well and let out a shriek of delight.

Despite being surrounded by the Guides, there was room next to Shem for one more figure. Calla, with her long black hair, looked radiant and very young next to her graying husband. She stood watching with him, his hand grasping hers tightly but his concentration still focused on the army below as the lights continued to form all over the mountain tops.

Calla gazed over at the rock outcropping and smiled at her daughters who screamed in elation. Below her, Lek and Salema wept and held each other as Zaddick and Boskos stared up in awe at their mother.

Shem never moved but continued to watch the view below him, while Calla kept her other hand firmly on his arm as if she'd never again let go.

Peto dropped his eyes to look at his mother. He vaguely remembered her that way when he was a boy, and she blurred as his eyes grew wet. But she was different in many brilliant ways. For one, she was significantly taller and broader, as if her body finally matched the size of her spirit. Nearly as large as her husband had been, Mahrree was beaming at each of her grandchildren who stared back at her in wonder and at the scene growing around them.

Up by the sloping rock, another dozen figures were appearing. Peto, speechless, turned to watch. He recognized one of them immediately and nodded to Jaytsy to look.

A young Joriana Shin smiled back at them before she patted her namesake on her shoulder. Jori stared at her great-grandmother and slowly reached out to touch her face. Joriana laughed and caught her in a hug.

Several other people appeared and joined her as well to protect their young descendants, and Peto realized there would be many more introductions later. He looked up at Lilla just in time to see her embracing her father.

Mahrree caught Peto's eye. "Next to Joriana by the rocks is Kanthi and her husband Viddrow, then your great-grandparents Pere and Banu. And at the very end there, standing back just a bit, that's Lek Shin, the first general whose name you wrote down so many years ago. Behind him is his sergeant and my ancestor, Barnos Eno. Actually, Barnos Zenos."

Peto couldn't take it all in. The faces, more than twenty now, were distantly familiar as if he knew them from a dream he was struggling to recall.

His gaze locked briefly with Lek Shin, a young, slender man with gentle, narrow eyes and a hesitant smile. The first general wasn't like anything Peto had imagined for all those years, and here he was, worthy to be there that day.

Peto wondered momentarily about his wife Lorixania, if any of the dozens of faces surrounding his family might be her, and then he wondered about Barnos Zenos, who wore a slight smirk as if he were surprised to be there. He caught Peto's eye and raised an eyebrow, rather cockily.

Suddenly Peto wanted to know Lek and Barnos's story, suspecting that maybe they were friends during their lives, based now on how they stood together.

But that would have to wait, because his thoughts went to more recent relatives.

"I know who you're *really* waiting to see, Peto," Mahrree said quietly.

He couldn't answer her, still awestruck that his mother was standing there, powerful, radiant, larger than life, and talking as if she hadn't been dead for the past few days.

"The *wait* is almost over," she promised him. "Not everyone's here just yet. Turn around. The best is *still* yet to come!"

She looked down at Young Pere lying on the ground in shock, nodded to him, and released Jaytsy's hand to gesture to the large empty space created by the Salemites who had fled for the back of the temple ruin.

Peto spun to watch and Young Pere gasped. "LOOK!"

In front of them appeared not only one light but two, one a few feet higher than the other. Every set of eyes in front of the temple, and a few thousand more behind it, stared as the lights grew.

The lower one became a large black horse that Peto immediately recognized, and he finally found his voice. "YES!" he shouted as the light on the top took form, becoming a brawny young man. On the horse he sat, with dazzling white clothes, black hair, dark eyes, and a familiar grin.

Relf stared at the man, checked his astonished brother on the ground to make sure he was still there, then turned back to the man on the horse.

He chuckled at Relf's reaction and everyone in the area felt the sonorous sound. The rider turned the bridle-less horse to face the temple wall and he nodded at Guide Zenos.

Everyone now watched the guide.

Shem broke into a big grin. "Oh, how I've missed my brother!" he said as he wrapped an arm around his radiant wife and pulled her closer.

Perrin grinned back at him. "All is now ready, Guide Zenos! Everyone is in place," he announced. His voice traveled through the valley behind the temple, reverberating as it went.

Now new shouts arose.

"General Shin! It's General Shin! He's here!"

Shem looked to the guide who had formed at the very beginning. Guide Hierum smiled and nodded once back to Shem.

Shem gazed down on Perrin and said the words which sounded as if they had been prepared long ago, and had been waiting centuries for this very moment. "General Shin, Salem has been delivered here to safety, and you may now release the Army of the Creator, which has always been yours to command!"

The words hit Peto like an avalanche, and he collapsed on the stone. Suddenly it all made sense and suddenly it seemed to be so obvious. It *always* was.

"General," he gasped, "the *Creator's General—*" He clutched at his chest, feeling the parchment still hidden in his pocket. He looked up at Lilla to see if she understood as well.

All she could do was nod and sob loudly as her father kissed her cheek.

Worried, Deck kneeled next to him, his parents still on either side. "Peto! Peto, are you all right?"

"Never better." He struggled to catch his breath.

Mahrree chuckled down at him. "Just *wait*, Peto. The best is *still* yet to come!"

Deck and Grandfather Cephas helped Peto stand back up, and Cephas patted Peto's chest knowingly. The envelope warmed significantly under Peto's jacket.

"Peto," Deck whispered to him, "don't do that again! I thought you were having a heart attack. I'd hate for you to miss all of this."

Peto chuckled weakly. "*No one* will miss it, Deck."

"You're right," Deck said. "And is it just me, or do you feel old, too?" he asked, smiling at his young father and mother.

Peto looked up at his father who could have been his middle son's twin. "I've aged fifty years today."

Perrin saluted Shem and spun Clark around. He didn't even have to spur the horse. Clark knew exactly what to do. He took off in a fast run straight off the edge of the cliff and vanished.

The mortals stared after him in stunned silence.

Except for one.

"See Briter? I *told* you it was Puggah!" Fennic's happy voice rang from the rock.

Down in the valley, pandemonium had erupted. Groups of soldiers screamed and cried and collapsed on the ground as the hundreds of thousands of lights began to move down from the peaks to the valley floor. As the lights neared it was obvious what was at the front.

Soldiers.

Over one hundred thousand in white shirts and trousers, each with a shining sword in his hands.

But not everyone saw them.

"What's wrong with you?" General Thorne yelled as thousands of his soldiers threw down their weapons, cried out in fear, and ran to the woods. "It's just a land tremor." He turned his horse in a circle as many of his men panicked around him. "Not even a big one. Men, stand your ground!"

"Lemuel!" cried Poe as he stood up and grabbed the reins of the horse. "They're not terrified of the land tremor—they're terrified of the men in white!"

"What are you talking about? What men in white?" he looked around. "There's no such thing!"

"You don't see them?! Lemuel, how can you not *see* them?"

Major Twigg began to tremble as he focused suddenly on the approaching men in white. "I . . . I see them now, too. Where'd they come from? What are they?"

Another soldier standing nearby shrugged, "I don't see anything, General. Maybe the sergeant major and major are suffering from trauma, sir."

Hili's mouth dropped open. "Trauma?! *Look at them!*"

From his position Poe could see the edge of the forest where the mountain began to rise, about seventy-five paces away. All along the edge, forming a bright ring, stood soldiers in white with their swords readied. Men from the Army of Idumea who wanted to escape dropped their swords and long knives before the white soldiers and were allowed to pass between them.

"No!" Thorne shouted. "They're surrendering to nothing!"

"*Nothing*?!" Poe shrieked. "Lemuel, *open your eyes*! We're hopelessly outnumbered! They're surrounding us!"

Lemuel kicked Poe in the face, knocking him to the ground again. "Poe, you're crazed! There's nothing out there!"

Major Twigg trembled even more, unsure of what to do. He watched enviously as soldiers surrendered to the white army and ran into the forest.

As Hili tried to get to his feet again, another soldier grabbed Thorne's leg. "Sir, sir! I see them! White soldiers, everywhere!"

Four more soldiers rushed over to him, clawing at him. "Sir! What do we do? Help us!" They pulled so hard that Thorne slid off his horse.

"Stop it!" He slapped one of them as he righted himself. He went to take the reins of his horse again when he heard a new rumbling coming from the direction of the cliff.

"Puggah just . . ." Barnos Shin finally started but faltered. He was the first to be able to utter anything, his arm motioning feebly to the cliff.

His cousin nodded. "I know," Bubba Briter said. "He just . . ." and he, too, lamely waved at where their grandfather had vanished.

Peto came to himself enough to turn around. "What is he doing?" he asked his mother, forgetting, almost, that she was radiant and vibrant and not *entirely* mortal. But his curiosity about what was happening overruled his astonishment at her new form.

She sighed in her same, familiar way. "Negotiations. He never felt it was his strongest skill. This shouldn't take long. Never does with him."

Assistant Ahno wrung his hands as he always did. Having one shackled high up on the large wardrobe made his position a little more awkward, but it was the only thing he could do all alone.

The screams of his fellow Salemites had ended abruptly last night when the officers made good on their insistence that they didn't need any prisoners.

Ahno had courageously waited for his horrible moment up in his room, but it never came. Perhaps they forgot about him.

Everything was hauntingly still and quiet, as it had been for the last several hours. No one would come back to Salem to find him. Even Guide Zenos had said, when he asked for a volunteer to learn how to lie to confuse the enemy, that whoever stayed would likely not be rescued.

But Ahno had wanted to do something daring and brave for the last act in his life. Sitting for years taking inventory of the warehouses wasn't it.

Now nothing was happening, or it *was,* just not around him. For the last few hours his emotions vacillated between terror, relief, and boredom. Right now it was tedium flavored by fear. And he was hungry.

Something seemed to change. He looked around and noticed a light coming from underneath the door, as if someone had lit a lamp near the crack. But it was still morning and there was no need for light—

The door swung open to reveal a beautiful young woman in

radiant white. She stepped into the room while Ahno gaped.

"My darling, I'm so proud of you!" she gushed. "You are truly the bravest man in Salem. Especially right now. You happen to be the *only* man left. Would you like to see how it all ends? I have a fast way of getting there that doesn't require walking or horses."

Ahno, speechless, could only nod at his radiant bride.

Instantly the chains fell off his wrists.

Faster than he could blink, he was somewhere else—the ancient temple site.

Around him, his children and grandchildren shrieked in astonishment, and he shrieked back at them, flabbergasted.

Ahno's young wife laughed at their reactions. "Told you I could find him. And it's the Last Day. Everyone faithful will witness it. Your father," she said to her family as she gripped her husband's hand, "is one of the most faithful men ever. And now here, among all of the Salemites, he's still the bravest man in Salem. Tell me," she turned to him, "isn't this better than dying?"

She kissed him on the cheek, and Ahno whimpered and crumpled in place. Soon he was propped back up by ancestors in white whose names he didn't immediately remember, but who were strong enough to hold up the hefty man.

"I'm not missing it," he whispered, a smile growing on his face. "I'm not missing it!" Finding his strength, he grabbed his wife and planted a kiss on her lips.

She laughed in delight. "Hungry, my darling?" She patted his large belly.

"Starving! Do I have time for a snack?"

One of their daughters, coming out of her shock, immediately rummaged in her pack and produced a sandwich.

Ahno sighed in relief as he took it. "What a perfect day."

Two more soldiers near General Thorne screamed, dropped their swords, and ran straight for the forest. But several other soldiers readied their stances and stood near General Thorne, prepared for whatever the rumbling would produce.

Twigg could do nothing more than shake, while Poe remained on the ground trying to evaluate what to do next.

Lemuel stepped in front of them, watching as the clusters of soldiers between him and the cliff began to separate as if to allow something unseen to move between them.

The rumbling became more distinct with the obvious sound of horse's hooves, but no horse and rider were visible. In the space between the soldiers a shimmering appeared, distorting the air around it like a mirage on a hot day.

Lemuel took a hesitant step forward trying to focus on what was rushing toward him.

The shimmering took shape.

A large black horse, galloping.

A rider, dressed in a white shirt and white trousers.

"I see him!" Guide Zenos announced and everyone looked to the valley again.

There appeared the white rider and the black horse down below, far too quickly.

Shem smiled faintly. "I told you, Lemuel. And he still outranks you."

Lemuel staggered as he saw the bright man on the horse, and he stepped back quickly into one of his soldiers.

The soldier, who a moment before hadn't seen any white soldiers either, gasped in terror and collapsed behind Thorne.

The horse and rider, imposing and enormous, stopped abruptly about ten paces in front of Lemuel.

Hili, still lying on the ground, whimpered when he saw the man. "It's *him!*"

General Thorne took a deep breath, puffed up his chest, and boldly looked the rider in the eyes. "And just who are you supposed to be?" he demanded.

The rider glared at him, slid off the saddle-less horse, and strode over to the general.

Lemuel leered at him. "*Private Shin.* I should've known. What a neat little trick, scaring my men. You Salemites are full of all kinds of deception. 'There won't be any Salem army to attack you!'" he mimicked. "Remember telling me that? So what's the next little ruse, Private?"

But Hili, too stunned to get to his feet, was tugging on Lemuel's leg. "That's . . . that's not *Private* Shin. I know that face. Colonel!?"

The rider looked down at Hili and nodded kindly. "That's right, Poe. And I thank you for taking such good care of the private for me. Well done, Sergeant Major!"

Poe beamed up at him. Perrin turned to General Thorne and his demeanor hardened. "And it's not colonel. I've been promoted by the Creator. It's *General* Shin, and Lemuel, it's over. Don't make me kill you."

General Thorne stared at him. The voice was wrong; it wasn't Private Shin's. It was deeper. And the eyes weren't quite right either. They were deeper, too, somehow. But it wasn't *him.* There wasn't any way it could be. Nothing like this had ever happened before so it couldn't happen now.

"It's a trick," Thorne concluded. "I saw the burial stone with dozens of names around it. You're just another grandson. Jaytsy said she had seven boys. You're another one of them, sent here to scare me. Well, I'm going to show Zenos it's not going to work!"

In an instant, Thorne slashed with his sword at General Shin with speed and ferocity that should have decapitated him. But the sword bounced harmlessly off General Shin's neck and fell to the ground.

Thorne stared at it, baffled.

A nearby soldier threw down his weapon and ran for the distant forest. Two dozen men followed him, and hundreds more began to back away cautiously.

Twigg crumpled to his knees and whimpered.

General Shin remained immovable. "It won't work, Lemuel," he said calmly. "No matter what you want to believe, you can't change the fact: I *am* Perrin Shin, the man you called Colonel, the man Poe first knew as Captain. You're right. I died nearly two years ago. But now I'm back. This isn't a body of flesh and blood but a perfected body that can never again be hurt or destroyed. Everyone in white is in the same perfected condition as I am. It's hopeless. Shem was right—you cannot win. Please, son, let's end this now."

Unmoved and unimpressed, Thorne bent over and picked up his sword, all the while keeping a wary eye on the man in white. He pointed his blade at Perrin. Peering at his neck, which wasn't even red where Lemuel had hit him, he concluded, "It's just a trick. Some kind of flesh-colored body armor—"

Another rumbling from the south startled him, and he spun anxiously to see a swath of soldiers separating as another shimmering began to form. A majestic horse, this time brown, appeared with another massive rider dressed in white.

"It's no trick," the young man on the horse said as the mount stopped directly in front of him. "Lemuel," said the deep, gravelly voice, "I come with a message from your Grandfather Cush. He's not ready to join us but he begs you to stop. Call it all off now and mercy can still be extended to you. If not, you'll be as miserable as Qayin."

"And what do you know of my father?" Thorne yelled at him, but the slight tremor in his voice suggested his confidence was beginning to crack, that something about all of this might be more than a mere illusion.

"I know that Qayin, along with Gadiman," the man began evenly, but his voice was making the hair on every soldier's neck stand on end, "ordered my and my wife's death. But as you can see, nothing can ever hurt us again." He slid off his horse as another ten soldiers dropped their swords and bolted for the trees, followed by a few hundred more.

"Get back here!" Thorne yelled to the fleeing soldiers. "It's just another grandson! The hills are crawling with them!"

The man smiled vaguely as he walked over to him, big and burly. "In a way. I have a great-grandson named after me, but I'm the original Relf Shin. And Lemuel, that story you told Perrin years ago about falling asleep in a class at the university, your professor marching you angrily to report you to your grandfather Cush, then I getting you off and letting you spend the day in my office?" He shook his head sadly. "We both know that never happened."

Lemuel took a hard step backward. Only two people in the world knew he told that story to Colonel Shin. Only one knew it was a lie.

He staggered, about to take another step back from this man

whose voice made his arms break out in goose bumps as if he were back in Command School again, when he remembered who loomed behind him. Anxiously, he turned to face the other Shin.

"I had a feeling that story wasn't true," said Perrin.

"I still think it's too bad he couldn't be wearing his uniform," Hycymum Peto sighed loudly.

Hycy Hifadhi stared at her great-grandmother who stood next to her.

Her cousins and siblings eyed Hycymum as well, who mystifyingly didn't seem too concerned about the terror below them in the valley. She smiled eagerly around at her descendants who couldn't quite grasp what was happening and didn't know yet how to respond to all their new relatives.

Hycymum nudged her great-granddaughter. "Ah, Hycy, you should have seen your Puggah on the platform in Edge in his uniform. So impressive! I suggested he wear the blue today because it would be more intimidating to that silly Thorne, but," she sighed again, "everyone's to wear *white*. Still, white *is* a timeless color, and quite noticeable. And you have to admit, you can't find finer linen than this. Feel the hem on this sleeve, Hycy. Beautiful, isn't it? Look at my Cephas! Isn't he dashing in white? I hope your son will grow up to look just like him!"

Unsure about anything, Hycy peered over to her aunt Jaytsy and Muggah.

Mahrree shrugged an apology and Jaytsy giggled between her tears. "That's my grandmother, all right!"

Cephas Peto smiled sweetly at his wife.

Hycymum nudged Hycy again. "I can't wait to get my hands on those cocoa beans your explorers brought back. No one in Salem has figured out quite what to do with them, but I've been thinking for *years* about how to add some sugar and milk. But I'm still working on the name. Does shokolot sound appetizing?"

Hycy finally found her voice. Not only did it seem fantastic to be speaking to an ancestor, it seemed fantastically absurd to be discussing fashion and recipes when they were waiting for a battle.

"I . . . I'm not sure, Grandma Hycymum. I'm . . . I'm kind of having a hard time thinking about anything else right now—" She waved vaguely to the valley beyond them.

"Oh, of course, dear! I was just planning for later."

Mahrree snorted.

Her father heard her. To his daughter, he said, "After all, what's an event like the Last Day without *refreshments?*"

Mahrree laughed with her father.

Peto watched in awe as his mother and grandfather laughed together. He looked at Jaytsy, and, judging by the amused and amazed expression on her face, she was thinking the same thing.

"There's going to *be* a later?" Hycy asked her great-grandmother.

"Oh, most definitely. My Mahrree was right. Then again, she always was. The best is still to come. Just because it's the *Last Day* doesn't mean it's *the end*. My goodness, you poor thing. What do you *think* is next?"

Hycy shrugged dumbly.

Her family stared in amazement right along with her.

Thorne was firming his grip on his sword, trying to hold on to something solid, when he heard whimpering behind him.

It came from Poe, who was staring up at the man pretending to be Relf. "It *is* him! I met him at his mansion in Idumea. Lemuel, that *is* High General Shin! Much younger, but I remember his face, his voice, *that glare*—"

"Hili, enough from you!" Thorne shouted.

"You can't fight it!" Poe cried, getting to his feet. "You're wrong, Lemuel! You've *always* been wrong, about *everything*! You couldn't even kill Zenos!" He pointed furiously to the cliff. "The ONE MAN who *DESERVED* to die and you even *failed* at that!" He looked as if he was ready to kill Thorne himself, fumbling at his waistband for his long knife. "Give it up, Lemuel! Just stop! The sky is gray!"

"*NEVER!*"

Before Poe could draw his knife, Lemuel plunged his sword into his chest.

Stunned and silent, Poe buckled in place, sliding off of Thorne's blade.

"Poe!" Perrin cried and dove for him, catching his head before it hit the ground.

Thorne held high his sword, Poe's blood sliding down the blade. "It still works, men! The day is still ours!"

Perrin cradled Poe as he struggled to breathe, his forehead against Poe's while the surrounding soldiers stared in dismay that the general had so readily wounded his trusted sergeant major.

Thorne gave all of them a challenging glare, waiting for the next man to oppose him.

"Poe, it'll be all right," Perrin assured him. "You can go. I'll find you and bring you home to us, I promise."

Poe shook violently, trying to meet Perrin's eyes. But Lemuel had, once again, been too accurate in his aim. "The sky's gray, I see it. Tell her," he managed before he went lifeless in Perrin's arms.

Major Twigg slapped a hand over his mouth, his horrified eyes growing wet.

Perrin tenderly laid Poe down and stood up to face Lemuel.

But Thorne refused to acknowledge him, acting as if he'd conveniently vanished.

However, he couldn't ignore that the crowd was parting again, and a tall, older man in a blue jacket was pushing his way through.

"I knew it!" Thorne snarled when he recognized the officer. "I've been getting reports about you all yesterday and this morning, that you were sneaking around my soldiers, trying to subvert them yet again. And then you had the nerve to camp with us last night?! Just whose side are you on, man? You're a disgrace to that uniform, Jon Offra! It's about time you faced me. Where'd you get that old jacket, anyway? And just what do you think you've been doing—"

But Jon didn't hear any of Lemuel's dressing down as he stared at Perrin.

"He's real, isn't he?" he gasped at his old colonel, now much younger and grinning at him. "Teman, is what I see before me real?"

Teman, who had gamely kept up at a jog, panted as he stopped next to Jon. He stared up at Perrin who winked happily at him.

"The man I knew for many years . . . Much younger now, but yes, Jon, yes—he is real!"

Jon was already extending a cautious finger, intent on poking

Perrin's forehead, but Perrin instead stepped up and embraced him.

"Oh, Jon—magnificently done, all these years. I can never thank you enough, and we have so much to catch up on, but later. First, let me ask you this: Would you like to do one more thing for me, and *with* me?" He released Jon who gawked at him.

"Of, of, of course. All right, then. What is it?" Jon hadn't noticed that behind Perrin, Thorne was tipping his head meaningfully to some of his guard several paces away.

But Perrin knew. "All will be explained to you. So that's a yes? All right, then—I'll let happen what's about to happen. Just look at me, Jon. Eyes on me—"

Perrin flinched, because two of Thorne's guard had come rushing up behind Colonel Jon Offra and cut him down on either side, slashing Perrin's old colonel's jacket in pieces, along with the colonel who wore it.

"Whaaa?" Teman cried as he clapped his hands on his face, devastated that his charge—and friend—had fallen. "But . . ."

"HA!" Thorne bellowed, hollow and angry and confused, but ready to take the strange victory. "You just let him die!"

Relf cleared his throat, and it echoed in the valley. "Not so fast, Lemuel. Not so fast—"

There was a flash, so bright and blinding that no one in blue could see properly for a moment, as if lightning had struck the very spot where Offra's crumpled body lay, but silently, beautifully silent. When they could see again, there stood a third figure in white, tall and lean and blond. He grinned at Perrin and Relf, who returned his smile.

"They were right! Not a moment's passed here, has it?"

Lemuel stared at the ground where Jon's body had been, but nothing remained. Not even the blue jacket. He couldn't help himself. "Who's *they*?" Lemuel demanded. "Who was right?"

Jon chuckled. "*Who*, he asks. Not worth wasting the time to explain—Teman! My dear friend, Teman!" He pulled the small, stunned man to him, embracing him enthusiastically. "Oh, Teman. You've been so good to me. I was so confused, but, oh! how I see things now! Hours have gone by, maybe even days, but no time here? Everything is so, so, *so clear*. It's . . . it's . . . glorious! So much to share with you, but there's no time left here, is there, General Shin?"

Complete and whole, in body and mind, he snapped off a sharp salute to Perrin.

"Thank you for your willingness to help, General Offra," Perrin said. "You understand your assignment?"

"I certainly do. I have one request, General."

"Name it, General."

Jon kept a tight hold on Teman. "Can he come with me? Not like I need him anymore, but I've grown rather attached, you see."

Perrin chuckled. "Teman, want to stay with him?"

Teman, looking very unsure but also very curious, shrugged. "I promised to take care of him until the Last Day. The Last Day isn't over yet, is it?"

Jon gave him a squeeze. "Then hold on tight," and suddenly they weren't there anymore.

Every soldier who saw what had happened was frozen in astonishment. Someone mumbled, "Lightning men. He died, then became a, a *lightning man* and stole that old Salemite—"

Even one of Lemuel's guard who had killed Jon staggered in confusion, and stupidly stomped the ground in front of him, as if Jon and Teman might have fallen through some trap door as in the plays at the amphitheater.

Relf leaned over to him and said, "If I were you, I'd drop my weapon and *RUN*."

He did, and hundreds more took the advice, screaming and wailing and rushing to get far, far away.

But only those who had seen what had happened to Colonel Offra, who was no longer a colonel, and no longer dead, and no longer even there. None of the soldiers fleeing bothered to explain why to the men they plowed through on their way to the forests, throwing swords and weapons far away from them.

Ignorant soldiers who saw only the strange lightning flash which carried no thunder readily picked up the discarded weapons and stepped up to take the places of those who had fled, closing in again on the knot of generals—Thorne and Shins—now glaring at each other.

It took Lemuel a moment to compose himself, blinking rapidly as if coming out of a bizarre dream which could be the only explanation for what had just transpired. He glanced down at Poe Hili at his feet, bleeding and still very dead, and nudged him with his boot as if to make sure.

"Lemuel, please—" Perrin began, but still Thorne wouldn't look him in the eyes. Instead he addressed the new set of soldiers who stood before him, itching and ready and conveniently oblivious.

"Men!" he shouted, "Those who still want glory, follow me! The men in white may not die but the Salemites on the hill still bleed!" Thorne ran for his horse, and Perrin sighed.

Relf regarded Poe's body sympathetically, then looked up at Perrin and put a hand on his shoulder. "Negotiations seem to be over, son. General, your command?"

Perrin nodded sadly at his father. "We proceed as we discussed. Come to me at the temple ruin when you're finished."

Relf straightened up, smartly saluted his son, and mounted his horse. She automatically turned and cantered back to the southern end of the valley where more marching soldiers in white had nearly reached the valley floor. Some men scattered in front of General Relf Shin, throwing down their weapons and racing for the trees, but thousands more stood their ground staring coldly at the general riding back to gather his troops.

Clark trotted over to Perrin. He mounted and watched the shouting figure of General Thorne riding hard for the cliff, several hundred soldiers running after him, thirsty for blood.

General Shin looked around at the dazed soldiers remaining. They were afraid to look at him, catching him only in the corners of their eyes, then recoiling to realize he was still there, and still very real.

"Head to the forest in the east," he said kindly to one trembling young man. "Find a man in white named Hogal. A woman named Tabbit will guide you to him. They'll watch over you until it's over. There are about three hundred with them already."

The soldier dropped his sword and took off running, followed by several more men.

Perrin turned to Major Twigg who continued to stare at the sergeant major's body. "Major Twigg," he said gently.

Twigg looked up at him and flinched at his brightness.

"Go to the forest, Major."

Twigg shook his head almost imperceptibly. "I've sworn undying allegiance to General Lemuel Thorne. I serve only him, to my death."

The words came automatically out of his mouth, but his eyes seemed to want to recall them.

"Why, Twigg? What has he done to deserve your loyalty?"

Twigg became his own isolated land tremor. "I've sworn undying allegiance to General Lemuel Thorne," his voice quavered as he repeated the oath. "I serve only him, to my death!"

"Twigg, Twigg," Perrin implored, "you've sworn allegiance to a *fraud*. And you will die in that allegiance. Save yourself! Drop your sword and *run*."

A tear trickled down Twigg's face and he said again, as if in explanation. "I've sworn undying allegiance to General Lem—"

"You *outrank* him, Twigg," Perrin interrupted. "He's only a *captain*. He's not worth fighting for. Twigg, GO!"

It was too much for the major, the notion of disobedience to what he'd been so thoroughly conditioned to believe. "I've sworn undying allegiance to General Lemuel Thorne. I serve only him, to my death. I've sworn undying allegiance . . ."

Perrin hung his head as Twigg continued reciting the oath, as if it held power to somehow protect him.

Still mumbling, Twigg looked up at the sky that Poe had said was gray. It was, indeed, clouding over and rapidly turning a dark gray.

But it was *still* blue.

That's what they always told him. Everyone said it. It was even on the tests he took when he was young: the sky is blue. Ignore the clouds. Ignore the dark. Despite what you see, remember, it's *still* blue.

"I've sworn undying allegiance . . ."

Perrin tried one last time. "Twigg, even Poe saw the sky was *gray*. It's all been a lie, *always*. But you don't have to believe it anymore."

" . . . I serve only him . . ."

Perrin sighed, glanced over at the lifeless body of Poe one last time, then faced the cliff ahead of him.

"Now, Clark."

There wasn't even a flash and they were gone.

" . . . to my death."

The ground rumbling around the Shin, Briter, and Zenos families drew their astonished attention away from Grandmother Hycymum's musings about what beverages should be served 'later,' and directed them to look back to the cliff side.

Suddenly General Perrin Shin and Clark appeared at the end. Clark galloped the forty or so paces to the temple site before stopping. The general slid off the horse and looked up at the guides.

"Thorne's coming. He's sending up several hundred men first. There are about a hundred on the trail. Looks like they camped on the cliff side. But the rest of our army will soon be clearing the valley."

Guide Zenos nodded. "I see them beginning." He smiled. "You're right—a bird's eye view is a great way to see it."

Perrin sent a complicated facial twitch at him then turned to his family. "I doubt all of you want to watch this—"

"Puggah!" a voice rang from the rocks and Fennic tried to make a dash for him, but he was caught by a stout man with black hair.

"Fennic, STAY!" Perrin ordered. "All of you, stay back! Grandpa Pere's in charge over there, so you do what he says, all right?"

Fennic stared at the large man holding him, who smiled kindly. "I used to be a general too, you know. Stay with me and I'll let you watch, if you really want to."

Fennic nodded as Pere Shin sat him down on a rock behind him.

Perrin turned back to his family at the ruined temple. "Last chance to join them."

None of them could say a word. They still hadn't gotten over his sudden appearance and the fact that he was standing right in front of them, younger and stronger. There were a few doubts that this glorious being had even been their white-haired Puggah. No one knew what to do but stare.

Until Cambo's gasp spun Perrin back around.

"Puggah, they're coming!" Lori cried.

Over the edge of the cliff came the first soldier, sword drawn and looking for a fight.

Perrin strode for the edge of the cliff and drew his sword. Where it came from, Peto couldn't discern. He wasn't holding one a moment ago nor did he wear a sheath.

The soldier charged. Without a word, Perrin lunged with the sword and the man fell instantly.

Lilla screamed and hid her face in her father's shoulder.

Lori whimpered as suddenly three more, then five more, then dozens of soldiers poured over the edge of the cliff racing toward the general.

"Puggah!" someone at the temple site cried, but it wasn't necessary.

Now General Shin had two swords, and as the yelling men rushed him, he easily dispatched one, then another. A quick step here and another man fell. A twist and thrust to the right and another body folded. A quick jab, a spin, another step and three more bodies were added to the pile of dead soldiers growing at the edge of the cliff. No one could pass the general to get to the vulnerable mortals behind him.

Jaytsy, Lori, and Hycy held their faces as another man and another fell dead under General Shin's quick blades.

Lek, still on the ground, gripped his head in his hands as Salema kneeled by him using him as a shield, watching the bloodbath and hiding whenever her grandfather deftly decapitated another soldier.

Young Pere hid his face in his hands, unable to witness soldiers dying in front of him, but Peto observed his young father with analytical admiration. "Saw that move before. And that one. Never saw that one, though. He's gotten faster on that step. Whoa, didn't see *that* coming," he muttered his commentary to Young Pere and Deck.

The rest of the family stood in shocked silence as Perrin took a few steps back to lure the soldiers to a new area not littered in bodies.

Only once did someone else mumble.

"Nope, I definitely can't fix *that*, Uncle Perrin," Boskos whispered in awe.

Professor Slither found his lazy morning disturbed in a most unusual manner.

For the past few days he'd enjoyed sitting in a cushioned chair at the northeast gates, a bottle of Thorne's private mead next to him, and a box of sweet rolls on his lap, watching the world try to climb over the boulders to invade Salem. He and Wanes had spent many amusing hours observing folks trying to hoist furniture over the rocks, not believing there was plenty of tables and sofas and wardrobes in the north for the taking, according to excited reports from the other side of the mountain.

But last night there had been another group of villagers, this time returning with warnings about treacherous and filthy trails, and armed and murderous Salemites, and even a most ludicrous report that Guide Lannard had been 'scared to death' and the army scattered.

None of those returning bothered to deliver a report to the fort, however, but continued on south as fast as their legs could carry them. Since it was only a handful of scared people here and there, Slither and Wanes decided to ignore them, as did everyone else who realized that there was now less competition for the best properties.

Slither didn't want a new house in the north. He had Thorne's mansion all to himself, while his old protégé Wanes enjoyed the run of the fort, and between the two of them they decided they could probably rule the entire village themselves once it emptied out which, at the going rate, would be in less than a week.

But Slither's entertainment this morning was being interrupted in the oddest of ways. The sun had been up for over an hour now, lighting the way for the next wave of villagers moving north who were ignoring a handful running back south. But for some reason the forest began to brighten.

Slither set down his mug and leaned forward, trying to see what was happening. There were several screams of surprise, and people scurried back down through the trees to the fort. In their panic to rush past him, someone rudely knocked over his jug of mead.

Slither attempted to get up but found the cushions had shifted so that he was trapped.

Behind him, he heard running footsteps. "What's going on?" Wanes panted. "I saw something bright coming out of the canyon a few minutes ago, but I can't tell what it is."

Slither shrugged. "Seems to have spooked the villagers . . ."

The bright presence was now making its way through the forest, sending thousands of people before it, fleeing.

Something pricked in the back of Slither's mind, an idea shoved hard away, and he glanced up to Wanes whose face was ashen.

Through the trees the brightness became more distinct, and the two men realized the light was actually people, men and women, dressed in dazzling white, and heading for the fort. One man in the lead purposefully approached the gates. Behind him tagged along an older man, not in white. His eyes flicked around frantically, trying to take in everything as if he'd never seen such a place before. But he kept up behind the tall man in white who strode rapidly, too rapidly, to Slither and Wanes.

Panicked, Slither grabbed blindly for Wanes's hand, hoping to use it to help him get out of his chair so he could run in terror like everyone else. But Wanes had gone rigid, staring at the young man who was focused on reaching them.

Slither collapsed into his chair helplessly, because something about the man in white was familiar.

"Wanes! Slither!" the man exclaimed, his voice rattling them to their bones. "How appropriate the two of you are here together."

Wanes trembled but said sternly, "Who are you? What do you want?"

The man stopped and folded his arms. "Your surrender. It's over. Today is the Last Day, and you're about to meet your destruction."

Slither gulped, more ideas shoving their way past the muck of his mind, insisting on being first and foremost, but they couldn't be right. They *mustn't* be correct . . .

The older man had caught up, and the sharp, determined expression on the face of the man in white softened as he saw him. Quietly he said, "Over there, Teman. About twenty paces out of the fray. But watch!"

Bobbing his head, he trotted away and stood anxiously in the middle of the training field.

Slither had been staring at the blond man in white, feeling something oddly familiar about him. He pointed, not noticing how violently his hand was shaking. "I . . . I taught you, didn't I?"

The man shifted his solid gaze. "Nothing useful, Slither. You were always determined to deceive everyone and anyone to get what you wanted. You even went so far as to rewrite The Writings to secure your position in the mansion." He shook his head in disgust.

"How can you say that?" Slither whispered, realizing that his and Thorne's private workings were no longer private.

Wanes licked his lips. "Who are you?"

"You should know me," the tall man said. "You chased me out of your fort on a few occasions, refusing to offer aid to an obviously needy officer."

Wanes was sagging under the words. "No, no, no, no . . . cannot be . . ."

"I'm no longer needy," he said with a sly grin. "I'm also no longer mentally imbalanced."

"But you died!" Wanes said, as if the man had forgotten such an important detail about his own life.

The sly grin grew. "Only a few minutes ago, actually."

"He can't be," Slither whined quietly. "Oh, he *can't be* . . ."

"That's what I thought, too," the man said, reflective. "How could I have died, so close to the end? That was my first thought, I must admit. Then suddenly I understood, the first of many fantastic and marvelous things. I needed to die today so that I could stand before you like this." He gestured to his body, radiant and powerful, and Jon Offra grinned at himself. Not like a madman, but like a perfected being.

Neither Wanes nor Slither could respond, too astonished.

What happened next dropped Wanes to the ground, as if he'd been knocked down by an unseen fist. Another being appeared, right next to Jon Offra, and the older men blinked, wondering where he came from.

The new man tipped his head at the prone colonel. "Wanes, how many people have lost their lives because of you? Care to make a guess?"

Wanes's jaw moved up and down uselessly until he produced, "I . . . I . . . I didn't kill anyone!"

The second man scoffed as Offra shook his head and elbowed his new companion. "As if lying right now is going to help him in any way."

The second man nodded in dismal agreement. To Wanes he said, "It was your *brilliant* idea to eliminate the aged of the world, to convince tens of thousands of people, even children, to commit suicide. That's *killing someone*. And Slither," he turned to the fat man quivering in the cushioned chair, "masterminding the news that everyone who died would be receiving a mansion of pure gold? In a few minutes you will see *exactly* where those who were as greedy as you ended up. And yes, Wanes, you killed my wife."

Wanes's mouth dropped open. "Who, who, who is your wife?"

The second man responded with, "One of many who sent appeals to you, who begged to be allowed to live. But you didn't listen to any of those appeals, did you? You rejected each and every one of them." He took a step closer and Wanes cowered, raising an arm above him to shield himself from the brightness of the man. "My wife was Teeria Rigoff. She was caring for several other injured and elderly people, and you sent them all to their deaths. She was forced to breathe in the herbs, executed by the very soldiers who years ago served me. I am here today to exact justice for that act."

Wanes burst out with a high-pitched, "Rigoff? Colonel Milo Rigoff?"

Rigoff glared. "Recently promoted to General Rigoff, and given power by a Being who delights to share in what He has."

Wanes stammered again. "I, I, I had no idea your wife, *your wife* was in such a situation—"

Offra and Rigoff exchanged glances of weary forbearance.

"You can't lie your way out of anything anymore," Offra declared. "We all have seen what you've said and done. There are thousands of witnesses and no more hope for secrecy."

Suddenly Slither realized who stood in front of him, throwing such accusations. "Creet! Offra? *Colonel Offra?* You, you went mad!"

Offra nodded and tipped his head as if having completed a fantastic trick. "Yes, I did, because I knew the truth and could no longer stand the lies of the world. But oh, how much clearer everything is on this side!" He seemingly forgot where he was and looked happily around him. "Everything falls perfectly and neatly into place, and suddenly the world makes sense." His gaze dropped back to the two men, and his smile vanished as he remembered who sat before him. "And I, too, have been promoted. It's General Offra, and Rigoff and I have been sent by our commander to demand your surrender."

Wanes took one last stab at bravery. "Who's your commander? I demand to know who demands this!"

To his astonishment, the men in white chuckled. "Oh, wouldn't he like to know?" Offra said to Rigoff conspiratorially.

Rigoff nodded and grinned. "It'd *kill* him to know. Kill them both, wouldn't it? But they'd never believe us, would they?"

Both of them abruptly turned back to Slither and Wanes, their expressions somber.

"Surrender," was all Offra said, and it was as if his voice echoed from the canyon.

Wanes wasn't one to back down, ever. He didn't get to his position without being tenacious to the point of stupidity. "Surrender?! Why?"

General Offra turned to Slither, who was trying to appear as small as possible, "What day is today, Slither? You should know. You rewrote all those sections in The Writings and eliminated all the references to such a day ever coming, didn't you?"

"The Last Day!" he whispered in terror. "Creet, it's real!?"

General Rigoff turned to Wanes. "Do you surrender?"

Wanes licked his lips. "Surrender to what?"

"The Creator," Offra said.

"No such being!" Wanes insisted.

Offra and Rigoff looked at each other and nodded. Instantly swords appeared in their hands.

Slither screamed.

A few moments later Offra and Rigoff nodded a *Well done,* to each other and turned to see the rest of the men in white with them chasing soldiers and villagers. Behind the line of white soldiers were the women, trying to speak to and console those who didn't run but surrendered in astonishment and curiosity to the glorious figures before them.

But one brilliant woman was striding for Offra and Rigoff, and Milo grinned as she neared.

Teeria sent back a smile, but it faded as she took Milo's hand and gazed at the bodies of Slither and Wanes.

"It's true," she said sadly. "There's no satisfaction in revenge. Only in forgiveness."

"This sets them on the right path," Milo said. "*If* they choose to take it. But that's up to them now."

Jon nodded officiously to Milo. "General, we need to clear the fort." He smiled at his hand in Teeria's. "There'll be plenty of time for that later."

Teeria chuckled. "For you, too, Jon. There will be an interested woman, I have no doubt."

He blushed and bobbed his head. Remembering his terrified mortal in the field, he beckoned him over. "Teman, come on. More work to do, then you can introduce me to your wife who'll be waiting for you back at the ancient temple. This is Milo and Teeria Rigoff, by the way."

Teeria took Teman's hand and smiled. "Jon, how about you and Milo take care of the fort? I think Teman may be more comfortable out here with me. This is perhaps a bit much?"

Teman nodded timidly, astounded. "I'll wait . . . wait right here, Jon."

"All right, then," Jon said, solid and powerful, and the two generals strode for the fort where a handful of furious soldiers poured out, blades waving, but only for a moment.

Teeria walked serenely to a cluster of villagers who were unsteady and confused, with Teman in tow. "Would you like to know what's happening here?" she asked kindly, "Or would you rather take on them?" She gestured to a line of men in white, each armed but walking calmly toward a group of men who were frantically searching their packs and wagons to find weapons.

"There's no need to fight," Teeria called out to them, and motioned to another group in white, unarmed but smiling gently. "We'd much rather teach you and help you, but the decision is yours. Today is the Last Day, and this is your Last Chance."

"It's true," Teman piped up, seeing how he could help. He was still a mortal, after all, and other mortals just might believe him. "There's a better way, and it's not yet too late."

A few weapons were dropped, and a few hands went up in surrender, and shining swords vanished as the men and women in white closed in, smiling.

At the far south end of the valley, General Relf Shin turned his horse around and nodded to the soldiers dressed in white at the edge of the trees, waiting for his command. Relf gazed over the valley before him and saw new flashes of light to the east, to the west, and to the north near the cliff where hundreds of soldiers were racing up the long path to the top, Thorne shouting at them to hurry.

Relf raised his sword and thrust it high above his head. It sent forth a brilliant stream of light, outward and upward, yet silent. It blinded momentarily the mortal soldiers clenching their weapons and wondering when to strike.

In the distance, three brilliant more streams from the new lights answered; they, too, were in place and ready.

He brought down his sword, the motion releasing one more burst of light as a signal, and his horse began to trot again toward the middle of the valley. Another sword appeared in his other hand.

The soldiers of the army of Idumea took that as their moment, cried out, and rushed High General Relf Shin.

Serenely he held out his swords on either side, slashing them across the chests of the men. Each man the swords touched dropped in a lifeless heap. Soldiers who rushed his horse, intent on wounding the mare, found their blades bouncing harmlessly off her.

Behind Relf, the rest of the white soldiers left the forest and began to march across the valley, plunging their swords into the soldiers who charged at them. None of the Idumean soldiers got out more than one futile attempt at slashing a man in white before he fell dead.

In each quadrant of the valley the same thing was happening.

Across from General Relf in the north, at the base of the cliff, several men had cried out in terror as the gray speckled mare appeared with the young figure of General Graeson Fadh on top of it. They, too, had been blinded momentarily as his sword flashed, but now Fadh trotted due south, silent and composed, his swords out on either side of him cutting down soldier after soldier.

In the east rode a calm, young General Brillen Karna, in similar manner, his white horse trotting directly west toward General Gari Yordin, whose appearance caused many men to scream, "Major Yordin?!" His brown and white horse trotted evenly toward the middle of the valley as men fell behind a quiet Roarin' Yordin.

The white soldiers continued their methodical slaughter behind the four riders, destroying all those who refused to acknowledge the truth, even as it cut them down.

In just a few minutes the four generals, unimpeded, would meet each other in the middle of the valley.

Anoki Kiah had been moving goods from an abandoned building

to a massive structure which he recently acquired when he saw the figures in white. He blinked, then blinked again. Idumea was virtually emptied, but he knew it was only a matter of time before people started coming back, wanting something more fashionable than the plain clothing of Salem.

He peered through the windows to see several more people in white, nearly glowing, coming to his building. For a moment he thought he had his first customers but something in the air told him he wouldn't be selling anything that day. He dropped the bundle of coats he carried and stepped outside.

One of the men headed directly for him, a determined look on his face and a meaningful squint in his eyes. The rest of the men and women behind him stopped to wait.

"Anoki Kiah." The slow drawl wasn't a question, it was a statement.

Anoki nodded, wondering how the man knew his name. He was young, about Anoki's age, but also seemed old somehow.

The man shook his head slowly. "Your father was a deceitful man. So was your brother. And now you."

Anoki shrugged. "Not sure what you're talking about."

The man in white folded his arms. "You pretended always to be something you weren't. Your life was one lie after another."

Anoki held up his hands. "Did Wanes send you? Because I'm not stealing anything. Just appropriating. Big difference—"

"It began with your first abandonment," the man drawled. While his voice sounded lazy, his tone was sharp. "*Corporal* Kiah."

Anoki narrowed his eyes and took a stab at innocent denial. "Uh, what are you talking about?"

"You abandoned your first post. Took your pay, took some goods, and vanished."

"I just—really, is this an issue *now*? That happened years ago—"

"Then you abandoned a young woman and a daughter."

"Versa had the baby?" Anoki was startled. "A girl?"

The man in white stared hard at him.

Anoki cleared his throat. "Figures. Guess old Thorne won't be too pleased about another girl." He coughed a laugh. "Well, good luck to her with *that*."

"Do you feel any regret, any at *all*?" the man asked him. "You abandoned another of Thorne's daughters, too. She gave up her life, so distraught she was. Any remorse for that?"

Anoki shifted uncomfortably. "That was her decision, not mine. I had nothing to do with that."

"Kiah, Kiah, Kiah . . . I always hated men like you."

"And just who are you?" Anoki demanded. "What kind of authority do you have—"

"You abandoned your post years ago, soldier!" the man cut him off. "As a sergeant major, I'm here to force you to account for your pattern of abandonment. And as part of the Creator's Army, I have been given the authority to extract justice for *all* your crimes."

Anoki paled. "Sergeant major? Creator?"

"Men called me Grandpy Neeks during my time in the world. Maybe it was because I believed in dragging them out behind the woodshed to *teach them a lesson!*"

Anoki gulped.

"You disgust me," Grandpy growled. "Tell me, soldier, what's the punishment for abandoning your post?"

"Uh, lashings."

"Uh-huh," Neeks drawled. "So what should be the punishment for abandoning a wife and a baby? For causing another girl so much distress that she thinks death is her only option?"

"Uhh, well in the world there isn't any—"

Sergeant Major Grandpy Neeks smiled vaguely. "Oh, but there *is*." A sword appeared in his hand.

Kiah never served a customer.

Grandpy turned and faced one of the men in white who approached. "What'd you think of that?" he asked.

Sergeant Major Sheff Gizzada nodded in approval. "No resistance whatsoever. The general said there'd be a large group hiding down the road, and then he wants us to clear out the rest of Idumea. We've done that before, after all." Gizzada grinned. "Shall we, Neeks?"

"Of course."

The sergeants began down the road, their soldiers following, much as they had more than twenty-five years ago. But this time, none of the sergeants would fall as they had when they took over the Administrators' building and destroyed Qayin Thorne and so many others, since all of the sergeants were in white and glowing.

Up ahead was someone who knew Idumea well—Dormin, the last son of King Oren, the last descendant of all the kings. Also in white, he nodded a greeting to the sergeants' army, and a segment of twenty men broke off to follow him into the city where his family had once ruled.

"As I suspected," he said to the two sergeant majors, "they're hiding in all the usual places. When we're finished, we'll join up again?"

"As the general directed," Grandpy said, saluting away Dormin and his army.

Grandpy leaned over to Gizzada, "Thinking of *after we're finished*, will you be cooking? I mean, not that we really *need* to eat, but it just won't be Paradise without a Gizzada sandwich. And there are still all those mortals who will need feedin' once this is all over—"

Gizzada grinned. "I've already asked about that, and I've already been told: whatever I want, however I want. There are a lot of ingredients Hycymum Peto and I have been talking about since we've been in Paradise, and oh, the plans we have for them! I can hardly wait. You can be my head taster, once we clean up this city properly."

Grandpy Neeks called to Dormin who was marching away. "Hey, Dormin! Ever have a Gizzada sandwich?"

Dormin turned around and grinned. "They were invented after I died, but I heard all about them. Sheff, are you going to be cooking later?"

Sheff Gizzada pointed at him. "Oh, you know it. So men, the sooner we're done, the sooner I get to experimenting, and you're all invited. It'll be a free lunch, boys, all the time."

That got them all running.

Perrin quietly took out another yelling man, then another, and another. It was so pointless, so tragic. All they had to do was drop their weapons and run to the trees and they would be spared. But they wouldn't do it. Even with the awesome display of force, power, and absolute invincibility in front of them. Not even the general's simple white uniform was affected. He remained spotless as he spun yet again with swords that gleamed without a stain or drip of blood. Two more men fell. Three more men rushed to take their places. In an instant they were down, lifeless.

Peto finally closed his eyes, unable to watch anymore. He had been keeping count but it was close to one hundred now, with more and more senseless soldiers coming over the edge sure that somehow they would be the one to destroy the—

Peto swallowed hard and opened his eyes again. "That's who he is," he whispered. "Who he's always been . . . Dear Creator!" he gasped. "*My father* has always been—"

He couldn't say the word.

It was too incredible. For a brief moment he remembered when he was fourteen and his traumatized father, unsure of who Peto was in their dark house, pointed his sword at him. Peto had seen the determined look in his eyes, stopped only by his mother's intervention.

He looked back up at the temple ruin wall behind him. Shem was watching Perrin with a sad smile, tears trickling down his face.

The Deliverer.

That's who Shem had always been. He had delivered them to safety before the coming of the—

Peto shook his head in amazement as he looked back at his father. Perrin had stepped closer to the edge of the cliff and calmly beckoned the next batch of soldiers to come at him. With fierce roars, two men rushed him. Perrin stepped up, stabbed both of them in the bellies, pulled out his swords, spun and kicked one, then the other off the edge of the cliff. He needed to keep the area clear for the next foolish men to rush him.

"I think you're looking for us," said a sweet-faced woman in white with a friendly smile. She took the hand of the trembling soldier who, unarmed, ran past the line of white soldiers cutting down everyone else in their path as their wide circle closed in to the center of the valley. The soldier nodded hesitantly as the woman led him through the trees to a small clearing. There sat more than five hundred men, stunned and staring at the smiling man in white clothing explaining to them what was happening. He turned to the latest addition.

"Welcome, welcome, my boy! Always room for another one. Dear, any others?"

She shook her head sadly. "Not that I see, Hogal."

He nodded back to her soberly. "Then come sit with us, Tabbit. We have plenty here to begin with."

"That's right, today's the *last day*," Thorne mumbled under his breath as he scaled the front of the cliff with the assistance of a rope a soldier tied to a tree at the top. The brawny soldier had been pulling Thorne up the cliff, until he plummeted to his death past the general, wearing a fresh sword wound in his chest.

Thorne had ignored that body, just as he had ignored the other bodies that rained down on him sporadically. Most were now falling to the right of him.

"Today is *your* last day, *Zenos*!"

He secured his hold on the rope and climbed another few steps, grasped the rope higher with his good hand, and pulled himself up again. It was slow work, but he'd be there just as those killing his soldiers at the top would be tiring. "Try to humiliate me in front of my men! I'll show you humiliation, *Guide*," he sniggered as he raised himself another level.

Further to his right, a few dozen paces away, the soldiers rushed up the switch-backing trail. But he was going to surprise Zenos further down the cliff.

"This *is* the last day," he murmured again. "The last day my kingdom is denied me. I'll take it all, Zenos. Your lands, your people, your sons . . . It's all going to be mine, you stupid, *stupid* sergeant!"

In the western part of the valley, a group of soldiers were still unsure of what to do, the men in white closing in on them.

But suddenly there was a woman, brilliant and glowing, with a blond ponytail and a fierce demeanor.

"Really, boys—it's time to give this up. Simple enough: drop your weapons, then run up the slope to that man there. My husband will care for you. Call him Rector Yung. See him smiling and waving? You'll not find a friendlier face among those of us who are perfected." She jerked a thumb to the warriors in white nearing, then to her own hard demeanor. "Now, enough of this nonsense!" she chastised them, and a few hung their heads in remorse, as if their grandmother was taking them to task, not a young woman with old and angry eyes.

"Now it's time to act like real men. Surrender to the Creator who is actually trying to help you, and walk away from this battle. Only the cowards will remain here, pretending to fight. That's right, run boys. Drop that ugly steel and get out of here . . ."

In the valley, the four generals were coming closer to each other, leaving swaths of dead soldiers in their wake. Behind them the ring of white soldiers began to tighten as they neared the center of the valley. None of the Creator's soldiers made a noise or cried out in joyful victory as hundreds and thousands of their fighting descendants fell.

Major Twigg didn't even try. His sword hung uselessly by his side as he stared at the general in gleaming white slowly ride to him. He looked up into the grim expression of Relf Shin and was still muttering, "I've sworn undying allegiance to General Lemuel—" when General Shin's sword sliced neatly across his chest, dropping him lifeless to the ground next to Poe Hili.

In the middle of the valley, about thirty paces away from Hili's body, the most brutal of Thorne's soldiers formed a ring, three men deep and twenty men across. They had already decided: the main victor in the ring would lay claim to Salem, the second man would have Idumea, and whoever else survived would have that valley. They watched with determination as the four horsemen came at them in opposing directions. The cluster in the middle braced themselves as the generals closed in.

"Now!" cried someone. With screams they ran for the generals, swords flailing.

In moments, the entire valley fell silent.

Deck was sitting on the stone steps, his arms around his sons Viddrow and Holling who held their heads, unable to watch anymore.

Deck's parents had their arms around Cephas and Cambo, while Jaytsy leaned against her mother and wept. Lilla kept her face buried in her father's chest.

Lori and Hycy crouched next to Salema behind Sam and Wes who sat near Lek, using their husbands as shields from the view.

Hycymum had gone over to join the other ancestors at the rock face to complete the wall of ancestors that prevented the younger ones from seeing the destruction.

Fennic had hidden behind the rock his Great-Great-Grandpa Pere put him on the instant he saw Puggah's swords.

Peto sat next to Young Pere, keeping a hand on his back while Grandpa Cephas braced him up on the other side.

Young Pere buried his head in his knees, quietly sobbing, while Relf, Barnos, and Nool stood arm in arm with Boskos and Zaddick.

When the first soldiers appeared, so did the elder Boskos Zenos, who now stood in front of the young men to partially block their view.

"Why won't they stop?" Zaddick whispered in morbid astonishment. "Why don't they see they can't win?"

Young Pere's head came up. "Because they each think they are different or special somehow," he cringed as another three men went over the edge. "The laws of nature, the rules of the Creator—those are for *other* people. Not them. But no one is above the laws," he said sadly. "No one can beat the Creator's power."

Two more men, three more, one more. Each met the same fate. At least now they weren't piling up in front of the temple site but were stacking in the valley below.

Lori looked to her right and screamed. "Puggah!"

Peto leaped to his feet and spun to Jaytsy.

"It's him!" she announced.

Lemuel Thorne was heaving himself up on the tableland.

Relf Shin's mare carefully picked her way over the bodies to reach the center of the valley, the other horses meeting her there.

Relf nodded at Yordin, Fadh, and Karna.

They each nodded back. This wasn't a victory to rejoice over. Each of the fallen men had ancestors weeping for them along the hillsides and on top of the cliff.

To the generals, Relf said, "He wants us to come to the ruin when we were finished. There's one last general to deal with."

Lemuel Thorne locked eyes first with Jaytsy. He balanced at the edge of the cliff between General Shin and his family taking refuge at the temple, the twenty or so paces open as if reserved just for him.

Jaytsy met his gaze and tipped her head at her mother.

Thorne shifted his glare to Mahrree but regarded her with confusion. He didn't recognize the large, young woman nor did he care to. He instead watched the young men rising to their feet to see the man who had done so much to destroy their family names.

Lemuel's chest heaved when he recognized Peto and Deck, then realized many of the young men resembled them in some way. His eyes lingered on Zaddick and Boskos before his attention was captured by Lek, who got up angrily, his demeanor uncharacteristically fierce.

The empty space next to Lek was suddenly filled by a body dropping from the ruined wall above.

"Lemuel, don't do this!" Guide Zenos commanded. "Drop your sword, now!"

One more grandson struggling to his feet caught Thorne's eye. Young Pere, supported by his father and great-grandfather, stared hard at General Thorne.

For a brief moment something like fear flickered across Thorne's face as he glanced over to see General Shin dispatch another soldier, then another. There *were* two of them. But that didn't matter. All that was important was that the man who he hated for so many years now stood within striking distance.

Thorne turned back to Zenos, thirty paces away on the stone steps. "I didn't come all this way to be disappointed, Zenos! Welcome to *your* last day!" and he started for the ruins.

"No!" Young Pere cried out. He dropped on all fours and did his best to scramble for one of the many swords dropped by fallen soldiers behind Perrin.

Peto lunged for his son. "Young Pere! No!" But from somewhere Young Pere found speed and strength that kept him just out of Peto's frantic grasp.

Shem saw Young Pere's sudden motion. Even though Thorne was fast approaching, Shem yelled. "Perrin! Young Pere!"

General Shin spun to see his grandson crawling fast for a sword, Peto scrambling to catch him.

Perrin glanced behind him as another soldier rushed him, but the four generals appeared directly between him and the soldier, giving him the time he needed.

"Stop!" Shem cried as Young Pere was in reaching distance of a weapon. Lemuel Thorne was now just twenty paces away from Shem and gaining. "No, Young Pere, you're not the Destroyer!"

Lemuel was fifteen paces away, fourteen . . .

Young Pere saw a white boot step on top of the sword he was about to grasp. He followed the white trousers up to see his grandfather looking down at him.

"No, you're not the Destroyer, Young Pere. I am."

With one leap Perrin hurdled over Young Pere and Peto to bear down on Lemuel.

Shem's eyes bulged as Lemuel ran up the first step, the second, his sword raised high above his head, an angry cry coming from his mouth—

"Perrin—!" Shem called.

Suddenly Lemuel stopped on the step below Shem's, a look of disbelief on his face. Shem recoiled to see the tip of a sword protruding from Thorne's chest.

Perrin, behind Thorne, pulled out his sword and spun Lemuel to face him, holding his weakening body by the shoulders.

Lemuel stared in bewilderment at Perrin, the light dimming in his eyes. "Colonel?" he gasped, as if finally recognizing him.

"Yes, Lemuel. I told you in your dream that my face would be the last you'd see. Remember? Good-bye, son."

Lemuel fell on the steps of the temple, dead.

Lek dropped onto the steps, unconscious.

No one at the ruins made a noise but stared at the lifeless form of General Thorne while Boskos knelt down to help his older brother, who was already coming around.

"He's dead!" came a startled voice from near the cliff side. "Thorne's down! The general's dead!"

The stream of soldiers rushing over stopped in a surprised heap.

Perrin nodded at the four generals. They nodded back, raised their swords and chased the remaining soldiers back down the trail.

Perrin turned back to Shem. "It will be finished in just a moment, Guide Zenos," he said soberly.

Guide Zenos, tears in his eyes, nodded. "Excellent work, General Shin." Then he took a deep breath. "But Perrin," Shem whispered, "that was just a *little* close."

Perrin smiled grimly. "No one's faster than me, remember?"

The four generals reappeared again on top of the cliff side.

General Relf Shin nodded once to his son. "It's finished, General," he said, walking over to the family once again speechless at who was approaching them. "Except for one more thing," Relf pointed at Peto who was still on the ground next to Young Pere.

He got clumsily to his feet, staring in surprise at his grandfather.

Perrin walked over to his son and pulled open his jacket. There were no more swords in his hands as he pointed at Peto's shirt pocket. "No more waiting, son."

Feeling his legs grow weak again, Peto turned to his grandfather, unable to speak.

"Would you like some help, Peto?" Relf rumbled.

Peto nodded. Relf reached over to Peto's pocket and pulled out the parchment envelope. Lilla began to weep all over again as the family watched breathlessly, wondering what it all meant.

Relf opened the envelope, pulled out the parchment, unfolded the sheet he originally folded, and handed it to Peto.

"It's best that you read it, Peto. I still can't make out all of your handwriting." Relf put a bracing arm around his grandson.

Perrin chuckled softly as Peto's hands and voice trembled:

"'This is written by Peto Shin, under direction of his grandfather, High General Relf Shin. While Relf Shin lay in the storage room of the old garrison, trapped by the land tremor, he had a dream, many times. He saw that his son, Perrin Shin, would become the greatest general Idumea'—and Relf crossed out and wrote here, *'the world* would ever see. He would lead a battle that would bring about an ultimate end to conflicts in the world. Peto will live to see the day.'"

He could barely get out the next words. "Signed by Peto Shin and Relf Shin, the 37ᵗʰ Day of Planting Season, 335 . . . thirty years ago . . . today."

It was more than he could take. Peto began to weep, and Perrin stepped over to him and wrapped his arms around him.

"Fantastic job, son. You carried it magnificently, all these years. Your children and grandchildren will never forget!"

Jaytsy came down a step and gently took the parchment out of her brother's hands. "Peto! This was when we were in Idumea? You *knew*, all the way back then?"

Peto pulled partially away from Perrin, not wanting yet to release his father. "I didn't know *everything*, Jayts. And it wasn't until today that I finally understood why. Can you imagine being a fourteen-year-old boy and discovering that your father was the Creator's *Destroyer*? Remember the line from Guide Pax's prophecy—"

And he was vaguely aware that up on the temple wall, Guide Pax was waving down at him.

"—The line, 'The Deliverer will ensure the safety of the Creator's people, until the coming Destruction'? Our father, Jayts—HE'S the Destruction!" He waved his free arm over the scene of carnage beyond them, disbelieving.

Perrin tipped his head. "I prefer *The Destroyer* myself. Much better title."

Jaytsy clapped her hand over her mouth. It seemed wrong to giggle at such a moment like this, but the giggle was forcing its way out anyway.

Perrin saw her struggle. He laughed and pulled her into a hug with her brother. That seemed to be the signal.

"Puggah, *NOW*?" a small voice from the rocky slope called out.

Perrin called back, "Yes, Fennic. NOW!"

A new kind of commotion broke out all over the temple ruin and behind it. It began with more than a dozen children rushing down the rocky slope between their ancestors and over to the temple site.

Perrin released his children and crouched with his arms wide open, ready to receive the onslaught. Morah reach him first, with Young Shem a close second and everyone else third. Whoever couldn't fit in Puggah's arms rushed into Muggah's.

Behind the temple site, the thousands of Salemites erupted into laughter and dove into the joy they felt when their ancestors first appeared. Now there was time for reunions and introductions.

Peto stepped back from the assault of children to find his nephew Cephas reading the parchment Jaytsy still held. She started to hand it back to Peto.

"Here," he said taking it out of her hands and giving it to Cephas. "It's for everyone."

Cephas gingerly took the prophecy as several more family members huddled around him to see it themselves.

Peto moved back to watch them. After all these years of keeping it secret and sacred, it was time to reveal it to eyes that now could understand. The moment nearly consumed him. He would be exhausted by nightfall. Peto felt a heavy but bracing arm around him. His grandfather Relf smiled at the cluster of descendants.

"Could you have ever imagined *this*, Peto?" he squeezed his grandson's shoulders, probably leaving bruises. "At the time we were both thinking of him as High General of Idumea, but it wasn't until I passed that I learned what the Creator really intended. I couldn't reveal it to you or to him, or even to Shem that day on the ball field when you were sixteen and he told you not to go to Idumea to play kickball. I just had to watch and hope you'd have enough faith to see it through. And you did! Remember when I told you I wished I could be there by his side?" Relf sighed happily. "We both were, Peto!" He kissed his grandson on the cheek and embraced him.

"But Grandfather, I have a question."

"Sure, Peto."

"Why? Why . . . did you have that dream, give me this parchment? Why?"

Relf gripped Peto's face with both hands. "Why? To give you hope, Peto."

"Hope? That's all?"

"Peto, hope's *everything*! I've got a few more people to introduce myself to. But I'll be back. Enjoy the day, son!"

"I am, Grandfather."

Relf walked over to Lori and Sam whose children now joined them, and Peto looked over to Jaytsy to say something to her, but found her embracing Grandmother Joriana. Then Peto saw the face he was really looking for.

Lilla rushed over to him and flung her arms around his neck. "This was it, Peto! We waited, and waited, and suddenly, and THIS and *now!*" She wept incoherently into his neck.

Peto chuckled and kissed her neck. "Thank you for carrying it with me, Lilla. I could never have done it without you."

Lilla bounced away from him. "Calla! I have to see Calla!"

"I think you may have to wait a moment."

Shem was waiting too. He stood near the wall watching as his daughters swarmed his wife. When the grandchildren had rushed to Perrin and Mahrree, Calla had easily hopped off the ruined temple wall as the other guides vanished to meet their families. Shem didn't even get a chance to hug her before her sons caught her. Shem just smiled and stood back, continuing to watch as his daughters sprinted from the slope to touch their mother and then embrace her.

Peto couldn't quite read the look in Shem's eyes. It was certainly immense relief and joy, but there was also something else that Peto didn't understand.

A moment later Calla gently pushed her children into the waiting arms of their grandfathers Zenos and Trovato, and turned to her husband.

But he could only shake his head. "Ah, Calla. Just look at you! You're as young as one of your daughters."

Calla beamed. "I thought you'd appreciate the twenty-year-old version of me. I always felt a little sad you never saw me younger. I saw you once, when you were twenty-two and stopped in Norden, but—" She looked at him shyly and held out her arms.

Shem didn't move. "Calla, can you ever forgive me?"

"For what, Shem? For fulfilling the dream I had ever since I was a girl to watch you in action? For letting my last day be so memorable? *I* got to die in battle," she said rather proudly. "You never did that." She stepped up to him and wrapped her arms around him.

He reluctantly put his around her.

"Shem, what's really worrying you?"

He sighed sadly. "I can't get over how amazing you look! And you . . . you're stuck with an old man, Calla."

She chuckled. "Only until you're seventy-two. Then you'll become that twenty-two-year-old I fell in love with when I was younger."

"But that's still eight years from now. Wait—there still *will* be years, right? I mean, I'm still alive, right?"

She twisted a lock of his graying hair in her fingers and giggled. "Obviously. And remember—I've always loved an older man."

Shem finally began to smile. "So you can put up with me like this for a while? While you look like *that*?"

"Let's put it to the test," and she pulled him in for a kiss. A moment later she stepped back. "Oh, yes. I can *definitely* put up with that. Can you?"

Shem couldn't speak.

Peto and Lilla chuckled. Calla and Shem were going to need some more time.

Lilla squeezed Peto's hand. "Papa wants me to meet his mother, but I wanted to check on Young Pere first."

"Go ahead. I'll find him. Don't keep your father waiting. He's been waiting for five years already."

Lilla bounded off happily to her father while Peto looked around for their son. He didn't see him in the swarms of laughing, crying and hugging people that now flowed freely around the temple site.

But he did notice his grand-nephew Briter. The seven-year-old squeezed between Shem's legs to hug his Grandma Calla. She kissed his forehead and he darted away, running over to his Muggah to grab her around the waist. Mahrree kissed his head and Briter dashed off again, back to Calla to pat her arm, then back the Mahrree to rub her back. Each time he made the jog he seemed to believe more and more they were truly back. By his fifth trip he was grinning and dodging out of his grandmothers' playful pinches.

Peto chuckled at his joy until something else caught his eye.

On the first stone steps laid the still body of Lemuel Thorne. Everyone moved well away from it as they passed.

But one person was approaching it. Versa stepped onto the stair and cautiously knelt by Lemuel's head. She shifted the position of her baby to face him.

"It's a girl, Father," she whispered. "Granddaughter. No surprise, right? She doesn't have a name yet, but I think she looks just like us. I just thought . . . you might want to know." Her lower jaw trembled as she touched his gray-streaked blond hair and gently brushed his cheek.

Peto started to walk over to her, but someone else was faster.

"Versa," said a quiet voice above her.

She looked up. The misery in her face was replaced with a bright smile. "Uncle Fadhy!" she cried. She stood up and threw her free arm around General Fadh's neck.

He laughed and picked her up off the ground. "You've grown, Versa!" he said, kissing her cheek and setting her back down. "You've turned into a wonderful woman! I know—I've always been watching you. Even when you were a mischievous *boy*!"

Versa laughed and cried out again as another person rushed up to her. "Aunt Fadhy!"

"Wait!" General Fadh said. "Give me the baby before you crush her between the two of you." He eagerly took the newborn from her arms as his wife embraced Versa.

Graeson chuckled and looked at the newborn with tender eyes. "Ah, Lemuel—what you gave up. She's beautiful. They all were." General Fadh kissed the baby and breathed in her scent.

Shaleea Fadh squealed at the baby. "Versa, can I hold her next?"

"Of course! Now you're a *Great* Aunt Fadhy!"

Graeson handed the infant to his wife. "Versa, I'd rather we be honorary grandparents, if that's all right with you? Thought you could use some . . ."

Now the tears Versa fought poured down her face. "I would *love* that, Grandpa Fadhy."

Peto nodded in approval and looked back down at the body of Lemuel Thorne.

It was gone.

The wall of fallen soldiers had also vanished, too. Peto jumped up to the top stairs of the temple ruin and looked down at the valley.

It was clean.

He smiled. There was nothing left to cause anyone more sorrow.

He noticed another man in white coming to him, holding the parchment as he climbed the steps.

"This is what you were holding, wasn't it?" General Brillen Karna said as he handed it back to Peto. "The day I brought the news that your grandparents were killed by Guarders, and you were in your bedroom?"

Peto took the parchment and nodded. "Yes, sir."

Karna chuckled. "And I thought you loved that *ball*. Excellent work, Peto. You would have made a great general as well."

Peto chuckled. "Seriously, how could I *ever* follow in *his* footsteps?"

"You have a point, Peto. None of us could." Karna patted him on the shoulder and turned to make his way to Perrin who was now laughing with Boskos about the 'ugliest flower in creation' that grew on the slippery slopes of the Back Door.

Peto surveyed the area again, looking for Young Pere.

Instead, his interest was captured by another reunion occurring with the Zenos family. The extended family had now joined Shem at the front of the temple site, where hundreds of people and ancestors in white paused in their introductions to see a visibly weakened Shem watch as one last ancestor made her way from the rock face, carrying Plump Perrin. Her smile grew as Boskos Zenos the elder jogged over to her to take the toddler.

"Our boy, Meiki—the Deliverer! I could never have imagined— *our boy!*"

She made her way up the steps. "I always knew, Boskos, from the day he was born," she said as she walked over to Shem.

Calla and Lek were supporting him on either side as he tearfully watched his mother come to him.

"The Creator whispered to me who my son was to become. I knew he would need constant help." She now reached him and held his face in her hands.

Even with his wife and son on either side of him, Shem would be a melted puddle in a moment. His face was already drenched.

"That's why I needed to be on the other side," she said, kissing him tenderly.

"Yours was always the voice in my head." Shem could barely get the words out. "When I was little, I thought you were my imagination.

But when I was five I realized my mother never left me."

Peto chuckled and wiped away a tear of his own as Shem's mother put her arms around him, keeping him from collapsing in joy but still reducing him into a leaking, mushy blob. They were lost to his view as the rest of the Zenos clan became one large, embracing mass.

Still searching for Young Pere, Peto finally noticed him resting on the ground and propped up against a tree, but he wasn't alone. Another general in white, Gari Yordin, sat in front of him, deep in conversation.

As curious as Peto was about the nature of their discussion, he took his time getting there, not wanting to interfere. Barnos came over, took the parchment gingerly from his father's hands, and Peto continued to meander over to his son and the general.

Yordin took Young Pere's face in his hands, kissed him on the forehead, and grinned. Young Pere nodded and Yordin slapped the ground, causing a small land tremor. Yordin noticed Peto approaching and stood up.

"Peto Shin! Where's that parchment? I want to see it!"

"Sorry, General, I just handed it off to one of my sons. I think it's in that group over there."

"Excellent!" he said, reaching to shake Peto's hand. "That son of yours has had an interesting couple of years, hasn't he? Quite the *worldly* education, I guess you could say," Yordin said.

"Yes, sir, that he has."

"You're lucky to get him back. No, wait. I have to revise that. You see, the past two years I've been getting quite an education myself," Yordin said, his eyes softening. "I learned not too long ago that there is no such thing as luck. What I should say is, you're *blessed* to get him back." His eyes were shinier than normal.

Peto put a hand on his shoulder, "You'll get them back too, General. It may take some time, but we have a thousand years to work on Eltana and your son. We'll help you get them all back."

Yordin cleared his throat of growing emotion. "Young Pere already promised me he would. And my grandparents will help."

His demeanor changed abruptly. "To the parchment!" he announced in Roarin' Yordin fashion as he marched away. "I want to see it! Who's got it?" he bellowed good-naturedly to the crowd. "My turn! General's orders!"

Peto chuckled and looked down at Young Pere. He was staring at the cliff side that was now clean. Peto sat down next to him and waited for his son to speak.

"Papa," Young Pere whispered. "They're gone now. Just before General Yordin came to talk to me, I still saw them. I was counting them, but there were so many."

"It's all right. The Creator did the cleaning for us," Peto said, putting an arm around his son.

Young Pere continued to stare at the now-empty site.

"I was like one of them, Papa. Not so long ago. So blind. So determined to believe what I wanted to, despite all evidence to the contrary. That should have been me, Papa, lying dead out there."

"No, Young Pere. It shouldn't. You opened your eyes and tried to remember what you used to know. You turned around, recognized your mistakes, and now you're fixing them. You've been given another chance, as all of them would have been given. They just . . ." he shrugged, unsure of how to think about those who had fallen but had never had as many opportunities as his son.

But an idea came clearly to his mind—a marvelous suggestion that he knew he'd understand better in the very near future. "While they didn't make it *yet*, we're not going to give up on them. They'll still have another chance, just as you were given another chance. They will someday get to feel joy just as you get to now."

Young Pere's shoulders began to shake. "It's too good, Papa. It's just too good."

Peto smiled. "Yes, He is. We deserve none of this and still He gives it to us. He loved us before we even knew how to love Him back."

Young Pere leaned against his father and Peto kissed him on the head. "Thank you for being with me today, son."

Peto noticed Perrin slowly making his way over to them. "I hate to interrupt, but there's someone I've been wanting to see . . ."

Young Pere looked up and gasped a sob when he recognized his grandfather, but Perrin reached down and easily pulled him up in a gentle embrace. "I'm so glad you listened to me, boy!"

Young Pere lost all strength in his grandfather's arms. So often he had heard his voice in the world, and so often he had ridiculed it, ignored it, argued with it, and many times convinced himself it was nothing more than his imagination.

But it wasn't. It never was. It was always his grandfather, even in his darkest, most stupid, and most terrifying moments. Perrin Shin was always there trying to reach him, to turn him.

Young Pere couldn't look at him. Not because he was too dazzling in white, which he was, but because Young Pere realized what a glorious Being he was. And the understanding that he had summarily dismissed his promptings on so many occasions filled Young Pere with such regret that he couldn't imagine how he could ever make it up to his Puggah.

But Perrin wasn't thinking anything like that as he embraced his grandson and kissed his neck. "So many times I feared you might not make it. So many times I thought I would lose you. I just couldn't bear that. Thank you for listening, Young Pere."

"No Puggah—I'm sorry. So sorry I didn't listen earlier. I should thank *you*. Thank you for being so . . ."

"Tedious?" Perrin suggested.

Young Pere snorted a laugh between his sobs.

Perrin grinned. "Let's see . . . and aggravating, stubborn, annoying, tiresome, useless—"

"Stop Puggah, please! I feel so awful about saying and thinking those things."

Perrin held his grandson's face in his hands. "But you were right. I *was* all those things. And *so were you!* We could make a good team, you and me."

Young Pere allowed his grandfather to support him as he wept. "Thank you, Puggah."

Perrin kissed him on the cheek. "For my grandson, anything."

Peto cleared his throat gently. "You two a team? No one could tell you two apart! Aside from the ears, that is. It's almost a little . . . *unsettling*. Except Puggah glows—"

"Whenever I looked at Young Pere," Perrin said, regarding his grandson, "I thought I was watching a younger version of myself. Unfortunately, that was true in far too many respects."

Peto's eyebrows furrowed as he looked at his father. "Really? Are you sure?"

And then he knew.

He understood more than he ever had, more than he wanted to.

And then he realized that none of it mattered anymore.

"See what your boy can still become, Rector Shin?" his father said.

Peto didn't even notice his mother standing by his side until she put an arm around him. "Don't worry too much about the past, Peto, especially since there's so much for us to do in the future."

Perrin grinned. "That's right! And Young Pere, there's something I've been wanting to ask you."

Young Pere swallowed hard, and said meekly, ready for anything, "Yes, Puggah?"

Perrin leaned in and whispered, "Ready to race the old man?"

"Wait," Shem said some time later as his family had drifted away to meet extended family and friends. Since *everyone* was there, there were a lot of people to become reacquainted with. Hours had passed, but it was as if time had stood still when the sun broke out, the air warmed, and the Last Day felt as if it was going to last marvelously forever. There were even refreshments over by the surgery tents, set up by Hycymum Peto.

But Shem was rooted to the steps of the ruined temple, and Calla, who was beginning down them, stopped to see why her husband wasn't following.

"Wait. He called him 'son,'" Shem said, startled to remember that moment when the Destroyer ended General Thorne's life on the wide stone stair he now stood upon.

Calla tilted her head. "Do you mean Perrin?"

"Yes," Shem said, his tone growing tighter as a worried knot formed in his gut. "He never called Lemuel 'son' before. He referred to Deck that way, and a couple others he claimed as his own, but *never Lemuel . . .*"

His gut twisted again as he remembered Versula Thorne at the garrison thirty years ago, greeting Perrin in such an intimate way by kissing his neck after his parents had been killed. Then Perrin's urgent pleadings to not tell Mahrree how Versula acted, his promise to Shem that there was nothing between them, and hadn't been for over twenty years before that . . .

More than fifty years now—

As if he heard him or read his thoughts, Perrin, dozens of paces away talking with a large cluster of Salemites and their relatives in white, stepped away from the crowd and glanced up at Shem. One facial tick was all Shem needed, and Shem's jaw dropped nearly to the ground.

Calla came up the steps again since it was clear that he wasn't about to move. "Shemmy, are you all right? What's wrong?"

It was another minute before Shem could stammer out, "I don't believe it . . . oh, no, no, no . . . I, I *can't* believe it . . . I, I won't—" Of everything he'd experienced that endless morning, this was the most impossible.

Calla took his arm. "Believe what, Shemmy?"

His eyes met Perrin's again, and while he appeared so young and vibrant, there was something weary that flashed in Perrin's countenance.

Because Guide Zenos needed to know, because his future calling required him to have understanding . . .

Perrin shrugged apologetically, regretfully.

Guiltily—

Shem collapsed on the stone step.

His wife kneeled next to him. "Shemmy? What is it?"

The only thing he could think to say as he slowly toppled over was, "Well, I'll be a slagging Zenos—"

And then . . .

Perrin and Young Pere walked slowly back to the deep gulf, taking their time because the person between them didn't want to see them go. But they would return again tomorrow because they spent every day there. The three of them stopped before the edge of the vast ravine where their companion could travel no further.

At the beginning of the bridge spanning the gulf, Guide Zenos looked up at them from the book he was writing in. As the last mortal guide—until he turned 72 and his aging, mortal body would be changed in the twinkling of an eye to a perfected, ageless one—he stood as sentry. On the other side of the bridge was Paradise, and no one got there without passing Guide Zenos first.

Shem smiled experimentally at the spirit between Perrin and Young Pere.

Qualipoe Hili smiled back.

Shem grinned and walked over to him.

Poe's chin trembled. "I'm sorry I refused to see it earlier, Shem. I was so willing to believe the lies, even when I knew the truth. Please forgive me. I've wasted so much time, was angry for no reason for so long—"

Shem embraced Poe's spirit as best as his physical body would allow. "It's all right, Poe. I forgave you long ago. I'm so pleased! Do you think you're ready?"

"I want to cross next week. I think I'll be ready."

Shem looked at Young Pere and Perrin.

"He'll be ready, Guide," Perrin said confidently. He put his arm around Poe's shoulders and hugged him. Perrin's perfected condition allowed him to touch Poe's spirit better than Shem could.

Shem grinned again. "Excellent! It'll be a grand celebration!"

Poe turned to Perrin and tried to touch the collar of his linen shirt, but his fingers sank through it. "I understand it will be some time until I'm prepared for the next step to *this*, but I'm looking forward to it."

Shem smiled and held up his hand that had developed more wrinkles in the past few years. "I still have a little while too, Poe."

"At least I won't be *there* anymore," Poe nodded to the dark, cold desert from which they had just walked. He turned to the bridge. In the distance beyond the gulf he could see the other side and the faraway light just beyond the hillside. He nodded with hope. "That's where I'll be next week. There's nothing I want more than that existence."

Young Pere and Perrin grinned at Shem.

Guide Zenos sighed happily. "That's what we need to hear, Poe. I'll be delighted to let you pass."

Poe hugged Perrin, then shook Young Pere's hand although he couldn't quite grasp it. "Be sure to tell her, all right?" he reminded Young Pere.

"Don't worry," said Young Pere. "There's no way I'll forget."

"I heard about that," Shem said. "From the Great Guide. It's remarkable progress, really."

Young Pere grinned. "I know. I can hardly wait to tell her."

"We need to go now," Perrin said to Young Pere. He turned and squeezed Poe's arm. "Until tomorrow?"

Poe nodded and took a few reluctant steps back. Perrin raised his eyebrows at Guide Zenos.

Shem rubbed his forehead and closed his eyes.

"Come *on*, Shem," Perrin whispered. "You know you're just jealous. But your time is coming, remember that."

Shem opened his eyes and smirked. "*You* remember that, Perrin. *Then* that will be something to witness."

Young Pere rolled his eyes. "Just say it, Uncle Shem. He'll keep teasing you until you do."

Shem sighed heavily before he whispered, "On your line . . ."

Perrin and Young Pere stepped up to the edge of the bridge.

Poe chuckled.

"Prepare . . ."

The two men in white were nearly identical in their stance. Except that one glowed.

Shem's last word came out as a whisper. "Run!"

The two men bolted across the bridge, side by side. The man who didn't glow shouted, "You cheated again, old man! You started early!"

The man who glowed chuckled. "No cheating allowed here, Young Pere! Pick it up, boy!"

Mahrree pulled the ear of corn off the stalk, tapped it three times against her leg, and handed it to the little girl standing next to her.

The girl with the blond braids put it in the basket.

Jaytsy, on her knees harvesting tomatoes, looked up at her dazzling young mother dressed in white, and snorted.

Mahrree pulled off another ear, tapped it again, and handed it to the little girl. She didn't take it.

"Rose? Rose?" Mahrree sang. "Over here, sweety. The corn?"

"What?" the three-and-a-half-year-old said. "Oh, sorry. I was talking." She took the ear from Mahrree.

Jaytsy sat back on her heels and watched her mother as she stepped to another stalk of corn.

"You were talking, huh?" Mahrree said. Pull. Tap, tap, tap.

Jaytsy rolled her eyes.

"Yes," Rose said. "To the butterfly."

"Ah," Mahrree smiled. "And what did the butterfly have to say?"

"The big flowers down the road are blooming again. She's going to tell her friends." Rose took the corn and put it in the basket.

Mahrree pulled off another and tapped it against her leg.

Jaytsy pushed back a lock of graying hair and started to laugh. "You're doing it *again*, Mother!"

"Doing what, Jayts?"

Jaytsy stood up and mimicked her mother. Pull, tap, tap, tap.

Mahrree bit her lip. "I was? Old habits die hard, even after you've died."

"Aren't you supposed to be *perfect?*" Jaytsy teased.

Mahrree gave her a teasing glare back. "My body may be perfect," she said, standing taller, and when she did she was really quite tall, "but my mind and soul have a long way to go yet."

Jaytsy giggled. "That's for sure, Mrs. Tap-Tap-Tap."

Rose wrinkled her nose. "Why do you do that, anyway?" she asked Mahrree.

"Because years ago we had to," Jaytsy explained.

Mahrree nodded. "To knock the bugs out."

Rose pulled a face. "But that's not nice. The bugs get to eat, too."

"That's true, Rose," Mahrree admitted, "but it used to be different. The bugs didn't eat *their* corn, they ate ours. And sometimes they would invade in such great numbers we'd have almost nothing left of our crops."

Rose's mouth dropped open. "But that's not nice! Why didn't you ask them to stop?"

Jaytsy giggled. "We couldn't then. Not back in *that* world. The bugs wouldn't listen to us. Neither would the deer and the raccoons. They could eat an entire garden that wasn't theirs in one night."

Rose's eyes grew big. "That's *really* not nice."

Now Mahrree giggled. "They just didn't understand us, like we didn't understand them. Rose, I *never* had a conversation with a passing butterfly in that world."

Rose's face fell. "That's sad. What about the birds?"

Jaytsy and Mahrree shook their heads. "Only sometimes could we talk to the dogs, cats, and horses," Mahrree said.

"And most of the time, the cats ignored us," Jaytsy added.

"But that's so sad!" Rose said.

Jaytsy smiled sympathetically. "And realizing a family of bears was bedding down in your back garden for the night, or that a mountain lion was spending the afternoon napping on your front porch? Those were never good things either."

"Why not?" asked Rose who was fond of cuddling up to anything large and furry. They were fond of her, too.

Jaytsy pursed her lips. "I think we'll explain that to you when you're a little older. But you don't need to worry about that because that's not the kind of world you live in. Isn't that nice?"

Rose nodded happily. "I love the animals. And I also love being in the gardens!"

"Well guess what?" Jaytsy leaned over to her. "Muggah used to hate gardens."

Rose's mouth dropped open. "Muggah, why?"

Mahrree smiled. "I hated the sun, the heat, the dirt, and especially the weeds. There was nothing worse than kneeling in the dirt pulling weeds."

Rose scrunched up her face again. "Weeds?"

Mahrree sighed. "Ah, Jaytsy, the existence this child has! Yes, Rose. Weeds were plants we didn't want in the garden."

"How'd they get there?"

"Lots of ways. Sometimes their seeds were already there, or they blew in with the wind, or birds dropped them. And we couldn't let them stay because they'd take over the garden and destroy it."

Rose was astonished.

Jaytsy smiled at her expression. "They always seemed to grow faster than the seeds we planted. If we didn't pull them out they'd suffocate the plants we needed to grow. Some were vines that twisted around the plants, others had big leaves that kept the light off the leaves, and some even had nasty thorns that could hurt you."

"What are thorns?" Rose asked.

Jaytsy looked over to her mother for an explanation.

Carefully, Mahrree said, "Rose, thorns were on lots of plants. Sharp little pokey parts that could stab you if you grabbed them wrong."

"That's bad," Rose shrank back.

Mahrree knelt by her. "Not entirely. Back in that world we had roses just as we do here. They smelled sweet and came in lots of colors, but their stems were filled with sharp thorns. We just learned to look past the thorns and focus on the beautiful flower at the end of them."

"Roses like me?"

Mahrree tickled her. "*Exactly* like you."

Something caught Jaytsy's attention, and she looked down the adjacent road, smoothly paved and coated in gold. "Mother, I think I hear something."

Mahrree raised her eyebrows at Rose. "I hear it too."

Rose jumped up and down. "A race!"

"Come on!" Mahrree took Rose by the hand and led her to the road. Mahrree assumed the position standing in the middle of it, with her arms outstretched.

On the side, Rose clapped her hands, waiting.

"There is NO way," a voice called from down the road, "that this is *fair*, old man!"

Perrin, grinning, rounded the curve to the straightaway where his wife stood waiting. He jogged easily, without even a hair out of place, as his grandson, panting heavily and sweating profusely, tried vainly to catch him. Perrin coasted past his wife, slapping her hand as he finished. He even had time to kiss Rose on the forehead before turning around to watch his grandson puff in behind.

Young Pere wearily slapped his grandmother's other hand and fell on the ground in exhaustion.

Jaytsy came through the corn stalks with a tall glass of water. She chuckled as she handed it to Young Pere. "When are you going to learn?"

He sat up. "Thanks, Aunt Jaytsy. One of these days—mark my words—one of these days, I *will* tie him!" He gulped down the water.

Jaytsy shook her head sadly. "In about forty-nine more years, Young Pere."

Perrin nodded. "That's right. And until then, I'm keeping him in shape." He ruffled Young Pere's hair. "He can never catch perfection, but he's becoming exceptional as he tries. He'll still be running the miles from the Dark Deserts when he's a great-grandfather."

"I can hardly wait," Young Pere chuckled ruefully as he rested his head on his knees to catch his breath.

"Race me! Race me!" Rose jumped up and down.

Young Pere looked up. "Are you *serious*, Rose? I never beat you! You're almost as quick as Puggah."

"I know! Race me!"

Young Pere smiled and finished his water. He gave the glass back to Jaytsy and struggled to his feet. "All right, Rose. Take it easy on me, all right?"

"You can carry the corn."

"What?" Young Pere exclaimed. "Now I have to carry the corn, too?!"

Mahrree chuckled. "I'll get it, Young Pere. You just race Rose."

Rose stepped up to an imaginary line.

"On your line . . ." Mahrree announced.

Young Pere joined Rose.

"Prepare . . ."

They both crouched.

Perrin reached over and slipped a finger into the waistband of Young Pere's trousers.

"Run!" Mahrree cried.

Rose took off running but Young Pere lost his footing as his grandfather held him back.

"Now that IS cheating, Puggah!"

Rose looked back and giggled as Perrin let Young Pere go.

He ran with great drama after her. "Oh no! She's beating me *again!* Look at her go!"

Rose squealed in delight as she ran down the road and turned left to a house with a short white fence around the front garden.

Her mother came out of the front door and grinned. "Run, Rose, run!"

"I'm winning, Mama! Do you see? I'm winning again!" She rushed up to the gate and slapped it.

Her mother stepped out of the gate to see Young Pere limping to the yard.

"She's just too fast, Versa. I don't know what you're feeding her," he panted with great theatrics, "but she's going to beat Puggah next year, I know it." He collapsed on the bench in front of the fence. "Mind if I take a nap here until dinner time?"

Versa giggled. "That's what it's here for."

Young Pere flopped on the bench and covered his eyes with his arm. "So what were you doing outside?"

"Oh, you know," Versa said casually. "I *was* waiting for the best husband the world could offer me, but then I heard a race coming and decided to watch that instead."

"Oh," Young Pere said quietly. He sat up and took a more formal position. "So, do you mind if I, uh, just sit here until that *best husband* comes home?"

Rose sighed loudly. "Papa, you're so silly."

Versa smiled and sat next to him, allowing him to put his sweaty arm around her.

"You *are* silly, you know that?" she said, kissing him.

Young Pere grinned and rested his head against hers as they watched their daughter run back to Mahrree and Perrin who were walking arm in arm up to their house.

"So how did it go today?" Versa asked.

"Very well. More than well, actually. Poe's ready to come out next week."

Versa turned to him. "Young Pere, that's wonderful!"

"He faced Shem today and you could see the difference in his eyes."

Versa sighed and leaned back against her husband. "I knew the two of you could reach him. You've already had so much success, especially with former soldiers, and now—"

"Versa," he interrupted gently, "there's something more."

She sat up and looked at him. "What is it?"

Young Pere took her hands in his. "Versa, he opened it."

She stopped breathing. "Are you sure?"

He nodded. "Poe went to see him this morning like he does every day. Of course he didn't acknowledge him. He doesn't see anyone yet. But this morning your letter was finally opened and sitting in front of him on the sand."

Versa's hands covered her mouth. She glanced over at Perrin who was nearing.

He smiled to confirm Young Pere's news.

"It took only six moons . . . Do we know if he read it?" she asked breathlessly.

Young Pere shrugged. "But Versa, it was *still* open in front of him. Shem spoke to the Great Guide about it. He says it's remarkable progress. Qayin, Nicko, Amory, Lannard and the others are still screaming in the pit with their eyes closed. But *he* opened his eyes, then crawled up and accepted Guide Hierum's outreached hand to get out of the pit . . . It really is amazing."

With tears bubbling in her eyes, she asked, "So he may not need the full one thousand years."

Young Pere shrugged again. "Remember there are still many, many steps to take. Crimes he has to pay for if he wants to leave, victims who need to forgive him, but . . ." He offered her a small smile when he saw the hope still shining in her eyes. "The Creator has softened so many hearts here. Many have a greater capacity to forgive. You're right, again. He'll probably make it out much sooner."

She jumped to her feet. "I need to read it again! The copy I made of it. Just to remember—"

Young Pere was already waving goodbye to her. "I knew you would," he smiled as she darted back to the house.

"Hey!" Perrin called after her as she jumped up the steps. "Where is he?"

Versa turned around on the porch. "Sleeping, finally. So don't you get any ideas, Puggah. But I promise, when we have dinner tonight at Lilla and Peto's, the Little Spewer is all yours."

Perrin rubbed his hands together. "Good! I have an experiment today."

In the house, Versa rushed to her and Young Pere's bedroom and opened the cabinet. She pulled out the copy of the letter she had written and sat down on the bed to read it again, trying to imagine what he might have thought and felt as he saw her words.

To my father Lemuel Thorne, from his daughter Versa.

I'm writing this letter to you in the hope that someday you will want to read it. I want you to know that I think about you every day, as I did when I was a child, and I also hope for you every day.

I also want you to know that you have a granddaughter. Her name is Rose and was born just two days before the Last Day. She was with me at the temple ruin and she looked upon your face. She's very sweet, unlike me, and is one of the greatest joys of my life.

Father, you also have a new son-in-law who loves me more than I deserve. You already know him, and I think you will be pleased to learn that Young Perrin Shin is now truly your son. He helped me birth Rose and has claimed her as his own. Rose adores him with all her heart, just as he adores her.

There is also something more. Father, you have a grandson. Yes, an actual grandson. Young Pere and I have chosen to call him Lemuel Shin, in hope of you. It's our desire that someday you will be able to meet him. Grandmother Versula was able to leave the dark desert and join us shortly after he was born. She said he reminded her of you. Except for his eyes. He already has his father's and great grandfather's dark brown eyes.

Father, my husband and grandfather go to the dark deserts every day to work with those who are tired of fighting and want to come home. They come to you each week, but you have yet to see them. They left this letter in front of you. They will continue to visit you until you are ready to see them. Perrin wants nothing more than to bring you home.

And when you are finally ready to leave, no matter when that may be, I will be waiting to walk with you across the gulf to bring you home with Perrin.

I love you, Father, as I always have.

Your daughter, Versula Thorne Shin.

Versa sat on her bed retracing the words, wondering how far he may have read. A noise in the bedroom next door caught her attention.

"No, no, no," she heard an urgent low voice, "you're not supposed to get up yet. But, since you're stirring, come here, Lemuel. That's my boy! Guess what? We're going to try something new at dinner. Yes, we are!"

She heard her son giggle as his great-grandfather probably tickled him. Versa walked quietly down the hall. She peeked into her son's bedroom to see Perrin sitting on the soft chair bouncing his great-grandson.

"Tonight will be the great spew test. Now your Grandpa Peto could spit anything green all the way past the table. But my mother said I was even worse than him. So tonight is the test—can little Lemuel spew further than either of us? You're nine moons old now, so you should be ready. And to test it, your great Aunt Jaytsy gave me some green beans. Now what makes this interesting is that your *other* grandfather loved green beans, so you might too. And he liked them raw. I never understood that. When he was your father's age, he'd walk by a farm on the way to the fort, grab a handful from the vines growing along the fence, and eat them all the way to the fort."

"Really?" Versa interrupted.

Perrin looked up, momentarily startled that he was discovered at having snatched yet another baby from his crib. "Yes, really. I thought Jaytsy was the only person who did that, but I saw him do it a few times too. He also liked them cooked, without any butter or pepper to hide the flavor. Strange," Perrin said with a concerned expression and a playful wink.

"I like raw green beans, too."

"He'll be happy to hear that someday. I'm sure."

Versa sat next to him as Lemuel snuggled into his Puggah. "Thank you for going to see him. The Creator certainly knew what He was doing when He paired you and Young Pere together. I still find it amazing you want to see him after everything—"

Perrin shook his head. "When I see him, I feel only sorrow for what he's experiencing. And to be honest, I feel much of his agony is my fault."

Versa wrinkled her nose. "Your fault?"

Perrin sighed. "I could have done more, you know that. After that first year, when he came back from Idumea before the attack on Moorland, he really was trying to be different. He was making an effort to be conciliatory, but all I saw when I looked at him was Qayin and everything else I detested. I failed to see just *Lemuel.* I had taken dozens of soldiers under my wing, trained them up properly, gave them what they were lacking—"

"Like you did with Poe Hili," Versa said.

"But I didn't with your father. Versa, I was afraid of him. I never would have admitted that in the world. Colonel Perrin Shin wasn't afraid of anyone, but I *was* afraid of Lemuel Thorne. Of what he could do to me. Of what he meant to me. Of who he may have been. Things might have been different if I had just seen *him*, accepted him. He looked to me for guidance, I knew that. But I kept pushing him away, ignoring the opportunities until it was too late. For that, I am deeply sorry. For him, for you, for our families . . . for the whole world. I *could* have made a difference in the world just by making a difference with Lemuel."

Versa slipped her arm into his and leaned against his shoulder. Little Lemuel was sucking on his thumb and slowly closing his eyes again, resting against Perrin who he occasionally mistook as his own father.

"Puggah, you're taking far too much blame," Versa told him. "I don't know that even you could have undone all the damage Qayin did to him. You had my father for a few brief years; Qayin had been molding him for twenty-two years before that. You can't dwell on what should have been."

Perrin kissed her on top of her head. "You deliver that line so convincingly, Versa."

"I've been practicing it! But it's true, and you know it as well as

I do."

"Versa, years ago your father gave Jaytsy a kitten as a thank you. Or rather, as a way to get her feeling maternal and thinking of him or something," Perrin smiled faintly. "The moment I saw that tiny thing I wanted to destroy it. I've always hated cats. That Qayin described Guarders as cats didn't help much, either. I saw all kinds of implications in that tiny gift.

"But my family begged me to let the kitten stay, at least for the night. Then it stayed for the next day, and the next, and I began to notice something: I really didn't understand cats. I had a hatred of them because when I was younger someone told me cats were bad. That's all it took for me to form a lifelong intolerance. But as I watched The Cat, as he came to me, purred for me, I began to realize I actually *liked* him. I had formed a prejudice against cats without ever giving them a chance to prove themselves.

"I did the same thing with Lemuel. He was a cat, I hated cats, therefore . . ." He sighed. "I wept when The Cat died. Only Mahrree knows that. He was fourteen years old and had become my friend. I confided in him all kinds of things and in return he brought dead mice which he dropped on my desk. Great relationship," he chuckled. "We had dozens of his descendants living all around us, for which I was grateful, but none of them were quite like The Cat. I had truly learned to love him. Just as I've learned to truly love Lemuel."

He smiled at Versa. "So, I can't dwell on the past, just fix the future. You're right. You know, Young Pere said he's always saying that to you, and now you've got me saying it too!"

Versa laughed.

Perrin's smile faded. "I want to make it up to him, Versa. I'll continue to see him every week until he's ready to acknowledge my presence. And then I'll see him every day until he's ready to leave. What may have taken me just a few years to accomplish in the world when he was younger will likely take me hundreds of years here, but I'll never quit on him. There's no greater work that I could be doing."

"I've told Young Pere this," Versa said, "but Puggah, I want to go with you on occasion. Maybe he'll hear my voice. Maybe if he hears from me that I forgive him and still love him, perhaps he'll realize that others can forgive him, too."

Perrin kissed her head again. "You're amazing, you know that?"

"It's Paradise, Puggah!" Versa exclaimed. "Tends to rub off on you, you know? The Creator takes all pain away. All that we suffer is what we're too prideful to release."

"You're absolutely right," Perrin said. "There you go, making me say it again."

Versa smiled back. "You Shin men are just so easy to train."

"I think Mahrree might disagree with you."

Versa laughed with him.

After a moment Perrin sobered again. "But Versa, you're right—those in the pit screaming are those who still refuse to acknowledge they caused all their suffering. But *he's* already doing that, Versa. Lemuel couldn't have crawled out of the pit without first feeling remorse, and he had to feel some measure of humility and meekness in order to accept Hierum's hand to pull him out the rest of the way. I'm sure one of his first regrets was you. He loved you once. And it will be because of your efforts that he'll eventually take the hand of Shem to cross the gulf and come home to us."

"And your efforts and Young Pere's. But thank you, Puggah."

"Anything for my granddaughter."

Mahrree stood at the bedroom door. "I'm sorry about the baby, Versa, but Perrin insisted he heard him waking up."

Versa nodded. "He was, so Puggah's not in trouble. He never is, is he?"

Mahrree chuckled at that. "Haven't you listened to *any* of the stories I've told you about him?! By the way, the basket from Jaytsy's is on your kitchen table, and Rose is still outside attempting to put her 'sleeping' papa in her wagon to bring him to the house. So far she's managed to get a hand and a leg in."

Perrin stood up and handed little Lemuel to Versa. "I think we can help her with the rest of him, can't we?" He kissed Versa on the forehead, then kissed Lemuel. "We'll see you tonight at dinner at Peto and Lilla's, right?"

"Get Young Pere in the wagon and we'll pull him over."

Mahrree came over, kissed her great-grandson, and smoothed his blond hair. "Versa," she said softly, "I'm very happy to hear about your father. If ever you think it might be helpful for me to go see him, just let me know."

"Thank you, Muggah," Versa smiled. "But to face *you*? That may still be a few years . . . decades . . .”

“Centuries?” Mahrree suggested. “I’ll still be ready.”

Back outside, Perrin and Mahrree saw that Rose had already managed to get her father, likely with his help, into her little wagon and was pulling it slowly but proudly up to the house. “See you at Grandma Lilla’s house!” she called in a very grown-up voice.

Young Pere opened his eyes, winked at his grandparents, and went back to ‘sleep.’

Arm in arm, Perrin and Mahrree ambled between the flawlessly laid out flowerbeds that lined the gleaming golden path. Nearby were the houses of their children and grandchildren. In many ways it was just like it was in Salem. But in many other ways it was far grander, more extensive, and exquisitely more beautiful. When nature cooperated, and the inhabitants—both mortal and immortal—respected its power, the effects were breathtaking.

Paradise was flushed in vibrant hues where plantings grew in grand abundance and reverberated with a harmony that defied description. So often when she was still in the world, Mahrree had tried to imagine what this life could be like, but her mind was too small to comprehend it. She realized now that if she could have imagined it, she never could have continued in her life on the world. Even at its best and most peaceful, life in Salem would have seemed desperate in comparison.

Mahrree chuckled as Perrin joyfully sucked in his breath as a herd of zebras trotted across the path in front of them toward a grassy field. Several of the herd acknowledged Perrin and, grinning, he nodded back. They would be bedding down in the Shins front garden later that evening.

In the far distance was the city that radiated its own light. Leading up to it were gently rolling hills dotted with gardens of carefully aligned produce and without a weed as far as the eye could see. Fruit trees, berry bushes, and grape vines grew on their own in intricate patterns that from a distance created a colorful tapestry along the hillsides as they weaved in and out and around each other. Sometimes the great grandchildren liked to run between the vines and shrubs in the natural mazes that also held surprises in the forms of other creatures also enjoying the abundance.

Mahrree smiled to herself remembering her astonishment as one of her great granddaughters, Lori and Sam's Maggee, came to her through an organized tangle of sweet pea blossoms. She was riding on the back of a tiger who smoothly deposited the little girl at Mahrree's feet.

Between the orchards and vineyards and gardens were vast grasses of all kinds where a variety of animals and creatures fed and rested. Every animal Perrin and Mahrree had ever dreamed about from Terryp's writings roamed freely and gently through the lands. They had fascinating histories as well. Perrin and Mahrree knew, because they frequently found Terryp sitting among them learning their stories which he shared with the Shins on a regular basis. Just yesterday they saw him deep in conversation with a silverback gorilla. The gorilla was thoughtfully stroking his chin as Terryp asked him questions. Terryp would tell the Shins the answers tomorrow when he stopped by for his weekly midday meal with them.

The Shins knew the histories of their pets, too. The Cat, their dog Barker, and Clark, who had their own families, frequently came by for a visit and a chat. At first, that startled Mahrree and Perrin, but soon talking with animals became common place, and it seemed tragic that they couldn't do it during their lives. They did it *before* their lives, after all, they just picked it up again in Paradise.

Hearing Barker's experiences as Shem's "spy" during his early years in Edge gave them new and surprising perspectives, for which Shem repeatedly apologized. Clark, of course, shared amazing tales of how he experienced all of Perrin's adventures, and provided his recommendations on how horses could have been better trained in the world. The Cat, however, never said much whenever he dropped by, usually with some kittens in tow to show off, but would settle in for an extended scratch behind the ears while Perrin chatted. Occasionally, for old time's sake, he would bring Perrin a mouse—alive and protesting to escape—and snickered as he trotted away.

Bordering every grassland, pasture, and garden were flowers of every shape, color, and variety imagined and unimagined. Their fragrances mingled in the air giving every spot in Paradise a unique and intriguing scent. Mahrree gazed ahead at the distant city which sparkled like gold. To call it a city was insufficient; Idumea was nothing like it. It was filled with glorious structures of magnificent architecture, waterfalls and statues, trees and flowers and designs and creations beyond the ability and imagination of mortals.

As an a newly immortal, Mahrree still found herself astonished and amazed. It wasn't until the Last Day was over that the last of veil slipped from her mind and she comprehended—and remembered—every last detail of her premortal life.

She could understand why there was the delay: The Last Day needed completion first, and that meant securing all the mortals, including the surrendering soldiers and the startled Idumeans. Everyone who chose not to fight was allowed to live their rest of their natural lives in Paradise. No one was quite sure how they got there—they just suddenly were there, in this astonishing place, someplace that was no longer their world. Their old planet still existed, but was now empty of life since it was all here, as well as all of their books and paintings and accomplishments. All of it went with them.

And in this Paradise the immortals helped the mortals begin a new life and learn of the Creator's ways. There were no swords but there were plows, no weapons but all kinds of tools for building and creating.

And there were schools for all ages and all levels. The re-education of the Idumeans was a top priority, especially once they realized that the Creator they'd been told about by Lemuel was nothing like the Loving Being of Light. They could glimpse Him in the distance, and always they turned away, too overwhelmed at the prospect. For now.

And no wonder they were overwhelmed, because Mahrree was as well, even though she was immortal. Because it wasn't just the Creator she now lived with; He didn't exist alone, nor could He have. He was her Father, and if there's a Father there must also be a Mother.

The moment Mahrree saw Her she remembered, and collapsed in joy and excitement when she once again was with her Nurturer.

There had always been Two of Them: their Father and their Mother, her Papa and Mama. The time she got to sit between Them and hold their hands and tell Them of every last detail of her mortal life was the grandest moment of her entire existence. They asked her so many questions, and wept when she wept, and laughed when she laughed, and hugged her frequently and welcomed her Home with joy, as They did with every child, each of them, as they were ready for it.

Mahrree *knew* Them—oh! how well she knew Them! She was astonished that could have so easily forgotten Those who had raised and loved and taught her for an eternity before sending her off on her Test. But They had closed that part of her mind which recalled her pre-existence for a reason: had she been aware of Them, she would not have been able to bear being away from Them. Existence with her Papa and Mama had been pure and loving and wonderful—everything the world wasn't. She would have done all in her power to let her life end so she could rush back to Them.

But *that* also would have been misery, realizing that all she had planned with her Papa and Mama before her mortal life, all that she had wanted to learn and try and accomplish and experience while in the world would never happen because she gave up too soon. She understood why ignorance had to be part of the Test—there was no other way.

A list appeared in her hands when she sat down between her Beloved Parents, just as she had predicted to Perrin it would. A long scroll of what she wanted to try, what goals she hoped to achieve, what she was willing to do, and even what trials she would allow. She remembered with perfect clarity discussing her very specific Test with her Parents before her life—even planning it with them. Now she was there to discuss the results and receive her grade.

As They squeezed her and whispered, "Well done, our sweet Mahrree!" she knew she'd passed the Test. She even remembered that she had a different name before her life in the world, but she, as most others, kept the worldly names they'd been given. At least, for the time being.

Before Mahrree and Perrin now, in the distance, was the Creator and Nurturer's city, made for Their children there and those who would someday—or year—still return from the Dark Deserts. There were many neighborhoods of varying glory and readiness, some nearer to the Grand City, others further away because their inhabitants weren't yet ready to be so close to their Creator and Nurturer. But there was constant movement closer and closer to the Grand City, open paths just waiting to welcome back Their children who grew more ready every day to go Home.

The Shins would be in the Grand City tomorrow morning to deliver Perrin's report of the previous day's progress in the dark desert. Mahrree would spend time in the vast library or visiting with her mother and father who enjoyed living in their mansion in the city where they helped prepare homes for the ones still to return. Her mother never once asked why Perrin and Mahrree chose to live near the desert. It didn't matter where they lived—they could be in each other's home in an instant.

The Shins, along with their children and grandchildren and the Zenos families, had all wanted to live close to the cold dark desert where so many who they loved and wept for still existed. It wasn't visible from the Grand City unless one chose to be there and cross the great gulf to visit those who were willing to listen.

There were many distances and depths there as well. The deepest, darkest place was the pit where those who caused the greatest destruction and sorrow screamed and wailed and thrashed in fury for years. There were many other plains of existence, up until the desert reached a spot where, in the far distance, a faint light from the Grand City could be seen on the horizon. It was there that those like Poe Hili sat reading, studying, learning, and waiting for their probation to be over. Mahrree would go next week with Perrin and Young Pere to watch Poe finally pass Guide Zenos who stood as sentinel, then accompany him on the bridge across the gulf to bring him home.

"Mahrree?" her husband pulled her out of her thoughts. "Poe?"

She smiled. "Yes, I'm thinking about him. Sometimes I still remember him as that little boy in silk sitting on our front doorstep. I hope he won't mind doing it again. I have so many more stories of Terryp to share with him now."

Perrin grinned. "He's looking forward to it. But he won't be ready for silk for a while yet. Nor do we have silk. I don't think he'll be disappointed by that, though."

Mahrree laughed. "We'll have to tell your parents to set out another seat at their former army gathering next week. Poe will be a wonderful addition."

"Grandpy Neeks will want to be by his side, I'm sure. He told me that he and Poe were very close in Grasses."

The only reason Poe had remained in the dark desert so long was because of his hatred of Shem. He had made up for his crimes long ago by becoming one of the few honest and noble men in the army. But he had struggled to accept that Shem Zenos wasn't the loathsome sergeant deserving of death he had been told to believe.

Mahrree had gone to visit Poe a few times to explain how it *had* to be her who Thorne killed that evening at the temple, that only her death would have had the effect it did on the soldiers. It had been prophesied over one hundred years before. She also tried to help Poe understand that Shem never could have succeeded in riding to Idumea to deliver the message to them about Edge's disaster, that it truly was Poe's calling, and his act in taking that risk to save Edge was the turning point in his life to becoming the excellent man that he was.

He believed her, mostly, but it still took him over three years in the deserts to understand that his life played out as it had meant to. Had he not been in Edge to help Young Perrin Shin, Young Pere would have died too soon, either by the hand of Lemuel or in the dungeon. Poe had come to accept—and be grateful—for that under-standing, but for the past couple of seasons his last remaining fury was still firmly aimed at Shem Zenos.

Until now. He was ready to live in peace with everyone else, be-ginning next week.

Others had left the dark deserts over the past three and a half years. Priscill had been released, greeted joyfully at the bridge by her mother and two sisters, just days after the Last Day. It didn't take much to help her learn what she'd missed, and soon she was ready for Paradise and the Grand City.

Unlike Anoki Kiah, who still remained in the pit, screaming.

Others had been working for a long time to be released. From the day Asa Cush died, Relf Shin the elder had visited him in the dark deserts, waiting patiently by the pit for his old friend to stop wailing, then encouraging him to climb out so they could talk. Still, after more than twenty-eight years, Cush hadn't been quite ready to join the army of the Creator when the Last Day came. But a full season later he, too, took the walk across the gulf, Relf Shin by his side, to be with his wife and great-granddaughters.

It took longer for his daughter Versula Cush Thorne to emerge. Requesting to see Perrin and Mahrree, then asking for their for-giveness for her desire for Perrin over the years, was a most humbling test for her.

But first, Versula had to make her confessions to Mahrree, who tried to assuage Versula's guilt but eventually realized she needed to just let the poor woman get it all out.

"I was jealous of you, that you won him over when I couldn't. I'd been with Qayin for ten years when I heard Perrin had finally married, and even though I knew nothing of you, I sent north to Edge every bitter, horrible emotion I could."

"I never felt it," Mahrree tried to say. "Never knew——"

But Versula, whose eyes were squeezed tight in an extreme effort to get out all her words, plowed onward. "I told the women I knew that you had tricked Perrin in some way, or that he'd grown desperate, or that he'd gone stupid to settle for a mere Edger. Every woman of stature in Idumea had the most vile reports of you, courtesy of me."

"I didn't know it, though——"

"Then when you came to Idumea for The Dinner, and I saw you sitting so nervously at the table, I almost felt sorry for you because you had no idea how much poise and power you actually possessed, and then I envied you all the more for it. I realized then that Perrin hadn't been deceived but had snagged for himself the most perfect companion. So I hated you even more.

"When I approached him after the dancing, I'd hoped that maybe my words to Perrin, my touching the old scar I'd given him, might have angered you. But I could see in your eyes you had no idea of our past. I'd been expecting that you knew all about us, and that it ate at you, and that you were jealous of me. But you had no idea. None at all! There was no anger or envy in your expression, and I was almost humiliated for my past thoughts of you.

"And they were some horrific thoughts, I'm very sorry to say. I'd spend hours fantasizing about how to get Perrin back, going so far as hoping the Guarders would kill you, that I could somehow implicate my husband—I had no idea, I promise, of his involvement with the Guarders. But I would have found some way to blame your death on him, then receive the sympathy and praise of Idumea for exposing Qayin, then rush to the side of Perrin and comfort him in his grief. I imagined us together again, making a new family together, even going so far as to convincing your son to change his name to Perrin, and being so kind to your daughter that she would have wanted to marry

Lemuel to keep us all together. At the time I was convinced Lemuel was Qayin's, so there wouldn't have been any complications. When Lemuel contracted the pox, I went up to Edge not to be with him but to try to see more of how Perrin felt about you, about how I might possibly undermine all that you had together, to find a way to take it for myself . . ."

By this point Versula was nearly heaving in contrition, and Mahrree wanted nothing more than to embrace her, but knew that would throw the miserable woman off her course. The embrace would come later.

"I'm sorry. I'm so, so sorry, Mahrree. Can you ever forgive—"

"I already did, a long time ago. It's buried and gone, and we never have to remember any of it again."

It was the private conversation between Perrin and Versula that Mahrree watched from a distance, however, which was even more difficult. Both of them appeared to be mortified by events that had occurred decades before but which needed to be resolved before they could continue on in peace. Although they stood facing each other, Versula shielded her eyes as she spoke and Perrin rubbed his forehead as he responded, both of them focused on the dark sand at their feet, scuffling it around and expressing sentiments each wished past circumstances hadn't forced them to confront. Eventually they shook hands like awkward teenagers, nodded to each other with immense relief, and Perrin jogged lightly away to return to the safety of Mahrree's side with yet another burden forever shed.

Versula didn't watch him flee nor did she glance over to Mahrree. But Mahrree watched Versula and noticed something shift in her.

When Mahrree had first met Versula at The Dinner in Idumea, she'd been taken aback by the woman's grace, poise, and, well, *majestic* demeanor. Mahrree had felt like a frumpy dog in comparison. But there had also been a coldness to Versula, and something empty in her eyes.

But as Versula walked away that day in the deserts, now able to reside somewhere brighter, some of that natural majesty returned to her and she could hold her head up once again.

Mahrree never asked Perrin what they said to each other. The past had been fixed and set away forever, never needing to be revisited.

A week later, Mahrree smiled welcomingly at Versula as she

crossed the gulf with her parents, and the tentative smile Versula gave back to her was filled with warmth and gratitude. They could enjoy Paradise together.

That had happened eight moons ago, only four weeks after their shared great-grandson Lemuel Shin was born. Versula Cush came across the gulf and went straight to Young Pere and Versa's home to weep in joy over her new great grandchild, then weep again, harder, with sorrow about her own son.

Mahrree marveled again at Lemuel Thorne's progress. He, like so many others who caused such devastation, had earned himself a position in the deepest pit. But he screamed in terror, fury, and shock for only three years. The original founders of Idumea still hadn't stopped after more than three hundred years.

But Lemuel stopped one day, opened his eyes, and looked around. He saw the company of people he was keeping and he gripped his head in agony.

Guide Hierum, who kept constant vigil over those who confined themselves to the pit, watched him with fascination and reported it to Thorne's family. Only a few days later Lemuel slowly began to pull himself out of the pit, the weight and agony of his guilt making his progress almost imperceptible. But eventually he was out, having meekly accepted Guide Hierum's hand at the end, and was laying on the edge of the pit staring into darkness.

That's where Poe found him. Each week Poe, who always had a view of the distant city and had been trying for seasons to change his heart toward Shem, walked back to the darker depths of the desert to see who else he could find and perhaps convince to listen to men and women like Perrin and Young Pere, and Mahrree and Teeria Rigoff, who spent their time teaching them.

When he saw Lemuel Thorne, grief etching his features, Poe felt compassion for the man who murdered him. It was the first big step in his own releasing process—feeling sorrow for the grief of someone else and freely forgiving his actions. He tried to rouse Lemuel, but Lemuel saw and felt nothing, not even his former sergeant major shaking his shoulders.

The next day Poe brought Perrin and Young Pere to Lemuel's prone spirit, but they had no success with him either. It was too soon. Lemuel's eyes were distraught, probably seeing from another perspective the pain and horror he caused in the world. He needed to see it all and understand the very depths of suffering he caused before he could begin to try to fix any of it.

It was regret that moved him from the pit. It would be a desire to pay for his crimes that would eventually let him see those who could help him accomplish that.

His mother Versula visited him before she left the dark desert. He didn't acknowledge her either, but maybe he felt her arms around him, because after that he crawled a few paces away from the pit and sat up.

That was when Versa wrote her letter to him and had her husband and grandfather set it in front of him.

Today he opened it.

How far he read, Guide Hierum couldn't tell them, but his eyes had rested on the parchment for hours until he stared back out into the darkness, anguish on his face once again.

He would make it out someday, Mahrree was sure. She examined her feelings about him once again. If he were ready today, she could face him happily. Her feelings about him had changed completely since the Last Day. Now living in Paradise with the Creator and the Nurturer, she had a fuller understanding of Lemuel Thorne. Some people had been deliberately evil, embracing the Refuser's influence and knowingly trying to undermine the Creator's plan.

But Lemuel had never understood the concept of the Creator. And for the couple of years that he was under Perrin's command, he had been changing, watching Colonel Shin and wanting to emulate him. If he hadn't been laboring under the pressure of Qayin to secure Jaytsy at any cost, and wasn't under the influence of Gadiman and Genev to find ways to undermine Mahrree, Lemuel just might have been able to become a different man.

He had moments of love and compassion; Druses had told them how often Lemuel kissed and snuggled his oldest daughter when she was a toddler, how he could make her laugh like no one else, and how his love didn't begin to diminish until he realized he would never have a son to carry on his name. That, again, was Qayin Thorne's influence: daughters were worthless, only sons brought honor to their fathers. So much of Lemuel was destroyed by Qayin. He was a product of an evil man, with few glimpses of what he could be.

But the mercy of the Creator was that all of His children would have an opportunity to know the complete truth, and He was granting them that time to learn it, but only if they chose it. Just as in Salem, no one was forced to believe anything. It was their choices that revealed the true natures of their hearts, and Lemuel Thorne's heart was revealing itself by feeling grief. It made Mahrree hope all the more that Lemuel could succeed. She felt that someday—or some *century*—the two of them could sit down and maybe even laugh about the past together. Back in the world, less than four years ago, Mahrree never would have imagined such an outcome. But now she actually looked forward to the day she could call Lemuel Thorne her friend.

"Not another lost son?" Perrin broke into her musing.

She frequently forgot he was an expert in reading her.

"He already has someone from mortal life who loves him as his mother," she replied. "And now he has you acting as his father. He has millions of brothers and sisters, but what he doesn't have a lot of are friends. I will be—no, I *am*—his friend."

Perrin kissed her.

In fact, everyone had pretty much forgotten about familial designations, because once they arrived they remembered with acute clarity that they really were all family: brothers and sisters whose true parents were the Creator and the Nurturer. Physical designations of mother and father were given primarily to help others understand who was responsible for caring for whom. And there were plenty of sons and daughters in need of parents. At the Last Day all those who had died and were faithful were restored to a perfected state, but that also included myriads of children, many whose parents were not yet worthy to leave the dark desert. Many had been abandoned or abused by their parents, some had even been killed by them, but now they were ready to finish growing to maturity and needed parents to care for them.

Perhaps one of the most wonderful moments was to watch the Nurturer lovingly assign those children to couples who had always yearned to raise a family. Mahrree and Perrin frequently visited Hogal and Tabbit Densal, along with the seven children they had been given. Each week the Shins were put on the spot by the Densal children who were eager to practice their debating skills. Watching Hogal and Tabbit talking, laughing, and planning with their four sons and three daughters put a lump in the Shins' throats, every time.

They weren't the only ones realizing their dreams of raising a family. General Fadh and his wife, while still honorary grandparents to Rose and Lemuel Shin, were also now Graeson and Shaleea Hifadhi, proud papa and mama to five children of their own. Two were girls whose mortal father was Lemuel Thorne, their mothers leaving them to die in trash heaps shortly after Lemuel sent them away. The Hifadhis, who took their family's original name, along with their extensive extended family, had two more blond daughters along with their three sons.

Milo and Teeria Rigoff also had restored to them the two babies Teeria lost before she could carry them to full term. She was allowed to be expecting with them again, and five moons after The Last Day, twins were born to them—a girl and a boy.

Brillen Karna and his wife also had a family of their own. They now had the joy of being parents to a set of young triplets, born years ago too early to a young woman so addicted to vials that she didn't even realize she was expecting, and a teenage boy who died during one of Brillen's attacks on General Snyd.

The leaders of the Moorland offensive frequently came to Colonel Shin for advice, but now it was for parenting ideas and weekly Play Like Children game days.

Mahrree thought that after three and a half years of watching the former commanders and their children playing with her large family massive games of Get Him! and Tie Up Your Uncle—Perrin always in the middle directing the activity—it would eventually become commonplace. But it never was. Mahrree found herself weeping for joy at some point of the evenings, every single time.

Maybe it would be when Brillen, far younger and stronger than elderly Shem, would outsmart with his teenage son the sergeant who had once run him ragged all night through the roads of Edge on a false Guarder chase.

Or maybe it would be when Hogal and Graeson huddled with their sons to conspire against Perrin, Peto, and Deck, with much eyebrow waggling and false gesturing.

Perhaps it would happen when the girls, led by the two Tabbits—Densal and Briter—would yet again beat the boys at Track the Stray Bull (using real and obliging bulls).

Or maybe it was when the children, winded and resting for a few minutes, would be entertained by a dubious story about one of their fathers from Uncle Gari Yordin. He was still without his son and wife, but he was making progress with them in the dark deserts. Perrin and Young Pere frequently accompanied him. Some year the Yordins, too, would come home and be a whole family again. In the meantime, Gari was never alone, spending time with his grandparents and friends, and working with his grandfather in the dark deserts teaching other soldiers weary of fighting themselves. No one was ever lonely in Paradise.

Not even Jon Offra. He, too, frequently joined the Play Like Children evenings, and would help Gari Yordin make even taller the tall tales he told about the former officers. And when he wasn't in the dark deserts searching out and teaching those who were ready to listen, he was in the company of Mahrree's old student Sareen, who used to own a bookstore filled with questionable books during her last years in Edge, and who had perished during the land tremor.

Jon, along with his companion Milo Rigoff, had found her in the dark deserts, not too far in, and Jon remembered how she'd been kind to the mentally confused colonel on the occasions he'd wandered to Edge. When no one else would listen to him, she'd take him in, feed him, and share with him stories about the Shins until he'd fall asleep on her cushioned chair by the fire. She'd taken in a lot of lost souls over the years, teaching them out of her books in *her ways*—usually not to their benefit. She'd rescued a lot of starving vial heads, and on three occasions, Jon Offra.

In the dark desert, they started talking, Jon thanking her for her kindness, and he started teaching her, but in the ways of the Creator. Jon and Milo rushed back to tell Mahrree and Teeria who they'd found, and the next day Sareen's former teacher and her former schoolmate hurried to meet her. Every day they worked with her, Jon and Milo accompanying them, and after a few weeks Sareen was ready to face Guide Zenos at the gulf.

Shem had blushed then, remembering that it was Sareen who had stolen his first kiss during the first Stronger Soldier Race, but she merely laughed when she saw him squirming.

"I'm over that crush," she told him with her girlish giggle. That giggle, which Mahrree had found so annoying when Sareen was her teenage student, had been gone for many years. But now it was back, with fresh innocence, and Mahrree delighted to hear it.

"Took me a few years—all right, decades, I'll admit—to get over the 'unattainable Shem Zenos.' I've realized I was infatuated with the *idea* of you, not actually *you*. So don't worry, sergeant." She critically eyed the grandfather up and down. "I've moved on," and she beamed at Jon Offra who, for the first time since coming to Paradise, seemed confused. Even when she slipped her arm into the crook of his, he blinked, unsure.

But Mahrree and Teeria, who were there to walk Sareen across the gulf, giggled, because they'd observed how attentively Sareen had listened to Jon when he spoke, and how earnestly he watched her, looking for signs that she needed more explanation.

Perrin and Milo Rigoff snorted softly and sent Jon looks of congratulations.

Poor Jon still didn't understand.

But he'd learned a few things in the ensuing seasons, his mind perfecting more each day so that he could comprehend that someone was actually interested in him. Once Sareen would be ready for her own perfected body—which would be soon because she was progressing so well—their future could continue, too. Everyone had a future, if they desired it. Life didn't end with the Last Day. It merely shifted to a new venue, and every mortal who desired love and marriage and a family would get that.

But Mahrree most loved watching her parents and her little sister. The baby who had been born early when Mahrree was two years old, taking only one gasp of breath before dying, had been restored and returned to her parents Cephas and Hycymum.

Mahrree sobbed almost as loudly as Lilla when she watched her parents tenderly take the little girl they never got to raise, her tiny body now perfected and breathing. She needed to grow up, too. Mahrree spent time each day with her sister in a friendly competition with her father, trying to get her to smile, laugh, then walk, talk, and now teach her to read before her father could. Although she was only three and a half, the same age as her best friend Rose, she was definitely Cephas Peto's daughter and already knew the alphabet and how to sound out a few words.

She wasn't being raised alone, either. Mahrree and her baby sister now also had two brothers, trash boys from Idumea who had been thrown into the river when they were just five and six years old when Lemuel held Idumea.

It was one of the great ironies that Mahrree still marveled at. For Lemuel to throw those children, already abandoned by their parents, to a watery grave was reprehensible. But then again, because of his actions, the sweet-faced boys, now eight and nine years old, became the sons of a very proud Cephas and the most attentive big brothers to their baby sister.

And they absolutely loved everything Hycymum cooked up. To them, their mother was the most amazing woman ever to be born. Nothing made them happier than to work by her side in the kitchen, eating everything she could dream up of making. Hycymum could hardly wait until they became teenagers with appetites to match. Sheff Gizzada was a frequent fixture in her enormous kitchen, creating with Hycymum feasts that all of Paradise came to marvel at and enjoy.

Everything in Paradise was restored—not only families, but abilities. Blind people could see, deaf people could hear, those who lost limbs or had been lamed were as perfected as anyone else in white. Even Lemuel Thorne would eventually have the use of his right arm again, once he came to himself.

No one found themselves alone, not even Druses Snyd Thorne. At the Last Day she had been mortified when, as the ancestors appeared, Creer's beautiful and young wife suddenly manifested in front of him. Creer had been holding Druses firmly, but let go of her as if she were a log on fire as soon as he recognized his wife. The only thing keeping Druses from feeling completely horrible was watching the sweet reunion between Creer and his wife.

Then his wife turned to Druses. With a warm smile she said, "Thank you! Thank you for making him smile again. For giving him someone to care for." Druses couldn't respond because she was so startled that Creer's wife was now embracing her. Her mortification lasted less than three minutes.

Her brief romance with Creer wasn't a complete loss. She realized that she *could* love someone again, and that she wanted to. Every man who ever served in the army suddenly felt it his duty to search Paradise for the perfect match. And she had plenty of men to choose from,

from the past three hundred sixty-five years. Despite all the help she received, and didn't always want, she found the perfect man all on her own.

It was at an extended family gathering, two seasons after the Last Day, that Druses came to the back garden filled with Shins, Briters, Zenoses, and many others. She signaled to Shem that she would like to make an announcement, and Shem called everyone to silence.

Bashfully, Druses beamed and said, "All of your efforts to find someone for me have been appreciated, but now are no longer needed. He found me." She motioned behind her, and through the gates emerged a man that made Shem's mouth drop open and Perrin start to laugh.

"Grandpy Neeks?!"

Grandpy grinned back at Perrin. "And why not?" he said, putting an arm around Druses. "This poor woman here has only known officers. I decided she best realize that enlisted men are where it's at!"

"Agreed!" Shem said, slapping him on the back.

Druses told the crowd that she and Grandpy had starting talking at one of Relf and Joriana's gatherings for former soldiers some moons previous, and it took off from there. As Grandpy (his given worldly name turned out to be Boniface; Perrin could see why he stayed with Grandpy) and Druses gazed dreamily at each other in the Shins' back garden, Mahrree knew it was right.

It was just that, well, even in his perfected and young state, somehow Grandpy still had that weather-beaten look about him that made him appear to be perpetually about fifty years old.

"You see," the former sergeant major told the crowd, "I've always been called Grandpy, but never got to be one. But now," he stepped over and gingerly lifted six-moons-old Rose from a stunned Versa, "I finally get to fit the title."

Grandpy Neeks turned out to be a wonderful father to Delia and Priscill, and yet another grandfather to Rose and now little Lemuel. Rose adored Grandpy and inexplicably called him Leroy.

The Shin and Zenos descendants were also happy beyond their expectations. So far each of the grandchildren of age had found someone to share the rest of their lives with. Even Zaddick had found a spicy young woman from the world who had made it through the Last Day.

But the first wedding was Young Pere and Versa's, taking place less than a season after the Last Day. Versa would have had it sooner but Young Pere still couldn't believe she *really* wanted *him*. Even as they walked down the aisle together between their families to stand before Guide Zenos, with Young Pere cradling three-moons-old Rose in his arms to formally claim her as his own, he had mumbled to Versa that she could still change her mind and take another look around for someone more worthy.

She answered loudly that she couldn't understand why he still didn't believe he was the best possible husband for her and father for Rose.

That's when the wedding became the most unusual the Shin-Briter-Zenos families had experienced, because for once it wasn't Shem or Calla or Lilla who cried the most, it was Young Pere. He started to sob as he neared Shem, Versa wiping the face of her soon-to-be-husband since he was holding baby Rose, and his tears became contagious.

Of course Shem teared up, recognizing how remarkable it was that the two of them should find each other and choose to become a family.

But Peto being so overcome with emotion that not even Lilla could successfully quiet him was completely unexpected.

It wasn't until Perrin began to join them, with loud throat clearing which didn't hide the fact that he was weeping but rather instead drew attention to it, that the rest of the extended family—ancestors and mortals—was reduced to gentle laughter and sniffles.

Mahrree fought her own tears only so that she could watch the strongest men she ever knew weep. Only Perrin, Peto, and Young Pere knew just how far Young Pere had come to feel so much joy on such a day. It had been just over a season before that he lay on the floor above the dungeon waiting to die by Lemuel's sword. Then, three moons later, he was becoming a husband and a father, surrounded by family he feared he would never see again.

"It was an exceptionally emotional day. You have to admit that," Perrin interrupted Mahrree's thoughts again. "Quite the peaceful ending for such a turbulent couple. But why do you have to think about *that* so much?"

The image of her husband gruffly sniffing and wiping away his copious tears was in her mind again. So was Shem's comment of, "Now as soon as Grandpy Crybaby over here is ready, we can organize a new family," which got Perrin going even harder.

Mahrree laughed. "Because it was such a wonderful day! I can't help it that remembering your crying is part of that memory."

"Yes, you can."

"True, I can. But I *like* remembering it. It was so *sweet.*"

Perrin groaned.

Mahrree giggled. "Don't worry. Your reputation as The Destroyer is still secure. Even if you now cry at weddings."

"That's *right* I'm The Destroyer!" he said with a firm nod of his head. "And don't you ever forget it, woman!"

"Yes, and now you destroy pies, cheesecakes, chocolate—"

"Because I can!" he proclaimed proudly, patting his firm and perfect abdomen. "Chocolate? Is that the name Hycymum finally decided on?"

"The name my brothers finally agreed on! They came up with another strange name for something else made of chocolate she's been working on, this fluffy stuff they want to call 'moose.'"

Perrin pulled a face. "Moose? As in the large deer?"

Mahrree shrugged. "They seem to think the brown texture of it is moose-like. I don't get it either, but I learned long ago there's not much logic in the minds of little boys. My mother says that whatever they want to name her creations, she's happy with."

The only thing Perrin couldn't enjoy in Paradise was steak. The reasons why were obvious; how can you carry on a conversation with an animal then ask to devour its haunches? Like everyone else, Perrin ate grains, fruits, vegetables, and items willingly offered up by animals, such as eggs and cream. And he apologized to every creature he could find for his previous life. They were all quite accepting. And it was true—the cattle in the world ran from him because they could see the hunger in his eyes. But he had retrained that appetite.

Perrin and Mahrree had reached the long drive that led up to Lilla and Peto's mansion, which was *not* made of solid gold. Only the roads were paved in gold, since that metal was prevalent everywhere and not valuable in any way except to clearly mark the roads. Several large houses they had passed belonged to their grandchildren. Now many of the Shin descendants were waving and calling over to Perrin and Mahrree on their way to the Shins for dinner. In many ways, very little had changed. They still ate—although they didn't need to, but they enjoyed it so why not—with their extended families. Perrin and Mahrree spent one day a week having dinner at the Shins, another having dinner at the Briters, another eating with the Zenoses, another day hosting everyone at their mansion, then the other three days of the week they invited over someone they knew in the world. Sometimes it was Mr. Hegek and his family, or Roak, the former owner of the Stable at Pools, and his wife and daughter. Roak had once again several hundred horses who liked to hang around in the vast, lush meadows that surrounded his house. Or Perrin and Mahrree would visit with Relf and Joriana and the former soldiers they hosted each night, or would drop by Cephas and Hycymum's to laugh with the children. Occasionally they just cuddled together quietly on the front porch, nibbling on another fantastic fruit they never had in the world—pineapple, banana, mango, or kiwi—naming all the species of animals that wandered by their home or bedded down in their garden for the evening.

Life in Paradise was easy, yet challenging. Gentle, yet exciting. Perfect, yet still with room to improve.

For example, in Paradise there was no need for doctors, because the healing power of the Creator and Nurturer cured all injuries and illnesses of the mortals an instant after they were afflicted. Midwives were also not necessary, because childbearing in Paradise was such a delightful experience.

A short time after the Last Day, Eraliz Briter, Holling's expecting wife, felt pains again—well, not so much pain, because pain no longer existed there, but she felt *changes*, pleasant and warm. When Salema, Jaytsy, and Lilla realized she was actually in labor, and *enjoying* it, they couldn't help but protest that it wasn't fair.

Soon their Nurturer arrived to teach them the ways of birthing a child in Paradise. Within minutes the tiny girl was delivered, with Eraliz literally laughing out her child and Holling remarking that it was so easy he wouldn't mind giving birth to the next one.

But Salema was worried—the child was small, born too soon.

And again, the Nurturer taught them there was nothing to fear, for the baby coughed and spluttered and breathed easily, all on her own. Paradise wasn't a place of death and grief; it was full of life and happiness.

But the lack of need of doctors and midwives didn't mean there wasn't anything for them to do; there was knowledge to be gained. Indeed, many mortals discovered their previous work wasn't needed. Farmers needed only to gather in the crops they wanted for that day, no weeding or watering or planting necessary; soldiers' skills weren't required in a place with no war, and law enforcement was unheard of since crime wasn't heard of, either.

Yet some professions remained; scouts and rescuers, by countless scores, were needed to find and teach those in the dark deserts, and in a place where so much needed to be taught, teachers were required everywhere.

Mahrree had plenty to do, but even more to learn from the greatest teacher of all, the Nurturer.

She taught all subjects to whomever wanted to learn, but in brief bits, because the pure knowledge She could bestow quickly overwhelmed the mortals and astonished the Perfected Beings.

Mahrree attended nearly every course available, even sitting in on the medical classes attended by thousands of students, including Boskos, Salema, and Doctor Toon. She sat in admiration as the Nurturer, in a short fifteen minutes, poured into each of them so much light and truth that Her audience would spend hours each day for the next week discussing Her words, trying to grasp it all, and feeling their own minds expand in ways they didn't know possible. Then, eagerly, they'd rush back the next week for another fifteen minutes that would take them another fifty hours to fully comprehend.

It wasn't only the medical classes which were so thrillingly comprehensive; every lesson taught was an experience in headiness, and Mahrree sucked in more about history, archaeology, anthropology, and a variety of other -ologies she didn't know even existed.

It was early in their time in Paradise that Mahrree discovered something: she had longed to be a teacher in the world not so much because her father was one, but because she so missed her Mother, the Greatest Teacher by whom she had sat for ages, absorbing all she could before her time for the Test.

During her life she'd felt a longing because something was missing, even when she was sure she had everything and everyone she needed. Only once she returned to Paradise did she realize she'd been homesick for her perfect Mother and Father.

Mahrree frequently went to the Nurturer to ask Her questions, to clarify answers, and to learn how to teach. There was time, *always* time, for every child and for every request.

There was also a division of labor, Mahrree discovered, so that while the Nurturer cared for and taught those in Paradise, the Creator oversaw the progress and deliverance of those in the dark deserts. It had been that way, always; the Nurturer preparing Their children for life and welcoming them home again, while the Creator oversaw that life and lent assistance to those requesting it.

Over all, it balanced, Mahrree discovered, and beautifully. Just as everything in Salem had balanced, or tried to, knowledge and experience and duties balanced also in Paradise, and perfectly.

Mahrree started up the lane to the Shin's home, but Perrin caught her hand and pulled her back.

"Almost forgot the tradition," he reminded her.

Together they walked over to a tall, clear obelisk, the point several feet higher than Perrin's head. Encased in the clear, pure stone that looked like glass but shimmered more like diamonds was the prophecy written by Peto and signed by his grandfather. To keep it preserved for eternity, and to allow anyone to read it who wished, it remained on permanent display by the roadside, the promise of hope unfolded and suspended flat, the envelope below it. Together they nodded thankfully, respectfully to it. It was completed, yet still continued.

"Puggah!" cried a happy voice.

"Maree!" Perrin cried back, scooping up the four-year-old who had run to his side. "Where's your sister? Where there's one of you, there's two of you."

"I'm right here!" Maggee giggled, peeking around Mahrree.

"Are you our escorts this evening?" Mahrree asked her great-granddaughter, taking her hand.

"Yep!"

"Wonderful," Perrin said, kissing Maree and patting Maggee on the head.

And so The Destroyer walked with the most dangerous woman in the world, accompanied by their great granddaughters, up to the house for dinner.

The Last Day

It would be another perfect night.

Dormin, the last son of King Oren, shook the hand of Shem who stood as sentinel at the great gulf. In his bright white clothing, Dormin lit up the entire area.

Shem smiled cautiously at him. "Are you ready for this? I mean, *really*?"

"Why shouldn't I be?"

Before Shem could respond, a man jogged up to them and exclaimed, "Are you really him? The last son of the king?"

"Yes, this is him," Shem said. "Allow me to make the introductions: Qualipoe Hili, this is Dormin, last descendant of the kings of the world."

Dormin grinned and shook his hand. Being perfected, he could touch Poe's spirit better than Shem could. "You shouldn't regard me with such . . . I don't know, admiration? Exactly what has Shem been telling you?"

Poe grinned at Shem, something he recently remembered how to do. "He told me how you were one of the best scouts in the forests for 15 years, and how the Yungs brought you out of the world—"

"They're eager to see you again," Dormin broke in. "You see, the Yungs remember you from before our life in the world, but as of yet you don't remember everything as you once did. But after you leave here tomorrow, much more will come back to you. Even your memories with the Yungs, your memories with me—we used to be friends, quite a long time ago."

Poe sighed wistfully. "That's what Perrin's told me, and while I feel I'm learning and remembering so much, I understand I've barely begun to scratch the surface of what I used to know. I can see why it comes back slowly. Every day I'm overwhelmed with what's poured into my mind. I can't wait for it to be perfected, to take in even more. To remember the Yungs, to remember you and learn of your experiences in the world—" Poe's eyes lit up. "Shem told me how he confronted you in the forest above Edge as the Yungs were getting you out, and how you tried to kill each other, which was kind of hard for you to do since you weren't even armed."

Dormin threw back his head and laughed. "Well, of all the things to know about me—thanks a lot, Shem! No, I wasn't too skilled at the beginning, that's for sure. And Shem and I became great friends after that."

Shem beamed at Poe, who smiled back.

Dormin continued. "Shem's always been too generous with his praise. I wasn't the best scout, but I did enjoy helping people escape the world my family created. Now, I understand you have something to show me?"

Poe nodded eagerly, and Shem waved them away.

Into the desert Poe led Dormin, the light fading the further in they went. They passed numerous souls sitting in the sand or wandering aimlessly. But some were talking with those dressed in white, while others were reading or praying. Still others were refusing to hear, or to see, or to try.

It grew darker until finally they came to the pit where Guide Hierum kept vigil. If one didn't want to hear the screaming, one didn't have to.

Dormin didn't want to. Most of his ancestors were in there, including his brother Sonoforen, who Shem had killed so many years ago before Sonoforen/Heth could carry out his planned murder of Relf and Joriana Shin.

Dormin wasn't there to see any of his ancestors who had established Idumea and ruled it cruelly and stupidly for over a hundred years. He was there to see someone else. Even though he'd been told about it, still he was startled at the sight.

"He's actually *out*," he whispered in astonishment.

Poe stopped next to him. "'Remarkable' is the word everyone's been using."

Dormin crept closer to the motionless figure sitting rigidly some paces away from the pit. Dormin crouched to see him, face-to-face, but was met with a blank stare.

"Lemuel Thorne," Dormin said.

There was no response.

"Look at him," Dormin whispered. "Not so fearsome now, is he? If people of the world back then could see the shadowy slip of a being he is now, they never would have cowered in fear of him. They never would have followed his orders." Dormin cocked his head. "Truly pathetic. Worse than I expected."

Poe shifted. "Perhaps . . . perhaps this isn't the best thing after all—"

"No," Dormin said, straightening up. "No, I only meant that I didn't expect to find him so . . . diminished. It's as if he's hardly there. As if what's left of him is so battered and destroyed from the inside out that if there were a breeze, it'd blow him away like a dandelion. How fragile. How utterly brittle."

Dormin steeled himself. He'd come for a reason.

"Are you sure you're ready?" Poe asked in the same cautious tone Shem has used.

Dormin regarded him. What a contrast Poe was to Lemuel. He'd be leaving the desert soon to begin his new life in Paradise, but already he shone. For as diminished as Lemuel was, Poe was solid, and full, and powerful, and . . . well, he radiated light himself. It wouldn't be long before he reached the next stage of having a perfected body.

Dormin felt inadequate next to Poe. While Dormin's body was perfected, his mind still had hundreds of years to go.

"I'm ready," he decided. Again he squatted in front of Lemuel and reached out to put a hand on his right shoulder. "Lemuel Thorne, I am the first innocent man you murdered, on a dark night in the forests above Edge. You were furious that Colonel Shin and his family had escaped from the village and were on their way out. But you were also terrified, a mere captain, desperate to prove your worth. Reckless for success, you used Relf Shin's sword on me, claimed I was Shem, and then believed that lie yourself for many years to come. That was the beginning of your very long downfall. But as you can see—or *could* see, if you'd allow yourself to—your decapitation of me wasn't a permanent change. I am again whole, perfected, and completely at peace. You, however, are not. So as the first man you murdered, I say: Lemuel—I forgive you. I want you to find peace as well. I hold for you no ill will."

He thought he should say something more, but nothing else came. Staring into Lemuel's pale, dead eyes was unnerving.

Poe kneeled next to Dormin and placed his hand on Lemuel's other shoulder. "Lemuel, I am the last innocent man you murdered, before Perrin ended your life. I, too, hold no ill will toward you, and I forgive you. I once considered you a friend, and now I want you to know that I think of you as my friend again. I get to leave tomorrow, but I will return to visit you, with Perrin and Young Pere and Versa. Lemuel, we want to help you—"

Poe sounded as if he wanted to say something more as well, but Dormin noticed he'd been looking into Lemuel's unresponsive eyes.

The two men exchanged fragile smiles. Together they stood up and looked down upon what used to be General Thorne.

"I didn't realize I was still carrying that weight," Dormin murmured to Poe. "Not until I unburdened it just now."

"I feel it, too," Poe said quietly back. "That immense lightness. If I feel any lighter, I'll probably *float* out of here tomorrow."

Quietly the men chuckled, then sighed as they gazed upon their murderer.

"Nothing," Dormin whispered. "Nothing at all. I feel nothing toward him at all. Just . . . pity."

Poe nodded in agreement. He crouched again to say, "We mean it, Lemuel; we forgive you. Read your daughter's letter that you opened. She forgives you too."

Lemuel's right shoulder twitched.

"Mahrree, where's the last piece of pie?"

"It should be in the cabinet."

"It's not."

"It should be, Perrin. Why are you looking for it anyway? You're not planning to have pie for breakfast again, are you?"

"Why not? It's mostly berries after all. Berries are good for breakfast."

"Not drenched in sugar!"

"Mahrree, what does it matter? I can eat anything I want for breakfast."

"It's not a very good example to your great-grandchildren. What are you teaching them?"

"That when you get a perfected body, you can eat pie for breakfast."

"Perrin, we've been through this. Pie for breakfast isn't any better than cheesecake!"

"Why not? I still don't see what's wrong with cheesecake for breakfast. It's cheese and eggs—might as well be an omelet."

"Omelets aren't saturated in sugar."

"They could be, Mahrree. They could be."

"I can get you something better to eat."

"Pie is fine. If I can find that last piece."

"Well it was in there last night, on a plate."

"On a *plate*? Not the tin?"

"No, I took it out of the tin to wash it. It was on a plate in the cabinet."

"Oh."

"Perrin . . ."

"Yes?"

"Did you eat the piece of pie on the *plate* last night?"

"No. Not at all."

"Perrin . . ."

"My father ate it."

"Relf ate it?"

"Yes, when he came over last night. I mentioned how good the new berries were this season and, well, I thought the piece on the plate was *your* piece."

"So you gave Relf what you thought was *my* piece, but it was actually your breakfast?"

"Seems that way, doesn't it."

"Serves you right for being generous with 'my' pie!"

"At least *he* enjoyed it."

"Don't worry—I have something else."

"Oh Mahrree, what is *that*?"

"Breakfast pie! My mother brought it over earlier. It's a new experiment. She knows how you like to sneak pie for breakfast. The boys loved it."

"This doesn't look right."

"Sure it does. It's eggs and cheese and pie crust—she calls it 'Keesh'."

"Any sugar?"

"Of course not, Perrin! It's like pie omelet. Just what you wanted."

"No sugar? Sounds like it's not living up to its potential. Mahrree, I really don't think I can eat that."

"Just try it. Joriana had some yesterday and said it was very good."

"Now I see why my father came over for the berry pie."

"Come on, just one bite?"

"Why can't your mother name these things something more appetizing, like . . . 'burrito'?"

"*That* sounds appetizing? Sounds like a donkey disease. Come on, Perrin, just one bite?"

"One bite."

"Well?"

"Needs sugar. And many other different ingredients. Like berries. And no eggs or cheese or . . . are those onions? She ruined it with the onions. There is no room in *pie* for *onions*. This is . . . this is just *wrong*."

"Where are you going?"

"To get some real pie."

"And where is that?"

"Hogal and Tabbit's. Tabbit knows how to feed a Shin man pie."

"My parents went over their right after they came here. My mother had a few more keeshes with her."

"Oh, poor Hogal. We better hurry. Mahrree, are you coming?"

"Always!"

Centuries later . . .

Sometime later—no one bothered to count the centuries, because after a while you realize it doesn't matter how long it takes, just that it *takes*—Mahrree sat on her back porch as the light slowly dimmed. Before her was the endless meadow where Perrin's favorite herd of zebras were bedding down for the evening. A grizzly bear meandered through them, nodding to the herd on her way to her cave just inside the edge of the trees. The zebras chortled her a good night.

Mahrree didn't watch them alone. On the stairs was her company for the evening. One of the men seated a couple steps down chatted easily. Qualipoe Hili had been there before, perhaps thousands of times, talking over old times, sharing stories of now, and discussing plans for the future.

But joining them tonight and positioned stiffly on the bottom step was someone new, and despite the encouraging smiles of Mahrree and the gentle prodding of Poe, he spoke haltingly, worriedly. Still, he persevered because he'd recently made promises, and he wasn't about to break any of them.

And so, very slowly, he became less tense as he related stories which, back in Edge, hadn't been at all amusing. But with the passing of centuries and the perspective of eternity, they took on a different tone. So much so that he found himself smiling as he related them.

And on more than one occasion Mahrree laughed.

And so did Poe Hili.

And finally, without being able to stop himself, so did Lemuel Thorne.

The Last Day

At the edge of the meadow was a forest. Trees of all varieties intertwined; trees which in the world wouldn't have grown together, but here climate didn't matter. So while some argued it was more of a jungle, Perrin still called it The Forest at the Edge of My Meadow.

Underneath the thick boughs which canopied him, he watched. The grizzly ambled past him with a grunt of acknowledgment, which Perrin almost forgot to return until the sow rubbed up against him, nearly knocking him off his feet. An attention-getting trick she'd learned from The Cat.

But Perrin couldn't pull his eyes away from the scene playing out before him. From the trees he watched as the three of them chatted, then laughed.

And he marveled.

And he wept.

And finally he got to say, "Welcome home, son."

Epilogue

And so the land rested. A few well-placed land tremors took down the rest of the buildings, but not until after some artifacts were recovered. Books. Writings. Journals. Paintings. A wide beam with the words "Shin-Briter-Zenos Eztates" carved on it.

Then everything grew over again.

Rivers flooded. Trees multiplied. Forests reclaimed their lands. A crater filled itself with a new mountain. A large hill eroded. The earth reset itself.

But ruins and carvings remained.

And then that world was ready.

Again.

An eon and two epochs later, plus or minus a million years if time were measured there, the Creator watched as they took their places.

The Nurturer ushered in the last of them and nodded to the Creator that all were present.

The Creator looked at the entities who sat before Him. They had no beginning, they had no end. But they most certainly had a middle. And now in that middle they were facing—as we would perceive it if were we to observe that realm—their Placement Exam, deciding the next several eons of their progression. This was not the first assessment the entities had prepared for with figurative hand-wringing and last minute meditations and fits of anxiety, nor would it be the last. But this exam was a most decisive one.

The Creator of the Test, the Organizer of their Cosmos, and the Father of Them All had called together His vast array of intelligent beings to the ethereal Testing Center located in an unspecified corner of the galaxy.

The entities were fresh with the glow from their Nurturer and the Mother of Them All, and Her messages which would have translated to a kiss on the cheek, a squeeze of reassurance, and encouragements such as, "You have worked so hard, I know you will do well!" and "I have faith in you!" as well as additional reminders such as, "Be good to each other!" and "Remember who you are!"

They had been anticipating this moment—the revelation of what kind of Test to expect. Many came prepared with the metaphorical #2 pencils and pages with circles waiting to be filled in thoroughly and fretting if they should have brought blue books as well. Others reviewed lessons and quizzed their siblings. A few more squirmed and chewed on what would have been fingernails were they corporeal. And still others sat rigidly and looked at their Creator to hide their apprehension.

The Creator leaned back on His cosmic chalkboard with a calm smile and regarded His beloved charges. They had come as far as they could, and learned as much as possible. They were ready for the next challenge.

He made a noise equivalent to one gently clearing his throat and all beings looked to Him instantly.

"My children, I am pleased to present to you your new test. It will be unlike anything you have ever experienced before." He radiated light and hope. "It will be glorious. And it will be terrifying. You will find love. And you will find loneliness. You will learn what you can become, and what you already are."

The combined silence of millions of thoughts trying to comprehend the magnitude of these unfamiliar words quieted the cosmos.

The Creator continued, "This is not to be a test of theories and knowledge, but a test of application and will."

Somewhere a metaphorical pencil snapped in two, and a few erasers were nervously bitten off and chewed.

"How do we prepare?" asked a hesitant voice.

"You are already prepared, my son."

"How will we be evaluated?"

"By what you choose to do with every thought and option placed before you, my daughter."

One of the sons stood up. "Will everyone pass the Test?"

The Creator had been waiting for him to rise. In the back, the Nurturer lifted her chin slightly. She'd anticipated this, too.

"The Test is designed to allow all to succeed," the Creator told this son, and all the others. "It is Our will that all of you do. It is to be open note, and I will even give you the notes. I will also start the test with you before leaving you on your own. You can all succeed." He smiled at them.

A sense of relief filled the region.

But the son was not finished. The Creator knew he would not be. "But some will fail, will they not? That is a purpose of a test—to have some fail."

He regarded him sadly. "Yes, some will fail. That is not a fault of the Test and it is also not its purpose. Failure need not be permanent. It means only that the lesson has not yet been learned correctly, and must be attempted again."

The son folded his arms. "If this test is the most important," he glanced at his siblings, "then why not make it so that we cannot fail? So that everyone succeeds?"

Some nodded in agreement while others furrowed their eyebrows in dismay.

The Nurturer looked at the Creator with the message, *It's happening.*

Yes, it is, He sent back.

And just as it should. Her gaze shifted to see another son take to his feet. She had expected this.

"But, Father, is not the test an examination of our will? Our ability to choose?"

The Creator nodded encouragingly at the son. He was a Great One.

The son continued, "Then designing it for unequivocal success would destroy its purpose. It would destroy the Test itself." He turned to his brother. "It cannot be anything but what the Creator has designed. We have to trust the Test."

His skeptical brother eyed him. "There must be other ways . . ." his voice trailed off as his brother shook his head.

The Creator had not been surprised by this exchange, but had expected it and was counting on it. In truth, nothing surprised Him, for

He knew it all. And this knowledge guided His creation of the Test.

As it always happens . . .

"You may each succeed," He repeated, "for I will give you the answers and the help you need. All you must do is ask for help. But I cannot give you help unless you ask for it."

Some of them smiled in understanding. Others looked at Him with hope. Only a few still seemed doubtful.

"It will not be a fair test," declared the son still standing with arms folded. "We are all so different. How can one test fairly assess each of us?"

The Creator waited for his other son to respond.

"It *will* be fair," he began. Then the Great son thought and added, "But it will not be *equal.* Each of us will experience something different, but it will be exactly what each of us needs." He looked to the Creator for confirmation.

The Creator smiled.

Another voice asked, "So we are to prove ourselves to you?"

"You have nothing to prove to me," the Creator said kindly to a daughter. "This Test is for you. You are to prove yourself *to* yourself."

The skeptical son shook his head, but a sense of understanding permeated the space.

"You will not be tested here, but on a place your Nurturer and I have created for you. And you will all have a turn there, in one form or another. Your involvement in the Test will change over time, but you will always be there. Even though there is space enough and to spare on the world I have created, your physical existences will be limited in time."

Understanding vanished as new words such as 'world' and 'time' and 'physical' mystified them, but the Creator merely nodded.

"You will come to understand," He assured. "The real challenge is this: While you are in the Test, you will not remember Me nor your Nurturer nor your existence with Us."

A collective gasp resonated in the universe.

The skeptical son threw his arms up into what would have been the air. "It is not fair!"

"It will be fair," the Creator promised in His steady and compassionate tone. "I will spend a period with you there, to teach you and to give you Writings to guide you. It will be filled with the same knowledge your Nurturer has already given you. Then I will leave, but I will never be far. You can then help each other. But I also give you this promise: as you progress in that sphere you will begin to remember some of what We have temporarily caused you to forget. As you choose to come closer to Me, I will then be able to come closer to you. But you may also choose differently. You may also choose to move away from Me instead, to forget even what you learn in that sphere."

His gentle voice developed an edge of warning. "If you do move away from what you have learned, you will find only darkness and sorrow. But you also do not need to stay in darkness." His voice softened again. "You may change your direction. And you may even progress to a time where you can again hear My voice and receive My guidance, if that is what you choose."

A murmur of discussion passed among the beings.

"You choose to succeed or fail. And when you fail you may try again and again until the Test is over. Our Savior, who has already gone through this test in another world, has paved the way for you to repent and come back to Us. He has already shown this will work. It worked on all other spheres and with all other generations. This is the Plan." The Creator looked at his Great son who first understood the purpose. "Will you take the Test?" He asked him.

His son nodded. "I will! And I will help all others that I can."

The Creator expected this and was pleased. He also knew what would come next. He turned to His skeptical son. "Will you take the Test?"

His son shook his head. "I have no faith in the Plan." He looked at his brother. "I refuse. I believe there must be another way."

The Creator regarded this son with great sorrow and great longing. "This is The Way, and you are already failing the Test."

A few others took to their feet and said, "Then we choose to fail too!"

The skeptical son looked at them with a flicker of appreciation, but not with any happiness.

The Creator surveyed His charges. "If there are any others who choose not to take the Test, you may say so now."

A few others rose and a spirit of defiance filled the space. Many of the other entities tugged on their metaphorical robes to pull them down. Messages of, "You do not know what you are doing!" and "Stay with us!" filled the space.

The Creator looked sadly at them, knowing that this pattern had occurred before, and would occur again. "So this is your choice. But you may no longer remain here. You must leave when your siblings do, and reside where I choose for you. But you will not have the same existence as the others."

"I would not want that existence!" cried the refusing one. He also had once been Great, but no longer. He had been diminishing for some time. "And given the opportunity, I am sure I can convince the rest of them they do not want that existence either. Whatever is the reward at the end of the Test surely could not be worth the trial that comes before!"

The heaviness of his words sat upon them all.

The Creator nodded slowly. "Then so be it. You may have the opportunity to try to convince them as they take the Test."

Many of His children regarded Him with shock. How could He allow this? What would it do to the Plan, the Test?

Others twisted to look to their Nurturer, but She was smiling sadly and nodding at the Creator.

"It will be well," He calmed them. "This," He gestured to his rebellious ones, "is part of the Test."

The cynical son looked with thinly veiled hatred at the Creator. "I will destroy you. I will destroy you all!"

Another son leaped to his feet, large in stature, and the Creator immediately turned to him, as did the Nurturer. He was another Great One.

"No, you will not!" he declared. "I will . . . go against you, there, in that . . . place!" He struggled to find words for behaviors and places he did not yet know.

Another son stood, close in size and temperament. They were always together.

Just as it should be.

"And I will stand with him!" the second announced. "I will . . . protect him!"

The Nurturer caught the Creator's eye.

They must stay together, the first and his . . . guard dog.

Epilogue

They will. The Creator sent the message back. *It is how it always is. The Deliverer and his Destroyer. Together.*

The Nurturer's eyes glowed.

"You will fail!" shouted the refusing one at his brothers.

"No, they will not!" Up stood a daughter, and another, and a son, and another daughter . . . until dozens surrounded the brothers in defense.

"We stand with them."

The Nurturer beamed.

The Creator beamed back.

As it has been before.

The refusing one scowled and stared at each of them. "I will remember you. And you. And you. Each of you. I will find you, and I will come after you, and I will destroy you—"

"Enough," the Creator said. He did not yell or shout, just spoke. And the cosmos fell silent.

He turned to the Refuser. "You will leave now, and take those who wish to be with you. You can no longer remain here."

The Refuser glared at the very first, the Greatest one among them, with the first look of loathing. Then he turned to those Great Ones who promised to defend them, and extended the same threat. But already he was leaving, with others following. They climbed over the feet of their siblings to follow him out of the Testing Center.

Many of their family tried to pull them back, and others sobbed quietly.

The Nurturer covered Her perfect face with Her perfect hands and wept. Even though She knew this was coming, still She wept.

The Creator sighed sadly and shed a few tears. He had hoped, until the very end.

They knew who would leave and who would remain. A Parent knows a child's heart. A Parent cannot, and will not, change that heart, but still weeps for it.

But one who was leaving hesitated and looked back at the Great Ones.

"Stay with us!" they cried, and the hesitating one looked to the Nurturer for guidance.

She nodded gently. "Come back."

Oh, how She loved this one; one who had always struggled, who had frequently doubted, but who had always tried anyway.

Still he wavered, now bombarded on all sides by those telling him where to go.

The Deliverer and the Destroyer beckoned him, loudest of all.

The Creator and the Nurturer locked eyes.

If he stays, he will cause them so many problems.

Yes. They will need many problems to solve.

Finally the hesitating one took a step, back to his family.

Cheers and cries erupted, and a few others turned from the Refuser and came back to the Great Ones.

Oh, they will have so many problems—

As many as they need.

The rebels left with those they still kept.

The guard dog/destroyer wrapped an arm possessively around the brother who returned, oblivious to what future pain this one would cause him. But also not knowing what joy they would later—*much later*—share again.

The Creator gazed with empathy upon His remaining children. There were far more that had remained than had left, but the empty seats scattered around the expanse filled Him with grief. Even if only one chair was empty, He and the Nurturer would weep for the one who was gone.

He sighed deeply again, and smiled again. There was work to do. "You who continue are my elect and my chosen. One of your brothers has already said he will take the Test. And now I ask each of you: Will you take the Test?" The Creator looked at a being in front of him.

She nodded and smiled. "I will!"

The Creator shared her smile, and asked another son, another daughter, and all of them. Were time measured, attending to each would have taken decades. But since they had no time, He had each of their answers in no time at all. They all would go.

"All is prepared to begin the Test. You," he gestured to the first Great son who stood, "will go at the first, to help establish Our way, and to teach Our families. And you," he gestured to the Great daughter standing next to him, "will also go at the first, to nurture and mother those families. I will also need daughters and sons to begin with you. Who is ready to go down with me?"

The shout of jubilation reverberated throughout the cosmos and a rush of souls came to him.

The Creator smiled at his children, and His gaze stopped on the two brothers and their siblings who had declared to fight the Refuser.

"Your time will not be yet," He told them gently, and their hopeful expressions faded. "I need Great ones at the beginning, but also Great ones at the *end*. I need those who can deliver, and can sacrifice, and can rescue, and can destroy."

They did not understand all that He told them. He knew they could not, but still they looked at Him with renewed enthusiasm and willingly stepped back from those wishing to be the first families.

They would be among the last families.

The Creator caught the eyes of the Nurturer again, who now stood with all those who would wait. She would prepare them for their time in the world, and welcome them Home again.

There was always a pattern. There were always roles to play. No soul was forced into one of millions of parts, but the test was about one thing: what part would each choose to play.

The Creator smiled and sent a complicated wink to the Nurturer that would been interpreted by mortals as, "Hold down the fort. I'll be home for dinner—I promise."

Mahrree winked back at Perrin.

Five points:
1) a defense,
2) a reason,
3) the purpose,
4) Jon Offra wasn't supposed to be here, and
5) why there's a discussion about pie near the end of the book.

I: Well, *of course* I got it wrong! What happens when we die? What happens in a few million years? I don't know. No one does. That's why this is a work of "fiction" and not a "how to get to Paradise" book.

I know there are a lot of people who will argue my take on what happens after we die. Go ahead. I expect discussion because, as Shakespeare put it, death is "the undiscovered country," and we're all going to have a different opinion about what we'll discover there.

But please do not construe anything I've written here as doctrine from *any* religion. While I borrow from my own LDS (Mormon) background, I also insert a great deal from "The Gospel According to Trish," which is doubtless fallible and wrong, because the last time I checked I wasn't a guide or prophet.

I've literally sat and thought for hours about, "How *should* it be when we die?" and that's what I wrote here. I believe in God the Father (and also Goddess the Mother—our Nurturer—but in "The Gospel According to Trish," Her duties and focus are on our siblings who are in the spiritual realms; the earth is God the Father's domain—His job—and He's who we address in prayer. If we prayed to Heavenly Mother, I think She'd sigh patiently and say, *Go Ask Thy Father. That is His Job. I am already busy with thy siblings over here.*).

I believe our Heavenly Parents are more fair, and loving, and just, and caring than any of us can fathom. What might our existence with such benevolent Beings be? This book incorporates the best scenarios I could imagine, and therefore will be woefully inadequate because I have a mortal mind, and it's banging the edges of its understanding that I get a headache trying to ponder it all.

When I get to the other side, I'll likely smack my forehead and go, "Now THAT'S how it should have been! Of course I got that wrong! Can I go back and revise my book?"

So please, if you have any issues with my idea of what happens after we die, or you believe something else, or your religion has taught you something else, great! Not a problem. In fact, I want to hear your theories, because I'm gathering them up and when I die and get over there, I'll pull them all out and make a chart.

I am banking on the assumption that when I get to the other side, they'll let me bring one piece of paper, full of questions; on the top of the list is, "1) *Dinosaurs*. What's the deal? 2) *Atlantis*. What's the deal?" and so on. I'll add all your speculations to my list and hope to find you so that we can compare notes. I'm expecting that you'll get there with a piece of paper, too.

On second thought, perhaps I should just commit the list to memory, because I have a feeling that there we'll remember everything with alarming clarity. See? I'm already revising.

I did consult near-death experiences in my research as to what our next life may be like. But I'm skeptical about experiences that have been published and publicized, because I wonder what the financial motivation may be to share such intimate and private moments. I either felt I was reading something sacred that shouldn't have been shared, or I was being fed an embellishment that no longer resembled the original experience. I ended up not incorporating information from any of those.

I've been intrigued, however, by a few accounts from the 19th century. Those rang truest to me, primarily because there was no gain to be gotten from the teller sharing details with a few select friends. I let my imagination play with those more seemingly-pure accounts to augment my vision of Paradise.

I repeat again, this series is fiction (although it feels very real to me at times). It's all conjecture and you may take it or leave it as you will.

But, you may ask, do I *really* believe that after a few million years of growth and learning and development, tutored by omniscient Gods, that people like Perrin and Mahrree and you and me could in some eon become gods ourselves and start another similar cycle all over again? Yes, I absolutely do. Why couldn't we? What better future could any of us imagine? Sit and ponder that for a few hours, then let me know what you come up with.

2: The entire reason I started this series was because of one clear, stark image that popped totally unbidden into my mind, probably back in 2003, maybe even earlier. I was in my backyard in rural Virginia, pulling out thorny bushes on a hot, summer day. The image was of an old woman, standing by herself, in a sacred place like a temple, and seeing an entire army coming against her. She knew her grandson was among them, and she stood her ground, hoping he'd notice that she willingly sacrificed herself.

The image so startled me that I quit pulling out the thorny blackberry bushes and instead stared into the forest behind my house, engrossed and fascinated for probably fifteen minutes just reveling in the scene, trying to draw as many details from it as I could until I could get no more.

For years I wondered about that image, because it frequently drifted back into my mind, usually when I least expected it. Who is she? What's happened? And why is she doing this for her grandson?

I distinctly remember driving with my family in Utah a few years later, heading west out of Sardine Canyon with Brigham City just coming into view. Now, you can see the Brigham City Temple where I was looking, but back then it wasn't there. At that moment, emerging from the canyon, I suddenly knew there was a whole story about the woman, and I felt that I needed to start writing it.

I did, perhaps just a few days later, late in the spring of 2009. Because I'd never before written any fiction (English majors rarely do, weirdly), it was going to be a short story. Yeah, really—a "short" story. I drafted fifty pages by early summer before I realized this woman had a husband, and for another fifty pages he was some nameless guy in the background, along with his captain. A week or so later I understood he was part of the story, too, and I shelved nearly one hundred single-spaced pages and started all over again.

I hadn't yet typed one word about the nameless grandson.

The short story was growing into a trilogy. Yeah, really—a "trilogy." But then *they* took it over—these nameless characters who wanted their stories known. And it took me about fourteen months of constant writing, probably 50-70 hours a week, to finally get to the page where Mahrree stands at the temple, knowing her grandson Young Pere (they eventually got names) is out there, and hoping this act of self-sacrifice might get him where he needs to be. Talk about a tingly moment. I was shaking when I typed those pages, realizing I'd come full circle and was going on to expand it.

All in all, I drafted the entire series, a couple thousand pages, in about fifteen months. Then I started revising, and that's taken a few years, because while I'm a fast writer, I'm an excruciatingly slow reviser.

3: It wasn't until I typed the last words General Relf Shin says to Peto that I figured out *why* I was writing all of this:

> "But Grandfather, I have a question."
> "Sure, Peto."
> "Why? Why . . . did you have that dream, give me this parchment . . . why?"
> Relf gripped Peto's face with both hands. "Why? To give you hope, Peto."
> "Hope? That's all?"
> "Peto, hope's *everything*!"

This series was to give me hope, to give others hope, to give us all perspective. I started writing this series for personal reasons, as therapy and escape from situations I was going through. But since I've published, I've heard from others who say it's given them hope. And hope's everything, I've discovered on many, many occasions.

4: Jon Offra died before Book 6, after Perrin sent him back to the world. He went around terrifying soldiers until he one day vanished. That's how it was written.

Except Debbie Beier didn't like it.

Debbie was a friend of mine from Virginia who later became a beta reader. But around Book 4 she developed cancer, her second round of it. When her prognosis turned grim, she emailed me asking if I could tell her how the series ends, since she wouldn't live to see it completed. Heartbroken, I spent many hours condensing the next four books into a few pages. Debbie approved of everything except for one thing.

"You shouldn't kill Jon Offra. That's wrong. Every part of me feels that's wrong. He has to live."

"But, Debbie," I wrote back, "he's *supposed* to die. It's in his name: Offra is 'sacrifice' in Swedish."

"I don't care—it's wrong. Make him live. As the dying wish of a friend, make Jon live."

How was I to argue with that?

It's not a simple task to weave a character into four books when he was already "gone." Over the next many months as I revised each book I had to work him in, until suddenly he became very important. Debbie was right—his story wasn't over yet, and with each line, I'd whisper, "Yeah, you were right, Debbie. You were right."

Jon lived until the very, very end, when he died for about ten seconds. I think Debbie would approve. In fact, I think Debbie wrote his story for me.

5: About the dialogue at the end of Book 8, where Mahrree and Perrin argue over pie. It may seem odd, but it was vital, so it stays. (I've broken so many "rules" in my novels already, it seems like it doesn't matter if I break a few more by sticking random conversations in wherever I feel like it.)

When I first wrote of Perrin's passing, it was less than two months after my sister Judy (Yudit) died from cancer. She was the most dynamic, powerful, amazing woman I've ever known, and the fact that she was gone in 2009 tipped everything wrong. Her family struggled immensely, her husband and children mourned deeply. After watching and experiencing that, I skipped ahead in the series' future and wrote about Perrin's dying, over Thanksgiving break that year. I took all that raw sadness and converted it into words.

Bad, bad timing. I was so despondent. It was the worst Thanksgiving ever. I sobbed, for fictional people, for real people, for myself. My sister would never know of my books. (My parents didn't either; as I was writing, they were declining with memory issues, and both died a few years later without knowing what I was trying to create.)

After driving my daughter back to college on that Sunday after Thanksgiving, I was deep in thought on the two-hour drive home, sorting everything and pondering about the next life. (See, I told you

I spend hours wondering about what's next.) The idea of Perrin and Mahrree, reunited and resurrected and bickering about pie came to me, and by the time I'd reached home, I'd thought through this whole little scenario. Even though it was late at night, I couldn't rest until I saw Perrin with Mahrree again, and took that nugget of hope and thought about Judy and her husband and children together again. It may sound silly, but it felt marvelous to write them together. I sobbed all over again, but this time with hope for a future that's still coming.

And that's why there's pie near the end of this book.

Because I'm sure there's pie in Paradise.

Meet me there and we'll go looking for it, probably at Gizzada's restaurant.

The Last Day

Excerpts of The Writings
(ancient/Salem version)

We are all family.
We have always been a family.
We have always been progressing.
We have always been. *(Guide Hierum's first writings)*

Before the Last Day even the aged of my people will strike terror in the deadened hearts of the fiercest soldiers.

On the Last Day those who have no power shall discover the greatest power is all around them.

On the Last Day those who stayed true to the Plan will be delivered as the destroyer comes.

I have created this Test, I have given this Plan, and I will reward my faithful children.

I warn you that we cannot continue in the ways we are now. Our lives and existence on this world are not forever. An end will come.

In the arguing among our people I see the seeds of antipathy and apathy that will grow to destroy the world we are striving so hard to create. We're drifting from the structure the Creator left us, and if we continue on this path our descendants will not be found faithful at the Last Day when the test ends. What we do today affects our children and their children. For their sakes, we can't continue down this way you are planning. I know your secrets, and they will destroy us all. I beg you to abandon this!

You know as well as I do that the Last Day will find each one of us facing either the reward of Paradise to enjoy the company of our family and friends for the next one thousand years and beyond, or the misery of the Dark Deserts to endure the torture of knowing we failed to do His will.

When that Last Day comes, no one knows but our Creator, and its arrival will surprise those who fight against the Creator's people.

On that day do not be one of those surprised to find yourself on the wrong side.

On that day do not find yourself with a blade in hand ready to charge your brother or sister.

On that day be one of the many standing with the guide, having seen the signs and recognizing what is coming.

Before the Last Day will be a land tremor more powerful than any ever experienced. It will awaken the largest mountain and change all that we know in the world. Those changes will bring famine, death, and desperation to the world. And that desperation will cause the world's army to seek to destroy the faithful of the Creator.

Be among those faithful to the Creator!

Be among those standing firm for what you know, having not so quickly forgotten His words to us!

Be among those who see the marvelous deliverance from the enemy the Creator will send us! For He will send deliverance before He sends destruction to those who fight Him!

Don't destroy His structure for our survival. What you're planning to do will ruin— *(Guide Hierum's last words)*

Guide Pax's vision, upon seeing the future of Salem:

The inhabitants of this new city will live in peace until the end comes, when the enemy will threaten to annihilate them. But before that time the Creator will send one to prepare them. From the highest ranks of the enemy will He call one to mark the path of escape for the valiant.

The Deliverer will ensure the safety of the Creator's people, until the coming Destruction.

Shin-Briter-Zenos Family Trees (Year 365)

Jaytsy and Deckett Briter Family (and ages)

Salema(27)
>> *married to* Lek Zenos:
>> --Briter (7)
>> --Fennic (5)
>> --Perrin (called Plump Perrin--1)

Cambozola [Cambo] (25)
>> *married to* Tessina:
>> --Decker (5)

Pere [Bubba] (24)
>> *married to* Alixan:
>> --Raishel and Reikel (twins) (4)

Holling (22)
>> *married to* Eraliz:
>> --Jaysie (2)

Viddrow (20)

Cephas (19)

Suzi (17)

Tabbit (16)

Banu (14)

Atlee (12)

Yenali (10)

Young Shem (9)

Peto and Lilla (sister to Calla) Shin family

Lorixania [Lori] (twin) (25)
> *married to* Sam Cadby:
> --Ensio (5)
> --Annly (4)
> --baby twins Maggee and Marey

Joriana [Jori] (twin) (25)
> *married to* Con Cadby:
> --Cori (5)
> --Gersh (4)
> --baby Peto

Relf (23)
> *married to* Mattilin:
> --Grunick (3)
> --baby daughter

Barnos (21)
> *married to* Ivy
> --baby daughter

Hycymum [Hycy] (20)
> *married to* Wes Hifadhi
> --baby son Jothan

Young Perrin [Young Pere] (19)
Kanthi (twin) (17)
Nool (twin) (17)
Kew (15)
Hogal (14)
Sakal (13)
Centia (11)
Morah (9)

Shem and Calla (sister to Lilla) Zenos family

Lek (26)
>*married to* Salema Briter:
>--Briter (7)
>--Fennic (5)
>-- Perrin (called Plump Perrin--1)

Boskos (24)
>*married to* Noria:
>--Utolian [Toli] (4)
>--Calia (2)

Zaddick (22)

Meiki (20)
>*married to* Clyde

Ester (18)

Huldah (16)

The Last Day

Mahrree's Family Lines (vines) charts

Perrin Shin's
Family Lines
(Vines)

>~~~<

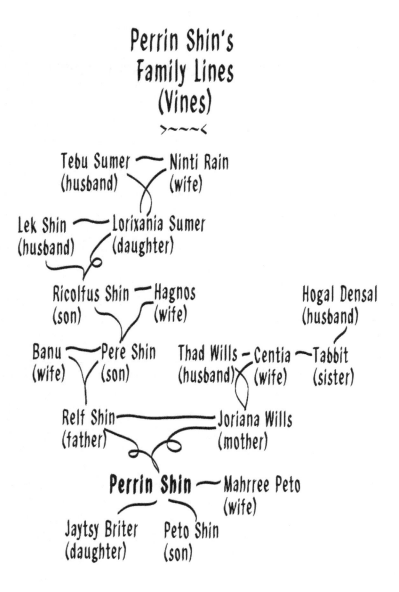

Tebu Sumer — Ninti Rain
(husband)   (wife)

Lek Shin — Lorixania Sumer
(husband)   (daughter)

Ricolfus Shin — Hagnos   Hogal Densal
(son)   (wife)   (husband)

Banu — Pere Shin   Thad Wills — Centia — Tabbit
(wife) (son)   (husband)   (wife)   (sister)

Relf Shin————————Joriana Wills
(father)   (mother)

Perrin Shin — Mahrree Peto
                  (wife)

Jaytsy Briter   Peto Shin
(daughter)   (son)

Mahrree Peto Shin's Family Lines (Vines)

>~~~<

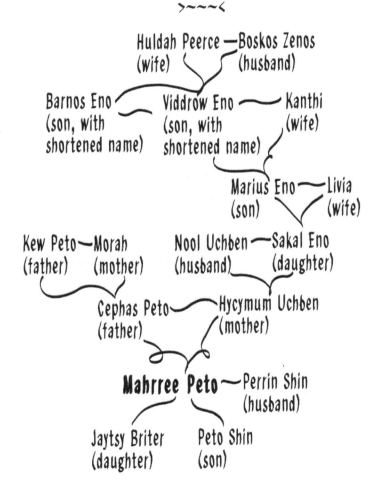

Huldah Peerce (wife) — Boskos Zenos (husband)

Barnos Eno (son, with shortened name)

Viddrow Eno (son, with shortened name) — Kanthi (wife)

Marius Eno (son) — Livia (wife)

Kew Peto (father) — Morah (mother)

Nool Uchben (husband) — Sakal Eno (daughter)

Cephas Peto (father) — Hycymum Uchben (mother)

Mahrree Peto — Perrin Shin (husband)

Jaytsy Briter (daughter)

Peto Shin (son)

Deckett Briter's Family Lines (Vines)

>~~<

Yenali
(mother)

Lilla — Holling Briter — Cambozola Briter — Sewzi Fleur
(wife)   (uncle)   (father)   (mother)

Atlee
(son)

Jaytsy Shin — **Deckett Briter**
(wife)

Shem Zenos's
Family Lines~Partial, showing
connections to Petos and Shins

>~~~<

Boskos Zenos —Huldah Peerce
(husband)   (wife)

Alkimos Zenos
(son, with brothers Viddrow
and Barnos Eno in the world)

Sophia Nash
(wife)

Dikha Zenos — Doxa Pram
(son)   (wife)

Ergon Zenos — Ester Guava
(son)   (wife)

Boskos Zenos
(father)

Tebu Sumer — Ninti Rain
(husband)   (wife)

Kiraxania Sumer
(daughter, with sister
Lorixania Shin in the world)

Max Neu
(husband)

Hines Leberts — Dannie Neu
(husband)   (daughter)

Zaddick Dedek — Emiko Leberts
(husband)   (daughter)

Meiki Dedek
(mother)

Shem Zenos — Calla Trovato
(wife)

Acknowledgements

I never thought I'd get here. Nine years or so ago, when I seriously started writing this, I had an idea of where it *might* go. But I never actually thought I'd finish it. Such an immense project, and who was I? Some dibbling, dowdy, middle-aged hausfrau with no experience and no real help. (I mean *professional* help. I needed professional help—yeah, yeah, I left that one wide open, didn't I.)

But friends and family stepped up, not really comprehending what they were getting into, not understanding the scope of this monster I needed them to help dissect. I think we're all just gazing at the carnage thinking, "Holy cow—what'd we get into? Is it over yet?"

Yes, amazingly, it is. And it wouldn't have come this far without all those who encouraged and promised me it was good even when it was bad. (Except for Jennifer Merrill—she *always* let me have it straight ["this is so wrong—what were you thinking?"], then immediately promised she was still my friend, even though I need to fix, oh, about 1/3 of the book.)

So thank you one last time to Barb Goff, Paula Snyder, Cheryl Passey, Dallin Crump, David Jensen, Jennifer Merrill, Freddy Thomson, Bob Golding, Stephanie Carver, Arlyn Collett, and Tulah Cook. (I hope I didn't forget anyone. I'm sure you'll let me know if I did.)

Will you be onboard for the prequel(s) and short stories?

You'll get back to me?

Um, ok.

Thank you, readers, for your charity in overlooking errors and typos. This isn't my full-time job, unfortunately, writing novels all day long. It's a hobby which I squeeze into crevices of real life, and sometimes I run out of crevices, run out of time, then family and work are bouncing behind me, eager for my attention, and I have to pat my books on the head and say, "That's all we can do, friend. Time to send you out into the published world." They'll never be perfect, no matter how often I go through them and have friends help me edit. There'll always be misteaks and issews. That's how you'll know I wrote them.

Writing is a lonely endeavor, which is fine for introverts like me who enjoy sinking down into a constructed world that obeys them.

But there are moments in that world that you yearn to share with someone even though they'd never understand the thrill of, "I finally figured out how to get Young Pere and Nelt away from General Thorne!" Or why I'm sullen and quiet because Calla just died and there was nothing any of us could do. You just gulp down your emotions and make tacos for the kids.

There were times that I threw my fists in the air in triumph, but no one knew it. And if they did, they wouldn't understand why. There were times I slammed shut my laptop because I couldn't get the words right, the timing right, the solution right, nothing right . . . I can't write! And no one knew it, nor would they understand.

It's a weird thing, to live a life in the middle of another life without anyone noticing. It's not bad; in fact, it's quite addicting. But I wish to share it. Now that I'm finished writing the series, I can share it all, every last detail—but again the timing is all wrong. You'll read things and be shaken or excited by them, but I was shaken and excited by it months or even years ago. We can't experience it together. I don't know how to fix that. Maybe it doesn't need fixing.

I appreciate my family's willingness to let me live so fragmented in many different worlds. I hope I was in theirs long enough each day, although I'm sure I frequently wasn't. I have created multiple families, and again, I don't know if I need to fix that. I hope I don't. All have taught me so much, and I've been better for everyone because of that.

If nothing else in my life, at least I can say that once I wrote over 4,500 pages, and a few of people liked the stories, and I accomplished something I never thought I could.

Now, on to the prequel of Lek and Lorixania . . .

The Last Day

About the author . . .

Trish Strebel Mercer has been teaching writing, or editing graduate papers, or changing diapers since the early 1990's. She earned a BA in English from Brigham Young University and an MA in Composition Theory and Rhetoric from Utah State University. She and her husband David have nine children (and now adding grandchildren) and have raised them in Utah, Idaho, Maryland, Virginia, and South Carolina. They used to live in the rural west and dreamed of the day they would be old enough to be campground managers in Yellowstone National Park. Now they live in rural Maine and pretend they already are.

forestedgebooks.com

(If you're like Peto and flipped to the end of the story to see the ending of Young Pere, I promise that they'll all live happily ever after because every story has a happy ending if you wait long enough. Now go back and finish the book.)

Made in the USA
Las Vegas, NV
14 January 2022

41443156R00420